MORIA TRIED TO SMILE,
AND SOMETHING INSIDE OF HER SNAPPED.

She was in his arms, he was holding her close, oh, God, oh, God, he might have lost her, she might have been struck by the rattler and died, she was so delicate, even lancing the punctures and sucking the poison might not have saved her.

His mouth came down over hers, he held her closer, until it seemed as if he were crushing her bones, as if he had to take her inside his own body to protect her, to hold her forever, never to lose her, not ever.

Quinn kissed her again, and his body took fire and it spread to hers, consuming her, consuming him. This might be the only moment in all eternity that they'd be together, that they'd have each other; what had just happened had brought it home to both of them that any quirk of fate might separate them forever. And she learned what it was to love a man and be loved by him . . .

Books by
Lydia Lancaster

Desire and Dreams of Glory
Passion and Proud Hearts
Stolen Rapture
The Temptation
To Those Who Dare
Love's Hidden Glory

Published by
WARNER BOOKS

Love's Hidden Glory

Lydia Lancaster

WARNER BOOKS

A Warner Communications Company

Love's Hidden Glory

Book One

Book One

1

The edge of the silver breakfast tray dug into Rose O'Riley's side as she shifted its weight to free her right hand to tap on her mistress's bedroom door. This morning there was no quick "Come in" in answer to her rap, and Rose's face tightened. If Eugenia were still asleep it meant that she'd had a bad night, and it was a crime to have to wake her, but orders were orders and William Northrup didn't issue orders to have them disobeyed. Rose's fifteen years at the Northrup estate would mean nothing if she deviated from following the master's orders by as much as a fraction. She'd be out of this house by nightfall, with no letter of character to help her obtain a new position.

All the same, if it hadn't been for her love for Eugenia Northrup, Rose would have carried the tray back to the kitchen and let William Northrup do his worst. She hated him for his coldness and his arrogance and his total disregard of the human rights of his fellow creatures, a hatred that had doubled and redoubled in the ten years since he had brought Eugenia to Retreat as his bride.

For Eugenia, every day started with breakfast in bed at seven, into

9

her riding habit and ready for the trainer when he brought her horse around at eight, two hours of riding, whether she was sick or well, whether she wanted to ride or not, whether it was fair or foul, excused only if there was a driving rain that made riding impossible. Even in the winter, when there was snow on the ground, unless there was so much that the horses couldn't be taken out, Eugenia must ride.

Rose forced a smile onto her face as she turned the knob and pushed the bedroom door open. Eugenia had enough to contend with without having to see a sour expression the moment her eyes opened in the morning. She carried the tray inside and placed it on the chiffonier and crossed to the tall windows that looked out over the Hudson River and drew back the drapes, dreading to turn around and see Eugenia's face. When she did, she winced.

There were shadows under Eugenia's eyes, shadows so dark that they looked like bruises. Even as she felt Rose's touch on her shoulder, the strain, the utter misery of her existence, came back into her face the moment she emerged from sleep.

"Is it seven o'clock already, Rose?"

"That it is, my heart. I tried to hold the hands of the clock back but the pesky things kept right on going with a will of their own." Rose's movements were gentle and practiced as she fluffed the pillows and reached for a wrapper to drape around Eugenia's shoulders, its delicate pink bringing a touch of color to the pale face and making her look younger than her twenty-nine years. It was paler than usual she was this morning, no color at all except for those shadows under her eyes, and may God strike that devil dead for bringing the tragedy into those eyes that should have been as clear and sunny as the April morning promised to be.

"Eat it while it's hot." Rose uncovered the bowl of porridge. "There isn't a lump in it, I saw to that, and the milk is warmed, and the coffee's good this morning, I had a cup myself instead of tea. Eat your muffin too, there's no preserves like we make right here at Retreat. It's going to be a beautiful day, to be sure, and you'll be wanting your strength to enjoy your ride."

Like an obedient child, Eugenia lifted a spoonful of the porridge, but Rose could see the effort it cost her to swallow it. She followed it with a bite of the muffin and a sip of coffee.

"It is good, Rose."

"Didn't I tell you? I'll just lay your things out while you eat, every bite, mind you, or I'll have to hold your nose to make you get it down."

Mother Mary have mercy, what would William Northrup do if he could hear the two of them, nattering away as though they were friends instead of mistress and servant? A shudder went through Rose's body as she removed Eugenia's riding habit from the wardrobe and carried it to the window to examine it with an eagle eye for any flaw, for any speck of lint or trace of soil. Eugenia had to present herself for inspection every morning, in the dining room where her husband took his breakfast in stately solitude, and he wouldn't miss a speck of dust even if it were so small that anyone else would need a magnifying glass to find it, and his displeasure would ruin the day not only for his wife and Rose, but for every living soul in the house.

The riding habit was pristine, even William Northrup would be able to find no fault with it. And this room in the early morning belonged to Eugenia and Rose, William knew nothing about their friendship when his ears were too far away to overhear. He never entered Eugenia's room in the morning, and thank all the saints for that one blessing.

Still struggling with her breakfast, Eugenia steeled herself to face the day. How was she to do it, how was she to get through another twenty-four hours? The thoughts she had been pushing into the background surfaced and she gagged on her coffee and had to snatch up her napkin and pretend that it had gone down the wrong way and that she'd choked rather than gagged, so that Rose wouldn't have her heart torn out with sympathetic suffering to match her own.

"It's all right," she gasped, and tried to smile, but she saw the flinch in Rose's answering smile and knew that her own must look ghastly. "I can't eat any more, but it was good. I'll get up now."

Get up now, wash, get into your riding habit, let Rose brush your hair and arrange it, or William will be displeased. And, oh God, what horse will I ride, what horse did he order for me, now that Rora's dead?

Aurora! Eugenia's shoulders began to shake uncontrollably, and she put her hands over her face and the tears came, floods of tears to scald her eyes that had already been scalded dry the day before and the day before that, burned so dry of tears that it was impossible that there could be any more. But still they came, drenching her face, seeping out between her fingers.

Rose's arms enfolded her, held her close, rocked her.

"Don't, girl dear, don't! The good beast isn't suffering, she's at peace, and she wouldn't want you to grieve like this. She'd want you to remember all the good times, all the sunny paths, all the wonderful jumps, all the rabbits that scurried out of your way while you laughed to see them go, and the violets under her feet in the spring and the leaves in the fall. Mavourneen, you've had all that, nothing can take it away from you, it's yours and it always will be."

Eugenia heard her words, but they were drowned out by the memory of Aurora's agonized shrilling as the mare struggled to regain her feet, her right foreleg broken. And Eugenia was running again, running from the garden where she'd been inspecting the gardener's expert pruning of the roses against this summer's blooming, her mind black with dread, trying to deny what she heard, trying to blank it out even as her feet raced faster to the ring where Morris, the trainer, had been putting Rora over the hurdles. And knowing, all the time she tried to blot it out, what had happened and that time couldn't be turned back so that it had never happened.

She'd told Morris, how many times she'd told him, not to force Rora over that last hurdle so fast, not to push her, to let her find her own rhythm, that Rora could do it if he didn't throw her off. She'd told him but William had told him to do it, to force her to his will, to smooth out her performance until it was perfect. Because Rora had to be perfect, just as everything William owned had to be perfect, in the eyes of his fellowmen, including his flawed wife.

As Eugenia reached the ring, Rora was struggling to her feet, her eyes rolling with agony and panic. Pat, the young stableboy, was pelting toward the house to fetch the master, his own eyes bulging out with terror.

Her arms around Rora's neck, her face pressed against her darling's warm, sweet-smelling coat, Eugenia's eyes widened with protest as William strode toward them, a pistol in his hand.

"No, William, no! Please don't!"

"Control yourself, Mrs. Northrup." William never raised his voice. "Stand away. She must be destroyed."

Convulsively, Eugenia's arms tightened around Rora's neck. Ruthlessly, without haste, William pulled her away. "Go back to the house."

Eugenia held her ground, her eyes streaming and blank with grief. "William, let me hold her!"

And then the report filled the air, filled the world, there was nothing but the report that sent the bullet into Rora's brain.

"Come, mavourneen, come back to the house. It's over, the dear creature isn't suffering anymore, come with me." Rose, drawn by the commotion, was beside her, supporting her, urging her away while Rora still twitched on the ground, her eyes glazing in death.

It all came back, relentless in its clarity, every detail etched in Eugenia's mind for all time. Rora was dead, she'd never ride her again, never press her face against that warm, sweet coat again. The sleek chestnut body, the muscles rippling with eagerness to be set in motion, was buried in the pasture, the soft whicker of greeting when Rora saw Eugenia coming was stilled forever.

"Child dear, you must get up. He'll be waiting." Rose never used William's name if she could help it, the very sound of it tasted bitter on her tongue.

Rose choked back her cry of outrage as she slipped Eugenia's nightgown off her shoulders and saw the bruises on her breasts, on her upper arms. Livid, the purple already turning black, they stood out against the milky flesh, mute evidence of the torment that devil

13

had put her through last night. Hastily, Rose pulled a fresh chemise over Eugenia's head, pretending that she hadn't seen.

Why was it, as faithful as she was, and with all the candles she burned and all the prayers she raised to the saints, that her darling still had to suffer as she suffered under the hands of the monster who walked the earth in the guise of a human being? If it wouldn't have been a deadly sin, she'd have prayed that William Northrup would be struck dead. But you couldn't pray for someone's death; the penances Rose had undergone after the horror of the priest when she'd had to confess that she wished that she could pray for it, proved that. All the same, where was the sin in praying that something would happen so that Eugenia would be set free?

Maybe if she were allowed a statue of the Virgin in her room so that she could concentrate better on her prayers, something would happen. But William Northrup allowed no idols in his house, he made frequent inspections of the servants' quarters to make sure that no such papist obscenities were housed under his roof, even turning out closets and looking under the beds and chairs. Some of his servants might be Irish Catholics, because they would work the hardest for the poorest wages, but no evidence of their faith was to be allowed, except for the rosaries that they refused to give up, and even they had to be kept out of sight and not left lying about where the sight of them might bring some comfort in passing by.

Eugenia was ready at last. She left the luxurious bedroom, a setting fit for a queen, and descended the broad staircase to the black and white tiled central hallway below, its crystal chandeliers dark now, the modestly draped statues dim in the half-light. Her blue velvet habit was perfection, her plumed hat sat at exactly the correct angle on her silver gilt hair, her boots gleamed with polish, her hands were perfectly kept under her gloves, because William would know, in his uncanny way, whether or not they met his standards even though they were covered.

The dining room was also in half-gloom in spite of the brilliance of the April sun outside the heavily draped windows. An enormous room, richly paneled, capable of seating forty guests at its mahogany table, it had been designed for candlelight, not sunlight. And alone in all this glory William Northrup sat at the head of his table finishing his breakfast. Fully dressed, impeccable as he always was, at forty-five the master of Retreat was still a remarkably handsome man in spite of the coldness of his face and eyes.

He rose to his feet as his wife entered the room. "Good morning. You are three minutes late." Courteous, his manners without flaw. Eugenia wondered for the thousandth time how he could present such a face to the world after what he had put her through. Why, now of all times, when she was so torn apart with grief over the loss of the only living creature available to her, outside of Rose, who could give her comfort, had he inflicted himself on her last night with the full force of his brutality, when at other times he would leave her alone for days or for weeks, blessedly alone even though she never ceased trembling inside from wondering what new cruelty he was devising to torment her?

To the world at large, William and Eugenia Northrup were an ideal couple, fond of each other, their lives contented and happy even though they had had to face the disappointment of being childless. No one except Rose knew the extent of William's wrath because the girl he had selected from dozens of other suitable girls to be his wife had proved to be barren.

Eugenia had been seventeen when William sued for her hand. Her sister Laura, eight years older, had already been married for five years, and lived in Baltimore with her husband, Daniel Gateman, and was the mother of three fine boys. Eugenia and Laura were all that were left to their parents. Their three brothers had all been drowned in a tragic boating accident when they'd been caught by a storm when they'd had their small craft out on the river several years before. Their loss had all but ruined their parents' lives, and from that day on their only thoughts had been to see both of their daughters married and secure so that they could die in peace and escape the grief that had shattered them beyond recovery.

Although the Randolphs boasted a flawless ancestry and could trace their origins to the early days of the settling of America and before that to a substantial position in English society, Bertram Randolph's business acumen had deserted him after the death of his sons, and he had failed to maintain his fortune as it should have been maintained. Although the family continued to live comfortably in their New York City mansion without betraying to the public that their fortunes were waning, there would be virtually nothing left for Laura and Eugenia to inherit.

When Laura had married well, half of their burden had been taken from them, and marrying their younger daughter to William Northrup had seemed a blessing. William was tremendously wealthy, the only heir of the last of a long line of Dutch patroons. His mother, a Drees, had married William's father, Stephen Northrup, and brought her fortune to add to his.

This fortune had grown and been turned over intact to William when not only his mother and father but his two sisters and his older brother had all been carried away in an outbreak of cholera. William, the youngest, was the only one of his family to survive. His natural hardiness of both mind and body had enabled him to add still more to his fortune, doubling it so that when he had finally gotten around to selecting a wife, he was a catch that half of New York society was eager to pull in.

But to the chagrin of New York's elite, William had shown no sign of wanting to relinquish his single state until he had reached the age of thirty-five and met Eugenia Randolph shortly after she had been presented to society. Eugenia had never been dangled in front of William at all, not only because she'd been too young but because it had never occurred to either Rebecca or Bertram Randolph that William Northrup would be interested in a girl who could bring him so little.

Eugenia was lovely, her face a perfect, classic oval, her silver blond hair a perfect foil for her dark blue eyes. Her disposition was gentle, and she was given to dreaming. Her friends often exclaimed, "Oh, that Eugenia! She'd rather read about Sir Lancelot than find a knight in shining armor of her own! She'll never catch a husband unless she comes down to earth!"

That wasn't exactly true. Eugenia had as many romantic hopes as any normal young girl. Her problem was that she wasn't sure that she could measure up in the marriage market. She hadn't failed to notice the vicious intensity with which families competed to obtain the most eligible of young gentlemen for their daughters. It smacked of the auction block. The whole process made her feel a little ill.

Besides, it wasn't a Sir Lancelot she wanted, or a man rich in worldly goods, but someone gentle and kind like her sister's husband, Daniel Gateman. Everyone had been astounded when the beautiful Laura Randolph had chosen Daniel, who wasn't handsome at all and who possessed only a moderate fortune, but Eugenia understood it very well. If Daniel had had nothing at all, Laura would still have chosen him, and it was only a pity that there wasn't another Daniel Gateman for Eugenia.

She went through the usual cases of puppy love, all of which came to nothing. The young men liked a girl who flirted, who made them believe that they were the most exciting men in the world. Eugenia was beautiful, but there was always a part of her that was withdrawn from them, a part they couldn't touch. And so they turned to girls who knew how to pamper their egos, and Eugenia turned back to her books, always telling herself that someday another Daniel Gateman would appear and then it would be her turn to find the love and the lifelong happiness that Laura had achieved.

When she met William Northrup at a ball a few weeks after her debut in society, it didn't occur to her that he might be the man. In the first place, he was far too rich and far too handsome, and in the second place he was old, a full sixteen years older than she was. Also, she sensed a coldness about him—despite his attentiveness. She saw the envious glances that were directed at her when William asked her to dance, but she was glad when the number ended, and relieved because all of her other dances were spoken for. And then she had put him out of her mind, certain that he would play no part in her life.

After she had returned home with her parents, she was astonished when Bertram Randolph told her that William Northrup had asked his permission to call on her.

"But why would he want to do that?" Eugenia blurted out. "He's old, he can't possibly have any interest in me!"

"He isn't old, Eugenia," her father told her, frowning. "For a gentleman, he's in the prime of life. And you are an attractive young lady, so you shouldn't be surprised that any personable gentleman should wish to call on you."

Panic rose in Eugenia's breast. "You didn't tell him that he could, did you?" What on earth would she say to him, how could they find any common ground to conduct even an ordinary conversation? The sixteen years between them loomed as uncrossable as sixty.

Rebecca Randolph had spent a lifetime learning to conceal her emotions, but Eugenia was a sensitive girl and she saw the worry in her mother's eyes.

"Eugenia, dear, I hope that you realize what a wonderful opportunity this is for you. There isn't an unattached young lady in society who won't envy you! It's time you were thinking of the future. Mr. Northrup is eminently eligible."

Eugenia's initial emotion at the prospect of being courted by William Northrup was one of bewilderment. She couldn't for the life of her understand what a man of such wealth and prominence could see in her. There were dozens of girls who were better qualified than she was for William to choose from.

What Eugenia didn't know was that William Northrup was looking for particular qualities in a wife, qualities that Eugenia possessed in abundance. The first and most important was that boys were predominant in her family. Her mother and her sister had each produced three boys; good.

Second, and almost as important, William wanted a wife who would be tractable, who would always bow to his wishes without question. And third, in order to ensure that she would remain tractable, it was necessary that her family was neither wealthy enough nor powerful enough to interfere in case their daughter showed signs of unhappiness under his domination.

William had done his research carefully. He knew, to the penny, exactly what Bertram Randolph was worth, that Eugenia's parents would be so gratified that he'd chosen their daughter for his wife that they would never dream of questioning his removing her entirely from their society. His wife was to be his, as much his possession as his money, his estate on the Hudson River, his paintings and statues and horses, not to be shared even with her own family. Once they were married, she was to be his alone, another acquisition to be put on display when it met his convenience and his fancy to display her.

It was true that there were other eligible girls who were more beautiful than Eugenia Randolph, but William was an expert at seeing the potential in many things that other men might have passed by. With his money and resources, he knew that he could transform her into the beauty of the decade, that he could make other men drool with envy because he was the one who owned her. It was essential to William that he should always be envied, that other men should look up to him as invincible in every aspect of his life.

Another thing that Eugenia didn't know about was William's single-mindedness of purpose once he'd made up his mind to acquire something he wanted. Having made up his mind, he set about winning her, and with his striking, dark handsomeness, and the charm that he could call up at will, there was little chance that he would fail. He sent flowers, and small but very expensive gifts that would be acceptable to a young lady of breeding. He took her, in company with her parents, to the best establishments for dinner, for drives in the country in an equipage that brought gasps of admiration from street urchins. He conducted them on a tour of his estate, Retreat, the widespread lawns impeccably kept, the mansion commanding a view of the river that was unparalleled, the stables and his champion horses enough to strike less fortunate people dumb.

He was unfailingly kind and considerate with Eugenia. He asked her her preferences, he sprang to fulfill her slightest wish as though his only desire in life were to please her and make her happy. It would have taken a far more experienced girl than Eugenia to see through this surface charm to the iron will underneath, to realize that by marrying him she would deliver herself into a life of total slavery.

What Eugenia saw, and little by little came to believe, was that in spite of being almost twice her age, William was the most handsome, the kindest and most gentle man she could ever have dreamed of marrying. That he actually wanted to marry her filled her with bewildered gratitude. All of her friends looked at her through new eyes that were filled with envy. She was to be Mrs. William Northrup, the mistress of Retreat! Her life would be a fairy tale, something that most mortals are only privileged to dream about.

She fell in love with William; she could not conceive how she had managed to exist before he had come into her life. He was her world.

Only Laura attempted to cast a note of caution.

Gina, darling, I don't wonder that you're ecstatically happy, having accomplished what countless other females have attempted to accomplish over the last fifteen years. But I am concerned, because your head seems to be completely in the clouds. Your William is probably everything that you're convinced he is, that most unique of creatures, the perfect man. Nevertheless, you must remember that he's a great deal older than you, and that older men who marry young wives have a tendency to become overbearing, to treat their wives as children. You must take care that this does not happen in your case. Naturally, being so much younger, you'll be inclined to look up to him, to believe him to be right in all things, but this might not always be true. Don't, I beg of you, forget that you are a human being in your own right, that you have a mind and intelligence of your own and the right to exercise them.

Enough of such direful warnings! In this case, I hope that a word to the wise will be sufficient. Now for happier things. Daniel has agreed that we shall attend your wedding! I am already in a flurry of packing. I can hardly wait to see you again. Your loving sister, Laura.

William had begun his courtship in mid-December of 1853. And in spite of convention, he pursued his courtship with such fervor that they became formally betrothed on February 14, 1854. Eugenia's betrothal ring was a sapphire that exactly matched her eyes, set all around with diamonds. And in spite of Rebecca Randolph's horrified protests, he insisted that the wedding must take place on the fifteenth of June of that same year.

Caught up in the prenuptial excitement, Eugenia's head, just as Laura had cautioned her, was in the clouds and she forgot the feeling of firm ground underneath her feet. Her days were passed in a dreamlike haze of happiness. How could she, of all the girls in the world, be the one who was so fortunate, so blessed by fate?

The arrival of Laura and Daniel and her young nephews early in June only increased her excitement. Laura was radiant, her dark-haired beauty so vibrant that if Eugenia hadn't been so radiant herself she would have paled into insignificance beside her older sister. But Eugenia had been so transformed that Laura gasped with disbelief when she saw her.

"Snow White and Rose Red!" Laura said, enfolding Eugenia in a hug that left her breathless. "They could use us for the illustrations in that fairy tale! Eugenia, if I were inclined to be jealous of little sisters, I'd be green with envy! I take back everything I said in my letter. If William Northrup can make you look like this, he must be everything you say he is and a whole lot more!"

Not even Laura, much less Eugenia, had any inkling of what this most brilliant of all weddings was costing Bertram and Rebecca Randolph. Their fund of ready cash was pitifully low, and an affair of this magnificence all but stripped them clean. William knew, and was satisfied to leave it that way, making no offer to help defray the expenses. If the Randolphs were left almost totally without funds to fall back on, outside of the house that they were determined to maintain until they died, for the sake of their pride, all the better. When Eugenia left for an extended European honeymoon she had no idea that she left behind parents who were virtually impoverished.

William took her to Paris, to Rome. Every day was filled with delights that she had only read and dreamed about, every night was filled with lovemaking that left her breathless and filled with wonder. Because William was an accomplished lover he brought her to the heights of ecstasy. He was generous, as well, buying her so many Paris gowns that they had to purchase more trunks to hold them all.

When she remembered Laura's warnings, Eugenia had to laugh. William was the most perfect husband in the world, and she worshiped him next only to God.

They returned from Europe in mid-September, just in time for Eugenia to revel in the changing colors of autumn as the countryside turned to flame along the Hudson River. And she had ample time to enjoy the season, as well as the riding lessons that William insisted she have with his trainer, Morris. If the man had any other name, Eugenia never learned it. A thin, taciturn man of indeterminate age, Morris knew horses, and how to teach. Outside of that he made no conversation at all.

It never occurred to Eugenia, with her gentle nature, that for Morris or any of the other servants at Retreat to enter into a casual conversation with her, on any subject, would be looked upon by William as a serious infraction and lead to that servant's dismissal. And by the time she learned it, it seemed of little importance. William was right in all things, and all she had to do was accept it.

In the matter of Rose O'Riley, William indulged her although it was against his better judgment. He would have preferred for her to have an older, more experienced ladies' maid to care for her intimate needs, but Eugenia had taken a liking to Rose, who was only a little older than herself. Most of the other servants at Retreat were middle-aged and solemn and Eugenia felt a little intimidated by them, but the Irish girl always had a smile for her and was so naturally friendly that Eugenia asked for her and William consented.

In the privacy of Eugenia's bedroom she and Rose became friends in spite of the fact that one was the mistress and the other a servant. It was Rose who explained to Eugenia how impossible it would be to foster any sort of human commerce with any of the other servants.

In answer to Eugenia's question of "Why?" Rose's answer was, "Because Mr. Northrup wants it that way."

And of course, if that was the way William wanted it, then it must be right, even though her own mother had conversed in a casual manner with her few servants about such things as the weather or to ask after members of their families. Retreat was, after all, a world of its own and must have its own rules.

She had been a little worried about managing a household as large as this, although William had told her not to concern herself. The mistress of any house, large or small, was expected to manage it efficiently and Eugenia had received all the proper training from her mother. But she found, immediately after her arrival, that she had almost nothing to do. Mrs. Lindstrom, the housekeeper, was so efficient that Eugenia was consulted only about menus that had already been drawn up, needing only her approval. Everything else at Retreat ran like well-oiled clockwork.

So Eugenia entered into an ideal existence of riding, which she developed a passion for, of being called on or calling on ladies of the few neighboring estates, of being a perfect hostess when she and William entertained and a perfect guest when they were entertained. The ingress of affluent people to the Hudson River Valley was not yet in full swing—that did not happen until after the Civil War—and so Eugenia's duties were light and she liked it that way, being supremely happy with things just the way they were.

The only shadow on her happiness was that she had not yet conceived. But even that failed to mar her contentment until William began to show his own concern. If William wanted a child, a son, then she must give him one. Producing his heir was the only thing she could do for him in return for all he had done for her.

She had long consultations with Rose, who knew a good deal of folklore, having emigrated from Ireland, where folk medicine was still practiced by all except the wealthy. She swallowed nauseating concoctions, and she prayed, and Rose burned candles. None of these things were effective. When winter set in, and her riding was curtailed, she had a wild hope that perhaps her riding had kept her from conceiving, but as the winter months passed she had to give up that hope as well.

William continued to be kind to her, to lavish her with everything a woman could possibly desire. The physicians he consulted told him that there was nothing to worry about, that it was not unusual for so young a bride to remain childless for one or even two or three years after marriage. Eugenia was healthy, her family had been prolific, and William was at the peak of his virility.

And so the winter passed. Vanderbilts and Astors were guests at Retreat, and they were guests at Vanderbilt and Astor mansions in New York City. They were intimate with every illustrious family in New York, if only for business reasons connected with William's own enterprises, but only when William chose to be. The periods when William preferred to remain at Retreat and see no one, have contact with no one, came often. Sometimes it was hard for Eugenia to understand her husband's moods, but as long as he loved her, it didn't matter. Mama had warned her that gentlemen had moods and could be difficult and that it was a wife's duty to remain serene and accept it. All things taken under consideration, she was still the most fortunate woman in the world.

2

Eugenia welcomed the first mild days of spring with eagerness. She had become an expert horsewoman, and she loved the sleek, beautiful creatures that were at her disposal. The fact that William seldom rode with her was a disappointment that she choked down. A superb horseman himself, her husband seldom had the time or the inclination to ride. His business affairs were so demanding that he often worked in his study until the small hours of the morning, or was away from home entirely for days or even a week or more at a time.

On the anniversary of their wedding, they gave a ball, and William's gift to her was a sapphire necklace and earrings to match her engagement ring. She had no idea of what they had cost, or that many of the gentlemen who attended the ball wished that they had that much money to invest in something more worthwhile than baubles. Their respect for William rose another notch, and William knew it and took satisfaction from it.

Summer merged into autumn, autumn into another winter. Eugenia saw almost nothing of her parents. For some reason, they never seemed to appear on the guest lists of any of the places Eugenia and William were invited, and except for special occasions such as holiday balls and their anniversary ball, William told Eugenia that they would feel out of place among their other guests.

Eugenia missed them, they had been a close and loving family, but a wife's first duty was to her husband and she deferred to William's judgment. She had no way of knowing, and William did not choose to tell her, that her father was in such financial straits that he and Rebecca could no longer afford to entertain or even to accept invitations that would have to be reciprocated.

Eugenia and Laura wrote to each other regularly, however. Laura's letters were filled with trivial bits of information about her three sons.

> And now for a bit of earth-shattering news. I am to become a mother again! And why are you such a slowpoke? Or are you keeping the news from me as a surprise? Here I am, expecting my fourth child, and if this one is another boy I'm going to scream because I want a daughter to dress in ruffles and to spoil rotten. And now, I must tell you about. . . .

Laura's letters were always long, it was her nature to talk incessantly and the trait spilled over onto paper. As the cost of postage, which inhibited most people from writing more than one closely worded page, meant nothing to either her or to Eugenia, they were able to indulge themselves as much as they pleased.

Sighing, Eugenia folded this last letter and lay it with the others that she read over and over. Three sons, three fine, healthy boys, and another child on the way, while she herself couldn't produce even one child for the man she worshiped. But she mustn't complain. She had William, and this magnificent estate, she had the love not only of William but of Laura and her mother and father, and even of Rose. Except for this one thing, she was the most fortunate of women.

The second year of her marriage passed, and then the third and the fourth. William wasn't as attentive to her now. They had had separate bedrooms from the start. William had explained to her that allowing her the privacy of her own room was a mark of his respect for her, and that she would sleep better if she didn't have to share a bed where he was inclined to restless tossing as he mulled over business problems.

Eugenia didn't personally know of any other married couple who had separate bedrooms. Her mother and father had always shared a bed and she knew that Laura and Daniel did also. But she accepted William's decision with gratitude, as proof of his love for her. Didn't his lovemaking, when he came to her at night, prove that he loved her as few women had ever had the privilege of being loved?

But during this fifth year of their marriage, William's visits to her bedroom, which had slackened off during the last two years, dwindled to only an occasional visit. Sometimes two or even three weeks went by without him taking her in his arms. And they attended fewer social functions, they entertained less frequently. William seemed withdrawn, preoccupied, often cold.

"Darling, is anything wrong? Have I done something to displease you?"

"Nothing is wrong. We aren't newlyweds anymore, Eugenia. I am a busy man, you must find ways of amusing yourself as other wives do and refrain from clinging to me as though you were a child."

Eugenia choked down her hurt. She didn't cling to him! She tried to be the most understanding and considerate of wives, she only had to know if it were any fault of hers that they seemed to be growing apart. But she had had little experience with men, and probably William was right in this as he was in everything else.

"Shall I accept the Martindales' invitation to their gala? And we owe the Vancouvers a dinner, what would you like me to do about that? Would two weeks from Friday be convenient for you?"

"Decline the Martindales' invitation, I shall be tied up with business matters. And postpone the Vancouvers, I'll let you know when it will be convenient. Excuse me, I have papers to attend to."

With growing despair, Eugenia realized that something was seriously wrong with their marriage, and with a chill that penetrated to her core she knew that it was her failure to conceive. The realization that there was nothing she could do about it, that she was completely helpless in the matter, only deepened her depression. Why, out of all the women in the world, should she be the one who was childless, when William had such an overwhelming need for heirs to carry on his name? She would have given her life for him without a second thought, but she couldn't give him the one thing he wanted.

On top of Eugenia's worry about her marriage, she had another worry that preyed on her mind continually. Bertram Randolph's health was failing. Her mother had written her that he might not live until spring. Rebecca made no reference to their financial affairs. Money was never discussed in polite society, even between mother and daughter. Finances were the exclusive province of men. But worry over his declining fortunes, added to blood pressure that was already too high, had put a strain on him that was too severe for a man of his years. His heart was bad, his appetite had fallen off until he had no interest in food, and he had bouts of severe indigestion that left him weak and trembling.

Bertram died on the first day of June. Rebecca, torn by her grief and totally incapable of coping with all the details, welcomed William's offer to see to everything. Eugenia herself was devastated. She'd loved her father, who had always been kind to her in spite of his grief over the loss of his sons. She blamed herself because she hadn't seen more of him during the years since she had married, she should have been there to comfort him. She'd been too wrapped up in her own happiness to realize how much he must have needed her, and so she felt guilt along with her grief.

"Mama, you'll come and live with William and me, of course. You can't go on living in this big house all alone."

Rebecca didn't tell Eugenia that there was no way she could continue living in her house, that there wasn't the money to maintain it and that it was already mortgaged to the hilt. Neither did she tell Eugenia that William had already decided for her. Entirely dependent on her husband all of her married life and on her father before that, she took it for granted that now that Bertram was dead she must abide by whatever her son-in-law saw fit.

"You'll go and live with your daughter Laura, of course," William told her. "With all of her children, she'll welcome your help, and your life will be filled with your grandsons to assuage your grief. I'll arrange for your journey myself, and take care of salvaging whatever I can for you from the sale of your house and furniture so that you won't feel that you're a burden to Daniel."

So when Eugenia asked her to live with her and William, Rebecca told her that she had already decided to go to Baltimore and make her home with Laura. Exactly six weeks after Bertram was buried, Eugenia said good-bye to her mother, leaving her feeling more alone and desolate than she had ever felt in her life.

On the day after her mother's departure, William produced a surprise for Eugenia that he told her would help her over the sharpest edges of her grief. He took her hand, a gesture so unusual lately that her eyes filled with tears, and led her outside the house.

There, by the mounting block, Morris was walking the most magnificent young mare that Eugenia had ever seen. Half Arab, the mare's coat gleamed red in the sunlight, as sleek as satin. Her mane was long and thick on a finely arched neck, her head was delicately molded, her feet dainty and dancing as she tossed her head and snorted as she fought against Morris's restraint.

"William!" Eugenia's cry of delight came from her heart. "Do you mean she's mine, actually mine? I can't believe it!" William did love her, all of her doubts and fears had only been her imagination, built up out of her guilt at being childless. No man who didn't love his wife dearly would present her with a gift like this! "When can I ride her? May I ride her now?"

"She isn't ready for a lady to ride, Mrs. Northrup." Morris touched his cap, his forehead beaded with perspiration as he attempted to keep the high-spirited creature under control. "She needs gentling and smoothing out. I'll have her ready for you as soon as I can."

"See that you do that!" William's voice was sharp as he spoke to his employee. "And see that you don't break her spirit in the process! I won't have her ruined."

"What is her name? Oh, you beautiful creature!" Eugenia was already beside the mare, reaching her hand to caress the silken forehead. The mare tossed her head and reared, her eyes rolling.

"Easy, Mrs. Northrup! Have a care for her teeth!" Morris warned, hauling the mare back down to all four of her feet, and perspiring even more profusely as he struggled to calm her.

"Her name is Aurora, after the goddess of dawn," William answered her, ignoring Morris's difficulty. "And once she's been gentled, you'll own the finest mount along the Hudson! I took a great deal of care in selecting her for you, a mare worthy of my beautiful wife."

Morris held his tongue. It wasn't for him to argue with his employer, but in his private opinion this mare would never be fit for a lady to ride. She was too wild, too spirited, it wouldn't be safe, Mr. Northrup must have left his wits behind him when he'd chosen this mare for his wife.

William's wits had been entirely with him when he'd chosen the mare. He knew horses, few men knew them better. There was a wild streak in this particular animal, as beautiful as she was. She'd never be reliable, and for a woman to ride her would be foolhardy. She'd be certain to be thrown. And if she were thrown, and if she were badly injured, she might die. Sometimes, it had often happened, there were internal injuries that didn't show up immediately, and the thrown rider died much later.

William had reached the end of his patience. He'd married to beget children, sons. Outside of her failure to produce those sons, Eugenia was a tractable girl, beautiful, and a wife other men envied him. But the one bald fact remained: She had produced no children, and by now William was certain that she never would.

He knew that the fault was not his. He had fathered a child, by a casual mistress he'd kept, over a period of years, more to elevate himself in the esteem of other men who took such things for granted than because he felt a need for loving companionship from any woman. He hadn't loved Lila, or even felt affection for her. She'd been decorative, and filled the purpose of letting his peers know that he was a normal man even if he hadn't seen fit to marry. Lila, on her part, had worshiped him, had accepted what he was willing to give her, and never asked for more.

When Lila had become pregnant, William had felt neither pleasure nor displeasure. Bastard children were an accepted thing among gentlemen of his station, and would only serve to further elevate him in the estimation of other men, who felt that a man who didn't father children was no real man at all. He could well afford to educate the child and give it a start in life.

But fortunately or unfortunately, Lila miscarried, and lost her life in the process. William never had a chance to find out whether he had fathered a son or a daughter. The only thing he was certain of was that the child had been his, because Lila had been faithful to him, she'd loved him with a single-minded love that precluded any possibility of the child being fathered by some other man.

He had felt no grief over Lila's death. It was time that he selected a wife and fathered legitimate children. He'd arranged for Lila to have a decent burial, and then turned his attention to the market in eligible girls.

But his wife, the wife he'd chosen with such care, was barren. And as long as she lived William would be burdened with her, burdened with a woman who was of no use to him. Divorce was impossible, because to rid himself of her by legitimate means would be a public admission that Eugenia was less than perfect. An accident, however, would be a convenience to him. There was still time for him to get heirs, if he could rid himself of this barren wife. There were other ways he might accomplish it, but a riding accident would be so aboveboard that there would be no suspicion at all, but only sympathy for his pretended grief.

"Don't go near her, Mrs. Northrup. She's wild," Morris said. "This one's going to take a lot of work, and I still have my doubts." Then he clamped his mouth shut, afraid he'd said too much, because

31

to express doubts about any choice of William Northrup's wasn't a wise thing to do. "It'll be weeks before I can get her into shape so that you can try to ride her."

Eugenia went back to the house, bitterly disappointed. Aurora was so beautiful! And she needed distraction right now, she needed a challenge, something that would engross her so completely that she'd be able to forget her aching loneliness for her mother and sister, her gnawing grief for her father.

To occupy her mind, she wrote a letter to Laura and her mother, but it was difficult to write as if all were right with her world because her mother and sister shouldn't be burdened with her own troubles while they too were trying to adjust to the loss of their husband and father. After she'd finished the letter, she went back to the stables.

Morris was in the ring, exercising another horse and putting it through its paces, and the stable was deserted.

She approached Aurora's box stall, moving slowly and gently so as not to startle her. "Hello, beautiful girl," she said. "Hello, my Rora."

Aurora pranced sideways, her ears flattened against her head.

"Now that's no way to act, darling! I like you, and I want you to like me. We're going to have wonderful times together." Eugenia made no attempt to enter the stall or to reach inside and stroke the nervous animal. She simply stood quietly, speaking in a low, soothing voice.

William had bought this mare for her, a gesture that filled her heart. She must learn to ride her. It was something she could do for William, something that would make him proud of her. She knew how highly he valued her horsemanship when he showed her off to his friends. Not to learn to handle Aurora would be letting him down. And all else aside, she herself had an overwhelming desire to make Aurora her own.

"You just wait and see, you're going to like it here. You're going to be my Rora and I'm going to be your Eugenia. As soon as you're gentled, no one else will ever ride you, we'll belong to each other."

William would think she'd taken leave of her senses, standing here talking to an animal. But it eased the ache in her heart, and she sensed that her voice, her reassurances, were quieting the mare as well. At least Aurora had stopped sidling away from her, and her ears had come up as though she understood her words, although her eyes still rolled nervously in Eugenia's direction, alert for the least threatening movement.

"It's all right. I'm not going to touch you until we become friends. I'm going to come and see you every day when no one else is here, and I'll bring you apples and carrots and lumps of sugar. We mustn't let Morris see, he doesn't approve. It'll be our secret."

There was something about the beautiful animal that touched her deeply. Some sixth sense told her that Rora had been hurt, that she'd been mistreated, that what she needed was kindness and gentle care until she learned to trust human beings again. She had no way of knowing how accurate her feeling was, that William had chosen Aurora because he'd learned that a brutal master had beaten her and so abused her, in his attempt to break her to his will, that her heart was filled with fury against all two-legged creatures. Possessed of an unconquerable spirit, Aurora had fought back until her master had gotten rid of her, defeated and afraid that she'd kill him. A bad horse was a bad horse and the only thing to do was get shut of it.

During the days and weeks that followed, it tore at Eugenia's heart to watch as Morris tried to smooth out Rora's rough edges. "Do you have to be so harsh with her? The bit is too high, you're jerking it too hard, you're hurting her mouth!" Eugenia protested.

"I know, ma'am, but she's got to learn to behave, she's got to learn who's master."

"She only needs time. Take all the time you want, don't push her so hard. Remember what my husband said about not ruining her spirit."

Morris remembered, but he also remembered that William had told him to have the mare ready for his wife to ride within a month, and for him to accomplish that he was going to be forced to use harsh measures.

33

Aurora backed up and pivoted and reared, and he yanked her down again, so hard that blood trickled from the corners of her mouth.

"Stop it! Stop it, I say!" Eugenia raged. "That's enough for today, can't you see she's in a panic? Cool her out and take her back to her stall!"

"Yes, ma'am." Damn the creature! And damn William Northrup for buying it, he who should have known better, and expecting him to work miracles!

Eugenia still rode every day, just as she always had. William kept a large stable in order to have mounts available for guests who had come in carriages. Eugenia was especially fond of Beau, a black gelding with one white stocking, himself so spirited that it had taken her nearly a year to perfect her horsemanship so that she was able to handle him. She enjoyed riding Beau and until Rora had been brought to Retreat she'd never imagined that she'd want another horse, but now she was in a fever of impatience to ride Rora, to make her her own so that Morris would have no more need to misuse her in his attempt to gentle her.

She used every opportunity to visit Rora's stall. The day after her first visit, she took a lump of sugar and held it out on the palm of her hand. Rora backed to the far corner of the stall, trembling. After a few moments of coaxing, Eugenia laid the sugar lump on the top of the half-door and backed away several paces and waited. It took an agonizingly long time for Rora to sidle up to the sugar, a tentative step at a time, investigate it with flaring nostrils, and finally pick it up with her velvety lips.

"Good girl! See, I mean you no harm."

It was two weeks before Rora would accept a lump of sugar from her hand, before she'd accept the apples that Eugenia proffered her.

"Mrs. Northrup!" Morris shouted when he entered the stable unexpectedly shortly after Rora had learned to accept Eugenia's offerings. "What under the sun are you doing? You'll lose your hand, that mare bites, she fair took a chunk out of my shoulder only yesterday!"

"Because you were abusing her!" Eugenia flared back. "And don't concern yourself about my hand. Rora isn't going to bite me."

"You're spoiling her! It's discipline she needs and not coddling! If anything happens to you I'll be held responsible."

"If something does, I'll tell my husband that you had no idea that I was in the stable."

Morris's expression of worry lightened, but there were still lines of apprehension around his eyes. "She's a difficult one, ma'am. I'm not sure you'll ever be able to handle her. But I'm doing my best."

"I know you are. Don't worry, Morris. Rora and I are friends."

Eugenia continued her visits to the stable. Little by little, she gained Rora's confidence until the day came when she was able to enter the stall and stroke the mare's neck, with Rora trembling but not backing away. The next day, Eugenia brought a brush in with her and spent half an hour brushing the silky coat. Rora's nostrils flared and her ears went back, but Eugenia brushed gently, talking to her until she calmed, and after that she accepted the attention calmly. Eugenia was making headway, and she was elated. She was going to have two victories, one in making William proud of her and the other in winning the heart of this mare who had already won hers.

On the first morning after the month William had given Morris to gentle Rora, he rose from his breakfast table and accompanied Eugenia when it was time for her morning ride. Morris had brought Beau around, but as Eugenia prepared to mount he put his hand on her arm and stopped her.

"Beau? It's been a month, Morris. Aurora should be ready for Mrs. Northrup to ride by now. Go and saddle her and bring her around."

Morris's consternation showed on his face. "Sir, do you think it's wise? There are still rough edges. . . ."

"Do as I say! Mrs. Northrup is an expert horsewoman, and she has waited quite long enough."

Morris had no alternative. Eugenia herself was elated, although small shivers of apprehension crept up and down her spine. Could she ride Aurora, could she possibly do it? But William was determined, and Eugenia lifted her chin. She'd ride Aurora for William if it killed her! In this, at least, she wouldn't let him down.

Aurora had never had a sidesaddle on her back, it was completely unfamiliar to her. She backed and sidled, her eyes rolling, while she was being cinched up. Two stableboys had to hold her so that Morris could complete the saddling. Their eyes round with fright, they followed Morris at a discreet distance to the mounting block. Aurora was trembling, her eyes wild. With William frowning with impatience, with one boy holding Aurora's head on either side and Morris in front to try to keep her steady, Eugenia mounted.

Aurora stood stock-still, but every muscle in her body was quivering. Eugenia gathered up the reins. "It's all right, Rora, it's only me. Let's see what you can do."

Gently but with confidence, as she knew was necessary, she touched Rora with her heel and lifted the reins. "Up, Rora!"

Aurora took a tentative step forward, and then another. Eugenia touched her with her heel once more, and neck-reined her to the right, again lifting the reins in the signal for Rora to trot. Aurora was still trembling violently, but she responded. Her gait was so smooth that Eugenia felt her spirits soar. She neck-reined her to the left, then right again, and the mare's response was perfect, although her ears were still laid back and she was still trembling violently.

"All right, Morris. Let's take her to the ring and I'll put her through her paces."

They walked, trotted, neck-reined right and left, turned in circles. Rora had stopped trembling; the mare seemed to realize that carrying Eugenia was far removed from being ridden by anyone else. Eugenia's hand on the reins was gentle but steady, not hurting her, only directing her. Eugenia lifted her into a canter. Keeping close beside her on his mount, Morris's face registered his astonishment. The stableboys, who had run to follow them to the ring, stood just outside with grins splitting their faces from ear to ear. And standing at a distance, William was rock-still, his face expressionless, before he turned on his heel and went back into the house.

Eugenia and Morris kept Aurora in the ring for half an hour, and then even Morris conceded that it would be safe to take her out on the bridle trails that wound through the estate.

"I never saw anything like it," Morris said, his voice filled with wonderment. "I would have sworn that she'd throw you, Mrs. Northrup."

"Rora knows me. She knows that she has nothing to fear from me," Eugenia told him. Gaily, she lifted the mare into a full gallop. Morris paled, and then his face turned green as Eugenia reined Rora from the path to jump a fallen log. The jump was as smooth as silk. Eugenia felt as though she were soaring, flying, her elation filled her to the point of ecstasy. Rora was hers at last, her very own! They belonged to each other.

They returned to the house two hours after Eugenia had first mounted. Eugenia's cheeks flew bright banners of excitement, her eyes sparkled, she was more beautiful than she had ever been in her life.

Her elation carried her on flying feet to William's study, where for the first time she neglected to knock before she entered, but burst in with words already tumbling from her lips.

"Oh, William, it was wonderful! Aurora is the most perfect mare in the world! I love her so much, I can't thank you enough for giving her to me, I'll love you forever!"

Impulsively, she ran around the desk where William was going over some accounts, and leaned over and put her arms around him. Smiling, William rose and encircled her with his own arms and kissed her.

"You're positively radiant," he said. "I'm glad that it went well. I knew that the mare was ready for you to ride. Morris is too cautious."

The gesture of affection made Eugenia's cup of happiness run over. She ran on and on, like a child who'd been given her dearest wish at Christmas. William finally hushed her and pushed her away.

"Run along now, take your bath and make yourself beautiful for lunch. Afterward, we'll go for a drive. We'll stop in at the Vancouver place, there's something I want to talk over with Jacob and you can visit with Estelle while you wait.''

This additional treat was almost too much for Eugenia. Rose had a hard time keeping her tears of joy from showing at this transformation of her mistress, who had been so sad only this morning. And for months before that, the poor lady had looked like a wraith and Rose's heart had bled for her, but now! If it wouldn't be a sacrilege Rose would say that she looked as radiant as Mary must have looked the first time she'd held the Holy Infant in her arms.

Eugenia and William spent a delightful afternoon. Eugenia savored every moment of the carriage ride. She liked Estelle Vancouver, who wasn't as overbearing and proud of her name and her wealth as many of the other women Eugenia knew, even though Estelle was acknowledged as the supreme social arbiter of the Hudson River Valley. At least ten years older than Eugenia, she was far different from her even older husband, who must be nearly William's age but whose stolid pomposity grated on Eugenia's nerves. Eugenia sometimes felt a little sorry for the woman because she suspected that Estelle's marriage had been one entered into for advantage to both sides rather than for love. Not in the least pretty, but with a kind dignity that Eugenia found heartwarming, Estelle had three children, two daughters who took more after their father than they resembled her, and an extraordinarily handsome son who was still a little boy.

She and William returned home to dress for a leisurely dinner. In the candlelight, Eugenia's eyes sparkled and glowed, her cheeks and lips were rosy. This was like a second honeymoon, except that it was even better than the first because now she was sure that William loved her in spite of her failure to give him children. And she had Rora, her own Rora, the whipped-cream topping on top of dessert.

She knew that William would come to her that night, and she prepared for bed with special care. She put on her most beautiful nightgown, of the softest shell pink, sheer and lacy, almost indecent, and she asked Rose to brush her hair until it lay around her shoulders like a shimmering cape, instead of plaiting it in two long braids for the night as she usually did.

William entered her bedroom a few minutes later. He was naked under his dressing robe, and he shed it the moment he closed the door behind him. Eugenia gasped. In all of their married life, she had never seen William naked before. He'd always blown out the lamps before he had gotten into bed and pulled the covers over him. His erection was enormous, and Eugenia couldn't tear her shocked eyes from it.

He crossed the room, his stride purposeful. His hands on her shoulders were rough.

"Get out of that rag!" In another instant, he'd ripped the nightgown from her body. The lamp on the nightstand was still lighted, and he stood looking down at her with an expression of contempt that froze her blood in her veins.

"My wife!" he said. His voice was filled with outraged scorn. "My beautiful wife! So perfect, so exquisite, and so useless!"

Then he was on her, tearing at her, rending her, forcing her terrified and rigid body to accept caresses that she had never dreamed of, performing acts on her that filled her with agony and revulsion. He used her brutally, until she screamed, again and again, until his brutal, bruising mouth covered hers and stilled it.

When he was finished, he left her without a word, without a backward glance, as if she were some piece of spoiled and soiled merchandise that was beneath his contempt. She was covered with bruises where his hands had gripped and held her mercilessly. Her body ached and throbbed, filled with pain. Her trauma was so deep that she couldn't even cry. She just lay there, hurting, wishing that she were dead.

The William Eugenia had married was gone. In his place there was a stranger, by turns indifferent or cruel as the mood struck him. In public, even in the presence of the servants, he was always polite to her, only the coldness of his eyes reminding her of the hatred he held for her. The nights he came to her room to use her as he had used her the first night after she had ridden Aurora brought home his hatred of her even more forcibly. Eugenia lived in dread of those visits, alternated by an almost frenzied wish that he would come and get it over with, because then there were almost sure to be a few nights of respite in between.

But she couldn't be sure even of that. He kept her off balance, so that she never knew what to expect. Once, he visited her five nights in a row, with the consequence that she was barely able to walk for the pain that lashed through her every movement.

He took care never to leave a bruise where even the servants would see it, except for Rose, from whom the marks and bruises couldn't be hidden. He knew that Rose wouldn't dare mention the bruises to the other servants for fear of instant dismissal. It suited William's purpose to let Rose stay on even though he knew that the Irish girl loved his wife and brought her comfort. Another personal maid might prove less loyal and quit her post, but not before she'd spread all she knew among the rest of the household staff, and William was fully aware of how gossip spreads among servants of different households and eventually comes to the ears of their employers. It wasn't the scandal that William feared, but the humiliation of letting anyone know that he held the wife he had chosen to be less than perfect.

Eugenia had no one except Rose to turn to. No wife, especially of a man like William Northrup, would talk about the things he did to her to any of her friends. Even if her pride had allowed it, it would only have made things worse for her at home because her few women friends were the wives of men who were friends and associates of her husband and any coldness on their part would bring repercussions down on her. Even if she'd been willing to take that risk, the men themselves were all in one way or another dependent on William's goodwill and would lift no hand to help her.

In her desperation, she finally wrote to Laura, pouring out her unhappiness and asking her if she could go to live with her and her family in Baltimore. No woman, even a woman who had failed to give her husband a son, should be forced to endure what she had to endure. Eugenia had never been a fighter, she'd never had any reason to be. Her life had been sheltered, so far removed from strife of any kind that now she had no idea of how to cope with it. But she had spirit, although up until now it had remained untapped for lack of any need to draw upon it.

She waited for Laura's reply, and despaired when none was forthcoming. Had her sister, her own big sister, whom she'd loved and looked up to all her life, deserted her? She couldn't understand it, and she spent hours weeping alone in her room.

But Laura had not deserted her younger sister. Far from that, she'd taken immediate action. She and Daniel arrived at Retreat, without notice, less than a month after Laura had received her sister's letter. They'd come without letting Eugenia know, for fear that William would find a way to circumvent them if she'd written that they were coming.

Eugenia's heart leaped when she heard their voices as she entered the house after her morning ride. Her riding crop, which she never used on Rora, clattered to the floor of the entrance hall, and in another second she was in Laura's arms, laughing and crying hysterically.

"Madam, control yourself." William, entirely master of the situation, spoke in a voice of ice. "You're making a spectacle of yourself. I suggest that you go upstairs and bathe and change, and return when you have your emotions under control."

"Just who the devil do you think you are, God Almighty?" Laura burst out, her eyes flashing. "Don't you dare speak to my sister in that manner! Eugenia, I'll come with you, and we'll start packing your boxes. We've come to take you home with us."

William did not so much as acknowledge that she had spoken to him. Let the two women go through the gesture of packing Eugenia's things. The boxes and trunks would never leave this house, and no more would Eugenia. He bowed his stiff, correct bow as they turned to ascend the staircase, and not until they had gained the upper hallway and Eugenia's bedroom door had closed behind them did he turn back to Daniel.

"Come into my study. Do you prefer brandy or whiskey?"

"Neither, thank you." Daniel, not fully aware of the power that William wielded, was in no more of a mood to be friendly with his sister-in-law's husband than Laura was. He'd always liked Eugenia, and he loved Laura and would have walked through fire to get her what she wanted, in this case to get Eugenia away from William.

"Have your own way." William closed the study door behind them and nodded to a comfortable leather chair. Daniel refused it. Sitting down while William continued to stand would put him at a disadvantage. "It's better that we get down to business without the social amenities," William said, his voice pleasantly conversational. "Let me apprise you of the facts, Daniel. There is no way you can remove my wife from my house. The law is clear that a man's wife may not make any move without his permission, that if she leaves him against his will he has the legal right to force her to return to him and to conduct herself as an obedient wife. If you were to take her, I'd see that you were prosecuted to the full extent of the law for kidnapping my legal spouse. Beyond that, I would ruin you and all the rest of your family, including your parents and your uncles and your cousins."

With that, William went on to explain, in full detail, just what steps he would take to bring about this ruin. By the time he had finished, Daniel's face was white and he was trembling with rage. It took all of his control not to attack the man physically, and only the certainty that William would take pleasure in having him arrested and imprisoned for assault held him back.

"Now that you understand the situation, you and your wife are to remain here for a period of two weeks, as you would scarcely have made such a long journey to visit us without staying for at least that long. We will entertain for you, and there will be invitations extended to us in your honor, even on such short notice. We will explain that an unexpected matter of business brought you to New York City and that of course you took advantage of your opportunity to visit your relatives. Have I made myself clear?"

He had, indeed, made himself clear. All of Laura's rage was of no avail, she saw how helpless they were. The fact that both she and Daniel were forced to act as if this were an enjoyable visit rubbed salt in their wounds. Every night during the time that William forced them to stay, Laura was physically ill by the end of the evening, so that she retched and then lay weak and trembling on her bed. It tore at Daniel's heart to see her, and he raged at his own helplessness. If he were any kind of a man, he'd find an excuse to call William out and kill him.

"Don't be an utter ass!" Laura burst out, her face as white as paper. "You know as well as I do that William Northrup is a dead shot. Oh, God, why did my father ever give Eugenia to him, out of all the men in the world? Don't you think I'd kill him myself, if I had any chance of getting away with it? I'm only afraid that Eugenia will find a way to kill him, and then she'll hang!"

Somehow, the two weeks passed. Rose used every artifice at her command to disguise the paleness of Eugenia's face, the circles under her eyes, to conceal any trace of unhappiness from William's friends so that William wouldn't punish her for not presenting a serene face to the world. And all the time, every moment she could steal from her duties, she prayed, fingering her beads and calling on the Holy Mother to intercede for her mistress.

And then Laura and Daniel were gone, and Eugenia was left alone with William. For three weeks he did not enter her bedroom. The suspense of waiting turned Eugenia into a nervous wreck, so that she could hardly speak without stammering, or walk for the trembling of her legs. During every day of those three weeks William was gentle with her, courteous, every inch the doting husband, until her teeth ached from being gritted together.

"Rose, I can't stand it any longer! I'd rather kill myself than wait for him to exact his revenge on me! I'll find a way, you must help me, if you love me at all, you'll help me."

"Heaven forgive you!" Rose gasped. Her plain, homely Irish face was filled with terror, her carrot-colored hair prickled at her scalp. "Taking your own life is the deadliest sin of all, the only sin that can never be forgiven!"

Rose's words, as horrified as they were, wouldn't have stopped Eugenia from committing suicide, but her own will to live did. Her

43

latent courage surfaced, and she determined to fight back with every ounce of her strength.

When William did enter her room, she was ready for him. Her face white and her eyes blazing, she warned him to keep away from her.

"Don't lay a hand on me, William! You are never to lay a hand on me again!"

William laughed at her, mocked her. "So even a cornered mouse will show its teeth! Behave yourself, my dear. Such histrionics are unbecoming. Get into bed, but first remove your clothing. I hadn't thought to find you still fully dressed, and it displeases me."

"Be displeased and be damned!" Eugenia spat at him. "I mean it, William! Don't touch me, don't come near me!"

His face livid with anger, William lunged at her. Her dress, her undergarments, were ripped from her body and tossed into a corner. Eugenia struggled, she fought and bit and kicked and clawed, but her strength was no match for his. When he had her naked, William bore no mark of the struggle except for a few scratches on his face.

He threw her onto the bed. "Stay there, you bitch!" he told her. "Unless you want me to take a horsewhip to you, and don't think for one moment that I won't do it if you continue to behave in this fashion!"

Contemptuous, his face showing his scorn, he began removing his dressing robe. Letting it drop, he turned to throw himself on top of her. But Eugenia had not yet stopped fighting. She was off the bed, backing away from him. As he lunged for her, his face contorted with rage, she snatched up the heavy china pitcher from the washstand and hurled it at him. It was filled with water and awkward and her aim was bad. It struck him, not on his head as she'd intended, but on the most vulnerable part of his body. And Eugenia was strong. Her years of riding had built her strength, and the blow had a terrific impact. William's throat opened to let out one agonized scream, before he fell unconscious to the floor.

A steady stream of doctors, the finest to be had, came and went. Mr. Northrup had met with an accident, he'd fallen and injured himself. Not one of the servants except Rose knew what had actually happened, and neither did the physicians, who were puzzled by the nature of the injury but who didn't dare to question William too closely. However it had happened, the results were clear.

William was impotent. His sexual life had come to an end. He would never father a child.

The sexual loss troubled him little. William had never been a highly sexual man. Sex to him had been a matter of relieving infrequent urges, and of continuing his family line. It was the irrevocable loss of any hope of fathering a child, even if he could find a means to rid himself of his barren wife, that made him vow to spend the rest of his life punishing Eugenia. He intended to make her life a living hell, and he did.

There was no escape. Her husband held a sword over her head, and any attempt to get away from him would bring it down not only on her but on her family as well. Everyone she loved, her sister, her mother, Daniel and her nephews, would suffer. Daniel would be brought to complete ruin, disgraced, never to recover either his reputation or his modest fortune. William told her that he could and would see that Daniel was sent to prison, that it would be a simple matter to pull the strings that would make him appear guilty of any number of frauds. His family would be plunged into poverty and humiliation such as she could scarcely imagine.

Eugenia was completely helpless. She couldn't even contemplate suicide any longer, because William had assured her that if she were to die, he would still carry out his threats.

"Take the utmost care of your health, my dear," William told her, his face hard and his eyes glittering with a coldness that froze the marrow of her bones. "Make sure that you meet with no accident." It was ironic that only a short while ago he had planned for her to meet with an accident, that he'd given her Aurora with the conviction that she would be thrown and that if she weren't killed outright he would be able to expedite her departure from this world and make it appear that her death was the result of her injuries. "The lives of your loved ones depend on it."

And although he could no longer use her sexually, he could, and did, abuse her physically, inflicting on her every cruelty and obscenity he could devise short of the completion of the sex act itself. She was tortured, humiliated, degraded, stripped of her last grain of self-respect. All she had in the world to keep her from going mad was Rose, without whose comfort she would have surely gone mad, and her hours of riding Aurora. William couldn't take that away because her riding the magnificent mare was important to keeping up his image in the eyes of his peers. But Eugenia was never sure, when she woke up in the morning, if Rose and Aurora would still be there.

She knew that William allowed Rose to stay on only because if she were dismissed she might talk, and that he allowed her to keep Aurora because of his pride, reveling in his possession of the most beautiful woman and the most beautiful piece of horseflesh along the Hudson River. But how could she be sure that his thirst for revenge might not sway him to risk the damage to his pride, if his brooding caused his mind to snap?

Slowly, on this April morning of 1864, Eugenia left her bedroom and went down the broad staircase of her prison to enter the dining room for William's inspection.

This morning William did not even glance up. "The horses are waiting," he told her.

Mind and body numb, Eugenia went outside to ride whatever horse William had ordered for her.

3

Liam Donovan's hands were steady as he held the two horses, a rawboned gray hunter called Ranger, for himself, and a beautiful creature named Beau, for the mistress of the house, whom he was to escort on her daily rides.

This was Liam's first day at Retreat. The day before yesterday, William Northrup had interviewed him and told him that he'd give him a trial, and that if he proved satisfactory the position would be permanent.

Liam had good reason to bless his years of experience in handling blooded horses in Ireland, on Sir Malcolm Carlysle's estate. As much as he hated the Englishman who had taken over old Sean Harrigan's holdings after the Irish lord had gone down into bankruptcy under the ruthless English rule, the post had been a good one. Liam had worked for Sir Malcolm nearly all of his adult life, he'd married his Molly, who was Lady Carlysle's personal maid, there, and their daughter Moria, who was the only child with whom they had been blessed, had been born in the cottage that Sir Malcolm allotted to his head horse trainer.

47

It was Liam's politics that had finally driven him from that snug haven. He supposed that it had been bound to happen sooner or later, in spite of how careful he'd been. The English authorities were always on the hunt for the members of all the subversive groups who were determined to wrest Ireland from the English yoke and drive their overlords from their shores, and every Englishman who owned property in Ireland was equally on the alert to weed any such rebels out of his own ranks of servants and see to it that they hanged. And Liam, Irish to the last drop of his blood, had been active in his own branch of the dissidents, his determination to drive the English out the ruling force of his life.

The English rule was insufferable, the Irish groaned under their iron-shod feet, and any Irishman worthy of the blood that ran in his veins belonged to some organization to fight back. No matter how many were caught, others sprang up to take their places.

Unfortunately, not all of those who were taken proved stoic enough to stand up under torture and threat of death, when hope was held out for their lives if they would inform on others. And Liam had been informed on; poor Paddy Sullivan, if ever a man had wanted to be a hero it was Paddy, but his slight, skinny frame and his frightened nature had cracked in the end. Paddy had been born frightened, it had taken more courage than most men are ever called upon to dredge up for him to join the movement in the first place.

A tap on his bedroom window in the dead of night had brought Liam to full wakefulness, every sense alert.

"Paddy's taken, and he's talked. Get your family and get out, they'll be here to take you at first light. I've a cartful of straw, hurry man, for the love of Mary!"

Liam didn't like to think back on the weeks before he'd managed to secure passage in one of the floating coffins that transported impoverished Irish immigrants to the land where the streets were reputed to be paved with gold, and where milk and honey flowed free for the taking. Riding in the wooden-wheeled cart, half suffocating under the straw, had been a nightmare in itself, with their ears straining every step of the way for the sound of pursuing hoofbeats.

They'd made their way in slow stages and through the kindness and courage of others of their ilk to Cork, putting their friends in jeopardy until the journey was accomplished. But escape from Ireland had been essential; if Liam were taken, his life would have been forfeit, and there were Molly and Moria to think of. Sir Malcolm himself would leave no stone in Ireland unturned in the search for him.

Liam had little money saved, but it was enough to secure steerage passage for himself and Molly and six-year-old Moria.

The passage from Cork to New York had been a never-ending scene from Hades. The ship was old and leaked at the seams, the immigrants were packed together below the waterline with scarcely room to move, the food was not only half spoiled but pitifully inadequate. Sickness ran rife and a good many died, men, women and children and babes in arms, God had no favorites when it came to choosing which of his suffering children he'd snatch to his bosom to put an end to their misery.

There were storms that blew the ship off course, one of them so severe that even the captain gave up hope before it blew itself out and allowed the battered ship to limp the rest of the way to harbor.

Liam and Molly and Moria were little more than hollow-eyed skeletons when they debarked. Weak from malnutrition and the dysentery that had swept through the immigrants, they could hardly stand on their feet. Liam had only enough left in his pocket to secure them shelter in a tenement that wasn't fit for human occupancy. The three of them had one room hardly larger than a closet, their bed with a mouse-riddled straw mattress, their blankets whatever clothing they weren't wearing. But they were alive, and they were free. The English law couldn't touch them here.

It took Liam a week to find work loading and unloading drays, the heaviest kind of work, from dawn until dark, for barely enough to keep food in their stomachs. Molly, her dark curls lusterless, her eyes sunken and bleak, struggled to keep Moria clean, struggled to make palatable meals from the potatoes and vegetables she bought wilted and half rotten from the stalls, sold for next to nothing because otherwise they would have been thrown away.

But Liam was strong, a lithe, whipcord six feet of muscle and sinew. Being on solid land again, having better food, no matter how poor it was, restored his strength so that he could put in the long hours of work, and he worked so hard that his work was steady. He and Molly and Moria were no worse off than most of the other immigrants, all of whom found out, with stunned disbelief, that all the tales they'd heard of America were only that, tales to lure them into lives of near slavery at starvation wages. As long as Liam had breath in his body, he could manage to put food in their bellies.

The day they were able to move into better quarters was a milestone. Their new home had two rooms, on the second floor of another tenement, but two rooms, and a few scraps of furniture that they had bargained for in the secondhand stalls. There was a coal stove, there was a real bed, battered but serviceable if you didn't mind its lumpiness, and a cot for Moria in the kitchen.

Water had to be carried, the toilet was an odoriferous outhouse in the back of the tenement, but at last, for the first time since they'd fled Ireland, Liam and Molly had privacy to go into each other's arms, something both of them had refused to do, no matter their agony of longing, while Moria had had to sleep in the same room and the same bed with them.

Liam's constant dread of being without work, Molly's that she would become pregnant, weighed heavily on them. Holy Mother Mary knew that Molly wanted more children. Liam deserved a son, and it was against God's law not to be fruitful. But how could they manage to feed another mouth, when Moria herself was lacking in the ordinary decencies of wholesome food and adequate clothing? Beautiful Moria, so beautiful that it made a lump come to their throats just to look at her.

Molly was a pretty woman, or she had been pretty, back in Ireland when she'd tended Lady Carlysle. Her face had been plump and rosy, her blue eyes had held a sparkle, her dark curls had gleamed with silky life. Liam had thought that she was the prettiest girl in all of Ireland. And Liam himself was extraordinarily good to look at, one of those dark Irishmen with soot-touched blue eyes and a shock of curly hair, lean and well-built and with a zest for living that had attracted the glances of half the colleens in the county. Every time Molly had looked at him her heart had beat faster, and longing to be in his arms had been a fever in her. Except for the constant dread of his being taken, she'd counted herself the luckiest girl ever born.

But Moria! Even at six, Moria was so beautiful that strangers gaped at her in the streets. Her hair was raven black, it was long and thick, lying around her shoulders like a satin shawl. Her skin was so fair that it seemed translucent, her eyes, Liam's eyes, so blue that only Mary's holy robes could match them. Her feet were high-arched, her ankles dainty, her hands graceful and delicate. Every movement was like poetry, and her smile was as radiant as an angel's.

It broke Molly's heart that Moria was growing up without any schooling. Molly herself could neither read nor write, although her accent was good because of her close association with Lady Carlysle, who had detested the Irish brogue and insisted that her house servants speak in what she termed a civilized manner. Liam could read and write, his ambition and drive had made him learn, mostly self-taught except for the help he'd received from his parish priest when he'd been a lad. And he could speak English as well as Malcolm Carlysle, owing to his daily contact with Sir Malcolm and Sir Malcolm's friends. And so Moria had little Irish accent, and her grammar was good, but outside of that she was growing up ignorant.

So Liam, no matter how bone-weary he was, set himself to teach his daughter to read and write, and all he knew about the world. Things were going to be better for Moria. Both Molly and Liam were determined about that. Someday, these lean years would be forgotten, and they'd be able to give her and whatever other children God saw fit to bless them with the things they deserved.

The firing at the steamer *Star of the West* by the South, on January 9, 1861, when the steamer attempted to bring supplies to Fort Sumter, had little impact on Liam. He was too busy trying to earn a living here in America to give much thought to American politics. His dream was to be able to return to Ireland someday and take up the fight there where he'd been forced to leave it off.

Until President Lincoln called for seventy-five thousand volunteers on April 9 of that same year, Liam had given no thought to the fact that slavery existed in the South. There were slaves in the North, but he had never come into contact with them and so hadn't stopped to think about it. But this War Between the States brought it home to him that human beings were kept in bondage here. Ireland was denied to him, but here was something to fight for, a cause to fire an Irishman's soul.

"It isn't our quarrel," Molly said, fear leaping into her eyes. "For the love of Mary and our Moria, let the Americans do their own fighting."

Liam leaned forward, his eyes alight. "A man has to do what he knows is right, girl dear, and I wouldn't be Liam Donovan if I didn't want to do something about those poor black devils."

"But there isn't any need for you to go! This war will be over by Christmas, even sooner, everyone says so. The Southerners haven't got a chance. They don't need you, and Moria and I do! It was bad enough being afraid you'd be killed in Ireland, but I couldn't bear it if I lost you now for a cause that has nothing to do with us."

In spite of her arguments, and in spite of his love for her and for Moria, Liam chafed under the restraint that kept him from rushing off to volunteer. But if he did, how would Molly and Moria live, here in this alien country that had little welcome for the Irish?

"If Saint Patrick could drive the snakes out of Ireland, why can't he drive slavery out of the United States?" Molly demanded, and immediately feared for her soul. All the same, she couldn't bear the thought of Liam going off to fight. Weren't all the years she'd already spent in fear for his life enough for any woman to bear?

"Saint Patrick has enough to do helping the Irish patriots. It's up to us here in America to do something about the slaves on this side of the ocean." Liam's words, his stubbornness, sent Molly into despair. All she had to cling to was the hope that the war would be over before Liam found a way to join the army and go off and get himself killed.

Liam too was in torment. On top of his longing to do his part he had to endure the taunts and jibes, the insults, of people who looked at his strength and accused him of being a slacker.

"Damned Irish, you come to this country and expect us to support you, you take jobs away from honest Americans, but you won't lift a hand to repay us! We shouldn't never have let you come in the first place! Someday we'll get smart enough to ship the lot of you back where you came from!"

The insults were unendurable for a man of Liam's spirit. He often returned home at night with skinned knuckles and a swollen eye or discolored jawbone. Not that he didn't win the fights, except when he was so outnumbered that even an Irishman couldn't overcome the odds. And then Molly would look at him with growing despair, knowing that it wouldn't be long.

It wasn't even as long as she'd dared to hope. Liam burst into their rooms one evening with his face alight.

"I'm going, Molly! Saint Patrick has answered my prayers! A man, a rich man, is paying me to take his place! Five hundred dollars, girl dear, to do his fighting for him, enough to tide you over until we win the war!"

Five hundred dollars! With the war so nearly over, Liam could go with a clear conscience. Molly and Moria would want for nothing. He'd be back long before the money was gone, and with the new freedom, times would boom and soon they'd be living off the fat of the land. Only the fighting remained to be done and that wouldn't take any time at all.

Molly knew that there was no use in protesting, or in tears. Liam wouldn't be Liam unless he was the way he was, itching to get into a fight, burning to make the world a fit place to live in by stamping out oppression. From now on, all she could do was spend every hour she could spare on her knees in front of a lighted candle, praying that he wouldn't get himself killed for his convictions. And she still had Moria. Whatever happened, she'd have that much left.

Liam went through a brief period of training and then he was gone, Molly didn't even know where. Her knowledge of American geography was scanty, the South was another country, completely unknown. Her knees became sore from her hours of prayer, her eyes became darker with dread as she waited out the weeks, and then the months and the years.

There was a handful of letters, only six in all. Tattered, rumpled, weeks or months in reaching Molly. Moria read them to her. They contained no names of places where Liam was fighting. As far as Molly was concerned, he was someplace in limbo, and even when a letter arrived she had no way of knowing whether or not he was still alive. Moria learned to walk to the nearest place where the lists of the dead were posted, and read all of the names so that she could tell her mother that her father's wasn't on it. Not yet.

What Molly did know, what she couldn't escape knowing by now, was that the war wasn't going as well as the North had been so sure it would go when it had started. The Southerners could fight, and they did fight. Their men were brave, seemingly without fear. They had good officers, and they had a deep determination to preserve their way of life. Battles were lost by the Union armies, victories won by the South. And always, in every battle, men were killed. Hundreds of men, thousands. And even Liam did not have a charmed life. Southern bullets knew nothing of Saint Patrick or any of the other saints, they'd kill an Irishman just as fast and as surely as they would kill any other man.

Molly conserved the money Liam had left her. She made every penny do the work of two or even three. Going without became not only a habit, but a way of life.

To make the money last, she took in washing. This meant walking long blocks to pick up the bundles, pulling them home in a rickety cart she purchased secondhand, carrying buckets of water up the stairs, heating it on the coal stove, and spending hours over the washboard. Her hands became chapped and sore from the strong lye soap, her muscles ached from lugging the wet wash down to dry in the tiny area behind the tenement. Her arms and legs became numb from hours of ironing with sadirons.

Moria helped her pull the cart and with the ironing when Molly would let her. Molly never let her put her hands in the wash water no matter how tired she was. Moria's hands had to be preserved, they mustn't be ruined as Molly's were. Moria did her share, without complaining, by sitting on the back step of the tenement and watching to see that no one stole the clothes on the line.

And then Moria became ill, chilled from watching the clothes in bitter weather. At first she was only unnaturally quiet, her usual cheerful spirits listless. Two days later she was running a raging fever and had difficulty in swallowing the soup Molly made for her from the wilted vegetables and scraps of meat clinging to bones that the butcher gave her.

Molly did everything she knew to do, used every ounce of folk medicine she had ever heard of. But Moria's condition worsened, she tossed her head in fever and pushed the spoon away, her eyes dull and glazed.

Doctors were scarce. Many of them had gone with the armies to treat the wounded soldiers; the ones who remained were, for the most part, old and overworked. Nevertheless, Moria had to have a doctor. It took Molly a full day to find one who was willing to come to the tenement.

It was December of 1863. The weather was raw; Molly's feet, innocent of any protection except shoes that had holes in the soles, were soaked, her shawl was wet through from the sleet that poured from a relentless sky, driven by a wind that cut to the bone.

Whether the doctor did Moria any good or not was something Molly never knew. Her daughter had influenza, and the man had little to offer except advice and a small amount of quinine for which he charged an exorbitant price. By the time Moria's fever broke, Molly's fund of cash had dwindled alarmingly.

The days of frantic worry on top of the way her strength had been sapped left Molly defenseless when the same illness struck her. Moria, barely able to stand on her feet, nursed her mother. She was young and resilient, and her strength returned even though she had to get out of bed before she should have, but Molly's ebbed.

Liam returned home on the twentieth day of February, in 1864. He had been with General William Rosecrans when Chattanooga was taken in September of the preceding year, and come out of that battle without a scratch. But on the twentieth day of that same month, the Union forces were routed at the Battle of Chickamauga, and Liam was one of the casualties. A bullet had caught him in the calf of his left leg, cutting to the bone. He'd nearly bled to death before he'd been carried from the field. The camp hospital tent was enough to make the surgeons despair. Infection had set in, and there was one black day when Liam's leg would have been amputated except that the surgeons didn't have the time. By the time they did have the time, the infection had begun to abate. They called it a miracle. But Liam no longer believed in miracles, and put it down to his own strong constitution.

He kept his leg, but he was no longer able to march. He was left with a limp severe enough so that his officers decided that he would be more of a handicap than a help. He was discharged from the army and left to make his own way home as best as he could. The getting home took so long that Molly was dying when he got there.

Skeleton-thin, his eyes hollow from fatigue and hunger, Liam looked down at the wasted body of his wife and for the first time in his life he felt total despair. He wanted to put his face in his hands and weep. Being Liam, he did not. Molly needed him, Moria needed him. He sent Moria back to bed and took over the nursing of Molly himself.

"Liam?"

It was the middle of the night. Liam woke from his fitful sleep, all he got anymore, and turned and took Molly into his arms. Her body was burning up.

"Yes, girl dear. Can I get you some water? Do you think you could swallow some broth?"

Molly shook her head. "I'm not hungry, Liam. Liam, promise me

56

that things will be better for Moria. Promise me that she won't have to live the rest of her life like this. Promise me!''

"I promise, Molly girl, you know I promise! Moria's going to have the best. I'll see to it. You can depend on me, I'll crawl through hell to see that she has everything you want for her!''

"I know you will." Molly rested her head on his shoulder. "She's so beautiful, Liam! And she's good. She deserves the best. She deserves everything we ever dreamed of for her in this new country. Don't take her back to Ireland! She'll only have you now, promise me you won't go back to Ireland and get yourself killed and leave her an orphan!''

Liam swallowed, his heart torn. But Molly was dying, and his promise was all he could give her. He'd brought her to this, and she was paying with her life. He'd have sworn away his soul to bring her comfort now.

"Liam?"

"I love you."

"And I love you." Liam kissed the tears from her cheeks, his own intermingled with them, but Molly never knew that, because her eyes had closed and she sighed once and died.

Liam nearly lost his mind from grief. He hadn't realized how near Molly was to the end, he hadn't even run to fetch a priest. Not that he believed much in such things anymore, he had seen too much, endured too much, to believe any longer that a higher power looked out for people here on earth. But Molly had believed, her faith had been her greatest comfort.

Father O'Brian did what he could to ease Liam's guilt, telling him that Molly's life had been so blameless that the last rites hadn't been necessary to get her into heaven. There was no money for a mass, there was barely enough to light a candle.

The Irish immigrants, most of them nearly as badly off as Liam himself, came for the wake and dropped what they could spare into a bowl, and two or three who had become affluent through means that were questionable, having to do with graft and politics, saw to it that

Molly was laid to rest in the Catholic cemetery and a mass said for her soul.

It was one of these who came to the tenement a few days after the funeral and told Liam that a man named William Northrup was looking for a horse trainer.

"It can do no harm to see the man," Michael McCarthy told him. "He can't do worse than turn you away. The trainer he had maimed a horse so that it had to be destroyed, and Northrup booted him out on the spot, so he needs a new trainer. And you're qualified, with all your years with Sir Malcolm. That leg of yours won't hinder you in the saddle, will it?"

"No, it won't. But who is this Mr. Northrup?"

"He's rich. He's about as rich as a man can get and not be struck down by heaven. He's unscrupulous, he's made more money than I can count by having his finger in every pie that cheats the government by selling shoddy supplies to the army. People, even the wealthiest and most influential, are afraid of him. All the same, it would be a job. For meself, I'd like to have his money, but I wouldn't want to be caught without a chance to have me sins forgiven when it comes me time to die, if I had his black soul in me instead of the faultless one I own!"

The homely, stocky Irishman, only a year or two older than Liam, insisted on taking Liam out to have a drink for luck, and found him a ride in a wagon to take him to Retreat, Michael himself not being without influence for all his faultless soul. Liam liked the man, and he was grateful, especially for Michael's words of warning.

And now he was here, with Moria looked after by a Mrs. Murphy in her boardinghouse, assured by Michael, who had recommended her, that the woman was good-hearted and would see that the child came to no harm. One of Michael's warnings had been not to tell Mr. Northrup that he had a child, as it would mean the loss of his chance to work at Retreat. It was a pity, because Moria would have loved the cottage that was assigned to him, all by himself, as befitted his rank of horse trainer.

But he couldn't think about Moria now. His concern this morning and on all subsequent mornings was to do a good enough job so that Mr. Northrup would keep him on, and to please Mrs. Northrup so that she would lodge no complaints about him with her husband and bring about his dismissal.

Liam had not yet seen the mistress of the house. He expected a vain and snobbish woman in her early or mid-forties, the same kind of person that William Northrup was. He knew from hard experience that pleasing women like Mrs. Northrup wasn't easy, that he would have to watch every word he spoke.

His jaw muscles were knotted as he waited, telling himself that he must make no mistake, that this was the best opportunity he was likely to have for a long time. No matter what he might have to put up with to keep this job, he must bear it. His promise to Molly tormented him. Moria had to have her chance, and there was no way he could keep his promise unless he started somewhere, and that somewhere was here.

The front door opened, and Mrs. Northrup came out, accompanied by a small woman of about thirty who wore a maid's uniform. This second woman had the map of Ireland on her face and hair that proclaimed her nationality at first glance. Liam didn't have to hear her speak to know that when she did her lilt would be like music to his ears. He'd have one ally at Retreat, provided that he could ever get close enough to her to make her his friend.

His gaze returned to Mrs. Northrup then, and he felt a shock travel through his body. She was young, and she was beautiful. He'd have wagered the last cent in his pocket that she wasn't yet thirty. And compounding those two surprises, there was the additional shock of seeing that her face was the most tragic he'd ever seen. Even Molly, on her deathbed, hadn't had that look of utter hopelessness in her eyes, of grief that was more than a human soul could endure. Molly had been loved, she'd had that. And Molly had still clung to her faith that someday things would be better, even if she herself would not be here to see it. This woman had nothing.

"Have a nice ride, Mrs. Northrup." The maid's words were formal, perfectly correct between servant and mistress, but her voice was a caress. Whoever the little Irishwoman was, she loved her mistress with a deep and abiding love. And if an Irishwoman, a servant, loved her, then she must be a person worthy of love.

"Thank you, Rose." Eugenia reached out and touched the maid's face with her fingers, and then turned to Liam. The brief, almost furtive gesture touched him deeply. He'd do his best for her, because with a mistress like this one, his lot would be a great deal more smooth. And he knew, instinctively, that Eugenia could use a friend.

"Your name is Mr. Donovan, I believe," Eugenia said. Her voice was contralto, low and sweet, but it held no real interest. She was only being polite.

"It is, Mrs. Northrup." Without consciously thinking about it, Liam's voice slid into a gentle brogue. Suffering was close enough to him that he recognized it in others, and God knew that he didn't want any other living creature to suffer. There'd been enough of that in the world, it was time that things changed, that that God the priests talked about looked down from heaven and saw what some wicked men did to others. "And a beautiful day it is, and beautiful creatures for us to ride. Would there be any particular path you'd like to take? I'm not familiar with the estate as yet, so I'm afraid you'll have to direct me this first time."

"Any path will do." Liam noticed the grace with which Eugenia mounted Beau, the practiced ease with which she laced the reins through her fingers. She had a good seat, Liam had never seen any woman in Ireland with a better. "We'll turn to the left there beyond the stables."

"As you say, Mrs. Northrup." Liam swung himself into Ranger's saddle, and felt an unexpected pride that, mounted on a horse, he was still the equal of any man. As his politician benefactor had surmised, in the saddle his limp was no handicap at all. If Eugenia hadn't been oblivious to everything except her own pain, she would have noticed what a handsome man he was, how broad his shoulders, how straight his back, how capable his hands as he reined Ranger around to take the path she had indicated.

Beau was a beautiful horse, almost as beautiful as Rora had been.

Eugenia had always loved him, and she'd gone on loving him even after Rora had come to Retreat. But Rora was dead, and now nothing else mattered. With Rora's destruction, her last reason for living had been taken from her.

"What a fine estate this is, to be sure!" Liam said. He knew that it wasn't his place to make light conversation with his mistress, that he was breaking a cardinal rule, but still the tragedy in Eugenia's face drove him to it. "I've never seen a better. Would you be liking a little canter, now that the horses are warmed up?"

Eugenia looked at him and, without even nodding, lifted Beau into a canter and then into a headlong gallop that took Liam so by surprise that she was far ahead of him before he collected himself to take after her. The woman had taken leave of her senses, she was mad! Beau was almost flat to the ground, his long legs covered the distance so rapidly that Liam wasn't sure that he'd be able to catch them.

Seated on Beau, Eugenia's eyes were blind with tears. She urged the gelding to run faster and faster. There were woods just ahead, the trail curved sharply, time and again, with trees so close on either side that going at this speed was hazardous, the danger of being caught against the side of a tree or by an overhanging branch so great that she had never allowed Aurora to gallop here at all. If she didn't pull Beau in, she would be in danger of losing her life.

Sanity returned to her as she realized what she was doing, that unconsciously she wanted an accident to happen to put an end to a life that was so miserable that she couldn't bear to face another day. She would be out of it at last, but Laura and her mother and Daniel and the boys would be left to face the consequences of William's wrath if Eugenia used this means to escape his vengeance. She clenched her teeth and began trying to pull Beau in, but Beau had the bit in his teeth and he was unmanageable. As well trained as he was, and as used to Eugenia, he had never been treated this way before and he had gone into a panic.

Eugenia didn't hear Liam's shout as she sawed at the reins, she was concentrating all of her efforts in trying to stop Beau, while at the same time she still had to fight back her overwhelming urge to set him to running even faster until she should be swept from the saddle and killed.

Frantic, Liam urged Ranger on, using all of his skill and mastery to catch the runaway horse in front of him. His thoughts raised to a prayer to Mary, to Jesus, to all the saints, in spite of his new doubts that they would listen even if they existed at all. He knew, with his Irishman's intuition, that Eugenia had done this deliberately, that for some reason of which he knew nothing the woman was trying to kill herself.

Eugenia was beyond thinking at all, now. When Liam's arm reached out and swept her from her saddle, all she experienced was a vague surprise. Then she was lowered to stand on her feet, and her knees buckled under her, and she fell to them, her hands over her face.

Liam swung down to lift her. Instead, he found himself holding her, while she collapsed in his arms, sobbing as if she would never stop until the world came to an end. All of her grief, all of her misery, came pouring out while Liam held her against his breast. His lips were pressed against her hair, and the sweet smell of her engulfed his senses. May God forgive whoever it was who did this to her, he thought, as he held her closer until some of her trembling subsided and her sobbing tapered off at last.

"I'm sorry," Eugenia gasped, her voice small and still filled with despair. "You would have been blamed, I didn't think. . . ."

"It's all right," Liam soothed her. He still held her, and his arms were trembling now with the desire to protect her from whatever it was that was hurting her. There was no disloyalty to Molly in the thought. Molly, with her soft heart, would want him to do everything he could to help.

Eugenia lifted her face at last, and looked at him. Her face was still drenched with tears, her eyes soft and swimming. Her mouth trembled, sweet and sad and vulnerable. Liam stood up, lifting her with him. He brushed first at her dirtied riding skirt and then at his trousers.

"Are you all right now? I see Beau up ahead, praise the saints that he didn't go running back to the stable and send them out searching for us. I'll fetch him back, if you think you can stand and wait for one little moment."

"Thank you. You're very kind."

This time Liam lifted her into the saddle, his hands tender as he settled her and made sure that she was steady enough to ride. "We'll walk the horses for a bit, to cool them out and settle them," he told her. "You'll not be wanting to go back to the house, I'm thinking, until you can go back with no trace of what happened on your face."

For the first time Eugenia looked at him and saw what she was looking at. A tall man, broad-shouldered, his face ruggedly handsome in spite of lines of suffering that were etched around his mouth and eyes. A kind man, a man who cared about her, who cared whether she lived or died. And for the first time in years, except for her love for Rose and for Rora, she felt an emotion other than grief or despair. She felt gratitude, and her lips moved in a silent prayer of thanksgiving that Liam Donovan had come to Retreat, because she felt that his strength and kindness would give her strength.

"A gentle trot, now, you'll be understanding," Liam told her, unexpected laughter crinkling his eyes. "We'll not be wanting a repeat performance of what just happened. And don't be afraid that Beau will get away from you again. I'll be right beside you."

They were the most beautiful words Eugenia had ever heard.

4

The process of Eugenia's coming out of the depth of despair was so gradual that she herself was hardly aware of it until it was already an accomplished fact.

Unless the weather was so inclement that riding was impossible, she continued to take the daily rides that William had made mandatory. The first morning that she realized that she was looking forward to it was only mildly surprising to her, and even then she put it down to the fact that getting away from this house that was permeated with William's presence even when he was absent from it was better than staying inside. Rose knew what was happening before Eugenia knew, but Rose was wise enough to hold her tongue and only pray that at last her mistress would find some measure of happiness even if it was a clandestine one that must be hidden from the rest of the world.

Gradually, Eugenia came to realize that Liam Donovan's unfailing kindness to her was making her life at least bearable. They had their love of horses in common, and Liam used this to full advantage in an effort to bring one of her rare smiles to her face. He told her about the horses he had ridden and trained in Ireland, about the champions that had brought honor to their owner only because of his training of them.

Interlaced with this, there were tales of the Irish gentry, of the English landlords and their trampling of the rights of Irishmen into the dust. Even anger at injustice half the world away was better than Eugenia's sadness, and as time went on her anger was aroused and she expressed her approval of Liam's activities that had ended with him having to flee Ireland in order to save his life and protect his wife and child.

"Ireland is the most beautiful place in the world," Liam told her. "The air is so soft it's like a lover's kiss, and the rains no more than gentle mists to make you feel the joy of living. And green! Lady dear, you've never seen green until you've seen Ireland! An emerald it is, just as the poets say, set down in the midst of the sea, 'tis no wonder Saint Patrick chose it above all the rest, to bring it his blessing."

"Is it true that there are no snakes in Ireland?" Eugenia had a horror of snakes. When she saw one as she rode through the meadows and woods, she shuddered and had to use conscious will to keep from communicating her unease to her mount.

"To be sure it's true, and didn't the blessed saint drive them out himself so as not to have the devil's spokesmen in his chosen land? The only snakes there are two-legged ones—the English who oppress us—and with Saint Patrick's help they'll be driven out just as he drove out the serpents." He didn't believe it himself, but he liked to see the smile his words brought to Eugenia's lips.

"I hope it happens soon," Eugenia told him. "I'll add my prayers to yours, Mr. Donovan."

When was the first time she'd called him Liam? She couldn't remember. It had come about so naturally that she hadn't even noticed. And little by little, she extracted Liam's own story from him, she came to know his sweet Molly, his beautiful daughter, Moria, whom he managed to see only two afternoons a month, and over whom he agonized because of their separation.

"Not that she isn't all right, mind you. But it breaks my heart that I can't do more for her, that I can't keep my promise to Molly. But times are hard, and this is the best I can do, there's no other work I know that would bring me in more money, considering that I get my keep here."

"And are you happy here, Liam? Outside of not having Moria with you?"

"I am that, and how could I help but be? It's a beautiful estate and the master paying me no mind as long as I do my work, and horses that any man would be proud to handle."

His eyes said more, but there was no way he could tell Eugenia that a large part of his liking Retreat was because of his daily contact with her. Her sweet smile and gentle voice were something to look forward to during the long nights when remembering Molly and missing Moria were almost more than a man could bear. And the smile came more often now, the saints be praised, and he knew that Molly would be glad that he was the one who was able to bring it about. If William Northrup should drop dead, Retreat would be a paradise on earth, doubly a paradise because Eugenia would allow him to bring Moria here to live with him.

Of Eugenia's story he knew nothing from her own lips. It was not a subject that any woman could talk about with a man, much less a servant. But there was Rose. His fellow countrywoman learned early in Liam's employment that he was a man who could be trusted, that he was the only person available to Eugenia who could lighten her burden and give her an incentive not only to go on living but to enjoy life as much as it could be possible for her to enjoy it as long as William Northrup lived.

"The devil!" Liam raged. "He's as bad as the English who trample our faces in the dirt. He's worse, because as bad as the English are, I've heard of few who'd treat their wives the way William Northrup treats his. Thank God she has you, Rose, else she'd never have survived."

"And don't think I haven't prayed and that I'm not still praying that he won't live much longer!'' Rose told him. ''Only my prayers aren't heard, and how could they be when it's a sin to pray them?''

''No sin,'' Liam growled. ''How could it be a sin to want to rid the world of a man like that? If it's a mortal sin to pray that William Northrup will die, then I'll be right next to you in hell.'' His fists were clenched so hard that the knuckles showed white, and the muscles along his jawline knotted.

It was Rose who warned Eugenia not to let William see that she was happier these days. ''He'd not rest until he learned the reason, and that would be the last of Liam Donovan at Retreat. Watch yourself, lest he notice.''

It wasn't hard to heed Rose's advice, because when William forced himself into her company she was never happy. The only difference now was that when she had to endure the worst of his abuse, she was able to project her mind away from her bodily pain and her humiliation to the next morning when she'd again ride with Liam, when the warm breeze would be on her face and Beau's perfectly muscled body moved with hers in perfect harmony.

As for William, it would never have entered his mind that Eugenia could have any interest in a horse trainer, a servant, much less in an Irish immigrant, the scum of the earth. To William, such people were of no more account than the slaves in the South; of even less account, because they had no monetary value in their own right, as slaves did.

He and Eugenia still entertained, when William saw fit, and they still visited William's friends and attended balls and other social functions. William still had a driving need to show off his beautiful wife, to make other men envy his possession of her. The fact that directly after any of these affairs William subjected her to more than his usual abuse behind her closed and locked bedroom door was something that not one of those friends could possibly have guessed. All of the bruises he inflicted were on Eugenia's body, never on her face or arms where they could be detected, and on her soul.

Eugenia and Liam had fallen into the habit of dismounting and resting for a while, sitting on the spongy moss with their backs against the trunks of trees, a proper distance apart, while Liam brought animation into Eugenia's face with his tales of Ireland. Liam had come to Retreat in April. It was the tenth day of September, a day so perfect that it was possible to believe in God's mercy no matter what went on in the world, that things came out into the open between them.

Eugenia had been subjected to harsher than usual abuse the night before. Some remark she had made at the Vancouvers' party had aroused William's anger, an innocent remark to the effect that Eugenia thought it was a pity that the immigrants from other countries were misled in what to expect when they arrived in America. The remark had brought shocked disapproval from her host and the other guests. Only Estelle had given her a glance of sympathy, and even Estelle hadn't dared to take her part while she was under Jacob's disapproving gaze.

On this tenth morning of September, Eugenia's body was such a mass of bruises and pain that it took every ounce of her courage to sit in the saddle without crying out. Rose had ranted and raved to think that she had to ride as usual, but the daily ride was mandatory and William took nothing but pleasure in forcing Eugenia to undergo further pain. Any additional suffering he could inflict on her was only an extension of her just punishment for having denied him the ability to father children.

Eugenia almost fainted with relief when Liam drew rein in the densest part of the woods through which the bridle path wound, and she had to hold her face expressionless so that he wouldn't see the pain she was suffering. But when he lifted her from the saddle she cried out, unable to hold back her half-scream of agony. Her senses reeled and for a moment her eyes dimmed, and then she recovered enough to see that Liam's eyes were as black as thunderclouds as he continued to hold her as gently as he could so that she would not fall. And in another instant, his mouth was over hers, in a kiss that held an eternity of love and longing.

Shock drove the pain from her body and made it stiffen, and then she seemed to melt, and her lips went soft under his as she returned his kiss with a longing that matched his own. The kiss went on and on, through one eternity and then another, before they drew apart to look into each other's eyes, stunned by the wonder of it.

Liam spoke first. "What are we going to do?"

"There's nothing we can do. I'm married to William, there is no way I can leave him, no way I can get away from him."

The hopelessness of it made Liam groan. If he were a rich man, if William Northrup's long arm wouldn't reach out to smash Eugenia's family along with themselves, he would have put her back into the saddle and they would have fled to the ends of the earth to some place where he could love and cherish and protect her for all the rest of their lives.

But there was no way, and both of them knew it. All they could do was endure it. Once again Liam raged at the injustice of a world that set a few men above all others so that the others had no control over their own destinies.

"We have this," Eugenia told him softly. Her eyes were shining. She loved him! And he loved her! The wonder of it made up for everything else. As long as they had this, then she would be happy, even William would not be able to destroy one ounce of her happiness.

But Liam was a man, and the bitterness in him for not being able to change things was like gall, even worse than the bitterness he'd known in Ireland. If he could change things by cutting off his arm, he'd do it, but the days of such sacrifice were past and God no longer looked with favor on such things, if He looked at all.

Their lips came together again, filling them with awe at the waves of passion that filled them until there was no room for more. Liam held her as if he could never let her go, until he remembered the pain he must be causing her, and, groaning, loosened the pressure of his arms.

"Did I hurt you? I'm sorry. . . ."

"It doesn't matter. I'd rather be hurt a hundred times worse than not be in your arms. Hold me, Liam, go on holding me, never let me go!"

Love's Hidden Glory

But their time for riding was almost up, and there was no way that they dared be late in returning to the stables. William knew everything that went on at Retreat, there was no way of hiding anything from him. Or, rather, there was no way of hiding anything from him except this one thing, and they must count that as a blessing never to be forgotten.

There were other ways they could be together. Simply because love between them was so impossible that no one would dream of suspecting it, there were ways. William was often away from home overnight, sometimes for several nights in succession. And Liam had his cottage to himself.

Only Rose knew of the nights when Eugenia crept from her bed, put on a dark hooded cape to make herself virtually invisible, and made her way through the midnight hours to Liam's cottage, where they lay in each other's arms until dawn streaked the sky.

In the beginning of her marriage to William, Eugenia had thought she knew what it was to be fulfilled. Now, with Liam, she knew that she had known nothing at all.

Her body sang with the love with which Liam filled her. She drew him deeper and ever deeper inside herself, she knew the supreme joy of giving every atom of herself to the man she loved. His mouth on all her secret and sacred places, his hands turning her to fire as they learned every inch of each other, told her the reason she had been born, the reason she had gone on living when life had been insufferable. The ecstasy that consumed her made her willing to walk through the fires of hell just to experience it one more time. And every time, no matter how many times there had been before, the ecstasy was more intense, her happiness soared to new and undreamed-of heights.

And to her shame, a part of Eugenia's happiness was the fact that by loving Liam and giving herself to him as she'd never given herself to William, she was hurting William in the most desperate way that a man could be hurt. Something like this would destroy him because it would destroy his image of himself, the image that he was omnipotent, that he controlled every aspect of his life. And if

71

anything happened to William, if she were sure that he was so close to death that he could lift no hand in retaliation, she'd take the greatest of satisfaction in telling him.

But, mostly, she didn't think of William at all on those nights of purest happiness. There was only Liam, and that was the way it would always be.

If it hadn't been for Moria, Liam would have been supremely happy, even knowing that there would never be anything he could do to take Eugenia away from William.

But there was Moria, who lived in a shabby boardinghouse, even helping Mrs. Murphy with the bedmaking and the cleaning and the kitchen work because she had to do something to fill her time in a section of the city that was so rough and wicked that she was safe only indoors. The weeks and months were passing while he seldom saw her, while he had done nothing and could do nothing to keep his promise to Molly.

"She's beautiful, Eugenia," Liam told her as they lay, sated and fulfilled, in each other's arms. "Molly was the prettiest girl I'd ever seen, but Moria is something created by the harp strings of the bards. I wish you could see her. I wish you could know each other because I know you'd love each other."

"I wish it too, Liam. I'd love her because she's your daughter even if she were ugly."

"She shouldn't be living as she is. I ought to be able to do more for her. What chance will she have, except to marry some hod-carrier and end up pinching and scraping and growing old before her time even if she's lucky enough not to get a man who'll drink up his wages even before he gets them home?"

The misery in his voice tore at Eugenia's heart. If only there were some way she could help him!

Liam went on, his voice bleak, "She deserves an education, a chance to take her rightful place in the world. The blood of Irish kings runs in her veins. The Donovans weren't always horse trainers, my line sprang from cousins of royalty. When I think of what might become of her, I get sick to my stomach, and all because I'm not able to change things."

"There must be a way. There has to be a way," Eugenia told him. She thought of giving him some of her jewels to sell, but William would be sure to notice that whatever she gave him was missing, and find out who had sold them and Liam would spend years behind prison bars.

In the end, not knowing where else to turn because there was no one else, Eugenia turned again to Laura.

It wasn't possible for her to write to Laura. William had forbidden all correspondence between her and her family, and all mail entering and leaving the house was scrutinized by him. But there was Rose.

Rose memorized what Eugenia wanted to say to her sister, word for word, her love for Eugenia making the task easy. And on Rose's afternoons and evenings off, which occurred twice every month, Rose went to the village and wrote the letter herself, and asked Laura to send her reply in care of the priest, who could be trusted. That long-suffering man agreed to take part in the deception because there was little he didn't know about conditions at Retreat, Rose having had to confess so often, and he thought it a pity that the poor lady could not correspond with her own sister. The fact that William Northrup was a Catholic-hater salved any pangs of conscience that he might have felt in helping a wife deceive her husband, but he never knew what was in the letters and so his conscience was spared a great deal more than he knew.

Laura's reaction to the letter was one of elated satisfaction. Here was a problem she could get her teeth into, and the chance to do William Northrup a disservice. Laura was an intelligent woman, and capable of going to any lengths to get what she wanted. In this case, she wanted Eugenia to have Moria, and she was determined to find a way to foist Eugenia's lover's child off on William.

As eager as she was to strike back at William as well as help her sister, it was a matter that could not be hurried. Plans must be made, plans so foolproof that William could never find out. Laura directed all of her thoughts and energies to making those plans. Within a month she was able to write to Eugenia, in care of the priest, and give detailed instructions.

Laura had found, by going through the casualty records, that a Lieutenant Compton of the Union Army had been killed in action and left a motherless child, a little girl the same age as Moria.

The name of the child is of no consequence. As so often is the case, this being a man's world, the records do not give her given name, but only state that the child is a female. Actually, the little girl was taken in by a distant cousin who lives in Boston, but this fact is not available in any records, I made very sure of that. One more orphan was of no concern to the officials.

Daniel and I know a lady, who used to live here in Baltimore and who now lives in New York City, who will be delighted to take your Moria into her home and coach her thoroughly in everything she will need to know. It's a blessing that the child is old enough to be able to carry it off, if she's as bright as your Liam says. She will acquire the right accent, she will be able to name Baltimore's streets and public buildings, be able to supply details about her parents that only a real daughter could know. We have already contacted Mrs. Franklyn, who is eager to enter into our plan because her son gave his life on the battlefield but not before he'd told his mother of the boots that disintegrated after a week's wearing, of blankets that melted in the rain, of rotten salt pork, and defective weapons supplied to our forces directly or indirectly by William's hand.

You remember old Mrs. Theodore Armitage, of course. She was and still is one of Mama's friends, although she is now so old that she never leaves her house and is cared for by her servants, being alone in the world since her husband died. Mama will write to her, when the time comes, telling her of this child who is a war orphan and how much she needs a home. She will ask Mrs. Armitage to write to you, telling you of the case, a letter that she is certain to copy almost word for word from the heartrending description that Mama and I will send her, as she used to ask Mama to help her compose her correspondence, not being blessed with the gift of putting words together as we are. Mrs. Armitage will explain that she thought immediately of you, as she knows that you are childless and could give the little orphan a good home, a child of impeccable lineage although she is now destitute, the small family home having been sold some years ago in order to pay off gambling debts incurred by Lieutenant Compton's father when he lost all sense of responsibility, owing to his grief over the death of his wife, and turned to gambling for solace.

As soon as your Moria is letter-perfect in her role, you must tell your friends, at some large affair, about the little girl of whom Mrs. Armitage wrote you. You must say how heartrending it it that such a child should be homeless, while you yourself have not been blessed with children.

We happen to know how much William's reputation has suffered because of his dishonest dealings with our armed forces, and this might just be the factor that will turn the cards in your favor. Added to that there is the reputation he has built up and so carefully preserved that he adores you and gives you everything that you might wish. Faced with the opportunity of proving himself patriotic and warmhearted, with the alternative being to prove himself unpatriotic and coldhearted, he will find it hard to refuse you, especially as he will be able to elevate himself in the estimation of his peers at so little cost and inconvenience to himself.

We've done the groundwork. The rest is up to you. You can pull it off if you play your cards exactly right. By no means ask William to consider taking the child until you are in the company of those of his friends whom he most wishes to impress.

Good luck, and God bless you, and may William Northrup rot in hell while you and your Liam bask in the comfort of having Moria with you. Your loving sister, Laura.

Five months from the February day that Rose had relayed to her, by memory, every word that Laura had written, William entered Eugenia's bedroom after they had returned from a dinner party at the Vancouver mansion, his expression sardonic.

"Madam, I would not have given you credit for such deviousness. You couldn't have timed your heartrending story more conveniently, I could almost believe that it was deliberate."

"But, William, you agreed that we should take the child! You told us all that you were delighted with the idea!" Eugenia had learned well how to act a part in the months since she and Liam had found each other, drawn together out of their mutual loneliness and need. "I was so happy when you said that we'd do it, a child will fill my life, even though she might sometimes be a bother."

"She'll not be much of a bother, my dear, I shall see to that." William's expression turned cruel. It would suit him to let his wife grow to love the child, and then make sure that she had little opportunity to enjoy the brat's company. There would be governesses, private academies, he would see that Eugenia's social calendar was so full that she'd have almost no time to spend with this orphan. The child herself could be punished, confined to her room for minor infractions. It would be one more weapon he could use to punish the woman who had ruined his life.

His first reaction had been to mentally curse that senile old woman, Mrs. Theodore Armitage, who had suggested taking the orphan to Eugenia. Eugenia had received the woman's letter without William's having bothered to read it, as he had been sure that no personal messages would be exchanged between Eugenia and her family through a third party. Family differences were never discussed among friends, and Eugenia still received occasional letters from people she had known before he had married her. There had been no way that he could forbid it without letting it become known that he was holding his wife a prisoner, although he had made sure that Eugenia discouraged too much of such correspondence by being late with her replies.

Now he looked at Eugenia, his eyes cold and glittering. The bitch had outwitted him, but she would pay for it. "You may write Mrs. Armitage that you will take the child. And now we will change a subject which I find boring. I only ask that you keep the waif out from under my feet. Remove your nightgown, if you please."

Eugenia paid that night in full, and then in full twice over, for the privilege of having Moria brought to Retreat. And she knew that she would pay again, and yet again, whenever William chose to make her pay.

During the four days she was confined to her bed, unable to walk after the abuse William wreaked on her that night, she considered it well worth the price. If her death would have made Liam happy, then she would have died without an instant's regret, except that she must go on living in order for Liam to have Moria here, and to protect her family. Bodily pain was nothing compared to the love she bore for Liam, and in bringing about the reuniting of father and daughter she was giving him the greatest gift that it was possible for her to give.

5

Moria's eyes were wide with disbelief at her first glimpse of Retreat. Her father had described it to her, many times, when he'd visited her, but still nothing in her experience had prepared her for its magnificence.

The weeks just past had been filled with bewildered confusion. First Papa had told her that he was taking her to stay with Mrs. Franklyn, who was to teach her things, and that she was to learn as fast and as thoroughly as possible. And her name wasn't to be Moria Donovan anymore, it was to be Moria Compton, who used to live in Baltimore, and whose father had been killed in the war.

But Papa was Papa, and it was wrong to lie and pretend that he wasn't and that she was someone she wasn't. Father O'Brian was always drilling it into everyone how wrong it was to lie, to deceive, and Sister Teresa and Sister Agnes, too.

She must never, never let it slip that Papa was Papa. Papa was only the horse trainer at some magic place called Retreat, where she was going to live in a mansion, while Papa lived in a cottage and was never allowed to set foot in the big house. She wouldn't even get to see him until her first riding lesson was arranged. It was all very strange, and she didn't understand.

"Girl dear, you're going to have everything that any girl could want. You'll have beautiful clothes to wear, dresses such as you've never dreamed of. And you'll marry a rich man, when the time comes, an important man from an important family and you'll never lack for anything."

"I don't care about that. I only want to be Moria Donovan. I only want you to go on being my Papa."

"Darling, your mother wanted this for you. She made me promise, when she was dying, that I'd see to it. A deathbed promise is sacred, you understand, and mustn't be broken. And I want it for you too. If you love me, if you love the memory of your sainted mother, you'll do as I ask. It's all for the best, or I wouldn't ask it of you. You're going to be happy, your new mother is the loveliest lady I've ever known, she's sweet and gentle and she already loves you although she's never seen you. And you'll love her, because there's no way on this earth that you'll be able to keep from it."

"I loved my mother, my real mother. I don't want another mother." Moria's eyes filled with tears. She was trying to understand, but it was hard.

"Of course you loved your mother, and so did I. I loved her more than anyone in the world except you. But your mother won't mind if you love Mrs. Northrup, she'd want you to love her because she's going to be good to you and give you everything she wanted for you. She'll be looking down from heaven and she'll be sad if you don't."

"She can't look down from heaven. She's in purgatory." How could Papa have forgotten that?

"Then your doing as I ask will shorten her time in purgatory, because our prayers for her will be more effective if we do as she wanted, and because we'll be making Mrs. Northrup happy."

Moria still didn't understand, but because she loved her father more than anyone else in the world, she'd do as he asked. She'd have to confess, though. And she didn't think that Father O'Brian was going to like it.

"You won't be going to mass or confession," Liam had to tell her, and this shocked her more than anything else. Not go to mass, to confession? But she'd go to hell if she didn't! How could Papa love her, if he wouldn't let her save her soul by going to mass and confession?

"It isn't that I don't want you to go to mass and confession." How was he to explain it to her, this girl-woman whose religion had been her only comfort since Molly had died and they'd had to be separated? "It's the master of Retreat who makes the rules, and he'd never accept a Catholic girl, he'd have you out of his house before you got your foot in the door. You must never mention Catholics, girl dear, not ever. The Northrups are Lutherans and that's what you'll have to be too."

Moria's face, already pale, turned deathly white. Lutherans! Of all the Protestants, Father O'Brian disliked the Lutherans the most, because Luther had been the one who'd caused all the trouble and made Mother Church lose thousands, millions, of souls. She couldn't do it. Everything else she could, and would, because her father asked it of her, even though she knew it was wrong, but she couldn't do this. Father O'Brian said that the first duty of any Catholic was to look to the salvation of his own soul.

"You'll still be a Catholic, Moria." Sweat beaded on Liam's forehead. "The Holy Mother will know that this is something you are being forced to do, that you have no choice in the matter. It's like when the Catholics were persecuted in England, back in the days of Black Cromwell, and had to hide their beliefs in order to survive. You can pray to Mary when you're alone, and you can have your rosary, there's a maid at Retreat, as good a Catholic as anyone I've ever known, and she'll keep it for you so you can say your beads when you're behind your locked door. She'll pray for you too, and help explain to Mary why you have to do it."

Well, maybe. But all the same it didn't seem right.

Moria liked Mrs. Franklyn. The widow took her to her heart, and being herself so softhearted, so sensitive to suffering, Moria was drawn to her and wanted to please her and make her as happy as she could. It must be dreadful not to have anyone at all. Moria had lost her mother and she'd been lonesome for her father when he'd had to go away, but she still had him, even if she was going to have to pretend, now, that she didn't.

So Moria plunged into her lessons. She spent hours practicing a Baltimore accent, only slightly southern, but southern enough so that no one would ever take it for Irish. Mrs. Franklyn drilled her until she was ashamed of herself for working the child so hard, but she knew how important it was for every trace of Irish to be removed from Moria's speech.

And there were the other lessons, the lessons about Baltimore and the Maryland countryside. There was so much to learn, and such a short time in which to learn it! Sometimes Moria didn't get to bed until ten or eleven at night, and once her head was on her pillow she wasn't able to sleep for the facts that kept roiling and moiling around in her head. And always, she must remember that she was Moria Compton, that she knew nothing about Ireland, that she had no father. She must cry when Lieutenant Compton's name was mentioned.

When the day that was to change her entire life finally came, Mrs. Franklyn took her in a hired carriage, well ahead of time, to the train station, where they lost themselves in the crowd and then mingled with the disembarking passengers at the exact moment. Mrs. Franklyn wore a pink silk rose on her bonnet, and another on the bodice of her black mourning dress, and Moria was also wearing black, as befitted a girl who had recently lost her last remaining parent. Mrs. Franklyn carried a carpetbag and Moria a small valise, packed with clothing a great deal better than she had owned since they'd come to America but washed many times and showing tiny tears that Mrs. Franklyn had mended, and some of them just a little too small for her, so that they would look as if she had begun to outgrow them. Moria must always remember, she must never dare to forget even for an instant, that Mr. Northrup was a very smart man, that no detail would escape his notice and then there would be the direst of consequences, the least of which would be that Papa would lose his position and he and she would be destitute again. Moria wouldn't mind, all that much, being ragged and going hungry, as long as she was with Papa, but it mustn't happen to her father.

At the train station, the thirteen-year-old girl saw the lady who had a wealth of fair hair under a bonnet that was so beautiful that other women looked at it with envy stop in her tracks and look back at her and then hurry forward. In another moment she was enveloped in gentle arms and drawn close to the lady's breast. The lady smelled sweet, her expression was softly glowing, her eyes were filled with joy.

"You're Moria," Eugenia said. "I'd have known you even without Mrs. Franklyn's pink roses. I'm Mrs. Northrup, and I'm so glad you're here at last!"

Papa had said that Mrs. Northrup would love her. Now, only seconds after they'd met, Moria's heart went out to her with a love that was to last a lifetime. She felt warmth grow and spread until her whole body glowed with it, she felt as if she had come to a safe haven, a place where she belonged, for the first time since she had left Ireland when she'd been six years old.

Then, over Eugenia's shoulder, she saw a tall, very handsome gentleman whose face wasn't smiling at all, whose eyes were cold, and the warmth was replaced by a chill that made her tremble.

"Come along, Eugenia. Mrs. Franklyn, I have arranged accommodations for you until you return to Baltimore. You can find a cab just outside that door." Disdainfully, he extracted a few bills from his pocket and handed them to the woman he thought had escorted Moria to New York, gave her the address of the room he had engaged for her, and promptly forgot that she existed.

William nodded to a manservant who stood a respectful distance from him to take Moria's bag, and put his hand under Eugenia's elbow and propelled her along, leaving Moria to tag after them, suddenly terrified that she'd lose them in the crowd. But Eugenia looked back and resisted William's urging long enough to hold out her hand to her, and Moria took it, and she was safe again as long as the gentleman didn't look at her with those cold eyes.

"I'm sorry that we can't stay in the city long enough for you to see something of it, but my husband has to get home," Eugenia told her. "But never mind. There will be other opportunities. We'll have a wonderful time shopping together, there are so many things I want to buy for you! And I'll have to see what you brought with you so I can tell what you need, in any case."

"I don't need anything, thank you."

"Nonsense! Every young girl needs things, even if only for her own pleasure! And we'll shop for them together. and have a lovely time." Would William allow it, or would he insist on accompanying them, to put a damper on any enjoyment she might have? But she wouldn't think about that now. It was enough, at this moment, that Moria was here, that tomorrow Liam would see her and know that everything had gone without a hitch.

How lovely the child was, Eugenia thought, filled with pleasure. And how lovely her voice sounded, sweet and clear and soft. She was everything Liam had said she was, and her only sadness was that he wouldn't see her until her first riding lesson. They would be left off at the front door before the carriage was driven around to the carriage house.

The drive along the Hudson River filled Moria with delight. She had never dreamed that it was so beautiful. She was already happier than she had ever been, except for the presence of the unfriendly man opposite her in the carriage.

But William paid no attention to her, not even speaking to his wife during the long ride. It was as if she were invisible to him, and looking at him out of the corners of her eyes, Moria wished that she really were. How wonderful it would be if only her father and Mrs. Northrup could see her, could know that she was living with them at Retreat!

But that was childish and silly. Father O'Brian would scold her for indulging in fantasies. She looked at Mrs. Northrup instead, and Eugenia still looked just as Moria thought a queen would look, only surely she was more beautiful than the queen of England, and kinder, and more wonderful in every respect. She must never forget that she must never mention Queen Victoria, who had so little compassion for her Irish subjects that her father and all the Irish immigrants Moria had come into contact with despised her for her cold heart. She was glad that Mrs. Northrup wasn't a queen, and that her heart was warm.

For a moment, she felt a pang of guilt that she should love another woman so much, after her mother, but then she remembered that Mama would want her to love this new mother and be happy with her. So it must be all right, and anyway her father was going to pray for her in church.

She smiled, and Eugenia's breath caught, and, like a real mother, her mind projected into the future as she saw how exquisite Moria would be when she was eighteen or nineteen, of the excitement of her being presented to society, of all the parties and balls and the beaus she would have, and then a wedding so spectacular that no one who attended it would ever forget it. Moria in white, her raven hair contrasting with the white lace of her veil, her eyes so blue that even those in the last rows of the pews in the church would murmur with wonder.

Beside her, Moria wondered if all this were really happening or if it were only more of her romantic imaginings that Father O'Brian and Sister Teresa and Sister Agnes so deplored. The whole thing, from the day she had been taken to Mrs. Franklyn, was like a dream. The carriage was luxurious, a landau with the top let down on this hot July day so that it was open to the sky and they could catch the advantage of any breeze. The cushions were red, of real leather, and there were lamps at the front that could be lighted if they were overtaken by darkness. Moria had never seen a carriage like this, such vehicles had never ventured into the slums of New York City where she had spent her life after she'd left Ireland.

And the horses! Moria could still remember the horses on Sir Malcolm's estate, but that had been a long time ago and she could only remember that they had been beautiful. But there was no doubt in her mind that these horses were fully as beautiful, a team of perfectly matched blacks, each with one white right stocking. How had they ever found two horses that looked so exactly alike, how had it been possible? Their harness was red, to match the upholstery of the carriage, the brass fittings gleaming like gold in the sun.

These weren't the horses her father was in charge of, of course. These were carriage horses, and the coachman or the grooms took care of them. Papa was in charge of the saddle horses, but right at this moment Moria couldn't believe that even Papa's horses could be more beautiful. If it hadn't been for the man in the seat facing them, she would have wished that the ride could go on forever. No, not forever, because then she would never see Papa again, but long enough so that when they arrived at Retreat it would be time for her first riding lesson.

And then the drive was over, and the carriage turned down a long drive lined on each side with oak trees, and the mansion stood before them, and Moria's breath caught in her throat and she was filled with panic.

This was where she was going to live. This palace, this castle! It was built of stone, and it was so large that she'd never learn her way around it, she'd become lost, and never be found until some servant stumbled over her skeleton in some dark passage years from now.

Servants! How many would there be? It must take an army of servants to care for a house like this, and Moria's terror increased. All those servants, and she must never, never, make a mistake and let it slip that her father was her father. Only the one named Rose O'Riley was safe. She'd better just not say anything at all, but only nod and smile if she were addressed by any of the others. She could not imagine speaking to any of them of her own volition. She didn't even know how to address a servant, Mrs. Franklyn had forgotten to tell her things like that.

A liveried manservant helped first Eugenia, and then Moria, step down from the landau. Moria's knees almost refused to hold her, she had to stiffen them to make sure that her legs wouldn't go out from under her. But then Eugenia took her hand, and smiled at her again, and led her to the great double doors that were already standing open to welcome them. A dignified woman stood just inside, and Eugenia nodded to her. "Mrs. Lindstrom, this is Miss Moria Compton. Has her room been checked to make sure that everything is in readiness?"

A thrill ran through Moria's body from the top of her head right down to the tips of her toes. Miss Moria Compton! She was a lady!

"I'm very pleased that you've come to stay with us, Miss Moria," the housekeeper said. Her voice was kind, and Moria liked her. Miss Moria! Moria's head swam and she prayed that she wouldn't faint. No, not faint, ladies swooned, and had smelling salts held to their nostrils and their stays loosened, she knew that much from stories her mother had told her about the gentry in Ireland.

Only she wouldn't swoon, she dasn't. She might say something she shouldn't before she was fully conscious again, and then her wonderful Mrs. Northrup would be in trouble and Papa would lose his position and maybe be sent to prison for his part in this deception. So Moria smiled and said, "Thank you, Mrs. Lindstrom. I'm very glad to be here," and Eugenia beamed approval and she knew that she'd conducted herself properly and the first hurdle had been crossed without plunging them all into disaster.

The entrance hall was so vast that it could have been used to hold a ball. The black and white tile floor seemed to stretch out forever on all sides, the furniture was richly carved, there were masses of flowers on the gleaming tables, and a few marble statues were placed to the best advantage, all of them sculpted with draperies and blind, blank eyes. Wasn't it a pity that the sculptors weren't able to make eyes that looked real and alive, when the statues themselves were so lovely to look at!

Her own eyes went to the staircase, that rose and then divided, one branch going to the right and the other to the left to reach a broad gallery on the second floor. There was a crystal chandelier hung in the middle of the ceiling high over the staircase, gleaming in the light from the open door, its prisms sending out rays of every color of the rainbow. Moria could have stood there looking at it forever because she'd never seen anything so enchanting.

"We'll go right on up, dear," Eugenia told her. "You'll need a bath after your dreadful train ride, trains are so dirty and uncomfortable, and then you'll have a nap before dinner. I hope you'll like your room. I had it fixed up just the way I thought you'd like it."

"Then it must be perfect," Moria said. Eugenia's heart swelled. Every response Moria made was exactly right. Maybe she'd been the daughter of a horse trainer and a lady's maid before she had been transformed into Miss Moria Compton, but she was a lady to the core, it had been born in her. Once again, Eugenia breathed a prayer of thanksgiving that she'd been shown the way to bring this child into her life and into her heart, and she blessed Laura for thinking of such a foolproof scheme that even William had been deceived.

Moria ascended the staircase side by side with Eugenia. They took the turn to the right. The gallery was softly carpeted so that their footfalls made no sound, and there were portraits along the walls, stern-looking men, and stiff-looking women who all looked just a little bit subdued by their husbands. Mr. Northrup's ancestors, of course. Looking at the portraits, Moria felt another of those chills. And taking as long a look at the ladies as she dared, she hoped that Eugenia would never look as they did, as though life had frightened them. She had no way of knowing that Eugenia had looked like that, many times intensified, until the day that she and Liam had discovered their love for each other.

They turned into another passage, and Eugenia led her into a room that stopped her in her tracks. Surely there must be a mistake! This room must be the most special guest room in the house, governors and even presidents might have stayed here except that it was so obviously decorated for a young girl.

A four-poster bed dominated the far side of the room, its white dotted swiss tester matching a bedspread that had deep ruffles that reached the floor. The same material curtained the windows, with rose overdrapes that matched the rose of the bows that decorated the canopy and the ruffles on the bed. There were two comfortable chairs, one a slipper chair of rose velvet, the other an armchair upholstered in pale blue. There was a dressing table with a mirror so large that she could see her reflection right down to her waist, and there were tortoiseshell toilet articles on it, beautiful against the embroidered runner under them. The wardrobe that stood against the wall was large enough to be used as a room, there was no way in the world that it could ever be filled with clothes.

There was a fireplace of pink-veined marble, its fire pit hidden now by a silk fan painted with peacocks and flowers, so beautiful that she knew she'd study it by the hour as soon as she had the time. In her mind, she was already naming the peacocks Beauty and Galahad, and they would talk to her when no one else was around because they were enchanted. Her imagination again! Maybe it was a good thing that she wasn't going to be going to confession; Father O'Brian would make her say a hundred Hail Marys.

Eugenia was delighted with the delight she saw in Moria's eyes. "I thought you'd like it. My room, when I was your age, was decorated very much like this. I thought it would make you seem more like my daughter, right from the start."

All of the trouble she'd had with William over the preparing of this room had been worth it. Not that she would have had her way if Estelle Vancouver hadn't taken such an interest. William could hardly forbid it when Estelle knew that he could well afford anything, and agreed with Eugenia that her plans for the room were perfect.

Moria couldn't answer Eugenia, her heart was too full. Instead, she put her arms around her and laid her head on her shoulder. Eugenia's eyes flooded with tears. "Thank you, God," she whispered. "Thank you for this day, and for all the days that will follow. As long as I have Moria and Liam, I'll never trouble you again with my earthly woes, but I'll find the courage to bear them on my own." It was a large order to live up to, but she was going to try.

Moria's inspection of her room was interrupted by a tap on the door, and a uniformed maid entered as soon as Eugenia bade her. "Yes, Dora? What is it?"

Dora was young, grown-up to Moria but still no more than eighteen or nineteen. For one half-second, Moria felt that she was glad that there was at least one young servant at Retreat, and then something in Dora's eyes brought foreboding to her heart. Her intuition, her inherited Irish intuition, told her that this girl resented her, although for the life of her she couldn't fathom why.

The fact of the matter was that Dora resented anyone who came into good fortune, that she was bitter because she herself had been put out to service when she'd been eleven, brought to this house by her own father, who hired her out as a scullery maid in order to pocket her infinitesimal wages to drink up at the saloons. Her father had died of drink when she'd been fourteen, and she'd exulted at his death, but that hadn't changed her circumstances and her bitterness had grown over the years, until she was filled with it, poisoning her to the core.

Gaunt, scrawny, Dora's eyes were small and mean, her homely face sullen. Physically unattractive, no man would have married her even if she hadn't been held in virtual slavery here in this house where married servants were forbidden and where there were no young men to want to marry her even if she had been pretty. She hated Eugenia because Eugenia had been born rich and beautiful, because she'd married into still more wealth. Everything had been given to Eugenia at birth, while Dora had nothing.

And now this young upstart, scarcely older than Dora had been when she'd been brought here to scrub pots and pans and floors until her back ached and her hands turned raw, had been brought to Retreat to be a daughter of the house, brought here through no virtue of her own but merely because she was one of the lucky ones, the ones Dora hated. The world was unfair, and Dora resented it and everyone to whom it was more fair than it was to her.

"Mr. Northrup has instructed me that I am to take care of the young lady," Dora said. Her face and voice reflected her satisfaction with this arrangement, not because being Moria's personal maid would be a pleasure to her but because she'd be able to find a myriad of petty little ways to make Moria's life uncomfortable.

Moria's heart sank. She didn't need a maid at all, the whole idea was silly, she was perfectly capable of looking after herself. For this young woman, whose animosity she could feel, to have charge of her deflated her high spirits of a moment ago, but then she shook the feeling off, reproaching herself. It was probably all in her imagination, anyway. The girl was only a servant. Even the word "only" that came into her mind made her feel ashamed. Servants weren't "onlys," they were human beings, the same as she was. Probably all Dora needed was someone to be kind to her and to recognize her as, and treat her as, a human being.

"But I'd already arranged for Mabel to look after Miss Moria." Eugenia spoke without thinking, her voice filled with protest.

She recovered herself quickly. If William had decreed that it should be Dora, there was no use in protesting. "All right, Dora. Miss Moria will want a bath before dinner, and there is her unpacking to do."

"Yes, Mrs. Northrup." The malice in Dora's eyes was more apparent than ever as she relished bringing bad news. "Mr. Northrup also instructed me to tell you that you and he are dining with the Vancouvers this evening and that the young lady will have a tray in her room. He asked me to tell you to be ready at six o'clock, the carriage will be waiting at that time."

Eugenia gasped with dismay. Dining out, and William had said nothing to her about it! The invitation would have been taken directly to him in his study, as was all the mail that came to Retreat, and was usually relayed to her later in the day if any of it concerned her, with instructions on how to handle it.

A glance at the mantel clock told her that it was already a quarter past five. It would be all Rose could do to prepare her bath and have her ready on time. Eugenia knew that William's giving her such short notice was no oversight; it was his way of showing her that although she had had her way about bringing Moria to live with them he was still very much the master and her destiny was in his hands to do with as he saw fit, and that Moria was of so little importance that she need not be considered at all.

"I'll have to hurry, darling, but I'll see you tomorrow morning." She would have liked to assure Moria that she'd come in when she

Lydia Lancaster

returned this evening to make sure that she was comfortable and able to sleep in a strange bed, but she knew that tonight William would be certain to prevent it. On Moria's first night under their roof he'd show his mastery by coming to her bedroom and subjecting her to all the abuse of which he was capable.

She kissed Moria's cheek and held her close for a moment, and then she sped to her own room, where Rose, who had ways of finding out everything that went on in this house, already had her bath ready and her dinner dress laid out. "Haines told cook and cook told Mrs. Lindstrom and she told me that the carriage had been ordered for six o'clock," Rose said, grinning. *"He* didn't even tell Mrs. Lindstrom that you wouldn't be dining at home until ten minutes ago!"

As she slipped into her bath, Eugenia thanked the Lord one more time for the loyalty of the servants toward her, and most especially for Rose. William was undoubtedly looking forward to reprimanding her for being late, but this time she'd fool him! The victory would be a small one, but any victory over William was worth savoring.

In her own room, the room that was to be hers until she was grown-up and married, Moria drew on all her inborn dignity to cope with the maid who had been assigned to her. She'd be kind, but her instinct told her that she must also be firm, or she would lose the battle before it was joined. "You may unpack while I'm having my bath, please. There isn't much, there will be plenty of time."

"As you wish, Miss Compton." The words were respectful, the tone resentful. "I'll have hot water brought up immediately."

The tub was behind a Chinese screen that stood in one corner, an oval-shaped tub of painted enamel, decorated with pink roses. One end was higher than the other to give the bather's head a place to rest. Moria had never imagined anything so luxurious. By the time two menservants had brought up kettles of steaming water and filled the tub, and Dora had unwrapped a cake of rose-scented soap and brought towels that were so large and thick that they would completely envelop her, Moria was almost numb with the impact of it all.

Her hair caught up and pinned on top of her head, Moria

92

luxuriated in the warm water. There had been a round wooden tub in the cottage in Ireland, a smaller, rusted, tin tub in the two-room flat in New York, but never a whole tubful of such warm water, to say nothing of the French-milled soap that smelled like a whole gardenful of roses. This was the stuff that dreams were made of, and she stayed in the tub, feeling delightfully wicked, until her skin began to shrivel and the water became cold.

Dora's hands were efficient but unnecessarily rough as she dried her charge, and Moria was forced to speak to her about it. "Gently, Dora! It isn't necessary to take my skin off along with the water." Her voice was light, and held a hint of laughter, but it had its effect and Dora's ministrations became more gentle, although her face tightened. Snippy young miss, falling into good fortune and it had already gone to her head, but what else could you expect? Dora's lips pressed together until they formed a hard line, and her initial dislike of the girl who had been handed a fortune on a gold platter deepened.

The nightgown and robe that Mrs. Franklyn had provided for Moria looked shabby and out of place in this room, but they were clean and only slightly mended. The felt slippers were just a fraction too small, as though she had outgrown them since her supposed father had died. Dora left her to fetch up her supper, and Moria's face flamed with embarrassment when the two men came up to carry out the tub and empty it. No man except Papa had ever seen her in her nightgown before. But the servants didn't look at her, and she told herself that she'd have to become accustomed to strange ways. Once again, she had no idea that Dora's instructing the men to remove the tub while Moria was in her nightgown was deliberate, something that was never done in this house, and intended to fluster and embarrass her.

Moria was kneeling beside the silk fan in front of the fireplace, examining the peacocks more closely, when Dora returned with her supper. Moria had to order herself not to gasp at the sight of the silver tray, of the silver-covered dishes. The china was so fine that it was translucent, the silver gleamed in the rays of the westering sun that entered through the windows.

"Will you eat in bed, or at the table?"

"At the table, please." Moria almost added, "I'm not sick!" but she thought better of it. How did she know whether or not ladies sometimes took their suppers in bed as well as their breakfasts? Mrs. Franklyn had neglected to tell her that, she'd have to ask Mrs. Northrup or the maid Rose O'Riley when she saw her. She mustn't make any mistakes, she had been drilled and drilled in the importance of not making any mistakes. "Put the tray on the table in front of the window, please."

Dora thumped the tray down on the table and made a good deal of trouble in arranging the china and silver. Moria wanted to cry out for her not to scratch the finish, to be careful not to crack the delicate plate or cup and saucer, but once again she held her tongue. Maybe the maid was in a bad mood about something that had nothing to do with her, and tomorrow she'd be completely different.

"Will there be anything else?" This time Dora neglected to say "Miss Compton" or "Miss Moria."

Moria ignored the lapse. "I don't believe so. Thank you, Dora. I can manage by myself now."

She waited until she was alone before she lifted the first silver cover. Roast chicken, covered with some kind of sauce that smelled heavenly. Unable to resist, Moria stuck her finger in the sauce and licked it, rolling her eyes with delight. Another dish disclosed biscuits, as light and fluffy as clouds, and another fresh green peas. Beautiful, tiny, garden-fresh green peas, not wilted from a cart and ready to be thrown away! And there was butter, and strawberry preserves, and a square of strawberry shortcake with whipped cream.

Moria ate the shortcake first. After all, she was only thirteen, and she had an irrational feeling that if she didn't gobble it down Dora might come and snatch the tray away before she got to it.

Sated, feeling almost uncomfortably stuffed, Moria rose from the table at last and went back to her inspection of the room. This whole huge, beautiful room was hers! Everything in it was hers to use, to look at, to touch and enjoy. If only Papa could see it! Where was his cottage, on this vast estate? How long would it be before she could see it and know how he lived, too, know what objects he saw and touched and used every day of his life?

And when she saw him, how was she to keep from showing her delight, from throwing herself into his arms and clinging to him? The difficulty of accomplishing everything that was expected of her overwhelmed her, and her eyes filled with tears.

Her fingers ached for the feel of her rosary, she needed to pray for help and guidance, but how could she pray without her beads? Papa had taken them with him the last time he'd seen her, because she daren't bring them with her other things. She hadn't even been able to bring the tiny statue of Mary with her, the one Mama and Papa had bought for her on her eighth birthday, scraping the pennies out of their small fund although they'd been ill able to afford it. One of Mary's feet was chipped, and Moria supposed that that was why it had been sold so cheaply. But Father O'Brian had blessed it for her, and Moria loved it all the more because of the hurt foot. It made the Holy Mother seem closer to her, because didn't she herself often hurt her toes running barefoot in the summer to save her shoes for mass?

She averted her face when Dora came to remove her supper tray. She wouldn't let the maid see tears in her eyes. "Thank you, Dora. It was delicious. I won't need you again tonight."

"As you wish, miss." The door closed behind Dora again, a little more loudly than was necessary, but Mr. Northrup was well away from the house by now and so there was little danger in it.

Left alone, Moria stood at the window and watched until the sun set in a blaze of glory. How much more beautiful the sunset was here, on the banks of the Hudson River, than it was in sooty New York City! She longed to run outside before it was fully dark and see what she could of the estate. Maybe she'd come across Papa's cottage.

But she didn't dare leave this room, no one had given her

permission. Eugenia hadn't even had time to come back and let her see her in her party dress. The house loomed dark and quiet around her, unknown territory, filled with unimaginable dangers.

When it was entirely dark, Moria moved at last, to slip out of her robe and between the lavender-scented sheets, her head on a down pillow so soft that she knew she'd never be able to sleep, and she felt so desolate that her whole body was one dull ache.

She'd never be able to do it, she'd let Papa down, she'd let something slip and betray him and Mrs. Northrup, and she'd rather die. The irony of being poised at the gates of heaven, knowing that her feet were bound to slip and plunge her downward into Hades, taking Papa and Mrs. Northrup with her, was too agonizing to bear, and the tears came at last. She cried herself to sleep, aching and numb.

She didn't hear the door to her bedroom open two hours later, or the light footsteps that crossed to her bed. She knew nothing of the gaze that fell on her face as it lay in a shaft of moonlight, or the picture she made with her raven hair spread across her pillow. But she felt the gentle fingers against her cheek, and even awakened so abruptly, in a strange place, she felt no fear but only a deep sense of relief.

" 'Tis Rose O'Riley, girl dear," Rose whispered. "And you're as beautiful as Liam and my mistress said you were."

Moria felt something being placed in her fingers, and Rose closed her fingers around hers so that she wouldn't drop it in her half-sleep. It was her rosary. "I had a feeling that you'd be needing your beads this night. And here I am to pray with you."

Then Moria was in Rose's arms, and she was crying again, but this time she knew that everything was going to be all right. Rose O'Riley was here, she had a friend, and with Rose's help and the help of Blessed Mary, she could do whatever she had to do.

6

Moria's knees were shaking as she followed Dora out into the garden, where several ornamental tables and chairs were sheltered under a rose arbor, all of them occupied by ladies sipping tea or cold lemonade as their tastes dictated on this sweltering August afternoon, and nibbling at tiny three-cornered sandwiches and fancy iced cakes.

If it was this hot here on the banks of the Hudson River, how must it be back in the city, in those narrow, airless streets that had been Moria's home ever since she had been brought to America? Poor Mrs. Murphy's face must be as red as the pickled beets she was so fond of serving to her boarders, and she'd be mopping at her forehead with her apron while huge perspiration stains grew under the armpits of her dress.

But thinking about Mrs. Murphy and her pickled beets didn't help at all. Moria was perspiring too, although she knew that ladies weren't supposed to perspire. She could already feel the moisture gathering damply under the armpits of the lavender dress that had been finished for her only yesterday. You'd think that a little breeze

97

would work its way up under its voluminous skirt, but no breeze would have a chance against the ruffled pantalets and the four petticoats. By the time she reached the arbor she'd be dripping like a fountain, and Eugenia would be disgraced by her lack of gentility.

An unbidden memory of her childhood in Ireland came back to her, and she had to blink to keep tears from coming into her eyes. When she'd been four and five and six, she'd run through the warm summer days in nothing but a dress and one thin shift, with the air cool on her bare legs and the grass tickling her toes. Cool and damp and green, and she wished with all her heart that she were still in Ireland, that the knock had never come on Papa's window in the middle of the night and sent them fleeing for their lives.

If she were still in Ireland, she couldn't be faced with this ordeal of being put on display to Eugenia's friends, who were going to look at her as if she were a creature from some heathen country, not quite human, and who would find her no more than an object of curiosity, something to be examined and found lacking and perhaps, if she were lucky, to be pitied a little.

It was that last word in her thoughts that made her chin come up. Pitied she would not be, not today and not ever! To these women who were waiting to pass judgment on her she might be Moria Compton, but she was Moria Donovan and the blood of Irish kings ran in her veins and nobody pitied an Irishman except at the risk of his life. She was her father's daughter, and he expected her to carry this off and she was going to carry it off and if these women didn't accept her it would be to their shame, not hers.

These last three weeks, since the day she'd been brought to Retreat, had been the loneliest in Moria's life. She had yet to see her father, her riding habit hadn't been finished, and except for a half-hour here and fifteen minutes there when Eugenia could steal the time to pay her a flying visit, there had been nothing to do except stand for dress fittings and have her piano lesson, or wander in the gardens, not daring to pick a flower, and wish that Mr. Northrup would be called away for a year or two years or forever, and never come back, because he was the one who kept Mrs. Northrup too busy to see her and kept her from seeing her father.

The rose garden was just ahead of her now, and Moria's face paled even under the flush brought on by the heat as she saw a dozen pairs of eyes raise from their cakes and teacups and fasten themselves on her. Don't let me trip, she prayed. Hail Mary, full of grace . . .

Eugenia had risen and come forward to take her hand. She looked beautiful in her summer dress, a blue that matched her eyes, her high-piled hair partially concealed under a lace cap. The visiting ladies all wore bonnets, lavishly trimmed, and their afternoon gowns were so elaborate that if Moria hadn't known that the war was still going on and a good part of the country impoverished, she'd have thought that there was no war at all. The aristocracy, the privileged few, lived in a different world and knew nothing of the plight of the poorer classes, and Moria suspected that they wouldn't have cared if they had known. That was one of the things that made Papa so bitter, and so determined that things must be changed.

"Here she is at last," Eugenia said, and her voice was filled with love and pride. "Ladies, this is Moria Compton, my ward. Moria, this is Mrs. Vancouver, Mrs. Linkbetter . . ." the minister's wife, Moria remembered, asked out of duty ". . . Mrs. Armstrong, Mrs. Simmons, Mrs. Schuyler . . ."

Moria felt faint, not from the heat, but from the effort to remember all those names and connect them with the proper ladies. Mrs. Vancouver was the most important, both Eugenia and Rose had impressed that on her. If Mrs. Vancouver accepted her, the rest would follow suit and she'd have nothing to worry about.

Moria smiled at Mrs. Vancouver, her face lighting up and her eyes eager, as though there were nothing in the world she wanted more than to be privileged to know the lady. But it wasn't all feigned. Estelle Vancouver, Eugenia had told her, was kind, and if Eugenia liked her, then Moria liked her too.

"How do you do. I'm very pleased to meet you," Moria said. She curtsied. She'd practiced until her knees had creaked, even

99

though she was naturally so graceful that practice wasn't actually necessary once she'd learned how to do it.

Mrs. Vancouver beamed, her plain face filled with pleasure. The child was delightful, even prettier than Eugenia had told her. Such grace, such gorgeous hair and eyes, such beauty in one so young! Perhaps her patriotism, when she'd backed Eugenia's bid to take the orphaned girl, hadn't been a mistake after all in spite of Jacob's displeasure with her for making her sentiments known. It would have been dreadful if the child had turned out to be socially unacceptable, plain and awkward and an embarrassment to Eugenia and William.

Moria's smile deepened, and encompassed each of the ladies in turn. And each of the ladies, in their turn, were as captivated as Estelle Vancouver, although each of them waited to see what Estelle's reaction was before they expressed their own.

"Sit here beside me." Estelle moved over a trifle on her wicker bench, where she had been sitting in solitary splendor, as became her rank.

"Thank you, Mrs. Vancouver." Why, the child's voice was as sweet as she'd thought it had been, however impossible it seemed! She'd fit in, there was no doubt of it. Estelle could hardly wait to get home and tell her husband that, once again, William had managed to obtain possession of something priceless, something that would further the envy of him already felt by his peers. Being a trifle put out with Jacob at the moment, Estelle would take pleasure in the telling.

Moria accepted a glass of lemonade and an iced cake. Her manners were perfect, she managed them as daintily as the ladies themselves. The lavender of her dress complemented her fair skin and black hair and brought out the intense blue of her eyes. Those of the ladies who had daughters of comparable ages felt twinges of uneasiness, but Estelle was clearly entranced and they had no choice but to follow her lead or suffer the anger of their husbands, all of whom had business dealings with both Mr. Northrup and Jacob Vancouver.

Fortunately for Moria, Estelle felt no jealousy because her own daughters, a great deal older, had never been the beauties that Moria was. She herself had never been pretty, but she knew beauty when she saw it, and she appreciated it. And her son, Anthony, more than made up for any lack of comeliness in her two girls.

Anthony was fifteen now, and Estelle was well aware that he was the handsomest young man in the Hudson River Valley. Just thinking of her son made her heart glow with warmth. His hair was so light that it shone like silver in the sun, his eyes were brown and melting when he wanted to charm someone, the lashes so long that it was a shame they had been bestowed on a boy when so many girls were lacking. With a son of such perfection, she had no reason to be jealous of Moria's beauty.

Helping Eugenia present this child to society, smoothing her way, would be more of a pleasure than a patriotic duty toward a war orphan. So Estelle beamed at Moria, and patted her hand, and urged her to take another pink cake, and the other ladies smiled, twittering and beaming and congratulating Eugenia on her good fortune.

"Eugenia, your ward is perfect! Absolutely perfect! What a joy she will be to you, how happy I am that you have her! But you mustn't be selfish, you must let us all share in the pleasure of taking her under our wings. We must arrange parties, outings, see that she is introduced to all of our young people."

To everyone who mattered, Eugenia thought, and she winced. In a way it was a pity that Moria would be forced into the company of boys and girls who were growing up in the image of their parents, selfish, shallow, thinking of nothing but their superior station in life. But Moria was Liam's daughter, and Eugenia had faith that she wouldn't be spoiled by it, and it was a great deal better than for her to have been snubbed and ignored.

In Moria's bedroom, which overlooked the rose garden, Dora stood at the window with her face pinched with jealous spite. Look at the little snip, sitting there beside Mrs. Vancouver, as smug as a cat with a saucer of cream! In all her life, Dora had never had a dress to compare with the one the upstart orphan girl was wearing, let alone had the privilege of sitting in a rose garden with women like Mrs. Vancouver and those others who were twittering and fussing over her as though she were a princess of the blood!

If only Mrs. Vancouver had taken a dislike to her! Then it would have been different, because if Estelle Vancouver hadn't accepted her, then none of the Hudson River Valley would have accepted her, she would have been put in her place and it would no more than serve her and Eugenia Northrup right.

She wouldn't watch any longer, she couldn't, it made her sick to her stomach. Dora turned from the window and began sorting and straightening the underclothing in Moria's chiffonier. Not that Miss Moria would complain if they weren't straightened. So far, she hadn't complained about anything. But the fuss those ladies were making over her, she'd be spoiled rotten and she'd start complaining, and treating Dora like dirt, and Dora's face grew harder and more bitter as she worked.

She removed a pile of new petticoats and pantalets to refold, all of them of a quality that rubbed salt into her wounds. The lawn was so fine that it felt like silk under her fingers. Fit for a princess, and her with no more right to things like this than Dora had been at that age, than Dora had now or ever would have! The other servants seemed to think that it was an honor for her to have been chosen to look after Moria, but to Dora it was the ultimate humiliation to have to serve a chit of a child who had no right to be here at all.

Something that was caught in the folds of a petticoat fell to the floor as Dora shook it out, and she stooped to see what it could be. A necklace of some sort, one that Dora hadn't seen before, a new bauble bought to further spoil her who was already being so spoiled that within a month she wouldn't be fit to live with!

Then Dora's eyes widened as she saw that it wasn't a necklace. She picked it up, and it seemed to burn her fingers. A young woman of no religious convictions herself, who attended the Lutheran services every Sunday only because Mr. Northrup required it of all his servants except the few who, like Rose, were Irish Catholics, she still knew a rosary when she saw one, and this was definitely a rosary, and why would a rosary be in Moria's chiffonier unless Moria had placed it there between her petticoats to hide it?

There was only one answer, as far as Dora could see. Her mind racing, she told herself that Protestant girls didn't own rosaries. Even if a Protestant girl might by some inconceivable stretch of the imagination have a rosary for any legitimate reason, something she'd found, perhaps, dropped by a careless papist, her still having possession of it would send William Northrup into a rage that might well end in Moria's being banished from Retreat. She should have turned the tainted article over to him the moment she'd arrived, or thrown it into the nearest trash container.

There was another possibility, one that Dora hardly dared to hope for. What if Moria were masquerading under false colors, what if the orphaned girl were actually a Catholic? In that case, her banishment from Retreat would be violent and immediate. Even thinking about it made Dora purr inside. But if it weren't true, the mere existence of the rosary, found in Moria's possession, was bound to cause trouble, a great deal of trouble.

Her face grim with satisfaction, Dora left Moria's bedroom and sped down the servants' staircase to make her way to Mr. Northrup's study, to present him with her find. If nothing good ever happened to her again, this would make up for it. The very foundations of this house would shake the moment she placed the rosary in Mr. Northrup's hand and told him where she had found it.

In the rose arbor, Moria drew a deep breath and got to her feet. Her ordeal was over, she had been excused. She'd passed this test with flying colors, but her elation was for her father and Eugenia rather than for herself. Now, she knew, the ladies would discuss her for at least another half an hour before their carriages took them back to their respective homes, but Eugenia's smile, brilliant and loving, assured her that nothing detrimental would be said about her.

She was glad that she'd been excused, because there was something she had to do. How could she have been so careless, how could Rose have been so careless, that neither of them had noticed that Moria's rosary was still lying in plain sight on her bedside table when Rose had left her room last night after they'd prayed together, as Rose came every night, when the rest of the household was settled and there was no danger, to pray with her?

She must retrieve the rosary and find Rose right away and give it to her, before Dora found it. She'd snatched it up last night and concealed it in her chiffonier between two petticoats, so the maid hadn't seen it this morning, but there had been no chance to place it safely in Rose's hand since then. Immediately after she'd had her breakfast, with Dora puttering around her room, she'd been forced to spend hours being fitted for her rapidly growing wardrobe, and then there had been a music lesson because William Northrup had lost no time in obtaining a piano teacher for her. Worrying about the rosary now, Moria thought that both she and Rose had been so concerned about this tea party this afternoon, when she'd have to present herself for the inspection of the ladies who could smooth her path by accepting her or make her living at Retreat a burden and a fiasco for Eugenia by rejecting her, to have remembered about the rosary.

The piano itself delighted Moria. Like everything else that William Northrup owned, it was the finest that could be had, a magnificent instrument. Its tone was beautiful, and the notes that tinkled under her fingers as they touched the ivory keys filled her with joy. Mrs. Drinkwater, her teacher, was a timid little spinster, afraid of her own shadow and terrified that she wouldn't be able to please Mr. Northrup with Moria's progress, but she knew music, and Moria was quick to learn, it was as if her fingers knew instinctively which keys to touch. Her hour-long lesson and her two hours of practicing afterward, with the door to the music room closed so that the sound of her scales wouldn't disturb Mr. Northrup, gave Moria nothing but pleasure. Instead of being the strict discipline which William had intended it to be, something to keep Eugenia and Moria apart, it was the one element in Moria's new life that kept her from dying from sheer boredom.

So the fittings and the lesson and the practice had taken up the time until she'd had to dress for the tea party, and until this moment there had been no opportunity to retrieve the rosary and find Rose.

She started to run up the staircase, remembered that a lady never runs, and slowed her pace. She breathed a sigh of relief when she saw that her room was empty. In another second, she'd opened the drawer of the chiffonier and her fingers were searching for the rosary.

It wasn't there. Disbelieving at first, and then frantic, Moria removed every article of clothing in the drawer. She even shook them all out and refolded them. Still more frantic, wondering if she might possibly have put it in a different drawer, she examined them all.

Had Dora taken her petticoats to be laundered, even if they didn't need it? Moria rechecked. Her heart sank when she determined that the same petticoats she'd concealed the rosary between were there, there was no possibility that they had been taken from her room with the rosary still caught between them.

It was no use. She'd put it right here, in the middle drawer, and it was gone. There was only one faint hope. Had Rose remembered it, and come in and searched for it and taken it away?

Grasping that tiny straw, her heart pounding, she sped down the corridor to Eugenia's room. Rose had to be there, she just had to! And it had to be that Rose had found the rosary and taken it. Dora disliked her, and it would be dreadful if she had found it. Moria would have liked to use a stronger word in describing Dora's dislike of her, a dislike she couldn't understand because she'd never given the maid any reason to dislike her. Sometimes she was sure that Dora actually hated her. But Sister Teresa and Sister Agnes said that you must never jump to conclusions about what other people thought, that it might all be in your own head and everyone should be given the benefit of the doubt. All the same, Dora didn't like her, no matter how much benefit of the doubt Moria gave her.

Rose let out an exclamation of alarm when she saw Moria's pale face and frightened eyes. "Girl dear, whatever is it? Did something happen in the garden, didn't the ladies like you? You never spilled your tea on one of them!'' To Rose's thinking, that was the most dreadful thing that could have happened, for Moria to have ruined one of the ladies' gowns and never be forgiven for it.

"No, no, of course I didn't! I was ever so careful. It's my rosary, Rose, it's gone! We forgot it last night, and I put it in a drawer and now it's gone! Did you find it?''

Rose crossed herself. This was a dozen times worse than spilling a cup of tea, or forgetting one of the ladies' names, or anything else Moria might have done in her nervousness a the trial she'd just been put through. "You're sure, then, that you put it where you thought you did? You didn't hide it under the clock or in the fireplace?''

"No, no, I put it in the drawer!''

"Dora has it, then, and no good will come of it! Thank Our Lady that *he* isn't home, or she'd have given it to him already! But we can be sure that she will give it to him, the minute he sets foot back in this house. Listen, mavourneen, when you're called to explain, you must tell him that the rosary is mine, that I dropped it when I brought you a message from my mistress, and that you dropped it in the drawer for safekeeping until you could give it to me. That's all you need to remember. God forgive our lies, but that's our story and we'll stick to it and there's no way that Dora, or *he,* can prove otherwise! And for the love of Our Lady take that terrified look off your face! You're an innocent child, you've done no wrong. It'll be all right as long as our stories match. Now get back to your room and if Dora comes in, pretend you haven't missed the beads or even given them a thought. I'm taking my own beads to Liam this minute, in case *he* takes it into his head to have my room searched to make sure there's no rosary of mine among my possessions when it was supposed to have been dropped in your room.''

"You'll get in trouble. You aren't supposed to carry your rosary with you around the house,'' Moria protested.

"So I'll be laced out, but that's all that will come of it. I'll survive, girl dear, I've survived worse than that and no doubt I will again. Go along now, and put a smile on your face! You're supposed to be happy because the ladies liked you, remember?''

She gave Moria a hug and then pushed her from the room. Dora! She'd have to keep a sharp eye on that one, there was no doubt of it. It was a pity that the girl didn't break her leg and end up lamed so that *he'd* dismiss her from his service! Crossing herself again and begging forgiveness for such an unkind thought, as deserved as it might be, Rose took her own rosary from the little box Eugenia had given her to keep it in, inlaid with mother-of-pearl, and hurried to find Liam.

William returned late. He was in an expansive mood. He'd spent the afternoon with Jacob Vancouver, and as their business discussion had lasted longer than he had thought it would, Jacob had invited him to stay for dinner. And at dinner, Estelle had run on and on about how lovely, how charming and how utterly perfect his ward was.

"You'll be the envy of everyone! If I'd known what a jewel your Moria was I'd have taken her myself, in spite of the fact that I already have two daughters and I'm a little old to start raising another. We ladies have plans for her, you can be assured of that! Everyone adores her, she'll be a credit to you, a credit indeed! Every lady there this afternoon is already planning some gala or outing in her honor. Indeed, she's a paragon, and I can't express how fortunate I think you are to have her."

William had been a little surprised by Estelle's enthusiasm, but he couldn't help feeling pride. It seemed that once again, even though this time he'd been hoodwinked into it, he'd come into possession of a treasure that other men would envy him. Still piqued by the way Eugenia had forced him into a corner so that there had been no way he could refuse to take the child without lowering himself in the esteem of his peers, and more than a little certain that Laura, Eugenia's sister, had had a hand in it although for the life of him he couldn't discover how when no correspondence was allowed between them, it looked now as if it were going to turn out to his advantage.

Moria was a beauty, William conceded that. He'd never seen a lovelier child, her manners were perfect, and if he chose to have it that way he could make her into the toast of the Hudson River Valley in a few more years when she was old enough to come out in society. The more of a success she was, the more it would reflect on him to his glory.

Settled in his study for a last glass of port before he retired, and having already decided that tonight he wouldn't visit Eugenia in her bedroom, William reflected on this new development. It pleased him enormously that Estelle and the other ladies had been so taken with his ward. Far from being only the minor nuisance that he had thought she would be, she could become one of his most valuable assets, envied him as much as Eugenia and his incomparable estate and all the priceless objects it contained. Therefore, he was not in the mood Dora might have wished when she tapped on his study door with the incriminating rosary in her hand.

"In Moria's chiffonier, you say? Hidden there in a drawer?"

"Yes, sir. That's where I found it, Mr. Northrup. And of course I knew it was my duty to bring it straight to you."

"Quite right. I'll look into it. Send Miss Moria here to me in my study, Dora. If she's already in bed, get her up. I'll wait."

Smug with triumph, Dora got Moria, who was feigning sleep, out of bed and helped her to dress.

"But what does he want, Dora?" Moria's pretended bewilderment was so convincing that for a few seconds Dora felt a qualm. But the facts were the facts. The rosary had been in Moria's chiffonier, and now she was being called to account for it.

It took every ounce of Moria's strength to keep from trembling as she faced Mr. Northrup, who was scowling at her, his face even more cold and stern than usual. William held the rosary between his forefinger and thumb, as though even touching it were distasteful to him.

"Is this yours, Moria? It was found among your possessions." William could scarcely mention undergarments to a female, even one so young. "In your chiffonier."

"The rosary, sir? No, sir, it isn't mine." Behind her back, Moria's fingers were crossed, and she hoped that she wasn't condemning her soul to Hades by these lies she was forced to tell. "It belongs to Rose, she dropped it by accident when she came to bring me a message from Mrs. Northrup."

"Did she, indeed? Dora, go and fetch Rose."

Her face properly expressionless, but with a smug look in her eyes, Dora relished getting Rose out of bed. Her expression became even more smug as Rose appeared to be bewildered, with no idea at all of why she had been summoned to the master's study at this hour of the night, and Dora did not enlighten her. It was better that Rose be completely unprepared for what lay ahead of her. Dora's jealous hate extended to the Irish girl simply because Rose was Eugenia's maid, more privileged than the rest of the staff, and because Eugenia was fond of Rose. In all her life Dora couldn't remember anyone having been fond of her. She led the way back down to the study like a jailer leading his prisoner to his execution.

William was standing in front of his desk, the rosary still dangling from his fingers, when the two servants were bade to enter.

"So there it is!" Rose exclaimed. "I've been searching high and low for it, Mr. Northrup, and that's no exaggeration." William's name was bitter on her lips, but this time she had no choice but to use it. "I was afraid I'd lost it forever! Might I ask where you came by it, sir?"

"You may, indeed. It was discovered in Miss Moria's chiffonier. Do you have any idea of how it might have come there?"

Rose pondered for a moment, and then seemed to recollect something. "I took a message to Miss Moria early in the day. I expect I might have dropped it then."

"It's difficult for me to understand how such a thing could have happened. I had thought that every servant in this house was aware of the rule that rosaries are not to be carried about the premises, but kept out of sight abovestairs in the servants' quarters."

"I'm that sorry, Mr. Northrup! I'm afraid I dropped it in my pocket and forgot about it. I'll not be so careless in the future, I promise."

"Indeed you will not!" William's voice was like ice. "You will be docked a month's wages for your infraction. I take it that you do not consider this penalty unjust?"

A month's wages! Moria wanted to cry out in protest, but a glance from Rose warned her to hold her tongue. And then she was comforted by the thought that the loss of a month's wages by a servant in this house held no such consequences as the loss of a month's wages would to a workman in New York City, whose family would go hungry from the loss.

"No, sir, I do not."

"You may go now, all of you," William said. He returned to his chair and picked up his glass of port, holding it to the light of the lamp in order to admire its color. Damn all Irish servants! They were almost more trouble than they were worth. Still, Rose seldom did anything to annoy him, and she could be counted on to hold her tongue about things she knew, as long as she remained in his employ. Her devotion to Eugenia was to his advantage, and far outweighed his anger that she had dared to ignore his rules.

Safely out of earshot after they'd left William's study, Rose turned to Dora. "You should have brought my beads to Mrs. Lindstrom, if you didn't know they were mine, and not caused Mr. Northrup all this trouble," she said, her tone severe. "Now, you'd best get your charge back to bed, the little love has had a long day of it and she needs her rest."

Dora gave her a glance of pure venom. Nothing could have satisfied Rose more. But all the same, she'd keep an eye on that one. She was out to cause trouble, and that was as sure as the fact that Saint Patrick had driven the snakes out of Ireland.

7

It had come at last! Today was the day she was going to see her father. Today, this morning, in just a few minutes!

All the while Dora helped her get into her riding habit, that had been finished only yesterday afternoon, Moria quivered with anticipation, her legs actually shaking. Seeing her trembling and the unusual shine in her eyes, Dora felt a spiteful satisfaction. So the chit was frightened, afraid of horses! Her very fear would make the most gentle mount skittish, and maybe she'd fall, maybe she'd be hurt. Even if that didn't happen, if she was afraid to ride, if she didn't do well at it, Mr. Northrup would be displeased and make his displeasure felt not only by Moria but by Eugenia as well.

"Dora, do hurry! The skirt is all right, the seamstress made sure that it hung perfectly."

"Mr. Northrup will inspect you to make sure that you present a proper appearance." Dora's mouth was prim. "He doesn't tolerate less than perfection."

Moria already knew that, and she had come to dread it. Every morning, as soon as she'd breakfasted in her room and dressed, she had to present herself in William's study, while his cold eyes appraised her from head to foot. Eugenia, also, had to suffer these daily inspections, hers while her husband was still at breakfast and Eugenia ready to ride. Up until today, Moria had always passed the inspection. Dora made sure that no least detail of her toilette was overlooked, because the blame would fall on her, with serious consequences.

Ever since the day when Moria had been presented to the ladies in the rose arbor, William had taken a greater interest in her and her progress in her lessons. Several times he had come to stand behind her while she practiced at the piano, making her so nervous that her hands trembled. But she'd gritted her teeth and done the exercises without mistake, fearing that if she didn't perform adequately Mrs. Drinkwater would be the one to suffer his displeasure and Moria didn't want the timid little woman to be humiliated and frightened. William had never made any comment, but only watched and listened for a while and then left, apparently satisfied.

Barely managing to contain herself, Moria stood still so that Dora could give a final twitch to her riding skirt and wipe an imaginary speck of dust from the toe of her boot. The cost of the boots alone would have kept her and her father and mother for weeks, maybe for months, back in New York City when they had first come to America.

Dora squinted her eyes and adjusted Moria's plumed hat a fraction of an inch, until it was at exactly the right angle. Moria's hair was caught back with a ribbon of the same royal blue as her habit. The riding gloves felt tight on her hands, but Eugenia had assured her that that was the way they were supposed to feel. She was getting used to wearing gloves anyway. Every time she stepped out of the house she was expected to wear gloves, even for a stroll around the garden. Being a lady was a deal of bother, and most of it nonsensical, but that was the way things were and she had to conform. There was too much at stake for her to offer the least hint of rebellion. Her father depended on her, and so did Eugenia, and she couldn't let them down no matter how much she wanted to be free, to be herself, even for a few minutes in a day.

"You'll do," Dora said, after an agonizingly long pause. "You'd best get downstairs, Mr. Northrup will be waiting."

Her legs trembling, her knees like water, Moria descended the staircase. She'd hoped that Eugenia would come to her room to fetch her and be beside her through this most crucial of all inspections. If she didn't pass muster, if she were sent back to her room to wait another day, she'd die. She'd waited so long already, she couldn't bear it if she had to wait another five minutes.

The study door was closed, as it always was. Any servant who carelessly left it open would suffer for the infraction far beyond reason. Moria lifted her gloved hand and tapped, very softly, holding herself back from pounding for admittance and then dismissal so that she could see her father at last.

"Enter." It was typical of William to use that word, a command rather than an invitation. Moria opened the door and stepped inside. As always, this inner sanctum of the master of Retreat filled her with dread. The rich Oriental carpet, the book-lined walls, the massive leather furniture and the heavy draperies all reflected the character of the man who inhabited it, completely masculine, completely cold and unbending. Nothing was ever out of place, no speck of dust would have dared to intrude.

William was seated at his desk, and Moria's heart leaped when she saw that Eugenia was standing beside him. And then it sank again as William ignored her to speak to Eugenia, his voice cold.

"It's out of the question, my dear. Your presence at the lesson would be a distraction. Donovan is perfectly capable of teaching our ward to ride and to see that she comes to no harm without you standing on the sidelines. He has his instructions, you may rest assured that the lesson will go well if the child has any natural aptitude at all."

"It's just that I'd like to watch, even for a few moments." There were two spots of color in Eugenia's cheeks, and her voice held more insistence than it usually did when she spoke to her husband.

Not that she ever displayed any fear of him, or even awe; it was more that she was resigned to the point of not caring.

"I'm sorry. I cannot grant your request. Learning to ride is a task, not an outing. I'll excuse you now."

Her chin high, Eugenia left the room, but she managed one brilliant, encouraging smile at Moria before the door closed behind her. Moria took a deep breath and stood very straight, waiting for the appraisal that she knew would be thorough and merciless.

She had to hold her breath for a long time, because William had turned his attention to some papers that were spread out on his desk. But at last he looked up, his eyes raking her.

"Turn around," he said. "No, slowly! Very well, you are excused. I'll have a report from Donovan after your lesson, it won't be necessary for you to return to the study."

Moria's breath expelled with a whoosh and for a moment she was afraid that William had noticed, but apparently he hadn't because his attention was on the papers on his desk again. Slowly, she opened the door, stepped through it, and closed it behind her again very softly.

And then she ran. There were no servants in the entrance hall, there was no one to see her. She struggled with the massive front door that never stood open even in the most sweltering weather.

But then she had to slow her steps, because there was a gardener scything the lawn. Her blood pounding with impatience, threatening to burst through her very skin, she walked toward the stables and the ring.

There he was, holding a medium-sized mare, while a rangy gelding was tied to a rail beside them. He was waiting for her, he was looking toward her, and Moria thought she would die of the effort to keep on walking, not to run, not to scream his name and throw herself into his arms and cling to him and never let him go.

"Good morning, Miss Compton."

"Good morning, Mr. Donovan."

She couldn't bear it. It wasn't right that she, that anyone, should be expected to bear this. But the ring was in sight of the house, the gardeners were out and about, and the stablehands, and it had to be borne whether flesh and blood could bear it or not.

But there was love in Liam's eyes as he looked at her, love and pride and admiration but most of all love, the love she couldn't live without. And there was love in her eyes as she placed her booted foot in the stirrup Liam made with his hands to lift her into the sidesaddle.

"Her name is Serena, and her disposition matches her name. There's nothing to be frightened of, Miss Moria."

"I'm not frightened, thank you, Mr. Donovan." The words burned her tongue. She'd been instructed to call him Liam, but it was indecent for a daughter to call her father by his first name and she couldn't bring herself to do it, even if William did not approve of servants being addressed by titles, as though being called Mr. or Mrs. or Miss would make them seem more than they were.

"Papa..."

"Be careful. But it's all right, darlin', they can't hear us, they're too far away. Holy Mary, but you're lovely! I'd give the next fifty years of my life if your mother could see you now, every inch a lady, just the way she always dreamed!"

"I don't feel like a lady. I feel like your little girl. Oh, Papa, I've missed you so much! It's worse here than it was when I was living with Mrs. Murphy, because then I knew I could only see you twice a month for a little while, and you were a long way away so there was no use in thinking about it. But here, you're only a tiny way away, I could get to you in two minutes, and I still can't see you, and sometimes I think I can't stand it!"

"Hush, hush, the worst of that is over now. You're starting your lessons, you'll see me for an hour every morning right after Mrs. Northrup has her ride. And mavourneen, as soon as you can keep your seat in the saddle, the three of us will be riding together, through fields and woods, out of sight and earshot of everybody, we'll be alone and it'll be like heaven, don't you see?"

From her high perch on the mare, Moria closed her eyes and let her mind project into the future. Heaven! Oh, yes, it would be heaven, she'd be the happiest girl in the world and she'd never ask for another thing, not if she died for it!

But first she must learn to ride, and she must learn as fast as she could so that it would happen sooner. She opened her eyes again and her smile was radiant. "What do I do first, Papa?"

"None of that," Liam told her as severely as he could manage, all the while that his heart was breaking because he couldn't take her in his arms. "Call me Liam, you must never call me anything else because who knows what ears might be listening even though we can't see hide nor hair of another soul? My name is Liam, Miss Moria. And first you hold the reins, like this, laced through your fingers, don't you see, and the top ones guide your beast and the bottom ones control the bit, for when you want to stop her, by turning your hand so. And to start, you lay the reins against the right side of her neck and kick her with your heel, and then she'll turn to the left. . . ."

"Ass-backward," Moria said. Liam had to choke back his laughter. He hadn't heard Moria say those words since she'd been a toddler back in Ireland, when she'd picked them up from His Lordship himself, who'd been complaining about some workman who did everything ass-backward! Molly had been hard put to break her of the habit because Moria had been entranced with the expression.

"Not ass-backward, at all, at all. She moves away from the pressure against her neck, don't you see, and so if you lay the reins against the right side of her neck she moves to the left. After you kick her, of course."

"Kick her!" Moria's face registered horror. "Oh, I couldn't do that! Why, she's a nice beastie, she hasn't done anything to deserve being kicked, the very idea!" Impulsively, she leaned forward until she could bury her face against the top of Serena's neck, and breathed deep of the clean, horsey odor that she remembered so well from her early childhood. Papa had always smelled like that after he'd been working with Lord Malcolm's horses. It smelled good, it smelled like home.

"Sit up now, there's my girl. Back straight, and get that heel in

116

your stirrup down, and turned in a bit like so, and your toes turned just a wee bit out. That way you'll keep your foot where it belongs, in the stirrup and not slipping out, and if you should take a tumble it won't be caught and you won't be dragged. Only you aren't going to fall, I'll be right beside you."

"Sidesaddles are silly," Moria said. "I wish I could ride astride like a man the way you used to show me back in Ireland."

"And so do I, mavourneen. Whatever idiot of a man decreed that females must ride sidesaddle should have been hanged, and I hope he was! No woman is as secure in the saddle as a man, they have to be better riders altogether from a ridiculous perch like that and God forgive the moron who said it must be so!"

"It's all right, Papa. I can do it, I can learn. Eugenia says it really isn't that hard."

"Liam. Call me Liam." Liam's face was impassive, but his thoughts were far from calm. Eugenia had ridden since she'd been younger than Moria. In the circle she'd moved in, every girl learned to ride at an early age, even city girls. She'd perfected her equestrianism here at Retreat, under expert tutorship, but she'd also been a natural rider, one who'd been born with the ability, and Moria had never been on a horse in her life.

There was the additional fact that Serena wasn't as docile as Liam had led his daughter to believe. No piece of horseflesh at Retreat was anything but spirited, William Northrup would tolerate nothing but the best. He'd have liked to ask for a gentle mount to be bought for Moria's lessons, but Eugenia had warned him that his request would not only have been denied, but that her husband would consider it an impertinence for him to as much as mention it.

Moria's eyes were shining. "Let's start the lesson, Papa . . . Liam. The sooner I learn, the sooner we'll all be able to ride together, you and Eugenia and I!"

"Hold her steady while I mount Ranger. No, no, don't pull back on the reins, just hold her. You'll have her backing up, else."

But Serena was already backing up, her ears twitching nervously. Moria's face took on an expression of such ludicrous surprise that

Liam couldn't help laughing. "Ease up," he told her. "There, that's right. Another minute and you'd have backed clear to the front door, and what if our lord and master had seen that! I'd have been out of a job before you could turn her around again, and then where would we be?"

He'd attached a leading rein to Serena's bridle, and as soon as he was mounted he leaned over to take it. "Just sit there and concentrate on holding the reins properly and keeping your balance. Keep your back straight. Put some weight on the stirrup, your foot and leg has to be steady in it. We'll just walk around the ring for a bit until you get the feel of it."

Although Serena was a relatively small animal, Moria felt very high up as they walked around the ring. She glanced down only once. The ground was a long way down, if she fell she'd get a real jolt, and besides, her riding habit would be dirtied and Mr. Northrup would be displeased. But keeping her balance wasn't so hard after all, and after the first few minutes she got the feel of it and was able to maintain the correct tension on the reins.

"It's almost like being in a rocking chair!" she told her father. "Let's trot, I'm tired of walking and so is Serena, she'll think I'm a moron and she won't like me!"

"Take care not to fall, then," Liam advised her.

"Poo! I'm not about to fall off!" But the actuality of trotting made Moria bite her tongue and flush at the audacity of her words. Trotting was different, she felt wobbly, she almost lost the stirrup. This was harder than she'd imagined it would be and she was about to disgrace herself and disgrace her father and disgrace Eugenia. And then, so quickly that she was filled with amazement, she got the feel of it, and she felt steady and secure, and minutes later Liam released the leading rein and she was on her own.

Turn right, turn left. Turn all the way around in a circle. Pull down to a walk, lift to a trot again. Serena didn't seem to mind being kicked, and in any case she didn't have to kick her very hard because she was eager to go. The rhythm delighted her, the exercise brought roses to her cheeks and made her eyes sparkle as though diamonds were scattered in their sapphire blue. Looking at her, Liam's heart swelled with pride. Molly, do you see her? Do you see how I'm keeping my promise to you? We're going to do it, Molly girl, our Moria's going to be and have everything we ever dreamed for her!

He found no incongruity in believing that Molly's soul had been saved even though his own faith had been so badly shaken that he no longer believed in such things for himself. If there were any God at all, then Molly was in heaven, even if all the rest of what the priests said was a pack of nonsense that any man with eyes in his head to see the evils of the world could never believe in.

Lost in his reverie, he was taken unaware when Moria kicked Serena more sharply, so caught up in her excitement that she couldn't restrain herself, and Serena broke into a canter. For one heart-stopping second, Moria was jolted off balance, and she swayed and slipped in the saddle.

But then she was upright again, and she had the feel of it, and it was as smooth as silk, and she threw back her head and laughed, her creamy throat pulsing. Keeping pace with her, Liam beamed with pride. She was going to be a rider, this girl of his, it was as plain as the Irish of his face. And how could it be otherwise, with it born in her and pulsing through her blood, and her the daughter of the best horse trainer ever to come from the Old Sod?

He saw William Northrup a split second before Moria did. William had come down to the ring to see for himself how the lesson was going. He stood just outside the rail, his face showing nothing of what went on in his mind. Liam's heart lurched. Don't let it make her nervous when she sees him, he prayed.

Moria saw him at that exact instant. Her heart lurched just as Liam's had done, but she lost no atom of control. She smiled at him, a smile so radiant that any heart capable of human emotion would have been warmed. William only nodded.

They drew up when they came abreast of him. "It's going well, Mr. Northrup. I think the lass has natural ability."

"Carry on, then." Without bothering to nod this time, William returned to the house. Arrogant bastard! Liam thought. He might have said something, told Moria that she was doing well. God rot his soul, if there wasn't a devil, as the priests said, then there ought to be, to carry such as William Northrup down into the depths of hell to burn forever for the sins they committed on earth.

A glimpse of blue in an upstairs window caught his eye, and he smiled at Moria, nodding his head toward the house.

"Mrs. Northrup is watching you, love, and you can be sure she's as proud of you as I am. Only a few minutes more and our hour will be up. Let's give her something to be proud of! Smartly, now, keep your heel down and your back straight, and smile!"

Moria was already smiling. She lifted her right hand to wave at Eugenia, and in her enthusiasm she kicked Serena a good deal more sharply than she had kicked her before, and the mare responded by breaking into a full gallop before Moria was ready for it. The stirrup flew out from under her foot, and Moria went sailing off Serena's back.

She landed on her own back, her arm almost wrenched out of its socket because her hand had instinctively tightened on the reins. Her fall was broken, but not enough so that every ounce of breath wasn't jolted out of her. To make it worse, she couldn't see properly, and it took her another instant to realize that her hat had come down over her eyes from the jolt of her landing.

Liam's heart leaped into his throat and he was off Ranger before the gelding stopped. And then he felt relief so great that he could have wept, because Moria was laughing! She couldn't help it. Imagining the picture she must make, sprawled ignominiously in the dust, her hat down over her eyes, sent her into gales of mirth so that she almost choked with it.

"Are you all right?" Liam was running his hands over her body, searching for broken bones that he was sure weren't there or she wouldn't be laughing like this, fit to kill.

"I feel like a fool. Eugenia must be so ashamed of me! Oh, Papa, do you think *he* saw?"

"Not a chance of it, mavourneen. He's already back inside."

Liam helped her to her feet and began brushing at her habit. "Nothing's broken, praise the saints, and your habit isn't even torn, it's only a little dirty and we'll have that off before you go back to the house. Come on, girl of mine, back into the saddle! You were old enough before we left Ireland to know that when anybody falls off a horse they have to get right back on again!"

She wasn't afraid. This daughter of his showed no trace of fear as she stepped into his cupped hands and regained her seat on Serena's back. Her gloved hand stroked the mare's neck, and her voice was filled with apology. "It's all right, Serena. It wasn't your fault. I'll do better this time, just be patient with me and I'll learn!"

Serena snorted and her ears twitched. Liam handed her the reins and they resumed the lesson, this time with Moria a deal more careful not to kick the mare too hard.

Upstairs in the window that looked out toward the ring, Eugenia's heart began to beat again—it had stopped when Moria had fallen. She was all right, she was back in the saddle, she was handling herself beautifully. Beside her, Rose put her arm around her.

"No harm will come to her," Rose assured her with absolute confidence. "Didn't I spend half the night at my beads, praying for her? And she isn't even frightened, bless her heart! Just thank Our Lady that *he* wasn't still at the ring to see it happen!"

"She's wonderful, isn't she, Rose?" Eugenia's voice was trembling, but it was with pride now rather than from fright.

"That she is. She's something special, that one, something so special that there's never been another like her and likely there never will be again. It was a blessed day when she came to Retreat, and we should both wear our knees out giving thanks that she was born into this world to bring us joy."

Liam was helping Moria dismount now. The lesson was over. Rose took her arm from around Eugenia's waist. "I'll just go down to the kitchen and scare you up some tea. You and the lovely lass will be needing it, and I could do with a sip myself. And I'll just stop on the way and shake Dora up so that she'll have a good steaming bath waiting for our Moria after you've finished the tea, because her bones will be needing it after that tumble, for all she's only thirteen and as supple as a cat falling off a roof!''

Because not to have left Retreat on his semimonthly afternoon and evening off would have raised questions in the minds of the other servants, even if William might not have noticed, Liam was obliged to take his time off away from the estate. He didn't dare risk any mention of his changed habits, because little escaped William's notice and he might have questioned him as to why he no longer left Retreat.

Without Moria to visit at Mrs. Murphy's boardinghouse, Liam put his free time to the best use he could think of. Ireland and the plight of the downtrodden Irish still weighed heavily on his mind, so he sought out his political friend, Michael McCarthy, and learned where meetings of loyal Irishmen took place. At the first meeting and every one he attended after that, he didn't waste his time in merely listening, but he got to his feet and talked.

"They need help, and they need it now, and they need every bit of help we can give them! Dig deep into your pockets, you Irishmen, give everything you can. If you can only afford a few pennies, they will still be welcome and put to good use. If you can donate a dollar, try to make it a dollar and a half. Every gun that can be bought, every penny that can be spent for food to feed our starving countrymen will get to them. I have friends there who can squeeze the last mill's worth from every copper penny they get from this side of the ocean. None of it, not one cent, will go into some politician's pocket!''

Laughter greeted this last assurance, and a sally of good-natured ribbing was directed at Michael McCarthy, whose pockets were well lined and well they all knew it. In this case, not one penny that was collected would stick to his fingers. Powerful he might be, in his small way, but stealing from Irishmen was not a sin he cared to commit, not if he had any hopes of salvation. Besides, Mr. McCarthy held the old-country Irishman's plight nearly as dearly as Liam himself.

Liam was eloquent in his speeches, so eloquent that more than one Irishman gave more than he could afford. Every penny of it was counted in the presence of every one of them, and the amount written down, and Liam himself saw to the sending of it to his friends, who would praise the saints at its receipt. Bullets, guns, payment for the printers who risked their freedom and perhaps their lives in getting out pamphlets to be passed around. Food for the starving, rent money so that an impoverished potato-grower wouldn't be evicted at the failure of his crop to the blight, and his cottage pulled down around his head to make sure that he and his family couldn't sneak back in to find shelter from the weather.

Liam's reputation as a speaker grew. The first gatherings he attended had to find larger quarters for their meetings, but Michael McCarthy took care of that. There were halls to be had, warehouse rooms, Michael knew them all.

There was some danger in what Liam was doing. If any word of his activities were to get back to William Northrup, his employment at Retreat would come to an end. William would never tolerate an employee who had an overriding interest outside of the estate and his duties to his master. And William was fed steady streams of all sorts of information by a network of spies, as he deemed no bit of information on any subject that might touch him too small to be dismissed without taking it under consideration. Liam could never be sure that the next time he returned to Retreat there wouldn't be a message waiting for him to present himself to Mr. Northrup, and that he'd be told to vacate the premises without further notice.

Nevertheless, he took that chance. His patriotism still burned inside of him, and the impossibility of going back to Ireland to take up the fight against the English in person was never far from his mind. As stories of English cruelty grew and spread and made their way to America, he might have gone mad if it hadn't been for Moria and Eugenia. Mad enough to return to Ireland, even if he had to lay down his life for the privilege of fighting on for however short a time might be left to him before he'd be taken and executed.

At least he was doing something. The steady flow of money that was collected through his efforts was badly needed and greatly appreciated. When he received a hastily scrawled, nearly illegible letter from a friend in Ireland, sent to him through Michael McCarthy, telling of the raiding of an English supply depot or the ambush of a patrol, his heart sang.

"You're doing all you can, darling. You're doing more than most men who had to leave Ireland. I'm proud of you, you'll never know how proud I am!" Eugenia told him.

It was early December, and the nights were raw and damp even though there was still no snow on the ground. In spite of the cold, Moria's riding lessons continued, and for more than two months the three of them had been able to ride out in the mornings and spend two hours out of eyesight and earshot of the house and the immediate grounds.

What joy those rides had brought them! Moria's eyes would shine like the topmost candle on a Christmas tree the moment they turned into the now leaf-denuded woods. They were alone, they were together, there was no one to spy on them.

For Moria, those two hours every day with the exception of Sunday were heaven itself. Her love for her father and for Eugenia knew no bounds. They were perfect, they were as near to being saints as any human being could be, and they were hers! They filled her heart to overflowing. As long as she had them, both of them, she could have been happy living in a prison on bread and water, much less living in what was still to her the utmost luxury in the world. And besides Papa and Eugenia, like an extra helping of frosting on a cake, there was Rose, who was a never-ending source of love and comfort.

Moria was happy. She couldn't imagine anyone else in the world being as happy as she was. She didn't even worry about the state of her soul anymore, because didn't Papa and Eugenia, and even Rose, assure her that no sin adhered to her?

She'd return from the morning rides with her cheeks red from the cold, her eyes shining and laughter bubbling from her lips. Eugenia also blossomed like a rose in midsummer, no matter how raw the wind or cold a misty rain. They'd enter the house hand in hand, or with their arms around each other's waists, to find hot tea and muffins with strawberry or raspberry preserves waiting for them in Eugenia's room, while Rose saw that hot baths were prepared for them. These brief hours after their rides were almost as precious to Moria as the rides themselves, marred only because Liam couldn't share them. But Liam lacked for nothing. His cottage was snug and warm, his food hearty and plentiful. The fact that nearly every penny of his salary found its way to Ireland to fight for the cause posed no hardship on him. His physical needs were taken care of at Retreat, and knowing that Moria's future was assured left him with more peace of mind than he'd ever dared hope for.

And there was still his dream, his great dream that he mentioned to no one, not even to Eugenia or Moria: the dream that when Moria was grown, when she was married and secure for all the rest of her life, he'd return to Ireland and take up the fight with his own two hands until the last Englishman was driven from Ireland's shores.

How he would live without Eugenia when that time came, he didn't know. Eugenia filled his heart and his life. It was hard for him to imagine that there had been a time in his life when he hadn't known of her existence. He thought of her the moment he woke up in the morning, his last thoughts were of her as he fell asleep at night. Although he still grieved for Molly, he knew that she wouldn't begrudge him his happiness, although it often bothered him that she'd be grieved that they were forced to live in sin.

The only cloud on his happiness, and Eugenia's, was that with winter setting in, William less frequently absented himself from Retreat overnight. During the past month, they'd had only one night together in Liam's cottage, a night filled with such bittersweet love and longing and passion that it still filled their hearts when they remembered it.

But there was tonight. Eugenia had sent Rose to him this afternoon to tell him that William was going to be away from home overnight. It was only by accident that Eugenia had learned of it. William often left the house for however long suited him without apprising her of his intentions. But shortly after noon today Eugenia had been passing William's study when Fredrich Harshay, William's valet, had been leaving the room, and she'd heard William say, "Not the new shoes, Fredrich, they're a little tight. I've written my bootmaker about his mistake." His voice had shown the degree of his displeasure, and the bootmaker would feel it in his pocketbook. "And the maroon dressing robe, not the green."

"Very good, sir." Fredrich bowed before he pulled the door closed behind him.

Eugenia's heart had leaped and begun to beat hard against her breast. She'd had to control herself by taking a deep breath before she'd asked, "Is my husband going to be away tonight, Fredrich?"

"Yes, Mrs. Northrup. For one night only, he will return sometime tomorrow. If you'll excuse me, I must see to the packing and order up the carriage."

Ten minutes later Rose had been at the stables to deliver the message to Liam. Tonight, after nearly a month of frustration, Eugenia and Liam would lie in each other's arms again.

Moria was lying in her bed, her eyes open. She hadn't been able to get to sleep, although it was now after one in the morning. Mr. Northrup was away, and she missed her father, and tonight, when there'd be virtually no danger in it at all, why couldn't she slip out to Papa's cottage to see him? She'd only stay a little while. He'd be glad to see her, even if she would have to wake him by tapping at his bedroom window.

No one would be awake at this hour. It would be perfectly safe. How surprised Papa would be, and how pleased! She wanted to talk to him about the party she was invited to three days from now, Anthony Vancouver's sixteenth birthday party. It was going to be a grand affair, every young person within miles would be there, and a good many from New York City, including parents who would have to accompany their sons and daughters.

Every young person who counted, Moria reminded herself, and her giggle was like tinkling silver bells in the darkness of her room. And she was one of them, she counted! She'd received her engraved invitation two weeks ago, and she'd known about the party even before that because it was all that Estelle Vancouver had talked about for the past two months. Anthony's sixteenth birthday, second in importance only to his eighteenth, which would be second in importance only to his twenty-first!

In spite of the fact that Eugenia and Estelle were close friends, Moria had yet to lay eyes on Anthony Vancouver. On the occasions when she'd accompanied Eugenia to Belvedere, the Vancouver estate, Anthony had either been away at school, or amusing himself on business of his own away from home.

But if she hadn't seen Anthony yet, she'd heard a great deal about him. He was reputed to be so handsome that every female heart, whether it was six or sixty, fluttered when he walked into a room. The girls of her own age whom Moria had met rolled their eyes and sighed when they mentioned his name, until Moria thought that they were as witless as sheep and ought to be slapped into having better sense.

All the same, she couldn't help being curious. And she wanted Papa's reassurance that she'd find herself at ease at such a large party, even though Eugenia had already told her that a dozen times. But most of all, she wanted to see the inside of Papa's cottage. In all the months since she'd come to live at Retreat, she had never been inside it.

She'd do it! No one would see her or hear her. Quickly, before she had time to lose her courage, she slipped out of bed. The carpeted floor took the worst of the chill from her bare feet, and she reminded herself of how her toes had used to curl away from the freezing boards of the floor in the two-room walk-up she'd lived in with Papa and her mother, before Molly had died and she'd been sent to live with Mrs. Murphy. Was she still the same girl, or was she somehow a changeling, someone entirely different?

Silly goose! she scolded herself. Find your clothes, hurry! Her hands trembled with eagerness as she threw her warm, fur-trimmed coat over her nightgown and located her slippers. She wouldn't bother to dress, the coat would hide her nightgown and after all it was only Papa, it wasn't as if she were visiting some other gentleman in the middle of the night.

There was no betraying creak of her door when she opened it to slip out into the dark hallway. William Northrup would not tolerate a door or a hinge or a stair tread that creaked, everything in this house ran smoothly and in perfect order.

Walking silently, groping with her hands against the walls of the hallway, she gained the staircase and went down, guiding herself by the banister. The front door, like the door to her room, opened without a sound. Then she began to run, as fleet as a young deer, around the house to the back and then in a straight line toward the stables and her father's cottage a short distance behind them. This was adventure, this was the sort of thing that gave spice to life and made it worth living!

The cold air burned her lungs, but she breathed deep of it, savoring it. There were stars in the sky, pinpoints of brilliance in the winter night. The tree limbs were bare, etched a darker black against the darkness. It would be prettier when there was snow on the ground, but although Moria loved snow, just as she loved green grass and spring flowers and the heat of summer days, now she dreaded a snowfall heavy enough to keep her from her daily rides with Papa and Eugenia. And tonight of all nights she was glad that there was no snow on the ground to show her betraying footprints to the first servants who would be abroad in the morning.

She was here! Papa's bedroom was in the back. He'd described his cottage to her in every detail until she knew it almost as well as he knew it himself. And tonight she'd see it with her own eyes, Papa would light a lamp and take her on a tour of it, all two rooms, and she'd see the things he saw every day, touch the things he touched.

She crept around to the back, suppressing another giggle as she thought of how surprised he'd be to find her outside his bedroom window in the middle of the night. The window was just here. There was a curtain over it. She raised her hand, icy from her cold run, to tap on the pane.

And then her hand stopped, frozen, in midair before it touched the glass. Papa was awake, she heard his voice, murmuring. Was he having a dream, talking in his sleep? She'd best rap hard, then, and wake him in case it was a nightmare and he wasn't awake at all, only she'd never known that he talked to himself.

Her breath stilled, caught in her throat, suffocating her, as she heard another voice, a voice she knew as well as she knew her father's and her own.

"Darling, it's been so long! I thought he'd never spend the night away from home again, I've almost died from wanting you!"

"I know, love, I know. Hush, hush, it's all right. We're together now, we have these hours."

"Yes, yes! It makes up for everything, I can bear it forever, after tonight. Liam, Liam, I love you so!"

"And I love you. You're my heart, you're my life."

The bedsprings creaked as weights were shifted, as Liam drew Eugenia closer into his arms, and then there was silence as he kissed her, a kiss that extended into eternity. There was a sobbing moan as Eugenia murmured his name again, over and over, Liam, Liam, Liam . . .

Her face as white as the snow which had not yet fallen this winter, Moria forced her frozen limbs to move, to turn her around, to take her away from this place. Her father, her father and Eugenia! They were together in Papa's cottage, they were in bed together, they were making love together!

At the window close to the back door where Rose was keeping watch to let Eugenia back into the house before the servants began stirring, Rose's head jerked up as she saw a swiftly moving figure racing toward the house. Holy Mary, she'd dozed off, someone was out there, how could she have been so careless? Who was it, and what had they seen?

And then her heart lurched as she recognized the figure. It was Moria! And coming from the direction of her father's cottage, and a blind man could tell what she'd been up to, slipping out in the middle of the night to go and see him, she who'd mourned because she'd never seen the inside of Liam's house!

She got outside just in time to catch Moria in her arms, her own grip as strong as iron, before Moria rounded the corner of the house on her way back to the front door by which she'd left. The girl's eyes were wide and blank with agony, her face a death mask in the surrounding darkness, the grief in her something that spilled over and engulfed Rose as well.

"Moria, mavourneén, don't! Hush, child, hush, it's all right." She said the words even though Moria wasn't making a sound, it was as if the child had been struck incapable of speech.

But she was capable. It came out in a hoarse whisper, tearing from her throat, fraught with the full agony of her shock.

"My father, my father and Eugenia . . ."

"Moria, they love each other. They love each other with a love that was made in heaven itself. You don't understand, how could you, only just finding out, and like this! But I'll tell you, love, I'll tell you and then you'll understand and you'll know that the love between them is right and good, and no sin at all."

"She's married. She's married to Mr. Northrup, and you say it isn't a sin?" To Rose's horror, Moria began to laugh, hysterical laughter born of her shock. "It's a sin, it's a deadly sin, it's adultery. . . ."

Rose clapped her hand over Moria's mouth. "Don't say it, don't ever think it! And for the love of Mary herself, be quiet! Do you want to rouse the house, do you want them discovered, and *his* rage to destroy us all?"

Moria was shaking, every inch of her was shaking, her teeth were chattering. She threw her head back and the pulse in her throat throbbed as though it were going to break through the skin. For one heart-stopping moment, Rose was afraid that the girl was going to open her mouth and scream, but then Moria slumped in her arms, as limp as though there wasn't a bone in her body, and if Rose hadn't been holding her she'd have crumpled into a heap there on the ground and still been there in the morning, to be found when the first servant stepped through the door.

"Come," Rose said, her voice low but filled with command.

"Come with me, now, and be silent! Come with me, mavourneen, and I'll tell you all about it, so that you'll understand, and then things will be the way they were before and all your grief will dissolve as though it had never touched you. Trust me, Moria, trust me!"

Moria's eyes were still wide but without comprehension, but by Mary's mercy she allowed Rose to lead her into the house and up the servants' staircase to Rose's own snug room, which she shared with no other servant because of her status as Eugenia's maid. The door closed behind them, without making a whisper of a sound. Not daring to strike a light, Rose led Moria to her rocking chair and sat down and drew the girl onto her lap and held her close and began to rock.

"Listen to me then, mavourneen, listen to Rose, my Moria. . . ."

8

The belle of the ball! That's what she was, she'd overheard Mrs. Dangerfield, who was third in importance only to Eugenia and Estelle themselves among all the wealthy and important families who lived along the Hudson River, say it to Mrs. Gogh, and if Amy Dangerfield said it it must be true.

You'd think that Mrs. Dangerfield's comment would have caused Moria to put an exclamation point after it when she repeated it to herself, but she didn't feel like putting an exclamation point after it. It was too soon after she'd discovered the shattering truth about her father and Eugenia for her to want to put an exclamation point after anything.

It wasn't that she didn't understand. Rose had made it very clear to her. She'd known, ever since she'd come to Retreat, that William Northrup was a cold and emotionless man, one she'd disliked, but she'd had no idea, Eugenia had never dropped as much as a hint and neither had Rose or her father, of the enormity of his bestiality. He'd made Eugenia's life a living hell, doubly so because she hadn't even been able to escape from her torment by killing herself because of his threats against her family if she should.

"She was dying, mavourneen, my Eugenia was dying when Liam came to Retreat, and he gave her back her life, he made it worth living again. She loves him, her love for him is as good and as pure as if she were married to him, and his for her is the same. They filled a need, each for the other, that cried out to be filled. It isn't as if Eugenia is *his* wife anymore, in that sense of marriage. She isn't, and she hadn't been for years before your father came.

"*He* can't, you see. It was an accident that made it so, an accident that Eugenia caused, defending herself from him. If she wouldn't have hanged for it, I'd wish she'd killed him instead of only rendering him impotent! Holy Mary knows that I've wanted to kill him myself, many's the time, but I'm as helpless in the matter as Eugenia is, and so she must bear it, and I must bear it, and now you must bear it too.

"And think how much harder it is for your father, because he's a man, strong and filled with pride and courage, and he can lift no hand to free the woman he loves from the man who still makes her life a torment every day she lives! It's enough to kill him, but he has to accept things the way they are for your sake and for her sake even though it's eating the heart out of him.

"Resent their love for each other, condemn it? No, no! Only thank God that their love for each other is there, and strong enough so that they can bear what they have to bear. They deserve every ounce of happiness their love for each other brings them, and a thousand times more! It's not adultery, you're only thirteen but you're old enough to understand that. Liam is the only man in Eugenia's life, and she's the only woman in his. Do you think he could face the priest, at confession, if it were otherwise?"

Luckily for Rose's own peace of mind, she had no idea that Liam had not been to confession since he'd returned from the war, already bitter and with his faith shattered, even to have it shattered still more by the loss of Molly. And Moria didn't know it, either, and so they both thought that it must be all right.

Rose had talked and talked that night, holding Moria in her arms, rocking her as if she were three instead of thirteen, almost fourteen. She'd talked until her words had finally begun to penetrate the fog of shock that had shut them out at first, until Moria had begun to comprehend what she was telling her. And Moria'd been able to cry at last, cry for the insolvable plight that her father and Eugenia found themselves in.

And she understood. She understood so well, and she still loved them as much as she'd loved them before, but things were different now, they could never be the same again. She was no longer the little girl in a fairy tale come true, thinking that the world was a beautiful place where all your wishes were granted. She wasn't a child anymore, she'd grown up that night, been forced into awareness of things the way they were, and the way they were was a web of lies and deceit that weighed her down and drove out the last vestiges of her childhood. She knew that no matter how well things seemed to be going on the surface, they were all walking on a tightrope over a bottomless chasm, and their feet might slip or the rope might break at any moment and plunge them all into Hades.

All around her, young people and their parents were laughing and chattering, their faces animated and happiness radiating from them in an almost visible warmth. These were the chosen, the elite, the ones whose feet were in no danger of slipping off a tightrope. Every girl was wearing a new gown, the hoops almost impossibly wide, the materials impossibly beautiful, until they looked like creatures from another and more perfect world. Their faces were eager and their eyes gleamed with the excitement of the occasion. Before the evening was over, every one of them would have worn out a pair of dancing slippers, worn the soles right through. And every one of them, with the exception of Moria, wished that the slippers might be worn out from dancing only with Anthony Vancouver.

Even in this brilliant assemblage, Moria stood out like one perfect rose in a garden of modest daisies. Although she was the youngest girl to have been invited, her beauty set her apart, made her the focus of all eyes. Her card had been filled within minutes of her arrival, while Eugenia smiled with delight and William looked coldly satisfied that his ward was presenting a good account of herself.

Eugenia had waged a running battle over Moria's dress for weeks before the ball. Mrs. Chatterton, the seamstress, had wanted to trim it with yards of ruffles and lace, with ribbons and bows. Eugenia had thrown all the patterns aside and sketched a gown herself.

The dress was of the palest shell pink, with only three flounces of rosebud embroidery at the edges. The neckline was only slightly off the shoulder, but it accented the gentle slope of Moria's shoulders and the creamy whiteness of her throat. She wore a single strand of small pearls and simple pearl earrings in her newly pierced ears. They had been pierced especially for this occasion, and she had stood stoically during the ordeal, without as much as a wince. She knew, from experience, what must be borne and that crying or whimpering would not change it.

Against the background of the gown and the modest pearls, Moria's porcelain skin and the cascade of raven hair that hung down her back almost to her waist stood out like a masterpiece painted against a neutral background. Her hair was held back by a circlet of pink rosebuds, plundered from William's precious hothouses. Her beautiful brows, the brilliant blue of her eyes, her delicately molded lips, all seemed to have been stroked in by a master's brush.

"She looks like a portrait, like a Renaissance portrait!" Amy Dangerfield exclaimed. "Really, it's amazing!"

"I would have thought that Eugenia would have taken more pains with her dress," Mrs. Gogh remarked, not without a touch of malice because Willemina Gogh's rather plump fifteen-year-old daughter did not show to advantage with this ward of the Northrups in spite of the elaborateness of the dress, which had cost Mr. Gogh a small fortune.

Moria was glad that she appeared to advantage tonight. If she hadn't appeared to advantage, Mr. Northrup would have been angry and then he'd take it out on Eugenia. It seemed as if everything Moria did, as if every move she made and every word she uttered hinged on the necessity of winning and keeping William Northrup's approval, and the strain was almost more than she could bear.

And there was the additional strain of appearing perfectly normal when she rode with her father and Eugenia. Rose had impressed on her that it would be unkind, even cruel, of her to let them know that she was aware of their real relationship. They both wanted to protect her, to keep her as innocent and happy as any girl of her age could be.

"It would only hurt them to know that you know, even if you understand and still love them," Rose told her. "They have so little happiness, don't do anything to take away even a drop of it! They're the same people they were before you knew, after all, you see. You're old enough to understand that for all you're still a child."

"I was a child before I found out. I'm not now," Moria wanted to say, but she held her tongue. Rose was so worried, she loved Eugenia and Liam so much, and she loved Moria too.

"I won't let them know, Rose. I promise."

She'd kept her promise, but at what a cost! In spite of being almost fourteen, old enough to understand, her nights had been sleepless, filled with shame and foreboding. The shame was dissipating as she understood more with every day that passed and with every glance between Liam and Eugenia that she intercepted, but the foreboding would not go away. She nearly wore her rosary out, seeking comfort in prayer, and she was worried that heaven must be growing tired of her importunings for forgiveness for the two people she loved the most in all the world.

She was dancing with a freckle-faced boy with ears that stood out from his head, whose face was bright red with the honor of dancing with her. He kept stepping on her feet and the necessity of keeping a smile on her face was becoming more of an effort every moment.

There! The number was over at last, before every bone in both her feet was broken. All she had to do was let him escort her back to Eugenia without limping. It would be disgraceful to limp, but whoever had made up that rule of polite society had never had his feet trampled by a well-meaning boy with calf eyes, it was a man who'd made the rule, she'd be bound.

"Thank you, Miss Northrup."

"Miss Compton," she corrected him. His face flamed more hotly than ever, but how could he think straight when this entrancing young lady had him under such a spell? "You'll dance with Anthony next," he said unhappily.

"Yes, his name is on my card." Moria conjured up another smile, and the boy felt as though he'd been tippling his father's brandy.

Eugenia reached for Moria's hand and smiled at her. "You looked lovely on the floor. Are you enjoying yourself?"

"Oh, yes. Of course I am. It's a lovely party."

"And here's Anthony, come to claim you. He'll be escorting you in to dinner, this is the last dance before the collation."

The thought of food, no matter how exotic, made Moria feel slightly ill. She was afraid to dance with Anthony Vancouver in spite of all the lessons she'd had, she was sure that she couldn't dance well enough to please him, and he was older than she was, a young gentleman already, while she was still considered a little girl in spite of the fact that she was budding out in front in a most embarrassing manner. She shouldn't be here at all, it was only because she was the Northrups' ward that she'd been invited.

But there was no escape, no place to run and hide. Eugenia was still holding her hand, and there, looking at least eighteen instead of the sixteen he had attained only today, was Anthony Vancouver himself, bearing down on her.

For a moment her eyes misted, and she saw the scion of the Vancouver family through a blur. She'd been introduced to him when she'd arrived, but that had been such a brief encounter that she hadn't had time to evaluate him, and her occasional glimpse of him since then, as they'd whirled past each other on the dance floor, had left her with an impression only of very fair hair and brown eyes, of a pair of broad shoulders and a height that was already that of a grown man. Her hand felt clammy in Eugenia's, and to make matters worse Mr. Northrup was looking at her as if he expected her to commit some unforgivable social gaffe.

So she smiled. That was something she'd learned a long time ago. When things were hard, when situations arose that she wasn't sure how to handle, she smiled, and then it was usually all right because her smile disarmed whoever it was she was nervous about.

Coming toward her, Tony Vancouver received the full impact of her smile and for a moment he was so startled that he almost stopped dead in his tracks. He wasn't looking forward to dancing with the little girl who was the ward of Eugenia and William Northrup. As a matter of fact, he was sick and tired of the subject of Moria Compton and how beautiful she was, how charming, how unutterably perfect. As if the brat were some kind of an *objet d'art,* something Mr. Northrup had searched the world for and for which he'd paid a fabulous price, to add to his collection of his other priceless objects!

But now, face to face with the girl who had become an annoyance to him even before he'd met her, that smile of hers set him back on his heels. There was something about it that melted away his antagonism toward her, if only momentarily. He pulled himself together before his step as much as faltered. She was only a child, for Criminy's sake, hardly more than a baby! But at least she didn't look so terribly young, she was as tall as several of the older girls, and there was a hint of a developing figure. He wouldn't look a complete fool dancing with her, and in a few minutes the ordeal would be over except for the inexplicable fact that his mother had insisted that he must escort Moria to dinner, overriding his objections because he wanted Veronica Hamilton for his dinner partner.

Veronica! Now there was a girl who really was a girl! She was almost exactly his own age, she'd be sixteen next month, and with her already ripe figure burgeoning out of her décolletage, and her full, lush lips curved in a smile that made gooseflesh pop out over every inch of his skin, Veronica of the auburn hair and knowing hazel eyes was enough to make any young man need to take a cold bath before he disgraced himself in his tight pantaloons by a manifestation of desire that would turn him into a social outcast.

But his mother had stood firm, and once Estelle Vancouver had made up her mind there was no appeal. He was to dance at least two dances with the Northrups' ward, one before and one after he had escorted her in to dinner.

"Miss Compton, I believe that this is our dance."

"Yes, it is." Moria smiled at him again, and accepted his arm to be led to the dance floor. Eugenia and Mr. Northrup were still watching her, and she could feel the eyes of almost everyone in the ballroom cutting into her as well. She tilted her chin and her smile became even more brilliant. And then, as she turned to step into his arms, she felt a wave of emotion that nothing in her previous existence had prepared her for.

She hadn't dreamed that Anthony Vancouver was this handsome! His shoulders were so broad, his limbs so muscled and lithe, and his eyes, of a deep brown that contrasted startlingly with his fair hair, made her feel as though she were drowning in them. It was all she could do to tear her own eyes from his face, and a shudder, like a thousand pricking needles, ran up and down her back as he placed his white-gloved hand precisely where it belonged at her waist.

The music started, a Viennese waltz, and Moria breathed a prayer of thankfulness for all the lessons that William Northrup had insisted she `suffer through. Not that she didn't like dancing, any motion requiring such grace was a delight to her and she had learned easily, as easily as she'd learned to ride and was learning to play the piano adequately enough to be acceptable. But this dance was something else. It wasn't Mr. Boyer, her dancing master, who had her in his arms, but Anthony Vancouver!

"I hear that you like to ride," Tony said. He had to say something, his mother was watching him and he'd have to suffer the consequences if he wasn't polite to the little girl. His first small shock, when Moria had smiled at him, had worn off, and the dance was only an onerous duty, although at least, to his relief, she could dance, and didn't stumble or trip over her own feet or over his.

"Yes, I do. I enjoy it very much." Moria's tone was as polite as his, giving no indication that her voice struggled to lilt into song rather than its ordinary conversational level. "Eugenia and I ride nearly every day."

Tony's eyebrows, dark as contrasting to his fair hair, shot up, and Moria's heart skipped several beats. She had an irrational desire to touch his eyebrows with her fingertips, to smooth them, to savor the texture of them with her sense of touch.

"You call Mrs. Northrup 'Eugenia'? Does she allow that?"

"I'm sorry. Of course I call her Mrs. Northrup when we're in company. I'm afraid I forgot. She likes me to call her Eugenia when we're alone."

"And I suppose you call Mr. Northrup 'William,' when you're alone?"

Moria tripped. Call Mr. Northrup William! She could feel her body go numb at the very idea. "Of course I don't! I'm sorry. Did I step on your foot?"

"You did, but I expect I'll live." Under the surface of his polite smile there was annoyance at her clumsiness that Moria could feel as though the wave of it were something palpable.

"I'll try not to do it again. But really, it was your own fault for startling me like that, suggesting that I might call Mr. Northrup by his first name!" To Moria's horror, she began to giggle because the idea was so ludicrous.

Tony's smile became even more strained. Moria Compton was nothing more than a baby after all. She might look older than she was, but thirteen was still thirteen. Under his smile, he gritted his teeth. Thank God, the waltz was ending. Now all he had to do was get through the midnight supper, and then he could dance with Veronica and if he couldn't persuade her, this time, to slip away from the ballroom and meet him in his mother's sewing room upstairs for a few stolen kisses and a caress or two that would send her blood to boiling as well as his own, his name wasn't Anthony Vancouver.

He was making great strides with Veronica, he'd already managed to go just about as far as it was possible to go with a young lady of breeding. Not as far, by a long shot, as he'd gone with several pretty young tavern maids up in Boston, while he was at Harvard, where he'd started this autumn, one of the youngest students there. Their beds were not soft or comfortable, but their bodies were soft enough to make up for it, and their willingness to give him what he wanted warmed his heart even remembering it. And he'd gone as far with a few chambermaids at the houses of his friends, although there was no maid in his own house with whom he'd care to indulge. Estelle Vancouver employed no female servants under thirty, and those she employed were far from comely. As much as she doted on her handsome son, Estelle was no fool. She was all too aware of what went on in some of the houses of her friends where pretty female servants were employed, between the servants and the young sons of the house.

No tavern maids or upstairs maids being available to him this evening, he looked forward to whatever pleasure he could derive from a few stolen kisses. Veronica had a way of parting her lips and darting her tongue into his mouth and making contact with the tip of his own that was enough to make him seek a few moments of seclusion before he appeared in company again, lest the evidence of his tryst be too apparent.

Moria managed to finish the dance without stumbling again. But her heart was beating too fast, she was afraid that Anthony would see it through the thin material of her dress. Why couldn't she have been born a year sooner, why couldn't she be fourteen-almost-fifteen or, better still, fifteen-almost-sixteen, instead of only thirteen-almost fourteen? She'd never catch up with Anthony Vancouver, he'd always be too old for her, consider her a child! First impressions had a way of lasting through a lifetime, her father had told her that, and Anthony's first impression of her, that of a thirteen-year-old child, would stay with him no matter how old she became. A great sadness came down over her, a feeling of despair that she was convinced would never lift.

And so she smiled, and watching her, Eugenia's heart melted with love and pride. Even William could find no fault with their ward tonight, although her heart had stood still when Moria had stumbled that one time. But William hadn't noticed, he'd turned aside to talk to Jacob Vancouver when it had happened, and so it was all right.

To Moria, forced to sit at the table with Anthony and the adult guests, the rest of the evening was an agony. Why had she been chosen to be Anthony's partner, rather than allowed to stay with the other young people who were served buffet style and allowed to find nooks of their own, chattering and laughing with no adult eyes on them?

She remembered her table manners, she made no mistakes, and these important adults smiled at her and murmured to each other of what a delightful child she was. But Anthony spoke to her only when it was absolutely necessary in order not to appear as a boor, and she didn't fail to notice how his eyes constantly sought out and remained on Veronica Hamilton, the enticing, beautiful girl with the auburn hair. A grown-up young lady, old enough for Anthony. The food stuck in Moria's throat, and she smiled.

She didn't notice, or remember, who she danced with after supper. She went on smiling, and young male hearts went on beating too fast while young male thoughts mourned because she was so young that they'd have to wait for a year or two before they could think of courting her. And then it was three o'clock in the morning, and the last dance, and Anthony came, dutifully, to claim it while Estelle and Eugenia smiled with happiness. Anthony was surly and sullen, barely able to contain his fury because there had been no opportunity to slip away with Veronica because his mother's eyes had constantly been on him.

Across the room, where she was dancing with George Dangerfield, Amy Dangerfield's pudgy husband, who was paying her extravagant compliments, Eugenia's smile became strained as she saw her husband's eyes on her as he stood on the sidelines, keeping himself apart from the few other guests who were not dancing. Always aloof, caring nothing for the goodwill of his fellowmen, William had danced the obligatory courtesy dance with his hostess, once with Eugenia herself, and then had drawn in on himself as he always did at these affairs, not even joining the card games in Jacob Vancouver's game room, where some of the other gentlemen had gathered to spend a more enjoyable evening than in piloting their wives and the wives of their friends around the dance floor.

William's eyes were hooded, but she knew their expression as well as if she could see them. Tonight, after the ball was over, he would pay a visit to her bedroom, to exact punishment on her for being so beautiful and so popular, for attracting other men to her, for gathering compliments from men and women alike. Always, after an affair like this, William felt driven to punish her, to wreak every pain and humiliation on her that his mind could devise. His lovely, his perfect wife, the wife who had betrayed him by failing to produce a child for him, who had rendered him impotent so that he could never sire an heir! She must be punished, and punished again and again, for the admiration that was heaped on her by his friends and acquaintances even though that admiration for her was something he sought out to feed his ego.

Eugenia felt suddenly cold although the ballroom was overheated in spite of the chill of the December weather, crowded as it was with dancing couples and the flames of hundreds of candles in crystal chandeliers, reflected hundreds of times over in the mirrors that lined the walls.

I'll bear it, she thought. I'll project myself back to this ball, to how lovely Moria is, to how everyone is enchanted with her. No matter what he does to me tonight I'll be able to bear it, because tomorrow, unless it snows and we can't ride, I'll be able to tell Liam about Moria's triumph. I'll remember every detail, I'll rehearse it all in my mind while William is abusing me.

The fact that she had learned to send her mind away, to endure William's abuse without expression or whimpering or crying, drove William to near madness. It was a defense that he had not yet been able to break down, although he swore to himself that he would, and make her suffer a hundredfold over for having cheated him of that measure of his revenge.

But in Eugenia's heart she knew that the indignities, the bestialities that William inflicted on her, were growing harder and harder to bear. She couldn't bear to have him touch her, even in the most casual way, much less endure the things he did to her behind her closed and locked bedroom door. After knowing Liam, after having experienced the beauty and ecstasy of his lovemaking, William's hands on her were an abomination. And now with winter drawing in, William would spend more and more time at home, and there would be fewer and fewer opportunities for her to slip away to Liam's cottage to renew her strength and courage in his arms while he lifted her to the gates of heaven.

Liam's brows knitted together in a frown as he studied Moria, who was riding on one side of him, while Eugenia rode on the other. There was a light dusting of snow on the ground, not enough to force them to cancel their rides, but he knew that that would happen any day now.

"So you think young Tony is a handsome lad?" he asked, his eyes not leaving her face. "You liked him, I take it?"

Moria tossed her head. "He's all right. I guess he's handsome. All of the other girls were drooling over him, it was disgusting."

And you weren't? Liam wanted to ask, but he was wise enough to hold his tongue.

"The more fools they," he said instead. "The boy's reputation is of the blackest, as I have good reason to know, such things having a way of coming to my ears. He plays fast and loose with all the lasses, not the ones in his own class you understand, he'd not dare that, although even there he goes as far as he dares. But less fortunate girls aren't so lucky. Mind you keep your head on your shoulders, Moria, if you happen to come into contact with him again. Playing with Anthony Vancouver is like playing with fire, and I'd not like to see you singed."

His words were like a blow to Moria's midsection, they knocked the wind out of her, but outside of a slight, sharp intake of breath she gave no sign.

"It isn't likely I'll be seeing him. I'm still a child, as far as he's concerned. He certainly won't be calling on me!"

145

Her words were light, but Liam, and Eugenia as well, detected the faint tinge of bitterness in them. Moria had a bad case of puppy love, and it would be up to them to keep her from being hurt. Like all the very young, no warnings about the object of her affection's character would be effective. Love was not only blind, it was deaf as well. Eugenia's concern bit through the pain of her body. William's punishment of her after the ball had been severe. It had been nearly dawn before he'd done with her, leaving her bruised and quivering with agony. Even now, after a day to recover, she had to hold back cries of pain with every movement of her horse under her.

But this was her concern, and hers alone. She would not, not if the effort killed her, let either Liam or Moria know what she had gone through two nights ago, what she was still going through today. With iron courage, she forced her attention to the problem of Moria's crush on Anthony Vancouver. This was the first time she'd heard that Tony's reputation was bad, that he played fast and loose with girls who had no defense against him.

But she'd protect Moria. Thank God that the child was still so young, too young for Tony to turn his predatory attention toward her! By the time she was old enough to attract him, she would have outgrown this childhood crush, Eugenia would see to that! And Tony would be away at Harvard most of the time and during his brief vacations he'd spend his time with friends of his own age and Eugenia could make sure that Moria accepted no invitation to any affair that would include him.

An hour after their ride ended, after they'd bathed and were having tea and hot muffins in Eugenia's bedroom, Eugenia's pain-clouded eyes brightened and sparkled.

"*He's* going to be away overnight," Rose told her, pouring herself a cup of tea and helping herself to a muffin. She enjoyed this privilege of taking tea with Eugenia and Moria all the more because she knew what a fury William would feel if he had known of it. "Fredrich Harshay just told me, while I was bringing up the tray."

Her eyes met Eugenia's, which were glowing, and she thought,

Mary protect her, how can she let even Liam make love to her this night, as bruised and hurt as she is?

But Eugenia wasn't thinking of her bruised and hurting body. She was thinking of a few hours of heaven.

9

Moria's back was straight and her head was high, she sat her horse as if she had been born in the saddle, every detail of her toilette and her riding costume was perfect. Beside her, keeping perfect pace with her, Eugenia presented as beautiful a picture as her ward, a picture to bring gasps of admiration and even of awe from all the onlookers.

Moria's horse was black, pure black, there wasn't a white hair to mar the perfection of his coat, which was as sleek and shining as a piece of highly polished coal. He was, beyond any doubt, the most magnificent animal ever to be seen along the banks of the Hudson River, with the single exception of the horse that Eugenia rode.

Eugenia's mount was palest gold. William's agent, who had spent months in searching it out, had taken a strand of her hair with him to make sure that the colors would be as perfectly matched as possible. Moria's riding habit was black, Eugenia's the same pale gold as her horse and her hair.

For an entire year after the acquisition of the two horses, Jazir and Kamil, the animals had been schooled by Liam, schooled to the

149

point where they worked in perfect unison, until every step was the exact duplicate of the other's. Eugenia and Moria had spent countless hours of grueling work learning the routines, learning to handle their mounts with such expertise that there was no possibility of error.

It was William's whim to mount his two female jewels on horses that were as perfect as his wife and his ward. Today was the crowning point of his lifetime career of exacting envy and admiration from all who knew him. No other man of his acquaintance, perhaps no other man in the world, could boast two females of such perfection, could boast two horses so perfectly complementary to them.

His friends, his most carefully selected friends, thirty in all out of all the people he knew, had been invited to Retreat on this Fourth of July in 1868, to be overwhelmed by a demonstration of Eugenia's and Moria's horsemanship on the magnificent mounts with which he had provided them. Neither of them had ever ridden Jazir or Kamil except on the immediate estate, where no alien eyes could catch a glimpse of them. Their time had been spent in the ring, in those hours and hours of daily practice. The effect, William knew, would stun everybody present, and his fame as a connoisseur of beauty would spread not only throughout the Hudson River Valley but throughout all of New York State and the entire eastern seaboard as well.

Several of the guests who lived in the city had arrived the evening before, and the others had arrived in time for a leisurely, late breakfast with those who were already there, as had been stipulated in the invitations. They all knew that William had something extraordinary planned for them besides the fireworks display that would take place after dark, and the ball to follow, but none of them had any inkling of what it might be.

Seated at the breakfast table where William reigned at its head, Tony Vancouver had to use all of his willpower not to fidget in his chair. He only toyed with the ham and eggs on his plate, with the slice of melon, and the sight of biscuits covered with preserves nauseated him. Tony was not only out of sorts because his parents had insisted that he attend this boring affair, but he was suffering from the hangover of all hangovers, having spent the evening before at a tavern where not only the spirits were of excellent quality and his male companions convivial but the tavern maids were more than ordinarily winsome to look at and accommodating.

He'd arrived at home in the small hours of the morning, his own personal valet watching to let him in without waking his mother and father. The few hours of sodden sleep he'd had had done little to mitigate his throbbing head and queasy stomach, and right at this moment he heartily wished William Northrup in hell. Damn the man, why did his mother think that the sun rose and set at the Northrups' command, and that they themselves, and Tony along with them, had to jump at their slightest nod?

To make it worse, the Hamiltons had not been invited, and so of course Veronica was not present. Of all the young ladies in his social class from whom he could choose, Veronica still held first place, and any holiday celebration spent without her could be counted as a dead loss.

What the devil was this all about, anyway? Tony lifted his coffee cup and almost gagged at the liquid that had gone lukewarm and was oversweet to boot. He'd learned, in his crowded years of dissipation, that having something heavily sugared after a night spent in carousing often mitigated his discomfort, but this morning it wasn't working. He'd have to take it easy for a while. As much as he liked to overindulge, he had no intention of ruining his health and turning himself into a wreck before he was thirty.

His father's eyes were on him, those slightly protuberant eyes that never missed a thing. He'd better pull himself together or the old man would corner him and put him through a grueling series of questions that he'd be hard put to come up with enough fictions to answer so that his activities would not be severely curtailed during the next several days. Jacob Vancouver did not approve of overindulgence, whether in spirits or in females. The staid, stodgy Dutchman didn't realize that this was a new age, that the end of the war, back in '65, had ushered in new freedoms, a new way of life for those with the youth and courage to grasp it. The world was for the young, it was time that the old were put on the shelf where they belonged so that young men of vision could take over and shape things to their own liking.

His mouth curved in a pleasant smile as he acknowledged his father's glance, and Jacob looked at him for only a moment longer and then turned his attention to William, who was coolly refusing to answer any questions about what was in store for his guests. Letting his glance flicker over the other breakfasters, Tony realized that Eugenia and Moria had left the table. They must have something to do with the surprise, then, and God grant that they weren't going to play the piano and sing, or worse yet, put on some amateur patriotic skit in honor of the day!

No, it wouldn't be any of those things, and that at least was a blessing. Nothing like that was ever presented in the morning, and in any case it would be too trite for William to offer to them. Tony shrugged mentally. He didn't give a damn what it was, all he wanted was to crawl back into bed until his stomach settled and get a few more hours of sleep. Was there any possibility that he could get out of the horseback ride and the picnic that he knew was planned when whatever was to come first, the surprise, was over with? Looking at his father again, he decided, his mental shrug turning into a groan, that there wasn't.

William rose to his feet. "If everyone has finished, we will go out to the ring. I have something to show you."

Horses, then. Tony might have known. But at least good horseflesh was better than being expected to enthuse over some new painting or piece of statuary. Like many young men, Tony thought that old masters should be shelved, pushed into the background to make way for the new.

The guests speculated among themselves as they strolled toward the ring. And then, as though a hand had been clapped over every mouth, there was complete and total silence followed by a concerted indrawing of breaths.

At the far side of the ring, Eugenia and Moria were mounted side by side on two horses that drew gasps of astonishment from every throat. Not only the horses, which were so utterly magnificent that they took the breath away, but their riders, evoked waves of awe. Moria in black, Eugenia in pale gold, their habits matching their mounts and their hair, were a spectacle the like of which none of them had ever witnessed.

Their gasps faded and breaths were bated again as the two horses moved forward. Their trots were identical, not a fraction of an inch deviated the height to which they lifted each foot. They turned to the right in perfect unison, then to the left, and then they backed away and turned and moved forward again.

Dazed, the spectators saw Moria rein Jazir to the left, Eugenia rein Kamil to the right, while their mounts pranced to the rails, pivoted in place, and took opposite directions to meet again in the center. It was poetry in motion, their precision a thing of impossibility. It was like a pattern dance as the horses changed pace, as they went from walk to trot to canter, as they racked and paced. The performance went on and on, but none of the witnesses wished that it would come to an end. It was a triumph.

Now two boys ran into the ring and set up a series of hurdles. Their eyes alive with excitement, the guests were agog to see if such precision could be maintained during jumps, something that was surely impossible.

At the far side of the ring, Eugenia and Moria touched their mounts with their heels and lifted them into a canter. Side by side, they bore down on the first hurdle, sailed over it and on to the next. Even in the air there was no detectable distance between the top of the hurdles and the horses. They alit on the other side without breaking stride, still perfectly matched, in complete unity, and went on to take the second and the third in the same unparalleled manner.

When the third hurdle had been jumped, once again the magnificent beasts turned in opposite directions, to meet at the rail directly in front of the stunned guests, where, in that perfect unison, each horse thrust out one foreleg and bent the other and lowered its head in a bow.

The applause broke out then, wild in its enthusiasm. "Never saw anything like it, magnificent, unbelievable!" Ladies daubed at their eyes with their lace-trimmed handkerchiefs, gentlemen cleared emotion-clogged throats. Smiling, Eugenia and Moria gave the signal for their mounts to rise, and again in perfect unison, they trotted from the ring to where Liam and a stableboy waited to help them dismount and lead the animals back into the ring so that the gentlemen could examine and admire them at their leisure.

"Papa, we did it! We carried it off beautifully, we didn't make a single mistake! Wasn't Jazir wonderful, wasn't Kamil?"

"Be careful, Moria girl. Call me Liam." But Liam's voice was tender and filled with pride rather than reproach. On an occasion such as this it was no wonder that she'd forgotten, however briefly. And it was all right, the guests were making so much noise with their applauding and cheering that the stableboy hadn't heard. "Yes, it was wonderful! In all my years of training horses, I've never seen anything to match it, but it would have been nothing without you and Mrs. Northrup to set the beautiful beasties off. William Northrup is a proud man this day, but if he only knew it, he isn't half as proud as I am!"

Holy Mother, but she was beautiful, this daughter of his! She was more beautiful than even he or Molly had ever dreamed she would be, and their dreams had been without limit. At sixteen, Moria was so lovely that it was difficult to believe that she was made of flesh and blood as were other mortals. Her figure had grown into its early promise. Her waist was so tiny that any man's hands could span it, her breasts were firm and slightly pointed under her bodice, she moved with the lightness and grace of air, and her face was enough to melt the ice in the devil's heart.

Molly, were you watching, did you see? I did it, Molly, I kept my promise! She's everything we wanted, and more! Surely even Molly would understand that the means he'd had to use to obtain their goal were justified, that anything would be justified as long as it had this result. Their Moria, who was already the uncrowned princess of the Hudson River Valley, who on this very morning had brought the entire valley to her feet!

And Eugenia! She'd never been more beautiful than she was on this day, showing herself off as William Northrup's perfect wife, as the jewel of all wives. For all that she was thirty-two now, an age when many women were middle-aged matrons, Eugenia's beauty had grown rather than diminished with the years. Her body was as slender as it had been when she was eighteen, but her face had taken on character as well as beauty until now it hurt him to look at her.

Crowding around the two horses with the rest of the gentlemen, Anthony was stunned into sobriety. During the interval between his sixteenth birthday party and this Fourth of July celebration, he hadn't seen Moria more than half a dozen times. Not that his mother hadn't tried to arrange that they be thrown together, but because he had resisted her efforts with all the stubbornness and finesse that was in him.

But all that had been before he'd seen Moria on Jazir this morning, a Moria so beautiful, so desirable, that she drove every other thought out of his mind. She'd grown up while his back was turned, she was something he had to have, and he meant to have her.

Not to marry her, he wasn't that besotted, his head was still firmly attached to his neck. It wouldn't be necessary to marry her. But he could make her fall in love with him, he was sure enough of his own unique handsomeness and charm to be sure of that. He could get her so enamored of him that he'd be able to have his way with her, and the consequences of discovery wouldn't be so great that he'd not dare to do it. After all, she was only a ward, she wasn't the Northrups' flesh and blood. Mr. Northrup would be angry if they were discovered, but being a sensible man he'd realize that it was the girl's own blood, an unknown quantity, that had betrayed his generosity in taking her in and giving her not only a home but every luxury.

To marry her was out of the question. Her father had been a gentleman, by all accounts, but her bloodline couldn't compare to that of his own or of the Hamiltons'. When it came to marrying, to choosing the mother of his future children, it would be Veronica. Not only would he know exactly what he was getting, but she'd be able to continue exciting him for years, and in between times she was enough of a woman of the world to overlook any extramarital affairs he might choose to indulge in.

Only they wouldn't be discovered, of course. Anthony was already a past master at having affairs that went undiscovered. He knew how to be careful, how to avoid unwanted consequences, not even a tavern maid had ever been able to claim that he had fathered a child on her. An affair with Moria was in order, and it was the immediate order of the day, taking precedence over everything else, but there would be no consequences. He'd enjoy her, he'd ensure that she remained exclusively his until he tired of her, which probably wouldn't be long because as beautiful as she was, she was still overly young and lacked Veronica's fire.

Upstairs in Moria's bedroom that overlooked the ring, Dora let the curtain fall as Moria and Eugenia, hand in hand, began to walk back toward the house. Dora's heart burned with spite. All these months of being pampered, of being given everything without having to exert an iota of effort, and now this! From this day on Moria's reputation as a beauty, as someone unique, would be established so firmly that the world would lie at her feet.

Rose entered the room so quietly that Dora almost jumped out of her skin when she spoke.

"Did you see it? Weren't they something right out of this world? I'm fair to bursting with pride!"

Dora forced a smile, but Rose's eyes were keen enough to see the effort it cost her, the spite that still lingered on her face. And once again, she reminded herself that Dora would bear watching, that she'd do Moria a hurt if she had the chance.

"I just came to remind you that the dress Miss Moria is going to wear for the fireworks display needs pressing," Rose said, her voice bland. "It will go hard with you if the least wrinkle comes to Mr. Northrup's attention. And you'd better get about it, because you'll be expected to help the other ladies, the ones who didn't bring their own maids. Mrs. Crandall has already asked that her ball gown be pressed and you'll have to do it because none of the other servants are capable of doing it well enough, and I have to help with Mrs. Sweetbriar. Being the most competent servants in the house has its drawbacks, doesn't it, Dora?''

Satisfied that her barb had brought Dora some discomfiture, Rose hurried back to Eugenia's room. It wasn't true that Mrs. Crandall had asked that Dora press her gown. Rose, by far the more expert, had been asked to do it, but having seen the gown, a solid mass of flounces and ruffles that would take hours to accomplish properly, she'd decided to foist the task off on Dora as punishment for sins uncommitted if not already committed. She'd have to confess, of course, but the penance would be light, as Father Connoly already knew a good deal about Dora, though Rose and he would be inclined to think that the extra work was no more than she deserved.

Moria ran into her room, her gloves already stripped off and her face still flushed with triumph. One of the gloves fell to the floor as she sat down at her dressing table to catch her breath. My, but she was flushed, she looked as if she were running a fever! She'd have to collect herself before she joined the guests again or they'd think that she was still a baby, unable to handle a simple social triumph.

Her face sour, Dora stooped and picked up the glove. The chit hadn't even noticed that she'd dropped it, she expected other people to pick up after her as though they had nothing better to do. Her mouth was still pursed with displeasure as Moria stood up and asked her to help her remove her riding habit. As soon as it was removed, making Moria feel deliciously cool and free after the exertion of her horsemanship demonstration, her fingers went instinctively to the unusual bracelet that she wore on her left wrist.

Seeing the gesture, Dora's mouth pursed even more tightly. "You should let me throw that tawdry bauble into the trash where it belongs, Miss Moria. If Mr. Northrup knew that you were wearing it today he would have been displeased.''

Moria's whole hand closed over the bracelet in a protective

gesture. Throw it away, toss it into the trash! She'd almost as soon part with her rosary. The bracelet brought her good luck, if she hadn't worn it this morning she was sure that she'd have let Eugenia and Liam down, that she'd have forgotten the signals, or gone off balance, or even fallen off, and Mr. Northrup would never have forgiven her and he'd have made life miserable not only for her but for Liam and Eugenia as well for months to come.

The bracelet was unique. Although many people, including Dora, would label it crude, not fit for the ward of the Northrups to wear, it was Moria's dearest possession. It was fashioned of tightly and intricately braided horsehair, the strands taken from the tails of Jazir and Kamil. Even as her fingers savored its texture, Moria's mind went back to the first time she'd seen the man who had given it to her.

His name was Quinn Bradmore, and he had brought Kamil all the way from the Territory of Arizona to deliver the magnificent palomino to Retreat. The son of the rancher who had bred and raised the horse, Quinn had been twenty at the time of the purchase, and to Moria's then barely fifteen years, he was a grown man, an adult, as old as men in their thirties or forties, as all adults are to children so young.

Quinn was tall, he stood a little over six feet. His skin was tanned to the color of Kamil's saddle by a lifetime of exposure to Arizona's relentless sun. His shoulders were broad and well-muscled, his waist and hips narrow, and his gray eyes, flecked with green and gold, were luminous against the darkness of his face. His hair under the broad western hat he wore was brown, sunbleached at the edges, and when he smiled at her she thought she'd never seen a mouth so firm, teeth so white, or a smile so certain to ensure a lifelong friendship.

But at the moment, Moria's excitement over the arrival of the new horse, which was to be Eugenia's, had overridden her interest in a man already grown-up, no matter how different he was from any other man she had ever known.

"Where is he? May I see him? Liam, may I see him this very minute?"

"This minute, Miss Moria," Liam had smiled. He was thankful that in her excitement Moria hadn't forgotten and called him Papa. If she had, he would have had to take Quinn Bradmore into his confidence, a man he didn't know, and ask him not to mention it to anyone, and even though he'd been taken with Quinn the moment he'd laid eyes on him it was a risk he wouldn't have cared to take.

The new horse was in a fenced-off portion of the pasture, where he had the run of nearly two acres to himself. Another horse was yet to come, for Moria, and another section adjoining this one was already fenced off to receive him. William was taking no chances on disagreement between these two new horses and those he already owned that might result in kicking or biting or actual injury to horseflesh he'd paid a fortune to obtain.

Moria's face had registered pure amazement at her first glimpse of Kamil. Why, he was gold, palest gold, he was exactly the color of Eugenia's hair! She'd never known that there could be a horse of that color. And what a horse! He was magnificent, he was the most beautiful animal she'd ever seen.

"Oh, oh, oh," she exclaimed, her eyes wide. "Is he real? What's his name?"

Quinn's eyes had crinkled at the corners as he'd smiled at her. "His name is Rio del Oro. That means River of Gold, in Spanish. He's a palomino, and I brought him all the way from Arizona. He's too valuable an animal to have trusted to someone else for such a long journey."

"Mr. Northrup has renamed him Kamil," Liam told his daughter. "You'll have to remember to call him that, Kamil, to get him used to it."

Moria was already climbing over the fence, too excited to go around to the gate. With an exclamation, Quinn vaulted over the fence after her, and caught her arm.

"Easy, there! He doesn't know you, and he's mighty skittish after that journey! You would be too if you'd been cooped up in a cattle car all those days, when you'd been used to hundreds of miles of freedom all your life!"

"I'm used to horses, Mr.—?"

"Just call me Quinn." Quinn smiled. "The last name is Bradmore, but where I come from we don't bother much with last names. We're sort of free and easy."

His voice was nice, Moria decided. She'd never heard such a nice voice, and Quinn's accent, a western accent she'd never heard before, intrigued her. But once again she forgot the man in favor of the horse.

"I'm used to horses, Quinn. I won't startle him, I promise."

Watching her approach the palomino, Quinn had had to concede that she knew what she was talking about. She was used to horses. Moria had talked to Kamil as she'd walked up to him, moving slowly, and she knew enough to call him by his real name.

"Hello, Rio. Rio del Oro! That's a beautiful name, I like it better than Kamil. And you're beautiful, too."

The palomino sidled, and turned away from her. Moria put her hand on his flank as naturally as if she'd been raised on a ranch, so that he'd know she was there as she walked around to his head and spoke his name again. "Beautiful Rio del Oro! And you are gold, you're pure gold! I love you, Rio. I wish you were going to be mine, instead of the black horse Mr. Northrup has ordered for me. I'll love him, too, but I think I'm going to love you the best."

Rio snorted, and the snort turned into a whicker, and he sniffed at the hand that Moria offered so that he could get the scent of her, to learn that she was his friend, that she meant him no harm. In another moment, his head rested on her shoulder while she stroked his forehead, still talking to him.

"She's quite a young lady, isn't she?" Quinn asked Liam, who had followed them over the fence. "She really does know her way around horses."

"She does that, Quinn." The more Liam saw of Quinn Bradmore, the more he liked him. "And you can rest assured that I'll see that no harm comes to your horse, after you've gone back to the Arizona Territory. If you wouldn't be minding, I'd like to learn more about that place, when we have the time. Is it a big ranch you're after owning out there, now?"

"It's big," Quinn nodded. "We run cattle mostly; winters in the valley are like summers back here, warm and filled with sunshine, and the pastures are lush where there's water. It's a dry climate, but folks are learning to irrigate, the Indians who lived there irrigated, hundreds of years ago, so we can't take credit for more than our share of brains."

"And this Arizona Territory, it's big?"

Quinn laughed, although it was a friendly laugh. "You could drop New York State in a corner of it and lose it!" he said. "Yes, it's big, and all open spaces, there's no place like it, for my money. It's a hard land, a harsh land, but there's a freedom there that I wouldn't sell for a million dollars. We aren't getting rich. There are bad years, just like anywhere else. But we're getting by, and making a little headway year by year. Raising palominos is a sideline I persuaded my father into. I was sure there'd be a market for them. It was years of breeding that produced Rio. He's a champion, Liam. I hate to part with him, but we couldn't pass up what Mr. Northrup offered."

His eyes were on Moria all the time he was talking to Liam. She was the most beautiful girl he had ever seen. If she'd been a little older . . .

He laughed at himself. Even if she'd been eighteen or nineteen instead of fifteen, he wouldn't have a chance of courting her and winning her even if he could stay here in the Hudson River Valley indefinitely. William Northrup's ward! Moria was as far removed from him and his way of life as if she'd been a princess royal, next in line to a throne! All the same, he felt an unfamiliar twisting in the pit of his stomach as the muscles tightened, and an aching in his heart that he had a feeling wouldn't go away for a long time.

In the month that followed, while Quinn stayed on at Retreat to make certain that Rio was becoming acclimated and that his training was going smoothly, Quinn saw Moria every day, unless it was raining or storming. The black horse, Moria's horse, had arrived a week after Rio del Oro, and Moria and Eugenia started their grueling

161

task of mastering every pace and trick of riding that Quinn and Liam between them could teach them.

Eugenia Northrup was an expert horsewoman, Quinn had never seen a better, not even in Arizona, where girls were born to the saddle. But Moria was every bit as expert, even at her age. Blond woman and blond horse, black-haired girl and black horse, they made a picture that would stay with Quinn for the rest of his life.

He and Moria got to know each other well during that month. It wasn't all spent in training. After the two-hour session in the morning, and after Moria's other lessons, they were free to take other horses and ride over the estate. And often, Moria managed to divert Quinn onto another bridle path in order to give Eugenia and Liam some time alone. She did it so naturally, so seemingly without guile, that it took Quinn days to figure out what she was up to, and the knowledge of the love between Eugenia and Liam weighed heavily on his heart.

Not that he either blamed or condemned them. He detested William Northrup, everything about the man went against the grain. It was a crime that Mrs. Northrup was tied to him, that there was no way she could ever free herself from him. He liked Eugenia, he'd have given a great deal to see her happy, and he liked Liam better than any other man he had ever known, a liking that was reciprocated and that deepened with every day that he stayed on at Retreat.

But it was Moria who intrigued him, who fascinated him, Moria who filled his thoughts both day and the long nights when he lay awake thinking about her. He wondered if having known her would spoil all other women for him, if he'd go through the rest of his life unmarried because of the memory of a little girl he could never have.

Moria liked him, too. She trusted him, she teased him to tell her about Arizona and his life there. She confided in him, little things that he suspected she confided to no one else, not even Eugenia. She even let it slip, to him, how much she disliked Mr. Northrup, with no fear that word of it would ever pass his lips. The only thing she didn't confide in him was that she was Liam's daughter, and there were times when it was hard for her not to tell him the whole story. Quinn was her friend. Quinn was different from any other man in the world. She'd never forget him, there'd be an empty place in her heart after he left.

As the days passed, Quinn became more and more wrapped up in Moria. When she lifted her horse into a gallop, and her loosened hair flowed out behind her and her face was flushed and her eyes sparkling with the excitement of the race, she was so enchantingly beautiful that he marveled that she could be made of flesh and blood. When her silvery laugh rang out, something inside of him melted. Not given to flights of romantic fancy, nevertheless he found himself thinking of her as a fairy-child, as some enchanted demigoddess from another sphere, forever beyond the reach of ordinary men.

That was nonsense, of course. Moria was very much a human being, a young girl who gave promise of growing up into a woman who would set men's blood on fire. If she'd been older, he'd have gone through hell and high water to win her for himself, he'd have met William Northrup on his own terms to battle for her. But she wasn't older, she was still a child, and he was acting like a fool. His father would tell him to stick his head in the horse trough until he sobered up and could think sense.

A girl like Moria, on a cattle ranch? The wind and sun would wither her, the harsh life would destroy her, Arizona was no place for the delicate foster child of people like Eugenia and William Northrup.

Besides, there was no use in even thinking about it. Fifteen was fifteen, and at twenty, Quinn felt at least a dozen years older, the five years between them were a gulf that could never be crossed even if Moria's place in the scheme of things wouldn't have made it impossible. Deriding himself for his romantic notions, Quinn took to treating her like the child she was, teasing her, laughing at her, acting more like an indulgent uncle than a young man only five years her senior.

Still, on the day before he left to return to Arizona, he gave her a bracelet he'd fashioned from the hairs from Jazir's and Kamil's tails.

He'd spent hours making it; the braided, interlaced pattern was intricate and beautiful, it was the only piece of its kind in the world.

"I'd like to think of you wearing it when you're training Jazir," he told her, as he placed it in her hand when they said good-bye. "I'd like to think that it will bring you luck, just because I want so much luck for you."

Moria's eyes filled with tears, hot and stinging. She lifted the bracelet to her lips and kissed it before she slipped it over her hand onto her wrist.

"I'll wear it, Quinn, I'll wear it every day! I'll never get on Jazir without it!"

She was having trouble with the clasp, a tiny loop that slipped over a little knot so that it wouldn't be too loose and fall off. Quinn's fingers trembled as he helped her with it. The feel of the flesh of her hand against his own took his breath away.

"You needn't cry about it. I hoped it would make you happy. It's only a keepsake, after all."

"No, you're wrong. It's my talisman! As long as I have it, you'll be near me. And I'll like that, Quinn. You couldn't have done anything nicer for me. I'll treasure it always."

The next morning Quinn was gone, but Moria had never forgotten him. Not a day went by that she didn't think of him with an empty feeling of loss because he wouldn't be at the ring when she and Eugenia went for their training session. True to her word, she never rode Jazir without wearing the bracelet, she never looked at it or touched it without thinking of Quinn.

She missed him. She wondered if she'd ever see him again. He was special to her, very special, she treasured the memories she had of him as sweetly as she treasured the keepsake he'd fashioned for her with his own hands. Someday she'd make sure that she'd see him again, even if she had to travel all the way to the wild Arizona Territory, because she couldn't imagine going all through the rest of her life without seeing him again.

Her hand still protecting the bracelet that was still on her wrist, Moria looked at Dora now, and her eyes were bright and hard and filled with a threat that made even Dora step backward with a little chill of fright.

"If you ever throw this bracelet away, you'll be sorry. It's mine. You aren't even to touch it!"

She removed it only to take her bath, and then she put it on again to take her nap, removing it only when she dressed for the afternoon ride and picnic. As always, she wrapped it in a silk handkerchief before she laid it away at the bottom of her small jewel chest. And before she closed the lid she said, "Thank you, Quinn. It brought me luck, just as you said it would. I'll have my father tell you, when he writes to you the next time."

It made her happy to realize that the young rancher who had been her friend for just one month wasn't completely lost to her, even though he was so far away. Quinn had written to Liam on his return to his ranch, and Liam had answered, and although they didn't write to each other often, they wrote three or four times before the year was out. Liam read Quinn's letters to her and it was almost like being with him again.

Moria was in seventh heaven. The ride through the cool woods to the picnic grove was delightful, but her delight in the ride had nothing to do with the coolness of the woods or the beauty of the day, or even the brilliant company of guests. Her delight was entirely because Anthony Vancouver had reined his mount in beside her own Serena as soon as the party had set out.

"That was quite a performance you and Mrs. Northrup put on. I had no idea that you were such an accomplished horsewoman," Tony told her. His smile was frankly admiring, and Moria's heart did flip-flops.

"It took a lot of practice. We've been schooling Jazir and Kamil for a whole year," she told him. "But it was fun, even if it was so much work."

"Mr. Northrup is the most envied man in the whole Hudson River area today," Tony went on, pressing his advantage. "He always comes out a winner. I never saw a man shot with so much luck!"

165

His eyes told her, beyond any doubt, that having Moria for his ward was a large part of his luck.

He'd noticed her at last, he liked her! All of her father's warnings, unnecessary thus far because Tony had avoided her ever since his sixteenth birthday party, were forgotten as she felt the full impact of his eyes. And she wasn't too young for him anymore, she was sixteen, a lot of girls were married at sixteen, she was grown-up, old enough to be courted!

"Thank you, Mr. Vancouver. But I'm the one shot with luck, as you put it. How could any girl be luckier than to have Mrs. Northrup choose her for her ward?"

"It was probably ordained by heaven," Tony told her, his smile devastating. "Heaven knew that if you hadn't come to Retreat, I would never have gotten to know you."

Thank all the saints that she was a good enough horsewoman not to fall off her horse! Moria was positively light-headed with ecstasy.

"Pshaw, Mr. Vancouver! How you do run on!" Great jumping hoptoads, had those inane, silly words come out of her own mouth? Other girls talked like that, they were past mistresses of such ridiculous mouthings while they were flirting with young gentlemen, but she'd never talked like that in her life! But she had a notion that Tony expected it of her, that if she didn't act like a silly goose he'd think she was naïve and boring and his newfound interest in her would die an early death.

"It's no more than the truth." There was a ring of sincerity in Tony's voice. He, too, was a past master at flirtation, at getting what he wanted by the use of extravagant compliments. And he wanted Moria. For a moment he regretted that he hadn't discovered her sooner, until he reminded himself that she would have been too young, so it was just as well that he hadn't felt the full impact of her beauty until today.

It was only a three-quarters-of-an-hour ride to the grove where the servants had already laid out linen cloths on the ground, and brought hampers of fried chicken and baked ham, of rolls and cheese and cakes and fresh fruit. The cloths were laid with the finest china and crystal and silver, lemonade and wine were chilling in silver buckets of chopped ice. Blankets and cushions had been brought for the ladies and gentlemen to sit on to prevent their clothing from becoming soiled by contact with the ground. A smile flickered on Moria's lips when she saw it, a smile so wry that Tony was intrigued.

"What do you find so amusing?" he asked her as he helped her dismount while a groom hurried to lead their horses away.

There was no way Moria could tell him that she was remembering picnics she and her mother and father had had when they had lived in Ireland. Real picnics, not outdoor banquets attended by servants and all the luxurious trappings of a meal taken in a mansion! Her mother had packed bread and cheese in kerchiefs, and there had been nothing brought to drink, they'd used their cupped hands to scoop of water from a brook when they were thirsty. How good that water had tasted, better than the finest wines served at Mr. Northrup's table! And how delicious the crusty bread had been, and the cheese, because their appetites had never been cloyed by fancy and exotic foods. Bread and cheese, and water from a brook, and their love for each other, had made those simple picnics memorable beyond anything that Mr. Northrup had contrived for today.

Only, this picnic would never be forgotten, either, because it marked the day when Anthony Vancouver had discovered that she was alive, that she was a grown-up and attractive female. She would never forget it as long as she lived, although she doubted that she would remember for long what had been spread before them on the linen cloths.

Sitting together, Eugenia and Estelle were both acutely aware of Anthony's attentions to Moria. Estelle's face was beaming. Although Tony didn't know it, his mother was fully aware of his attraction to Veronica Hamilton, an attraction of which she did not approve. Not that the Hamilton family itself wasn't acceptable, but there was a wild streak in Veronica, she was too sexual, there was something there that made Estelle suspect that Veronica would not make a good and modest wife, a good mother to Anthony's children.

But Moria was perfect, and Estelle's fondest desire was that she and Tony should fall in love and be married.

Eugenia's thoughts were on an entirely different track. She didn't like this. Although no rumors about Tony's private life ever reached her ears, she remembered Liam's warnings, and she was afraid for Moria. All you had to do was look at her to see that the girl was enamored of the handsome young Dutchman, who was so handsome, so completely charming, that a girl far more worldly than Moria would be ensnared.

She'd have to tell Liam what was developing as soon as she could seek him out privately. Perhaps together, their influence would do some good.

Alerting William to what was so obviously going on right under their eyes would be useless. Nothing escaped William's attention, he was already aware that Moria and Anthony were giving every indication that they were attracted to each other. If William wanted to stop the affair, he'd stop it, but if he didn't, he'd lift no hand to help her to stop it.

"Aren't they a beautiful couple, Eugenia? Did you ever see such a beautiful young couple before, perfect for each other! Wouldn't it be wonderful if they should fall in love and marry?"

"Moria is far too young to think of marriage. I would never allow her to become engaged until she is at least eighteen, or even older."

"Come now! Why, I was married at seventeen! And so are a good many girls. You're being overprotective. You must begin to realize that Moria is no longer a little girl, she's a young lady, even though you hate to think of losing her."

Eugenia forced herself to smile. "We'll just have to wait and see. I, for one, refuse to be a party to matchmaking."

Sitting beside Moria, attentive to her every need, Tony resented every moment that must pass before nightfall and the fireworks display, before the dancing would start. If he couldn't entice her into a deserted part of the garden, and start sweeping away her defenses, then he didn't deserve to have her at all! He sensed that his battle was already half won, and he was confident that before this night was over, it would be completely won and he would only need to pick and choose the time and place for its culmination.

Around them, the talk was still all of Jazir and Kamil, of the unforgettable spectacle of Eugenia and Moria putting them through their paces, the magnificent palomino and the equally magnificent Arab that only William could have found. William was congratulated over and over, and he accepted the compliments graciously but as no more than his due.

William was well pleased. Everything had gone as well as he had expected it would. Today had established him, for all time, as a connoisseur beyond comparison.

In spite of appearing to give his entire attention to his guests, he had not failed to notice that Anthony Vancouver had singled Moria out. He was far from displeased. He and Jacob Vancouver had close ties, not only in business but in their Dutch lineage. Cementing the alliance between himself and Jacob would be an advantage to him. Jacob could be stubborn, and often was stubborn, about matters that William tried to convince him were advantageous. Having Moria and Anthony married would be a lever he could put to good use.

So while Moria thrilled to her conquest, and while Eugenia worried and agonized over the possible consequences, William turned matters over in his head and was satisfied.

The hours between the picnic and the pyrotechnics display passed, even though to both Moria and Tony they seemed to drag on forever. At a little before ten that evening, when the sky was brilliant from the bursts of skyrockets, Tony drew Moria away from the gathering into the dark seclusion of the rose arbor. Eugenia, who had been watching them rather than the brilliant display that was bringing gasps of admiration from their guests, half rose from her chair to hurry after them, but William laid his hand on her arm, holding her back.

"You must watch this next burst, Eugenia. The effect is very special, I ordered it specifically, made up to my own plans."

There was no way she could get away from him. Her heart heavy

169

with foreboding, Eugenia was forced to sink back into her chair and pretend to be as enthralled as the other ladies, who were gasping and crying out with delight.

"Do you know that you're driving me mad?" Tony asked Moria. "Do you have any idea of what just being near you is doing to me?"

They were facing each other, their faces no more than pale blurs in the gloom of the rose arbor. Tony put his hands on Moria's shoulders and drew her close, but not too close, he knew better than that, it wouldn't do to frighten her, to make her skittish.

"You're beautiful," he said. "You're the most beautiful girl I've ever seen. I'm going to kiss you. I have to kiss you, or I'll be taken away in a straitjacket and locked up with the maniacs for the rest of my life."

It was Moria's first kiss, and for a moment she thought she was going to die of it. Tony's mouth was warm and hard on hers, it told her even more than his words, it conveyed admiration and desire and love so overwhelmingly that if she hadn't been made of such sturdy Irish stock she might have swooned.

"We'll have to get back before we're missed. Your guardian wouldn't relish our causing a scandal at his own party," Tony told her, his voice husky.

Her legs shaking, her lips throbbing, her face feeling as though it were on fire, Moria let him lead her back to mingle with the spectators who were still admiring the last of the fireworks display.

And then there was the dancing. Waltzing in Tony's arms, Moria thought over and over, "I'm in love. This is what love is, this is what life is all about. I know at last, and if I'd never learned it, then I might just as well never have been born."

Watching her, Eugenia's heart ached. Across the room, William's hooded eyes concealed his satisfaction.

Moria went to bed that night with her cheeks flushed as though she were running a fever. She lay there, wide awake in spite of being so tired from dancing almost until dawn, her fingers pressed tightly to the horsehair bracelet that she had slipped on her wrist right before she'd gotten into bed.

Quinn will be happy for me, she thought. His bracelet has brought me the most wonderful luck in the world!

10

Liam and Eugenia lay in each other's arms. The only light in Liam's cottage fell across their bed from the window, where a moonlight night must have been bringing joy to lovers less star-crossed than themselves.

Their lovemaking had been fierce and sweet. Now that summer was in full swing, and traveling easy, William spent more time away from home overnight, but still it didn't happen often enough to satisfy their desperate love for each other. When it did happen, it was as though they had to consume each other so that they would never be alone.

Liam was a tormented man, and Eugenia, worried and tormented herself, wasn't able to assuage his torment as she wished she could. The fact that their love for each other knew no bounds, that they could never be together publicly, man and wife in the eyes of the world, had little to do with it. Their own state was something they were forced to accept, and they were resigned to it.

It was Moria who lay heavy on both their hearts. Moria, and her wild infatuation for Anthony Vancouver. Ever since the day William had shown off his two new horses with Eugenia and Moria putting them through their routine to the amazement and envy of his friends, the girl had walked about in a dreamworld of her own, one that even Eugenia and Liam found it impossible to enter to bring her back to earth.

"He's a scoundrel, Eugenia! The boy is no good, his heart is as black as Satan's. Nothing good can come from this. I have a feeling that Moria's life is going to be ruined."

"Perhaps it isn't as bad as we imagine it is, Liam." Heartsick herself, Eugenia attempted to ease Liam's misery. "After all, Moria is only sixteen, she can't possibly think of getting married for a long time yet. If she's anything like other girls, she'll go through half a dozen more severe cases of puppy love before she settles on the man who's right for her. And Anthony has competition, so much competition that it's a wonder it hasn't gone to Moria's head. Every young man in the Hudson River Valley is beating a path to our doorstep."

Her words were brave enough, but she didn't believe them in her heart, and neither did Liam. Although it was true that Moria was the most popular girl in the Hudson River Valley, that she could have her choice of dozens of young scions of illustrious families, she had eyes only for Tony.

Eugenia had talked to her for hours, telling her all she could, in decency, about what she knew of Tony. Liam had talked himself blue in the face. But all Moria did was look at them with those blue eyes of hers, and say that they didn't understand, that maybe Tony had sowed some wild oats the way every young man of wealth did, but he'd changed, his love for her had changed him, he was everything that was noble and wonderful and they were meant for each other and nothing could ever change it.

"Use the common sense the good Lord gave you, girl!" Liam raged, his face flaming with anger. "I tell you he's no good for you, he'll break the heart of any girl who's foolish enough to believe his black lies! I know things about him that would singe the hair right off your head!"

"But that was before he fell in love with me, Papa. He's different

174

now, he'll never be like that again. If you only knew him as I know him, you'd understand.''

"I understand that you're as stubborn as Paddy's pig!" Liam shouted at her. "And as senseless, to boot! You're only a little girl and you're getting in over your head and if somebody doesn't stop you you're going to drown and all the prayers in the world won't save you!"

A fine man he was, talking about prayers, Liam Donovan who'd turned his back on God and Mother Church years ago, after he'd seen things and heard things and smelled things during the war that no man could see and hear and smell and remain sane. He'd gone mad, that was what had happened, he'd gone mad with the terror that he could never make things better for Moria, that only the strong and the ruthless had any chance in a world dominated by the Evil One and not by the saints and Holy Mother Mary and God the way Molly and the priests had always told him, even though he'd not believed them even then, knowing things about the world and the people in it that his dear Molly was too innocent to be told for fear of breaking the heart of her.

Now Liam couldn't sleep, his days and nights alike were tortured by nightmares of what would happen to Moria, and it was all his fault for selling her to William Northrup. Because selling her it had been, even though it was Moria who was to reap all the benefit and not himself, never himself. What would Molly think of him now, letting her child, her beloved Moria, walk into a trap that would snap closed on her and she'd never be able to get out, not even if she chewed off her own leg the way wild animals did to get free?

He'd sold his Moria, and now there was no way to get her back, to save her from the situation he'd forced her into through no fault of her own. If there was any way he could gather her up and run with her, somewhere beyond William Northrup's reach, he'd do it even though it would tear the heart out of him to leave Eugenia.

But there was no place beyond William Northrup's reach. He'd proved that with Eugenia, he'd forced her to stay with him, to bear all the bestial abuse he could heap on her, because of his powerful arm that reached to every corner of the earth. And even if Liam dared to take the chance, even if he dreamed of taking Moria and getting them both to Arizona, that place of freedom that Quinn had convinced him must be the nearest place to heaven, then it would be Eugenia who would suffer the consequences.

Once again, he pushed away the thought that had come into his mind of its own volition hundreds of times. He could kill William Northrup, killing him was the only way to set them all free. He could kill him and he'd take joy in the doing of it.

Murder! He shuddered, pulling Eugenia closer into his arms, crushing her body against his as though to use her to make a barrier against the blackness of his mind. He'd come to that, then, that he'd murder in cold blood in order to protect those he loved from the consequences of what he himself had done.

But if he did it, driven to it by the desperation in his soul, he wouldn't get away with it, there was no way he could get away with it, a man like William Northrup couldn't be murdered without the law digging in and prying until they learned the last crumb of truth. The William Northrups of the world were sacrosanct, no one could lift a hand against them without being tracked down and hanged by the neck until they were dead. No matter his willingness to sacrifice himself for them, they'd never have another happy moment in their lives.

What would Eugenia do without him? She'd be devastated, her life would be empty and desolate, she might even choose to follow him into death. And Moria loved him as few daughters loved their fathers. Even if she should marry someday, she would never forget. The fact that it wouldn't be Anthony Vancouver she would marry, because the Vancouvers would never accept the daughter of an Irish murderer, wasn't enough to balance the scales. Moria's love for him might very well turn into hate, feeling as she did about Tony, if by any act of his she should lose him.

"Don't, Liam, don't!" Eugenia said. She pressed herself even closer against him, her arms enfolding him. "Don't torment yourself. Everything you did, you did because you thought it was for the best. And we've had each other all this time, we still have each other. Moria won't marry Tony. She's too basically sensible to go on loving him until she's old enough to marry. We have at least two years before we have to worry about it, and by that time she'll be in love with somebody else, someone worthy of her.''

"There's no one worthy of her! No mortal man could be worthy of Moria!'' Liam said, his voice filled with anguish. "I've ruined her life. I put money and possessions above all the honest values, I've put her immortal soul in jeopardy. Molly must be weeping to see it. My Molly, who trusted me to do my best for her! I promised her, I made a sacred promise on her deathbed, and this is what it's come to!''

"You made the promise in good faith, and it hasn't been broken yet.'' Instinctively, Eugenia pressed her mouth against his, her hands moving to caress him, to comfort him in the one way that was certain to ease his self-torture, the time-tested formula that always seemed to work for men. How different men and women were! A man's heartbreak, a man's cares, could always be alleviated by the warm and passionate body of a woman, while a woman who suffered heartbreak had no interest in the act of love at all, it seemed like a sacrilege to her.

Once again, as it had countless times in the past when Liam went into one of his dark Irish moods, it worked. And afterward, Liam slept, but Eugenia hadn't closed her eyes when she finally crept out of his bed, moving quietly so as not to disturb him, and made her cautious way back to the house, where Rose was waiting to let her in.

How lucky they'd been so far! All these years, and still no one on the estate suspected the love that she and Liam had for each other, no one had an inkling of the nights she spent in Liam's arms when William was away. Only Rose knew. No matter what the future holds in store for us, Eugenia thought, we've had that, and nothing can ever take it away from us.

Liam tried again, with Moria, the next morning. He'd had too little sleep, and in spite of the lovemaking so recently over, his mood was as black as it had been the day before. Of all the young men in the world, why had Moria had to imagine herself in love with Anthony Vancouver? Why couldn't she have been older, of a marriageable age, when Quinn Bradmore had come to deliver Rio del Oro, for instance? Liam had been taken with Quinn, he liked and respected him, and not being blind he'd realized right from the first that Quinn had been mightily taken with his daughter. William Northrup wouldn't have liked it, but knowing Moria, Liam didn't believe that even William could have prevented her from marrying the young rancher if she'd been of age and had fallen in love with him. And knowing Quinn, he was equally sure that Quinn wouldn't have let William prevent him from marrying his ward.

Arizona! The limitless blue sky, the endless range of open space, the very air impregnated with a freedom that few people on earth were ever privileged to experience! And a man like Quinn for his daughter, strong, honest, his integrity without question. If Moria had been eighteen instead of barely fifteen...

"You must be out of your mind!" Liam lashed at Moria. "Haven't you heard a word I've said to you, girl? Anthony Vancouver is no good, he has the morals of a tomcat! He doesn't know the meaning of right from wrong, he takes what he wants and that's the way he'll always be!"

Moria's face was pale as she reined Jazir in and turned to face her father, forcing him to pull up his mount as well. "I don't think you have any right to talk about Tony that way. What about your own life, your own morals? You and Eugenia..."

The moment the words passed her lips, she would have given anything to take them back. But it was too late. Liam's face had gone to the color of putty, there were white lines running from his nostrils to the corners of his mouth, and his eyes were stricken.

"Papa, I'm sorry! I know it's different with you and Eugenia, I know how much you love each other! But I love Tony the same way,

I love him as much as you love Eugenia, and you're wrong about him, I know you are!''

Liam didn't answer her. He reined Ranger around and touched his heel to him, lifting him into a headlong gallop, his blind eyes seeing nothing through the blackness that Moria's words had brought on him. She knew! How long had she known, how long had his example been poisoning her life? The sins of the fathers!

Eugenia, who'd ridden ahead in order to give him an opportunity to talk to Moria alone and try to pound some sense into her head, saw him coming, the pounding of Ranger's hooves beating against her heart and wounding it.

"Liam?"

He didn't hear her. He thundered past her, and knowing that it would have been useless to go after him even though Kamil could have overtaken Ranger easily, she turned the palomino around and cantered back to where Moria was still holding Jazir motionless, her face flooded with tears.

"What did you say to him?" Eugenia demanded, flags of anger coloring her face. "What did you say that sent him off like that, as if the devil were after him?"

"He goaded me!" Moria cried. "I'm sorry I hurt him, but he drove me to it! Why can't he understand, why can't both of you understand that Tony and I love each other as much as you and Papa love each other?"

For the first time since Moria had come to Retreat, Eugenia wanted to slap her. The impulse swept over her, and before she had time to control it she raised her hand and brought it across Moria's cheek with all her strength. The blow was so hard that Moria reeled in her saddle, and then the girl straightened her back and looked at her foster mother, her face as white as paper, the red mark left by the blow flaming against the whiteness.

"Don't you hurt him, don't you dare hurt him!" Eugenia shouted.

"Then don't you or he dare hurt Tony and me, either!" Moria flung back. Then she, like Liam, lifted Jazir into a gallop, headed

179

back to the house, the black's hooves flying, his nostrils extended, as the frantically unhappy girl urged him on.

Pat, the stableboy, who was now sixteen, heard Jazir coming and ran out of the stables where he had been spreading fresh straw. His mouth dropped open as Moria pulled Jazir up, so sharply that he reared, and Pat reached out to grab at his bit to pull him down again.

"Miss Moria! Has there been an accident, is someone hurt?" Pat burst out. It was the only reason he could conceive of to make Miss Moria come pelting back to the stable like this with such a look on her face.

"No!" Moria was out of the saddle before Pat could move to help her, and running toward the house. Inside, she flew up the broad staircase, her heart hammering, the blood pounding in her temples, her anger consuming her. It wasn't fair! How could they, how dared they, condemn Tony, when they themselves had been having an affair all these years! Her own guilt, knowing that she'd hurt them desperately, they who had already been hurt so much because they could never belong to each other entirely, only made it worse.

Rose heard Moria's boots pounding along the hall, and she hurried from Eugenia's room in time to catch Moria in her arms and draw her into her room. "Holy Mother, what's happened?" she demanded.

Moria began to cry, great convulsive sobs that shook her body. Rose reached up and removed her hat and stroked her hair back from her forehead, her hands tender and caring.

"It can't be that bad. Nothing can be that bad. Whatever it is, it'll all come right."

"They have no right!" Moria cried. "Rose, they have no right!"

It was Tony, then. Rose had thought as much. Moria and her father and Eugenia had quarreled about Tony.

"I'm going to marry him, Rose. I don't care what they say, I love him and I'm going to marry him!" And silently, Rose changed her statement. Knowing Moria as she did, knowing the stubbornness, that Irish stubbornness that was ingrained in the girl no matter how

180

sweet and gentle she was basically, Rose had a foreboding that it wasn't going to come right, that all of them, every one of them, was going to be hurt beyond enduring before this was over.

Moria was in a reckless mood that evening when Tony came to call on her. All the rest of the day, after the morning ride that had ended so disastrously, her hurt and resentment had festered inside of her. She was sorry that she had hurt her father, she still wished she could recall the words that had hurt him so much, but she had a right to live her own life, she had a right to take the happiness that Tony's love offered her. Liam and Eugenia were old, they didn't understand. But she was young, and she wanted to live, she wanted to experience life and everything it had to offer to the fullest, and they had no right to try to stop her just because they were old and cautious and afraid for her.

She herself wasn't afraid. Tony had changed, he'd never go back to being the way he'd been before he'd fallen in love with her. And Mr. Northrup approved of Tony's courting her. He hadn't said so, outright, but she knew that if he hadn't approved, Tony wouldn't have been allowed to call on her several times a week and spend so much time with her. And with Mr. Northrup on her side, there was nothing her father or Eugenia could do to stop the inevitable result of that courtship.

Looking at her as they walked in the rose garden, the roses full-blown and beginning to look bedraggled now that October had come as if they knew that their day was past and that a killing frost would soon cut them down, Tony sensed the recklessness of her mood, and his heart leaped in anticipation of how he could turn it to his advantage.

His seduction of Moria hadn't gone as well as he had anticipated. There was something untouchable about her, her very innocence made it almost impossible for him to draw her into a situation where they would have the time and the privacy for him to sweep down her defenses. But tonight was the night. The estate was large, there were countless places where they would not be interrupted now that he had her outside with no chaperone watching their every move.

William Northrup didn't enforce the strict chaperonage that was taken for granted with other girls. Moria was, after all, only his ward, not his blood daughter, and besides, he and Mrs. Northrup were away from home this evening.

Smiling, his smile filled with tenderness but his heart filled with elation that the end of his hunt was so near, Tony reached for her hand. "Let's walk for a while. It's a beautiful mild evening for this time of year, you won't get chilled."

Her own blood running hot with the residue of her angry resentment, Moria was sure that she wouldn't feel chilled even if the temperature should plummet. "Yes, let's," she said. "I could walk for miles!"

But that wouldn't be necessary, Tony thought with satisfaction. There were hidden sheltered places much closer than miles, and having been almost as familiar with Retreat as he was with Belvedere from early childhood, he knew them all.

Hand in hand, Moria thrilling to the contact, they strolled away from the rose garden, took a flagstoned path that led them away from the house and past the kitchen gardens, and then turned on to another, graveled path that would lead them to the remotest part of the immediate grounds, where a stand of ornamental bushes and shrubbery would give them shelter both from the slight breeze and from prying eyes.

He's going to propose to me, Moria thought, her heart beating faster and faster until it made her dizzy. He's going to ask me, and I'm going to say yes, and then everything will be all right because when Papa and Eugenia see how happy I am, they'll realize that they were wrong about Tony and they'll be happy for me. When I go back to the house tonight, I'll be betrothed!

She savored the word on her lips. Betrothed! How beautiful it was, there were only two words in the English language that were more beautiful, and they were the "I do" that she would be saying very soon.

They were at the stand of ornamental bushes and shrubbery now, and Tony drew her into the center of it. Moria's heart beat even faster. Tony put his hands on her shoulders and turned her to face him, almost exactly as he had that time the evening after her and Eugenia's triumph when they had shown off Jazir and Kamil on the Fourth of July.

Only it wasn't the same, because Tony's hands moved from her shoulders, moved first to her throat, his fingers caressing the ivory skin until she tingled from his touch, and then moved downward again, bringing a flush to her face as, startled, she realized where they had come to a stop.

She drew back, not timid or afraid, but only because her instincts were those of any decent young girl. "Tony, no."

"Yes, Moria, yes! Oh, Moria, you drive me mad! I can't see you without wanting to take you into my arms, to hold you, to possess you. Like this, and this, and this . . ."

The rush of blood through Moria's body astonished her. Hot blood, hot and racing, telling her to throw caution to the winds, telling her that this moment would never happen again, that she must grasp it and hold it or it would be lost forever. At the same time, her head told her that this wouldn't do at all, that if she let Tony go on, she'd lose not only her self-respect but his respect for her as well. The hot blood of passion was a legacy from her father, but so was the common sense, and she had the additional legacy of absolute morality from her mother as well.

But Tony's mouth on hers, moving and demanding, as demanding as his hands, was waging a battle with the common sense and the morality, and the stars above her seemed to reel through the sky as Tony's kiss deepened, as his hands became even more insistent. She loved him, she loved him!

The ground was soft and resilient as they sank down, first to their knees and then, at Tony's pressure, all the way. Every inch of the ground of Retreat was well kept, no patch of it allowed to harden or become weed-choked because of lack of rain or care. Somehow the tiny buttons at the back of her dress had been loosened, when had that happened? she couldn't remember, but they were undone and the bodice of her dress had slipped off her shoulders and Tony's

183

hand was there, his fingers stroking her nipple until it stood out hard and firm in a way she had never imagined. She was sinking, drowning, her emotions were closing in over her head and nothing mattered, nothing but her love for Tony and his love for her.

At the last instant, even as Tony's whisper of "Please, Moria, I won't hurt you . . ." fell on her ears, Moria came back to her senses. There was too much of her father and mother in her to allow herself to be seduced here on the grounds of Retreat. Her own sense of her own worth came to her rescue.

"Tony, stop it! Stop it this instant! I won't . . ."

"You will, you can't help yourself any more than I can help myself, it's too late." Tony's whisper was urgent, his hands and mouth even more insistent.

"I'll bite you!" Moria warned.

Tony either didn't hear her, in the depth of his passion, or he didn't believe her. But in the next instant he yelped with pain, his hand releasing her breast to fly to his face, and he cursed as he felt blood. Yes, it was blood, she'd not only bitten him but she'd bitten him hard enough to break the skin and it stung like the devil.

Instead of cooling his ardor, the wound served instead to inflame him all the more. "You vixen!" he cried, his voice a gasp. In the gloom of the sheltering copse, his eyes glittered, and he crushed her to him, his mouth on hers searing her own. Struggling, Moria managed to free one hand, she drew it back, the fingers curved, to rake his face.

Her fingernails never reached their mark. A horrified gasp, clearly audible even through Tony's labored breathing, made him jerk his head up and say, "What the devil!"

It wasn't the devil, it was Dora. Moria's personal maid had had the temerity to follow them, to spy on them! And to spy on them for just this purpose. Not only that, Dora wasn't alone, it wouldn't be just her word against Moria's and Tony's. Dora was cleverer than that, she'd brought along the fourteen-year-old scullery maid, a good-hearted girl who wasn't exactly retarded but who was definitely slow and just as definitely incapable of telling a mistruth when put to the question. To be asked by such an exalted personage as Miss Moria's own personal maid to take a stroll with her had turned Sally's head giddy with the honor and she'd been only too willing to risk the night air, which she was convinced was lethal, to accommodate Dora's request for company.

Dora's satisfaction with the result of her spying was monumental. She hadn't imagined anything as compromising as the sight of the two young people, Moria half undressed, her breast actually exposed and Anthony Vancouver's hand on it! It wasn't the first time that Dora had spied on them without their knowledge. She could move as silently as a cat stalking a mouse. But outside of a snatched kiss on the cheek, or of holding hands, she'd never seen anything that would have been worth reporting to Mr. Northrup.

Moria was on her feet, her eyes blazing. "How dare you! What do you mean, sneaking up on us like this? Get back to the house where you belong!"

"We're going, Miss Moria," Dora's voice held a smirk. "We're going right away. Come along, Sally."

This turn of events wasn't at all to Tony's liking. Stifling his curses, he asked Moria, "They won't carry tales, will they? They wouldn't dare!"

"Dora will dare. She hates me. I've never known why, but she does. She'll tell Mr. Northrup, and we'll just have to face it, Tony. Button my dress, please. If you hadn't been so blasted ardent, we wouldn't be in this pickle now! For a minute there I thought I was going to have to scratch your eyes out to make you turn me loose!"

Looking at her, his eyes fully adjusted to the dark, Tony thought bitterly that she'd have done it, too. She wasn't the easy victory he'd imagined she would be. Groaning, he realized that this time he was going to have to face the consequences of his folly, if what Moria said about her maid was true.

Only one thought brought him any consolation. His father would be furious if he were forced to marry Moria Compton. Tony knew, being endowed with a good brain buried under all of his tomcatting, that William Northrup was eager to have some control over his father's business ventures and that Jacob was as determined to prevent him from getting any kind of a foothold in his enterprises.

"I'm afraid we're in a compromising situation," Tony said. "If I'm not mistaken, we're going to have to face an unpleasant scene when Dora carries this tale to your foster father."

Moria's eyes were as brilliant as her smile. Tony marveled that she could laugh at a time like this.

"The way I look at it, it isn't that bad at all. I can see now that I'd never be able to control you, so the sooner we're married the better, so I won't have to try!"

Veronica was going to be as mad as a cat left out in the rain, but she'd just have to get used to the idea. Given a little time, she'd come around. There weren't many young men in Tony's present situation who could have it luckier, with Moria Compton for a wife and Veronica Hamilton waiting on the sidelines, ready and willing any time he wanted her. The chances were that the maid Dora had done him the biggest favor of his life.

Dora did her work well. Directly William and Eugenia returned home that night, she related everything she had seen, including the compromising position of the two young people on the ground entwined in each other's arms and Moria's bared breast with Anthony's hand on it. She related it all with downcast eyes and the air of someone who was reluctant to carry tales but who knew that her first duty was to her master. With Sally to back her up, William had no choice but to believe her.

Eugenia's face paled as she listened, and her heart was torn in two. How could Moria have been so foolish, whatever had possessed her to behave in such a manner, to allow Anthony such liberties? This would kill Liam. Their only hope was that William would fly into one of his cold rages and forbid Tony ever to see Moria again, a hope that was dashed almost before it was born.

"That will be all, Dora. Send Sally back to her quarters and go about your usual duties." William's voice was as emotionless, as impossible to read, as his face.

The moment Dora had shepherded Sally from the room, Eugenia turned to him, plunging in to try to salvage what she could from the situation.

"William, that young man must be forbidden our premises! No real harm has been done, Anthony didn't have time to finish what he had so obviously started, and Moria wouldn't have allowed it in any case. I know her, she's incapable of such behavior, Tony must have forced her, overpowered her, she's too young to have realized what he was leading up to. But we must certainly protect her in the future."

William's eyebrows rose. "No real harm, you say? With a woman like Dora with full information at her tongue-tip? Moria has been compromised. She will marry Anthony Vancouver at the earliest date consistent with custom. I believe that in this case, we might consider a June wedding. A month or two less than the usual year will do no harm, in order to have the wedding in June."

"You can't force her to marry Anthony Vancouver! You surely know of his reputation, you know what he is! Moria's life would be ruined! Dora won't talk, you of all people know that one word from you and neither she nor Sally would dare to open their mouths. All that's necessary is to forbid Moria and Anthony to see each other again!"

"My dear, if I'm not mistaken, Moria will be only too eager to enter into the matrimonial state with Anthony Vancouver. She's in love with the young man. The matter is settled. Our ward will find her happiness with the man of her choice, and a scandal will be averted. I suggest that you retire. It displeases me to see you in a state of emotional upheaval."

"You can't do it! Moria is my ward, as well as yours, and I won't allow it!" Eugenia cried. In her agitation, she rushed in where she knew better than to tread. This was one time she'd fight, and fight to the last ditch, no matter what William might do to her in punishment for daring to set herself against him.

"I should not need to remind you that, legally, you have no rights concerning my ward at all," William told her. "As my wife, your legal as well as your moral duty is to accede to my wishes."

Her mind screaming against the injustice of it, Eugenia turned and left the drawing room to find what comfort she could in Rose's arms.

11

If Eugenia and Liam had had any hopes that William would change his mind about allowing Moria to marry Anthony Vancouver, their hopes were dashed when William, without consulting Eugenia or saying a word to indicate what he was going to do, announced that he had legally adopted his ward. By the time Eugenia and Liam knew, the adoption was an accomplished fact.

Having Moria for his ward had pleased William, even though he had not considered legal adoption until it had become expedient in view of an alliance with the Vancouvers. Jacob might drag his heels at the idea of his son marrying a mere ward. An adopted daughter was a different matter. As William's legal daughter, Moria would stand to inherit a large part of his fortune, as well as having her name changed from Compton to Northrup.

With no blood heirs of his own, William was satisfied to let his fortune go to Moria. His own demise was so far in the future that there was no need to think about it, but the idea of leaving the bulk of his estate to the girl who had proved to be such a jewel in his crown, while cutting Eugenia off with barely enough to sustain her, if he should have the bad fortune to die before she did, gave him a great deal of pleasure. He had never forgotten, much less forgiven, the injury his wife had done him that had prevented him from siring a son.

Liam's mood, black enough before he learned of the adoption, became so much blacker that Eugenia was frightened. She lived in terror that he might lose control and do something so desperate, even kill William, that all of their lives would be ruined. His face was so grim, his eyes so smoldering with despair and fury that it terrified her just to look at him.

It hurt Moria, too. She loved her father, and she was sorry that she had hurt him by throwing his own affair with Eugenia in his face when he'd objected to her falling in love with Tony. She would have done anything in the world to take the black look off his face, anything except give up Tony now that it was settled that she was to marry him. And she hated hurting Eugenia, but it was her life and she could not and would not throw away her only chance for happiness just because Liam and Eugenia didn't approve of Tony, a disapproval that to her was blatantly unfair.

One month after Dora had unwittingly precipitated Moria into what she wanted more than anything else in the world, Retreat was the scene of an engagement party that was calculated to put even Tony's sixteenth birthday party in eclipse. Not only the engagement was to be announced, but the adoption. It took the entire month to prepare for the affair. The house was cleaned and polished even more thoroughly than William always demanded. The furniture had such a sheen that Moria was afraid to lay so much as a finger on it for fear of leaving a print, the crystal chandeliers were washed and every prism rubbed with a soft lintless cloth until the reflected rays from them dazzled the eyes. A chef was brought in from New York City, throwing the entire kitchen into a chaos of resentment and confusion.

Not that Moria cared about any of the preparations. Her days and nights were spent in a walking dream. Tony was with her almost constantly, except when she was forced to stand for hours being fitted for her ball gown.

William dictated what both she and Eugenia should wear. Their gowns were identical, except that Eugenia's was sapphire blue to exactly match her eyes, and Moria's the palest shade of shell pink, both fashioned from watered silk from a design of William's choosing, so elegant in its simplicity that all attention would be drawn to the wearers' beauty rather than to the gowns themselves.

Right up until the last minute, when the guests began to arrive, Eugenia harbored a faint hope that Tony would do something terrible, that he'd refuse to marry Moria or that he might even run away. As faint as the hope was, knowing Tony it was possible, but even that hope died when Tony arrived early, resplendent in evening clothes, his handsome face wreathed in a smile that would give the world cause to know that he was the happiest man on the face of the earth. That a good deal of his happiness was because William had apprised him and his father of the adoption was something that nobody else could know. When William made the announcement, he would appear to be as surprised as any of them.

Moria had never been more beautiful. Her happiness gave her a radiance that was almost painful to look at, because it served to remind the beholder that they themselves had never looked like that and never would. Dressing her mistress, arranging her hair, Dora's mouth was set in a grim, downward line and her eyes were hard and hot with hate. She'd intended to bring Moria to disgrace, perhaps even see her packed away from Retreat never to return. Instead, the girl of whom she was so jealous had gotten exactly what she wanted.

"Dora, do hurry! Why are you fumbling so? No, no, I won't have my hair in curls, I don't care what the fashion is, I look horrible in curls and you know it, they make me look like a silly wax doll! Just brush it away from my face, and let it hang down my back as it always does. No, wait, I'll have a coronet braid around my head and the rest will hang down my back, it will make me look older, really grown-up. Bother, I'll do it myself!"

The result, when Moria's fingers had fashioned the plaited coronet, might have been far from fashionable, but her instinct had been unerring. The simple style not only made her look older than her sixteen years, but it was so becoming to her that she was transformed. Dora's breath expelled sharply as she caught a glimpse of her own plain face, made ugly by the lines of discontent around her mouth, beside Moria's in the dressing table mirror.

"There, it's perfect! And I'm perfect, if I do say so myself! I couldn't have made it more perfect if I'd fussed another hour!" The words were spoken with no trace of conceit, only of satisfaction, because Moria wanted to be perfect for Tony, she had to be perfect for him, to make him proud of her and proud to be engaged to her. If only Papa could see her! For just a moment, her spirits flagged and she felt depression sweep over her, but then she tossed her head. If Papa could see her, he wouldn't be proud of her at all, he'd more likely want to rip her dress right off her and tear it to shreds because all this perfection was for a young man he detested.

And then she stopped thinking about such troublesome matters, she stopped thinking about anything at all but this night and what it meant to her, because a tap on her door told her that it was time for her to go downstairs, that the first guests were arriving. And as she rounded the graceful curve of the staircase, she saw that Tony was already there, so handsome that her heart almost stopped beating.

She floated the rest of the way down like a princess, to where Tony was waiting for her, and he held out his arm and she put her fingers on it, and the early arrivals who were still in the entrance hall knew that they had never seen a young couple more perfectly suited to each other.

Pressed into service to help handle the horses and carriages of the guests, Liam went about his duties with a grim face. Everything he had promised Molly that he would get for Moria had come true. She was the pampered ward of one of the wealthiest men in the country, she had servants at her beck and call, she was about to enter into marriage with one of the most aristocratic scions of the century. And there was a bitter taste in his mouth because he knew that once

Moria married Anthony Vancouver, all hope for happiness for her would be lost.

Inevitably, his mind went back to Quinn Bradmore, and to the Arizona Territory that Quinn had told him was so wild and so free. If this party tonight were to announce Moria's engagement to Quinn, he would have been the happiest man on earth, even if it meant that he would never see her again after she'd gone to live in the Southwest.

To add to his bitterness, he'd received a letter from Quinn that afternoon, delivered to his cottage after the post had been sorted at the house. In the letter, written in a strong hand that spoke of Quinn's character, he had asked about Moria, the daughter of the house, and although Liam knew that Quinn liked him and would have continued their acquaintance by mail even if Moria hadn't existed, it was plain that the young westerner was taken with her, that he couldn't get her out of his mind.

Liam would have to answer the letter, but it would tear his heart out to have to tell Quinn that Moria was engaged. There would be no point in telling him that he didn't approve of her choice. What would a horse trainer, one of William Northrup's servants, have to do with liking or disliking the choice? In those dark hours of the ball in honor of his daughter's engagement, Liam wished that he still had the faith of his boyhood so that he could throw his problem and his heartbreak on God's mercy.

But it was too late for that now, years and sins too late. Moria was lost, and her immortal soul with her, as the result of his own blind determination to get the best for her no matter what means he had to use. He was a liar, a cheat, an adulterer, he'd sold his own daughter, his Molly's beloved child, into the hands of Satan for a mess of pottage that had spoiled and rotted until the stench of it sickened him and he could no longer come face to face with himself without flinching.

When the last guests had arrived and their carriages and horses were cared for, Liam returned to his cottage, thankful to be far enough away from the house so that he could no longer hear the music and the laughter. The people inside, the fortunate guests who had been selected to attend this ball, were dancing on the grave of all his hopes for the future.

A tap on his door brought him to his feet. He hadn't lighted the lamp. Dark was his mood and the darkness of his cottage suited him. If God had done his business properly it would have been the darkness of Hades that surrounded him, not just that of an unlighted cottage, and Moria would still be in the care of some honest Irish family and none of this would have happened.

It was Pat, the stableboy, his hands filled with a tin tray loaded with delicacies from the kitchen. "You wouldn't go to see what could be had, so I brought you something," Pat told him. "It's a feast! This is quail, Liam, quail! I never tasted quail in my life before. Light the lamp, how can we see to eat in the dark? And there's pheasant, and ham, and roast beef, and cakes so light they're about to fly right off the dish, all frosted up so fancy it's a pity to eat them. Only we're going to, it'll be a lifetime before we ever see food like this again, and I went to enough trouble getting it without that Frenchie catching me and cutting my throat, so I'll enjoy it all the more!"

Liam's hands shook as he lighted the lamp. The sight of the exotic food nauseated him, but he ate a little to please Pat although every mouthful choked him.

"I've been buttering up Sally every day for a week," Pat confessed. "I knew I could talk her into snatching some of the goodies and slipping them to me. Did you ever taste the like! Man, I'd sell my soul to be able to have food like this every day of my life, the way the nobs do!"

Liam closed his eyes, and an expression of pain crossed his face. "Don't say that!" he commanded. "Don't ever think it, much less say it!" He pushed his plate away. "Take the rest along with you, lad, and finish it up. I'm going to sleep for a while before we have to bring the carriages around to the door after the ball."

He blew out the lamp again, and the minutes ticked into hours as he lay brooding on his bed in the dark cottage. Inside the

194

house, the dancing had stopped and the midnight supper was finished. William rose and tapped a knife against the side of his crystal wineglass. The demand for attention was hardly necessary. Everyone at the ball had been expecting this, and the murmur of conversation ceased immediately.

"This is an especially important occasion for the Northrup family," William said, while every breath bated and all eyes were fixed on him. "It is my great pleasure to tell you that my ward, Moria Compton, is now Miss Moria Northrup. As she has been my dearly beloved daughter for so many years, I deemed it time to make her status legal."

Murmurs of approval and pleasure broke out and swelled into polite applause. The guests' eyes went from William to Moria, and Tony, who was her supper partner, urged her to her feet while the applause deepened. Moria herself was stunned. Mr. Northrup was supposed to announce her engagement to Tony, and she had had no least inkling that she had been legally adopted, that she was now as much a Northrup as Eugenia. Tony hadn't told her, bowing to William's request that it should be a surprise. William Northrup's daughter! The full implication of the announcement was lost on her. In a few months she would be Moria Vancouver, so she attached no particular importance to being called Miss Northrup in the meantime.

William was smiling. Only Eugenia, herself stunned by the announcement, realized that his eyes were as cold and lacking in emotion as they always were. "But it seems that I have gained a daughter only to lose her all too soon. It is my even greater pleasure to announce that as of this evening, Miss Moria Northrup and Mr. Anthony Vancouver are betrothed, the wedding to take place on the twentieth day of June of next year."

Tony also rose to his feet, and put his arm around Moria. The applause was thunderous. It went on and on until Moria's face was pink with embarrassment, until Tony, smiling, kissed her cheek and motioned that it was enough.

Moria was happier than she had ever been in her life, tonight was the culmination of all her dreams. Tony gave every appearance of being enthralled with her, so much so that even men who knew a good deal more about him than he might have wished they knew gave him the benefit of the doubt. And their envy of William Northrup increased. To possess the two most beautiful women in New York State, perhaps in the whole country, and then to make an alliance with Jacob Vancouver that would give him a hold over the Vancouver enterprises, was good fortune almost beyond belief.

In the forefront of the well-wishers, a smile plastered on her lush mouth, Veronica Hamilton's heart seethed with rage. How dared Tony, how dared he! After all they'd meant to each other, after all of his promises, to betray her like this! Why, she'd all but let him go the whole way with her, there was scarcely an inch of her that he didn't know as intimately as he knew himself! She wished that she could kill him where he stood, but even more, she wished that she could kill Moria. That nobody upstart, the orphaned daughter of a mere army lieutenant! Her blood might be acceptable, but only barely, it was the trickery of fate alone that had brought her here to Retreat to usurp everything that Veronica had always considered as her own. Admiration, adulation, the undisputed place as the undisputed belle of the Hudson River Valley! And now she had Tony as well, and it was beyond bearing.

Even Tony, as inured as he was against the anger of young ladies whom he'd loved and discarded, felt a chill as he met the full impact of Veronica's eyes. But there was nothing she could do. The Veronica Hamiltons of the world do not attack either their ex-lovers or their ex-lovers' present sweethearts, it wasn't done. He'd only have to try a little harder, to exert a modicum more charm, when the time came that he'd want her back as his light of love, after his first pleasure in possessing Moria had paled.

"Darling, I've never been more pleased! I'm so happy for you!" Veronica exclaimed, as she kissed Moria's cheek.

"Thank you, Veronica. I'm happy too. I only wish that everyone in *'   'orld could be as happy as I am right now!"

*   ou, Veronica thought, so viciously that she had to turn
        Moria read her feelings in her eyes. Damn you to

perdition! He'll make you miserable, you'll never be able to stand his neglect and his philandering as I would have done. He'll break your heart, and I'll be right there laughing! And I'll have him back, and you'll know it, and the more you suffer for it the happier it will make me!

Eugenia's smile was as artificial as Veronica's as she endured her share of the congratulations. Her heart was so heavy that every second that passed seemed like an eternity. What was Liam feeling now, how was he bearing up? She wanted to go to him, the compulsion was so intense that she had to exert every ounce of her will to stay where she was, smiling the smile that hid her fears, and making the right responses.

She wouldn't be able to go to him tonight, after the ball was over. She'd seen the look in William's eyes, when he'd regarded her only a moment ago, sardonic, filled with grim promise. Tonight he'd come to her in her bedroom, and make her suffer once again all that he was capable of making her suffer. And she would have to bear it, because there was no escape.

What was to become of them, she wondered? How was it all going to end? Was Rose praying for them right now? The thought brought her a whisper of comfort, but not much. They'd prayed before, both of them, and this had still happened, Moria was going to marry Tony and she was still tied to William, and Liam would never find happiness, only the small dregs of comfort that she could give him.

Battered and bruised, her body screaming with pain that hurt less than the ache in her heart, Eugenia didn't ride the next day. Neither did Moria, although her reasons were entirely different. Moria was too tired after having danced until dawn and then lain awake for most of the morning, too excited, too ecstatically happy, to sleep.

Blessed Mary, where was he? Rose fretted for the hundredth time. It was past three o'clock in the morning, and Liam wasn't back yet. Knowing his mood, knowing that the way he was feeling he was capable of anything, Eugenia had sent Rose to wait at his cottage when she'd reported to her, when she'd retired at ten-thirty, that Liam had not yet returned.

"No matter how late it is, wake me and tell me when he gets back," Eugenia had said, her eyes dark with foreboding. "Promise me, Rose!"

"You don't need to make me promise. You know I'll do it." Rose herself was as worried about Liam as Eugenia was. And the minutes were still crawling on snail's feet, and there was no sign of the man, and Mary's ears must be tired from hearing all the Hail Marys and all the prayers Rose had poured out on them since her vigil had begun.

She paused in her pacing, and then hurried to the window. There was no light in the cottage, it would be disastrous if anyone were to discover her here, waiting for the horse trainer. Yes, she had heard something! She could just make out a bulky figure, moving slowly and laboriously along the path to the cottage. It couldn't be Liam, he was nowhere near that big, he never moved that slowly.

And then, her heart in her mouth, she realized that it wasn't one man but two, and that one of them was supporting, half carrying, the other.

She was out of the cottage in a flash, fearing the worst. "Is it Liam, then?" she demanded in a fear-fraught whisper.

"It's no other," came the answer, in a brogue as broad as Ireland was wide. "And it's in a bad way he is, I thought I'd never get him up that driveway! It's God's mercy that you're waiting for him, Rose O'Riley. I didn't dast to bring him the full way in the carriage, for fear we'd be heard, I left the horse well before the gatekeeper's cottage and prayed that he wouldn't hear us as we passed. Turn down the bed, for the love of Mary! And draw the curtains and make a light, he's needing attention."

"I'm all right." Liam's voice was hoarse, and the tone told Rose that he was far from all right, because it was laced with pain.

He͏͏͏͏ ͏͏͏rt pounding, she did as she'd been asked. She turned the l͏͏͏͏ ͏͏͏͏͏͏͏ as she could without it going out, but there was enough ͏͏͏͏ ͏͏͏͏ to see what damage Liam had contracted. "And who might you be, and what happened?'' she demanded as she helped the Irishman who'd brought Liam back strip the clothes off him and held up the lamp so she could look for injuries.

"Michael McCarthy, I am, and if I and me bullyboys hadn't interfered our boyo here wouldn't be back here at all this night, because it was outnumbered he was by a dozen to one and him plowing in with his fists to teach them all a lesson! And all because they wouldn't ante up as much as he was convinced they could afford and the patriots needin' every penny we can send them. He'll never be able to get on his feet tomorrow, and how's that to be explained to his high and mightiness, William Northrup?''

"I'm all right," Liam said again. "I only need a few hours sleep."

"The divil you do! Look at those ribs, man! Look at those bruises, and if one or two of them aren't cracked or broken it's only because Mary herself has a soft spot in her heart for you! And look at that eye, as black as a tar pit, and there's a tooth or two wriggling around in your head ready to fall out if you as much as wag your tongue! And your mouth is cut, and of your own doing because you didn't know enough to keep it shut. Can you get some water, Rose? We'd better be washing him off, and some bandages to strap up those ribs wouldn't be a bad idea. At least he's alive. You'd think that any Irishman would know that one Irishman can't lick a dozen Irishmen, no matter how strong their convictions that they're in the right!''

Rose's fingers were already probing at Liam's ribs, her face set in concentration. "Not broken, I think, but the bruises! He'll be so stiff and sore that moving will be an agony to him."

"Will you stop fussing over me?" Liam glared at them out of his one good eye. "I'll be fine!''

"And for a fact you will, in a month or two!" Michael McCarthy told him. "I don't know why I bothered to cart you home, you with that thick head of yours, bound to get yourself into more trouble than you can get yourself out of! Lay quiet now, or I'll bash you one meself and you'll have two black eyes instead of only one."

Rose brought a basin of water and some cloths. Her hands were gentle as she bathed the blood off Liam's face, as she patted the bruises on his ribs, but still she managed to study the man who had taken the trouble to bring Liam home and who was helping her the best that his great clumsy hands would let him.

"Not so tight!" she commanded, as Michael wrapped the bandages around Liam's ribs. "We want to help him, not kill him! It was good of you to go to all this trouble, Mr. McCarthy. Liam's talked about you, you're the political man he knows in New York."

Michael's homely face, a map of Ireland all by itself, broke into a grin. "Ward heeler is the name for it, Rose O'Riley. Only I'm a little more important than that, ward boss would be more appropriate. They can keep the Irish down in lots of ways, by pretendin' that we aren't quite human, but they can't keep us from runnin' things when it comes to politics! There never was an Irishman who couldn't outthink and outtalk any other man, and politics bein' the only way left to us, then that's the road we've taken and it'll get us where we want to go, as long as we keep puttin' one foot in front of the other. One of these days the Irish are going to run the city of New York, and it's comin' sooner than you think!"

"Your mouth is as big as you are," Rose told him. She stood back to survey her work, and concluded that she'd done all she could. Rest and nature would have to take care of the rest. "Go to sleep, Liam. It's near morning, you're going to need all the rest you can get."

"Thank you for bringing me home. Not that I wouldn't have made it on my own, mind you," Liam growled at Michael.

"Flat on yer face in the gutter is where you'd have made it!" Michael derided him. "With yer pockets stripped and yer head broken and maybe yer next stop the morgue and potter's field! Still, it was a good fight, I'm not denyin' that. I wouldn't have wanted to miss it."

"I should have taken a shillelagh. I just never thought I'd need one to beat sense into Irish heads when the need is so great."

"A grave error of judgment," Michael told him, his eyes mocking.

But there was fondness for Liam there, real fondness, and respect as well, Rose noted, and she felt her own gratitude to the man swell for all that he was as ugly as Paddy's pig with his reddish hair and his thickset body and his great clumsy hands with blunt-tipped fingers. But there was shrewdness in his eyes and real intelligence, and she didn't doubt that he knew what he was talking about when he bragged that someday the Irish would run New York City. Persecuted they were, and would be for a long time to come, allowed only the most menial, lowest-paying employment, prevented in most cases from even owning property, looked down on and held lower than the slaves on the Southern plantations had been held before the war; still they'd manage to pull themselves up by their bootstraps by sheer perseverance and singleness of purpose.

"I'm no beauty, and that's a fact," Michael told her, guessing at her thoughts.

Rose tossed her head, but she flushed. "Beauty is as beauty does. William Northrup's a handsome man, but I'd prefer even the likes of your homely mug any day of the week including Sundays."

"I'd best be getting along. It's a long way back to the city. See if you can sit on that idiot for a few days, until he gets some sense in his head. I hope to see you again sometime, Rose O'Riley. Come to the city on your time off and Michael McCarthy will show you a better time than you've ever had in your life. Here's me card, stash it somewhere so you'll know where to find me. It'll be a deal safer for you to come to me than for me to come to you, the way things are at this Retreat of William Northrup's. But if you don't come, I've a notion that I'll be back here lookin' for you."

"Get on with you! I've no time to listen to blarney!" Rose snapped. "But take my appreciation for bringing Liam home, for all that."

"I'll be seeing you again," Michael repeated, before he stepped outside the door. "I've taken a fancy to you, for all you're as skinny as a broomstick and have a sharp tongue."

Rose snorted before she closed the door quickly to keep in the light. When she crossed back to Liam's bed, she found him asleep, exhausted from the brawl he'd taken so much punishment in and from the long trip home.

Eugenia was still awake when Rose slipped inside her door. "Is he back? Is he all right?"

"He's back, and he's all right. Battered, but not fatally," Rose told her. "Lie back down, didn't I tell you he's all right? He's only been in a fight, but he's home now and only a little the worse for wear, nothing that a few days won't set right."

Eugenia was already counting the hours until she'd be able to get up and dress in her riding habit. It was four o'clock in the morning, it would be only three more hours, and she'd see him for herself, be able to assure herself that he was really all right.

"Don't tell Moria," she warned. "Let her be happy for as long as she can. And thank you, Rose. If I didn't have you, I wouldn't know where to turn."

"It's little enough I can do, and there's no need to thank me. I'm fond of the man myself. He'll be fine, trust me and go to sleep." She must get to bed herself, in William Northrup's house no deviation of routine was allowed, she'd have to be up almost before she laid her head on her pillow, and she'd suffer for her lack of sleep tomorrow.

Michael McCarthy, now! The nerve of the man, presuming that she'd want to see him again! She had troubles enough without adding him to her list. All the same, it had been interesting to meet him. Liam had talked about him so much, and now her curiosity was satisfied.

As tired as she was, and as emotionally drained by the long hours of waiting for Liam to come home, Rose didn't neglect to say her prayers before she finally lay down in her bed. This night, she added another name to her list, Michael McCarthy. After all, and for all that he was as ugly as a mud fence, he'd brought Liam home, and if he hadn't, if Liam hadn't got home at all or come crawling back in the morning, late and the worse for wear, he could have been discharged on the spot, and that would have killed both him and Eugenia, as well as separated father and daughter.

So Rose added Michael to her prayers, but not without a postscript that she was sure that Mary, as a woman, would understand, "Help the man to know his place and keep it, for all he seems to have a kind heart under all that brass. Amen."

12

The day of June 20, 1869, dawned as sunny and fair as if William Northrup himself had ordered heaven to provide it. No cloud or drop of rain would dare to mar this day when he would give his adopted daughter to Anthony Vancouver in a wedding ceremony that would go down in the annals of Hudson River Valley history.

Not that ordinary mortals would be permitted as much as a glimpse of the wedding. It was for that reason that William had decreed that it must be held at Retreat, where extra guards at the gatehouse made sure that only those with invitations would be allowed to enter the grounds. Only the most elite had received invitations, the *crème de la crème* of society. If this was not actually a royal wedding, it was planned to be the next thing to it, a wedding so brilliant that every man of William's acquaintance would look at him with awe and wonder what fate had touched him with a golden finger.

Myriads of workers hired for the occasion had transformed the grounds of Retreat into a fairyland. The wedding was to be held on the sweeping lawn, where row after row of gilt chairs had been

205

placed, under an awning to keep the sun from the ladies' delicate complexions. The posts that held the awnings were entwined with pink roses, the awnings themselves were pink silk, as were the cushions on the chairs. Other awnings protected long tables covered with pink silk cloths, where the same refreshments would be served to those of the assembled guests who were not eligible to have places at the banquet table inside the house, as were served to those more fortunate.

In front of the rows of chairs, a bower had been constructed entirely of white roses, as befitted a bride. Not one of the roses had been stripped from William's own rose garden, which was in its full glory of bloom, but had been brought in at a cost that made the guests' eyes pop with wonder, as familiar as they were with the lavish manner of living at Retreat.

Liam's face was white, his expression stony, as he stationed himself to supervise the disposition of the guests' carriages. Nothing he'd been able to say to Moria had shaken her faith in the rightness of her marriage to Anthony Vancouver. It was as though the girl were moving in a dream, sleepwalking through her days, touched by some feyness that nothing could penetrate. Both he and Eugenia had tried, right up until the last moment, to prevail on her to change her mind, to at least insist on waiting until she was eighteen.

Despite their hopes, Anthony Vancouver had done nothing, at least nothing that had come to public notice, that would cause Moria to have second thoughts about him, in all the months of their engagement. He'd made up his mind that this marriage was to his advantage, and he was careful to do nothing to jeopardize it. Eugenia and Rose had prayed until their knees were stiff from kneeling, but their prayers had fallen on deaf ears. Liam hadn't prayed. His days of praying were long past. He'd put his desperate arguments to Moria instead, arguments that had fallen on ears as deaf as those in heaven.

Frantic for Liam, equally frantic for Moria, Eugenia had no opportunity at all to seek Liam out and try to comfort him, on this day of the wedding. God be with him, help him bear up. What was to be was to be, and anything Liam might do, in his agony, would only make things worse than they already were.

In her room, Moria had been awake since dawn, and no amount of determination on her part had allowed her to fall back to sleep. But she wouldn't spoil this most important day in her life by having dark circles under her eyes. Her elated excitement would sustain her, she could go for twenty-four hours without sleep, for forty-eight, with no sign of fatigue on her face.

She forced herself to lie still in her bed, contenting herself with going over mental lists of everything that had been packed to accompany her on her honeymoon journey first to New York City, where she and Anthony would spend the night before they set sail on the Cunard Line's most luxurious ship for Paris. A honeymoon in Paris, with Tony! She was so happy that she couldn't bear it, she would burst, Dora would come in to wake her and find only her skin lying limp on the bed, the rest of her scattered all over the room from the force of the explosive pressure inside her.

Her trunks, her boxes! She must think of them, or she'd never be able to contain herself until four o'clock this afternoon when she'd actually stand in the bower and say the words that would make her Tony's wife. Had her violet lawn dress been packed, had Dora forgotten it and left it hanging in the wardrobe?

Of course Dora hadn't forgotten! She wouldn't get out of bed to check, she was going to lie right where she was and rest so that she'd be as radiant a bride as Tony deserved. Nothing had been forgotten. And even if it had, what would it matter? She'd buy new gowns in Paris, rafts and rafts of new gowns. Her wedding dress, hanging in the corner of her room with a muslin cover over it to protect it from the least speck of dust, had been made from a French design, after the very latest fashion.

How beautiful it was! The change in fashion had been dramatic. The huge crinolines that had been so lovely to look at and so hard to manage with any modicum of grace were gone. Now, a revival of the fashions of the 1770s was in the mode. Moria's wedding gown had a soft, bouffant overskirt, called a polonaise. Of creamy satin, it set off the lace underskirt to perfection. The neckline was edged with the same priceless lace, and the gathered back of the dress was inset with a wide lace panel. The backs of gowns, now, were more important than the fronts, more elaborate, and Moria's wedding gown was the epitome of the new style, so lovely that her breath caught in her throat every time she looked at it.

Dora wasn't to do her hair, or even Rose. A French coiffurist had been brought in, arriving yesterday morning, and Moria had had to endure nearly an entire day of letting the foppish man experiment with her hair until at last he was satisfied. No more teasing little kiss-curls framing face and forehead, her hair was drawn back and up, with a chignon so intricately arranged that Moria was sure it would all tumble down if she as much as turned her head, although Monsieur Corbin assured her that it would not.

And today she had to go through it all again, after she'd taken her breakfast in bed, after she'd bathed, after she'd counted off the minutes, one by one, until it should be four o'clock. Lying there, every inch of her body tense with excitement, she was more convinced than ever that she'd burst before the wedding ever came to pass.

One thing she kept firmly in the back of her mind, refusing to let it surface. Her father and Eugenia were both still completely opposed to this marriage. Eugenia went about looking as if the world had come to an end, and Liam was in such a towering rage that she had scarcely dared to speak to him during their daily rides. Only the fact that she was her father's daughter, with a mind as set and stubborn as his own, had enabled her to hold out against his opposition.

She wouldn't think about it today. And after today, she wouldn't have to think about it ever again, because it would be an established fact, she'd be Mrs. Anthony Vancouver, and then both her father and Eugenia would see how mistaken they'd been about Tony, when they saw how happy she was.

In her own room, Eugenia was also wide awake even though she had hardly slept at all last night. If there had ever been a miracle, she wished for one now. Let the house be struck by lightning and burn to the ground, let something, anything, happen to stop this wedding and what it was doing to Liam, tearing him to pieces. Like Moria, she counted off the minutes as they ticked by, although for a different reason: she was trying to hold them back while Moria tried to urge them on to a faster pace.

It was six-thirty now, and although the hours since she had awakened seemed an eternity, Eugenia wished that it were only dawn. She'd get up soon. There was so much to do. Closing her eyes, she prayed that she'd be able to convince Moria that her smile was genuine when she supervised her dressing for the ceremony. Let her have this day, at least, and let it be perfect, because if Eugenia was any judge, it would be one of the last happy days she'd ever have. Anthony might manage to behave himself for a while after the wedding, but honeymoons don't last forever, and before six months were out Eugenia was as convinced as Liam that Moria's world would be shattered.

A quarter to seven, seven o'clock. No lightning bolt was going to come out of the sky, nothing was going to happen to stop the wedding from taking place, and Eugenia knew that Liam would be as wakeful as she was, and going through even more intense agony.

At seven-fifteen Rose slipped into the room to see if Eugenia was awake. More likely, she thought, her throat constricted with tears, the poor lady hadn't slept at all!

If she had slept, she wasn't sleeping now. Eugenia's eyes were open, and there were dark shadows under them that Rose would have to use all her skill to cover, because it would never do for her to look as if she wasn't as fresh and happy as any mother of any bride who had ever been born when her daughter married not only the man she loved, but the social catch of the decade.

"Rose, go to Liam, see how he is. Go now, please."

"But you need to be up and about, there's your breakfast to see to and your bath . . ."

"Never mind! There's plenty of time. William hasn't left me anything to do, anyway." Eugenia's voice showed the bitterness that she usually managed to keep hidden. "Go now, make sure that he's all right and that he isn't going to do anything foolish, tell him that I beg him to keep control of himself!"

Her lips compressed, Rose did as Eugenia asked her. Slipping from the house, she hurried to Liam's cottage and rapped on the door, praying that his mood wouldn't be so black that she wouldn't have the heart to tell Eugenia when she reported back to her.

The door opened almost before she'd finished knocking, and she took a step backward so fast that she stepped on the hem of her skirt and almost fell. A strong, firm hand grasped her elbow and steadied her.

"Easy now, Rose, me love! To be sure it's no ghost you're after seeing, but meself."

"What are you doing here, Michael McCarthy? How did you get in, how did you get past the guards?" Rose's amazement was genuine; the guards had been posted last evening in order to make sure that no curious undesirables slipped into the grounds in hope of concealing themselves and catching a glimpse of the festivities.

"I walked past them, how else would I have gotten in? And doesn't meself have a position here, hired as an extra groom to help handle the beasts when the carriages arrive? Not that it didn't take some doing, mind you, and me hardly knowin' one end of a horse from the other, but I have me contacts, and I got meself hired, so as to keep an eye on my impetuous friend here and make sure that he doesn't start takin' potshots at Anthony Vancouver and Mr. William Northrup, or something equally disastrous."

The feeling of relief that flooded through Rose left her dizzy. She'd never been so glad to see a face before, as ugly as it was, split from ear to ear with a smug, self-satisfied grin.

"And how is he?"

"As sober as a judge, and a long sight soberer than a lot of them I've known in me life," Michael told her. "Not that Liam Donovan is a drinking man, he's the only Irishman I ever saw who never tips a glass, but on a day like this I couldn't be sure, so I thought I'd just come along and see to it that nothing happens. Liam, here's a lady to see you, you lucky dog! Are you decent yet?''

Liam was decent, fully dressed, his face so dark and grim that Rose's heart sank. But it was all right, Mr. McCarthy was here, bless the man, and she'd remember him in her prayers again tonight if he managed to keep Liam under control.

"I'm all right, Rose. You can go back to the house," Liam told her. He didn't look all right and he didn't sound all right, but Rose knew that he was all right, with Michael McCarthy beside him.

"I just wanted to make sure," Rose said, and left, anxious to get back to Eugenia and tell her that there was nothing to worry about.

When the door had closed behind her, Michael turned to Liam, grinning. "Now there's a fine figure of a woman, even if she is a bit scrawny for me taste. And what a blessing it is indeed that Mr. Northrup doesn't hold with married servants, else some other man would already have snapped her up and I wouldn't have a chance unless I saw to it that she became a widow and I couldn't do that, now could I, being a devout Catholic? The only problem is how I'm to court her, Mr. William Northrup's rules being so strict."

"Don't waste your time," Liam advised him. "Rose would never leave Mrs. Northrup. She's completely devoted to her mistress."

"And an unnatural way of living it is, then!" Michael told him. "God never would have created us male and female, if he hadn't intended for us to marry, and what a waste it is for a fine woman like Rose O'Riley to live out her life in the single state when there's many a man would jump at the chance of wedding her, sharp tongue and all."

A sideways glance at Liam told Michael that his friend was in no mood for philosophy. Devil take the man! Why, out of all the women in the world and so many of them single, had Liam Donovan had to give his heart to Eugenia Northrup? Not that Liam had ever confided in him about the matter, but Michael had eyes in his head and a brain to think with, and seeing how Mrs. Northrup's personal maid took such an interest in checking up on his welfare, it was only a matter of common sense to see how the wind blew. And a devilish coil it was, because there was no way in the world Liam could ever have the woman, all he could do was go on breaking his heart.

Of all the people in the world, Michael supposed that he was the only one outside of Liam himself, and Eugenia Northrup and Moria, who knew that Liam had passed his daughter off as a war orphan and foisted her onto William Northrup as his ward. Hadn't Michael himself been the one to direct Liam to Retreat, to apply for the position of horse trainer?

And a good position it had turned out to be, except for the complications that had followed, and that were all but destroying the man. But how could Michael have guessed that Liam would fall in love with Eugenia Northrup, and she with him, to the damnation of their mortal souls and the danger of discovery and retaliation beyond anything any rational man could think of if William Northrup should stumble on the truth about his wife and his horse trainer? To say nothing of what would happen if Northrup found out about the girl they'd foisted off on him, the girl of whom he'd become so proud because of her beauty and charm that he'd actually adopted her, given her his name, and shown her off to all society as his proudest possession?

And that was why Michael had taken such an unconscionable amount of trouble to get himself hired as an extra hostler to help handle the guests' horses and carriages, so that he could keep close by Liam and see that the man didn't break and bring the whole tangled mess tumbling about their heads, his and Eugenia's and Moria's.

How the man in charge of the agency through which William Northrup had hired the extra help had goggled, nearly choking when he'd recognized the name on the note that told him that Michael was to be hired. Not Boss Tweed himself, that one was too all-powerful to bother himself with one of his minions not yet high enough on the scale of things to be that important, but one of Tweed's lieutenants. Yes, Michael had friends in high places these days and he could swing more votes than you could shake a stick at, and he was getting higher on the scale with every year that passed, a far cry from the days when he'd been just beginning to make a place for himself in the vast network of Tammany Hall.

And so here he was, and it was a blessing that he'd thought of it, because from the looks of Liam the man's nerves were stretched to the breaking point. Somebody had to keep an eye on him, and Michael had been inordinately fond of him ever since those early days of their acquaintance. A familyless man himself, Michael had taken a brotherly interest in his smoldering countryman, until now Liam was more important to him than any other man he knew.

"We need men like you in Tammany, Liam lad. This William M. Tweed, now, he's gettin' so powerful that I don't like the looks of it at all, at all. I don't like the man, he's as crooked as a bulldog's tail, and I'm hopin' he won't pull Tammany down with him if ever he's caught up with. I'm keepin' my own nose clean, and I intend to be around to help pick up the pieces if Tweed ever does get caught, and we'll be needin' men like you to help us rebuild Tammany the way we want it to be, not a viper's nest of crooked politicians all out to milk the public. You don't have to stay on here, a word from me will get you a place, if I do say so meself."

Liam heard him with half his mind, but the words didn't penetrate. This was his daughter's wedding day, and William Northrup was the one who would give her away, give his Moria away to the last man in the world Liam would have wanted to see her marry!

And it was all because of him, because he'd lost his faith, because he'd thrown away his last shred of human integrity in his determination to see Moria have what he and Molly had wanted for her. Molly must be weeping, up there in heaven, if there was such a place. If there was, then Molly was there, but he'd never join her, and the chances were that Moria wouldn't, either, because Moria had also turned her back on all of Molly's teachings, on Molly's faith, and was going her own headstrong way to get what she wanted with as much determination as Liam had grasped the chance to bring her to Retreat.

"Get ahold of yourself, man!" Michael said, and this time his voice was sharp. "It isn't going to make that girl of yours happy if you go off your head and break up her wedding! She'd never forgive you. We all have to make our own mistakes, and Moria has as much right to make hers as you had to make yours.''

"I'm all right.'' Liam's voice was as wooden as his face. Looking at him, Michael hoped for the best. God love the man, but Michael wouldn't want to be standing in his shoes even if a million dollars was hidden in the sole of one of them!

In Eugenia's room, Eugenia's face regained a little of its color when Rose told her that Michael McCarthy was with Liam and keeping a close eye on him. "Not that I have any liking for the man, but I believe he's fond of Liam, he'll make sure that he's all right. Now I want you to eat some breakfast, every bite you can manage. Moria's depending on you, you mustn't let her see the state you're in, and spoil things for her.''

Eugenia forced a smile. "There. Is that better? I'll be fine, Rose, don't worry about me. After all, it isn't as if we're losing her entirely. We'll always be right here, in case she needs us.''

Right at the moment, Moria had no thought in the world of ever needing anybody except Tony. Sitting up in bed, she finished the last crumb from her breakfast tray and drained her second cup of coffee. She'd thought that she'd be too excited to eat, but the sight of the ham and eggs and biscuits had shown her that she was ravenous, as she always was in the morning. Now she stretched her arms above her head and smiled at Dora.

"Take it away. I'm stuffed! I'll have to skip lunch, or you'll never be able to hook me up in my wedding dress. Go and see if Mrs. Northrup is awake. No, I'll go myself. She's sure to be awake, she couldn't possibly still be sleeping on a glorious morning like this.''

Her father would be awake, he would have been awake at the first streaks of dawn in the sky. Liam had always been an early riser, and on this day of all days sleep would have deserted him before the first rooster crowed. Impatiently, Moria thrust her feet into slippers and her arms into the sleeves of a dressing gown, to run down the hallways and tap at Eugenia's door. She mustn't think about her father. She mustn't let anything spoil today. If her father was unhappy, she was sorry, but she couldn't sacrifice her life to him.

Eugenia smiled as Moria raced across the room and threw herself into her arms. "Eugenia, be happy for me, please be happy for me! I'm so happy that I can't bear for you not to be happy too!"

If Eugenia's heart was breaking, even Moria couldn't detect it as she folded her into her arms and held her close. Looking at her, Rose breathed a prayer to Mary, that this look of pure joy wouldn't disappear forever from Moria's face after she'd been married to Tony for long enough to discover for herself what he was.

It was time at last, although Moria had been certain that she would go mad with the waiting before the hands of the clock reached four. She was at the great front door of Retreat, and Mr. Northrup was waiting to offer her his arm to escort her down the long grassy aisle between the rows and rows of gilt chairs that had been occupied for the last hour by the guests who were held high enough in William's estimation to have received invitations.

The bridesmaids, Veronica Hamilton's sultry beauty standing out among them, caught their breaths as Moria came down the stairs where they were clustered waiting, and Veronica's eyes narrowed, and she dropped her lids over them to conceal the look of pure hatred that would have struck Moria dead if she'd had the power. Then Veronica opened them again, and she was smiling, completely in control of herself, even though her hatred churned inside her with such force that she felt sick to her stomach.

Through the open door, Moria could see Tony waiting at the bower, turned to watch for her, his face filled with eagerness. It was a dream, it had to be a dream, nothing could be this wonderful, this perfect. Only it wasn't a dream, she was real and Tony was real and the Reverend Moses Linkbetter, standing with his Bible open in his hands, was real, and now she was walking and her knees held her up after all, her only trouble was in keeping from running to get to Tony sooner.

It all took such a very little time that it was almost impossible to believe. Weeks and weeks of preparation, and in a wink of time it was over, and the words were said and there was a gold ring on her finger and Tony was lifting her veil from her face to kiss her, the first time her *husband* had ever kissed her!

There was a shower of rose petals, thousands and thousands of them, as she and Tony walked back down the aisle arm in arm, husband and wife, so that her wedding dress and her veil and her hair were covered with them and she had to shake and brush them off, with Tony laughing as he tried to help her. And there was the reception line, with all of the gentlemen kissing her, kissing the bride, and the matrons and the girls kissing her and wishing her happiness and that was the silliest thing of all because she was already so happy that one speck more would be more than she could bear.

Mr. Northrup was smiling. Why, he looked human, actually human, he looked as if he really liked her, as if he were proud of her! And Eugenia was smiling, and she pushed the thought of her father back into that dark corner of her mind where she had kept it for so long now, and locked the door behind it so that it couldn't get out.

Tony managed to keep his face discreetly polite as Veronica kissed his cheek. "Congratulations, Tony. I hope you'll be very happy." Veronica's voice was sweet, her eyes held nothing but candor and goodwill. And then her teeth, white and sharp, came together on the lobe of his ear as she bit it viciously, not quite hard enough to make it spurt blood but hard enough so that if Tony hadn't had the quickest of reactions to the unexpected he would have yelped, and he could feel a drop of blood oozing from his earlobe.

"You vicious little bitch!" he hissed at her, his mouth smiling as he kissed her cheek in return. As unobtrusively as he could, he pressed his handkerchief to his ear and there was blood on it when he took it away. No one noticed; nearly every eye was on the bride, so radiant that her image was burned into their memories for the rest of their lives.

"I hope the ship sinks before you get to France!" Veronica hissed back. "Nothing would make me happier than to see both of you dead!"

"Cunard ships don't sink, my dear," Tony told her, his mouth quirking. "And if by some calamity ours should happen to founder, neither Moria nor I would go down with it. I'm an excellent swimmer, fully capable of saving both of us. But it won't happen. Amuse yourself by thinking of us on our honeymoon. I'll be thinking of you, you can be sure of that. And we won't be away forever. I'll be seeing you, after we return."

"Go to hell!" Sick with rage, Veronica turned away, determined that she'd get Tony back if it took her all the rest of her life. But it wouldn't take that long. She'd get him back, and she'd have her revenge on Moria even if she had to ruin her own reputation to do it.

Everything was ready, the boxes and trunks had all been sent on ahead, Moria had changed into her traveling dress, her hat was set at exactly the right angle, and the carriage was waiting to take her and Tony to New York City on the first leg of their honeymoon.

Moria stood in the middle of her bedroom, her eyes misted as she looked at every familiar object. She'd been happy here, this room would be forever bound up in her memories. How awed she'd been the first time she'd seen it, likening it to a room in a fairy tale castle, and imagining that the peacocks on the silk fireplace screen could talk.

Downstairs, Eugenia and William were waiting to bid her their final farewells. She'd said her private good-byes to Eugenia half an hour ago. A lump in her throat threatened to cut off her breath as she thought of her father, who would not be able to kiss her good-bye and wish her happiness, even if he would have wanted to.

No! She wouldn't think of that. Tony was waiting, he'd be in a fever of impatience by now. And Dora was fidgeting. She was to go with them, all the way to Paris, to Rome, to London, because Moria had to have her own personal maid to attend her, as much as she would have preferred not to take her.

"You'd best be coming along, Miss . . . Mrs. Vancouver," Dora said primly. "I haven't forgotten anything, I was careful not to overlook a thing you might need."

"Of course you were," Moria murmured. Wouldn't you think the young woman whose life had been so drab and joyless would be agog with excitement at the prospect of all the traveling that awaited her! But Dora's face was as dour as always, as though Europe and England meant nothing at all.

One last look, and Moria took a step toward the door. And at that last instant, her eyes fell on a small object that lay on the floor in front of the chiffonier.

With a little cry, she darted back across the room and swooped to pick it up. Her horsehair bracelet lay in her hand. "Oh, Dora! You did forget something! Look, it must have dropped to the floor and you didn't notice it!"

"I didn't think you'd want it, Mrs. Vancouver. It isn't suitable for a honeymoon tour," Dora told her, her eyes expressionless.

Moria hesitated, but only for an instant. Dora was right. The bracelet had no place in the trousseau of a bride.

And then she made up her mind and slipped it on her wrist, her fingers, so long practiced, fastening the intricate loop that would keep it secure. She'd take it with her. Quinn had told her that it would bring her luck, and it had. It was a talisman.

Superstitious idiot! she laughed at herself. Anybody would think you were two days away from the Old Sod! Nevertheless, she couldn't leave it behind. It didn't show, under the sleeve that covered her wrist, but the feel of it there brought her a sense of security.

"All right, Dora. I'm ready," she said. And Mrs. Anthony Vancouver walked through the door, leaving Moria Donovan behind her forever.

13

The *Scotia* was a steamship, the largest in the world. Moria marveled that such a huge mass—three thousand, eight hundred and seventy-one tons—could stay afloat. But she had no sense of fear, only a sense of deep and abiding sadness as she remembered, over the span of years, the squalor and misery of the floating coffin on which she and Liam and her mother had fled Ireland. Although she'd been only six, that passage was forever engraved in her memory, the crowded steerage, with barely enough room to move between the hard planks that lined the bulkheads to serve as bunks, the pervading stench of sweat and urine and vomit, the smell of death.

But that had been long ago, and now she was seventeen, a bride, and the toast of the *Scotia* as it made its way to the other side of the world.

If all masculine eyes were on Moria, it seemed that every pair of feminine eyes widened and misted with unsatisfied dreams at the sight of Tony, so handsome that even Moria, who knew him so well, still felt a sense of awe as she struggled to realize the extent of her good fortune. They sat at the captain's table, Moria on his right,

219

while lesser beings looked at them with envy and wistful awe at their sheer beauty, Tony's bright hair and brown eyes a perfect foil for Moria's raven locks and camelia skin. Wealthy, privileged, young and beautiful and in love, it was no wonder that they were treated almost as royalty even among the other wealthy and privileged people aboard.

Dancing in Tony's arms, her feet seeming to float inches above the polished floor, walking with him on deck, lying in his arms after hours of such passionate lovemaking that she was left breathless and spent, Moria sometimes had an uneasy, disturbing impression that she was living in a dream, that something would jolt her awake and it would all disappear and leave her desolate.

But that was fanciful and silly. Her father would call her fey, and she laughed at herself and thrust the dark feelings into that same closet in the back of her mind where she kept her quarrel with Liam, refusing to let them out to disturb her. She was happy, and she'd be happy all of her life, because how could she help but be happy when she was Tony's wife, when she was the one he loved?

Paris was glorious. They had time to see everything, Versailles, the Cathedral of Notre Dame, St. Sulpice, which was almost Notre Dame's equal, St. Étienne-du-Mont with its combination of Gothic and Renaissance architecture. The Panthéon, the domed building in the form of a Greek cross, astonished her; the Palais Royal, built by Richelieu himself way back in the early seventeenth century, was like something out of a dream. And the Comédie Française was a revelation to her, to say nothing of the various and downright shocking bistros which Tony insisted on visiting, determined not to miss them now that he was in Paris, a privilege denied him before because he had been under the watchful eyes of his watchdogs, who reported to his parents every move he made.

"Little prude!" Tony teased her when her face flamed scarlet as some of the costumes and suggestive dances and even more suggestive language shocked her to her core. She understood French much better than Tony did, William Northrup had seen to it that she was proficient in the language as befitted his ward, while Tony had always gotten out of any studying it was possible for him to get out of. "To see your face now, nobody would believe you're the same girl who went to bed with me last night! What did they say, I missed that part . . ."

"Tony!" Moria's voice was agonized. "Someone might hear you!"

"What would it matter? They don't speak English. Come on, what was that last line?"

Whether the laughing, colorful crowd around them spoke English or not, Moria put her lips close to Tony's ear and whispered the words that he'd missed, her face more scarlet than ever. Tony whooped with laughter, delighted. Moria couldn't help but be glad that the joke lost a good deal of its impact in translation, even as she joined in his laughter. French was an incomprehensible language. How foolish she'd felt, when the clock in their *maison* bedroom had stopped running, when she'd had to tell the chambermaid to send a repairman because the clock did not march!

They had all the time in the world, the entire summer. Money was of no importance. Moria's wardrobe grew until more trunks had to be bought to hold her Paris gowns, her Paris hats, her Paris parasols and gloves and shoes. If she didn't return home with enough Paris creations to make the whole of the Hudson River Valley gasp with envy, she'd be letting Tony and the Vancouvers down, and William Northrup would be displeased. She might be Moria Vancouver now, but she was still William's adopted daughter, and she still had to live up to the image he had created of her. But Liam's face would go hard and cold, as he thought of all the arms and ammunition, all the pamphlets and recruiting for the Cause that could have been bought with the money wasted on clothes that she didn't need.

The delights of Paris savored to the last drop, they traveled on to Rome. Sometimes Moria felt that she had been traveling, living in strange and exotic places, all of her life. It was a dreamlike existence, made even more rapturously delightful because she and Tony spent nearly all of their time away from Dora, who at Retreat had seemed to dog her footsteps, her dour face always right over Moria's shoulder every time she turned around.

But Tony didn't like Dora, and unlike Moria, he had no compunctions about ordering her to make herself scarce. Born to ordering servants around with no regard for their feelings, Tony could tell Dora to leave the room, to stop fussing around and find something to do elsewhere, without a second thought.

"Why William Northrup ever chose that woman to be your personal maid is beyond me," Tony said lazily, after one of the times when he'd snapped at Dora to stop puttering and get out.

Moria, who knew very well that William had chosen Dora in order to cause Eugenia distress, bit her lip and only said, "You needn't have been quite so short with her, Tony."

"Forget her!" Tony commanded, drawing her into his arms. "If she were in the room, I couldn't do this, and this, and this. . . ."

No, he couldn't have, and Moria was glad that he'd sent Dora away, glad that Dora wouldn't dare enter their room in the morning before she was invited. This was another advantage to being married, to have a husband who would take over unpleasant tasks for her.

And then there was London. The antiquity of the streets and buildings overwhelmed her. St. Paul's Cathedral, the London Bridge, the Tower, where she couldn't help but weep for thinking of Lady Jane Grey, that tragic girl who had been queen of England for a few short days, against her own will, and lost her life for it before she had ever had a chance to live. Manipulated by the men who had dominion over her, Moria thought, just as Eugenia was manipulated by William Northrup. How lucky she herself was, to have found Tony, who would never manipulate her except to bring her happiness and delight! And Anne Boleyn, and the young Elizabeth who had been in such terror for her own life here, and Sir Walter Raleigh who had lost his, and all those others who had lost their heads or been condemned to live out their lives behind these walls until death at last released them.

Tony laughed at her and teased her. "They're dead, you sentimental little idiot, they've been dead for hundreds of years, but you're alive, and people will think I beat you if you don't stop that silly crying. I'll take you to Covent Garden, I could use some gaiety to erase the taste of this place from my mouth, and so could you.''

Regent Street, Westminster, the Haymarket and the excitement of the races, on which Tony bet and invariably lost and on which she bet and invariably won, her father's sense of horseflesh having been transmitted to her so that her judgment was almost infallible, and before the afternoons were over people were following her lead, and a Lord Fitzsimmons personally asked her, as a favor, to pick a horse for him, all the while eating her up with eyes that had been jaded for more than a decade.

Moria almost made a fatal error there. Congratulated on her good fortune, she laughed and nearly bit her tongue in two as she realized that she'd almost said that it was only the luck of the Irish. For almost five years, she'd been Moria Compton, and then Moria Northrup, watching every word lest she slip, and she still had to go on watching herself!

But she was Irish, it was bred into her blood and bones, and in spite of her happiness something inside of her ate away at her with the longing to set foot on Irish soil again. Not only for herself, although her longing was genuine, but so that she could tell Liam, after they'd gone home, that she'd been there, tell him what she'd seen and heard. No matter how angry he was that she'd married Tony, he'd be pleased that she'd thought to go to Ireland, pleased that she wanted to share her experiences there with him.

She'd been almost asleep, and beside her, Tony's eyes were closed, his face boyish and heartbreakingly handsome in the shaft of moonlight that fell across their bed. Their lovemaking had been especially wild and satisfying tonight, they'd reached heights Moria had never dreamed of and Tony seldom achieved. If ever there would be a good time to ask, it was now.

She slipped her hand into Tony's, and squeezed it. ''Tony? Are you asleep?''

''Yes.''

"No, you're not. You don't talk in your sleep."

And thank God for that, Tony thought.

"Tony, do you think we could go to Ireland? It seems a pity to be so near, and not see it."

Tony's eyes opened, and he stared at her with disbelief. "Ireland! What under heaven put that notion into your head? No, we aren't going to Ireland. It's a dirty, dreary place, we'd be bored to distraction, and uncomfortable in the bargain. Who wants to go to an impoverished country populated by grubby, ignorant people? Think of Paris and Rome, sweetheart, and go to sleep."

She didn't dare pursue the subject. Tony was selfish in many ways, self-indulgent, in spite of his charm. Moria wasn't so blinded by love that she didn't realize that. But he wasn't stupid, and if she insisted his curiosity would be aroused and how could she explain her longing to go to a place he had no interest in, a place that was eons removed from honeymoons and happiness?

Still, in spite of her common sense, she couldn't help but give it one more try. "They breed wonderful hunters there, Tony. I'd like to see them. I've heard that they breed the best hunters in the world."

Tony snorted. "Good Lord, and you with Jazir! There isn't a horse in the world that can touch him, unless it's Eugenia's Kamil. This is a honeymoon, not a horse-buying trip, especially horses we have no earthly use for. Go to sleep and don't turn into a nagging wife."

There was a note of warning in his voice that Moria couldn't ignore. The subject was closed, there would be no trip to Ireland. She lay awake for an hour or more after Tony had fallen asleep, fighting her disappointment. She was being foolish. A visit to a country she scarcely remembered wasn't worth having Tony cross with her, not even for the sake of having it help her to make up with her father. She'd find another way to make up with him, he couldn't help but relent when he saw how happy she was. And she was happy, this honeymoon was like a dream of paradise, more than any girl had any right to expect.

But the longest dream has to end sometime. What had seemed at first to be limitless, endless time slipped away, and June had melted into July and July into August and August into September, and now, unbelievably, it was October and she and Tony were on shipboard again, steaming across the Atlantic, and her sense of loss was an ache inside of her.

To make matters worse, she didn't feel well. Too many strange foods, strange drinking water, too much traveling and excitement, and this voyage was rougher than the first, the seas choppy as the season stretched toward winter.

It was intolerable to think that she might be becoming really ill and that these last few precious days would be spoiled, so she determined to ignore her queasiness. Nothing was less romantic than a woman who was ill, even the most doting husband couldn't help but be bored and annoyed at his wife's ailments, especially when he himself enjoyed the most robust of health.

So Moria laughed, and chatted, and danced, and flirted with Tony as if they weren't married at all, and flirted just a little bit with all of the gentlemen who were enthralled with her to keep Tony aware that she was desirable. As on the voyage over, they were the toast of the ship, sought after, the object of all eyes and interest.

But on the fourth day out, Moria had to admit that she was really feeling ill. She'd managed to get through the day without letting anyone notice, but after dinner she felt so tired that she was forced to tell Tony that she wasn't feeling very well and she wanted to go to bed.

A flicker of annoyance showed on Tony's face, so brief that Moria almost convinced herself that she had been mistaken. Then he was all concern, taking her back to their stateroom, summoning Dora to tend her.

"Shall I sit with you until you fall asleep?" he asked, his voice anxious, nothing but concern in his eyes.

"No, of course not. Shoo!" Moria said. She laughed. "I'm not a child, I know how to go to sleep without your help! Dora will be with me in any case."

"Then be sure to send her to fetch me if you should want me."

Tony kissed her forehead, and left with a proper show of reluctance. "And if you don't feel better, we'll have the ship's doctor take a look at you."

Once he'd closed the stateroom door behind him, Tony's face brightened. He'd been good for months, so good that sometimes he'd felt that all that virtue was suffocating him. It wasn't that Moria wasn't a delightful companion and an exciting wife. She'd fulfilled all her early promise of being a warm and passionate bed partner. He'd had to teach her, but she'd been an eager pupil.

Still, it went against his nature to be faithful to one woman, even a woman as beautiful and delightful as Moria. His enforced faithfulness, for all those months before their marriage and now all these months of their honeymoon when other beautiful and delightful women were readily available and more than willing, had been a strain. And when they got back to Belvedere, under the eagle eye of both his mother and his father, he'd have to do without again until they'd been married long enough so that people's vigilance would relax.

But there was tonight, and there was a moon that was almost full, and they were at sea, the most romantic setting in the world. And there was Mrs. Helen Forrester, a widow who'd been visiting friends in England and who was traveling back to the United States with only her maid as a companion.

Helen Forrester was probably in her early thirties, wealthy, beautiful, as exciting a conquest as Tony might ever hope to make. He'd never seen hair that exact shade before, a strawberry blond so bright that it seemed to catch all the light in a room. And her hazel eyes were warm and knowing, laughing with a secret knowledge that the two of them could share delights seldom experienced by ordinary mortals if only circumstances could be manipulated to permit it.

What a figure the woman had, to go with that beautiful face! Taller than Moria, almost as tall as Tony himself, her breasts were full and high and her waist small, her hips a flowing line under a couturier gown that clung to show off every curve, her matureness as compared to Moria's girlish freshness was exciting, promising thrills that even as sex-sated a man as Tony trembled to contemplate.

And she was available. It was written in every line of her body, in the sultry way she looked at him. She found him as attractive as he found her, and he knew instinctively that Mrs. Helen Forrester was accustomed to taking what she wanted. If he had been alone, if there had been no Moria to stand in their way, he would have been in her bed before the first evening was over.

But tonight it was Moria who was in bed, and the evening stretched before him, and there was Mrs. Forrester, talking to a bepearled dowager and her paunchy husband, her eyes filled with a question as he entered the salon alone.

He made his way toward them, stopping to talk to half a dozen people in the most casual manner before he reached them and waited to be invited to join them.

"Mr. Vancouver," Helen Forrester said, and Tony could see that she was tasting the sound of his name on her lips. "All alone? Where is your lovely wife?"

"She isn't feeling well. It's nothing serious, but she wanted to retire early."

"What a pity! She's the most gorgeous child I've ever seen. You're a very lucky man, I hope you realize that." Her words were correct, but Tony read her true meaning. He was a lucky man indeed, on this moonlit night, and he would be luckier before the evening was over.

He sat down and the talk drifted in general channels, the dowager chatting about London versus Paris fashions with Helen, while her husband probed Tony's knowledge of the world of finance. Half an hour later Helen asked to be excused.

"I'm afraid I've had too many late nights myself. I think your wife was wise to retire early, and I intend to follow her example."

"And I must get back to Moria," Tony said, also rising. "I'll escort you to your stateroom, Mrs. Forrester."

"And I'll stop by the first thing in the morning, to see if dear Moria is feeling better," Helen said.

Tony left her in front of her stateroom, watched her enter and be greeted by her maid, a middle-aged woman who looked so respectable that it made him shudder. Dutifully, he said good-night and turned in the direction of his own stateroom, only to veer off and spend the next half-hour waiting in the shadows of a lifeboat until he could be sure that Helen would be alone.

Dressed in a transparent, flowing peignoir over an equally transparent nightgown, Helen opened the door herself, just wide enough and long enough for him to slip inside. Then it was bolted behind her, and he turned to face her, his eyes alight and smoldering as he read the open invitation in hers.

The stateroom was in semidarkness, with only one lamp to shed a soft glow. There were two wineglasses on a low table, with a bottle of champagne in a silver bucket of ice. Helen had brought her own bed fittings, and a royal blue satin spread made Tony's blood run hot as he pictured the contrast of her pale, naked body against its darker color.

Smiling, Helen poured the champagne and sipped hers, and came into his arms with her lips still wet and wildly exciting as she raised them to his. His wineglass dropped from his hand as he gathered her into his arms and pressed the full length of his body against hers, every curve of her burning through his clothing and setting him on fire.

Outside the stateroom, Dora melted back around a corner and settled herself to wait. All during this long honeymoon, while she'd seethed with jealousy over Moria's happiness, she'd watched and waited for a chance to ruin that happiness. Knowing Tony's reputation, as every servant in the Hudson River Valley knew it, she'd been certain that her chance would come sooner or later. She'd had to wait a long time, because there'd been little opportunity as they'd traveled for her to spy on Tony, who hated the sight of her, a hatred she returned in full measure.

But this evening, Moria's indisposition had been a godsend. Her mistress had dismissed her as soon as she'd been settled in bed, and Dora had seized the opportunity to position herself where she could watch Tony's every move. She'd been certain that by this time he'd seize his first opportunity to make another conquest, and she had been right.

There was a smile on her face, bitter, triumphant, as she waited so that she could tell Moria, in the morning, exactly how long Tony had spent in Helen Forrester's stateroom.

It was amazing how much better Moria felt the next morning. All of the dizziness and nausea of last evening were gone. The stateroom was flooded with sunlight as she opened her eyes and realized, with flooding pleasure, how well she felt.

Propping herself on one elbow, she looked down at Tony, who was still asleep. How boyish he looked when he was sleeping! Even with his hair tousled from the pillow, even with his mouth slightly open, he was so handsome that she marveled for the thousandth time that he was actually her husband, that he belonged to her.

The long single plait of her hair hung over her shoulder and touched Tony's face. He wriggled, and brushed irritably at the spot that tickled, and then he opened his eyes. Moria's face, rosy and shining with happiness, smiled down into his.

"Good morning, sleepyhead! Are you going to waste the best part of the day lolling in bed?"

"I'm going to spend the best part of the morning in bed, but it isn't going to be wasted!" Tony had locked the stateroom door last night, when he'd come back after leaving Helen Forrester. He always locked it, because if he didn't, Dora would come barging in where she wasn't wanted, a habit so irritating that he took pains to prevent it. "Look at your hair! You know I hate it plaited like that!" Already his fingers were working at the braid, spreading the dark cape of shining black around her shoulders.

Moria's face flushed as his fingers worked next at her nightgown, unbuttoning the row of tiny mother-of-pearl buttons so that he could slip it off her shoulders. Here she was an old married woman, and she still blushed when Tony saw her naked. She'd known little of sex when she'd come to Tony as a bride, but what little she'd known had told her that married women, even in their most intimate moments, kept properly covered under the sheets, and under cover of the darkness of night, not in the rosy dawn in full daylight without a stitch on!

But it was a wife's duty to please her husband, and if this was what pleased Tony, then she was happy to oblige. No one would know, after all. And it hadn't taken Tony any time at all to convince her that if other married couples denied themselves this kind of pleasure, they were to be pitied rather than admired. She was glad that her body was beautiful, so beautiful that Tony wanted to see it, so beautiful that it gave him all the pleasure he deserved just because he was Tony, and her husband.

Her nipples stood up taut and hard, as pink as tiny rosebuds, at the touch of his fingers, and she gasped, flames shooting through her from the top of her head to the tips of her toes, when his hands traced and caressed the curve of her hips. How innocent she'd been, how incredibly naïve, before she'd married Tony! Even in her wildest imaginings of eternal wedded bliss, she'd never imagined anything like this, so close to heaven that even if she never got there it wouldn't matter because she'd already had heaven in the fullest measure.

She responded to him without reservation, giving as well as taking, doing all those things he'd taught her and delighting in the doing, because anything she did with Tony, anything he wanted, must be right.

They didn't hurry. That was one thing, the first thing, that Tony had taught her, that the act of love wasn't to be hurried, gotten over with as quickly as possible as though it were something shameful, but savored and enjoyed for as long a time as possible. How was it possible that it could be better every time, when the last time had been the acme of perfection? Drained at last, but feeling more vibrantly alive than she'd ever felt before, Moria marveled at it.

"I'll get dressed and out of the way so the bulldog can come in and help you. I'll meet you at breakfast, I'll be waiting just outside the dining salon door. It takes you women so long to make yourselves beautiful that I'll have time for a quick walk on deck while I wait,'' Tony teased her. His kiss was long and deep and filled with love.

"Hand me my nightgown and dressing gown, darling,'' Moria asked, when he let her go at last, and Tony laughed.

"Dora knows we're married, love. If she doesn't, it's about time she realized it! But all right. Cover yourself decently, I don't want that sour face of hers looking at you, anyway.'' One more kiss after he pulled her nightgown over her head and settled it, after he slipped her dressing gown around her shoulders, and then he was out of bed, so beautiful in his nakedness that Moria's breath caught and she wished that they were just starting instead of having it over with until at least tonight.

It took longer to dress after she and Tony made love, because she had to bathe thoroughly. What humbugs people were, even in this modern day and age! All the same, she was glad that that was the way it was, because their lovemaking was something that should be entirely private, something that no one else should even realize they had been doing.

Although she was so happy that she'd scarcely noticed Dora's dourer than usual face as the maid helped her to bathe and dress, she was forced to notice that something was bothering her when Dora dropped the hairbrush for the third time, after she'd spilled the bath powder and laid out the wrong set of undergarments. Dora's hand was trembling as she picked up the brush.

"For heaven's sake, Dora! What ails you?'' Moria demanded. "You can't be seasick, that only happens during the first days of a voyage!''

"I'm not ill, Mrs. Vancouver.''

"But something's the matter! Come on, out with it!''

"I shouldn't tell you. It's none of my concern.''

Thoroughly curious by now, Moria snatched the last of the hairpins and thrust them into her hair herself. "All right, now that you have me all agog, you'll have to tell me, or it'll bother me all day. Just what is troubling you?''

Her eyes downcast, giving every impression of reluctance, Dora found her voice. "It's something I happened to see last night, Mrs. Vancouver. Something that you should know, only I hardly know how to tell you."

"Stop that! Tell me what it is this instant!" Moria demanded. Drat the girl, why was she making such a big mystery out of something that was probably nothing at all?

"It's Mrs. Forrester, Mrs. Vancouver."

"Mrs. Forrester? Helen Forrester, that beautiful widow? What could she possibly have to do with you?"

"Not with me, Mrs. Vancouver. With Mr. Vancouver."

Thrusting in the last hairpin, Moria's fingers went numb. Blindly, she finished positioning it, willing her fingers not to tremble, willing her face not to show its shock.

"What about her and Tony?"

Dora let it burst out then, as though she'd rather have cut her tongue out, although Moria knew perfectly well that she was finding the most exquisite pleasure in telling her.

"Mr. Vancouver went to her stateroom last night. He was in there with her, alone with her, for more than two hours. I only happened to see him go in by accident. I was on my way to check on you one last time and I had to pass her stateroom to get to yours. I saw him knock on her door and saw her open it for him. She was wearing an indecent nightgown and peignoir, and there was a bottle of champagne on a table, and two glasses. Then she shut the door, and I waited, and it was more than two hours before he came out again, looking both ways to make sure the way was clear and nobody would see him, only I took care that he didn't see me. He was smiling . . ."

"Shut up! Shut up, shut up!" Moria screamed. "And get out of here, get out of my sight! You're lying, it's all a pack of lies!"

Only Dora wasn't lying, or else Moria wasn't any judge of character at all, and she knew Dora well enough to be sure that she was telling the truth. Trembling, nauseated, so sick that she could scarcely see her reflection in the mirror, Moria struggled to control herself. She must be calm, she must put the finishing touches on her toilette and go and join Tony for breakfast. He'd be wondering what was delaying her.

All of her Irish heritage, the blood of the Irish kings and queens that Liam had told her about during her childhood, came to her aid. Her chin came up, her mouth stopped its trembling, her face was composed as she rose and left the stateroom.

Tony looked perfectly normal. Young, boyish, his open face and frank eyes so handsome that it made her insides melt with agony.

"There you are! I was about to mount a search party! You're radiant this morning, Moria. Every man on board this ship will want to cut my throat because you belong to me."

He held out his arm and she placed her hand on it, smiling at him. "And all of the women will want to put poison in my coffee! Because you belong to me and not to them."

Laughing, they entered the salon. Still smiling, they took their places. Moria let her glance wander around the room.

She was there, two tables away from them. She was the most beautiful woman Moria had ever seen. And older, more mature, more experienced, more everything than Moria was or ever would be unless she managed to survive this, and grow a few years older herself.

"Good morning, Mrs. Forrester," she said.

Helen smiled, her face expressing the delight that she injected into her voice. "Good morning, Mrs. Vancouver. I'm so pleased to see that you're feeling well again. Perhaps we could walk on deck later this morning?"

"Perhaps we can. Only I don't believe I feel quite that well yet." Moria made a little moue, depreciating her lack of well-being. The orange juice she lifted to her lips tasted sour, bitter, and her stomach churned. "I'm afraid I'm not at all as well as I thought I was. I believe I'll have to go back to bed."

"Darling, if you didn't feel well you shouldn't have got up!" Tony reproved her. He patted her hand, gentle and tender, his face filled with concern. But Moria saw his eyes, she saw the look that passed between Helen Forrester and her husband, and she knew that everything that Dora had told her was true, and it was killing her to know, and she rose to her feet, her face white.

She had to tolerate Tony's arm around her as he helped her back to their stateroom. His touch sickened her, burned her, made her feel dirty, fouled.

Last night he'd been with Helen Forrester, he'd made love to her, passionate, flaming love, as only Tony knew how to make love. And this morning he'd made love to her, straight from Helen Forrester's arms, and she wished that she were dead.

Everything that Liam had told her about Tony was true, everything Eugenia had told her. Why hadn't she listened to them, why hadn't she believed them! This was their honeymoon, still their honeymoon, and Tony had already betrayed her, already been unfaithful to her at his very first opportunity! What would it be like, after they were home, when she wouldn't be with him every hour of the day and night?

And she knew what it would be like. There would be one woman after another, always another woman, because no one woman could satisfy Tony, would ever be able to satisfy him.

"Moria, you look like death!" Tony's voice was filled with genuine alarm as he opened their stateroom door to find Dora fussing around. "Dora, run and ask the ship's doctor to come immediately. And hurry, damn you, your mistress is ill!"

Moria turned to face him the moment Dora had left. Her face was white, so white that her eyes seemed almost black in contrast.

"Get away from me. Get out of this room. Don't ever touch me, don't ever come near me again! I know where you were last night, I know what you did."

"What the devil are you talking about?" Tony stared at her, his face the picture of perplexed innocence. But not before that one, fleeting, quickly hidden flash of guilt, of being caught out.

The enormity of what he had done filled Moria with rage, made her feel as though she were suffocating, as though she couldn't draw any air into her lungs.

"You must know what I'm talking about. You and Mrs. Forrester!

Or do you call her Helen, now that you're so intimate? No, get away from me! I meant what I said, I don't want you to touch me, ever again!''

"You're out of your mind. You must be much more ill than you realize, making a mountain out of a molehill just because I escorted Mrs. Forrester back to her stateroom!''

"You were seen, Tony. Seen going into her stateroom, seen coming out again more than two hours later! Seen visiting her when she was undressed, when she was wearing a transparent nightgown and peignoir! And you drank champagne, and you made love, while I was ill and asleep and you thought it was safe, that I'd never find out!''

"Nobody saw me because it never happened! Unless . . .'' The fury of Moria's attack had taken him off guard, or he never would have made that last slip.

"Yes, it was Dora. And I know she isn't lying, just as I know that you're lying now. You sicken me, I could throw up just looking at you!''

Moria's voice wasn't high-pitched or screaming, but its pure fury penetrated like sword points. Damn Dora, why hadn't he been more careful, why hadn't he realized that she hated Moria enough, hated him enough, to spy on him, to try to find any evidence at all that would ruin their marriage?

Tony reached out for Moria. She was upset and angry, which was only to be expected, considering her youth and innocence. But she'd get over it, he could convince her that it would never happen again, that he was sorry, that he'd rather cut off his right hand than hurt her. He'd simply have to be more careful until she was older, until she realized that for a man to have extramarital affairs was completely normal and to be expected and that other wives tolerated it for the sake of domestic harmony.

Moria struck out at his hands, and then her own flew to her mouth and she retched, again and again. The room spun around her, faster and faster, and she felt herself falling into darkness and she was glad, she wanted it to enfold her and hide her forever, where she

235

couldn't feel the hurt that was killing her. Dimly, she heard Tony calling her name, but she didn't answer.

She realized almost instantly, when she opened her eyes again, that she had fainted. She was in bed, her clothing loosened, and her forehead felt wet because Dora was wiping at it with a sopping cloth, and the ship's doctor was snapping his bag closed before he turned to check her pulse again.

"Congratulations, Mrs. Vancouver," he told her. "Do you want a boy or a girl? I'm sorry I can't put in a special order for you, you'll have to take what you get." His face smug, he seemed to think that his tired joke was humorous. "You'll be fine. Swooning in the early stages of impending motherhood isn't in the least unusual."

"I'm not pregnant." Moria's voice made it sound like a statement of fact. "I haven't been sick in the morning at all, until this morning. Just in the late afternoon, and then my dinner makes me feel nauseated, I have some indisposition that will pass."

"I can guarantee you that it will pass." Still smugly complacent, the doctor beamed at her. "In two or three more months. Morning sickness doesn't necessarily occur only in the morning, my dear. Women are contrary creatures and some of them like to be different. I'll leave a list of instructions and suggestions for your diet and exercise, and if you feel ill again I'll be right with you. One advantage of being on shipboard is that the doctor is right at hand, you never have to wait for hours until he can get to you."

He patted her hand, while Moria's body lay exhausted and her mind screamed with protest. Pregnant, she was pregnant! Now she was trapped, there was no way she could ever get away. She turned her face away as Tony bent over her. "Leave me alone!"

The doctor chuckled. "Pay no attention, Mr. Vancouver. Young ladies in your wife's delicate condition often have irrational fancies. They will pass along with the other symptoms. Let me be the first to congratulate you and wish you a healthy, bouncing boy. And you, young lady, behave yourself and don't take your feeling a little ill out on your husband. It'll all be worth it in the end and you'll be one of the happiest young women alive."

Moria turned her face to the wall. Yesterday she would have been the happiest woman alive, if she'd known that she was to become a mother. Today, everything had changed.

Tony left the stateroom with the doctor, no doubt to fill the gullible man's ears with tales of her flightiness, her childish imaginings, her quick temper and unreasonableness. He wasn't one to lose such an opportunity to place her credibility in doubt, in case she decided to confide in him. It was as if blinders had fallen from Moria's eyes and she was seeing him as he actually was, for the first time. Her father had tried to warn her, Eugenia had tried to warn her, but in her blindness she'd refused to listen to them. Because Tony was handsome, and charming, because every other girl in the Hudson River Valley had wanted him, because marrying him had seemed to her like a romance in a novel, she'd been determined to have him.

She lay with her eyes closed for a few moments, despair engulfing her. And then, almost without realizing what she was doing, she rose from the bed and went to her jewel case. In the bottom drawer, wrapped in its scrap of silk, was the horsehair bracelet that Quinn had made for her when she was fifteen. Still almost without thinking, she removed the silk cloth and slipped the bracelet on to her wrist. In some inexplicable way, it brought her comfort.

She returned to her bed then, and lay down with her hand and wrist nestled under her cheek so that she could feel the rough texture of the bracelet. Feeling it there made her feel that she wasn't entirely alone.

14

Moria and Tony had been home for nearly a week, but this was the first opportunity she'd had to ride over from Belvedere to visit Eugenia. She needed Eugenia, she had to see Eugenia, and her father too if it could possibly be arranged.

Not to tell them what had happened aboard ship, not to mention Tony's brief affair with the beautiful widow, Helen Forrester. Moria had had more than enough time to think, before the ship had docked in New York. There was nothing either Liam or Eugenia could do to help her. She was Tony's wife now, they had no more jurisdiction over her, nothing to say about how Tony treated her or whether or not he was making her happy.

It had been her mistake, and hers alone. There was no point in making her father and Eugenia unhappy by telling them the truth. And although she hadn't forgiven Tony, although she still hadn't allowed Tony to touch her, she still loved him. And Tony had told her, again and again, that he loved her, and maybe it was true. All of their passion, all of the joy they'd shared, couldn't have been sham. Tony was Tony, that was all, and, despairingly, Moria thought that he probably couldn't help himself, that his flaws of character had been inborn in him and that as long as there was no way she could leave him now that there was going to be a child who had to be considered, she might as well do her best to be happy with what she had. But the first glow was gone, the gilt had tarnished, and she knew that she would never again be truly happy.

"A baby!" Eugenia said. Her eyes went soft and shining. "Oh, Moria, you're going to have a baby!"

"Is there an echo in this room?" Moria teased her, and not even Eugenia, who knew her so well, could detect what an effort it cost her to be gay and teasing. "That's what I just said, Eugenia."

"It's just that I'm so happy! Moria, you're going to be a mother, you're going to have what was denied me! How I longed for a child, a child of my own, to hold and love and cherish!" Realizing what she'd just said, she hastened to add, "But then you came, and you filled my heart, but there were so many years before you came, and you'll be spared that, you'll have your child right from the beginning. Estelle must be beside herself with joy. Even Jacob must be happy, you'll be the most important person in the household now that you're about to present the Vancouvers with their heir."

"Estelle and Jacob don't know yet. I asked Tony not to tell them until I could tell you first."

Eugenia's face lit up. "Thank you, Moria. That's the nicest gift you could have given me."

"Gift! Good grief, here I've sat nattering away, forgetting all about the gift I brought you! And I have one for Papa, too, and for Rose. Yours first, but let's wait for Rose so she can see you open it and then she can open hers, and then we'll walk down to the stables so I can see Jazir, no one will think there's anything odd about that, or that I thought to bring Liam something." As an afterthought she added, "I got something for Mr. Northrup too. I was so anxious to see you that I left them all in the carriage. Can you imagine me coming in a carriage when what I really wanted was to ride like the wind to get here faster? But Tony, drat him, had to go and say I looked a little pale, and get Estelle to back him up that I must take the carriage so as not to overtire myself!''

Rose thumped against the door with her shoulder, her old signal that her arms were burdened with a tray and she'd appreciate someone opening the door for her. It was a standing joke between the three of them that Rose's shoulder must be black and blue from all the times she'd bumped the door.

''Tea!'' Moria cried as she let Rose in. ''And I'm ravenous. But first you must run and bring up the packages I left in the carriage. Be especially careful with Mr. Northrup's, it's breakable. I managed to find him a leather spirits case, with little glasses nestled in their pockets, it was the best I could do for a man who has everything already.''

It had been hard to find something for Eugenia, too, but a little antiques shop in London had provided the answer to her quest. It was a locket, very old, and the lavender-scented elderly lady who showed it to her had touched a hidden spring so that it opened to reveal a hiding place inside that only someone who knew the secret could possibly have found.

''There was a scrap of baby hair in it when it came to me,'' the old lady said. ''Some mother must have treasured her infant's hair all her life. It isn't a valuable piece, of course, I doubt that it's anything you'd be interested in.''

But it was exactly what Moria wanted. Now, as Eugenia held it in her hand, it already held a scrap of Moria's hair, and there was room for a scrap of Liam's, and later they would add a scrap of the baby's.

''And no one will ever know,'' Moria told her. ''It will be our secret.'' Eugenia's eyes were filled with tears as she slipped the locket around her neck, and her fingers trembled so hard that Rose had to fasten it for her.

Rose's face filled with reverent awe as she opened a velvet case and lifted a rosary from the satin lining. The beads were of smoothly polished wood, so beautiful in themselves that their very plainness proclaimed them to be something special.

"It's olive wood, from the Holy Land. I found it in Rome, in a little shop right by St. Peter's, and I carried it with me when Tony and I visited the cathedral so that you'd know it's been there." She didn't have to ask if Rose liked it. Her eyes were flowing over. A diamond necklace would not have meant so much to her.

There was one more package, long and slender, and Rose ran her fingers along it. "A stick," she said. "It must be a stick."

"A special stick," Moria told her. "It's blackthorn and it came from Ireland. I was determined to bring Papa something from Ireland even though Tony refused to make a side trip there. Do you think Papa will like it, Eugenia? Do you think he'll accept it, as angry as he is with me?"

"Come. We'll find out now." Her heart in her mouth, Moria followed her from the room and they went to find Liam. Seeing his eyes as he caressed the stick, seeing his eyes as they looked at her as if they'd been sick from the wanting to see her, Moria knew that she had been forgiven, and she felt that no matter what the future held for her, that alone would give her the strength to bear it.

All during the autumn and into the early winter Moria's figure remained slender enough not to betray her condition, so that she didn't have to remove herself from society. That pleased Tony, who would have been driven insane if he hadn't been able to attend every social function of the season. As happy as his parents were because of Moria's pregnancy, they would have raised the devil if he'd accepted invitations without his wife at this early stage of their marriage.

It was bad enough that Jacob insisted that he must learn something of the Vancouver enterprises now that he was a married man and about to become a father. The mornings and most of the afternoons as well were spent in going over long columns of figures, pages and pages of them, and reports so long that he was in danger of falling asleep from sheer boredom before he came to the end of them.

"You must understand it all, all!" his father told him. "I will not live forever and then it will all fall on your shoulders, and if you do not understand it all the Vancouver empire will fall into ruin."

There was nothing wrong with Tony's brain. It was only that these things held no interest for him. He chafed under the burden of it, and then made up for his boredom of the days by accepting every invitation for evening affairs that came their way.

It pleased him to see the admiration for Moria that ranged all the way down from callow, unshaven youths to doddering old codgers whose days of amorous adventure were long past. The lust they felt for her was so evident that it gave him a sense of possession that made him understand how William Northrup felt in his possession of Retreat and Eugenia. Moria had to do no more than enter a room full of people on his arm for every pair of eyes to fasten on her, the women's with jealousy, the men with a gnawing longing for something they could never have.

Of all the women, Veronica Hamilton had the most reason for jealousy and felt it the most fiercely, although her control was so complete that no one but Tony ever guessed.

"Has a little of the shine worn off yet, Tony?" she asked him while she was dancing with him at the pre-Christmas ball held at Retreat in Moria and Tony's honor. Her green eyes, made even greener by her spite, surveyed Moria over Tony's shoulder. "Isn't your dear wife letting herself go just a trifle? She's put on weight, I swear! She must be overindulging in your famous Dutch cooking."

Tony smiled down into her eyes, his own eyes candid and boyish and expressing nothing but pleasure in the information he imparted to her. "How observant you are, my love! No one else has guessed. Moria is going to be a mother."

Veronica's face paled, and then flamed. Even her control couldn't prevent that much of her emotions from showing. "You, a father! You certainly didn't waste any time, did you?"

"With a girl as beautiful as my wife, it would have been remarkable if I had wasted any time! You're the first to know, outside of the immediate family. Doesn't the honor please you?"

The moment the first shock of Tony's revelation had passed,

Veronica smiled. Tony's revelation did please her, far more than he could possibly have anticipated. Moria might still be lovely tonight, but, like Cinderella, the clock would soon strike twelve for her. She'd grow fat and ugly, she'd be unable to be a wife to Tony. And Veronica would be here, slender, beautiful, vibrant, able to do everything and give everything that Moria would no longer be capable of doing or giving.

Adultery! A shiver of pure excitement went through her. The consequences, if it should be discovered, were enough to make her tremble. But she knew that she was going to do it. Tony was hers, he'd belonged to her first, before Moria had snatched him away. And now she was going to get him back, even if she could never be his wife. And she'd make sure that Moria knew it, that Moria would suffer as she'd suffered, that Moria would suffer a hundredfold of her own suffering!

In the library, half an hour later, William showed off his latest acquisition. All during that autumn, Eugenia and Moria had had to sit for a portrait, the painting of which had been kept a secret until this moment. Now the portrait dominated the room, so beautifully executed, such a masterpiece, that his guests were struck dumb. The contrast of their coloring, the almost unbelievable beauty of their faces, made it a treasure beyond compare.

William raised his glass in a toast. "To my wife and daughter," he said.

The guests raised their glasses and drank, their eyes filled with awe, and William basked in their envy and was content.

As the weeks passed, Moria too was content. Her changing figure did not bother her, she carried her baby easily in spite of the slenderness of her body and her fine bones. Her years of horseback riding had imbued her with a strength granted to few women, and even during the final weeks of her pregnancy she remained active, although even Liam and Eugenia now backed Estelle Vancouver in insisting that she must give up riding for the duration. But she had ridden well into her sixth month, pitting her will against Estelle's and Tony's and Eugenia's, although Liam had been more sensible about it than the rest of them. Any girl with Moria's skill in the saddle could not help but benefit from the exercise, as long as she no longer galloped at a headlong pace, or jumped.

William's gift to her on learning that she was to become a mother had been Jazir. Liam had ridden to Belvedere leading the magnificent black, with the message that he now belonged to Moria and was to stay at the Belvedere stables. Moria's reconciliation with her father was still sweet, something she hugged to her in the dark hours of the night while Tony slept beside her, oblivious to the thoughts that he could never share. She had been able to present such a picture of happiness in her marriage that Liam had relented. Besides, he loved her so much that he wanted to remain close to her in case she ever needed him, he wanted her to know that she could turn to him, and she wouldn't do that if she were alienated from him by his own stubbornness.

At night, when it was impossible for Eugenia to come to Liam because William was at home, Liam would lie as wakeful as Moria, fingering the blackthorn stick she'd given him. She'd bought it on her honeymoon, mind, she'd remembered him in spite of the rift between them, and searched all of London until she'd found the one thing that he would cherish the most, something from Ireland.

"And isn't it beautiful!" Michael McCarthy exclaimed, rubbing his fingers over the wood before he relinquished it to Liam. "That's a fine girl you have, Liam Donovan, and don't you go forgettin' it! All your dark fears have come to naught, and now don't you think it's time you took a more active part in the great affairs that are shaping the politics of New York?"

"I've not much chance of that, tied to Retreat as I am," Liam told him. And tied he was, in spite of Michael's insistence that he could leave Retreat and take his place in the scheme of things. As long as Eugenia was here, as long as Moria was on the neighboring estate of Belvedere, he could not and would not leave. And now there was the advent of his first grandchild to hold him here as well. He'd continue to work for freedom from England's domination of

Ireland by making speeches and extracting every penny he could for the cause, but American politics he'd leave to Michael and his like.

But if Liam would not come to Michael, then Michael would come to Liam, and he did, with more frequency than was safe. How the brash Irishman managed to elude William's gatekeepers and make his way into the estate and to this cottage was a marvel. But Liam smiled as he realized that Michael came as much for news of Rose O'Riley as to see him, to talk about her and question him about her, and hope, every time he took the chance again, that this time he would actually see her.

Moria's pregnancy had advanced so far by early spring that in order not to disturb her, Tony had moved into another bedroom. Moria's lips curved in a faintly bitter smile as she realized how convenient this was for Tony. He could stay out as late as he pleased, confident that she would never know how late he returned. But Moria slept as lightly as a cat, so she knew that last night it had been after two when Tony had tiptoed into his room, closing the door so softly behind him that only ears as sharp as hers would have heard him.

She was sure that he was being unfaithful to her again, after the period of months after their return from their honeymoon when he had been forced to watch his step. And she realized that there was nothing she could do to stop him. She was too proud to complain of his unfaithfulness to her mother-in-law or father-in-law, and even if she did it would only make matters worse because Tony would resent it and even hate her for it. As it was he was sweet and charming to her, as long as she didn't rant or rail at him. It was to his advantage to keep her content. He was so attentive to her in public that she knew she was envied by nearly every woman she knew, and even in private he was solicitous of her comfort, mindful of her wishes.

At first she'd thought that her jealousy and hurt would destroy her. But serious reflection told her that she wasn't the first woman who had had to accept a situation like hers, and she wouldn't be the last. But just wait until after her baby was born! Once she was in condition to fight back, Tony's other women would find out that they had competition, and Tony would find out that she wasn't the gullible fool he thought she was.

Out of nowhere, a thought came into her mind. She wondered if Quinn knew that she was pregnant, if her father had told him when he wrote to him. She hadn't thought of Quinn for weeks, he was so far in her past that she almost never thought about him anymore. Only when she was troubled or upset, and then she'd slip the bracelet he'd made her onto her wrist, and it would bring her comfort.

Now, wondering where Tony was, she got out of bed and put the bracelet on. Her smile was amused as she realized that now that she was wearing it, now that she could feel it against her cheek, she was falling asleep in spite of her previous wakefulness as she'd listened to the old house creak around her and waited to hear Tony's stealthy footsteps when he finally returned home.

"It's my favorite scent," Veronica told Moria, as she sat sipping tea in Moria's bedroom. The table was set up in front of a crackling fire to chase the chill from this rainy May afternoon. There was a cold drizzle of rain outside her windows, and the old stone house with its thick walls retained the chill of winter long past the advent of the first spring flowers. It had been good of Veronica to brave the weather to come and visit her.

She came back to what Veronica was saying, she'd been daydreaming, her thoughts on the weather and the imminent arrival of her baby.

"It came from Paris," Veronica prattled on, lifting her wrist to hold it close to Moria's nose so that she could more fully appreciate it. "It's made of lilies of the valley and it's very rare. Tony always liked it too. He told me only last night that he still likes it better than any other scent I use. . . ."

So that was where Tony had been last night! With Veronica. And Moria could have sworn that Veronica had made the slip deliberately, that she wanted her to know! It was certain that she must have had some better reason to come out in the rain than to see Moria because she wanted to be with her. Veronica was not prone to good deeds, she was as selfish and self-centered as Tony. Moria was fully aware by now that Veronica had been determined to get Tony for herself before she had come into the picture, even though the other girl had done a magnificent job of hiding her jealousy and spite.

She twisted in her chair, a little gasp escaping from her lips.

"Are you all right?" Veronica demanded.

"I think so. It was just a twinge. I get them now and then." But Moria's face was pale, and there was a fine beading of perspiration on her forehead, and the room wasn't that warm even with the fire. Veronica had upset her more than she'd thought she'd be upset when she found out who Tony was seeing these last days of her pregnancy. She should have guessed that it would be Veronica, she'd simply assumed that Tony had taken up with Helen Forrester again, as the widow lived in New York City and it was fairly easy for Tony to make some excuse to stay in the city overnight.

Now she wished that it were Helen Forrester, rather than Veronica. Helen Forrester was old, way older than Tony, and as soon as she had her figure and her strength back she'd be able to put the widow in her place. But Veronica was another matter entirely, almost as young as Moria herself, and definitely a provocative beauty without a moral to her name, as well as being much more readily available to Tony.

Another twinge made her stiffen in her chair. This one had been harder than the first. Moria drew a deep breath. She must be calm, having a baby was a natural thing, there was nothing to worry about. All the same, she thought she'd better have Veronica call her mother-in-law.

"I think you'd better find Estelle and tell her that I need her," she said. It was probably nothing, but Estelle would know. She hoped that it was nothing, because she didn't want her baby to be born on a dreary, rainy day, what would it think of the world it had been thrust into? Silly goose! Here she was, being as fey as her father sometimes accused her of being!

Veronica left the room on flying feet, the picture of apprehension. Left alone, Moria got up out of her chair and began to walk, to pace the space between the fireplace and the huge tester bed. Let it rain, then! In Ireland, they'd call this a soft day, and think nothing of it, her father had told her that, and she even thought that she could remember it from her childhood there.

Estelle would come, and Estelle would send word to Retreat, and Eugenia would come, and Rose. And this May day would be the luckiest day in the year if it turned out to be her baby's birthday.

Estelle came hurrying into the room, out of breath because she'd ascended the staircase faster than she'd ever ascended it before. "You must be brave," she told Moria. "I'll help you into bed, I've sent Miss Hamilton home, this is no place for a young unmarried lady. I'm sorry that Anthony isn't home, I really don't know where he is, on some business for his father, I understand, and his father with him. But I've already sent a groom to alert Eugenia, and another to fetch the doctor, and everything will be all right. Just be brave, Moria dear, and try not to scream."

"I have no intention of screaming," Moria said. "And I'd like to finish my tea before I go to bed, please."

"Moria!" Estelle was agitated, shocked. But Moria was already gobbling down the last of the muffin spread with preserves, a slice of pound cake, and another full cup of tea. There was work ahead of her, the hardest work she'd ever been called upon to do, and she was going to need her strength.

Nine hours later, Jacob Reid Vancouver came squalling into the world, and he was beautiful. His hair was fair like Tony's, his eyes were blue now as all babies' eyes were blue, or at least that was what Eugenia and Estelle told her, but they might turn brown as he grew older. His eyelashes lay in silken half moons against his cheeks once he'd stopped protesting about being born. Moria held him and loved him and marveled at him and forgave him for every second of the pain she had had to endure to bring him into the world.

She hadn't screamed. Estelle was still marveling about that, agog to tell every one of her female acquaintances how her daughter-in-

249

law had gone through the entire ordeal of childbirth without screaming or shedding a tear. It made Moria laugh to see how wonderful
Estelle thought that was. She hadn't had time to scream or cry, she'd
been too busy.

How they'd all fussed over her, all except Eugenia, who had
better sense, and Rose. Estelle doing all the moaning and groaning
for her, the doctor hemming and hawing and acting as if there were
no way she could bring this baby into the world without him. And
then when he'd been born, the doctor had been downstairs, fortify-
ing his strength with some of Jacob's best brandy, and Rose had
said, her eyes glittering with satisfaction, "Leave him there! We can
do better without him, the pompous old fool!"

She called her son Reid, and everyone else followed her lead.
Reid was the name of some remote and respected ancestor of the
Vancouvers, but to Moria it was still a lovely name, and far more
desirable than Jacob. She shuddered to think of this perfect son of
hers going through life being called Jacob. So he was Reid, and in
time the only reminder that he had been named after his paternal
grandfather would be a name on legal papers, seldom seen and even
more seldom remembered.

Moria wished, with tears in her heart, that she could have named
him Liam.

Now, ten days after Reid had been born, she was sick and tired of
all this pampering and petting. She was stifled, she felt suffocated.
Let Estelle fume, let Tony put his foot down, let Jacob forbid it, she
was going to Retreat to visit Eugenia, and she was going to take
Reid with her.

Two hours later, she was there, and she'd come alone in spite of
Estelle's protests. Fortunately, neither Tony nor Jacob had been at
home to try to stop her, but she would have come in any case. It was
simply better this way, because Tony would have insisted on accompanying her when he couldn't talk her out of it, and then what
chance would she have had to show Liam his grandson?

Thank the Almighty that Dora was no longer around to spy on
her! Tony's intense dislike of the maid who had spied on him and

told Moria of his visit to Helen Forrester's stateroom had resulted in Dora's being relegated to the sewing room at Belvedere, and replaced by an older woman with a sweet disposition who was much more to Tony's liking and Moria's as well.

"Well, Father? What do you think of your grandson?" Moria demanded.

"I thank God for him," Liam said simply. "And I thank God that he was born in the United States, and will never know the oppression of the Irish." He touched Reid's cheek once, and slipped out of Eugenia's room. Rose had smuggled him up the servants' staircase with no one the wiser, and even if Mrs. Lindstrom or the cook had seen him they wouldn't have told. They knew how fond Moria was of the horse trainer who had taught her to ride, and they wouldn't think anything of the visit except to hope that Mr. Northrup wouldn't find out that Liam had been in the house, where he had no business to be.

He'd seen his grandson. And before Moria left, another tiny snip of hair, as fair as an angel's, was placed in the locket that nestled over Eugenia's heart, beside the lock of Moria's raven hair and the lock of Liam's, showing gray among the dark.

15

Moria never entered the drawing room at Belvedere without a sense of pleasure, even though the room itself was cavernous and gloomy, situated as it was on the northwest side of the house so that only the late afternoon sun ever had a chance to penetrate. The room didn't need sunshine now, because of the portrait over the mantle.

The portrait was large, as large as the one of Moria and Eugenia at Retreat, and painted by the same respected artist who had done the first. But this one had three figures, not two. Moria was in the center, with Reid, at nine years of age, standing beside her with his hand on her shoulder, while eight-year-old Gayle sat on a low hassock at her feet, looking up at her, so exact a replica of her mother that their friends marveled to see her.

How different Gayle's birth had been from Reid's, Moria thought, as she studied the portrait. For one thing, it hadn't been raining, but it had been a sizzling July day, with a relentless sun scorching an earth that cried out for relief.

And Tony had been at home, for a change, even Tony a little worried because Dr. Morrison had been concerned that this birth had

253

come so hard on the heels of the first. It was almost indecent, even though not quite close enough to cause a sensation. Still the doctor hadn't liked it, and Estelle had fretted and fussed, and Eugenia hadn't quite been able to hide her concern underneath the joy she felt that Moria was to have a second child.

How lovely Gayle was! Had she, Moria wondered, ever looked exactly like that, at her age? A fairy child, a child touched by the leprechauns to bless her, to set her apart from ordinary little girls. Every feature of her face, every line of her body, were identical with Moria's. Liam had told her so, his eyes filled with the pain of bittersweet memories.

But the physical resemblance did not extend to Gayle's personality. Sweet and charming when she chose to be, she was inclined to withdraw into herself, her mood sullen and hostile, and she was convinced that the Vancouvers were better than anyone else on earth. A born snob, Reid called her, his brows knitted with disgust.

Strangely, Jacob Vancouver doted on Gayle, much more than he cared for his grandson, the one who would carry on the family name. No matter how difficult Gayle was, Jacob was always on her side. Her arrogance, her moods and her snobbishness were to him signs of the Vancouver breeding of which he was so proud.

Moria spent uneasy hours pondering over the fact that Jacob should so prefer his granddaughter over his grandson. Could it be, she wondered, because as Reid had left his early childhood behind, his resemblance to Tony had decreased? Reid's hair had darkened, still blond but not nearly as fair as Tony's, and the eyes which had turned brown as Estelle had predicted had changed again before he was four to something more nearly hazel, with definite green lights in them.

But she was more inclined to think that it was Reid's independence that grated on the Vancouver patriarch. Reid was very much his own person, liking whom he chose to like without regard for breeding or wealth, respectful enough when Jacob talked about his ancestors but holding them not the least bit in awe.

Her eyes softened as they rested on Reid's face in the portrait. If she could have had her choice of any son in the world, there would have been no choice to make at all, because Reid was the joy of her life, her companion and her comfort. Reid's disposition was always sunny and agreeable, although he was a thoughtful boy as well, serious in all he did. He attended his lessons diligently, enjoying them, eager to learn. He had no sense of snobbishness at all, but treated everyone with whom he came in contact as equals, including the servants. He deferred to other people's wishes, but it was not from weakness but only because he liked pleasing them.

The relationship between Liam and Reid was something so special, so beautiful, that Moria's throat tightened whenever she saw them together. And that was often, because even Jacob conceded that there was no horse trainer in the Hudson River Valley who was as qualified to teach his grandchildren to ride. Each of the children had been introduced to their first ponies when they were four years old. Liam, borrowed from Retreat, had led them around on leading reins until they had found their seats and were able to manage on their own.

By the time they were six, they were riding the bridle paths between Belvedere and Retreat. William, nearly as proud of Gayle as he was of Moria, kept two ponies especially for them so that they could have fresh mounts to ride about his estate after they had ridden over from Belvedere.

As the children grew older, the ponies were replaced by horses, the first gentle mounts again replaced by animals with more spirit. William tolerated Reid, and even seemed pleased that his adopted daughter's son was so intelligent, but like Jacob, it was Gayle upon whom he doted.

When Moria and Gayle appeared together in public, they never failed to cause a sensation because of their carbon-copy resemblance to each other. And William made it a point to hold a good many affairs at which the children could be included, just to show them off. Moria was still very much his possession, and now Gayle was included as the third jewel in his crown.

Tony was fond of Reid, ruffling his hair whenever he entered the same room, asking him about his studies, even taking him with him on an occasional excursion to New York City or to neighboring towns and estates. But for the most part Tony had little time to spend with his children, and it was Liam who took a father's place in Reid's life. Reid adored the man whom he had no idea was his grandfather, he admired him, looked up to him, they were friends and companions, and Moria's heart swelled with gratitude because it brought her father so much happiness.

She was happy for Eugenia too, because Eugenia's life had become easier to bear as the years had passed. In his pride in Moria, who had taken the Hudson River Valley by storm, and now in his pride in Gayle as well, William had gradually stopped torturing and tormenting the wife he blamed with such unrelenting bitterness because she'd inflicted an injury on him that had ensured that he would never father a child of his own.

Eugenia herself never discussed it with Moria, but Rose told her. "The man hasn't come to her room for more than two years now," Rose said, her voice filled with gratification. "Ever since you and Gayle began setting this valley on its ear because you make such a picture together, he's mellowed. Your coming to Retreat was a miracle, Moria, a miracle from heaven. Our Lady answered my prayers after all, even though I was wicked enough to think that she didn't at the time."

Moria knew that it was true, because Eugenia was so much happier. The unbearable strain of never knowing when William would come to her room and inflict his sadistic tortures on her was gone from her face and eyes. But there was still a sadness there, and Moria knew that it was because William spent more time at home now, that he wasn't nearly as often away from Retreat overnight and so Eugenia and Liam had fewer opportunities to be together in Liam's cottage.

Liam's and Eugenia's love for each other had never wavered over the years, but had only grown stronger. Moria thought, aching, that theirs was a love story that should go down through the centuries.

Where had all the years gone! Standing in front of the portrait, thinking of two other portraits that now hung in William's library, those of Reid and Gayle, Moria looked at the painted likenesses of her children and felt a sense of panic. It was May of 1881, and soon she'd reach that milestone in any woman's life, she'd be thirty, her youth behind her, a middle-aged woman with nothing to look forward to except seeing her children grow up and marry and present her with grandchildren.

But she didn't feel old! She didn't feel a day older than she'd felt when she was seventeen and she'd married Tony. What she felt was cheated!

The word that jumped unbidden into her mind brought her up short, appalled her. But it was true, all the same. She felt cheated because she had been cheated. The fairy tale marriage she'd envisioned when she'd married Tony had not come true.

How stormy those first years of her marriage had been! She and Tony had quarreled incessantly about his affairs. Just as she'd sworn when she was pregnant with Reid, Moria hadn't taken Tony's unfaithfulness lying down. Gayle was actually the result of one of their more violent quarrels, when Tony had had the unbelievable temerity to take her by force in the mistaken belief that he could physically love her into forgiving him! But it had been the last time he had touched her for months, because she'd locked him out of her room.

In the eyes of the outside world they were an ideal couple, an ideal young family. In public, they gave every appearance of being happy. They had youth, beauty, wealth, two lovely children, they had everything.

Actually Moria had had next to nothing. It infuriated her that Tony could always cajole her, charm her, into forgiving him after enough time had passed. And she counted her friends among the dozens, her social triumphs as many. Over and over again she'd forced Tony to break off his recurring affair with Veronica Hamilton.

But her victories over Veronica had never lasted, and it was actually Jacob who had forced Tony to be more discreet, more careful not to be caught. Incensed because of his son's behavior,

Jacob had told him, his eyes icy, that if he didn't mend his ways he'd disinherit him and leave everything to Reid and Gayle.

So for a while, Tony had been careful, even to the point of breaking off with Veronica entirely for nearly two years. But then Veronica had married Ned Curtis, a nondescript young man from an impeccable family. They had a house in New York City, and the Curtis family estate was in the Hudson River Valley, one of those acquired by wealthy families who flocked to the valley after the end of the war.

As a married woman, Veronica was no longer suspect. Her husband was so gullible, so astonished at his good fortune in winning such a prize that she could have walked a man past him and up the stairs and into their bedroom and he would have accepted any innocent explanation she chose to throw him over her shoulder in passing. But there was no need for that. Edward Curtis thought that Veronica was so perfect that it would never enter his mind to suspect her of anything, and so she had more freedom than nearly any other woman in their social circle, more opportunity to meet Tony and go on with their on-again-off-again love affair.

If Edward was unaware of what was going on, Moria wasn't. The only thing that had changed was that she hardly cared anymore. She no longer screamed at Tony, or threw things, or refused to let him touch her, because she knew that there was no way she could win. Tony was Tony and he would never change and she had no choice but to accept him as he was. What she had now was a marriage that was pleasant on the surface, a luxurious home, the love of Eugenia and Liam, the children she adored, and no more dreams.

And it wasn't enough! Standing there looking at the portrait, she was surprised at the bitterness that welled up inside of her. What had brought it on?

This morning she had taken the children to Retreat and they had ridden with Liam. Eugenia wasn't feeling well, she had a slight cold, and Rose had insisted that she stay in bed. Moria had been concerned until she'd run up to Eugenia's room to see her before they'd started out on their ride, but Eugenia had been propped up on her pillows, only a little feverish, and she had laughed at her concern.

"Don't let the children come up, though. There's no use in taking chances. And no, don't kiss me, you foolish girl, I don't want you to catch my cold, either!"

It had been while Gayle had insisted that her indulgent brother help her gather handfuls of wild flowers that would be wilted and ruined before she could get them home that Liam had taken a letter from his pocket and given it to Moria to read.

Moria had recognized the handwriting instantly. Nobody but Quinn Bradmore wrote with such a bold, dark hand, and wrote such long letters. He and Liam still exchanged at least three or four letters every year, and this was Quinn's latest.

> *. . . we chased those horsethieves clear up into the moun-*
> *tains, into the ponderosa pine forest. Only my father could have*
> *tracked them, I lost the track half a dozen times but he always*
> *found it again. There were half a dozen of them, they'd got*
> *away with our best breeding stallion as well as a dozen mares.*
> *Dad was fit to be tied. I was mightily relieved when we*
> *managed to keep him from killing any of the skunks before we*
> *got them back to Phoenix with only two of them slightly shot. I*
> *expect they'll all hang but their deaths won't be on our heads,*
> *not this way. Dad is of the old school, he snorts that we could*
> *save a deal of trouble by using the nearest tree to sling a noose*
> *over, but I think he's glad that he restrained himself even if he*
> *won't admit it. . . .*

Quinn! Reading his letter, her blood racing with the account of the chase and the capture, Moria had pictured him just as he'd been when she was fifteen and he was twenty. Tall, whipcord lean and saddle-leather brown, he'd been the most romantic figure of her girlhood until she'd fallen in love with Tony and almost forgotten him.

But she hadn't ever really forgotten him. She'd remembered him every time she'd been sad or troubled, every time she'd needed extra strength to bring her through. When Reid was born, she'd been wearing his horsehair bracelet all during her labor, and thinking of how disappointed he'd be in her if she screamed and cried and made a fuss, she'd managed to give birth to her first child with such a show of bravery that Estelle still talked about it.

"Isn't he married yet, Liam?" Even here, Moria didn't dare deviate from her habit of calling him Liam, lest anyone overhear. The children were well out of earshot, but what if they should happen to come closer? "He never mentions a wife."

"Not yet. He's mentioned two or three different girls, over the years, but it looks as if none of them panned out." Liam's expression was guarded. There was no point in telling his daughter that he was convinced that Quinn was still unmarried because of her, that little things that Quinn had let slip out in his letters told him that Quinn still compared every woman he met with Moria, and found them lacking.

"He might have been killed! Those rustlers might have killed him!" Moria exclaimed, her face paling. "But, oh, Liam, how wonderful it must be out there! Why haven't you ever gone to visit him? You haven't had a vacation since you came to Retreat, you're entitled to ask for an entire summer off! Mr. Northrup wouldn't like it, but he knows he could never find anyone else as good as you are and he'd hold your place open."

"I've thought about it," Liam admitted. He didn't tell her how often he'd thought about it. But he was held here by invisible bonds. He couldn't go away from Eugenia, from Moria and Reid and Gayle, for that length of time.

The children had come racing back then, the wild flowers' stems already crushed in Gayle's eager hands. "Gayle, you shouldn't hold them so tightly! See, you're crushing them!" Moria reproved.

Gayle looked at the flowers she was holding, and her face showed distaste. "They aren't any good, after all," she said, and she dropped them to the ground, rejecting them.

"Spoiled brat!" Reid told her. "If you hadn't insisted on picking so many, they wouldn't have been crushed. Mother, I'll pick some for you.''

Belvedere's gardens were filled with cultivated flowers, as were those of Retreat, but Moria thought that none of the pampered blossoms were as lovely as those that were in her bedroom now. The cultivated flowers, like the cultivated, artificial society Moria moved in, were more showy and would last longer, and it was a pity that the wild flowers would fade and die so soon, just like her dreams.

Where was Quinn now, she wondered, at this very moment? It was earlier in the day in Arizona than it was here in New York State; it would be ten o'clock in the morning there while Moria was waiting for lunch here at Belvedere. Quinn would have been up for hours. What did he look like, now that so many years had passed? She couldn't conjure up an image of what he would look like at thirty-four, and it gave her a sense of loss so acute that she felt hollow and empty inside.

Tony wasn't at home for lunch today. The children were hungry, but Moria's appetite had deserted her. The years stretched before her, each one as meaningless, as empty, as the ones that had gone before. In spite of her love for her children, she took no credit for Gayle's beauty, for Reid's good disposition and intelligence. They were accidents of the genes, any woman could have given birth to children to equal them. And although she loved each of them dearly, she still felt that sense of having been cheated, of not having done anything worthwhile with her life.

Three days later, her mood as unhappy as it had been when she'd been brooding about Quinn and her own lack of direction in life, Moria looked up from the square of needlepoint she was working as Estelle entered her room, a little out of breath. She was heavier now with the passage of the years, and climbing the stairs too quickly brought a flush to her face.

"Moria, a groom just rode over from Retreat. Eugenia wants to see you. I'm afraid, from what the groom told me, that she isn't well.''

Alarm flooded over Moria, rising to make an acrid, metallic taste in her mouth. Eugenia wouldn't have sent for her unless she was really ill!

She went immediately, not taking a carriage but riding Jazir cross-country to save time. Jazir too had aged. He'd been three years old when William Northrup had brought him to Retreat. Now he was seventeen, old for a horse, although he was still fleet and powerful. Even so, Moria knew that she wouldn't be able to ride him for many more years, and that too gave her a sense of loss. Jazir and Kamil, the Hudson River Valley wouldn't seem the same after they were gone.

She galloped up to the stables at Retreat, careless of her father's hard-and-fast rule that a horse must never be run into a stable, but trotted slowly or walked so that it could cool out. Someone would cool him out for her, this was an emergency.

It was Liam himself who caught the reins as she pulled Jazir up, his face so grave that her heart caught in her throat.

"How is she?" she demanded. She was out of the saddle before he could move to help her, her eyes begging him to tell her that Eugenia wasn't as ill as she'd been led to believe.

"I'm afraid she's really ill, Mrs. Vancouver. Rose told me that the doctor says it's pneumonia. She was caught in that rain the day before you and the children came over to ride, and she was drenched. I should have been more careful, I should have realized that it was going to storm, and insisted that we turn back earlier. It was a cold rain with a wind driving it, you remember, and she was chilled to the bone."

His torment was there in his eyes, his blaming of himself. Moria's heart ached for him. "I'm going right on in. I'll tell you how she is before I leave. Watch for me, Liam."

She ran all the way to the house, ran up the graceful, curving staircase and down the hallway, only stopping to catch her breath and try to compose herself before she rapped on the closed door.

Rose opened the door for her, her face filled with relief. "Praise the saints that you've come! She's been asking for you."

"How bad is she? It can't be that bad, she was hardly sick at all two days ago when I saw her, it was only a little cold!"

"Her fever's raging," Rose told her. "The doctor's worried, I can tell that, even though he doesn't tell me anything, but only *him!*" Even now, in her distress, Rose could not bring herself to call William Northrup by name.

From the bed, Eugenia's voice was weak as she asked, "Moria, is that you?"

"Yes, darling. I'm right here." Moria's heart constricted when she saw Eugenia's face, flushed with fever, her hand lying on the counterpane so thin, so fragile, that it seemed transparent. "I came immediately I got your message. Jazir got me here in record time, I'll bet Kamil wouldn't have been able to keep up with him!"

"You shouldn't have . . . shouldn't have . . . run him," Eugenia whispered, distressed. "Liam won't like it. . . ."

"Liam's taking care of him now. He'll be all right, he's still very strong. Darling, how do you feel?"

"Not very well. I wanted to see you. I wanted to tell you how happy, how very happy, you've . . . made me. So very happy, Moria."

"Hush, Eugenia, hush!" Moria blinked tears from her eyes, willed them not to fall, not to distress Eugenia any more than she was already distressed. "It isn't important, I already know that we were happy together, no two people could have been happier! You're supposed to rest, not get all upset by trifles. It's just a silly notion brought on by your fever, you'll laugh at yourself in a day or two when you're feeling better."

Eugenia tried to smile. "I expect I will. Moria?"

"Yes, darling." Moria leaned closer to her.

"Liam. Tell Liam that I . . . love him . . ."

"He knows that! Please, Eugenia, don't get all upset! Just rest. I'll stay here beside you, see, Rose has already brought me a chair, and I'll hold your hand until you fall asleep. And when you wake up you'll feel better, and in a few days we'll be riding together again, and this time it won't rain and make you ill, it will be beautiful out, spring in the Hudson River Valley!"

"Tell Liam . . ."

Moria put one finger across Eugenia's lips, shushing her. "Go to sleep. I'll be right here."

The effort it had taken her to speak, the waiting for Moria to come, had exhausted Eugenia's strength, and her hand relaxed in Moria's and she went to sleep. Whispering, not wanting to wake her by removing her hand, Moria asked Rose, "How long has she been like this, been this bad?"

"Since yesterday," Rose told her. "I woke in the night, knowing that she needed me. Our Lady herself must have warned me, and I found her with the blankets thrown off, tossing with fever. She's been getting worse ever since, in spite of all the doctor can do." Rose's fear, her despair, was written all over her. "She's delirious a good deal of the time, she raves, she says things. I'm afraid that *he'll* be in the room and he'll understand."

Now a cold fear settled around Moria's heart, squeezing it. She hadn't thought of that, it had never entered her mind. But if Eugenia did talk in delirium, if she called out for Liam, it would be all over. Even if Eugenia lived, and looking at her, Moria was desperately afraid that she wouldn't, once William learned any inkling of the truth, she and Liam and to a lesser degree even Moria herself would suffer consequences that she didn't dare to think about. She didn't care about herself. She was capable of defending herself, but Eugenia and Liam would be fully vulnerable to William's wrath.

"He'd never forgive her, he'd never forgive either of them. You know how he is, Moria. Her life would be twice the hell he made it before he softened a little, these last two years. And Liam!"

"Stop it!" Moria whispered, her voice agonized. "It isn't going to happen! Eugenia's going to be all right, she has to be all right!"

"Moria? It was good of you to come." William had entered the room so quietly that neither she nor Rose had heard him, but Moria knew that their whispers could not have reached him and her heart lurched with relief. "I see that she's sleeping. That's fine, it's what she needs."

"What does the doctor say? Why isn't he here?" Moria demanded. She slipped her hand gently from Eugenia's, and rose to face

William so that she could study his face, search it for any grain of hope.

"I won't try to allay your concern by misleading you. Bloomington is quite worried." Dr. Bloomington! Even the name brought dread to Moria's heart, because he was the best man to be had, William must have sent for him from New York City as soon as he'd known that Eugenia was so ill.

"He's resting now. I had him roused in the middle of the night, with orders to get here immediately. The prognosis isn't encouraging. Eugenia is very ill, and while we must hope for the best we should be prepared for the worst."

The words fell on Moria's heart like stones. No, it couldn't be, not Eugenia! How could she bear it if Eugenia were to die? And she hated herself for her selfishness, knowing that Liam would suffer more than she would. If Eugenia were to die, Liam would be bereft, the larger part of him would be buried with her.

"Will you send someone to Belvedere to tell them that I'm going to stay here for as long as I'm needed? I can't bear to leave her."

"Certainly. I'll take care of it immediately. It's as well that you don't return to the children for a while, anyway." It was Gayle he was thinking of, Moria knew, and not Reid, but she brushed the thought away. This was no time to be petty, to pounce on small details that meant nothing at all. All that mattered was Eugenia, that she must get well. "And you mustn't tire yourself, Moria. I appreciate your being here, but you must take care of yourself, we can't have you taking sick too."

For three days, Moria stayed on at Retreat, her heart breaking all over again every time she saw Eugenia and how the disease was sapping her strength. William refused to allow her to remain in the room for more than an hour at a time, but she was there, ready to be with her in a few seconds, any time Eugenia roused enough to ask for her.

Twice every day, and again in the evening, Moria visited the stables, ostensibly to see Jazir and Kamil. Under the cover of seeing the horses she had the opportunity to talk to Liam.

There wasn't any use in lying to him, of holding out false hope. He'd know before the words were out of her mouth that she was lying. And her heartbreak was doubled by seeing her father age years in those three days, in seeing all the light go out of his eyes, while his fists clenched and the muscles along his jawline were rigid as he struggled to hold his emotions in check.

"Liam, she loves you! She loves you so much, you were the most important person in her life, you brought her so much happiness, happiness she'd never have known if it hadn't been for you! You have that to remember, you must always remember it, because she'd want you to."

"I know," Liam said, but his eyes were bleak, so filled with suffering that Moria had to turn blindly away.

Now, late in the afternoon of the third day that Moria had been at Retreat, Eugenia's fingers curled around the locket that nestled between her breasts, holding it so tight that her fingers must have ached. She refused to let go of it, she tossed and murmured in protest when Rose and Moria tried to loosen her grip so that they could change her nightgown to make her more comfortable.

"Let her hold it," William instructed them. "It seems to comfort her. You should be touched that she sets such store by it because you gave it to her." But there was a speculative, thoughtful look in his eyes, and Moria shuddered. He'd never noticed Eugenia wearing the locket before her illness, she'd never mentioned it to him after she'd shown it to him after Moria had given it to her, when he'd wanted to know what gift Moria had brought her from Europe.

The New York City doctor stayed on, relegating his other patients to other doctors so that he could give all of his time to Eugenia. Moria knew that William was making it well worth his while, but she also suspected that the main reason that William was so anxious for Eugenia to live was that if she died, then one of his most envied possessions would be gone. Although Eugenia had now entered her forties, she was still one of the most beautiful women anyone had ever seen, and her grace and charm still set her above all others in the Hudson River Valley.

Her suspicions were confirmed when William said, almost absentmindedly, "If our beloved Eugenia dies, you will have to be my hostess. It's what she'd want. You and Gayle will have to spend a great deal more time at Retreat."

He was already planning to exploit Gayle just as he'd exploited Eugenia and herself! She wanted to strike him, to lash out at him with all the hatred that was stored up inside her, but she didn't dare. He wasn't worth it, any more than Tony was worth hating. Only Eugenia mattered, and her father and her children.

Now, late in the evening of the third day, William came into Eugenia's room and sent Rose away. "She's asleep. There's nothing you can do for her. I'll sit with her while you rest. Tell Moria that she must rest as well, I won't be needing her."

Rose didn't want to go, but there was no excuse she could find for staying. Something about the look in William's eyes sent a chill through her right to her bones.

As though she sensed that neither Moria nor Rose were with her, Eugenia stirred and began to murmur as soon as Rose had left.

William leaned over her, straining to understand what she was saying. Her fingers, he saw, were still closely clasped around the locket that Moria had given her. "Yes, Eugenia? What is it?"

She opened her eyes, but there was no recognition in them. They seemed to be looking beyond him, over his shoulder, at something or someone that wasn't there.

"Moria, darling..."

"She's near. She's resting."

Eugenia didn't hear him. Her fingers tightened convulsively around the locket. "Liam. Liam, my darling, my darling..."

William stiffened. His face was cold, alert, as he waited.

"Liam. My love, my darling..."

She was sinking fast. Her eyes had closed again. She was scarcely breathing. Slowly, deliberately, William pried her fingers loose from the locket and removed it from her neck. He turned it over in his hands and studied it, holding it close under the lamp, searching the smooth surface as some instinct told him that there was some secret here, the same instinct that had made him one of the richest men in the world by sensing other men's most closely guarded secrets.

He kept on examining the locket, patient, persevering. And then the locket opened as he touched the exact place in exactly the right way, and he stared down at the four wisps of hair that were enclosed in it. Black, shining, Moria's. And fair, silky, Reid's. Another of black, but finer, smaller, would have been taken from Gayle's head when she was only an infant. And one more, as dark as Moria's, but coarser, with a little gray mixed in.

Liam. Liam Donovan, his horse trainer, his Irish horse trainer!

Eugenia's breathing had changed, he heard the rale in it, and he stared down at the four wisps of hair for another moment before he snapped the locket closed again and replaced it around Eugenia's neck, and noted, his face like stone, that even now, breathing her last breaths on earth, her fingers tightened around it. Only then did he stride to the door to rouse the doctor.

16

Rose laid Eugenia's body out, washed it and dressed it for burial. Fiercely, she refused to let anyone help her, even Moria.

"It's for me to do," she told Moria. "Pick the dress she'll wear, and then leave me."

Numbly, hardly able to think, Moria went through Eugenia's wardrobe. The darker dresses she discarded immediately, she couldn't bear to think of Eugenia being buried in a dark dress, it had to be something light and beautiful, not somber, something that would bring out all her startling, fair beauty.

And she was beautiful, because death had been kind to her as it is to so many, erasing the lines of strain and care and pain, making her look years younger and at peace, as though she were only sleeping.

"This one," she said. It was the dress Eugenia had worn in the portrait in William's library, a light cream-colored satin that brought out the delicacy of her complexion and the fairness of her hair.

"Yes, that one. Leave us now, Moria girl. I'll call you when I'm done, you'll be the first to say good-bye to her, before even *him*."

Moria wanted nothing more than to return to the room of her childhood, to throw herself across the bed and cry until she could cry no more, until sheer exhaustion would give her the respite of sleep. But that would be weakness. There were things that had to be attended to, she had to offer William Northrup any help she could give.

William was in his study, papers spread in front of him. His face was expressionless as he looked up as he bade her enter.

"Is there anything I can do?" she asked him. "I chose the cream satin, I hope you approve."

"A good choice," William said. "No, there's nothing, Moria, except for you to let the servants know that everything must go on as usual. Make sure that they aren't shirking their duties."

As if they'd dare! Moria thought. If the king of England or the president of the United States were to die in this house, the servants wouldn't dare to deviate by one iota from their duties.

She spoke to the servants, knowing that it was a useless gesture. Mrs. Lindstrom had everything well in hand. But they appreciated her speaking to them, and that made it worthwhile.

Rose's work was done, and Eugenia looked so lovely as she lay in the freshly made-up bed that Moria had an icy sensation that she might open her eyes and smile at her.

"How did he look?" Rose asked her.

Moria didn't know what she meant, and Rose went on, "Did he look any different? Do you think our dear lady might have said anything, in her delirium, before she died?"

"No. No, I'm sure she didn't. He's just the same as he always is." How strange that she'd forgotten the danger, but her grief had shut everything else out of her mind. But Eugenia hadn't said anything, how could she have? She hadn't spoken for hours, she'd been barely conscious, there was no way she could have said anything.

She looked down at the woman who had been mother and

sister and friend to her, and something inside of her broke, and she began to cry. Rocked in Rose's arms, she cried and cried, until she was spent, until her body was only a quivering mass of exhausted hurt that still went on hurting.

"Don't try to hold it in, girl dear. Let it go, cry it out. Dear knows I'm going to, as soon as I'm alone. Cry it out, and then rest, because you'll have to see Liam before you leave, and you mustn't let him see you like this."

"Rose, how will he be able to bear it?" Moria cried, her voice filled with despair.

"He'll have to bear it. We all have to bear whatever comes our way, that's the way of the world, the way it always was and always will be. But you can help him, by being as strong as you can, and just by being." Not by being here, Moria noted, but just by being.

She couldn't cry any more, but she couldn't rest, either. She lay down for half an hour but then she got up again, and moved around the room she'd loved so much when she was a child, a teen-aged girl, the room that she still loved, touching things, saying good-bye to them just as she'd already said good-bye to Eugenia.

She wouldn't be coming back into this room again. She'd come to Retreat, so that the children could continue their riding instruction with Liam, and so that Liam would have the comfort of seeing them, but the door had closed on one part of her life, never to be opened again.

She had already determined, and she knew that she would be strong enough to carry it out, that she would never play the hostess in this house, that William was not going to have the satisfaction of showing her off, of showing off her daughter, that he'd taken in showing off her and Eugenia. William Northrup would have to find some other means to satisfy his ego.

She bathed her face in the fresh, cool water that one of the servants had brought to fill the ewer. Her eyes were swollen, and she held a cloth over them until the swelling was reduced. She removed the dress she was wearing, and changed back into her riding habit.

It was time to leave. She hesitated, and then decided against saying good-bye to Rose. Rose was still in Eugenia's room, spending these final hours alone with her, and it was her right to suffer her grief without intrusion. She'd understand why Moria had left without saying good-bye.

Swallowing against the lump in her throat, she descended the staircase. William's study door was closed, and she didn't rap to tell him that she was leaving. If she did, he'd send someone to the stables to have Jazir brought around and she wouldn't get to see Liam, and she had to see him before she left. She didn't even dare to think about how he must be feeling, his desperate grief. And there was no one he could turn to, he wouldn't even be able to show his grief, but must keep it all bottled up inside him.

As though he had been watching for her, Liam stepped out of the stables at her approach. "You'll be wanting Jazir, Mrs. Vancouver? I'll saddle him for you, it will only take a moment."

Calling him Liam now was almost more than she could bear. "Yes, Liam. I'm going home. There's nothing more I can do here."

And then she broke. Her voice was anguished as she cried out, "What are you going to do now, Papa? I'm so sorry, I'm so terribly sorry! If only . . . if only . . ."

"Easy, Moria." Liam's face flinched. "Get ahold of yourself."

He reentered the stable, and Moria followed him to watch him saddle Jazir. The stable was empty except for themselves and the horses. Liam's hands were steady as he arranged the saddle pad, as he placed the saddle in exactly the right spot on Jazir's back and tightened the girth, as he slipped the bridle over Jazir's head and the bit into his mouth.

"I've given it a lot of thought," he told her. "And I've made my decision. You're married, gone from me, you're as happy as you can expect to be with a man like Anthony Vancouver. You have no need of me. You have the children, and you're certainly in no need of anything I can give you. I'm going back to Ireland, I'm going to take up my work there again. They have need of me there."

272

Moria stared at him, aghast. "You can't! You're a wanted man, it's too dangerous, how can you even think of it? You'll be putting your neck in a noose!"

"It's been over two decades since I left. There'll be no one in authority who will recognize me. I wasn't blessed with eternal youth, Moria." His smile didn't reach his eyes, which were bleak, but the bleakness was hard, with a flaming purpose behind it. "It's something I have to do. Don't ask me to stay."

Moria could find no words, she only stood there looking at him, as if she had, in these few moments, to memorize every feature and every detail of him, to etch his image forever in her mind so that she could never forget.

Liam's voice was softer now, filled with kindness. "There will be little danger of my being recognized and taken. I'll go under another identity. Michael McCarthy will arrange it all, there's nothing the man can't manage through Tammany Hall. And I won't go back as empty-handed as I left. Michael has promised me, more than once, that if I ever did go back I'd take money with me, no fortune you understand, but enough to help, to make itself felt wherever it might be needed most."

There would be no holding him back, and Moria realized, her heart breaking all over again, that she wouldn't try even if she could. As he'd said, he had to do this thing, he'd never know another moment's peace or happiness unless he did.

"Then my prayers will go with you," she said. "Papa, I love you! I love you so much! Only promise me that you'll be careful."

"That I will, Moria. Dead men are of no use to Ireland, it's flesh and blood it's needing, and the will to fight."

"When are you going?" She didn't want to know, but she had to know. "The children will miss you."

"Reid will miss me to be sure. But he's young, he'll get over it. And I'll miss you, and Reid, and Gayle, more than I can say. But I have this thing to do. I'll be going as soon as Michael can arrange it

273

for me. A few weeks, at the most. We needn't say good-bye today, Moria. We'll be seeing each other again.''

Yes, he had to go. He had to do the only thing that could quench the fires of his tormented soul, he had to go back and fight for the cause that had almost cost him his life and that had turned him into an exile. Moria could see the beginnings of that peace of soul in his eyes even now. He knew where he was going and what he was going to do, and it was his salvation.

"Eugenia thought of you, right until the end," she told him now. "She told me to tell you how much she loved you. She died with her fingers curled around the locket that holds our hair.''

"I never doubted her love, but thank you for telling me." Liam's eyes were clear as he led Jazir from the stable and helped her to mount. "Good afternoon, Mrs. Vancouver. Take care on your way home. Are you sure you don't want me to see you safely there, or I could send one of the boys?''

"Thank you, Liam. I'll be perfectly all right. Jazir could make the trip between Retreat and Belvedere blindfolded.''

She didn't look back as she trotted Jazir out of the stableyard, although her heart broke with the effort not to. She set Jazir's head toward Belvedere, and as she rode away from Retreat she left the last of her girlhood behind her.

It seemed, these days, as if the dull ache in her heart would never go away. It had been over a month since Eugenia had died, but the ache that had started with her death went on and on. The morning had not yet come when she could wake up without knowing it was there before she even remembered why.

How could Liam have stood there so calmly, his face betraying nothing, when the person he held most dear in all the world was being laid into the ground, still another man's wife? Moria had felt as if she must die of grief for him, the grief he dared not show. And Reid had pressed close against her side at the graveyard, his hand in hers, his face showing his own heartrending grief for his "other" grandmother, the one he'd loved the best. Gayle's face had been wooden, unreadable, as if she were too young to understand and was thinking more about presenting a proper appearance than grieving over her loss.

At least it hadn't been raining. The day had been clear and bright, with just enough crispness in the air so that if Eugenia had still been alive, she and Moria and Reid and Gayle would have spent the morning riding, savoring the fresh green scents, while Liam would have kept a sharp eye on the children's horsemanship at the same time that he pointed out a squirrel that their eyes might miss, or a mole poking its tiny nose from its hole.

"Miss Gayle, loosen your top rein just a trifle. And mind that sharp bend up ahead, I've seen many a more experienced rider than you go off when they took that curve at a gallop."

But Gayle would already have set Starbright into a gallop, refusing to be ordered not to do something, laughing with triumph when she took the curve without mishap and then reining aside to jump a fallen log. "Born to the saddle," Liam said. "It's only her recklessness that worries me, Mrs. Vancouver, not her ability."

Gone, all gone. She'd never ride with Eugenia again, the five of them would never be together on a spring morning, their hearts filled with joy.

She heard footsteps pounding down the hallway outside of her room. Someone was running, so fast that the very sound was alarming in this house where nobody except Gayle ever ran, defying Estelle's disapproval and sure that Jacob would back her up. But this wasn't Gayle, Moria knew Gayle's footsteps too well, and even before her mind leaped to the conclusion that it must be Reid, her son burst into the room and threw himself at her with such force that her elbow struck against a vase and sent water and flowers stewing across the carpet.

"Mother, it's Liam!" Reid choked out. His face was twisted, and he was crying, his shoulders shaking as he burrowed his head against her, clinging to her.

Moria's lips went so dry that she could feel them cracking. "Liam? Reid, tell me! What about Liam? Please, God, no..."

275

"It was a fire. His cottage caught fire. Mother, he's dead, Liam's dead!" Reid's grief was heartrending, but Moria's shock was so great that for a moment she couldn't move to comfort him. Father, father!

It wasn't true, there was some mistake, how could Papa's cottage have caught fire? Reid hadn't heard it right, or the message had been garbled, it was some other horse trainer on some other estate, or no one had been in the cottage, whoever it had been had gotten out.

Reid's eyes were open now, filled with stark tragedy, but there were sparks of fury underneath his agony. "Mother, they say he'd been drinking, they say he was drunk! They say he was drunk and overturned the lamp beside his bed while he was sleeping! But it isn't true, it's a lie, Liam never drank! And he was never careless, he told me, and Gayle, too, all the time, how we had to be especially careful about fire, that it was an unforgivable sin not to be careful! How can they say he was drunk, that he was careless? I don't believe it, I'll never believe it, Liam wouldn't have!"

It seemed to take moments for Reid's words to sink in and make sense. Liam, drunk? But he didn't drink, he hadn't had a drink for years, even one, since that time so long ago when Moria's engagement had been announced at the ball given in her and Tony's honor, and he'd gone off to New York City afterward and Michael McCarthy had brought him home so bruised and battered that he never would have made it on his own. That had been the last time Liam had ever touched a drop.

Could he have got drunk because of Eugenia's death, because he'd lost her forever? No! Liam had accepted her death, he'd closed the door on that chapter of his life and his eyes had been fixed on the future, on going back to Ireland. He'd told her that he had work to do there, that it was a thing he had to do, and there had been no trace of weakness in him. Reid was right. Liam hadn't been drinking, he hadn't been drunk, and furthermore he had never had a lamp close to his bed in his life. Just as Reid had reminded her that he had cautioned him and Gayle about carelessness with fire, Moria

276

could remember him cautioning her when she had been a little girl, and insisting that lamps must be placed where there was no danger of them being knocked over.

He hadn't been drinking, he hadn't been drunk. She knew it as well and as truly as though Liam himself had appeared before her and told her.

"I'm going over there. I'm going to ride over right now," Reid told her. His sobbing had stopped, and his face, although still as white as paper, was composed. "I don't know when I'll be back. Don't worry about me, Mother. I'll be all right."

"Wait for me. It'll only take me a moment to change. Go to the stable and have Jazir saddled for me as well as Jumper." With frantic haste, without bothering to pull the bell cord to summon Elsie to help her, Moria began stripping off her dress.

Estelle met her at the bottom of the staircase, her usually placid face startled. "You're going out? You're riding? With your dear mother scarcely in her grave? Moria, dear, do you think you should?"

"I'm going to Retreat. Liam has been killed in an accident."

"I know, dear. Reid is most dreadfully upset. He was very fond of Mr. Donovan."

"We were all fond of him. He was our friend. That's why I'm going." Before Estelle could open her mouth to voice another protest, Moria brushed past her and was out the door.

She and Reid rode silently, putting the horses to the fastest pace consistent with safety. Even now, Liam's training was so instilled in their minds that they took care not to violate his rules.

They could smell the acrid smoke as they approached Retreat, traces of it still heavy in the air. Reid's face went a shade paler, and he pressed his lips together, biting them. The odor made Moria tremble, and her own face was so white that if anyone else had seen her they would have thought that she was at the point of death.

"I'm going to the stables. They'll tell me what happened," Reid told her. "Pat will tell me the truth."

"All right, Reid." She wanted to reach out and touch him, she

277

wanted to call him darling, but this wasn't the time. This was something he had to do on his own. He was only eleven years old, but this morning he had become what he would be when he had attained full manhood, a person who could face things with no shoulder to lean on, who could bear his own loss and sorrow. "I'll be with Rose."

Mrs. Lindstrom opened the door for her. The housekeeper's face still retained traces of shock at what had happened. "Miss Moria! This is a surprise. Mr. Northrup is in his study, I'll tell him you're here."

"No, thank you, Mrs. Lindstrom. I'm going up to see Rose. Is she in her room?"

Startled at her thought, because it was the first time it had crossed her mind through the grief she still felt over Eugenia's death, Moria realized that Rose might not be at Retreat much longer. William Northrup wasn't one to keep on any servant who was no longer needed, and besides, Rose hated him so much that she wouldn't want to stay on now that Eugenia was gone.

She'd come to Belvedere, of course. Anything else was unthinkable. Tony would have no objection, he let her have her own way in everything as long as she let him have his, and Estelle was fond of her, she'd understand why she wanted Rose with her. Jacob wouldn't care one way or the other, he was too immersed in his business affairs to care what servants his wife and his daughter-in-law chose to have in the house.

Rose was kneeling beside her bed, her olivewood rosary in her hands. Her eyes were red, her face looked years older than it had the last time Moria had seen her, even after Eugenia's death.

"It's you, then," Rose said. She got to her feet and held out her arms. "I thought you would come."

"Rose, what happened? Reid said that they say . . ."

Rose's face was suddenly grim, and her eyes blazed with fury.

"They say it was an accident, they say he was drunk. Liam, drunk! But it's a black lie, there wasn't a drop in his cottage and there hadn't been for years, as who should know better than I? I saw

278

him yesterday evening, I went to see him late, before I went to bed, to ask him if he knew yet just when he'd be leaving. I thought he might take me with him to New York City, that Michael McCarthy might help me find a place to live, because I can't bear staying here now that Eugenia's gone even if he would let me stay on. I wouldn't be needing any help, I've saved nearly every penny of my wages all these years.

"And Liam wasn't drunk last night, he hadn't been drinking, he was making plans, thinking of nothing but getting back to Ireland and taking up his work there. He didn't die by accident, Moria. He was murdered."

All the strength went out of Moria as if someone had pulled a plug and her blood had drained out of her. Her legs went out from under her and she groped for Rose's rocking chair and sat down in it, her eyes blank with shock at hearing the words she hadn't allowed herself to think until this moment.

"*He* knew," Rose said. "I know he knew, although he never gave a sign. And who could ever tell what was going through that black mind of his, him who kept such a cold face turned to the world that it was as if he had no emotions at all? He knew about Liam and Eugenia, she must have let something slip in her delirium when she was dying."

She turned to her bureau, and picked something up and came back to place it in Moria's hand. "Look. Her locket. I left it on her, for her to be buried with, she would have wanted it, your hair and Liam's and Reid's and that last tiny scrap of Gayle's. She always wore it, she never took it off. And he didn't say a word, but when I went to his study yesterday to ask him if I should pack her clothes away and lock her room, he was sitting there at his desk, his face like stone, and he had the locket in his hand and it was open."

Her own face was like stone now. "I stole it, Moria. I crept downstairs after everyone was asleep, and went into his study and he'd left it in plain sight on his desk and I took it, because I wasn't going to let him have it. I didn't know then, it hadn't come over me, as numb as I was with Eugenia's dying, that he could have recognized that fourth scrap of hair, Liam's hair.''

She closed Moria's fingers around the trinket. "Take it. Keep it. Then let him search my room, let him turn it inside out, it won't be here. He'll not have it, the murdering devil! If he asks me about it I'll tell him the truth, that I gave it to you, and he can't do anything but order me from the house and I'm going, anyway. He won't ask you to give it back to him, he wouldn't want anyone to know he could be so hard and mean, not so soon after Eugenia's death.''

"He knew," Moria said. The locket was growing warm from the pressure of her fingers. "You're right, Rose. He must have known." He'd known about Liam and Eugenia, but he didn't know about her, that she was Liam's daughter. If Eugenia had let that slip, as well, he wouldn't have been planning to have Moria act as his hostess now that Eugenia was dead, he wouldn't have been planning to exploit Gayle as well.

"Yes, he knows. And he killed Liam, I'm as sure of that as I am that I'm still breathing. He murdered Liam, and may his soul burn in hell for all eternity!''

Looking at her, the locket seeming to burn her fingers with a fire as hot as that which had taken her father's life, Moria knew that Rose was right. William Northrup had killed her father, he had murdered him, because he'd found out, after all these years, about Liam's and Eugenia's love for each other.

"Where is he?" she asked. She was startled at the calmness of her voice. "My father, not Mr. Northrup."

Rose's face worked. "He's in the gardener's shed. They set up a board on sawhorses until a casket can be brought. He wasn't badly burned, it was the smoke that got him. Pat smelled it, he's always been a light sleeper, and he smelled smoke and he got up from his cot in the stableboy's cottage and checked the stables and barns, and then he saw that it was coming from Liam's cottage, and he broke the window to get in and he pulled Liam out, but it was too late. Liam was still in his bed, and the curtains beside his bed had just caught fire but the mattress and the blanket were still only smoldering. He never woke up, the smoke killed him while he was still asleep."

"Rose, pack your things. I'll have the coachman hitch up the pony trap and I'll drive you back to Belvedere with me. Reid will lead Jazir back. I'll come back here for you after I've seen my father."

Rose nodded. Whether she would stay at Belvedere with Moria, doing whatever could be found for her to do, or whether she would contact Michael McCarthy and go to live in the city was something she didn't know yet, and at the moment she didn't much care. She only wanted to get out of this house where a murderer lived, a man she couldn't bear to set eyes on ever again.

Moria found Liam where Rose had told her that she would find him. Reid was still there, standing beside the makeshift bier, his face tearing at her heart. And going to stand beside her son, looking down at her father's face, something inside her grew and swelled until it burst.

His face was cold when she touched it with her fingertips. Part of his hair was singed, around the temples, and his eyebrows were singed, although there were no other signs that he had been burned. He hadn't awakened when the fire in his mattress had started. The heavy woolen blanket had retarded the flames, only billowing out clouds of heavy, acrid smoke. Why hadn't he awakened, he who had a fetish about fire because of his lifelong work with horses?

There was only one answer. He must have been drugged. Something had been put in his food or drink that had sent him into such a deep sleep that he hadn't wakened when William had entered his cottage in the middle of the night to overturn the lamp.

"Pat told me that there was a bottle on the table beside his bed. A whiskey bottle. He said it was nearly empty and that he could smell whiskey on him when he dragged him out." Reid's eyes were dry and bereft. "Maybe he did get drunk, Mother. Maybe he drank, only nobody knew it." His voice sounded ragged, as though he had just found out that his lifelong idol had had feet of clay.

Damn you for this, too, Moria thought, damn you for destroying a boy's faith in his friend, the best friend he ever had!

She went to look for Pat, and found him sitting on a pile of straw in the stable, his eyes red although he was a grown man now.

"Pat, tell me everything you know," she demanded. "Did anything unusual happen last night, before the fire?"

Pat shook his head. "No, Miss Moria. I saw Liam earlier, a little while before he went to bed. He always liked a glass of milk before he went to sleep, and I'd fallen into the habit of going to the kitchen to get it for him, Cook left it sitting in the icebox for me to pick up, and she'd leave me a little something too, cake or cookies or a piece of pie although Liam never wanted anything but the milk. Last night was the same as always. He drank his milk and I ate the piece of pie Cook left for me, lemon it was, and I told him he didn't know what he was missing, and then I left because we both had to get to bed. It was a little later than usual, that's all, because Rose was with him late and I waited until she'd gone before I fetched the milk. I walked to the house with her, that's how I got in so late, she'd left the kitchen door unlocked when she went to see Liam."

A glass of milk left in the icebox for Liam. And William would have known that, because William made a point of knowing anything that he could turn to his own purpose. He would have checked up on Liam's movements, his habits, to determine how he could manage to murder him, and the milk had been made to order for him.

And a resolution was born in her, and took root and grew, and she vowed that he wasn't going to get away with it. For years, for nearly all of her married life, he had tortured Eugenia, made her life a living hell. For years, after Liam had come to Retreat and Eugenia had fallen in love with him, William had stood between them, guaranteeing by his very existence that they could never belong to each other fully, that their love would bring them as much pain as it brought them comfort and joy.

Moria hated him. She had always hated him, ever since she had learned the truth about him and the way he treated Eugenia. But that hatred paled to nothing now, as this new hatred, blazing so hot that it was like a white light all around her, surged through her body and forged its flesh and blood into steel.

He wasn't going to get away with it. She'd see him brought to justice, and she swore as she looked at her father's lifeless body one last time that she would see him avenged. Looking up into her face when a shudder passed through her, Reid wondered why his mother's face was so white and expressionless while her eyes burned with a fire he had never seen there before.

17

Tony stared at Moria as if she were a stranger, someone he had never seen before. A stark-raving mad stranger, asking of him something that he would not and could not give, not now and not ever.

"What possible reason can you have for making such a wild accusation?" he demanded. "How can you possibly have jumped to the conclusion that your own adoptive father, that William Northrup, murdered his horse trainer? You've taken leave of your senses, you're ill. You'd better go to bed until your mind clears."

Moria jerked away from his touch as he moved to feel of her forehead to see if she were running a fever. "I'm not sick, and I'm completely serious. William Northrup murdered Liam, and I want you to help me set things in motion so that he'll be arrested for his crime and punished for it. I want him to hang!"

"The man was drunk. He got drunk and set his bed on fire. That's an established fact. What's come over you, Moria? I know you were fond of him, but he was only a horse trainer, a servant. For the life of me I can't understand why you've gone so to pieces over his

Lydia Lancaster

death that you can stand here saying things against a man who had no reason in the world to harm him!''

"William Northrup had every reason to want him dead," Moria told him. She'd been afraid that she'd have to tell him the truth about Liam and Eugenia before he'd act to help her in her determined quest for justice, and the thought had sickened her to her soul. Such an admission, that her beloved Eugenia, whom the whole of the Hudson River Valley had looked up to and admired, had had a love affair of years' duration with Liam Donovan, the Northrups' horse trainer, tore at her vitals. But she had to tell Tony, or he would never believe her and he'd do nothing to help her see William arrested and made to pay for his crime.

"He had every reason," she repeated. "Eugenia and Liam loved each other, they'd been lovers for years."

Tony's eyes widened, and even his worldliness was shocked, a shock that showed in his suddenly slack jaw. "You can't be serious! Eugenia Northrup, and a horse trainer?"

"They loved each other. And William found out. Eugenia talked in her delirium just before she died, and called for Liam, and William found a lock of his hair in the locket I brought her from England. My hair was in it, and then his, and Reid's and Gayle's, the four people she loved. But she loved Liam the most of all, it was always Liam."

"And you knew it, and you kept quiet about it!" The first shock of Moria's revelation having passed, Tony looked at his wife with admiration. "I wouldn't have thought you capable of such deception, not with your overdeveloped sense of morality! What surprises me is that you went on loving Eugenia even after you found out that she was an adulteress, a woman who indulged in a cheap affair with her horse trainer!"

His smile turned to a look of pure astonishment as Moria's hand lashed out and struck him in the face, the full force of all her strength behind it.

"Don't you dare say that! It wasn't a cheap affair, they loved each other as few people have ever loved each other since the beginning of time! Don't you ever say that about Eugenia, or Liam, either!''

"What the devil!'' In all the years of their marriage, Moria had never been this angry, even when she'd learned about his one-night affair with Helen Forrester and his recurring affair with Veronica, and all the other lesser affairs that he still indulged in. She'd been angry, she'd screamed at him and thrown things at him and even struck him, but there had never been anything to match her anger now.

Comprehension dawned in his eyes, as he thought he had the answer, along with astonishment. "Don't tell me that you had a crush on him too! I know he was a handsome devil, but he was old enough to be your father!''

The words were out before Moria could bite them back. Her voice was filled with cold rage as she blazed back, "Damn you for that, Tony. *He was my father!*''

For the first time in his life, Tony was struck dumb. He stared at her, his face blank with shock. Her father! But that wasn't possible, Moria was an orphan, her father had been a Lieutenant Compton, who was killed in the war, and Eugenia had persuaded William to take her into their home after she'd learned about her from a friend of Eugenia's family. How could Liam Donovan, an Irish horse trainer, be Moria's father? He couldn't have been, there was no way that it could be true!

"He was my father, and William Northrup killed him, and I'm going to see him punished for it!'' Moria said. Her voice wasn't loud, but it held such a cold ring of truth that it snapped Tony back to reality. And the reality included his mother, because Estelle had chosen the exact instant when Moria had uttered that last statement to rap on their door and open it, her peace-loving nature shaken by what she'd been sure were voices raised in anger. A tiff, she must do something about it, if Tony was misbehaving again she'd really speak to him very severely, he shouldn't cause Moria so much grief, the girl was a good wife to him and a perfect daughter-in-law.

Estelle stood just inside the door, her hands clasped together and wringing, her face gone pasty and crumpled. There was nothing wrong with her ears, she never misunderstood what she heard, and she'd heard Moria say that Liam Donovan, the Northrups' horse trainer, was her father, and that Mr. Northrup had killed him!

"Moria, what are you talking about? Whatever can you mean?" she asked, her voice shaking.

Tony's reaction was stronger. His face as white as his mother's, he shouted, "Say that again, Moria! I can't believe I heard you right! Say it again so I'll be very sure what you mean!"

It was all over. She'd said it, and it was the truth, and there was no way she could retract her words, and now that it was out in the open at last she wouldn't have retracted them if she could. Liam was her father, and she was proud of it!

"Liam Donovan was my father," she said. "Lieutenant Compton's little girl, the girl who was just my age, went to Boston to live with a relative there. Eugenia's sister arranged the whole thing, so that my father could have me at Retreat, so that I'd have all the advantages he wanted for me. I had to learn my part, I was coached until I knew it by heart. William Northrup never had an inkling of the deception that was perpetrated on him. But he found out about my father and Eugenia, and he killed my father for it, and we've got to see that he pays for it. He murdered my father, he murdered him in cold blood, he drugged him and overturned the lamp on his bed. I can prove it, Rose knows, and we know how he did it, and if you ever loved me at all, if you have any feeling for me at all, you'll help me now!"

"For the love of God, be quiet!" Tony lashed out at her. "Don't you realize that if what you say is true that it will ruin us if it gets out? My wife, Eugenia Northrup's adopted daughter, the daughter of an Irish horse trainer! We'd be ruined, we'd be laughingstocks, it would destroy our children! Be quiet, and let me think!"

"There's nothing to think about. It is true, every word of it. And if you won't help me, then I'll find a way to bring William Northrup to justice myself. Rose will confirm everything I've said, to the authorities, and there's Pat, who brought Liam the milk that Mr.

Northrup had drugged, and who knew that Liam never allowed a lamp near his bed, who knew, as Rose and all of the other servants at Retreat know, that Liam never drank.''

With a strangled moan, Estelle crumpled into a heap on the floor, unconscious. Cursing, Tony knelt beside her. "Help me loosen her clothing, for God's sake! She will wear those tight stays, trying to have a waistline! Get those buttons undone.''

Her fingers numb, Moria worked at the buttons. "Find Rose. She'll know what to do. I'm sorry your mother overheard, Tony, but as long as you intended to refuse to help me, anyway, it would have all come out when I go to the police.''

"You're going nowhere!'' Tony's voice was vicious. "You're going nowhere and you're saying nothing! My God, the daughter of an Irish horse trainer!''

If Moria had had any love for Tony left in her, it died at that moment when she heard the revulsion in his voice. But she had no time to mourn for it. Her life had just one purpose now, and that was to see William Northrup hang.

Jacob sat at his desk, ponderous and immovable, his face without a trace of emotion.

"I have heard all the evidence, and there is only one conclusion to be drawn. This young woman's allegations are without foundation. Although the servant Rose O'Riley has for some unknown reason chosen to back up this young woman's wild accusations, they have been refuted by this young woman's former personal maid, Dora Sisti. This Dora Sisti has told me that Liam Donovan was in the habit of drinking, that he drank a great deal. She has told me that she herself had an illicit liaison with the man, and so she knows of his habits because of the time she spent with him. That the horse trainer managed to conceal his habit of drunkenness from everyone else at Retreat is not to be wondered at, as he would certainly have been discharged if it had come to anyone's attention.''

"She's lying! Can't you see that she's lying?''

"Dora Sisti visited the horse trainer on the evening of his death,''

Jacob went on imperturbably. "There are no restrictions placed on her movements after her hours of duty are over, my wife is much too lenient in such matters."

"Ask at the stables! Ask if she took a horse and buggy, or a pony trap!"

"We will not ask at the stables. Too many people know of this affair as it is, I will not have any more talk or speculation. Dora Sisti swore on the Bible that what she told me is true. She visited the horse trainer on the evening of his death, and he was drinking, he was in a state of sodden drunkenness before she left."

He fixed his protruding eyes on Moria, whom he had deliberately refrained from calling by her name or even his daughter-in-law.

"You will seal your lips and never utter another word of what you think you know. This family will not be ruined by a horse trainer. William Northrup and I have common interests, common enterprises. I will not allow him to be brought down to the detriment of my own name and fortune. If it is necessary, I will have you locked in your room, I will have you certified, by a competent physician, as being insane, and you will be kept under restraint here at Belvedere for all the rest of your life, not even allowed to see your children. If you will not give me your word that you will not make any attempt to pursue this matter, that you will make no attempt to contact the authorities or to tell anyone what you suspect, you will learn that I am fully capable of doing as I have said I will. There are rooms in the attic that are never used, you would not be the first person who was locked up in a family home, never to be seen again."

He meant it. He'd do it. With a strangled cry, Moria turned and ran from the room, to find Rose and let out all her grief and frustration.

"There's nothing you can do, mavourneen," Rose told her, her face hard and grim. "I know these people, I know what they're capable of. The Vancouvers and the Northrups have power such as common mortals can never fight. Lips can be silenced, officials can be bought, doctors can be coerced into signing papers."

"It isn't right!" Moria cried. "Rose, it isn't right!"

"Of course it isn't right. But you've yourself to think of, and if you don't care about yourself, there are your children. Even if you managed to escape and tell what you know, it would do Eugenia and Liam no good now. They're together in heaven, and you know that they would grieve to see you ruin your life and the lives of your children. Think of what it would do to them! You know how people in their society are, they'd be shamed, every chance of their finding happiness would be ruined for as long as they live."

Moria knew that everything Rose had told her was true. Not only would she be circumvented, locked up, her children kept from her, but now that she had had time to think she knew that she couldn't drag Liam's name, Eugenia's name, in the dirt, for the entire country to gossip about and laugh at. Let them spend eternity in peace, as Rose had said.

But there was one thing she could do, and she was going to do it.

There was no one in the entrance foyer, almost as large as that at Retreat, when she descended the stairs dressed to ride. But Tony, who was still closeted with his father, heard her even though she moved so quietly, because he came out into the hall and intercepted her.

He grasped her wrist, his fingers digging in cruelly, and held her. "Where do you think you're going? What mad scheme have you hatched now?"

"I'm going riding," she told him, and her voice was calm. "I need to get out of the house, to ride. I'm not going to the police, if that's what you want to know, or to tell anyone the things that I know to be true. Let me go, please."

Tony stared at her, trying to see by her face if she were telling the truth.

"See that you remember the consequences of any rash action, then. And don't be long, or I'll come looking for you." Right at the moment, he wanted nothing more than to have her out of his sight. His wife, a horse trainer's daughter! And she'd known it, she'd deceived him, she'd made a fool of him, and if she didn't get out of

291

his sight immediately he wasn't sure that he could control himself not to strike her.

Moria left the house without another look at him. If Tony didn't want to look at her, she felt doubly the same about him, the husband who'd betrayed her on their honeymoon, the husband who'd had one affair after another during all the years of their marriage, the husband who had now made this final, irrevocable betrayal by refusing to stand by her when she'd begged him for his help. As far as Moria was concerned, their marriage was dead. They'd continue to live under the same roof, they'd appear in public together, no one outside the immediate family would have any inkling that there was anything wrong between them. But Tony would never come into her bed again, she would never speak to him again except in public, the last vestige of her love for him had crumbled into ashes when he'd refused to help her bring William Northrup to justice.

She didn't push Jazir on the ride to Retreat. There was no hurry about what she was going to do. She knew that William would be there, it was too soon after Eugenia's death for him to be away on business, he had to give the appearance of a grieving husband, for his reputation's sake.

Pat came to take Jazir when she arrived at the estate, and she was in complete control of herself as she asked to see William and was invited into his study.

A look of genuine pleasure crossed William's face, which so seldom showed any emotion at all. Looking at Moria always gave him pleasure. She was his most prized possession, and the fact that she was now a married woman made her no less his possession. And now there was Gayle as well, an exact replica of her mother, and the mother and the daughter would dominate the Hudson River Valley society for years to come, their beauty a legend in their own time. William's mind was already filled with plans for exploiting their beauty to his own advantage, for managing everything so that no one would ever forget that they belonged to him, and men's envy of him would grow and his ego would be fed enough to satisfy even him.

He rose from his desk, extending his hand. "Moria! It was good of you to come. You didn't bring Gayle, or Reid?'' Reid's name was said as an afterthought, and Moria was fully aware of it, and it only strengthened her resolve.

She shook her head as William pulled a chair forward for her. ''I'll stand, thank you. What I have to say to you won't take long, but there are things that you should know.''

William's face froze. Was it possible that Moria knew about Eugenia and Donovan, that she was going to tell him about their love affair? For a moment he was so shaken by anger that he almost lost control, but then his mind, always logical, told him that as much as Moria had loved Eugenia, she would never betray her now after Eugenia's death.

''Yes, Moria? You sound very serious. Are you sure you don't want me to ring for refreshments? Whatever it is you want to tell me, you might as well be comfortable while you do it.''

There was no answering smile. Moria's face was colder than he had ever seen it, and there was an anger underneath the coldness that shook even him.

''This isn't a social visit, Mr. Northrup. I came to tell you that I know you killed my father.''

For a moment, William was so baffled that he could only stare at her, wondering if he could possibly have heard her wrong. Killed her father? What was she talking about? Her father had been killed in the war. Or, and the possibility disturbed him, had something set her to brooding about her father, had some tale of his wartime activities, of the way he'd made a considerable part of his fortune by supplying shoddy goods to the Union Army, come to her ears and in some obscure female way she blamed him for Lieutenant Compton's death?

''I'm afraid I don't understand you, Moria. You'll have to make yourself more clear.''

''Liam Donovan was my father, Mr. Northrup. He was Eugenia's lover, and that is why you killed him, but he was my father long before he ever met Eugenia. She and he together, with Eugenia's sister's help, concocted the plan to bring me here, to foist me off on you as an orphan, so that I could live here at Retreat and my father could see me every day, and I could have all the things that he could never get for me. And I was happy, you'll never know how happy I was except for my hatred of you! I always hated you, for what you did to Eugenia, who was the best and sweetest and most gentle woman who ever lived! I knew everything you ever did to her, and I hated you for it, but most of all. I hated you because you didn't die, because some accident didn't snuff out your cruel, sadistic life, so that Eugenia could be free to marry the man she loved, my father!''

William's face had turned to stone, but a vein in his forehead was throbbing, pounding so that pain shot all through his head. The girl was mad, raving, there wasn't a word of truth in what she was saying! Liam Donovan's daughter? It wasn't possible, he didn't believe it, he could not believe it, and retain his sanity.

Moria's lips curved, but it wasn't a smile. ''Yes, Mr. Northrup. I was born in Ireland. Liam Donovan was my father, and my mother's name was Molly. I was six years old when my father had to take us and flee for his life because of his activities against the British. We came to this country on one of the ships that were called floating coffins. I remember it all, every detail, even though I was so young. The crowding, the hunger, the sickness and the stench of that ship, and the deaths, so many deaths!

''We were Irish immigrants, poor Irish immigrants. My father could barely find enough work to keep us from starving. He and my mother wanted so much for me, never for themselves but only for me! Sometimes we were hungry. We lived in tenement rooms, and in the winters we were cold when there wasn't enough money to buy coal or wood. We were ragged, but we were never dirty, and we were proud.

''And then my father fought for this country, because he believed in freedom, freedom for all men. And while he was fighting, my mother became ill, nursing me through an illness that nearly killed me. My father was wounded, he was invalided home because he was of no more use to the country he had fought for in a war that made men like you richer and richer while the men who died for you were supplied with rancid, rotting food and with boots that disintegrated on their feet and with rifles that misfired. My mother died just a little while after he came home. But he promised her, on her deathbed, that things would be better for me. And so I was brought here, and you accepted me, after you'd seen that I would be an asset to you, another possession you could show off to the world. You exploited me, just as you exploited Eugenia, for your own selfish purposes. But it wasn't the daughter of a war hero you were nurturing and showing off as one of your most prized possessions, Mr. Northrup. *It was the daughter of your wife's lover, Liam Donovan, your horse trainer!"*

The vein in William's temple was throbbing more wildly now, so that Moria's eyes were mesmerized by it, wondering if it were going to burst. But she wasn't going to wait to see. She'd done what she had come here to do, she had destroyed the thing that Mr. Northrup held most dear, his belief that she, and now her daughter, Gayle, were the possessions that other men envied him above all others.

"Your jewels are flawed, Mr. Northrup," she said. "Flawed, and worth nothing." And with that, she left him, satisfied that this man whom she hated would never spend another peaceful moment as long as he lived.

His eyes glazed, his head filled with the pain that was driving him mad, William rushed from his study into the library where the portraits of Eugenia and Moria, of Reid and Gayle, dominated the room, on display for the purpose of adding to the envy of him of all his fellowmen. His hands were shaking wildly as he grasped the poker from its stand beside the fireplace and raised it over his head and struck at the portraits, his blows frenzied as he struck and struck again until they hung in shreds, until there was scarcely a scrap of them left to show what they had been. His breath came in painful gasps, rattling in his throat, as his blurred eyes surveyed the damage he had wrought, the destruction of what had been his life.

Only then did the poker fall from hands that had gone numb. It clattered to the hearth, and the noise of its falling made something inside his head explode, and then he, too, fell, to lie motionless on top of the instrument of the portraits' destruction.

"What did you do to him?" they shouted. "What did you say?"

Moria's hands were folded in her lap, and they were still, with no trace of trembling, just as her face was still and calm as she faced their rage. First Tony, and now Jacob, shouting the same question over and over. "We know you went there. We have already been told that. And you had no sooner left than he destroyed the portraits, and fell into a stroke!"

"I told him the truth. I thought he had the right to know," Moria answered them. "I told him that Liam Donovan was my father, and that I knew he had killed him. If he suffered a stroke, it is only just punishment. Maybe God is just after all, because if he'd died, then his suffering would be over, but now he may live for years and suffer every moment of them, suffer a tenth of the amount of suffering that he caused Eugenia, a hundredth part of the suffering that he should suffer because he murdered my father."

None of the tense, emotion-ridden people in Jacob's study knew that there was an eavesdropper just outside the closed door. Such a thing, at Belvedere, was unheard of. But there was one person in the house who knew that something extraordinary was going on, because she made it her business to know everything that concerned Moria. She knew, because all of the servants at Belvedere knew, that William Northrup had suffered a stroke after Moria had visited him, and that before he'd suffered the stroke he had destroyed Moria's portrait and those of her children.

"Taken with a fit, as though he'd gone stark mad!" was what the messenger from Retreat had said, and it had spread through the servants at Belvedere like wildfire.

Her ear pressed against the study door, Dora's heart leaped with an elation that she had never dreamed was possible. Here, at last, after all the years of her festering jealousy of the girl who had been set above her, a girl who by rights had deserved no more than Dora herself had been handed by fate, was the ultimate weapon that could be used to hurt her. Not only to hurt her, to destroy her, but to hurt her where it would do her the most damage, through her children!

Her eyes gleaming with spiteful fire, Dora crept away from the door and then sped up the servants' staircase at the back of the house, to go in search of Reid and Gayle, who had been sent to the schoolroom to assure that they would not overhear anything their elders were discussing.

Reid looked up from a sketch he was making, a likeness of Gayle as she sat in the window seat with a book on her lap. The likeness was uncanny, Reid had developed a talent that his tutors were certain could be developed into greatness if only his father and his grandfather would allow him to become an artist. But today Reid's heart was not in what he was doing. He was aware that untoward events were taking place, that his mother's adoptive father, the man he'd been taught from earliest childhood to call grandfather, had been taken with an illness that had affected his mind and that he'd had a stroke after he'd destroyed the portraits that Reid had loved to look at every time he'd visited Retreat. How beautiful his mother was in that portrait, as beautiful as a queen, and Grandmother Eugenia too. Surely they were the two most beautiful women in the world, and his heart had always swelled with love and pride every time he had looked at their painted likenesses.

Whatever could have made Grandfather Northrup do such a thing? It was so completely out of character that Reid could not fathom it. William Northrup was the most coldly emotionless man he'd ever known even though he had always shown pride and fondness for Reid's mother and sister.

Dora's face was a mask of spite as she said, "Children, I have something to tell you."

She'd have to leave Belvedere after she told them. The Vancouvers' fury would know no bounds. She'd be thrown out without a recommendation to help her secure another position, she'd have only her savings to fall back on until she could find something else, and that something else would without doubt be a much more menial position than she occupied here because the elite did not employ servants without a letter of character. But even if she starved to death, it would be worth it.

It didn't take her long to tell it, everything she had just learned. And the words were hardly out of her mouth, the first immobilizing shock of them worn off, before Gayle was screaming at her, her face contorted with rage.

"Liar, liar! It isn't true, you're making it up, you're a wicked, wicked woman!" Before Reid, his face gone white, could catch her arm to stop her, Gayle was out of the schoolroom and racing down the stairs to burst into Grandfather Jacob's study, something she would never have dared to do even as much as the old man doted on her if she hadn't been frantic with shock.

"Mama, Father, you're going to have to send Dora away, she's telling the most dreadful lies! She said that Liam was our grandfather, that he was Mama's father! She just told us, Reid and me!"

"God in heaven!" The words burst from Tony before he could stop them. "How did the bitch find out? Gayle, stop that screaming! What are we to do about it, Father, how are we to shut the woman's mouth before the whole country finds out?"

Reid had entered the study on Gayle's heels, and his eyes went from one adult to another until they came to rest on his mother's face. Moria's face was white, stricken. "Gayle, darling . . ."

"Say it isn't true, say it right now, this instant!" Gayle screamed.

Reid wanted to strike her. The strength of his impulse frightened him. In all his life, he'd never struck his sister, or even wanted to, even when she deserved it. He'd held his own against her, his natural good nature enabling him to tolerate her periods of unreasonableness.

"Shut up," Reid said. He said the two words with such force that Gayle's mouth dropped open and the words stopped pouring out of her. "Mother, is it true? Was Liam Donovan my grandfather?"

Moria was faced with the most difficult decision she'd ever have to make, but it took her only an instant to make it. She'd not deny her father, now that the truth was out. If she did, she'd never be able to live with herself again.

"Yes, he was," she said.

Gayle began to cry, completely hysterical. Reid stood there, his shoulders squared, and then he crossed the room to his mother and kissed her cheek.

"I'm glad," he said. "Mother, I'm glad! I'm proud that he was my grandfather, I couldn't have chosen a more wonderful grandfather if I'd been allowed to choose from every man in the world. I don't understand it, I don't understand any of this, but I'm proud and I always will be!"

Moria thought that her heart would break with love for him as their eyes met, two against the world. "And I'm proud that he was my father, and I always will be!"

"Reid, take your sister away." Jacob had risen to his feet. In her chair across the room, Estelle was weeping softly, her face crumpled, her hands twisting in her lap. This was all too much for her, her world had crumbled under her feet and nothing would ever be the same again. "Take her upstairs and keep her there. I will talk to both of you later."

"Yes, sir." Reid looked at his mother once more, a look filled with love and compassion and understanding, and then he put his hand on Gayle's arm and drew her toward the door.

Gayle's feet moved as though she were sleepwalking, but she dragged back just before Reid pulled her out of the room, and flung over her shoulder, "I don't believe it, it's a lie, Liam wasn't my grandfather, it's a lie, it's a lie!"

Yanking at her arm, forcing her to come along, Reid had a thought that was much too mature for his years. If he didn't hit his sister now, then he would probably be able to refrain from ever striking out at someone smaller and weaker than he was, no matter the provocation.

18

Dora was packing her meager possessions when Rose entered the attic room that she shared with three of the other female servants, two each to each of the two plain bedsteads that stood against the walls. Her straw portmanteau was open on her bed, and she was stacking underclothing in it haphazardly, almost frantic in her haste to have the packing finished so that she could flee Belvedere before Jacob Vancouver's wrath exploded over her head and destroyed her.

Rose didn't say a word. Words were beyond her. Furthermore, they were unnecessary. Dora would know why she was doing what she was doing, without being told. Her hand reached out and grabbed Dora's hair, so hard that some of the pins fell out, and she began shaking the younger woman as a dog might shake a rat. It was a good simile, Rose thought, because Dora was a rat, she was the lowest form of vermin that the good Lord had ever allowed to inhabit the earth.

The initial surprise that immobilized her dissipated by the pain she was experiencing, Dora began to fight back. But although she was younger and taller, even her panic at the attack was no match for Rose's fury, which lent her a strength that was awesome.

Still holding Dora's hair, Rose's other hand lashed out, again and again, striking first one side of Dora's face and then the other. The blows that Dora managed to inflict on her assailant were unfelt as Rose continued to mete out punishment that Dora had had coming for years. The bitch, the vixen, the devil's spawn! Even the devil wouldn't want her by the time Rose got through with her.

Dora's screams brought two chambermaids who had been working on the second floor. The first of them, a girl of seventeen or eighteen, added her screams to Dora's as she saw what was happening, until the older, a woman in her fifties, shoved her back through the door with the command to fetch Grimshaw, the butler, as fast as she could make her feet run.

Grimshaw, his portly body sadly out of breath, nevertheless wrapped his arms around Rose to drag her off her victim, while the older chambermaid subdued Dora, which was a great deal easier to do. Rose had had more than enough time to inflict all the damage that she dared to inflict unless she wanted to kill her and have murder on her soul.

Dora's face was unrecognizable, already swollen grotesquely, and covered with bright red splotches that would turn into a mass of black and blue by the time a few hours had passed. Rose's hand that had clutched Dora's hair still held a clump of it, ripped out of her scalp, and now Rose looked at the clump and dropped it disdainfully to the floor. It would be months before Dora would be able to brush her hair without more handfuls coming out, so loosened by the tugging that any brushing or combing would finish dislodging the hairs from their mooring. Half bald, her face battered, other parts of her body covered with welts and bruises, it was far less than she deserved but all that Rose had dared to inflict on her.

"I have some advice for you," Rose said, her eyes as hard as stone. "Get as far away as you can, as fast as you can, because if I ever lay eyes on you again I'll finish what I just started!"

"I'll have to report this to Mr. Vancouver," Grimshaw said, his face filled with shock. Two female servants, in this perfectly regulated household, actually inflicting bodily harm on each other! And the blame would be laid on his shoulders, beyond any doubt, for not keeping the staff under control.

"Report it, then. I wouldn't want to keep you from doing your duty, man dear," Rose said, before she stalked out of the room. She was breathing hard, her arms and legs were trembling from the tremendous effort of punishing Dora, and she knew that she, too, would be sent from Belvedere in disgrace, but if she had it to do all over again she'd do it. She only hoped that her actions wouldn't get Moria in any more trouble than she was already in.

In Jacob's study, the conference was still going on, if it could be called a conference, with Jacob doing all the talking and not allowing even his son to venture an opinion contrary to his own. The commotion abovestairs had not reached any of their ears through the heavy, closed door.

"You have shown, by your actions, that you are not to be trusted. The scandal of what has happened will rock this community from one end to the other. Speculation will run rife, there will be no end to the speculation about what could have transpired between you and Mr. Northrup to have brought on his fit. The damage you have wrought is all but irreparable. There is no way that I can allow you to remain here."

Moria had been sitting in silence, only her eyes blazing in her white face. Now she spoke, her voice as hot as her eyes.

"And what do you propose to do with me? Lock me away, as you threatened, so that I can cause you no more embarrassment?"

"Young woman, levity is not becoming in this situation. You may be assured that locking you up has crossed my mind. In your case, you are fortunate that I am inclined to be more lenient, not because of any compassion for you, who deserve no compassion, but because I do not choose to keep you under my roof, always wondering if something might happen that would enable you to foment still more mischief.

"It would be impossible, also, to keep your being locked up a

303

secret, and that would cause still more talk, which is to be avoided at all costs. But the choice must be yours."

"The choice?"

"Exactly. And the price for your freedom to go where you will, never to return or to communicate with any member of this family again, is simple. If you attempt any communication, if you let drop as much as one word of what you suspect about Mr. Northrup, if you cause the Vancouvers any more trouble at all, or tell anyone that you are Liam Donovan's daughter, I will seek you out and bring you back, and then you will in truth be a prisoner for as long as you live. Make no mistake about my ability to do this."

"You're willing to destroy my marriage, never see your grandchildren again? What if Tony should choose to go with us?"

"There is no danger that my son would make such a choice." Tony, standing across the room with his hands thrust into his pockets, refused to look at her. Their marriage, as far as he was concerned, had been finished the moment she had told him that she was Liam Donovan's daughter, and these last actions of hers made it impossible for him even to go through the motions that would lead the public to believe that they were still a happily married couple.

Jacob's protruding eyes were fixed on Moria's face, and his next words dropped like stones on her heart.

"Anthony will not go with you, and you will not take my grandchildren. They are Vancouvers, in spite of the tainted blood that runs through their veins. Every law in the land gives your husband the right to send you away, as long as he provides reasonable support for you, and to keep your children from you. I will give you until six o'clock this evening to make your decision. If you decide to go, you will be provided with enough money to sustain you in moderate decency. If you decide to stay, I will have quarters prepared for you. In either case, you will never see either of your children again." With that, Jacob stood up, opened his pocket watch to check the time, and snapped it shut again. "You have three hours," he said. "You will remove yourself to your room to make your decision. That is all."

Even now, Moria could not believe that Tony was going to stand by and let this happen. He might not love her anymore, he might never want to treat her as his wife again, but she was still his wife, she had borne his children, she had loved him as much as he had allowed her to love him.

"Tony! You can't allow this!"

Tony's eyes flicked across her face and then looked away again. His face was pale, his hair a little disheveled, but otherwise he showed no emotion.

"I agree with my father. Your actions have forced me to agree with him. Your action in marrying me, in allowing me to marry you, under completely false pretenses, have forfeited any right you might have had to ask for my support in this matter. I cannot risk the total destruction of this family, of my children, because of a misguided sense of loyalty to a woman who deserves no loyalty."

He rehearsed that speech, Moria thought, outraged. He knew what his father was going to say, and he rehearsed that speech!

"So it is to be divorce," she said.

"There will be no divorce. Divorce is unheard of in this family, as well as in all decent society." Jacob's words held a ring of finality. So stunned that she hardly knew that her feet were moving, she left the room, vaguely aware of Estelle's muffled sobbing.

Rose was waiting for her in her room. Rose's valise was already packed. Moria wanted to throw herself into her arms, to sob out her frustration and despair as if she had still been the child that Rose used to comfort so many years ago. But she wasn't a child, and there was nothing that Rose could do to help her.

"It's the money, of course," Rose said, when Moria had told her of Jacob's ultimatum. "He'll never let Tony divorce you as long as there's a chance that *he* might not recover, and all of his money will go to you. He put you in his will, when he adopted you. Jacob Vancouver will not let that fortune slip through his fingers if he can help it. As long as you're still married to Tony, the money will be his."

"Rose, will you come with me? If they'd let you stay on here I'd ask you to do that, to look after my children. But they won't, and I want you to come with me, wherever I decide to go. You're all I have in the world now, I couldn't bear it without you."

Rose's face was filled with sorrow as she answered. "No, girl dear, I can't go with you. I'm going back to Retreat."

Moria stared at her, not believing her ears. "Rose, you can't! How could you bear it, to live in the same house with William Northrup?"

"I have to go back. I know that now. I'd already decided even before all this happened. Moria, he swore that he'd ruin Eugenia's sister Laura and her husband, ruin their whole family down to the last cousin or nephew, if ever Eugenia did anything to displease him! If the man recovers now, he'll carry out his threat with more vengeance than you can dream of, knowing that Eugenia betrayed him with Liam, knowing that she foisted you off on him, Liam's daughter! I have to be there, to watch and wait, and to do what I can if he shows signs of recovering."

"But what could you do? He's so powerful, no one could stop him, if he ever does get better!"

"I don't know what I'll do. But I have to be there. Our Lady grant that I won't have to kill him to keep him from carrying out his threat. But Eugenia loved Laura, and she loved her nephews and Daniel, and there's her mother, still alive. For Eugenia's sake, I have to protect them, however I can. Clara Lindstrom likes me, and so do all of the other servants. They'll let me slip back in without a ripple, and *he's* in no condition to forbid it."

Wordlessly, they clung to each other, each of their hearts breaking, until Moria stiffened and cried out, "My children! I've got to see them!" She picked up her skirts and ran to the schoolroom, where she thought they would have returned after Jacob had sent them from his study.

The room was empty. Her heart pounding, Moria retraced her steps and went to Reid's room. The door stood open, he wasn't there. Down the hallway the door to Gayle's room also stood open, and there was no sign of Gayle.

Moria raced down the stairs, forgetting this time to pick up her skirts, so that her foot caught in the hem and she would have fallen headlong down the rest of the flight if she hadn't caught at the banister to save herself. She burst into Jacob's study without knocking.

"Where are my children?" she demanded. "Tell me where they are!"

"They're where you can't find them," Jacob told her, not bothering to rise to his feet. The omission told her more plainly than words that he no longer considered her a lady, that he regarded her as being unworthy of common courtesy. "You may rest assured that they are safe, but they will remain out of your reach until you have left this house or decided that you prefer to be locked away. I trust you have given the matter some thought. Have you reached your decision?"

"I'm leaving! What choice do I have? But I have the right to see my children before I go, I demand the right!"

"You will make no demands. I have here . . . deliberately Jacob picked up an envelope from his desk, ". . . sufficient cash for you to get to wherever you choose to go, preferably as far away as possible. When you are settled, you may let me know and I will send you a weekly allowance."

Moria knocked the envelope from his hand with such force that the banknotes flew around the room. "I'd rather starve than touch a cent from you! I'll make it on my own, damn you! Any food I bought with Vancouver money would choke me!"

What a fool she was, but even knowing that, she wouldn't retract a word. The Irish pride in her wouldn't let her. Vancouver money was tainted, as tainted as they themselves were, tainted with power with inhumanity, with cruelty to anyone who wasn't strong enough to fight back. But she'd fight back, she swore it on her father's memory, and she'd get her children back, if it took her all the rest of her life!

Five minutes later, Rose was also handing her an envelope. "As long as you bit off your nose to spite your face, you'll be needing

307

this. It's my savings. Wages for servants being what they are it's no fortune, but it'll carry you for a long time just the same. Take it, and no back talk! Do you think Eugenia and Liam would let me rest easy if I let you leave this house empty-handed?''

"Not all of it. Half," Moria said. Her eyes were so hot and dry that she felt as though they were cracking, but she wasn't allowed the relief of tears. "I'm strong, I can work, I'll survive."

"To be sure you will. But do you mind telling me where you'll be going, just so I'll be able to think of you being on your way there?''

Already turning out wardrobe and drawers, Moria hesitated over the jewelry that Tony had given her over the years since they'd been married. She'd be insane to leave it, it was worth money, a great deal of money. But once again that black Irish pride, her heritage from her father, got in her way. She'd take nothing he'd given her except such clothing as she absolutely had to have. Maybe she'd go hungry, maybe she'd go without shelter, but if she couldn't manage to exist without Vancouver charity, then she didn't deserve to exist at all.

She scooped up the pieces she'd dumped out on the dressing table and started to put them back into the jewel box, and then she picked up the one piece that she must not leave behind. Her hand shaking, she slipped it onto her wrist, the horsehair bracelet that Quinn Bradmore had given her when she'd been fifteen, just before he'd gone back to the Arizona Territory.

She knew, instinctively, where she was going. It sounded so far away, at the ends of the earth. But she was going, and somehow she'd build a new life there. Quinn was a man, capable and intelligent, and he'd been Liam's friend. He'd help her in any way he could. She wasn't quite as alone in the world as she'd thought she'd been.

They were interrupted by a tap on the door. It was Estelle who slipped inside and closed the door behind her, her face quivering, her eyes still red and swollen from all the tears she'd shed.

"Here," she said. "I know that you refused the money Jacob offered you, but you can't go with nothing. I have no money of my own, Jacob handles it all, but you can take this and sell it. If Jacob misses it, I'll tell him the truth, that I gave it to you, but he probably won't notice if I never wear it again."

A diamond and ruby brooch lay in the palm of her hand, the stones not large enough to be worth a real fortune, but still valuable.

"Take it," Estelle urged, as Moria hesitated. "It isn't from the Vancouvers. It came from my mother. I want you to have it, so that I won't have to worry about you. I can't go against my husband, and it wouldn't do me any good even if I did, but this is mine, to give if I want to give it."

Moria cried then, all the tears that had been dammed up inside of her and that she hadn't been able to shed. She went into Estelle's arms, and they clung together for a moment. Dear Estelle, kind Estelle, why couldn't Tony have inherited some of her goodness and kindness?

"God bless you, Moria," Estelle said, and then she was gone, slipping out as quietly as she'd slipped in, so that no one would know that she had seen Moria at all. Her last words, whispered just before she closed the door, were: "I'll watch over the children for you, and I'll never say a word against you to them."

Everything that Moria owned in the world was in the valise that she had brought with her, and in the reticule that hung from her arm. The plush seat of the train was hard and unyielding, uncomfortable after so many endless hours. She was a little hungry, because she was conserving her money, eating only what she must have to conserve her strength.

Beside her, Mrs. Ethel May Stover shifted her heavyset body to a more comfortable position, her middle-aged face filled with concern.

"Dearie, you'd better try to rest. We'll be in Chicago before too long, and you'll need to be fresh when we get there. Why don't you just close your eyes and try to sleep a little?"

Ethel May Stover was a kind woman, Moria thought, one of those women whose mission in life seems to be to mother other people, even people she'd never seen before. That she wasn't wealthy was proved by her clothing and lack of gentility, but Moria appreciated the kindness she'd shown her, insisting that she sit with her.

"It's always nicer for two ladies to share a seat, don't you think? Then none of the gentlemen will think they can take liberties with you because you're traveling alone. It isn't safe for a young lady as pretty as you, the way some gentlemen are! Just sit with me, and you'll be as safe as if you were in church."

Although some of the gentlemen had attempted to approach her under the guise of offering their assistance, none of them had managed to get past Ethel May Stover's bulk. And it was a blessing that Mrs. Stover had offered to help her find her way around when they reached Chicago, insisted that she'd see Moria on the right train to take her toward her final destination.

Moria was tired, the train was hot, the window wouldn't open, and she had forgotten the last time she had slept an untroubled sleep. First Eugenia's death, and then her father's, and now there was no way she could forget that every click of the train's wheels was taking her farther away from her children. When would she see them again, how many months, how many years? What were they thinking, had they been told the truth, that she'd been forced to leave them, or did they think that she had deserted them of her own will?

Reid would miss her. She wasn't sure about Gayle. Gayle loved her but she had always been a standoffish little girl, and Jacob had monopolized her and spoiled her so much that it was no wonder that she chose to give her first affection to him. She had resented it when Moria had tried to cut down on the amount of spoiling she received, as though Moria were infringing on her rights. And Moria hadn't forgotten, nor was she likely to forget, how Gayle had reacted when Dora had told the children the truth about their heritage.

But Reid had accepted it, and he'd been glad! He'd been proud that Liam was his grandfather, and he'd made it plain, in the few moments he'd been allowed to stay in the room, that no matter what happened, he was on his mother's side, that his loyalty was completely hers. How was it possible that two children born of the same parents could be so different? Or hadn't they been different in the beginning, was it only Jacob's spoiling that had made Gayle the way she was?

Mrs. Stover was right, she must try to rest. She was going to need all her strength in the days and weeks to come. Smiling at her new friend, she closed her eyes. She was sure that she wouldn't sleep, but her eyes were tired from hours of looking out of the train window at passing scenery that meant nothing to her except that it was alien, that it reminded her that she had left everything she had ever known behind her.

The clicking of the wheels, the rhythmic jerking, back and forth, of the train itself, were so monotonous that in spite of her conviction her mind began to drift.

Jerking awake, disoriented, confused, Eugenia realized, vaguely, that the strong scent Mrs. Stover wore must have caused her to dream about the lilacs in Eugenia's garden. But Mrs. Stover wasn't beside her now, and as Moria's eyes cleared she could see that the woman wasn't anywhere in the coach. And the train was slowing down, they were in a city, a big city, they were in Chicago!

Where on earth could Mrs. Stover be? For a moment Moria was panic-stricken, until she told herself that if the woman had regretted her offer of help, it wasn't surprising. Taking care of Moria would be a good deal of trouble when she must be eager to get home to her own home and family. She could manage by herself.

People were standing up, lifting their bags down from the overhead racks, and Moria did the same, only to have a gentleman lift it down for her. He looked respectable, and Moria thanked him and then asked him if he'd seen Mrs. Stover during the last several moments.

"The lady who was sitting with you? Why, she got off the train at the last stop! I helped her with her bag, she said that she didn't want to disturb you, and asked me if I'd help you with your bag and to say good-bye for her."

Still confused because of her dream-laden sleep, Moria tried to digest what the gentleman had told her. Mrs. Stover had left the train? But she'd said that she lived in Chicago, that it would be no trouble at all for her to help Moria when they arrived! It didn't make sense.

But there was no time to think about it now. The train had stopped, the steps were in place, and the gentleman was helping her to alight, and carrying her bag into the station.

"Is someone meeting you? There isn't?" His face expressed his disapproval at a young lady traveling alone. "Then may I find you a cab to take you where you're going? Do you live here, or will you be stopping at a hotel?"

"I can manage, thank you," Moria told him. Firmly, she took possession of her bag. She'd have to manage, she couldn't spend the rest of her life depending on strangers to help her.

The ladies' room wasn't hard to find. She must straighten her hair, make herself decent, before she checked to see about continuing her journey, and how long it would be before she had to board another train. And she needed to eat something, she was uncomfortably aware that it had been too many hours since she'd had nourishment.

There was a comb and brush in her reticule, in order that she would have free access to them without having to get into her traveling bag for them. But something was missing, and her heart slowed for an agonizing instant before it began to pound as though it were trying to force its way out of her breast.

Her money, the money Rose had given her, half of the wages she'd saved during all of her years of service at Retreat, was gone. All of it, except for a few loose coins. And a further, frantic search, while she removed every other article from her reticule to make sure, showed her that the brooch that Estelle had given her was gone as well: She and Rose had decided that she should wait until she reached Chicago to sell it. She was too well known in the East, and for Estelle's sake it would be better not to sell the brooch anywhere that Jacob might get wind of it.

There was no mistake. Except for her comb and brush, three handkerchiefs, a small bottle of cologne to pat on her face and wrists to refresh herself during her journey, and the comb and brush, her reticule was empty.

The scent of lilacs had been in her dream while she'd slept. There was no doubt that she'd smelled it in her sleep, when Mrs. Stover had leaned close, her bulk hiding what she was doing from the other passengers, and gone through her reticule. Moria was in Chicago, with nothing but the clothes on her back and in her suitcase, to stand between her and starvation.

For a moment she felt such despair that she wanted to give up. Would she have to throw away the last vestige of her pride after all, beg the stationmaster to telegraph Jacob and ask him to send her funds? What other alternative did she have?

She could scarcely stand on a street corner and beg! She pressed her fingers against her burning eyes, and took a deep breath.

She was still wearing her wedding ring. She'd meant to take it off, leave it behind, wanting no reminder of Tony. But in the confusion of packing and leaving, she'd forgotten.

She had no idea how much the ring was worth, but she knew that it was gold. As much as she hated the sight of it now, it would save her life. If Rose were praying for her at this very moment, her prayers had been answered.

Book Two

19

Moria had heard of Marshall Field's. The huge department store was famous even in New York, and she had heard both William Northrup and Jacob Vancouver express admiration for the man's expertise and the way he had recouped his fortunes after being burned out in the great fire. But she had never, by the wildest stretch of her imagination, thought of herself behind a counter in his store, selling gloves!

She'd been appalled at how little her wedding ring had brought when she'd been forced to sell it at a pawnbroker's shop. She had been close to tears as she'd accepted the few dollars, and she'd vowed with every drop of Irish blood in her that she would never again be as humiliated as she'd been when she'd had to enter the dingy establishment to sell the only thing of value that remained to her for enough money to keep from starving.

The cheapest accommodation she could find was a room scarcely larger than a closet, on the third floor of a tenement house in a section that would have filled her with terror if her memories of the places she had lived in New York City with her mother and father hadn't been so vivid. But a toughness had been instilled in her in those childhood days, and she'd been able to walk the shabby streets and endure the stares of its inhabitants without panic.

Her room had one small window that faced on a blank brick airshaft, through which no breeze ever managed to find its way. The furnishings consisted of a chipped white-painted iron cot with a sagging mattress, a straight-backed chair with a rung missing, and a washstand with a crazed water pitcher and bowl. The landlady, a hard-faced woman whose dustcap half concealed frowsy hair, demanded a week's rent in advance. But she'd accepted one of Moria's dresses instead, a dress of such quality that the woman knew she could sell it to a dressmaker and reap a profit that made it worth her trouble.

The room was like an oven at night, and in addition to the heat that kept her from sleeping, there was the scratching and scurrying of mice in the walls. Only mice, she hoped fervently, please, not rats! But the toothmarks on the bread and cheese she subsisted on until she found employment were tiny, surely not made by rats, and she spent nearly the last of her remaining cash to buy a tin box to protect her food from further depredations by the furry vermin, and by the cockroaches that scurried in every direction to disappear in cracks in the walls and floor as soon as she entered the room. Her first extravagance, after she had been accepted as a saleslady at Marshall Field and Company, had been to buy an apple to supplement her bread and cheese for supper. That apple, to her fruit-and-vegetable-starved appetite, was more delicious than the most elegant banquet she had ever attended as the adopted daughter of William Northrup or as Mrs. Anthony Vancouver.

It was neither Moria Northrup nor Moria Vancouver who applied for a position at Marshall Field and Company, it was Moria Donovan. Even if the Irish name worked against her chances of being accepted, she was determined to use it. She'd spent the greater part of her life denying her name and her father, and her resumption of her true identity did something for her that nothing else could have done in this time of her greatest need.

Irish surname or not, the manager who interviewed her recognized quality when he saw it. This young woman was a lady, and an extraordinarily beautiful one, from her Paris-imported hat to the tips of her custom-made shoes. The clothing she wore proclaimed wealth and breeding, her voice was soft and lovely to hear, her smile would melt the most exacting society matron who was determined to find Marshall Field and Company's gloves not quite fine enough for her. Moria was exactly the image of a saleslady that Marshall Field wanted in his establishment. Her hands alone, so graceful and beautifully shaped, so delicately white, would sell more gloves than any other saleslady had ever sold before.

The store itself was so elegant that it was no wonder that it had met with such success. A grand staircase, a full twenty-three feet wide, rose from the center aisle to the second floor. The elevators were finished with rich upholstery and wood and mirrors. On the fifth floor, an army of seamstresses made exclusive garments for those ladies able to afford them. On the second floor, a waiting room offered respite from the ardors of shopping, with comfortable chairs and sofas and potted plants and ferns adding to the air of refined elegance.

Only Moria's years of training in hiding her emotions enabled her to conceal her shocked dismay when she was told that her salary would be only eight dollars a week. "The sum is sufficient to support you adequately and still save a little every week," the manager told her, passing on Mr. Field's sentiments as he was expected to do. Mr. Field was an exponent of thrift, and he endeavored to instill that same thrift into every one of his employees from the two-dollar-a-week "cash" boys to the very top salespersons' salaries of twenty-five dollars. Merely being employed at Marshall Field and Company gave any person a respectability that more than made up for the lack of higher wages. Even the cash boys, on their two dollars a week, had to be immaculate, scrubbed and brushed, their shoes shined to a high gloss every morning when they reported for inspection.

Although she wouldn't have believed it a month ago, Moria found out that it was possible to exist on eight dollars a week, although she found it difficult to save that ten or fifteen cents a day recommended by Mr. Field. If the twelve-year-old boys who ran the cash from the sales counters to the cashiers for change were able to be little gentlemen on their two dollars a week, then she could certainly maintain her status as a respectable lady on her eight dollars.

So she could exist, she could support herself, but her plans to go to Arizona had to be scuttled. But on sober reflection, Moria had come to the conclusion that only desperation had sent her in the direction of Arizona in the first place. What right had she to impose on Quinn Bradmore, when she'd known him for only a few weeks when she'd been fifteen? A few letters exchanged between Liam and Quinn was hardly a basis for demanding his help. This was her problem, and hers alone. In that wild, new country, she would certainly have been no better off than she was here, there probably wouldn't even have been any employment, and if Quinn had felt obligated to help her because of his friendship with Liam, she would have died of shame.

She wrote to Rose, saving out the money for the stationery from her first week's salary. "I must be the most gullible fool ever born," she confessed. "But what's done is done and there's no use crying about it. And you are not to send me another cent. My position at Marshall Field and Company is highly respectable and pays a wage I can easily live on."

She didn't mention the amount of the wage for fear that Rose would insist on sending her the second half of her savings, and she couldn't allow that, not even if she were starving. It would take longer than she dared to contemplate to work her way up to a higher salary so that she could begin to repay Rose, as it was.

"It's a beautiful store, and the work is interesting, and even amusing as I cater to the vanity of stately matrons who'd like to look down their noses at me but at second glance don't quite dare. All of the salespeople are called Miss or Mr. or Mrs. and all of the lady patrons must be called madam. Everything is of the highest quality, Mr. Field has a fetish about quality, and it's a pleasure to handle the fine goods and a challenge to see how much I can sell."

She didn't mention what a blessing it was that her years of outdoor activity, of riding, had so strengthened her body that she didn't suffer the fatigue and backaches, the swollen feet and painful muscles, that many of the other salesladies suffered. She didn't mention the long hours, or the budgeting that she had to do to make her salary stretch from one week to the next, or her determination to save something, no matter how little, until she would have enough to consult a lawyer about demanding her right to have contact with her children.

"Tell me about Reid and Gayle, that's what I really want to hear," she wrote. "Anything at all, no detail could be too trivial."

Rose knew almost all there was to know about Reid and Gayle, and about everything else that had to do with the Vancouvers. She'd been surprised, but not actually dumbfounded, when Jacob had sent a message that he would like to see her and that he would send a conveyance to bring her to Belvedere at her earliest convenience.

What Jacob wanted was regular, daily reports on William Northrup's condition. A spy in the enemy camp, so to speak. With William incapacitated, unable to speak or move or even to hold a pen to let his wishes be known, Jacob was in a position to take advantage of his condition by manipulating the interests they held together in the partial partnership they'd formed when Moria and Tony were married. But if William were to begin improving, then Jacob would have to be a good deal more careful, because William would certainly ruin him if he were to learn of his activities.

And above and beyond that, Jacob hoped that William's condition would deteriorate, that he would grow weaker and die. Once he had William's fortune in his grasp, through William's will that left everything to Moria, there were no bounds to the heights to which he could rise!

And so Rose was a spy, although she reaped the benefit of being able to extract every iota of information about the children and the Vancouvers that she could conjure out of the messenger from Belvedere who was the go-between, the only reason that she agreed to the liaison between herself and Jacob at all. The small amount he

Lydia Lancaster

paid her for her services was set aside to save toward Moria's legal expenses when it should be time for her to fight for her rights.

It was easy for Rose to keep close tabs on William's condition. She had volunteered to care for his room, to change his bed linens and carry his trays, to spoonfeed him whatever he could manage to swallow and to act in general as his nurse. It was dirty and degrading work, often revolting, which none of the other servants were eager to undertake, and Fredrich Harshay, William's valet, had defected, little liking caring for a total invalid, and accepted a position as valet to a New York City millionaire who had offered him far more than William had paid him.

All of the main rooms at Retreat were closed up now, the furniture covered with dust sheets. The staff of servants had been reduced, as directed by Jacob, in order to conserve William's estate. There was no use in wasting money on servants who had no active master to serve.

Rose was diligent in her duties, never neglecting any item of care that would make the stricken man more comfortable. But all the time she was caring for him, performing the nauseating tasks that must be performed, she was praying that he would never recover, and begging Mary's forgiveness for praying it.

"But you know, as well as I do, that if that man were to get well, he'd find a way to ruin Laura and her family, and to hurt our Moria as well. If he has to suffer for a short time here on earth, it can count for nothing against the eternity of hell he'll suffer when he dies, so there's no point, now is there, in letting him get well?" Rose had complete confidence that Mary, being a woman and more logical than men were, would understand exactly what she was talking about.

She'd lift no hand to speed his recovery, even if she'd known how. But she'd lift no hand to make his condition worse, either, because that would be a sin she'd be brought to account for and it would be a waste if it turned out not to be necessary in order to protect Laura and Moria. And so she prayed, every day and every evening, that she wouldn't have to take steps in order to ensure that protection,

322

and if her prayers did not ask for William to die, surely it was no sin to ask that he shouldn't recover.

In the meantime, the vultures moved in, little by little, as William's condition remained unchanged. Business associates and lawyers all had their fingers in the pie. If Jacob hadn't been acting as watchdog for the estate there would have been little of it left to come to Tony, through Moria, when William died.

She wrote to Moria, blessedly ignorant that the address was one that would have filled her with dismay. The children were well. Reid missed her, he was polite to his father and grandfather but showed no affection for them. His affection was for Estelle, who was true to her word that she would care for them with all the love in her heart.

About Gayle she said little. It would only hurt Moria to know that Jacob was spoiling her more fiercely than ever, that he was teaching her that she must be so ashamed of the blood of the Irish horse trainer that she must forget that Liam had ever existed, forget that her mother had existed. Her Vancouver blood was dominant enough to overcome the Irish side of her ancestry, and that was all that mattered.

> *Reid rides every day that the weather permits. He takes Jazir, to give him exercise, and rides to Retreat, where he takes Kamil out to exercise as well. He is not allowed to take flowers from Belvedere, as Jacob and Anthony know why he wants them, but he carries armloads of them from Retreat to place on Eugenia's grave, and on Liam's. You have every reason to be proud of him. I can see Liam in him, even though their features are different and Reid's hair is light instead of black. The resemblance is there, in his expression, in the look of his eyes.*

Moria wept over the letter, the first one she received, and reread it a dozen times and wept again. Her heart swelled with an almost agonizing pride in her son, and her love for him doubled, if such a thing were possible. As for Gayle, her heart could only ache. And her determination was steeled to an even harder edge, that someday, somehow, she would have both of her children back.

Lydia Lancaster

* * *

It had taken the dowager, a woman in her late fifties whose overly ample figure spoiled the line of even the outrageously expensive dress she was wearing, almost an hour to settle on which pair of gloves she thought were the most becoming to her pudgy hands. Everything about the woman grated on Moria's nerves. Arrogant, overbearing, convinced that she was better than anyone else simply because her husband was one of the new breed of millionaires who had made his fortune in the meat-packing business, there was no way she could have ever gained admittance through the doors of Retreat or Belvedere.

"Madam, this pair is just a trifle too snug," Moria suggested. "A half-size larger will give you better service."

"Young woman, this pair fits perfectly!" This, after Moria had struggled to work the fingers of a size seven pair of the finest kid gloves onto a hand that was clearly a size eight, with the result that though they were on, the dowager couldn't bend her fingers at all. "Kid gloves are supposed to be snug, as a glove salesperson should know!"

Not this snug, Moria wanted to tell her. "Yes, madam. Of course, you are right." The customer was always right, there was no way that a customer could be wrong. "This pair is perfect."

The call of "cash!" went out from a counter directly behind Moria's, and one of the cash boys darted from his post on a bench along the wall where the cash boys waited for the call that sent them into action. Fresh-faced and eager, he was a new boy, barely twelve, determined that he was going to be the best and the fastest cash boy that Marshall Field and Company had ever employed.

Unfortunately, he was a little too eager. The dowager stepped backward without looking, to hold up one gloved hand in what she judged to be better light in order to admire it, just as the cash boy attempted to dart past her on his way to his destination. The dowager tripped over him, both went sprawling onto the floor, and even as the boy scrambled back to his feet and attempted to assist the dowager to hers, her cries of outrage brought the section manager hurrying to

324

the scene of chaos, an unheard-of disgrace in this establishment where such a thing had never dared to happen before.

"Beg pardon, mum, I'm sorry, mum, are you all right, mum?" The boy, agonized by the accident, looked as if he wished the floor would open up and swallow him. Terror was on his face as well, as it had every right to be.

"Clumsy oaf!" the dowager screamed, her voice so shrill that Moria winced. "You filthy, clumsy oaf!" The glove on her right hand had split, two of her fingers were puffing out from between the seams. "What do you mean, knocking me down?" Enraged, forgetting that no real lady would act in such a manner, she lifted her reticule and began striking the boy around his head with it.

"Stop that! It was an accident, a pure accident!" Moria cried. She was around the counter, her hand grasping the dowager's arm to stop her punishment of the terrified boy, before she had time to think. But she would have done it anyway, her sense of justice was far more outraged than the dowager's sense of dignity. "He didn't mean to do it, you have no reason to strike him!"

"Miss Donovan!" Mr. Percell, the section manager, fixed her with an icy stare. "Get back to your post, if you please. I will deal with this. Madam, may I convey Marshall Field and Company's most abject apologies for this unfortunate occurrence? I assure you that we regret it most profoundly!"

"You will discharge that boy immediately!" the dowager demanded.

"Certainly, madam. It is understood that he will be discharged. Marshall Field and Company would keep no such clumsy young man in its employ."

"That isn't fair! It was as much her fault as his, she stepped back without any warning, and stumbled right over him!" Moria said hotly.

"Miss Donovan, you will report to my office." The iciness in Mr. Percell's voice told her that it was all over for her as well as for the cash boy. "Immediately, if you please. Madam, allow me to escort you to the waiting room. I'll find a maid to help you repair the damage to your person, and then I myself will assist you in selecting another pair of gloves, without charge, of course, but only a small token of Marshall Field and Company's regret that such a thing should have happened. And if there is any other damage to your person or your apparel, Marshall Field and Company will make full restitution, along with our most sincere apologies!''

"Well, I should most certainly think so!" Only slightly mollified, the dowager allowed Mr. Percell to assist her to an elevator, giving both Moria and the unfortunate cash boy a look of pure venom before she accepted Mr. Percell's arm.

Half an hour later, Moria left the store by the employees' entrance. She had committed the unforgivable sin, she had taken the attitude that a customer had been wrong! Her employment by Marshall Field and Company was terminated, and she left without a recommendation, as it would be impossible for the store to give one under those circumstances.

Except for being an expert horsewoman and knowing how to dress and how to be a perfect hostess, there was nothing that Moria was qualified for except to work as a saleslady. But finding another position was harder even than she had known it would be. The first question a prospective employer always asked was if she had had experience, and the second was to ask her why her employment at Marshall Field and Company had come to an end. The better stores refused to consider anyone who had left such a prestigious position under a cloud, no matter what a good appearance she gave.

She tried the second-quality stores then, making the rounds of them. Her rent was paid only a week in advance, it was essential that she find something soon, or else she would be put out on the street. Barring asking Rose to send her money, and that was impossible, she might very well be arrested and jailed as a vagrant!

How could there be so many stores, in the department-store capital of the world, and none of them wanting to hire her? She traversed the length of Lake Street, applying first at one and then another, always with the same result. Tired, discouraged, near panic, she hesitated before she could work up her courage to enter still another store, with the name "Greenbaum's" on a sign that was faded by the weather.

The establishment showed signs of hard times. Some of the shelves and counters were scantily stocked, there were few customers, all of them of middle or lower classes, the merchandise couldn't begin to compare with that offered by Marshall Field's. She had a sinking feeling that she'd be wasting her time in even asking for an interview.

But she must have work, and she didn't dare turn away from any chance of finding it, no matter how hopeless it seemed. The door of the office in the back was ajar, and she tapped on it, squaring her shoulders.

The man who sat behind a plain oak desk, going over a scattered pile of papers, wore a green eyeshade and at first she couldn't make out much of his face. What she could see of it seemed to be a network of wrinkles, and a nose that would have proclaimed his ancestry even if his name hadn't.

"Mr. Greenbaum?"

He looked up, he got to his feet, he removed the eyeshade. A customer like this, a real lady, in his store? She'd come to complain, then, it couldn't be anything else. In the depth of his soul, Abraham Greenbaum sighed. Customers like this he didn't need, what did he have to offer them, no wonder she'd come to complain!

"Mr. Greenbaum, I'd like a position as a saleslady. I have experience, I worked for six weeks at Marshall Field and Company."

He wouldn't have believed it. This was a customer, not a saleslady. But a closer look at Moria's face, tense under her bright smile, told him that even Abraham Greenbaum could make a mistake. And why not? Hadn't Abraham Greenbaum made a mistake thinking he could run a department store, wasn't he on the verge of bankruptcy because he didn't know how to compete with stores like Marshall Field's? Even the poor people he didn't know how to attract, no matter how much he cut his prices, until there wasn't any profit at all and his back was against the wall.

"May I ask, if you don't mind, why you aren't working for Marshall Field's any longer?"

"I disagreed with a customer," Moria said. "Because she was wrong. She stumbled over a cash boy and fell, it was her own fault, and she hit him with her reticule and made him be fired. As so I was fired too because I said it was her fault, and I grabbed her arm so she couldn't hit the boy any more."

Abraham's face lit up with interest. An honest young lady, and what a lady, quality all the way through, and for being honest and for having compassion she'd been fired! A smile tugged at the corners of his mouth. In all his fifty-seven years, the last thirty of them trying to make a living in competition with stores like Marshall Field's, he'd never heard a story like this, a lady wanting a position as a saleslady, telling him the truth about why she'd been fired.

"Did the lady fall hard?" he asked.

"Yes, she did. And it was almost worth being fired, to see that *lady* go sprawling on her . . . dignity!" Moria said. And they were both laughing, she and this man she had never seen before this moment. They laughed so hard that their eyes watered, and Abraham wiped his with an immaculate handkerchief, started to hand it to her, recollected himself and fished another equally as immaculate from one of his pockets to proffer to her.

Moria accepted it and wiped her own eyes. "I'll try not to do such a thing again, the next place I work," she said.

"But you couldn't promise?"

"No, I couldn't."

"Good. You're hired. You can start now. What counter did you work?"

"Gloves and accessories." Moria held her breath, not daring to let it out for fear that he'd change his mind and say that he didn't need anyone to sell gloves.

"Go tell Miss Fitzgerald on gloves that you're on gloves, she's on corsets. You should maybe be on corsets, the customers might think that our corsets would make them look like you, but we'll start you

328

on gloves, a saleslady who doesn't know how to sell her merchandise I don't need.''

He was out of his mind, and he knew it. He couldn't afford another saleslady, he couldn't even afford those he had. And he felt compelled to be as truthful with this young lady as she had been with him. ''But don't count your lucky stars yet. The employment maybe won't last so long, me being in over my head and not very good at swimming. Can you live on eight dollars a week?'' Now he knew he was out of his mind. His other salesladies received only seven. But Mr. Field had paid her eight, he'd pay her eight, she'd sold gloves for Mr. Field and who could know, maybe she could sell them for him.

''I've been doing it.''

''You live with your family, then? You don't need to earn enough to support yourself?''

''No, I'm quite alone.''

This Abraham Greenbaum didn't like. A young lady, and a young lady of quality, or he was an Irishman, shouldn't live alone in a wicked city like Chicago, and besides, everything about Moria spoke of wealth, of privilege. There was a mystery here and Abraham didn't like mysteries, usually the answers were something he wouldn't want to know. But he'd said she had the job, and Abraham Greenbaum was a man of his word. Reba would be furious.

He told Reba that night after supper. They ate in the kitchen, they'd fallen into the habit of eating in the kitchen years ago, when no children had come to fill their house, eating in the kitchen was less work for Reba, and a dining room ought to be filled with children around the table, the extra chairs were a reminder that their house was empty.

''I hired a new saleslady today.''

''One of the others quit, then? Which one? She's maybe getting married?'' This in an excited, hopeful tone, because marriages were the next closest in Reba's heart to the bearing of children.

329

"That much luck I should have, one less saleslady to pay! No, no one's getting married. I hired the new saleslady extra."

"You're sick!" Reba reached across the table to lay her hand against Abraham's forehead. "And no chicken in the house, how can I make chicken soup with no chicken in the house?"

Abraham spooned another spoonful of sugar into his glass of tea and stirred it, around and around. "I'm not sick. I put her on gloves. She looks like she can sell gloves, she sold three pairs before we closed."

"What is she like? She must be something special for you to go out of your head and hire her when you should be laying off!"

"She's a girl. Young. Her hair is black."

Men! Even the best of them, and there was no doubt whatsoever in Reba's mind that her Abraham was the best man who had ever walked the face of the earth, were so stupid about some things that it was a wonder their wives didn't murder them in their sleep. "But what does she look like?"

"Her eyes are blue. She isn't fat."

"I'll come and see for myself," Reba said. "No more sugar, how can you drink your tea with so much sugar? I should fill your glass with sugar and pour in two teaspoons of tea, maybe, and then you'd be satisfied?" Reba moved the sugar bowl to her side of the table. "Tomorrow, I'll come."

Exactly fifteen minutes after Greenbaum's Department Store opened the next morning, Moria looked up from gloves and accessories directly into the eyes of a woman who was studying her as if she were intent on memorizing everything about her for some future use. The woman was short and plump and middle-aged, her cheeks were smooth and pink, her eyes were a soft, intelligent brown, but her most striking feature was her black hair, parted in the middle and coiled in a round chignon on the back of her head, hair that had a wing of white at each temple. Moria could only see a little of it under a hat that bobbed with artificial cherries and she had a sudden, intense wish that she could see the woman without that hat.

330

"May I assist you?" she asked. "We have some really beautiful gloves, I'm sure we can find you exactly what you want."

"The gloves are cheap," Reba said. "And there isn't much of an assortment, your stock is down and, anyway, gloves I don't need. You have a name?"

"Miss Donovan, Moria Donovan."

"Irish. Black hair and blue eyes and you aren't fat. Abraham did better than usual."

While Moria's eyes widened with bewildered surprise, Reba began to chuckle. "Now I've seen you I know why he hired you, but don't go jumping to conclusions, Moria Donovan. My Abraham doesn't chase young ladies, me he's married to and he knows it and I'm enough for him, or at least I've never had any complaints. You're alone in Chicago?" That much Reba had been able to extract from her husband. "Come to supper. We should get to know each other, before we lose the store and never see each other again."

In all her life, Moria had never enjoyed a meal as much as she enjoyed supper that night in the Greenbaums' kitchen. Reba had the dining room table set when Moria and Abraham arrived, but then she changed her mind, the table was too big and formal, how could you get to know someone from across a big dining room table so you had to shout to make yourself heard? If this Moria Donovan, who was a lady, thought she was too good to eat in the kitchen, then Reba didn't want to get to know her anyway.

"I'll wash, you'll dry. Tonight Abraham doesn't have to dry," Reba said. "And you'll learn something. Hands we use to wash, never a cloth, a cloth might have washed a dish with meat or milk in it, separate they must be kept, dishes and pans separate too."

"May I ask why?"

"Ask. How else can you learn? It's part of our law. Do I argue with rabbis?"

"It's for health," Abraham told Moria. "That's how it started. Milk and meat spoiled in the olden days, and tainted the food, and pork spoiled the fastest of all, that's why we don't eat pork or touch it."

"That makes a great deal of sense."

"Other things should make as much sense, like why my Abraham's store doesn't do enough business when he works so hard," Reba said.

"Your stocks are down. There isn't enough variety. The whole store needs repainting, redecorating. There should be softer lights, soft light is flattering. The merchandise is too cheap, of too poor quality."

"Rich people we don't cater to. They go to Marshall Field's," Abraham said. He spooned another teaspoon of sugar into the glass of tea he was still nursing at the kitchen table while the women washed and dried the dishes. "Our customers can't afford quality."

"Yes, they can. Not the quality they'd find at Marshall Field and Company, but good quality, all the same. There are thousands of middle-class women in Chicago, women who want nice things, and who will buy them if they're reasonably priced. Women who want to feel important, to feel that they're as good as the society women even if they don't have very much money. You could cater to them."

"Repainting, redecorating, building up stocks of merchandise I can't pay for?"

"Greenbaum's should make itself distinctive in its own way. Not only in making the store itself more attractive, but perhaps the salesladies could wear a sort of uniform. Not a real uniform, but a very attractive dress, all the same color, with Greenbaum's monogram on the bodice."

Reba clapped her hands together, sending splatters of water onto the floor. "Embroidery! My embroidery you should see, but the design?"

"We could work one out." Why was she so excited, Moria wondered, as excited as if any of this could come true? But it was a challenge, and she liked Abraham and Reba; even after having known them only a matter of hours she felt that they were the only real friends she'd ever had. "We could have boys, not cash boys like Marshall Field and Company, but boys who'd carry the ladies' parcels to the horsecars for them if they didn't want to wait to have them delivered. Their shirts could be monogrammed too."

"No lace. Lace on boys' shirts I will not have," Abraham said. "What am I saying? Lace on salesladies' shirtwaists we will not have, who could afford it? Or paint, or building up the stock?"

"Embroidery we can afford," Reba said. "I'll do it myself, if Moria can work up a design. It's a start, Abraham. It would be better we should do nothing, and see the store go under? The dresses we can make, from the same bolt of cloth at wholesale from our stock, let Moria talk!"

"The secret of selling to women is to give them what they want," Moria said. "That's the story I heard about Mr. Field, when I first went to work for Marshall Field and Company. He said to give the lady what she wants, and the rest would take care of itself. You could give ladies who aren't as wealthy as Mr. Field's customers what they want, a sense of being important, of being catered to."

As weary as she was after Abraham had insisted on walking her back to her room, because Reba had been aghast at the thought of her walking Chicago's streets alone after dark, Moria wrote to Rose before she went to bed. She had to tell Rose about being discharged from Marshall Field and Company, of finding a new position with Abraham Greenbaum, of how much she liked Abraham and Reba, and how much she wished that Abraham could afford to upgrade his store and his stock so that he'd be able to attract the trade of what was called Chicago's New Woman.

That the New Woman was invariably a member of the wealthier classes didn't mean that women of less means, middle-class housewives, didn't yearn for the same things. Fashion, beauty aids, pretty things for their homes. Campbell's, the leading dealer in switches and chignons and puffs, was too expensive for the less affluent woman, but Greenbaum's could put in a hairpiece department and sell at more reasonable prices.

What middle-class woman yearning for chic wouldn't love to be able to purchase Lillie Langtry bangs if the price were right? And elastic bosoms, if nature had not endowed them with the natural thing, as well as smart shawls and decorative combs for their hair? And lovely dresses copied from exclusive models only made up of less expensive material? She could turn her hand to designing dresses, she knew that her sense of line and style was good.

Her eyes heavy, she finally put down her pen. Dreams were what made the world go around. Didn't she herself go on dreaming, against all practical possibility, that someday she'd get her children back?

20

Quinn stood in front of Greenbaum's Department Store on Lake Street, his broad-brimmed hat pushed back from his forehead as he narrowed his eyes through the fine, cold rain that was nearly sleet, to study the sign stretched across the front.

If Rose O'Riley's first letter, written in answer to a letter he'd sent Liam, had jolted him on learning that Liam was dead, her second letter, in answer to his expressing his deep regret and asking about Moria, had jolted him even more. Moria, alone in Chicago! Moria, working at Greenbaum's Department Store! Moria of the long black hair and laughing blue eyes, who had had the world at her feet!

Rose's letter had been lacking in detail, owing to her reluctance to air Moria's affairs even to so old a friend as Quinn Bradmore, but it had conveyed one thing without doubt: Moria was in trouble, deep trouble. And so Quinn had come to Chicago in search of her. He'd taken time only to register at a hotel and leave his bag before he'd set out to find Greenbaum's, and now, raging with frustration, he found that it was closed!

But there was activity inside, workmen plying paintbrushes, laying strips of carpet, building new counters. Quinn tried the door, found that it was locked, and then pounded on it.

A painter, his cap well besplattered, as were his overalls, came to shake his head and shout, "The store's closed. Won't open for more'n a week or two, come back then!"

"I'm looking for Mrs. Vancouver, Mrs. Moria Vancouver," Quinn shouted back.

The painter shook his head. "Never heard of her. Come back when the store's open."

Cursing to himself, Quinn strode off in search of the address Rose had given him, that of the rooming house where Moria was staying. His jacket collar turned up against the rain, wind-driven off the lake with a chill and degree of discomfort that only an October day in Chicago could know, his hat brim pulled down over his eyes, he cursed the store that was closed, he cursed the weather, but most of all he cursed the lack of facts that were available to him. If Moria wasn't at the rooming house, how the devil was he to find her?

His father thought that he was out of his mind, and so did his sister and Chet Chambers, her husband, who'd both ridden over from their own ranch to tell him that he must be insane to go chasing off to Chicago in search of a woman he hadn't seen since she was a fifteen-year-old girl, a woman who was married and had two children and a husband who was still very much alive. But his mother had looked at him with her calm, steady eyes, and told him that if he had to go, then he might as well go and get it out of his system or else he'd never know any peace.

He knew that he'd disappointed his mother by not marrying years ago, that she would have accepted and loved any one of the half-dozen girls he might have married, but unlike his father and Mattie, she never nagged him about it. His father told him, bluntly, that he was a damned fool, and Mattie was still doing her best to be a matchmaker, shoving him into contact with first one girl and then another, never giving up hope that this last one would be the one to make him forget that society snob back East, that black-haired bitch who'd bewitched him until he'd taken all leave of his senses.

There had been many times over the years when Quinn had agreed with both his father and his sister. He must be out of his mind, to deny himself the comfort, the fulfillment, of a wife and children, all because he'd met a girl who had been little more than a child, all those years ago, a girl he could never have, anyway. He'd been crazy even to think about being able to have her, once she was old enough, if he had the guts to go back to the Hudson River Valley and win her and tell William Northrup that he and all his millions could go to blazes. But all the same he'd been going to go, and if he didn't succeed he'd at least know that he'd given it his best try.

Thoughts of failure had not actually played any part in his thinking. If a man wanted something, he went out and got it, if he was deserving of being called a man. Maybe the girl would have changed, maybe he wouldn't want her anymore, but he wasn't going to call it quits until he knew for sure, one way or the other.

The news of Moria's marriage to Anthony Vancouver, when she was only seventeen, had stunned him. Seventeen, she was still only a child, William Northrup must have been out of his mind to allow it! He'd been planning to go back that fall, after roundup, he knew that Liam would be glad to see him, that renewing their friendship would be satisfying in itself even if everything else went sour. But if there'd been any chance at all he would have been right in there fighting, and William Northrup and all the people like him, who built walls to keep people like him out, would have learned what a westerner was made of.

Seventeen, and married, gone to Europe on her honeymoon. And then her first child, a boy, when she'd been eighteen, and a girl when she was nineteen, and Quinn had set himself to forget the girl with the long black hair and the laughing blue eyes and the lilting laugh that had set his heart to throbbing with a hunger that had not yet, even today, been satisfied.

But not for lack of other sustenance. Quinn was very much a man, with a man's physical needs, and an ever more raging need to find solace for his loss. A man wasn't designed to live alone, nature itself had planned it that way, and when he hadn't been squiring one girl or another around, determined to fall in love with her and bury Moria's memory so deep that it would never rise to haunt him again, he'd found brief, temporary forgetfulness in the arms of other kinds of women—the dance hall girls and prostitutes who were only too willing to accommodate him when he was available.

The trouble was, none of it had worked. The memory of the girl with the black hair and the laughing blue eyes had still haunted his dreams, and he'd known that no other woman would ever satisfy him, and that if she was lost to him, then marriage was not for him. Whatever girl he might marry would be cheated because he could never love her as much as he loved the girl he couldn't have. And by the time he had reached his thirties, the dance hall girls and prostitutes seldom saw him. The encounters had been too unsatisfactory, had left him with an empty feeling that was worse than his original need.

His life was reasonably content, even so. He made it content. He loved the Arizona Territory, he loved the ranch and every aspect of the grueling work that went into it. He and his father bred the best horses north of the Rio Grande, one of Kamil's descendants was even now giving promise of being an even more magnificent animal than Kamil himself.

Kamil! Quinn snorted. His name had been Rio del Oro, no matter if William Northrup had preferred to rename him some near-Eastern name to match the black, Jazir, that he had had brought over from Arabia. Rio del Oro had been every particle as fine a horse as the Arabian, and the line still went on, the envy of every connoisseur of horses who laid eyes on them and dug down into his pockets until it hurt to pay for them, providing that Quinn was willing to sell.

It was a satisfying life, in spite of his inability to make it completely satisfying by acquiring a wife and children, and it would have gone on being satisfying if Quinn hadn't received the letter from Rose O'Riley that was in his pocket now, read and reread until he'd nearly read the words right off the paper. But now he had only one object, and that was to find Moria and give her any help he could give her, and to punish or destroy whoever had hurt her if that was what she wanted.

The street he found himself on appalled him. Moria, living on this street? His stomach a tight knot, he knocked on the door of the house Rose had said Moria lived in, determined that if he could do nothing else, he'd have her out of here and living in a decent place before nightfall.

The woman who opened the door was so slatternly that Quinn was even further appalled. "I'm looking for Mrs. Moria Vancouver. She has a room here, I believe."

"There's no Mrs. Vancouver here."

"Then where is she? Do you know where she's gone, her present address?"

"How could I know, when she was never here? You've come to the wrong place." The woman started to shut the door in his face, but Quinn's foot was in the way, holding it open.

"A young lady, black hair, blue eyes. A pretty young lady."

"Moria?" Uncertainty crossed the woman's face. "I had a young lady like that, with blue eyes and black hair, but her name was Moria Donovan, not Vancouver, or so she told me." Now avid curiosity filled her eyes. "Is she in trouble? Why would she take a room under a false name?"

Moria Donovan! Quinn's heart leaped. Of course it was Moria, it couldn't be anyone else. Ignoring the landlady's question, he asked, "Is she at home? I must see her immediately."

"She doesn't live here anymore. She moved."

"The address! Do you have the address?"

"No, I don't. She didn't say. She isn't in trouble with the law, is she? This is a decent house, I never would have rented her a room if I'd known she was lying about her name!"

But Quinn had already turned and was striding away, heading back to Greenbaum's Department Store, the only lead he now had. This time he pounded on the door and demanded entry until one of the workmen disappeared into the back of the store and returned with a small man, his suit as rumpled as his wrinkled face, who unlocked the door to put an end to the disturbance.

"I'm looking for Moria Donovan. She works for you."

"That's news? Only who's working for who? I'm working for her is more like it, and who are you?"

"Is she here?"

"Where else would she be? She and Reba, driving me out of what mind I have left! Who are you?" The question, repeated, was sharp, and Quinn realized that in spite of his agitated, flustered appearance the man in front of him was shrewd.

"I'm Quinn Bradmore. Miss Donovan knows me. May I see her?"

"I'll ask her if she wants to see you." Quinn had the very distinct impression that if Moria were to say that she didn't want to see him, the door would be locked again in his face and no amount of pounding would make it open again. To be on the safe side, he shouldered his way inside, and Abraham, in his turn, realized that if Quinn wanted to come in and see Moria, Abraham Greenbaum wasn't going to be able to stop him. Shrugging, spreading his hands, he gave up.

"Upstairs," he said. He led the way, up a staircase that was in the process of being carpeted with royal blue carpeting, whose banisters had been freshly painted with gilt paint. Then up a second flight, carpeted with the same carpet and with the same gilt-painted banisters, and down a stretch of carpeted hall to a room whose door stood open, and even before Quinn was close enough to see inside he heard a voice filled with laughing impatience.

"Clara Fitzgerald, if you don't stand still I'll stick this pin in you! Do stop fidgeting, you know that the fit has to be perfect!"

"I was only trying to see." This voice was plaintive.

340

"You can see in a minute, when I'm sure that it's going to fit without a wrinkle. There! Now you can look."

"Oh!" The second voice wasn't plaintive now, it was filled with delight. "It's so elegant! I knew it was going to be elegant, but it's even more elegant than I thought it would be!"

"That's the general idea." Moria's voice was filled with laughter. "Very elegant, and in the height of good taste, as becomes a lady. Greenbaum's own distinctive dress for its salesladies."

"Take it off, then. I have to finish embroidering that monogram before the seams are sewn up." This was a third voice, rich and comfortable, one that Quinn found pleasant on his ears.

"All right, Reba. It's coming off. You finish the embroidery, and I'll go light a fire under those workmen setting up the new counters."

Moria looked up as the two men darkened the doorway, Abraham in front, and she asked, "Abraham, have the mirrors arrived? The hairpiece counters have to have mirrors so the ladies can see themselves. They should have been here days ago!"

"Plain mirrors we could have had, your gilt-framed mirrors were harder," Abraham said sourly. "Moria, here's someone to see you. If you don't know him I'll call half a dozen of the workmen to throw him out."

A woman screamed, and Quinn, who had started to step into the workroom, a dressmaking room from what he could see of it, backed up with his face covered with confusion as a lady, it must be Clara Fitzgerald, clutched the half-finished dress she had just removed in front of her to conceal her petticoats and camisole.

"Beg pardon, ma'am."

"Well, I should certainly think so!"

"Quinn?" Moria's voice was uncertain, filled with disbelief, it sounded as if she were fifteen years old again, a child. "Quinn, is that you?"

She was hallucinating, it couldn't be anything else. She'd been working so hard, every day from the earliest hour she could prod Abraham to unlock the store until late into the evening, driving

341

herself to attend to every detail of everything pertaining to the women's departments herself, determined that everything must be so perfect that every middle-class matron and young lady in Chicago would swarm into the store intent on buying everything they saw. She was dreaming, and besides even if she wasn't this man wasn't Quinn Bradmore, his shoulders were broader, his face harder, he was too old, years too old.

"No. Of course I don't know him. Oh, Quinn!"

Her last two words were shrieked as she followed Quinn out into the hallway and looked at him with wide-eyed, still disbelieving recognition. "Quinn Bradmore! It's you, it really is, I'm not dreaming!"

Quinn's body felt like it was shaking in his effort not to sweep her into his arms, to hold her close, to crush her to him with such force that she'd never be able to get away. He would have known her anywhere, on the streets of London, on the streets of Shanghai! The years between didn't matter, they'd only made her more beautiful. Her hair was a little disarranged, one strand fell over her forehead and across her left eye and now she blew at it childishly before she tucked it back with an impatient hand.

"If you're dreaming, then we're having the same dream. I had one heck of a time finding you! The store was closed, and your landlady told me you'd moved without giving her your new address."

"I live with Mr. and Mrs. Greenbaum now. Reba, this is Quinn Bradmore, an old friend, I haven't seen him for years and years and I still don't believe this, it can't be happening!"

"He's pretty solid, for a dream," Reba said from just behind her. She was studying Quinn, and he had a half-amused, half-despairing conviction that if she found him wanting he might as well have saved himself the trouble of this trip to Chicago. "Where do they grow men so big, and so brown?"

"Arizona Territory, ma'am."

"Indians and cacti and rattlesnakes," Reba said. She was still reserving her opinion, but her blood was racing with excitement.

Unknown to anyone, even to Abraham and Moria, Reba was an avid reader of those lurid periodicals which depicted impossible exploits by a breed of men who could never have existed, the westerners who were so quick on the draw that they could shoot a rattlesnake in one eye before he could rattle, who could stop stampedes of long-horned steers and chase rustlers and bandits across barren wastelands and bring about justice with their flaming guns and their iron fists.

"Yes, ma'am. Moria, Mrs. Van . . . Miss Donovan . . ." Quinn winced. Why couldn't he get ahold of himself, what if these people, these friends of Moria's, didn't know that she was married, that her name was Mrs. Anthony Vancouver?

"It's all right, Quinn. Abraham and Reba know my whole life history."

"Which is one heck of a lot more than I know!" The words burst out before he could stop them. "Is there someplace we can talk? I have a lot to catch up on, and I've come a long way to find you. Rose didn't tell me much in her letter."

"She wrote to you, and told you to come?" Moria's voice was incredulous.

"I came on my own account. Of course I had to find you! If you were in any kind of trouble, I had to come."

Reba made up her mind, and she would never change it. "It's late, it's time to stop for the day. Mr. Bradmore, you'll come to supper, and you and Moria can talk yourselves out. Abe and I will stay in the kitchen and you can have the parlor, we won't bother you, you won't even know we're there."

"Thank you, ma'am. I appreciate it."

"You'll appreciate Reba's cooking even more," Moria told him. She turned to call back into the workroom, "Clara, are you decent yet? You can go home now, I don't believe we'll need another fitting. And, Quinn, I hope you won't mind if I work while we talk, we still have five more dresses to finish and time is running short, but it's all plain stitching now, it won't distract me."

"It looks like you're mighty busy around here. What are you

343

trying to do, turn this store into another Marshall Field and Company?'' Quinn was baffled at Moria's part in all this. If she were merely an employee, why was she living with Mr. and Mrs. Greenbaum, and taking so much of the work on her shoulders? From the looks of things, and from what Abraham Greenbaum had said, she was running the whole shebang!

He learned the gist of the story over supper. They ate in the kitchen, Reba's ultimate stamp of approval of him. If she hadn't liked him, they would have eaten in the dining room, with the best china and her prized heirloom linen tablecloth.

''And would you believe, when I wrote Rose that the store was in trouble and how I wished we could change it around, Michael McCarthy decided that it was just the investment he was looking for!'' Moria said, her eyes shining with as much excitement as she'd shown the first time she had seen Jazir. ''Thousands and thousands of dollars; Michael was telling Rose the truth when he told her that he was by way of becoming a wealthy man!''

''At interest,'' Abraham said dourly. ''Don't forget the interest! A Jew this Mr. McCarthy should have been, the head he has for business!''

''But we're on our way! There was enough for everything we wanted, enough to do it right.''

''Enough for what you and Reba want,'' Abraham said, his voice still sour. ''Me, I didn't want bankruptcy, which is what I'll get!''

His face belied his pessimistic words. His eyes, as they rested on Moria, were filled with love and pride. He didn't know what it was that he must have done right, but he must have done something right because Moria was here, in his house, she was the daughter he and Reba had yearned for all their lives, the daughter of their old age, this beautiful girl. My daughter, Miss Donovan. Your *daughter*, Mr. Greenbaum? So? And hadn't stranger things happened, hadn't the Red Sea parted to let his people through?

Ever since that first night when Reba had insisted that Moria come to supper, it had been so. Reba's heart had opened and taken Moria inside, and she had belonged to them. Within three days Moria had been settled in the biggest bedroom upstairs, the bedroom that had never been used because it had been intended for the children, for the little girls who needed more room for their pretty things than boys needed; the smaller, back bedroom had been going to be for the boys.

Reba had gone through the store like a whirlwind, and there'd been as little chance of standing against her. She'd picked out this bed, that bureau, the prettiest, most comfortable chair. She'd bought pictures for the walls, she'd sewn new curtains for the windows, she'd hung Moria's few dresses in the wardrobe herself, her fingers caressing the fine materials, her eyes marveling that such clothes should be hanging in her house even if there were so few of them. There'd be more, and of just as fine quality, when the store began to make a profit, when the remodeling paid off, when Greenbaum's image had imprinted itself on Chicago and the beauty-starved women who couldn't afford Marshall Field's stampeded through its doors.

They never stopped talking, those two, their heads were together every minute, talking, jabber-jabber-jabber, and laughing too, always laughing. Moria's laughter made Abraham's heart swell, because he had a very good idea that she hadn't laughed for a long time, ever since that wicked man had killed her father, and her husband and her father-in-law had turned her out and taken her children from her.

They knew it all, he and Reba, because Moria had told them. Reba had wept, Abraham had never seen her weep as she'd wept over the story. To think of having lived nearly all of your life as a lie, having had to live a lie, pretending to be someone you weren't! And then to fall in love with a scoundrel, with a man who wasn't worth the sole of your shoe, and have him turn out even worse than Liam Donovan had been afraid he would! Reba hoped that Jehovah would be able to think of more dreadful ways to punish Anthony Vancouver than she could think of.

As for William Northrup, it was a pity that he hadn't died when he'd had a stroke after Moria had told him the truth, only that would have been too good for him. And she'd love to meet Rose O'Riley. My friend, Rose O'Riley. My best friend, Rose O'Riley. And the children, Reid and Gayle, were Reba's grandchildren, and she grieved because she'd never seen them and probably never would, but that couldn't stop her from loving them, she who had never had a child or a grandchild before.

Abraham might not be a rich man, and he might not be a smart enough man to have a store like Marshall Field and Company, but he had friends, he knew a lawyer, and he badgered the man to find out everything about the laws that kept Moria from having her children for as long as the Vancouvers chose to keep them from her. What he had learned was that it was a blessing that Moria and Reba had the remodeling of the store to take their minds off their troubles. When he was a richer man, if the store didn't go bankrupt, he'd hire other lawyers, but even then he didn't think it would do any good. All the same, he'd get the best, so good that with enough money to fight there might be a chance.

In the meantime he comforted Moria and Reba as well as he could. "They'll grow up, and then they can come to you of their own free minds, and they'll do it. They won't forget you, Rose O'Riley will see to that, she and your Reid are close. He'll never turn against you, that boy of yours. And Gayle only needs a little unspoiling, but how could that happen with Reba here to spoil her even more?"

"I'd spoil her with the flat on my hand on her . . . on the back of her skirt!" Reba had told them. "That's the best kind of spoiling, it keeps them from being so spoiled that nothing can help them when they grow up. Moria, cry. That's what tears are for."

And Moria had cried, in Reba's arms, and then she had dried her tears and started scheming and planning how to help repay Reba and Abraham for giving her the one thing that no one else in the world could have given her, for giving her themselves. And when Michael McCarthy had invested in the store, making all she wanted for it possible, she had been so busy that she had time to cry only at night, while she counted down the long years until the day her children would be grown-up and could come to her of their own free will.

And when they came, as she must go on believing they would, they'd find a mother they could be proud of. Moria Donovan, of Greenbaum's Department Store! She'd be rich, she'd be famous, she'd be ready to give them everything that their father, that their grandfather, couldn't and wouldn't give them, a sense of real pride, not false pride, but pride in achievement, pride in decency, and more than all of that, genuine love. Her love, and the love of their adopted grandparents of whom they still had not even heard.

In the front parlor at last, with Reba and Abraham still in the kitchen, Quinn couldn't force himself to sit still on the stiff horsehair sofa. He got up and paced, turning every few steps to face Moria and try to reason with her, or if she wouldn't see reason, to beat her down until she'd do as he wanted.

"You're young!" he flung at her for the tenth time. "You're too young and beautiful to bury yourself in the lives of Reba and Abraham Greenbaum, no matter how much you love them. You could get a divorce from that bast—from Anthony Vancouver, it has to be possible! You can't spend the rest of your life married to a department store, no matter how much of a success you're determined to make of it. Mr. Greenbaum has financial backing now, he doesn't need you, he can go on from where you left off. Moria, I love you! I've loved you all these years. I want you. You belong to me, you belong with me, back in Arizona. We have all our lives in front of us, are you going to make us live them out alone?"

"I'm married. And I can't divorce Tony, there's no way. My children would be hurt, their lives ruined, if the entire truth came out, and even then I wouldn't have a chance. Tony and my father-in-law are capable of doing as they threatened, of locking me away, treating me as a madwoman, and they'd do it if I forced it on them. You have no idea how ruthless people like them can be, Quinn. You have no idea at all."

"They'll find out how ruthless I can be, when I go back there and beat them within an inch of their lives! If you can't get a divorce, there's no reason you can't be a widow!''

Even as his heated words burst out, Quinn realized the futility of them. If he were to use force on the Vancouvers, there was no way that he wouldn't be arrested, imprisoned, and if he so completely lost control of himself that Anthony Vancouver ended up dead, it would mean hanging. And the scandal would ruin not only Moria, it would ruin his family as well, it would destroy his mother.

"Then come with me without getting a divorce!" Desperate, Quinn was ready to grasp at any straw. "In Arizona, who would know that you were Moria Vancouver, that you're married? Only my immediate family would know, and they wouldn't tell."

"Quinn, are you honestly asking me to start living another life of lies? I couldn't do it, I couldn't bear it! And even if I could bring myself to do it, I couldn't do it to you. You'd always know that I wasn't really your wife, that we had no right to be together. And if we had children they would be illegitimate.''

Maddeningly to Quinn, Moria went on stitching at the seams of the dress she was working on. Her face was pale, but her hands were steady as she plied the needle, making stitches so fine and tiny that even Quinn's western-keen eyes could hardly see them.

"And how do you know that you love me? All you know of me is a memory, those few weeks we had together when I was a child of fifteen. There's no way that you can know that you love me, any more than there's any way that I can love you, with only those few memories we have in common.''

Quinn's face, his eyes, went so bleak that Moria's heart twisted. She didn't want to hurt him. She knew only too agonizingly what it was like to be hurt. But the whole thing was impossible, and Quinn ought to realize it.

She shifted the position of the dress so that she could work on it more easily, and the movement of her hand caught Quinn's eye, and with an exclamation that filled the parlor he grabbed her hand and held it up.

"You're wearing the bracelet I made you! You hadn't forgotten me, not for a minute, or you wouldn't be wearing it!"

Dear Lord, what was she going to do? She forced herself to meet his eyes, her own as truthful as her words.

"No, I never forgot you. I thought of you often. And every time there was any kind of a crisis in my life, I wore the bracelet. It gave me courage. I wore it first for luck. I took it with me on my honeymoon, and I put it on the first time I found out that Tony had betrayed me with another woman. I was wearing it when Reid was born, and Gayle. It helped, Quinn. It's been my talisman. But that doesn't mean that I can give up everything that I hope to be or have, in order to follow you to Arizona and start a new life as filled with lies and deceit as the one I've left behind me! If I cared less for you than I do, I might be able to do it. If I didn't love my children, I might be able to do it. But don't ask me, Quinn. Stop asking me, because all I can say is no."

In the kitchen, Reba fidgeted, bemoaning the fact that she couldn't hear through the walls that separated her from Moria and Quinn. The man loved Moria, Reba had seen that almost the first instant she'd laid eyes on him. Now she knew that he had loved her for years, ever since Moria had been fifteen, loved her so much that he'd come rushing to Chicago the moment he'd learned that she was in some kind of trouble.

And he was a good man. A good man and a strong man. If Moria had been free, Quinn Bradmore was the man Reba would have chosen for her, to cherish her and care for her, to protect her and keep her safe and to make her happy and to father her children. It was a tragedy that Moria wasn't free and that there was no way that she could gain her freedom.

But what if Quinn were able to talk her into going off to that faraway, wild Arizona Territory in spite of all that? And if he could talk her into it, didn't Moria deserve the happiness she'd find with him? What kind of a marriage had the farce between Moria and Anthony Vancouver been? No marriage at all! Bondage was a better word for it, and even a slave has the right to make a break for freedom, to hold on to that freedom once he'd attained it!

What will I do, what will Abe do, if Moria goes with him, Reba wondered, and her eyes were filled with all the tragedy of her persecuted race. The store would mean nothing, their lives would mean nothing, if they were to lose this girl who had become their daughter.

"If she goes, she goes," Abraham said. In all the years of their marriage, even before their marriage because there had never been anyone else for either of them, Abraham had known what Reba was thinking about without her telling him. "And we'll let her go, and we'll pray that she'll be happy."

"Happy she wouldn't be," Reba said, her mouth trembling.

They heard the sound of the front door closing, and a moment later Moria entered the kitchen.

"I finished the dress. There was very little to do on it. Reba, your monogram is beautiful on the bodice, Greenbaum's will be the talk of Chicago!"

"He's gone, without saying good-bye?" Reba asked.

"He asked me to apologize for him." Both Reba and Abraham could see the battle that Moria was waging to keep herself under control. "He wasn't in the mood for social pleasantries, I'm afraid."

"You turned him down, then," Reba said. She rose from her chair and held out her arms. And again, as she had on that other occasion when Moria had told her and Abraham her life story, she said, "Cry. And tomorrow we'll get back to work."

They got back to work, but their work was interrupted, again and again, because although Quinn had left the house in defeat that first night, he wasn't the kind not to go on fighting.

"It would be crazy for me to go back home without spending some time in Chicago while I'm here. And even crazier for me not to spend all the time with you that you'll let me have. It's been a lot of years since the last time I saw you and it may be a lot of years before I see you again. I want all I can get."

Moria's heart was torn in two directions. She wanted Quinn to stay, she wanted it so much that it frightened her, and at the same time she knew that the longer he stayed the harder it would be when they finally had to say good-bye.

In the end, she lifted her chin and decided that like Quinn, she'd take what she could get. Every moment they spent together would be something to savor, something to cherish after he had gone. She'd have these memories, even if she never had anything else.

There was no dress among those Moria had brought with her to Chicago elegant enough for the places Quinn insisted on taking her. Like an irresistible force, Reba bullied and shoved Moria to Marshall Field's, and overrode all her protests as she bullied and bribed a dress to be made almost overnight, regardless of the cost. An evening wrap was added, made of velvet and trimmed with narrow bands of fur, and satin slippers and an evening bag.

"We can't spend all this money on clothes for me, it belongs to the store, Abraham is paying Michael McCarthy interest on it!" Moria protested. But Reba vetoed her protests just as she vetoed Quinn's insistence that he should pay for what Moria needed as he was the one who would reap the benefits of escorting her to the finest restaurants in all her glory.

"It is for the store," Reba said. "We're going to be famous, aren't we? Being seen you have to be, and being seen so elegant that people will remember you, Miss Moria Donovan of Greenbaum's Department Store!"

Moria gave up, laughing. "And you claim that Abraham is the one with a head for business! All right, I'll be a walking advertisement! Only won't it be more an advertisement for Marshall Field's than for Greenbaum's, seeing that the clothes came from there?"

"The beautiful lady isn't from Marshall Field's. Marshall Field's hasn't anything like you!" Reba refused to give even an inch of ground.

And only that one dress and its accessories came from Marshall Field's. Three more were added, of Moria's own design, cut out and stitched up at a record-breaking pace by means of Reba drafting every one of Greenbaum's salesladies who could hold a needle. And the little Jewish housewife, who had no head for business, dressed herself in unaccustomed elegance of her own and made a distinctly uncomfortable Abraham escort her to a restaurant table only a few tables removed from Moria and Quinn's.

"Look at that beautiful young lady! Just look at that gown! Where have I seen her before? I remember! It's Miss Donovan, the fashion lady that Mr. Greenbaum has brought in to design ladies' apparel for his grand new store!"

Her purpose accomplished, Reba would finish her wine, all that she and Abraham would order because the restaurants weren't kosher, and leave as soon as her glass was drained. They took it on faith that the wineglasses had never contained either meat or milk.

Moria and Quinn spent their afternoons sightseeing, and Quinn shook his head in outright disbelief on Prairie Avenue, the street that was already being called "the street of the stately few." Marshall Field's home was among the grandest of them all, built in 1876 by the architect Richard Morris Hunt, who had distinguished himself by designing the homes of William H. Vanderbilt and John Jacob Astor, among other New York millionaires. Field's mansion was rather less ornate than some of the others on Prairie Avenue, perhaps because his taste was better than those of the wives of the new breed of millionaires, the meat-packers and the grain dealers and their ilk, but Moria knew, through Reba, that its interior walls were covered with yellow satin and that one room was furnished with Louis XVI furniture.

"And Reba told me," Moria told Quinn, her eyes sparkling with laughter, "that the library is filled with beautiful volumes, and that all of the pages have been cut to make it look as if they've been read!"

"I'd rather read one good book than own a thousand that I didn't have time to read," Quinn remarked. "Not that I'm much of a reader. But if I had that man's money, I'd end up the biggest and best horse breeder in the country."

"Mr. Field has horses," Moria informed him. "Fine ones, or so Reba told me."

Quinn's interest perked up. "How many?"

"Three or four," Moria admitted, deflated. And then, brightening, "But they come from his own breeding farm in Nebraska!"

The only answer she got from that was a disgusted "Humph!"

In spite of their aching hearts because the time they would have together would be so short, Reba's machinations added spice to their evening excursions. Moria played her part to the hilt, not only because it could benefit the store but because Quinn was so proud to be seen with her and because he took such delight in Reba's unexpected deviousness. He'd developed a fondness for the woman who had made Moria's life not only bearable but given it a new direction so that she could make something satisfying and worthwhile of it in spite of the debacle of her father's death and her being exiled from her children.

He still found it incredible that Liam had been Moria's father, but he was glad that it was true. That was where Moria got her fighting blood. It was a heritage to be proud of, and he was proud that he'd known Liam and been privileged to call him friend. As for Moria, his life would have been meaningless if he had never known her and loved her, even if he would never be able to have her for his own.

But he, like Moria, wasn't the kind to give up. If he failed this time, he'd come back again, and again and again right up until the time her children were grown if that was the way it had to be, and he'd have her in the end because he wouldn't settle for anything else.

They spent the last evening, before Quinn would have to board the train that would start him on his long journey back to Arizona, in Reba's front parlor, unwilling to share one moment of their last moments together with anyone else, even strangers in a restaurant. Reba and Abraham stayed in the kitchen, as they had on that first night, so that they could be entirely alone.

"Damn it, Moria, how can I go back and leave you here? It's more than you have any right to ask of me!" In spite of his usual control, his nerves were at the breaking point at the thought of leaving her behind now that he'd found her again, now that she needed him. "You'll be throwing your life away, and throwing mine away right along with it! If you knew how much I need you. . . ."

Moria was shaking inside, already feeling so empty and desolate that she could hardly bear it. She didn't dare to think of how much she'd miss Quinn, this man who had haunted all the years of her life since she'd been fifteen merely by being alive. Now, when his control broke and he caught her in his arms, when his mouth came down over hers in a kiss that set her body on fire, every inch of her flesh and blood screamed out for him. She'd been alone for so long, she needed a man, she needed this man! She hadn't been born to live alone, she needed love, Quinn's love, how could she live without him, how could she face the nights alone in her bed, aching for him, wanting him until she'd go mad with the wanting?

"Oh, God, Moria! I love you, I've got to have you!"

She couldn't think anymore. She had to have him, she couldn't bear it if she didn't have him, if she were left alone again. If they hadn't been in Reba's parlor, if Reba and Abraham hadn't been in the kitchen, it would have been too late, she would have let him sweep her up in his own overwhelming need and she'd have been lost.

But they were in Reba's front parlor, and sanity crept back into her mind at the last possible moment. It was impossible. She had to let him go, she had to send him away, even if she died of it.

Defeated, but only for the moment, sick with wanting her, Quinn had only one thing to say before he left.

"I'll be back," he said, his jawline rigid and his eyes fierce with his promise. "You can count on it. And you'd better be here, because if you aren't I'll find you wherever you are, if it takes me all the rest of my life! It isn't over between us, Moria, it never will be. You know that as well as I do."

Moria did know it, and for a moment she had to steel herself against running out of the house after him, against calling him back and agreeing to anything he wanted, even to going to Arizona with him. Her hand was actually on the doorknob when Reba spoke to her from the parlor doorway.

"He's gone? And again he didn't say good-bye! But I forgive him, how could he think of Abraham and Reba at a time like this?"

Moria glared at her, her hands clenched into fists, fighting against screaming.

"Don't you dare tell me to cry!" she said. "Don't you dare!"

21

If it hadn't been for her work in getting the store ready to reopen, Moria was convinced that she would have lost her mind after Quinn left. She insisted on going to the store with Reba and Abraham the next morning, even though Reba cried out in distress at the sight of her white face and the circles under her eyes.

"Let her come," Abraham said. "It will help matters if we don't open on time? But no climbing ladders or walking under them, Moria! At a table you'll sit, with a pencil and paper, not a sketch we have yet for those dresses you fooled me into thinking you were going to design to make me my fortune!"

Every week since the remodeling had started, Moria had intended to get at the sketches, to design dresses that the less affluent women of Chicago could afford but that would still be so smart, so chic, so becoming, that no one could tell them from models that cost three or four times as much at Marshall Field's. She knew that she could do it. And now she had to do it, and it was a blessing. How, she wondered, did people who didn't have work that they had to do manage to survive in times of devastating loss and sorrow?

So she sat at a table in the dressmaking room, surrounded by bolts and swatches of materials, and she sketched. No dress would be made for display, the ladies would choose from the sketches and Greenbaum's would guarantee the completion of the chosen model in such record time that they wouldn't believe it. Every model would be subject to change, to alterations that would flatter the individual figure, that would bring out the customer's best points and conceal her worst. A tuck here, a gather there, a different line to skirt or bodice, and the fortunate lady who had chosen a dress from one of Moria's sketches would think that she was more beautiful than she had ever dreamed she could be.

It was exacting work, demanding all of Moria's attention. When she got up to stretch her limbs, to move around to get her circulation going again, she was all over the store, making sure that everything was being done exactly as she had directed it should be done. The gilt-framed mirrors for the hairpiece counter weren't large enough, they must go back, larger ones must be found and delivered with all speed. How could a lady tell what she looked like in a mirror that was too small? Abraham, be quiet! Are you a woman, what do you know about it? The mirrors must be larger! No, you will not go bankrupt. You'll go bankrupt if you skimp on the things the New Chicago Woman wants in order to feel important and catered to and coddled, not by ordering larger mirrors!

No, no, no! The comfortable padded stools that Moria had insisted on for both the gloves and hairpiece counters were upholstered in a blue that clashed with the royal blue of the store's carpets, it looked more green than blue and it was the wrong material, what moron had changed the order for the material? I'm sorry, Abraham, you aren't a moron, you're only a man so you didn't know any better. Have them done over, and show me the material before you start, I want to see it!

Where are the pug-dog doorstops, where are the statuettes for the knickknack department? Send those vases back, they're revolting. I don't care if you did get a lower price by paying cash, with no refunds, make the dealer take them back, he'll find you what you want, if you're firm with him.

Driven to the wall, Abraham snarled, "Why don't you do it yourself, if you know so much?"

"All right, I will."

"A woman, a young lady, haggle with a dealer?"

"You just watch me!"

"How can I watch, when I'll be in my bed with a breakdown from going bankrupt buying doodads that our customers can't afford?"

"Give the lady what she wants, remember? And she wants doodads, she wants china and pressed glass that looks like cut glass and pretty little statues to put on her shelves, and she wants to see her whole face and head when she looks into our gilt-framed mirrors! And she wants to sit in a chair that looks elegant and matches the carpet while she's doing it!"

"This is what I get for hiring a saleslady Marshall Field's fired! Out of the kindness of my heart I hired you, and now you stab me!"

"Bread on the waters!" Moria shot back at him. "You gave a little charity, and you're going to get so rich you'll be living on Prairie Avenue and Reba will be a society queen!"

Moria had been progressing through the nearly completed store as she talked, with Abraham tagging along after her like a sad-faced dachshund, and now she stopped in her tracks. "You! Why are you hanging those pictures so high? Ladies buy pictures, not gentlemen, and ladies aren't tall! How can a lady tell if she wants to buy a picture if it's hanging so high that she has to crane her neck to see it? Lower them, lower them all, every one of them!"

"It'll leave nail holes," the workman complained. "And you won't like that."

"Then fill the nail holes and paint over them, but lower the pictures!"

"By the day we're paying him, and half a day lost lowering the pictures!" Abraham's face became even more lugubrious.

"And pictures sold that would hang there forever without being sold if we left them hanging so high!" Moria retorted, without giving him as much as a glance. "And I want a fern in here, right in that corner. A big fern, with a chair, no, two chairs, beside it, nice chairs. I'll pick the upholstery for them now. Gilt chairs, large enough so that large ladies can be comfortable in them. Large ladies get tired, and uncomfortable ladies don't buy, they're too busy being uncomfortable."

Bankrupt, Abraham thought, sinking ever deeper into despair. And he went in search of Reba, to tell her that Moria was a genius, that she was going to make them millionaires, if she didn't bankrupt them first.

Greenbaum's reopened in time to reap the benefits of the Christmas trade. The last week was frantic, with Reba worn to a frazzle trying to keep some semblance of peace between Abraham and Moria.

"The blue paint you got, the gilt paint you got, the carpeting you got, the gilt-framed mirrors you got, the ferns you got. But naked dolls?"

"They aren't naked. They're beautifully dressed in undergarments. Don't worry about it, Abraham, just trust me. I know they'll sell."

Abraham tugged at his thinning hair with such force that he was in danger of waking up the next morning bald. "By giving away material?"

"Scraps," Moria said complacently. Her idea was an original one that she was sure that the ladies would embrace with enthusiasm. Order a dress made for Christmas, one of Moria's own designs, and buy your daughter a doll exactly like Mama. Your choice of hair color to match your own. Patterns would be available for the dolls' dresses to match Mama's dress. Moria and Reba had spent countless evening hours cutting out the little patterns. On the ground floor, as the customers entered, there was a completed dress on a dress form, with a doll dressed in an exact duplicate standing on a marble-topped table beside it. Delight your daughter this Christmas, a beautifully hand-lettered sign invited. No charge for doll dress pattern or material.

"Bankrupt!" Abraham moaned, when he found Moria tying bows of red and green satin ribbon around the necks of the pug-dog doorstops, around the necks of ceramic cats.

"They'll sell," Moria told him.

"Bankrupt!" Abraham whimpered, when Moria brought in a street-corner calligrapher to write out calling cards in his beautiful Spencerian script, to be given free with orders of Greenbaum's finest stationery. The street price for calling cards was ten cents per dozen, but at Greenbaum's, the lady paid nothing, they were a token of appreciation for her patronage.

About the toy department, which Greenbaum's had never had before, Abraham couldn't even moan, he was struck dumb with shock, too numb to make a whimper. Dolls, sleds, cast-iron horses and wagons and trains and fire engines, hoops and hobbyhorses, Moria had made a clean sweep of the market, ordering in such quantity that she'd been given the lowest possible price, so that Greenbaum's in turn could sell at lower prices. Leaping in to avert an actual stroke, Moria assured Abraham that people would spend money on their children if the price were right. "We'll advertise: 'Don't pay too much, buy at Greenbaum's.' "

Abraham didn't suffer a stroke. He wept instead.

Greenbaum's had to hire three extra seamstresses to keep up with the orders for ladies' dresses, as the ladies went into raptures over the dolls, with choice of hair and eye color to match their own or their daughters', to dress in replicas of their own dresses. Almost overnight, the "Miss Moria Donovan" doll became famous. The "findings" shelves were stripped to fashion more bows for the ceramic statues, as harrassed stock clerks sped to the stockroom to bring out more of the whimsical pug-dog doorstops and ceramic cats. The calligrapher reaped what was to him a fortune, and to Greenbaum's a healthy profit in stationery.

"Aren't you ashamed of yourself, making so much money out of a Christian holiday?" Moria teased Abraham.

"And who persecuted us, down through two thousand years give or take a few years, so they should make a small atonement, enough profit so that we won't starve?"

The reborn Greenbaum's was launched in a blaze of glory as the curious came to look and stayed to buy. Abraham counted the sales with a sense of unreality. Such a thing couldn't be happening to Abraham Greenbaum. A merchant prince he'd be, if it kept up, and his head danced with figures as he cautioned himself not to count the chickens before they were hatched, maybe there wouldn't be a chicken left to make the soup he'd need when the bubble burst and he went bankrupt. Reba would be dressed in silks and satins and living in a mansion, on Prairie Avenue even, with servants at her beck and call and she'd never have to slave over a hot stove again, or wash another pair of long johns. A carriage she'd have, and a team of high-stepping horses, so that when she drove out people would point and stare and say, "There goes Mrs. Abraham Greenbaum!"

"Pish," Reba said. "What would I do in a mansion? With your digestion, you'd die if I didn't do your cooking! A new set of parlor furniture I want, and new wallpaper, we can afford that maybe, with all these sales. And no other woman is going to wash your underwear, Abe Greenbaum, you want I should have some other woman laughing because you're so skinny?"

If Abraham's astonishment at the sales threatened to overwhelm him, Moria was equally astonished and more than a little amused when she received an invitation, couched in the most polite language, to call at Marshall Field and Company, where she would be granted an interview in reference to the possibility that Marshall Field and Company might be interested in procuring her services.

Abraham's hair suffered still more mutilation when Moria read the letter aloud to him and Reba. "So hiring you right out from under me they're going to, how can I pay you what they will? So go, go, make your fortune, Jehovah forbid that Abraham Greenbaum would stand in your way!''

"Don't be ridiculous," Moria said. "Even Mr. Marshall Field doesn't have enough money to hire me away from you." Laying the letter down on the kitchen table, where they were sitting after supper, Moria rose and walked around the table and wrapped her arms around Abraham and kissed the top of his head.

Abraham squirmed. "Reba, what's she up to? Make her stop, it isn't decent, me a married man and you right in the room! Moria, you aren't going to work for Mr. Field?"

"Of course I'm not! And I'll kiss you whenever I feel like it. Reba doesn't mind, it saves her the trouble of kissing somebody as ugly as you are."

"Ugly, yes. But I'm used to him," Reba said complacently. "Twenty-five years it took me to get used to him, but I guess I'm so used to him now that I'll keep him, even if he is as stupid as a jackass. Moria leave us? Ha!" She replenished Abraham's glass of tea and pushed the sugar bowl toward him. "Go on, put in two teaspoons, put in three, four even, maybe it'll sweeten your disposition!''

Abraham spooned in five teaspoonfuls. Who was the head of this household, that Reba should tell him how many teaspoonfuls of sugar he could put in his tea? To drive home his point, he spooned in another.

"You'd better let Mr. Marshall Field hire you. Greenbaum's will be bankrupt in a few weeks and you won't have a job."

This time Moria kissed his cheek. "Then we'll starve together. But in the meantime, let's get busy with the after-Christmas campaign."

"After-Christmas sale?" Another tuft of hair was sacrificed to Abraham's consternation. "Are you determined to ruin me? It isn't enough that Mr. Garfield is dead, that that madman Charles Guiteau shot him, right at the Baltimore and Potomic Railroad Depot in Washington, D.C.? And now Mr. Arthur is president and how do we know what he'll do to the country? We just get used to one president so we'll know which way to jump, and now there's another, he could ruin business."

"Maybe Mr. Arthur will be a good man," Reba said, completely unruffled. She pulled the sugar bowl back to her side of the table. "Enough. You want I should be a widow because you sugared yourself to death?"

"Mr. Garfield had to be a good man or that Puck cartoons paper wouldn't have printed all those scurrilous cartoons about him! He never stoned cats, he always hanged his, one said! And even when he was a boy, he showed a great love of liberty, that one showing him truanting from school, yet! He must have been a good man or his enemies wouldn't have been so afraid of him that they'd print garbage like that! And a steeple on the White House he didn't build, even if he was a preacher, and if that cartoon was a lie, then so were all the others. But who knows from this Mr. Arthur?"

"Then you find out all about him that you want to know, and let Moria take care of the after-Christmas sale! Politics are for men but women know what women will buy and how much they'll pay."

"Mr. Abraham Lincoln assassinated! Mr. James Garfield assassinated! In Budapest my father should have stayed, why did he think things would be better here?"

"Because things are better here. Drink your tea."

"Mr. Marshall Field trying to take our Moria away! This is better?"

"Yes, it's better, because I don't have to let Mr. Marshall Field take me away unless I want to go, and I don't. No more tea, you've had enough." With that, Moria removed the glass from Abraham's hand just as he was lifting it to his mouth, and carried it to the sink. Both hands tearing at his hair, Abraham bemoaned the day he'd added another woman to a life that had been complicated enough with only one.

Dear God, what would she do without Abraham and Reba, Moria wondered, her throat tight and her eyes smarting from the tears that she refused to shed. Every doll that Greenbaum's sold, every hair ribbon for a little girl, made the ache in her heart grow. Cast-iron horses, paint boxes, balls, sold in such quantities for boys, tore at her insides. But Gayle was too old for dolls, Reid was too old for cast-iron horses, and the realization that this Christmas she didn't even know what they would want, and that she was not permitted to send them anything, was almost more than she could bear. How could she survive Christmas, so far away from her children?

She wanted Reid and Gayle, she wanted Quinn. On the afternoon of Christmas Eve, she was so depressed that she couldn't stay at the store. Its walls closed in on her, every shining, expectant face of a boy or a girl lacerated her soul until she thought that she'd die of it. Last Christmas Liam had been alive, Eugenia had been alive, they'd exchanged gifts. She'd given Liam a riding crop that had come from Ireland. He'd given her a box of three handkerchiefs of the finest Irish linen, the box with Eugenia's name on it as the giver so that no one would know, but she could carry one of the handkerchiefs with her always, and feel close to her father. She still had them, they were among the few things that she had brought with her. She still carried one of them every day. Soon she'd have to stop carrying them, so they wouldn't wear out and disintegrate.

She walked the streets of Chicago, acutely aware of the happy faces that surrounded her. Her hands tucked into a muff, she walked without noticing where she was going. A light snow had begun to fall, it would be a white Christmas, the children would be able to take their Christmas sleds out. How many times had she perched on a sled behind Reid, her arms around his shoulders, while he'd sent it flying down a hill while she'd screamed in pretended terror, and they'd both ended up in a snowdrift, covered from head to foot and laughing until their tears froze on their cheeks? Tony had been indulgent about her childish behavior, Estelle had prayed that none of their friends would see her daughter-in-law behaving in so undignified a manner, Jacob had ignored it if he had known about it at all. But Reid was too old for sleds now, or was he? She didn't even know! He was so grown-up for his years, but he was still a little boy, after all.

365

She was passing a church, a Catholic church. People were going in and coming out. Moria stopped and looked at it. She wanted to go in, she wanted to pray for Liam and for Eugenia and for her children. But she couldn't have even that comfort. She'd turned her back on her church years ago, when she'd been a child, because she'd been forced to attend the Lutheran church which William Northrup and Eugenia attended, keeping her Catholicism a deep and hidden secret. She hadn't been to confession in all this time. Forgive me, Father, for I have sinned. . . .

Dimly, she realized that a smartly dressed woman was looking at her, that she had turned to her male companion and was saying something about her. "No wonder she looks so lovely! It's Miss Donovan, Miss Moria Donovan, of Greenbaum's, wearing one of her own creations, without a doubt. Look at the line of that coat! It's exquisite."

Yesterday, a week ago, she would have been elated to overhear that scrap of conversation. But this was Christmas Eve, and she wanted her children, she wanted Quinn.

"So you're the young lady who has cut into the margin of my profits! Miss Donovan? May I ask where Mr. Greenbaum found you?"

It was Mr. Field! For a moment Moria was so surprised that she couldn't think how to answer.

"Mr. Greenbaum didn't find me, I found him. I applied to him because I was in need of employment, my former employment having been terminated at the request of my employer."

"Extraordinary! May I further impose on you to ask where you were employed before Mr. Greenbaum was so fortunate as to acquire your services?"

"At Marshall Field and Company. I sold gloves. But Marshall Field and Company didn't see fit to keep me on, much to my own good fortune. Good day, Mr. Field. And Merry Christmas!" Moria gave the merchandising tycoon her most brilliant smile, she had no grudge against him, he wasn't the one who had fired her although he probably would have if he'd happened to be in his department store at the time of the incident with the overbearing lady and the cash boy, and had happened to witness it. Besides, she hadn't known then that she had a flair for design, that she had a business head on her shoulders, so how could Marshall Field and Company have been expected to know it?

Her smile remained on her face for a few seconds after she walked away from the nonplussed Mr. Field. Abraham and Reba would be filled with delight at the story of this encounter, she'd have to repeat it over and over until they knew every word that had been exchanged by heart.

But the lifting of her depression was short. She went on walking, intent only on making herself so tired that she'd be able to sleep that night, this Christmas Eve night when her children were half a continent away from her to the east, and Quinn half a continent away from her to the west.

It had been dark for hours before she found herself at the corner of her own street. She had to go home, Reba and Abraham would be frantic, worrying them like this was a terrible thing for her to do after all they'd done for her—giving her a home, a family, a reason to go on living and trying. By this time, poor Abraham might be as bald as a billiard ball.

The front part of the house was dark, they'd be in the kitchen as they always were. Even in her present dark mood, Moria's mouth curved a little at the corners as she thought of Abraham's dreams of putting Reba in a mansion, along with swarms of servants. Reba would go out of her mind, what would she do in a drawing room, when even her own front parlor was too formal for her, when she'd rather be in her kitchen?

The front door opened even as she was reaching for the knob. Reba's voice was sharp with relief. "She's here! She's come back!" The next instant, Moria was engulfed first in Reba's arms, and then in Abraham's as he came hurrying from the kitchen. Reba had been in the dark parlor, watching from the window, more certain with every passing moment that Moria had been run down by a dray or kidnapped by white slavers, that she'd lost her memory and was wandering the cold, dark streets without knowing who she was or where to go.

"Where have you been? You wicked girl, wicked, to worry Abe so!" Reba scolded, even as her tears of relief drenched Moria's cheek. "Come back to the kitchen, you're frozen, you're an icicle; Abe, is the kettle still on, our Moria has to have tea, good hot tea! And our supper's ruined, it's shriveled to nothing, but I'll find us something. There's chicken soup, I thought of chicken soup when you didn't come home, just in case, it doesn't hurt to be prepared."

Her coat was taken off her, her hat. She was put into a chair at the kitchen table while Reba bustled around making fresh tea, dishing up bowls of chicken soup, and Abraham knelt to take off her shoes and rub her frozen feet. Every remaining hair on Abraham's head was standing on end, mute evidence of his emotions while he'd been waiting for her to come home.

"Where have you been? Would you mind telling, or is it a secret?" Abraham demanded. "If you weren't kidnapped or run down by a wagon, if you didn't lose your memory and forget your way home, you had to be somewhere!"

In spite of the dark mood she'd been in all day, imps danced in Moria's eyes as she answered him. She couldn't resist what she told him.

"I was talking to Mr. Marshall Field."

"Oy!" The sound was a wail. "And you've come back to pack your things, Abraham Greenbaum's house isn't good enough for you anymore now that you're going to work for Mr. Field? Reba, never mind my soup, to eat I'm too sick! Moria's thought it over, Greenbaum's isn't grand enough for her even if she promised! To Mr. Field she went, in answer to his letter!"

Moria couldn't bear to go on tormenting him. "Not quite that, Abraham. I met him on the street, quite by accident. You should have seen his face when I told him that his own store had fired me!"

Just as she'd thought, she had to tell it over and over, every word, every gesture, every expression. Reba laughed so hard that she had to wipe her eyes with her apron, and Abraham rubbed his hands with more glee than he'd felt in years.

"One thing's certain, as well as death and taxes!" he crowed. "Mr. Marshall Field knows who Abraham Greenbaum is now! Abraham Greenbaum is the one who has Miss Moria Donovan!"

The soup had grown cold while Moria had recounted her conversation with Mr. Field, but they ate it anyway. Even cold, Reba's soup was delicious. Halfway through her own bowl, Reba's eyes widened with a sudden recollection.

"The letter, Abe! We forgot the letter! With all this worry it flew right out of my head!" She rose from her chair and hurried to the shelf on which she kept salt and pepper, spices, matches, and she and Abraham fell silent as she retrieved the letter from where she'd put it where she wouldn't forget it.

Moria turned the envelope over and over before she opened it. It wasn't from Rose, it was from Reid. She knew his handwriting, precise, every letter strong and legible. He'd sent her short notes before, sent on by Rose enclosed in her own letters, but this one was special because it was a Christmas letter and it had come on Christmas Eve.

There was a single sheet of paper covered with the same dark, legible handwriting, and another one, blank on the outside where it had been folded. Moria unfolded it, and her breath caught in her throat.

Liam's face looked up at her from the sheet of paper. It was a pencil sketch, drawn from memory, and it was Liam, so like him that Moria's eyes filled with scalding tears and the likeness blurred until Abraham handed her his handkerchief.

It isn't very good, but I did the best I could. I thought you'd like to have it, Mother. I couldn't think of anything else to send you.

I miss you very much. Grandmother Estelle is good to Gayle and me, she does her best to make it up to us that you're gone. I don't see much of Father, he's away from home most of the

*time. I hope you're happy with the Greenbaums, they sound like
wonderful people and I wish I could know them. Thank them for
me for taking such good care of you. Have a merry Christmas.
Your son, Reid.*

Only a few lines, but Moria's heart was running over as she
studied the drawing of Liam again. How true Reid's memory was,
how true the pencil lines!

"A frame!" Reba said, leaning over so that she could study the
picture. "Abe, a frame we've got to have, tonight, it has to be
framed! Go to the store and bring a frame!"

"Oh, Reba, not tonight! It's freezing out, and it's snowing and
it's late!" Moria protested.

"He can find a cab. Abe, did you hear me?" Reba removed his
bowl of soup from in front of him. "The soup I'll have hot for you
when you get back. And I'll heat the sadiron, the creases have got to
be ironed out of the picture. A frame with glass in it, Abe, a gilt
frame, the best one in the store! Make sure it's the right size, and the
best!"

"Bankrupt," Abraham said. "A cab, on Christmas Eve? You
think I'm a magician, maybe, I can wave a magic wand and, presto,
here's a cab?" But he was already shrugging into his coat, wrapping
a muffler around his scrawny neck, pulling a knitted cap that Reba
had made for him down over his ears. A boughten hat was for warm
weather, when ears wouldn't freeze, in the winter Abe had to have a
woolen knitted cap, never mind how it looked, a ludicrous-looking
husband was better than one without ears because they'd frozen
off.

"Take out a picture if you have to!" Reba told him. "And don't
fall down on the ice and break your leg, who'd mind the store?"

She put the sadiron on the range, and snatched Moria's bowl to
reheat her soup. Moria was crying, her heart so full from Reid's
gift and Abraham and Reba's love that she couldn't hold back the
tears.

She tried to repress her sobs, her shoulders shaking. Reba put her now steaming bowl of soup back in front of her and thrust her spoon into her hand.

"Cry," she said. "Cry, Moria. But first eat your soup. It takes strength to cry enough to do any good."

22

"You're enough to drive a man mad!" Quinn said. The muscles of his jaw were knotted, and Moria could see the fury in his eyes and it made her tremble as the full force of it broke over her.

It was summer again, June, and the spring roundup was over, the fall roundup still in the future, and Quinn was back in Chicago to renew his campaign to either talk or force this maddening woman into going back to Arizona with him.

"I never stopped thinking of you, all these months. Your face was in front of me when I woke up in the morning and when I went to sleep at night. I almost broke every bone in my body because I was thinking of you when I was out on the range and a steer charged my horse and I wasn't paying attention to what I was doing and I was thrown and I'd have been trampled and gored if my horse hadn't turned the critter before it could get me. If I hadn't been riding a horse I trained myself I'd have been a goner. I cussed you so hard it's a wonder you didn't hear me all the way back here!

"My mother's worried, she thinks I'm going crazy, my father's convinced that I've already gone around the bend, my sister doesn't

373

speak to me anymore because I turned down her latest bid to match me up with another girl, and all for a woman who digs in her heels like a stubborn maverick calf and refuses to budge!''

"Quinn, nothing has changed. You knew that nothing would have changed before you made this trip. I wrote to you and I know you received my letters because you answered them. I'm still married. I'm still a mother. Abraham and Reba still need me.''

"What about me needing you? Don't I count at all? And Abe and Reba don't need you, from what I've seen Abraham's store is setting a record for making money. You got him off to the right start and he can go on from here without you a heck of a lot better than I can go on without you!''

"That isn't what I mean at all. Of course Abraham could go on making money without me, although I doubt that he'd make as much if I wasn't here to push him into trying new things, new ideas. But it would break their hearts if I left them. It would break their hearts twice as much if I left them to go off and live in sin.''

"What sin? Since when is it a sin to love somebody? According to your own faith you aren't married at all because you weren't married by a priest. In all conscience, you're free to marry me.''

"I'm married. I made my vows, no matter what church I made them in. And I'm married legally. And what about my children, what about Reid and Gayle? How could I ever face them again if I were living with you as your wife?''

"Trust a woman to come up with all sorts of ridiculous reasons why she can't do what she wants to do! Do you know what I think, Moria? I think that you won't come with me because you don't want to give up everything you've accomplished for yourself here in Chicago! How does it feel to be Miss Moria Donovan of Greenbaum's Department Store, the smartest, the most beautiful, the best-dressed woman in Chicago? Do you think that I haven't noticed that you're recognized everywhere we go? Recognized, and stared at, and admired and talked about and envied! The beautiful Miss Moria Donovan, there she is, but who's that man with her? Nobody, he isn't anybody at all!''

"Quinn, that isn't true!" Moria had been going through days of this, and she was near the breaking point. "If only I were free, I'd turn my back on everything I've accomplished without a moment's regret! I wouldn't even look back, except to wave good-bye to Abraham and Reba, and any tears I'd shed would be because of leaving them, not because of leaving what you call my accomplishments here in Chicago."

Maybe what she said was true, but all the same Quinn couldn't help but be disgruntled because of Moria's being so well known, because of the name she'd made for herself in such a short time. When he'd arrived a few days ago, Moria's campaign to sweep the June bride market had just been drawing to a successful conclusion. An entire trousseau for under fifty dollars! A traveling dress, a pair of slippers, a pair of gloves. Four white shirtwaists, four nightgowns, two ruffled petticoats, a linen suit, six chemises and four pairs of drawers. Even a bottle of scent was included, and, in spite of Abraham's continued moans of impending bankruptcy, two dozen calling cards, inscribed with the bride's new married name, were included as a wedding gift from Greenbaum's.

The wedding dress, not included in the trousseau, could also be ordered at Greenbaum's, a Miss Moria Donovan design, designed exclusively for each prospective bride. June, the month of weddings, flattened the pockets of the fathers of the brides, but this June of 1882, it fattened Abraham's pockets to such an extent that he even gave up moaning that the free calling cards would be his ruination.

If the campaign had been such a triumphal success, Moria had so much on her mind that she scarcely noticed how her fame was growing throughout the city. A letter from Rose early in the month had so depressed her that if it hadn't been for the absolute necessity of working, of applying all of her energies to designing the exclusive wedding dresses and haggling over wholesalers' prices so that the cost of the rest of the trousseau would offset the extra cost of the wedding gown, she might have given up to her despair.

The Vancouvers have given out that you have been in Switzerland at a private sanitarium all this time, that your health had suffered so much from the shock of Eugenia's death that it was necessary to get you away from familiar surroundings and under the most expert medical care. Anthony made a trip to Switzerland himself, as you know because I wrote you about it although I didn't know why he'd chosen that country at the time.

Now Anthony is returning to Switzerland, telling all his friends that you have recovered sufficiently to leave the sanitarium and that the two of you are going to spend the summer traveling through Europe. And Mrs. Edward Curtis, our sweet Veronica, is also traveling, although her husband has remained at home, and we don't need to be hit with a shillelagh to guess where she is and who she's with even if Mr. Edward Curtis is so innocent that he hasn't an inkling.

The blatant falsehoods being bandied about her were bad enough in themselves, but Rose had only been leading up to something far worse. Reid was to be sent to England in the fall, to complete his education there because he persisted in being loyal to Moria, his loyalty never wavering. He was to be exiled, sent away from his home, his family, his friends, to live in a strange country among strangers, because of her! Gayle, of course, would remain at home, only attending a young ladies' seminary when she became old enough, if Jacob could be persuaded to part with her for so long. Gayle was a Vancouver, her loyalty to the Vancouvers never wavering, the apple of Jacob's eye.

Everything Gayle wanted, she was given. She was already being groomed to take her place as the toast of the Hudson River Valley's society, the most beautiful debutante ever to grace that exalted company. Already, she received more invitations than she could accept, she was in constant demand, admired, petted, pampered, made to believe by all and sundry, not only by her grandfather, that she was better than anyone else by right of birth and wealth and breeding, by right of the Vancouver blood that ran in her veins.

Reid exiled, Gayle being ruined! And all of Moria's success, everything that she had accomplished through her own strength and courage and ability, could do nothing to help Reid, to help Gayle.

With the advent of his new prosperity, Abraham had consulted the best lawyers in Chicago about Moria's rights to her children. What he had learned had been discouraging. Far from being helpful, Moria's success in the business world would prejudice any judge against her, a woman in the marketplace, a female competing with men in a man's world! Not only had Tony been within his legal rights in putting her away from him and withholding her children from her, for what he judged to be good and sufficient reasons, but Moria's occupation would be held to make her unfit to be a mother.

Nothing but defeat and bitter disappointment could come from suing for her children, Abraham was told. And even worse, bringing the old scandals to light, as would almost certainly happen owing to the prominence of the Vancouvers, would further hurt Reid and Gayle. And so they were advised to forget it, to accept what must be accepted, because there was no way they could win.

Now Quinn's anger, his fury, because she couldn't simply pack up and go with him to Arizona, was almost too much for her to cope with. But there was no way she could do as he wished, and if he really loved her he'd know that she couldn't, and it wasn't fair, and in the end she exploded at him as violently as he had exploded at her, until Reba covered her ears and Abraham's hair became more and more sparce as he pulled more and more of it out by the roots.

"I can't do it, and I want you to stop asking me! It has nothing to do with my loving you or not loving you, you know that, but you simply won't admit it!"

"Maybe you want me to stop coming to Chicago, too!" Quinn shouted back. "Not that I wasn't a damned fool to come this time! Why am I wasting my life wanting a woman I can't have, will you answer me that, unless I'm as crazy as my father thinks I am? Well, I've had it up to here! I'm going back to Arizona, and I'm going to court the next girl my sister finds for me, and I'm going to marry her and have a family, and you can damned well stay here in Chicago and get richer and more famous every year until you're old and dried up, and what good will it all do you then? You can spend your declining years thinking of my sons who could have been yours, my daughters who could have been yours, my wife's husband, who could have been yours!

"Your children, Reid and Gayle, will be grown and married and no part of your life. Abraham and Reba can't live forever, and where will you be then? Alone with your money and your ex-fame, and how are you going to tell yourself that it was worth it, when you're old and alone?"

How could he be so cruel, how could he say he loved her when he could hurt her so much, when he could beat her with words? God in heaven, didn't he know how much she wanted to go with him, didn't he know that she'd sacrifice anything except her children to be with him for all the rest of her life? Yes, even her own soul! She'd sacrifice that gladly, but not her children, never her children!

Because they'd know—Anthony, Jacob would be sure to know—and they'd tell them that she was living in sin, living as another man's wife! And not only that, which would disgust Gayle and break Reid's heart, but to live in sin as Quinn's wife would negate any last possibility that she could ever find a lawyer who could help her regain her right to her children.

"Don't say any more, Quinn. Please, don't say any more!"

"I don't intend to say any more. What would be the use? If I had a brain in my head I'd rape you, I'd at least have that to remember, that I had you once!"

Too angry to even look at her, Quinn crashed from the house, his broad-brimmed hat pulled down over his eyes, his long stride taking him away from her without as much as looking back. And Moria wished that he had raped her, that she'd have had him once, before he went back to Arizona and she never saw him again. Her soundless prayer wasn't for forgiveness for her wicked thought, but that when Quinn married the girl his sister would find for him, he wouldn't let her know about it because she wouldn't be able to bear it.

Abraham and Reba didn't try to comfort her. They knew, with the deep, instinctive sensitivity of their race, that no words could bring her comfort, that only time and work could ease the aching of her heart. Their own hearts bled for her, they would have given the last drops of their blood to ease her heartbreak, but all they could do was be there, so that she knew they were there, that she wasn't entirely alone.

It helped. They had no idea how much it helped, that it was the one small factor that kept Moria going. That, and her work, which she plunged back into with such fevered frenzy that Abraham and Reba were afraid that she'd ruin her health, that she'd have a complete breakdown.

"It isn't too early to think about the reopening of school after the summer vacation," Moria told them. "We want our share of the trade."

"With you out to get it, we'll get more than our share!" Reba said. Her faith in Moria was unshakable.

"I have to inventory our yard goods. I'll work up patterns for little girls' school dresses, free patterns with the purchase of the goods."

Abraham opened his mouth and closed it again. He didn't moan "bankrupt." Who cared about bankrupt, at a time like this? Let Moria make patterns, let her make a million patterns and give them all away, if it would make her feel better, if it would ease her heartache for one little minute.

"Book bags, book straps." Moria ticked off on her fingers. "Sturdy shoes. Stockings. Hair ribbons. Slates. We'll open an entire department for them, I'll find room somewhere, on the ground floor, no, in the basement. People will walk downstairs to buy, they won't walk up for bargains in anything as prosaic as school supplies. 'Bargains in the basement, outfit your children for school at the highest quality for the lowest price.' "

A bargain basement? Moria was either stark-raving insane or she was a genius. It didn't matter which. She wanted bargains in the basement, she'd have bargains in the basement. But no ferns. Ferns didn't go with bargains, he had to put his foot down somewhere.

"Tea," Moria said.

"Tea?"

"We'll have an urn. And chairs. Mothers shopping for children, with their children, get tired. We'll have chairs for them to sit down in and rest, and offer them a cup of tea. How many cups and saucers will we need, how many chairs? And there should be little tables by the chairs, to put their teacups on."

Abraham closed his eyes. He was having a nightmare. In a little while he'd go down to the kitchen, after he managed to wake himself up, and make himself a glass of tea, Reba he wouldn't wake up to do it for him, a glass of tea he could make for himself even if he was insane to let Moria ruin him. Bargains in the basement, and tea? He wouldn't open his eyes yet, maybe if he kept them closed a little longer, when he opened them the nightmare would have gone away.

The bargains in the basement, the tea, brought the middle-class ladies of Chicago flocking to Greenbaum's. Where else could they shop with such convenience, such comfort, such pampering of their aching feet? And at no extra charge!

Counting his profits, Abraham made another substantial extra payment against the loan from Michael McCarthy, and hoped that Marshall Field was tearing out his own hair because he'd let Moria be discharged from his store and Abraham had got her. Not that he wished the gentleman any harm. Better he should remember him in his prayers, for so kindly discharging her so that she'd come to Greenbaum's looking for work.

He was getting to be a rich man. And he still got to sit in his own kitchen, with his shoes off, not in some drawing room in a mansion with his shoes on because of the butler, and a stiff collar choking him, and he counted his blessings, because what man had ever been blessed this much, to have Moria and to be getting rich until he went bankrupt the next time Moria got some insane idea?

"I thought you weren't coming back. I thought you'd be married by now, with your first child on the way."

"I ought to break your neck. I ought to strangle you. No, I ought to rope and hog-tie you and slap my brand on you and laugh when I smell your smoking hide while I do it! Are you ready to come back to Arizona with me?"

She was so glad to see him that she thought she was going to die of it. She wanted to go to Arizona with him so achingly that she thought she was going to die of it. She wished that he hadn't come, it only made it worse. How could she forget him if he kept coming, if he kept taking her in his arms, kissing her until her senses reeled, until every inch of her screamed with agony because there couldn't be more, there could never be any more? But if he hadn't come, she would have died.

"Moria, how much of this do you think I can stand, how much more of it can you stand? Our lives are getting away from us, every year we aren't together is a year lost, thrown away! Ask your husband for a divorce again, how do you know he'll refuse this time, he might have found someone else by now!"

"I have asked. My letter was returned to me. It had been opened and read, but there was only one word in reply, written on the margin. No. And Tony does have someone else, one woman in particular and dozens more on the side, but it will never make any difference, he'll never give me my freedom. As long as William Northrup lives and doesn't recover enough to change his will, so that there's a chance that I'll inherit his fortune, Tony will never agree to a divorce."

"Money!" Quinn's fists clenched, and the muscles along his jawline knotted and throbbed. "The Bible is right, the love of money is the root of all evil! I'd like to get those Vancouvers in Arizona for just an hour, get them on my own ground, and make them run back to the Hudson River Valley with their tails between their legs and a divorce in your pocket! What kind of man does the East breed, anyway? Where I come from, they'd have been strung up from the nearest tree years ago!"

"Do you really think that lawlessness is the answer to all the world's ills? Fists and guns and ropes? That would breed an even worse race of men; it's taken all the years from the beginning of the world for men to advance as far as they have. It's only a pity that it hasn't advanced far enough yet so that women have rights, so that they aren't merely the property of their husbands!"

"Why don't you crusade for it, then?" Quinn shouted at her. "You've managed to make a success of everything else you've tried your hand at! Put a little of that genius of yours to work at it, and maybe by the time we're in wheelchairs, you'll be able to call your life your own, and marry me!"

He was impossible when he was like this. There was no way to reason with him. Moria blinked back tears of frustration, determined that she wasn't going to cry. The unfairness of the world filled her with rage almost as strong as Quinn's. The slaves had been freed, when was it going to be women's turn? Maybe she would crusade, start a revolt! If every woman in the world were to go on strike, how long would it take for men to capitulate?

But even as she thought it she knew that it wouldn't work, simply because men were bigger and stronger and they could hit harder and shout louder. She didn't believe that there was more than a handful of men in the world who wouldn't beat their wives into submission if they felt that their own superiority was being threatened.

Quinn returned to Arizona in that late summer of 1883, left as angry as he'd been when he had come, leaving Moria's life an empty, aching shell. And as she had before, she threw herself into her work, she filled every waking moment with so much work that she had no time to think of anything else.

Abraham and Reba suffered for her, even as they looked with disbelieving eyes at the results of her labors. Rich! Not just a little wealthy, but really rich their Moria was making them, and Michael McCarthy's loan was paid off and the store still poured out profits and Moria became more beautiful, more talked about and admired and envied.

No sooner did other department stores plagiarize her innovations than she came up with something else that enticed back lost customers and added still more to their ranks, and by the time the other stores were able to follow suit Abraham's bank account swelled until he was almost afraid to look at the balance. Maybe it was wicked to have so much money. It wasn't as if he and Reba needed it. Their kitchen they needed, and each other, and enough not to starve. But both he and Reba took comfort from the fact that Moria would never be poor, that she could live out her life in luxury once they were dead and it all came to her. The will Abraham drew up was hard and fast, Moria was to have it all.

Moria couldn't have cared less about being wealthy, as long as no amount of money could buy her her freedom from Tony and the right to have her children with her. If she could have her children, if she could marry Quinn and they could all be together in Arizona and never have to think of the Husdon River Valley again, she would be happy.

But there was no use in thinking about it. For all she knew, Quinn might have carried out his threat, he might be married by now.

"Write," Reba urged her. "Even knowing isn't as bad as not knowing."

This time there was an answer so soon that Moria was almost afraid to open the letter. Her hands were trembling so hard that the words blurred because the paper shook. And then, after she'd read the letter once, and then once again, she laid it aside and went to her room and sat down in the comfortable rocking chair that Reba had bought for her, and began to rock with her hands folded so tightly in her lap that the bones ached.

It was over. Quinn wanted a clean break. He wasn't going to go on tearing his heart out over her, there was more to life than that, and if he couldn't have her, if she didn't love him enough to come to him and make a life with him, then he'd have to start building a life without her. He asked her not to write to him again unless it was to say that she was coming. The break was clean and final.

Moria didn't go to bed at all that night. She sat in her dark room and stared into the darkness at all the images that passed before her

383

eyes. Quinn, when she'd been fifteen and he'd been twenty, at Retreat, galloping along the bridle paths, her with her hair streaming out behind her, laughing, her eyes sparkling with excitement and joy. Quinn, finding her at Greenbaum's after Rose had written him, her astonishment at seeing him, the almost unbearable joy that had flooded her heart.

Quinn, laughing, joking, taking her sight-seeing, taking her to the finest restaurants, sitting in Reba's kitchen with a glass of tea, while he and Abraham talked about everything in the world, absorbing each other's experiences and viewpoints. Quinn, holding her in his arms, kissing her, his mouth and his hands fiery and demanding. And Quinn, angry, his eyes black with anger, shouting at her, accusing her, telling her that this time, when he left, he wasn't coming back.

And now it had happened. He wasn't coming back. She'd never hear from him again, she wouldn't even know whether he were alive or dead. His work was dangerous, he could be thrown, trampled, gored. He'd marry, and she'd never know the name of the woman he married, never know when his children were born.

She went to work the next morning. Pale, her eyes shadowed, she dressed and groomed herself with her usual care, and Reba and Abraham didn't tell her to go back to bed, didn't tell her to rest. Reba didn't tell her to cry. This was Moria's heartbreak, and she had to face it alone.

"What's that in your mouth? Take it out, put it out!" Abraham stared at Reba as if he were afraid that he was hallucinating. "Have you gone crazy, yet?"

Reba blew a moutfhul of smoke in his direction. "You know what it is, or else you're blind and stupid. All the ladies are smoking them. It's a cocarette, and it's good for the nerves, it's beneficial, it makes you feel good."

"There's nothing the matter with your nerves! And you're not a man, my wife is not a man, my wife does not smoke tobacco! Does

Miss Moria Donovan of Greenbaum's Department Store smoke tobacco, or tell other ladies that it's smart to smoke tobacco?''

''It isn't tobacco. At least, not all of it. There's Bolivian coca leaves, too. And it's Absolutely Not Injurious, it's a nerve tonic and an exhilarator.''

''Which is it, then, a nerve tonic or an exhilarator? It can't be both, how can something calm you down and pep you up at the same time?''

''Because it says so, that's how it can be.'' Reba blew another cloud of smoke in Abraham's direction. ''Better you should try it, your nerves could use it.''

Abraham began to cough, waving his hands in front of his face. His coughing went on and on, his face turned red, it appeared that he was choking to death. Frightened half out of her wits, Reba dropped the offending cocarette on the floor as she ran to pound him on his back.

''Abe, Abe, are you all right?''

Abraham went on coughing. Moria, upstairs in her room, going over plans for still another promotional scheme where Abraham would look over her shoulder and scream ''bankrupt!'' dropped her pen and papers as she ran for the stairs. She burst into the kitchen, white with alarm.

''What is it? What's the matter?''

As Abraham continued coughing, she added her efforts to Reba's, pounding in unison with Reba's healthy thumps on Abraham's back.

''Enough, yet! You want you should beat me to death, the choking won't kill me fast enough to suit you?'' Abraham's coughing subsided at last, and he slumped in his chair, gasping for breath and wiping his streaming eyes. ''Beneficial, she said! Good for the nerves, yet! Now you see what you're smoking, woman, you're smoking up the death of me!''

''It couldn't have been just the cocarette.'' Moria bit at her lower lip, her eyes reflecting her worry. ''You've been coughing a lot lately, Abraham, you've been coughing entirely too much. And it's summer, you don't have a cold. Reba, I think he must see a doctor.''

"Of course he's got to go to a doctor! Haven't I been telling him that until my face is blue? Abe, you're going to see a doctor, tomorrow you're going."

"It was the cocarette." Abraham was stubborn. "A cold I haven't got, just something in my throat, sometimes."

They took him to a doctor the next day, Moria on one side of him, holding his arm so that he couldn't make a break for freedom, and Reba on the other. Abraham's feet dragged. He spluttered. He wasn't sick, he only had a little cough, something was irritating his chest, there was nobody minding the store. Let Moria go mind the store, he didn't need two women to take him to a doctor, was he a little boy, a child?

"All men are babies when they're sick," Reba said, her words fraught with wisdom. "Walk faster, Abe. You should have let Moria hire a cab."

"Who needs a cab? The horsecars aren't good enough, and we only have to walk a few blocks? It isn't raining, my feet I won't get wet. Besides, it's only a little cold, a summer cold."

"We can afford a cab. You said yourself that you're getting to be a rich man."

"And cabs when they aren't needed would make me a poor man! I am walking fast. You want I should arrive at the doctor's house out of breath so he'll think I'm sick?"

They walked more slowly, but in spite of Abraham's holding them back as much as they'd let him, they finally arrived at their destination. After waiting for six other patients, who were ahead of them, to be seen, after Abraham's loudly voiced conviction that by the time he got back to the store his business would be ruined, Moria and Reba were left to wait while Dr. Gammadge closed his office door in their faces.

They waited for a long time. Reba fidgeted, twisting her handkerchief until it was in shreds, getting up to look out the window, sitting down again to further mutilate her handkerchief. "He's dying," she said, her face a mask of tragedy. "I killed him with that cocarette."

"Don't be silly. One cocarette couldn't kill him. They're harmless, it says so right in the ads. It's only a little cold."

"You said yourself it isn't a cold! He's dying, or why hasn't he come out?"

Moria too was worried, but she sat quietly, her hands folded loosely in her lap. Abraham couldn't be ill, not really ill! Reba's world would crash around her head, and her own as well. And she had a sudden, aching wish that she'd put on Quinn's bracelet before they'd brought Abraham to the doctor.

"Mrs. Greenbaum, Miss Donovan, will you step into my office, please?" Dr. Gammadge opened his office door and held it for them. Reba's face was as white as paper as she went in, her eyes flying to Abraham as he sat as though he were stunned in the chair in front of the doctor's desk.

"Tell me," Reba said. Her mouth quivered. "I got to know sometime, so tell me."

"Mrs. Greenbaum, your husband is ill."

"We're paying you to tell us that? Would we have brought him if he wasn't sick?"

"It's his lungs. He has a respiratory problem. Chicago's climate is definitely detrimental to his health. It will probably be safe for him to remain here for the rest of the summer, but I recommend that you move to a warm, dry climate as soon as possible, or else our cold, damp weather will aggravate his condition to the point where I could not be responsible for his well-being."

"It's a cold, only a summer cold," Abraham said. "Tomorrow I'll be all right."

"How serious is it?" Moria demanded. How could her voice sound so calm when she was hysterical inside?

"It could become very serious. I recommend that you take him to the Southwest. New Mexico, the Arizona Territory, somewhere where it's warm and dry the year around."

"Your practice you could take to the Southwest. My department store I can't," Abraham said. "Give me some pills, give me a tonic. For a little summer cold I don't need to move to the Southwest."

Reba thought, my kitchen, I can't take my kitchen to the Southwest. And her heart broke a little, but she ignored it. "We'll go. We can afford it. We'll sell out."

"Look what that cocarette did! It scrambled your brain!" Abraham shouted. "I'll sue the company! Sick it made me, and it ruined your brain! For their last penny I'll sue!"

Moria's heart sank. If Abraham wouldn't go willingly, there was no way that she and Reba could force him. Indulgent toward them in everything, Abraham was still the head of the household, the head of the family. She couldn't sell the store out from under him, she didn't have the authority, there were limits to what even Miss Moria Donovan of Greenbaum's Department Store could do. And she knew, just by looking at him, that it would take an earthquake or another Chicago fire to move Abraham from Chicago and his beloved store.

"Should he go to bed, rest?" she asked the doctor. "And what about medicines?"

"Bed rest would be of no avail. In fact, it might cause even more damage, constant lying down congests the lungs. He should live as normal a life as possible until you move to the Southwest, taking every precaution, naturally, that he doesn't overtire himself. He most definitely must stop smoking."

"There!" Abraham leaped to his feet, shaking with outrage. "You see how much he knows, this doctor? I never smoked in my life, the only smoke I ever had Reba blew at me yesterday. A little steam from the kettle, my feet in hot water, a mustard plaster, I need, not a doctor who tells me to stop smoking and move to the Southwest!" He jammed the hat he'd been holding in his hands back onto his head and stood up. "I'm going to the store. Tonight it'll be steam from the kettle and a bucket of hot water for my feet and how much do I owe you for not knowing what you're talking about?"

With both Moria and Abraham back at the store, Reba made her decision. The rift between Moria and Quinn didn't matter now even if he hadn't come last summer. Nothing mattered but Abraham and she knew what she had to do. It was a pity that the pony express had been discontinued. A letter by pony express she'd have liked to send, just to think about it getting there so fast, through deserts and hostile Indians, with hard-faced, tanned young men pushing their ponies at full gallop from one station to the next. But as there was no longer a pony express, she'd use the telegraph that had put it out of business and if Abraham killed her when he found out, at least it would be too late for him to stop her.

She couldn't force Abe to do what had to be done, and Moria couldn't force him. But Quinn was a man, as stubborn as Abe and twice as strong, and if he couldn't do it, then nobody could and at least she'd know that she'd done her best.

Equally unknown to Abraham, Moria was also moving to do something concrete. An accomplished fact, or one as near as accomplished, might prevail where reason failed, and a healthy enough profit might be the deciding factor. In a corner of the fitting room, where the seamstresses measured and pinned on ladies clad only in their underclothing so that no man dared to enter, not even the owner of the store, she sat at a table and wrote to Michael McCarthy. Michael would know how to go about contacting prospective buyers for the store, buyers with enough money to buy a going enterprise. She stressed the need for speed. Abraham wasn't going to die, she wasn't going to let him die if she had to hire someone to carry him to the train and get him to a climate that would agree with him. She'd lost her real father, under circumstances over which she'd had no control. Now she had another father, as dear to her in his own way as Liam had been, but this time she had foreknowledge, and she could do something about it and she was going to do something about it no matter how extreme the measures had to be. If Abraham thought that she was going to sit by and let his stubbornness kill him, he was very much mistaken!

Reba served one of the best suppers of her life that night, but she served it in the kitchen even though she felt like celebrating by eating in the dining room, with her prized heirloom linen tablecloth and the best china. She was the picture of innocence, of the obedient wife, always willing to let her husband make all of the decisions.

Moria, another picture of innocence, praised Reba's cooking, waited on Abraham, pushed the sugar bowl to his side of the table, and agreed with him that steam and a hot footbath were bound to do more good than harm.

The head of the household, the head of the family, sat in satisfied, smug complacency, convinced that he and he alone was in charge of his own destiny.

23

At Retreat, Rose offered Michael a cup of tea. They were in William's study, the only room downstairs that was not swathed in dust sheets, closed off to conserve on expenses now that they were no longer used.

Michael looked at his cup distastefully. How was it possible that an Irishwoman, who'd been born on the Old Sod itself, would offer another Irishman a cup of tea, after a journey from New York City in the pouring rain, and himself soaked to the skin and in mortal danger of catching pneumonia if he weren't offered something that would warm his blood better than tea? The thought of William Northrup's cellars, stocked with the best of wines, brandies, whiskeys, made him ache all over. Tea, was it! But he forced a pleasant smile as he prodded Rose's sense of hospitality.

"I could do with a drop of something in me tea," he said. "It bein' so wet and all, and me chilled to the bone."

"Mr. McCarthy, I am not a thief. Tea is considered a part of a servant's wages, but to use Mr. Northrup's whiskey would be an act of outright theft."

"And who would be the wiser? It's just sittin' there, covered with dust and goin' to waste, and that's a worse crime than stealing."

"Covered with dust it is not. Mrs. Lindstrom doesn't shirk her duties even though the master is paralyzed and can't give orders. And every bottle will be accounted for, either when he recovers or when he dies. Drink your tea while it's hot, if you're so chilled."

Sighing, Michael tasted the tea. He had to admit that it was good tea. Apparently Rose's conscience didn't extend to using servants' tea, at least for company, and he supposed that he was company. The devil knew that Rose refused to consider him a suitor, stubborn woman that she was, pigheadedly burying herself in this mausoleum of a house to nurse a man who wasn't in any condition to appreciate it and who wouldn't have appreciated it even if he had been in any condition.

Draining his cup, he put his hand over it against its being refilled. One cup for politeness' sake, but he was damned if he'd drink a second no matter the quality of it. He had a bottle in the buggy, and now he regretted his forbearance in not having availed himself of its comfort during the journey from the city, because Rose would have made her displeasure at smelling whiskey on him all too clear, and he was having a hard enough time with her as it was.

"I won't be visiting you again for a while," he told her. "I'm off to Chicago. Have you heard from Moria? I've a pocketful of offers for Greenbaum's Department Store in my pocket, and Moria and I will have to decide which one to accept. Providing we can pound some sense into the head of that pigheaded Jew, Abraham Greenbaum!"

Rose's mouth curled, and her eyes looked like a colleen's as they sparkled with laughter. " 'Pigheaded' isn't exactly the word you should use to describe a Jewish gentleman. I don't think he'd appreciate it. And yes, I've heard from Moria. It's a shame about Mr. Greenbaum. And to think of Moria having to live in that godforsaken wilderness! But she's determined to go with them, if there's any way to make Abraham go."

"And that's exactly why I'm going to Chicago. If Liam's girl needs help, I'm going to see that she gets all I can give. I'll help sell the department store and get Abe on that train, or Liam would haunt me all the rest of me life. I don't expect that you'll be after missing me, Rose?''

"I don't expect that I will. I've better things to do than miss a Tammany Hall politician, as crooked as a corkscrew and one who drinks too much to boot."

Michael winced. "My occasional drop isn't drinking too much. And even that drop is your fault, if you want to face the truth of it. If you'd marry me, I wouldn't need to drink, except to make myself agreeable when I go out with the boys. And I am not dishonest, Rose O'Riley. For a politician, I'm as pure as the driven snow. I only stay in the game to help those less fortunate than meself. But if I had a wife, I'd be able to turn me back on all of it with no regrets. William Northrup might live for years, and how is he, now that his name has been mentioned?''

"He's the same as he always is. The doctors come and look at him and go away again. He can't move or talk, although he can think, of that I'm as sure as I am that I'm breathing. I can see the evil thoughts rolling around in his head, his plans for revenge. And I can see him trying to move, straining till it's a wonder the effort doesn't kill him, and a pity too. So you're off to Chicago. Give Moria my love. She already knows that she has my prayers.''

"Come with me!" Michael urged. "You know you'd rather see Moria than anything else in the world. It's been years, woman, and her as dear to you as your own daughter! You're doing no good here, and you know it. We could make the journey our honeymoon, if you'd only give over this notion that you have to watch William Northrup night and day.''

"I do have to watch him. It's a promise I made Liam and Eugenia.''

"After they were dead!''

"It's still a promise, and God knows I made it, and what would Mary think of me if I broke it? I'd never have the nerve to pray for her to help anyone again! As long as Moria is safe, as long as her husband and her father-in-law leave her alone, I have to watch *him*

393

against the possibility that he might recover and do Moria harm. Eugenia would have expected it of me, and I'll not let her down any more than I'll let Moria down, or Laura and her family. And besides, I have to pray for *his* soul. He has to be made aware of all his black sins, and it's for me to remind him of them every day by praying aloud, so that he might be prevailed upon to repent."

Michael looked at her with awe. Reminding the man of his sins, was she! Helpless to bring about justice, to have William Northrup hanged for Liam's murder, Rose had still found a way to punish him—by always being here, by praying aloud for his soul to remind him of his sins! Was there no end to the woman's willpower, to her determination? If he wasn't a crazy Irishman, he'd know that he was better off without the likes of her, because how could any man call his soul his own with Rose O'Riley for a wife?

He stood up, there being no point in staying any longer, and the journey back to the city through the pouring rain something he'd as soon get over with even with the comfort of the bottle that he hadn't touched on his way to Retreat.

"I wanted to be able to tell Moria that I've seen you," he said. "And that you're looking well, for a woman of your age. Is there any special message you'd be wanting me to give her, before it's too late and you're in your grave a spinster?"

Rose ignored his jibes. She'd never been a beauty, so what did it matter if she wasn't getting any prettier as she grew older? There was nothing she wanted for Michael to tell Moria. They wrote to each other, Rose told her all she could find out about Reid and Gayle. She no longer told her anything about Tony, because what good could it do for Moria to be reminded of Tony's infidelity, to tell her that his often renewed affair with Veronica Hamilton Curtis had been renewed once more and that Edward Curtis seemed to be the only man in New York City and in the Hudson River Valley who wasn't aware of it?

Edward, with his weak chin and his Spaniel-doting eyes, still hardly believed his good fortune in having wooed and won Veronica Hamilton. It was enough to make Rose want to go to the cellars and filch one of those bottles that Michael was so interested in, only she wouldn't do it because drinking *his* whiskey would make her gag. And she had to keep her wits about her, she never dared to relax, to be less than fully alert, fully aware of the smallest change in *his* condition.

"Look at the pot on you!" she said. "Being a Tammany Hall politician will be the death of you yet, if you don't stop indulging yourself, Michael McCarthy. And don't think that I don't know that you have a bottle in your buggy! It's a blessing that the horse will be sober, else you might not make it back to the city without ending up in a ditch."

"I'll bid you good day," Michael said. "And I'd advise you to put an extra spoonful of sugar in yer tea every time you have a cup, to sweeten yer disposition! I don't know when I'll be callin' on you again, even after I get back from Chicago, your hospitality bein' so sadly lackin'."

With that, Michael clapped his hat on his head and stalked out of the study, crossed the great, elegant hall, its crystal chandeliers shrouded now, its statues covered, and went through the front door as he would never have been able to do if William Northrup hadn't been struck down for his wickedness.

In the buggy, he rummaged for the bottle, uncorked it, hesitated, and then slapped the cork back in without tasting as much as a drop to ward off the chill of the rain that was still pouring down. In the ditch, was it! And he as sober an Irishman as had ever walked the earth! Within reason, of course. And bad cess to a woman who could ruin his enjoyment of a drop, even when she was inside that great house and he was outside in the rain!

Rose held her back straight as she left the study and made her way up the servants' staircase to resume her watching over *him*. Struck down or not, unable to issue orders, it was still *his* house and she was still a servant and she always used the servants' stairs.

William's eyes were closed as though he were asleep when she entered his room, but he heard her come in and his eyes opened, gleaming balefully. The rain beat against the windowpanes, and

Rose steeled herself against worrying about Michael as he traveled back to the city. He was a grown man, he could take care of himself, but if ever a man needed a woman to make him take better care of himself Michael McCarthy was that man.

Her face was carefully impassive as she crossed the room to fluff William's pillows. "It comes to my mind that you'd better enjoy the rain, because there won't be a drop where you're going unless you repent your sins. Do you remember your wife's poor tormented body, covered with bruises? Do you remember how you tortured her? I'll pray for you, and you'd better pray too, you can pray silently even if you can't talk and God will hear you if you're truly sincere.

"There's one thing in your favor. When you murdered Liam Donovan, you only sent him to join Eugenia, and they're at rest now, together and happy. It's your own soul you must be thinking of, and how the fires of hell will never cool."

Her innermost thoughts, that tormented her day and night, tried to surface and she pushed them away, taking refuge in prayer. It would be so easy to put an end to all this, to set herself free from this prison of her own making. A pillow over *his* face, and who would be the wiser, and it no more than he deserved, less than he deserved, a thousand and a thousand times less than he deserved for his sins. And then Moria would be safe from him, and Laura and her family, and she, Rose O'Riley, would be free and she could marry a Tammany Hall politician if she wanted to, or join Moria, the choice would be hers.

But that would be murder, no matter how much *he* deserved it, and then she'd be no better than he was, her soul would be forfeit for all eternity. She wouldn't think about it, she'd have to pray special prayers tomorrow morning when she hitched up the pony cart and drove to the village for her novena, going to pray in the church every day, no matter the weather, no matter whether she felt ill or well. She would pray special prayers for *him* and for herself. And for Michael McCarthy, just in case he overindulged in that bottle on his way back to the city and ended up injured in a ditch.

She finished fluffing the pillows and drew the sheet smooth under William's chin. He was still watching her as she sat down in the rocking chair she'd brought from her own room, an indulgence she allowed herself even though she was a servant. His eyes were black with fury, and she could see him trying again to move, to flex a single muscle, to force his throat to speak. If sheer willpower could do it, William Northrup would manage to find a way to communicate with his lawyers and his henchmen and set in motion the forces that would destroy everyone Rose loved.

And it would be a sin to pray that he would never get well, that he would die without being able to speak or to write. Sometimes the rules the church laid down seemed unreasonable, but she had to abide by them just the same. Just as she had to pray now without her rosary, because of *his* rule that rosaries must be kept out of sight in *his* house. But there was no rule that she couldn't ask forgiveness for not having her rosary with her, and asking it aloud, because such a contingency had never occurred to *him* so that he could make a rule against it.

William's hate reached out from where he lay in his bed and seemed to wrap itself around her. She went on praying that he would realize the error of his ways and repent before it was too late. If her praying brought *him* discomfort, if it made him furious, that was no fault of hers and therefore no sin.

Moria answered the front door, marveling that she had heard the knocker over the shouting that filled the kitchen, Abraham's voice raised fully as loud as Michael McCarthy's as each of them tried to shout the other down. How could they keep it up, hour after hour, and not fall silent from sheer exhaustion? Her ears rang with it, she heard them even in her sleep, as she dreamed that they were still arguing, still shouting at each other, Michael's voice taking on a stronger brogue the angrier he became, and Abraham, driven to frenzy, lapsing into Yiddish that only Reba could understand. Reba, who added her voice to the uproar, insisting, demanding, so that of the four of them only Moria was able to retain any semblance of calm.

Michael had been in Chicago for nearly a week, and every day of that week had been like this, not only here at home during the evenings but at the store, where Michael bullied his way into Abraham's office, his face so red that Moria was afraid he'd go into a fit of apoplexy. Yesterday Abraham had hired a guard to keep Michael from entering the department store at all. What was it doing to business, when he had to shout so that every lady in the store could hear him? He was being ruined, he'd go bankrupt, if this Irishman didn't go back to New York and leave him in peace!

And Reba, his own Reba, this wife of his whole adult life, adding her voice to Michael's, nagging, nagging, never leaving him alone, telling him he had to accept one of the offers that Michael had found for him and go to the Southwest so he would get well and she wouldn't be a widow.

"So you'll be a widow! You'll be a rich widow, that's so bad?" Abraham shouted. "And a widow you won't be, because the doctors are wrong! A cold I've got, a summer cold!"

He broke off, choking and gasping for breath, his face red from the fit of coughing that overtook him, and Michael's voice went right on shouting, along with Reba's.

"Look at you, man dear, listen to you! You're wheezing and creaking like a wheel without grease! I've got you the highest bid any man could hope for, and I'm ready to stay here in Chicago for as long as I have to and keep driving the bids up, setting one against the other, it's a rich man you are, with a fortune waiting to fall into your lap and you'll never have to work another day in your life, and here you are, a pigheaded idiot, killing yourself instead of being sensible!"

"Pigheaded!" Abraham wheezed, his face going an even deeper red, a circumstance that Michael would have thought impossible. "You dare say that word in my house! Reba, throw him out, Moria, throw him out! I'll throw him out myself!"

"Pigheaded!" Michael repeated, his voice even louder than it had been the first time. "It's pigheaded I say you are and pigheaded you are, and I don't know why I'm wasting me breath on you except that Moria and your Reba want you to go on living. Why, I don't know, but women being the foolish creatures they are, they do, and that's why I'm here and that's why I'm not leaving until you stop your blathering foolishness and accept the highest offer and get on a train before you drop dead!"

Michael himself was forced to stop for breath, his throat was dry and he needed a drink, a real drink, not that foolish wine that was all Abraham Greenbaum kept in his house and didn't that prove that the man was crazy? Some good Irish whiskey, imported Irish whiskey, was what Michael needed, and here he was wasting his time on a man who was so pigheaded he wouldn't listen to reason and all he had to offer a guest was a thimbleful of wine!

If Michael was forced to stop for breath, Abraham had regained enough of his to resume where he'd left off. "So who asked you to come? Did I invite you, me, Abraham Greenbaum?"

"Moria asked me, that's who asked me! And for your own good, you blathering old fool! What's a man to do with the likes of you, that's what I'd like to know? Listen to me, Abraham Greenbaum . . ."

Moria stood in the doorway, looking up at the man who stood there, his wide-brimmed hat pushed back on his head as he listened to the bedlam that issued from the kitchen.

"Who's that?" Quinn demanded.

"It's Michael McCarthy. I asked him to come. Quinn, what in heaven's name are you doing here? You said you were never coming back, you said you never wanted to see me again!" Moria's heart was pounding until it almost suffocated her, she wasn't sure that she was awake because how could Quinn be here, when she'd resigned herself to never seeing him again?

"Reba asked me to come. Is Abe as bad off as she said in her telegram? She said he's dying!"

"He isn't dying. Does it sound as if he's dying? But he might die, he will die, years before he should, if we can't get him away from

399

Chicago to a warm, dry climate! Oh, Quinn! I can't believe you're here, I just can't believe it!''

She'd held up, by sheer strength of will, up until this moment, but seeing Quinn, having him here, knowing that he'd come to help even though seeing her again was the last thing in the world he wanted, was too much for her. The shock of seeing him, the surprise, because Reba had never opened her mouth about asking him to come, flooded over her and her shoulders began to shake and then she was crying, she who hadn't allowed herself to cry, who had refused to waste any of her strength in crying because she had needed it all to bear never seeing Quinn again, she'd needed it all to try to make Abraham see reason.

"Moria, stop that, cut it out!" Quinn's arms went out of their own accord and he gathered her to him, holding her shaking body close, stroking her hair, that glorious hair, while she sobbed as if she could never stop. "I'm here, and Abe's going to get out of Chicago if I have to carry him on my back, so there's nothing to cry about now, it's all over but the shouting."

What he'd just said struck them both at the same time, so funny—because the shouting was still going on, ear-splitting—that they both began to laugh. The shouting wasn't over by a long sight, but at least reinforcements had arrived, the reserves had been called up, and Abraham was so outnumbered now that he'd have to give in.

"Bog-trotter, potato-eater!" Abraham shouted. "Out of my house! No Irish Catholic is going to tell Abraham Greenbaum, a good Jew, what to do!''

"Moria's an Irish Catholic! Does she have to get out of your house too?''

Another fit of coughing, while Abraham fought to keep breathing just long enough to get his hands around that fat Irish throat. Put his store up for sale, would he? Help Reba and Moria stab him in the back, would he?

"Abe, Abe, breathe!" There was the sound of whacking on the back as Reba's anguished voice took over. "See what you've done, getting all upset! Are you trying to kill yourself right in front of my eyes?'' Whack, whack!

"Enough!" Abraham gasped. "It isn't fast enough for me to die a natural death?"

Quinn put his hands on Moria's shoulders and pushed her away from him, his face hardening with determination. "I think they need a referee. Wipe your eyes, it isn't going to help anything for them to see that you've gone to pieces. I got here as fast as I could, but it sounds like I should have got here a lot faster!"

He didn't need Moria to show him the way to the kitchen, Abraham and Reba's house was as familiar to him as the ranch house back in Arizona. He pushed back the memories that flooded over him as his long strides carried him past the front parlor, through the dining room, and into the room where he had spent the most enjoyable and the most frustrating hours of his life.

Michael was standing in the middle of the kitchen, his hands on his hips, his jaw thrust forward belligerently and the blood creeping up his thick neck until the pulses throbbed as he fought to keep his gentle Irish temper under control. "And who the devil might you be?" he demanded as Quinn loomed in the doorway. "Don't tell me, you're Quinn Bradmore, you couldn't be anybody else with the size of you, and those broad shoulders and that hat, this pigheaded Jew can't know that many Arizona cowboys that any other would walk into his kitchen without a by-yer-leave!"

"And you're Michael McCarthy. Abe couldn't know that many Irishmen that any other would be shouting at him in his own kitchen! All right, Abe, we've had enough of your nonsense. Pick out the offer you're going to accept and we'll get things moving. We want to get you settled in Phoenix before winter." Then he had Reba in his arms, while she clung to him, howling, her face awash with tears.

"You came, you got here!"

"Of course I came. What are friends for, if not to be there when there's trouble? And from what I've just been hearing, you're having plenty of trouble with this . . ." Quinn looked at Abe, who was still staring at him with open-mouthed incredulity, "pigheaded Jew."

"You sent for him?" Abraham stared at Reba as if she had suddenly turned into the devil. "Behind my back you sent for him, to help you make me do what I don't want to do and what there's no reason for me to do because of a summer cold?"

"I knew you wouldn't like it, that's why I did it behind your stubborn back! I knew that we couldn't get you to budge, and it's a good thing I did send for him because Mr. McCarthy can't talk sense into you, either, you pigheaded Jew!"

Abraham's face turned a sickly white, and he seemed to totter. His Reba, calling names, calling her husband names, as if she were a Gentile, as if she were on their side! And she was on their side, she'd betrayed him! The world had come to an end.

It would serve her right if he died of the shock. He'd been ready to capitulate. Maybe he hadn't sounded like it, but he'd been ready, his Reba he couldn't have worrying herself to death because of him so he'd be a widower before she was a widow. He'd just put up a fight so they wouldn't think they could tell him what he had to do, who was the man of the house, who was the head of the family? And now this! Maybe he'd die tonight, to teach them a lesson, it was no more than they deserved.

"Mr. McCarthy, you can take care of selling the store?" Quinn asked, before Abraham could find his voice, struck dumb by the enormity of it all.

"That I can, if he'll sign a power of attorney for me. Which the pigheaded fool won't do."

"Get it drawn up. I'll see that he signs it."

"Will he now?" Michael eyed Quinn, his eyes traveling the long length of him, the width of his shoulders, the hard, determined eyes and jaw. He pulled in his own stomach. Rose was right, he had a pot. How would it feel to be as flat and whipcord hard as Quinn Bradmore? There was a man, a real man, they didn't grow men like this in the East, in the cities. Maybe he ought to go to Arizona himself, but on the other hand, he was too old to grow any taller and he'd earned his pot, and how could he go on wearing Rose down from Arizona? "I don't have to get it drawn up. I have it right here."

With that, he pulled an envelope from his pocket and extracted a legal-looking paper. "And haven't I been sticking it under his hooked nose for days, and him pushing it away? We'll just see if you have any better luck!"

Quinn took the paper and read it, and then laid it flat on the kitchen table. "Reba, will you bring a pen?"

The pen was thrust into Abraham's trembling hand. Quinn's hand, heavy and relentless, pushed him down into his chair.

"Sign it," Quinn said. "Sign it, or you'll go to Arizona without signing it, and then there won't be anyone to mind the store and it'll go bankrupt without leaving you with a fortune in your pocket. But bankrupt or rich, you're going."

With a heartrending sob, Abraham signed. His signature was shaky, but it was legal. Quinn took the pen from his unresisting hand and signed his own name, in his bold, strong script, as a witness, and Moria added hers.

"We'll be scalped by Indians," Abraham said, glaring at Reba. "And it'll be your fault."

"I'll maybe be scalped," Reba said, her plump, pretty face complacent. "Moria maybe will be scalped. You, they wouldn't bother with, with more skin than hair on your head because you keep tearing out more of what little you have!"

And then she put her apron over her face and began to cry, great, gulping sobs of relief. Her Abe wasn't going to die, and he wasn't going to be scalped, either. If Quinn couldn't see to that, then she would!

Moria hadn't had any idea, any conception at all, of what it involved to travel from Illinois to Phoenix in the Arizona Territory. She'd had a notion that you simply boarded a train, spent several comfortable days on it, and there you were.

Nothing could have been further from the truth. One did not travel

403

from Chicago to Phoenix in a direct line. One traveled by train to California, to San Francisco, or, rather, to Oakland because that was where Quinn told her the depot was located. From there, one boarded a train to Los Angeles, and from Los Angeles one traveled by train to the town of Maricopa, in the Arizona Territory at last. And from Maricopa, one took a stagecoach to Phoenix.

"We'll see the world!" Reba said, her eyes shining. That the shine came from secret tears as much as from excitement was something for only her to know. Her furniture she could live without, furniture could be bought. Her heirloom tablecloth she was taking, and her best china. It was her kitchen she couldn't bear to leave behind.

"Will we live in a tepee?" she asked Quinn. How could she have a kitchen in a tepee? How could she learn to cook over a fire of a few sticks, on the ground, at her age?

"No tepees. A hogan, maybe," Quinn teased her, his face perfectly straight. "They're built on bent poles and plastered with mud. A little cramped, but they have the advantage of being expendable. When they get dirty, you burn them down and build another."

"Quinn! You stop that!" Moria demanded. "Of course we'll have a house, Reba. A beautiful house, just the way you want it."

"Made of mud." Quinn wasn't to be quelched. "They call it adobe, but it's bricks made of mud. It'll melt a little when it rains hard, but that isn't much of a problem because it doesn't rain hard very often, in Arizona. Except for the times we have cloudbursts."

Reba gave him a dirty look. She didn't believe a word of it, she knew when she was being put on.

The train was reasonably comfortable. Quinn had taken care of everything. The linens, the china, the silverware, were safely stowed and labeled, only their traveling bags were carried with them. It had all taken time, but Quinn had had no intention of leaving them to make their own way without him no matter how long it took. If Abe hadn't become ill, he would have kept to his promise that he'd never travel to Chicago again, never see Moria again. But Abe was ill, and

Quinn's first dismay at the necessity of transporting all of them to Arizona, where Moria would be on his doorstep and he'd never have a chance to forget her, had turned into a wild, desperate hope.

He'd wanted her in Arizona, he'd wanted her near him, where he could go on working on her, wearing her down. Half of the thing he'd wanted most was already accomplished. She wouldn't be able to get away from him now, any more than he could get away from her. And she loved him. He knew that. It was only her foolish scruples that had kept her from going with him a long time ago.

Arizona was another world, so far removed from Chicago, even farther removed from the Hudson River Valley and its stilted, unreasonable rules of a false society, that she'd have to respond. A new country, a new life, and all the past left behind her.

How many lives had been rebuilt in the West, how many secrets had been buried never to come to light again? The slate wiped clean, and a new life spread out in front of you for you to make anything you wanted of it! All it took was courage and determination. Moria had the courage, and Quinn had the determination.

Reba was so excited that she bounced on the plush-covered seat. "It's like the ocean!" she exclaimed, over and over. "From horizon to horizon, like the ocean, except for those pesky beasts that keep getting on the tracks! How can there be so much prairie, doesn't it ever end? How did the railroad men know where to build the tracks, why didn't they get lost in this ocean of grass?"

"Sit still yet, you're making me seasick," Abraham groaned.

It was as new to Moria as it was to Reba. This train wasn't as luxurious as the one she had boarded to take her from New York City to Chicago, but the ride was smooth because the tracks were so straight. The train to Chicago had had hotel cars, with their own kitchens, the kitchens taking up most of the space in the cars so that the windows had had to be open because of the heat from the stoves, and dust and cinders had flown in to lodge in the excellent food that had been served on sliding boards that pulled out over the lap and were covered with cloths.

405

This train had no hotel car. Meals, Quinn told them, were taken at trackside eating sheds. Moria's stomach told her that it was meal-time now, and she was worried about Abraham. They needed something to eat soon, because he had to keep up his strength.

Chicago to Omaha. Omaha to Ogden, Utah. Ogden to San Francisco. From Chicago to Omaha one berth cost three dollars. From Omaha to Ogden, eight dollars. From Ogden to San Francisco, six dollars. They were traveling by Union Pacific and Central Pacific. To think that this vast country was connected, from one coast to the other, by these shining rails! She'd known that, she simply hadn't thought about it, but now the magnitude of the task struck her and filled her with pride in the accomplishments of men. It made her feel small and insignificant, but at the same time it filled her with determination almost as great as theirs had been, to make the most of the life that lay ahead of her.

She wouldn't think about her problem with Quinn now. One problem at a time. Now, all she had to think about was getting Abraham and Reba to their destination and helping them make a new home, helping them find contentment in the alien and frightening land of the Southwest.

In spite of her determination, she was all too conscious of Quinn so close to her. His masculinity seemed to flow from him in a current so strong that it made her tremble. How was she to hold out against him, when they'd see each other so often, how would she be able to bear it when she had to keep on saying no? She steeled herself against the heartbreak of thinking how different her life might have been if she'd been seventeen or eighteen when she'd first met this man, if she'd fallen in love with him instead of with Anthony Vancouver, if she would have had the courage to defy William Northrup and marry him and go to Arizona with him!

But then she wouldn't have had Reid, she wouldn't have had Gayle. Was one thing given, only to have another taken away, was that the way it always had to be? The thought was depressing, she must shut it out, think only of what she could have, Abraham and

Reba, and her children when they were grown, and not of what was impossible.

The train slowed and stopped, passengers were already rushing to disembark and enter the eating shed, a low wooden building that actually was a shed. Reba's eyes were sparkling.

"I'm famished! Abe, come along, you want to starve to death before we get to Arizona?"

The long trestle tables were bare boards, the food that was slapped in front of them was unappetizing, to give it every benefit of the doubt. Soggy pancakes, fried ham, coffee. Ham! Oh, glory, ham! Moria hardly dared to look at Abraham, whose face had turned livid.

He wouldn't even touch his plate to push it away. "Moria, push it away," he said. "So I won't get to die in Chicago, minding my own store, I'll get to die on a train, of starvation!"

Quinn's face was impassive. "Drink your coffee. How about the pancakes and potatoes?"

"Fried in lard!" Abraham said, while Reba fought against tears.

"Probably. But the coffee isn't contaminated. Drink it."

Their hands trembling, their faces white and filled with distress, Abraham and Reba drank the bitter coffee. Moria tried to swallow a mouthful of ham, but it choked her. She couldn't eat when Reba and Abraham were going hungry. Why hadn't she thought of this, why hadn't Quinn?

"It's all right," Quinn told her. "I remembered. I have bread and cheese and fruit in my bag for them, and dried fruit for when the fresh runs out. I just didn't mention eating, because Abe never would have got on the train if I had. We'll find enough for them, it won't always be pork or ham at the eating sheds, there'll be fresh game, and beef. And there'll be a good hotel in Omaha and another in Ogden and we can resupply with things for them to eat on the train if the sheds don't have anything they can have."

"Abe, did you hear? Quinn thought of it! Such knuckleheads, we didn't think of it but he did!"

Hard-dying suspicion clouded Abraham's face. "Where did you buy the cheese?"

"The same place you buy it." Quinn grinned. And then the fifteen minutes allotted for eating was up and there was a rush to reboard the train, the passengers terrified of being left behind. "Next stop, it might be buffalo or antelope, you don't have any laws against them, do you?"

"From buffalo and antelope they didn't know when the laws were made," Abraham grumbled. "So how would I know?"

"If it isn't written in the laws, there aren't laws against it," Reba assured him. "You think the rabbis were stupid?"

"Fried in lard?"

"Boiled, then, or roasted," Reba's voice was firm. "And how do we know if they're fried in lard? We don't ask, we don't know, so it's all right."

Abraham gave her one venomous look and closed his eyes, opening them again only long enough to eat the cheese sandwich and the apple that Quinn thrust into his hands. So today he wouldn't starve, but when the bread and cheese ran out? In Chicago he should have stayed, he only had a cold, what would happen to his beautiful store, with some other owner? Change the name they'd better, why hadn't he told Michael McCarthy that they had to change the name, so the name of Greenbaum wouldn't be disgraced when his beautiful store was run into the ground and bankrupt?

But when he was offered buffalo steak, he didn't ask what it had been fried in. Wondering what it had been fried in didn't even keep him awake, sleeping on a shelf behind a curtain kept him awake, and not having Reba with him. At least he was able to get out of his suit. Reba and Moria weren't so fortunate, for there was no room for them to disrobe on their shelves, ladies were constrained to sleep in their clothing, it being impossible for them to remove it and store it in such cramped quarters.

Ogden was an adventure. What if Quinn hadn't been there to take care of them? Such a racket, with runners for different hotels clanging gongs and all shouting that their hotels were the best! But Quinn knew his way around, he secured comfortable lodgings for them, and Abraham and Reba were able to eke out a decent meal, by not asking.

It seemed as if they had been living on a train for all of their lives. The constant blast of the whistle and the sudden, grinding stops when cattle blocked the tracks were exciting. The insidious, sharp white saline dust that billowed into the train, covering every surface, including the passengers every time the doors were opened, was something to be borne. Reba's eyes were strained from reading the innumerable signs posted along the tracks, advertisements, she'd never forget Sun Stove Polish, she'd try that, if she had a stove in Phoenix.

Abraham kept his face buried in a newspaper nearly all of his waking hours. Newspapers were civilization. The advertisements were read and moaned over, who could advertise a price like this, like that? But if he was minding his store instead of being on this train going to nowhere, he could do it, and cheaper, he'd learned a thing or two from Moria, and now it was all gone.

Retired! He was too young to retire. Who retired, when they were making money? When he got over this cold, he'd go back. In the meantime, he placed a clean folded handkerchief over his nose and mouth so the dust wouldn't kill him before he could get over his cold.

If the dust didn't kill him, if not asking about the food didn't kill him, Abraham moaned, then was he going to drown? A ferry, yet, from Oakland to San Francisco! A boat, on the water, and he'd never swum a stroke in his life! How had his father and mother had the courage to get on a ship and sail across the ocean? Quinn would save Reba and Moria when the ferry sank, but he couldn't save all three, there wouldn't be time, he only had two arms.

He wavered between keeping his eyes shut so he wouldn't see it coming, and keeping them open so he'd know when they began to sink. And even when the ferry didn't sink, San Francisco was cold and foggy and damp, and what was to keep the cable cars that made Reba and Moria squeal with excitement from breaking loose and crashing back down to the bottoms of the hills, killing everyone on them? He coughed and coughed, the fog got in his lungs, in Chicago it had been better even when it rained.

Moria and Reba were ecstatic. San Francisco was like a fairyland. They wished that they could stay longer, for a week, two weeks, a month. Here was where hundreds of ships had been abandoned back during the gold rush, when the crews deserted and left them to rot in the harbor. Here were mansions on top of the steep hills, here were faces of every color, so that Reba stared wide-eyed at pig-tailed Chinese and shivered with delicious fear, excited and thrilled at being frightened as long as Quinn was with them so that they could come to no harm, even in Chinatown.

Moria reveled in the fog, in the cool air. She stuffed herself with seafood, and looked out over the harbor and dreamed of taking passage to the Orient on a sailing ship. And she was grateful, right down to her bones, that she and Quinn were never alone, that Quinn did not, even by an intimate look, indicate that he was going to renew his campaign to persuade her to go through a false marriage ceremony with him and live out the rest of her life in sin. She couldn't do that. She could never do that. But she knew that when the time came, it would all but kill her to go on saying no.

She wouldn't see much of Quinn, once they were settled. He had his ranch, he had his work to do, he couldn't ride in to visit Reba and Abraham often. The only trouble was that she couldn't decide whether that was a blessing or a tragedy. She only knew that it was something that she would face when the time came, because she had to face it.

She looked at Reba, and she knew that there was one blessing that she would never lose. She had Reba and Abraham and Rose, who were her comfort and her reason for living until the time came when Reid and Gayle would be of age and she could have them back again.

24

Quinn had told them that Phoenix was small, but Moria had had no idea how small. Twelve or so blocks long from east to west, seven blocks from north to south. Washington Street, the main street, boasted a town square midway of its length. Quinn called it a plaza. The street names going from east to west posed no problem. Van Buren at the northernmost boundary, then Monroe, Adams, Washington, Jefferson, Madison, Jackson and Harrison, patriotically named for former presidents.

The north-to-south streets were an entirely different story. Reba's eyes bulged and she stumbled over the unfamiliar syllables as though she were learning an entirely new language. And so she was.

Cocopa, Yuma, Papago, Mojave, pronounced Mohave. Cortez, Montezuma, Maricopa, Pima, Pinal, Aribiapa. They were all the names of Indian tribes, and once Moria's tongue had mastered them she marveled at the beauty of them, the lilting, musical cadence, sounding like poetry. And she thought, with her heart twisting with pain, of how Liam would have loved those names, how he would have loved this place, this Phoenix, as small as it was, as dusty as it

411

was, as dry and hot as it was, so dry that she was constantly thirsty and drank quantities and quantities of water and then felt thirsty again in just a few moments, her mouth and throat dry, her skin seeming to shrivel. It was the lack of humidity, Quinn told her; she'd get used to it, her body would adjust, all newcomers experienced the same thing.

"It will cool off soon. It's already September, nearly October, and then the cool weather will set in. I wanted to get Abe here and settled, to spend the warm dry winter here, but if you find you can't tolerate it in the summer we'll arrange to get you up to Prescott, in the mountains. It wouldn't have been advisable for the winter, it's cold up there, it even snows, although even there the air is drier than back in Chicago. You'll be surprised at how perfect the climate is here in Phoenix in the winter. Warm, sunny days, and nights cold enough so you have to have fires and sleep under blankets."

"I can't believe that it's ever really cool here!" Moria exclaimed. "Honestly, Quinn, how hot does it get here, how hot do you think it is right now?"

"Only about a hundred and four, I'd judge," Quinn said. "Not bad at all. In full summer it goes up a lot higher than that. One hundred and ten, one hundred and fourteen, even one hundred and fifteen and sixteen."

Moria gave him a look filled with disgusted reproach. Teasing was one thing, but did he actually think that she was a moron? No human being could survive temperatures like that. Ridiculous!

"You don't realize it's that hot because the air is so dry," Quinn told her, a little lamely. "You're perspiring even though you don't know it, it dries on your skin immediately and that keeps you cooler. Wear a hat. Don't ever go out in the sun without one. You'll have to get a sunbonnet, they aren't beautiful but they do the job."

A sunbonnet! Moria had already seen women in sunbonnets, ugly things, she wouldn't be caught dead in one, she'd get one of those enormously broad-brimmed straw hats the Mexican men wore, first! And she had a very good idea that she'd look attractive in a hat like Quinn's, even if the ladies of Phoenix would look askance at her.

Besides, he was only teasing her. It didn't get that hot, because it couldn't.

The town itself; a village, really, no more than that, with somewhere around twenty-five hundred people, was something that Moria had never conceived of, but at least she believed it now, where Abraham and Reba didn't.

"Mud houses!" Reba said. Her face was puckered. "Whoever heard of mud houses? I thought Quinn was making a joke, but he wasn't. Who could live in a house that will melt when it rains?"

"They're easy to repair, if they do." Quinn grinned. "Adobe is cheap. And they don't melt as much as you'd think."

"And they won't burn down." Abraham was still haunted by the Chicago fire back in '71; in a rough shed he'd sold what goods he'd managed to salvage, and starting over hadn't been easy, those had been black days, he'd never forget. Fire was a thing to be dreaded. "But there's brick, Reba." He might have a cold, but there was nothing the matter with his eyes, and he'd noticed the brick buildings that Quinn told him were relatively new as Phoenix grew and prospered, real brick to replace the adobe structures that had been the rule not very long ago. If Reba wanted a brick house, a brick house she'd have, although his soul cringed at the prospect of paying so much more when adobe was so cheap.

There was shade everywhere, giant cottonwoods, a tree that grew phenomenally fast and was favored above all others because in Phoenix shade was more important than what a house looked like. The beautiful trees were heartfelt relief after their stagecoach journey through the desert. Reba had shuddered at the desert vegetation. But Moria had been enthralled. The magestic saguaro, that Quinn told her grew only in Arizona, the ocotillo with its long spearlike branches, elephant ear and barrel cacti. Joshua trees, looking almost like gnarled old men, the graceful paloverdes, named for their pale green trunks, lacy and not much use for shade, but Quinn said that in the spring they would be covered with bright yellow blossoms. And that in the spring, if there was enough winter rain, the desert itself would be carpeted as thick as tapestry with wild flowers. Reba's

413

look at him had been venomous. It didn't rain in the desert, did he think she was ignorant, that was why it was desert, anybody knew that.

You could see for miles, the air was so clear that mountains seventy or eighty miles away looked as though they were in easy walking distance if you cared to take a hike. Reba didn't believe that they were that far away, any more than she believed that it rained in the desert. Westerners grew tall and strong and brown, but they also grew up to be the biggest liars ever born!

Moria was enchanted by the mountains that made a backdrop, like a curtain on a stage, for Phoenix. They looked like cardboard silhouettes, their color changing with every change of light, from blue to lavender to pale or glowing rose and yellow or dull brown. Camelback Mountain looked like a sleeping animal, its outline remarkably like the beast for which it had been named, a camel lying down. How Liam would have marveled! He'd wanted to come here, it had been his second most important dream, after his dream of returning to Ireland to take up the fight for independence from the British.

There was a bank, the Valley Bank. There were two major newspapers, one Democratic and one Republican, the *Arizona Gazette* and the *Phoenix Herald*. There were hotels, large and prosperous. There were churches, a Methodist church made of brick, a Baptist church built of wood, and a neat, pretty Catholic church built of adobe. There was a courthouse, the finest building in the county of Maricopa, two-story and built of brick in the form of a cross, eighty-by-sixty feet crosswise through the wings. It took up a full block on Washington Street. The jail was in the rear wing, with six wooden cells for lesser offenders, and four of boiler iron with grating doors for desperate criminals. Quinn was proud of the jail.   —

There were blacksmiths, livery stables, and an ice plant, owned by George and Samuel Lount, its machinery capable of turning out two and a half tons of ice a day, which sold for ten cents a pound. Barbershops offered hot baths first, shaves and haircuts second. And there were saloons. There were more saloons than Moria could count, even if she'd wanted to.

Phoenix was civilized, Phoenix was growing in spite of its heat, in spite of the lawlessness that had made Reba tremble all the way from Maricopa on the stage, after she'd been told that the stages were held up and robbed so often that there was a five-hundred-dollar bounty on every stage-robber's head. Reba had clutched the umbrella she'd insisted on carrying, on the alert, ready to beat any bandit over the head or jab his eyes out with its ferrule no matter how frightened she was, no matter that the driver and the guard were heavily armed and that Quinn had strapped his gunbelt around his lean hips. Guns she didn't trust or understand, an umbrella she understood.

"Look at the roadrunner!" Moria would exclaim. "Oh, Reba, just look at it!" The comical, ungainly birds that ran down the road in front of the stage made her eyes shine with excitement. But Reba was looking out for bandits, roadrunners she could see when they were safely in Phoenix. And she screamed when Quinn put a horned toad in Moria's hand at one of the stops, a little, flat brown toad, a ridge of serrated skin down its back culminating in a stubby pointed tail, a ruff of the same horns around its neck. It was adorable, and Quinn told her that little boys made pets of them. A pet, Moria wanted? She could have a cat. Or better a dog, a big dog with big teeth, in this wild country. An umbrella and a dog they needed, horned toads they didn't need.

A brick house, then. They'd have a brick house, but first they had to find an adobe house to live in until the brick house was built. Reba would use her heirloom linen tablecloth and her best china, they'd be civilized even if the temporary house was built of mud. And an icebox she'd have, seeing that a miracle had happened and there was ice in this desert, and a black iron range to cook on, and food they could eat, Abraham was too skinny, she had to start feeding him.

"Moria, get yourself one of those funny hats, we can't have you with fried brains. One of those big Mexican hats."

415

"She'll cause a sensation if she does. Everybody would stare at her," Quinn said, only moderately amused because Moria was already causing a sensation. When they'd registered at the Maricopa Hotel, the proprietor had had such a stunned expression at his first sight of her that Quinn had been afraid he was going to fall on his face. The stage driver, the guard, had nearly come to blows scrambling to pick up her luggage and carry it inside for her. The train conductors, the male passengers, had acted as if they'd never seen a beautiful woman before. Why hadn't it crossed his mind that Moria, in Phoenix, would be a sensation?

There were other pretty women here. Some of the ranchers' and merchants' wives and daughters were very attractive, and a good many of the Mexican girls were beautiful, lovely enough to turn any man's head, with their huge brown eyes and long dark hair and eyelashes, their creamy-dark, satiny skin and their lithe, graceful bodies. But Moria was something entirely else again.

When Moria walked down the street, heads turned and people gaped. Men looked first startled, and then disbelieving, and then their eyes glazed. Only yesterday, a young cavalry lieutenant had all but fallen off his horse in his hurry to dismount and dash to hold a shop door open for her, bowing from the waist, his hat swept off his head and his face scarlet.

"Lieutenant Daniel Haverly, ma'am, at your service!" A damned handsome cavalry lieutenant, at that, and years younger than Quinn. And he hadn't even noticed Quinn until he'd straightened up again, and then his face had turned green and every other color of the rainbow, but he'd stood his ground, his eyes wary and hard, filled with the challenge of one man for another over the sight of a beautiful woman.

Cowboys, ranchers, miners from the Tip Top silver mine up near Carefree, shopkeepers, liverymen, millers, saloonkeepers and hotelkeepers, the printers from the newspaper, were all first struck dumb at their first sight of Moria and then found their voices, falling all over themselves in their eagerness to be of service to her. Three days, and already Moria was the talk of Phoenix, the female

416

contingent filled with the whole range of emotions from admiration down to outright jealousy and spite, the men still not quite believing that she could be real, and unattached.

Once again, as he had a hundred, a thousand times over the last few years, Quinn cursed the conditions that the Vancouvers had laid down, that there could be no divorce, that there would never be a divorce. If Moria were free to marry him, there would be no problem at all, but having Moria apparently single was going to raise the devil. There weren't that many unattached females in the whole territory, there weren't anywhere near enough to go around, and for a woman as beautiful as Moria to appear in the midst of all the woman-hungry men was likely to start a minor war. Thank God for Abe and Reba! If they hadn't been here to act as watchdogs over her, Quinn wouldn't have dared to leave her alone in Phoenix.

"We have to decide where you're going to live," he told them. "It doesn't have to be in Phoenix, although that would be my first choice. You could settle at Hayden's Crossing. Back in '82 Charles Trumbull Hayden put up a flour mill there, there's a general store and a machine shop and a ferry over the Salt River, a regular little settlement. Or . . ." and here his eyes crinkled into laugh lines as he looked cornerwise out of them at Reba, " . . . you could try the Mormon settlement."

"Mormons!" Reba half shrieked. "Men with two wives!"

"Sometimes more than two. It's the general rule that they have as many wives as they can support. It makes it nice for spinsters and widows, they have somebody to take care of them." Quinn's face was perfectly straight. But then he added, in all honesty, "They're fine people. They're God-fearing and hard-working, they don't drink or smoke, they take care of their own and they don't bother anyone who doesn't want to be bothered. Maybe it wouldn't be such a good idea for you to settle with them, after all, come to think of it, think of the rush there'd be to convert Moria and add her to their ranks!"

"Two wives," Abraham mused, his eyes thoughtful as he mulled it over. "Not such a bad idea. When a man's wife stabs him in the back like Reba stabbed me—it's only a cold—he could marry

417

another wife and have one who knows who's head of the family, the man or the woman! Solomon might have had a good idea, a thousand wives, he never had to put up with one who didn't know her place, he just called in another one!''

"You try it, Abe Greenbaum, and you might as well have stayed in Chicago to die, because I'll beat some sense into your thick head with my iron frying pan and I maybe wouldn't know when to stop!'' Looking at her uneasily, Abraham couldn't be absolutely sure that she didn't mean it. As if there were any danger! But he wasn't willing to let Reba know that.

"All the same, it's something to think about," he said. "No more backstabbings, or maybe you'll be surprised!'' He wheezed a little, undermining the effect of his words, and cringed as Reba raised her hand to whack his back. "No whacking! I'm better, yet! A frying pan you won't need, the whacking will kill me without the frying pan!''

Reba desisted. It was true, wasn't it, she was sure it was true, that Abraham's breathing was easier, that he didn't wheeze as much. The hot, dry air was already benefiting him. A mud house she'd live in, and the heat and the rattlesnakes and the scorpions and the black widow spiders and the wild Indians she'd put up with, just as long as Abe got well. But another wife, no! And she wouldn't need a frying pan, she had her tongue.

Quinn left them to seek out a shave and a bath at one of the barbershops, stopping at the Wells, Fargo express office that had opened two years ago to check up on how much longer it would take before Reba's household goods arrived. He had to get back to the ranch, let his family know that he was back from Chicago, if they hadn't already heard, which they probably had. He didn't relish facing his father. Quentin Bradmore was a hard man, a man of inflexible morals, who made no attempt to conceal his disapproval of Quinn's hopeless romance with a woman who was married to another man. Having Moria here, right on his doorstep, was going to be a bitter pill for him to swallow. He only hoped that they wouldn't have a clash that would cause an open break between them. It would break his mother's heart, and Willa Bradmore's life had already been hard enough, coping with heat and dust and sand and sun and wind, with lack of feminine company to gossip with, with two strong-willed men and a daughter equally strong-willed.

And later he'd have to face Mattie, and he didn't like to think about what his sister would have to say about his bringing Moria here. But he might as well get it over with, and then get back here and get Abe and Reba settled in a house of their own. A married Catholic woman, Quinn thought, and a Jewish man and wife! It would be a miracle if the ranch house didn't explode tonight, just from the heat of the tempers inside it!

If his father and his sister had given him a hard time, Quinn didn't let any hint of it escape to Moria and Abe and Reba. But they knew, all three of them, without being told, and it saddened them. They didn't expect Quinn to take them to see his family, under the circumstances it would be impossible. They could only appreciate all he was doing for them, and hope and pray that it wouldn't entirely ruin his life. There was no way they could stop him, anyway, because if Quinn wanted them here, if he wanted to help them, he was going to do it.

He found them an adobe house, small and cramped, and got things started for the erection of the brick house that Reba wanted. Moria decided how large the parlor should be, how large the dining room. The kitchen was Reba's, and in spite of Moria's laughing protests and Abraham's tearing of what remained of his hair, the kitchen was to be larger than the parlor. Now, in October, with the weather cooling off, Reba wouldn't think about how in the summers she'd have to cook outdoors, with a range set up under the trees. Next summer was a long way off. There was furniture to buy, household goods, Reba had other things to do than to worry about next summer.

Abraham underwent a mild case of insanity and bought a horse and buggy. He could have rented a horse and buggy but that wouldn't have been the same. Marshall Field he wasn't, his store

419

he'd had to leave behind him, but he could drive out like Mr. Marshall Field and if it was only a buggy instead of a carriage it was a good buggy, the best.

He visited Hayden's Crossing and spent hours talking with the men at the general store. He drove out to the Mormon community and spent hours arguing with the men whose minds were so muddled that they didn't know right from wrong. He sought out every Jewish gentleman in the vicinity. There were a few, and that was a blessing he hadn't counted on. Alone he wouldn't be. He even toyed with the idea of starting a store in Phoenix, his cold was better and he wasn't too old. Even if he only started another store to prove to Reba that he wasn't too old, it was something to think about. With Moria to help him, even in Phoenix he could have a store and maybe not go bankrupt.

He found an eleven-year-old Mexican boy to wash his buggy every day. As the horse stepped out smartly, the buggy bright and shiny with its yellow-spoked wheels, Abraham's face was smug and proud because of the stares of admiration that followed his progress.

When Reba went with him he was more proud than ever. His Reba was a handsome woman. He'd had his doubts about marrying a woman ten years younger than he was, and the prettiest girl he'd ever seen, at that, so that he'd been afraid to ask her for over a year although he'd been so much in love with her that every day without her had been a sickness. Why would a beautiful girl like Reba, whose father was a rabbi, marry a scrawny, homely storekeeper who barely managed to keep afloat?

A hundred times he'd called on her, convinced that this time he'd have the courage to ask her, and a hundred times he'd lost his courage before he could get the question out. In the end, it had been Reba who had done the proposing.

"Abe, am I going to be an old maid then, a spinster all my life because you hang around all the time so other men can't get close enough to ask me? Or are you going to marry me?"

He hadn't believed it for a long time, that he could have such

420

luck, he hadn't believed it even after they were married. He'd wake up in the middle of the night convinced that he'd dreamed it, all covered with cold sweat from the terror of it. But she'd be there, she was always there, beside him in the bed, and he'd reach out and touch her just to make sure. She loved him, him, Abraham Greenbaum, she'd married him, when she could have had her pick of a dozen, two dozen, richer men who weren't scrawny and ugly.

And she was as pretty now as she'd been the day they'd been married. Plumper, he admitted, but that only made her prettier. Her face was smooth and unlined except when she smiled, and the smile lines were beautiful, they didn't make her look old. Her hair was still black, except for the two wings of white. He was so proud of her it threatened to choke him, he loved her so much that the thought that she might not have married him at all could still wake him up in the middle of the night covered with a cold sweat, so he had to reach out and touch her just to make sure that it wasn't all a dream.

So people stared, and admired, and envied him, Abraham Greenbaum. He had the prettiest wife in Phoenix, and the shiniest buggy, and the highest-stepping horse, and he had Moria on top of all that, the two most beautiful women in Arizona. So he'd had a cold and he'd had to leave his store and move to Phoenix because Reba nagged, because Reba stabbed him in the back, a man with a wife who was beautiful ought to count his blessings even if she nagged. When Reba drove out with him, he was so proud he felt like he was going to burst. When Moria went with them as well, he was a king, he was the king of the Arizona Territory.

And if Abraham were king, Moria was the crown princess, with a court. Quinn's premonition that she was going to be a sensation had been well founded. Not an evening went by that there weren't callers at the little adobe house, there were always one or two horses hitched outside, sometimes three or four. Moria didn't encourage the would-be suitors. They perturbed her, she wished that they wouldn't come, but she didn't know how to stop them. She couldn't tell them that she was already married, because that would have caused a scandal that would reflect on Abraham and Reba, and even more on

Quinn, who had brought her to the Southwest. She couldn't tell them that she was a widow because she had determined that she was never going to lie again.

Besides, if she were a widow, then everyone would wonder why she didn't either choose Quinn, or choose one of these new suitors who stormed her doorstep. A woman couldn't stay a widow forever, particularly not a woman as beautiful as Moria, in a country where women were at a premium. Widowed or married or unmarried, questions would be raised that couldn't be answered, and questions that weren't answered aroused suspicion in people's minds and she couldn't allow Reba and Abraham and Quinn to be hurt.

So she told them nothing, not even Lieutenant Daniel Haverly, who was turning out to be the most persistent of them all. Virile, handsome, his brown eyes filled with ardor every time he rode in from Fort McDowell to call on her, almost every other unmarried female in Phoenix and for miles around would have given her eyeteeth to be in Moria's shoes. Heartthrobbingly handsome in his cavalry uniform, the dark-haired lieutenant was the romantic figure of any girl's dreams. And speculation about Moria multiplied as the mystery deepened. If Moria wasn't going to marry Quinn, why didn't she choose Daniel Haverly? The two most desirable men in the Territory, and Moria had both of them, and seemingly, for a reason no one could fathom, she didn't want either of them!

She discouraged her suitors as gently but as firmly as possible. She wasn't thinking of marriage, Abraham and Reba needed her, she told them, and she wouldn't leave them. Her devotion to her adoptive parents was apparent, but it still didn't make sense. Parents or no parents, adoptive or not, all women married, unless they were so ugly that no man would want them.

"Miss Moria, you're enough to drive a man out of his mind!" Daniel told her, exasperated and desperate. This, after he'd attempted to kiss her and she'd fended him off, smiling but firm. "You know I love you. You know I want you to be my wife. You know I'd spend the rest of my life trying to make you happy. Cavalry life isn't so bad, there's some distinction in being the wife of an officer and I'll be promoted to captain soon. If you were my wife, there's no telling how far I could go, I could end up a general! But if you want me to, I'll pull out as soon as I possibly can. I'd be anything and live anywhere you wanted.''

"You'd be miserable away from the cavalry," Moria told him. "And it isn't that, Lieutenant Haverly. I'm simply not interested in getting married. I like you very much, I admire you and what you're doing to help civilize the West, but my best advice to you is to find some other young lady who will return your love and who will make you happy."

"I don't want any other girl, I want you!"

"Then I'm afraid that you're doomed to disappointment, Lieutenant." Moria refused to go riding with him, even when he offered to bring over the best horse he had under his command. She refused to attend any social function with him. She received him in the little adobe house when he called, but Abraham and Reba were always in the kitchen while she entertained him in the parlor, and they always joined them after a discreet half-hour, and sat there without budging until Daniel was forced to give up and say good night, seething with frustration.

If Moria had given any indication that she preferred Quinn to him, he would have been tempted to call Quinn out. But she didn't. She didn't ride out with Quinn either, or attend any social functions with him, and Daniel had no way of knowing that Quinn was treated as a member of the Greenbaum family when he visited them, that Quinn sat in the kitchen, while he was relegated to the parlor.

If fending off would-be suitors occupied a great deal of Moria's time much to her consternation, Phoenix itself was a never-ending source of pleasure to her. She was enchanted with the Mexican population, especially the children, who walked barefoot on the hottest ground, before the cool weather set in, and who were so shy but always smiling. The adults as well as the children were shy and diffident, but all of them, without exception, seemed to smile constantly, their voices so soft and musical that she never tired of listening to them, their friendliness something to warm her heart

after her years in the Hudson River Valley, where friendliness bore a price tag, and in Chicago, where no one seemed to care about anyone else unless they were family or close personal friends.

She set about learning Spanish as fast as she could. *Buenos días* and *adiós, mañana* and *cómo está usted* became as familiar to her as her native English. *Muchacho, muchacha, gracias.* Quinn spoke Spanish as his second language, Reba was picking up a smattering, but Abraham said that it was a waste of time because all of the men and most of the children spoke enough English to make themselves understood. Did he ask them to learn Yiddish? Then why should he learn to speak Spanish?

Moria bought a pair of huaraches, the woven Mexican shoes that were so comfortable. She bought a wide-brimmed Mexican sombrero, although she didn't wear it; it hung on the wall of her bedroom. She bought a full bright red Mexican skirt and a Mexican blouse, white and with very full, puffed sleeves and lace around its drawstring neckline. She bought a bright Mexican shawl. She wore none of them in public, it would have caused a scandal, but Abraham and Reba and Quinn loved to see her dressed in them when they were alone at home.

Her heart ached because she couldn't send a hat, huaraches, a serape, to Reid, because she couldn't send a Mexican skirt and blouse to Gayle, who would have been so beautiful in them that hearts would stop to look at her. She wanted to send them both kachina dolls and Mexican silver jewelry—bracelets and necklaces for Gayle, a concho belt for Reid. But they wouldn't have been allowed to keep them, they would either be returned or thrown away.

Reba bought Indian jewelry, heavy, beautiful bracelets and rings and necklaces, all set with turquoise. Her eyes gleamed at the sight of it, she had a jewel box full of it and she kept buying more.

"Junk," Quinn told her, and Abraham agreed.

"You want jewelry? I'll buy you pearls, I'll buy you diamonds. They're worth something, it's like money in the bank," Abraham told her. "Pearls and diamonds you can always sell. And you wouldn't have to sell them, I'm not a poor man, tell me what you want and you'll have it. Within reason.''

But Reba spurned the idea of pearls and diamonds, even of rubies, and went on buying Indian jewelry. When she drove out with Abraham she looked like a display counter but it suited her even though most of the Phoenix ladies smiled behind their hands. What did they know? Reba knew what was beautiful, what suited her. When the brick house was finished she'd have her kitchen. In the meantime she had her turquoise. And Moria told her that she was sure that someday Indian jewelry would be appreciated, that it would double and redouble in value until the pieces she was picking up now for almost nothing would be worth a small fortune. Diamonds and pearls were smart, maybe, like Abe said, but Moria was smarter.

Moria had nothing. She wanted her children, and she wanted Quinn. But there was no price tag that she could meet to pay for them. And so she hid her desolation behind a smile so that Abraham and Reba would think that she was happy, and she lived one day at a time.

The brick house rose with astonishing rapidity, simply because there were so many eager hands fighting each other for the privilege of helping to get it up for Miss Moria Donovan. Cowboys who, a few months ago, would have called another man crazy for suggesting that they lay bricks and mortar, miners from the Tip Top mine, printers and shopkeepers and liverymen and barbers vied with each other to be of the most help. They got in each other's way and drove the genuine bricklayers and carpenters to distraction, but the work went forward so fast that it was hard to believe.

It was a grand house, as grand as that of Ira Stroud on Monroe Street, which had up until now been acknowledged as the largest and grandest house in Phoenix. Reba had to have a house that was worthy of her, Michael McCarthy had gotten a price for the store Abe wouldn't have believed, payments on the dot, with interest, bankrupt he wasn't and before that happened he'd have another store.

There was a porch, there was a fanlight over the front door, a

425

white-painted, paneled door, the windows were tall, there was a fireplace in the parlor. Mesquite they would burn, Quinn told him, that was the best. A fireplace he'd never had, and he didn't know what good it would be to them because Reba would still want to live in the kitchen, but it made him feel good to have it. Didn't Mr. Marshall Field have fireplaces?

"You want a fireplace, have one in the kitchen too," Reba told him complacently. But he drew the line at that. One fireplace, there was no use in being foolish. For friends, they'd sit in the kitchen and make do with the black iron range. Close to the teakettle and the sugar bowl, and with no stiff collar and with his shoes off so his bunions wouldn't hurt. Mr. Marshall Field couldn't do that, his wife wouldn't let him.

And Mrs. Marshall Field couldn't pick roses in December, and she didn't have a jewelry box full of Indian turquoise jewelry. Reba had her kitchen and her turquoise and her flowers in the winter, from her own garden, not a hothouse, and Abe's cold was better, he hadn't wheezed for weeks, and if he kept on not wheezing she might let him have a little store as long as she and Moria could keep him from working too hard. Having a husband underfoot all day wasn't the paradise she'd thought it would be. Sometimes a woman had to be alone so she could clean her kitchen. Sometimes a woman had to have a kitchen without an Indian in it.

She didn't dislike the Indian. She didn't like him, but she didn't dislike him, either. It was just that he made her nervous, appearing without any warning, and Abe inviting him in. He sat there, looking alien sitting on one of her good kitchen chairs at her big kitchen table, and he ate. He ate her cookies, he ate her cakes, he ate her pies, he drank her tea and he used more sugar in his tea than Abe did.

He wasn't a young Indian, and he wasn't old. Fifty maybe, how could you tell? He wore a red calico shirt and faded denim trousers, he wore a white man's hat, disreputable and with a feather stuck through it. He wore moccasins on his feet. Quinn said he was a Maricopa. He wasn't tall and he wasn't short. He never smiled. His face was as expressionless as if it had been carved from stone. His black eyes, as black as the coal Reba had used to burn in her kitchen range back in Chicago, never seemed to blink as he sat there and ate, and ate, and ate.

They'd first seen him at Hayden's Crossing, in front of the general store, with a stock of turquoise jewelry spread out on a blanket while he sat cross-legged in a patch of sun. Reba being Reba, she had had to examine every piece.

"I want this one, Papa," Reba said. She'd taken to calling Abraham Papa shortly after Moria had come to live with them. "This necklace, and this ring." She'd beamed at Charlie and told him how wonderful she thought his craftsmanship was. "And, Papa, I want the bracelet, they match, they make a set. No, don't haggle about the price, they're worth what he asks, such beautiful work I wouldn't enjoy wearing if I thought we'd cheated him!"

Quinn told them later that Charlie was an outcast from his tribe. He'd had to run for his life when there'd been sickness in his village, an epidemic of dysentery, after the shamans, the medicine men, had singled him out as the witch who had caused the sickness.

In cases like that, the suspected witch was stoned and clubbed to death so that the sickness would go away. So Charlie—that's what he was called, no one knew his Indian name—had cut and run before the medicine men could catch him, because he'd had an uneasy feeling that he was the one they were going to pick because he'd complained that they hadn't cured a bellyache he'd had a few weeks before, that he'd been cured by the doctor at the fort and not by their charms. A man who claimed that a white doctor had cured him instead of the shamans was a likely candidate to be the witch who was causing the epidemic.

"Quinn, they don't!" Moria protested. "Not in this day and age, and so close to civilization! They couldn't possibly club and stone innocent people to death through such childish superstition!"

"They still did a few years back," Quinn told them. "It wasn't all that uncommon. It's part of their beliefs."

"But how does he live, how does he keep from starving?"

"Handouts, what he can scavenge. He sticks close to the settlement, he doesn't dare not to. I offered him a job on the ranch, but working isn't his idea of being a man, that's for women. He was a silversmith, and he sells a little jewelry to people who visit the settlement." He looked at Reba slyly, out of the corners of his eyes. "Gullible people who don't know any better than to buy it."

Reba slammed the iron frying pan down on the table so hard that it was a wonder that it didn't crack. " 'Gullible people'! I know who you mean, Quinn Bradmore! So I bought a few pieces from him, they're beautiful pieces and we'll see who's gullible when it gets valuable someday the way Moria says it will! Will he scalp us?"

"Not as long as you keep feeding him."

So Reba kept feeding him, not because she was really afraid that Charlie would scalp them, but because Abe kept letting him in and if he was a guest she had to feed him. She'd just have to put up with it, because Abe was going to go right on letting him in because Charlie listened to him while Abe went on and on about Judaism, trying to convert him. They knew that Charlie understood English, at least enough to get the gist of what Abe was saying, even if he never said anything himself but just sat there eating and listening.

Moria thought it was hilarious, she could hardly keep from laughing while Charlie ate and Abraham preached at him, determined to produce the first Indian Jew anybody had ever heard of. He hadn't ever gotten to be a rabbi, but converting an Indian would be almost as good.

Charlie had been coming for nearly six weeks now, just showing up, knowing that Abraham would let him in. Reba wished that Papa would hurry up and get him converted so that she could have her kitchen to herself again without an Indian in it.

He was here again today, in the middle of the afternoon, eating her pie, he'd had three pieces and it looked as if he was going to finish off the whole thing all by himself and there wouldn't be any left for supper. He wouldn't use a plate and a fork, he picked up the wedges in his hand and stuffed them into his mouth, his eyes unblinking, his face expressionless, listening to Abe.

"Reba, his glass is empty. And the sugar bowl needs more sugar," Abraham said.

Charlie looked at Reba. He looked at Abraham. He reached inside his shirt and brought out a necklace, fabulously studded with stones. He handed it to Abraham, who took it, not understanding. Then Charlie stood up and put his hand on Reba's wrist and started pulling her toward the kitchen door. The courtship had been completed, the deal had been made, he'd bought himself a wife.

Abraham, his face bewildered, still didn't understand. Reba was too flabbergasted to even try to understand. It was Moria who understood.

"Oh, my goodness! Charlie, let go of her! You can't have her, she's already married, she's Abraham's wife!"

"Abraham her father. She said so, she calls him Papa."

Abraham understood then. He was on his feet, his face contorted with outrage. But his outrage didn't begin to match Reba's.

"No, Abe, no! You're a sick man, I'll do it!" Reba said. Not expecting resistance, Charlie let her yank her wrist from his grip, and then her broom was in her hands. She brought it down over Charlie's head, once and then again and again. "Get out of here, you red devil! Get out and don't come back!"

Charlie went. Reba went after him. Doubled over with laughter, Moria tried to run after them to stop Reba but she was laughing too hard to run fast enough. Down the street they went, with people gaping, Charlie running for his life, Reba right behind him, showing a speed that no one would have suspected she was capable of, still belaboring him with her broom.

Moria, her skirts held up with one hand so she could run faster, finally caught up with them and grabbed the broom. "Stop it, Reba! He's going, you don't have to beat him to death, do you want to start another Indian war?" With one last look at Reba over his shoulder, Charlie yelped, "Who'd want you! You're a shrew! You can keep your cakes and pies!"

It was nearly midnight before Charlie dared to return to retrieve his horse. Reba had finally calmed down enough to put supper on the table, although Abraham was still so outraged that he couldn't eat. Reba's father, was he? He was cut to the quick, as well as insulted that Charlie had thought he could buy Reba with a piece of junk. He was so upset that Reba decided that she'd have to let him start a store, to prove to himself that he wasn't old.

Abraham and Reba were both asleep when Charlie came skulking out of the shadows. Moria had been waiting for him, to give him back the necklace. She'd fed and watered his shaggy, dispirited-looking horse earlier, it wasn't the poor creature's fault that his master had made a mistake.

Even in the darkness, Moria thought that she saw Charlie's face blanch, as dark-skinned as he was, when she slipped through the front door to confront him.

"It's all right. Take this, it's yours," Moria said. And then, as an afterthought and just to make sure that a mistake wouldn't be made a second time, she added, "I can't cook!"

Charlie took the necklace and stuffed it inside his shirt. He swung up on his horse, which had a saddle blanket but no saddle, and clamped his legs around its belly. He didn't deign to answer her, he simply rode off into the night and Phoenix never saw him again. Being stoned and clubbed to death as a witch would have been one thing, but being laughed to death was an entirely different matter, so he set out for parts unknown, only wanting to get far enough away so that no one would know the story that already had all of Phoenix in stitches. And going back into the house, still laughing, Moria thought, "Well, it was only a little lie! I can't cook nearly as well as Reba."

25

Mattie Chambers, née Mattie Bradmore, had made up her mind.
Quinn had brought the Greenbaums and that woman, Moria Donovan,
to Phoenix clear back last fall, and here it was March, and she had
yet to see the woman who had ruined her brother's life.

It wasn't that she mightn't have seen Miss Moria Donovan, as she
called herself. Mattie had been to town on half a dozen different
occasions, and it was only a happenstance that she hadn't seen
Moria on the streets or in a store. She'd certainly kept her eyes open
for her, hoping to see her, wanting to see for herself just what there
was about this particular young woman that could make Quinn so
insane that he was still a bachelor when he could have had any girl
in the territory. And Mattie had also attended every public social
gathering that there'd been, but Moria hadn't been at any of them.

She wasn't going to wait any longer. It was high time that she had
a look at Miss Moria Donovan, and gave her a piece of her mind that
would either send her scuttling back where she'd come from, or at
least make her tell Quinn that she wouldn't see him any more and he
might as well marry someone else.

431

Mattie loved her brother. They'd been close as children, as ranch children had to be close, isolated as they were from other companions and playmates so they had to depend on each other. But Mattie would have loved Quinn anyway, just because he was Quinn, head and shoulders better than any other male she had ever known until she'd fallen in love with Chet Chambers, and even Chet couldn't measure up to Quinn in lots of ways, she'd fallen in love with him because he was sweet and shy and kind and someone she'd known she could always depend on, a man who'd be a good husband, a good father to their children.

She still loved Chet, even if they had been married for twelve years and had four children. Chet and the children came first in her life and they always would, but Quinn came second, and she'd waited long enough, she'd waited too long, to see if there wasn't something she could do about an impossible situation that wasn't going to get any better unless someone did something about it. Part of it Quinn had told her, and part of it she'd guessed. Moria Donovan, indeed! *Mrs. Anthony Vancouver*!

She didn't hitch up the buckboard to drive to Phoenix from the Crazy C Bar M ranch. *C* for Chet, *M* for Mattie, it had been Chet's idea when he'd struck out on his own, his older brothers, two of them, and their wives already living at his parents' ranch. They'd wanted to be alone, make it on their own, she and Chet, and they'd done it, with a start on their herd from Chet's father and the other start on it from her father, all of which they'd paid back years ago. They'd done well, she was content with what they'd accomplished, content with her life, her only major worry was Quinn and what his love for a woman he couldn't have was doing to him.

So that March morning she saddled up her horse, Yucca, instead of taking a buckboard, because she wasn't going in to town to lay in supplies and she wasn't taking the children, no matter how hard they clamored to be taken along. She was going for one purpose only, and that was to confront Miss Moria Donovan in her own house, and see if anything could be salvaged from the shambles that Miss Moria Donovan, Mrs. Anthony Vancouver, had made of her brother's life.

432

She didn't need to get dressed up in her best bib and tucker for that, this wasn't a social visit, her saddle horse would be faster and she wasn't trying to make an impression. Her long split riding skirt and her boots and her western hat would do. She'd given up riding habits and sidesaddle soon after she and Chet had been married, because she'd so often had to help Chet on the range and you couldn't haze steers from a sidesaddle.

Besides her split skirt and her wide-brimmed hat and her boots, Mattie wore one other item that was as much a part of her normal riding clothing as the clothing itself, a holster and a gun. Not a small, ladylike gun, but something that meant business in case she met up with a rattlesnake or a two-legged varmint, although that last wasn't very likely these days now that the Territory was becoming so civilized. Quinn had taught her to shoot when she'd been so young that her whole arm had trembled from the weight of the gun when she'd aimed it, and there wasn't a man in the Territory who didn't know that she was a dead shot.

In addition to the handgun, there was a Winchester rifle in her saddle scabbard, and she was an even deadlier shot with that than she was with the Colt. Mattie was a westerner, a ranchwoman, not a la-di-da lady who'd been sent to an eastern finishing school the way some of the ranchers' daughters had been, and she wouldn't have wanted it any other way.

"Dan, you're in charge, but no bossing or bullying," Mattie instructed her offspring as she mounted up while they watched, their faces filled with disappointment. At ten, Dan was fully capable of being in charge. "Scott, you're Dan's deputy."

Eight-year-old Scott shrugged. It would be nice to get to be sheriff once, instead of deputy, but that was the way things were and he accepted it. Sam, at seven, was the problem, because Sam was fiery and argument-prone, he took more after Quentin Bradmore than either of the other boys and he resented having to take third place just because nature had made a mistake and made him the youngest of the three boys, with only four-year-old Gloria to boss around, and girls didn't count.

Gloria, a miniature of her mother, her hair more golden than sandy brown because she was still almost a baby, her tilted nose sprinkled with freckles, put her chubby fists on her hips and adopted a stance of authority.

"Don't worry, Mama. I'll make them behave!" she said. Her eyes were cool and level, missing nothing. Mattie chuckled as she gathered up the reins and set Yucca into a ground-covering lope that would eat up the miles between the ranch and town. There'd be no fancy eastern schools for Gloria, either, she was a ranch girl, her favorite game was roping her brothers whenever she could catch them unaware, with the small, lightweight riata that Chet had made for her. She'd make her brothers behave by the sheer force of her will, and never believe for a moment that they deferred to her because she was the youngest and a girl.

Mattie had no compunctions about riding out alone. The Indian troubles were over, even the Apaches had been subdued a few years back, after the settlers had gotten up in arms about their marauding and demanded action.

Yucca was a pinto, tough and wiry and tireless, so sure-footed that he never missed his step even in the roughest terrain. There was a canteen tied to the saddle, even if the early morning hour, just after eight o'clock, was crisp and refreshing. The summer heat wouldn't settle over the land for another two months, relentless and dangerous for those who didn't know how to handle it. Miss Moria Donovan, here I come! Mrs. Anthony Vancouver, you'd better have a good story, or you're going to find yourself in a mess of trouble as bad as falling into a nest of rattlesnakes in the spring, still sluggish from the winter and more dangerous than at any other time of the year. Enough was enough, and Mattie was loaded for bear.

Reba answered the door. Everybody in Phoenix, everybody in Maricopa County and all the other counties for miles around knew the Greenbaum house, the big brick house that had been put up faster than any other house had ever been put up because every fool man in the Territory had fallen all over himself to do Miss Moria Donovan a favor. Abraham Greenbaum's house, with its white-

434

painted front door and its green-painted shutters, with its huge brick chimney for the fireplace, and its tile roof because Abraham didn't want sparks from the fireplace to set the roof on fire.

Reba was wearing a cotton housedress and an apron. Her hands and arms were covered with flour up to the elbow because she was baking molasses cookies, Abraham's favorite, redolent with cinnamon and ginger and nutmeg, the aroma permeating the house and wafting through the front door to make Mattie's stomach stir with sudden hunger in spite of the ranch breakfast of steak and eggs she'd consumed at dawn. There was a smudge of flour on Reba's nose, where she'd scrubbed at an itch with the back of her hand. Her plump face was beautiful, her dark eyes, under the two startling wings of white hair, widened with shock at the sight of a young woman who was the image of Quinn, standing on her doorstep armed to the teeth.

"I'm Mattie Chambers," Mattie said, quite unnecessarily. She might have looked like a woman and she was certainly attractive in spite of her strong face, but she was all Bradmore. "I've come to see Miss Donovan."

Abraham wasn't at home, he was out in the buggy, and what could Abe have done even if he had been home, a sick man he was and he wouldn't know one end of a gun from the other even if he could bring himself to shoot a woman, and Quinn's sister at that, even to defend Moria. Reba wished that she had her rolling pin in her hand, or better yet, her umbrella. She should scream, maybe, warn Moria, who was upstairs. Only she couldn't scream, because that would bring Moria running.

And then it was too late to do anything, scream or push Mattie Chambers out of the door and lock it, because Moria appeared at the landing of the stairs. "Who is it, Reba?"

Mattie, in the act of putting one foot inside the door, taking it for granted that she'd been invited in because out here nobody ever said you couldn't, froze in her tracks, her eyes widening. She'd never seen anyone so beautiful in her life. That wealth of black hair, piled high on Moria's head, the skin as satiny as the petals on a cactus flower, her dark-fringed eyes so blue it didn't seem possible, eyes that were looking at her now with sudden recognition, came as near to striking Mattie dumb as she'd ever been in her life.

Moria finished descending the stairs, every movement so graceful that Mattie felt oversized and awkward. She smiled, and if Mattie thought she had been beautiful before, now her heart turned over and her throat tightened. Of all the women in the world, why had it had to be this one, this Moria Donovan, whom Quinn had chanced to meet, because what man who wasn't already in his grave could possibly not fall in love with her?

"You're Quinn's sister, you're Mattie," Moria said. She held out her hand, and her smile was genuine. "I'm so glad to meet you at last! Come in. Reba, are any of those cookies done yet? Mattie, would you rather have tea or coffee? You rode in, you must be hungry. Come into the kitchen, the parlor is for company and you aren't company because you're Quinn's sister."

"This isn't a social visit. I wanted to talk to you."

Moria's eyes filled with pain, such deep pain that Mattie flinched.

"Of course you want to talk with me. In your place, I'd have been here a long time ago. You love Quinn. Please believe me when I say that I love him too. We need to talk, Mattie. I need to talk to you as much as you need to talk to me."

Hardly knowing how it had happened, Mattie found herself sitting in Reba's kitchen. Checkered blue and white gingham curtains, handsewn, covered the windows. Pots of geraniums were on the windowsills. Everything was scrubbed to an immaculateness that made Mattie wince to think of her own young brood stampeding in to wreak a chaos of dust and mud, of spills and scatterings and shouting young voices, and yet this kitchen seemed to tell her that it would welcome muddy feet, that it would welcome spills and scatterings, that this was the heart of a house that had been built for love and happiness.

The cookies, warm from the oven, were the most delicious Mattie had ever tasted. The coffee was strong and full-bodied, rich and satisfying. Reba Greenbaum, now that she was convinced that

Mattie wasn't going to shoot Moria at sight, was warm and welcoming, and Moria was lovely and beautiful and nothing at all the way Mattie had thought she would be. For a woman who had come to beard a lioness in her den, Mattie wasn't doing very well.

Nevertheless, Mattie being Mattie, she wasn't going to capitulate without putting up the best darned fight of which she was capable.

"You call yourself Miss Donovan," she said. "But as I understand it, you're still married. Your legal name is Mrs. Anthony Vancouver."

Moria's face went a shade more pale, and her eyes, those incredible blue eyes, were shadowed with tragedy, with a hurt so deep that Mattie almost wished that she hadn't come at all.

"You already know that. Quinn has told me that you know."

Mattie put down the cookie she had half eaten and faced Moria squarely, her own eyes resolute. "Then why in God's name don't you leave him alone? Why don't you let him go? It isn't right, what you're doing, keeping him from finding someone else, keeping him from marrying and having children!"

"I've asked him to go. I've told him to go. Do you think I enjoy hurting him, ruining his life? I love him, Mattie! I'd do anything to make him happy, even give him up because there isn't any hope for us, there isn't any hope at all. My husband will never give me a divorce."

"How could you leave your children, go running off with another man, when you knew all along that it was hopeless?" Mattie challenged her.

"I didn't. I left my husband because I was forced to leave him." Apparently there were things that Quinn hadn't told even Mattie, things that he considered he had no right to tell. But having met Quinn's sister at last, Moria thought that she was entitled to know everything there was to know.

She knew, instinctively, that Mattie could be trusted, that given the right circumstances, she and Mattie could be friends, the kind of friends that only a few people are ever privileged to have.

And so she told her. Sitting there in Reba's kitchen, forgetting the aromatic coffee, the cookies that only Reba could make, she told her all of it. She started at the beginning, and she ended with today.

"Oh, my God!" Mattie said. She wasn't blaspheming. "Moria, how did you bear it, how can you bear it? I'd have killed them, I swear I would have! William Northrup, and that husband of yours! Snakes like that don't deserve to live, they're vermin!"

"No, you wouldn't have. You have children, four beautiful children. You know why I couldn't, even if I could have otherwise. Murder is a dreadful thing. I know. My father was murdered. And no matter how ruthless he is, how heartless he is, William Northrup has murder on his soul, and he's paying for it in his own way. And no matter how selfish and self-seeking Anthony is, he's paying and will go on paying in his own way. And I wouldn't change places with them, even if it would bring me what I want more than anything else in the world."

"All the same, I'm glad that William Northrup was struck down with that stroke! It wasn't as much as he deserved by a long shot, but at least he's suffering! And as for your husband . . ." She broke off, at a loss for words. "Oh, Moria! I'm so glad I came! I was going to tear you to pieces, I was going to tell you what I thought of you and try to drive you away!" Appalled at her intentions now that she'd met this woman her brother loved, Mattie choked and came to a stop.

Her eyes filled with tears, Reba jumped up to dump out their cold coffee and refill their cups. "Nobody could blame you," she said. "How could anybody blame you? You didn't know. But now you know, and it's a good thing. Moria needs friends, she's young, Abe and I aren't enough no matter how much we love her, our daughter she is, sent to Papa and me in our old age. She needs friends like you."

"And she has a friend like me!" Mattie held out her hand and Moria placed her own in it. Mattie's grip was strong, so strong that it almost made her wince. But her own grip was strong, too, in spite of the fact that her hands were soft and white and delicate in contrast to Mattie's square, sun-darkened hands, used to the roughest and hardest kind of work. "That is, if she wants me!"

"I want you," Moria said. She would have wanted Mattie for a friend even if she hadn't been Quinn's sister. Just knowing Mattie, having her for a friend, would give her strength, would give her courage to go on even when it seemed that there was no use.

"Come to the ranch and see me," Mattie said. "Quinn will bring you, I'll tell him to. The boys will be flabbergasted by you, it might even strike them dumb for a few blessed seconds! But don't be surprised if Gloria is a little jealous. Up until now, she's been convinced that she's the most beautiful woman in Quinn's life!"

"I'll come. I'll be glad to come."

"And you, too, and Abraham," Mattie said, turning to Reba. "I could kick myself for not having got to know you months ago. No wonder Quinn is so fond of you. Now that I've met you, I feel as if I have a whole new family."

"And you come back. Bring the children," Reba urged her. "This kitchen needs children. A kitchen is the heart of a house, but what's a heart without children? Papa and me need children, alone we were until Moria came to us, and even she isn't a grandchild!"

They stood on the porch and watched her ride away, their hands clasped. "What a woman!" Reba sighed. And Moria, her face breaking into a grin, said, "Imagine the sensation if she were to walk down the streets of Chicago, with that gun on her hip! Reba, we have a friend, a real friend."

She only barely caught Reba's low mutter as they reentered the house with their arms around each other. "I wonder if she would have shot you if she hadn't decided she liked you?"

Amused, Moria couldn't help wondering, too.

It was so early that dawn had barely lightened the sky when Moria stood on the front porch, her eyes wide with disbelief. Quinn, standing beside her, watched her face as his pleasure matched her own.

He'd started out while it was still full dark, riding his own horse and leading this one, a close relative of Kamil. No one but Quinn had ever ridden Caballero, and he'd trained the magnificent palomino himself, putting more work into it than he'd ever spent on any other horse because this one was worth it.

Caballero was a darker gold than Kamil, and there were even darker mottled markings on his hindquarters. He was large, sixteen and a half hands, and every line of him was perfect. His head was beautiful, and his eyes showed spirit and intelligence.

"Oh, Quinn! I don't believe it, I can't believe it! Am I really going to ride him?"

"You are if you're going to visit Mattie. He's a powerful lot of horse, but you can handle him. It's time you had a horse of your own, you must be tired of riding around in Abe's buggy."

The look in her eyes made the battle he'd had with his father about giving Caballero to Moria more than worthwhile. Quentin Bradmore had been in a towering rage when Quinn had saddled the golden horse, the most valuable horse they'd ever owned, to take to town so that Moria could have him for her own.

"Caballero's mine. I can give him to whomever I want," Quinn had said, his voice even, struggling to control his own temper. "I raised him, I broke him and trained him, he's been mine since the day he was foaled. I'm sorry if you don't approve, but I'm giving him to Moria. Don't worry that she won't know how to handle him. She's the best horsewoman I ever saw."

His face white under the saddle-leather tan that a lifetime in Arizona had given him, Quentin had turned and stalked back to the ranch house, his silence even greater testimony to his outrage than his shouting had been.

Quentin could have sympathy for a woman whose father had been murdered, whose husband had been unfaithful to her and then betrayed her by refusing to help bring the murderer to justice. He could have sympathy for a woman who had been forced to leave her home and her children. But for that woman to have hypnotized his son so that Quinn would not look at another woman was something that he couldn't forgive. Because of Moria Donovan, Moria Vancouver, he had no grandchildren of his own name, and as much as he loved Mattie's brood, it wasn't the same. Besides, it was immoral.

His own face set, Quinn had finished saddling Caballero and then led him to Phoenix, their pace easy so as not to tire the horses. They'd have time to let them rest while he had a second breakfast with Moria and Reba and Abe before they set out to visit Mattie. The first time, only Moria was going. Next week, Quinn would take Abe and Reba, he'd bring a buckboard so that Abe wouldn't have to risk breaking a buggy wheel, and a tough team that could stand the trip better than Abe's buggy horse, soft now from only pulling Abe around Phoenix and the near vicinity, a town horse, pampered and spoiled.

Reba had baked cookies. They were for the children, a big bag of them, tied to Quinn's saddle. Cookies for the children, for the first children she'd ever been able to think of as belonging to her even if she hadn't seen them yet. Grandma's cookies. Quinn ate four of the ones Reba had held out for their breakfast, and downed his third cup of coffee. "A good breakfast, Reba. All it needed was bacon or ham to make it perfect."

Reba refused to be ruffled. "Bacon and ham Mattie'll give you. You take care of Moria, don't let any bandits or Indians or rattlesnakes get her. And kiss the children for me."

"If I kissed Dan or Scott, they'd shoot me. I wouldn't be able to catch Sam to kiss him. You'll have to settle for Gloria."

It seemed to Moria, as they left Phoenix behind them and settled into the slow, easy, mile-eating lope that western horses were trained for, that she was happier than she'd been since the day she'd boarded the train for Chicago, with the future black and unknown before her, as empty as her heart. Just to be in the saddle again, on a horse like Caballero, on a perfect March morning, with the desert air crisp and dry and so pure that they could see for nearly a hundred miles, was enough to elate even the most depressed spirits. The Hudson River Valley seemed like another world, Arizona was a world apart, far removed from anything she had ever known.

Caballero snorted and pranced, uneasy because of the sidesaddle on his back, Willa Bradmore's saddle—Quinn's mother had never learned to ride astride. And he was uneasy because of the woman on his back, when nobody but Quinn had ever ridden him before. But Quinn was beside him, speaking to him in his familiar, authoritative voice, and the hands on his reins were competent and confident, and after the first few miles he settled down, enjoying Moria's lighter weight and her soft, caressing voice.

The Crazy C Bar M ranch house was low and sprawling, built of adobe, and rooms had been added on as they had become needed. It was neither graceful nor beautiful, it was utilitarian, but Mattie's hand was evident in the flower beds along the porch, nurtured with precious water, the most precious commodity in this arid country where water was more precious than gold. Calendulas, cosmos, iris, and there was a climbing rosebush alongside, covered with brilliant red roses in clusters.

Women not only perpetuated the race, Moria thought, not only followed their men into wilderness and desert, but stubbornly, implacably, they managed to bring a touch of beauty where none had been before, a touch of grace and civilization where none had been before. It made her feel proud to be a woman, to belong to that sisterhood that managed to survive, and persevere, wherever the dictates of men led them.

Then her attention was entirely taken up by the three boys who raced to meet them. Whooping, their faces filled with excitement, and after them, her short legs churning, her plump face filled with fury, a little girl, screaming at the top of her lungs that she had to be the first because she was the girl. "You aren't being *polite*!" Gloria screeched.

Quinn leaned from his saddle and scooped her up into his arms, and her face immediately beamed brighter than the sun. "You are first! Aren't you always?"

Even as Gloria crowed her triumph, the boys stopped, their heels digging into the dirt of the yard as their jaws dropped and their faces registered astonishment. The youngest, Moria struggled to sort out their names, it would be Sam, burst out in a voice laced with accusation, "You're riding Caballero! Uncle Quinn never let me ride him, he never lets anybody ride him!"

"Shut up, Sam!" That would be Dan, he was the oldest, ten, Mattie had told her, almost Reid's age when she'd had to leave him. Her throat felt tight, her heart felt as though a fist were squeezing it. He even looked a little bit like Reid, in his coloring, in his steady, level eyes. "Uncle Quinn can let anybody ride Caballero he wants to, Caballero's his."

"Not anymore, he isn't. He belongs to Moria now. And maybe, if you're real polite and mind your manners, she might let you get up on him before we leave, if you don't mind a sidesaddle." Quinn's face was straight but his eyes were filled with teasing.

Moria found her voice. "The sidesaddle can be removed. And you shall all ride Caballero, before we leave." She almost added that she or Quinn would lead him, and bit the words back just in time. That would be a fine way to make friends with Mattie's boys, that would, insulting them the first time she met them!

"Me first!" Gloria demanded, her voice confident. But this time her uncle shook his head, and he was adamant.

"Not you, sugar. You're just a mite too little. You'll have to wait a few years."

"But that's not *fair*!"

Mattie came out of the house, her face lit up with a smile, eager and almost as excited as her sons. "Who ever said anything about fair, kitten? You take what you get! Moria, I'm glad to see you. And on Caballero! Darn it, Quinn, you never let me ride him!"

Moria laughed even as she dismounted. "Then you'll ride him today, but you'll have to stand in line. The boys asked first."

The house was dim and cool, its yard-thick walls an effective barrier against both heat and cold. Moria had to see it all—the parlor, which was almost never used; the dining room, which was used only for company; the children's bedrooms. But they ended up in the kitchen, just as they would have in Reba's house. Only this kitchen, while not as elegant as Reba's, had something that Reba's lacked, it resounded with the voices of children, gabbling, squabbling, laughing, as they crowded around Quinn and Moria, shy but eager in their excitement, the boys' faces as awestruck by Moria as Mattie had said they would be, Gloria just a little jealous at first until Moria lifted her up onto her lap and gave her the first cookie out of the bag that Reba had sent them.

The warmth of the snuggling body made her heart twist again. She'd held Gayle like this, when Gayle had been four, before Jacob Vancouver had managed to ruin her, before he had made her believe that she was better than anybody else because she was a Vancouver, before William Northrup had helped ruin her because she was beautiful, the third beautiful jewel in his crown, one of his three most precious possessions.

The mood was broken by Chet's entrance, his shy face filled with welcome. Immediately, he and Quinn were involved in ranch talk, in talk of cattle, and grazing, of branding and disease prevention and rain and drought, of what the market price of beef was likely to be this fall.

They left in the middle of the afternoon, after Dan and Scott and Sam had had their rides on Caballero, after Mattie had waited in line to take her turn, hauling herself up by clutching the golden mane just as the boys had done and riding bareback around and around the dooryard. Moria was entranced. Someday she'd try that!

She felt an almost physical sense of loss as she and Quinn turned their horses' heads back toward Phoenix. It cost her an effort to smile at Quinn, to tell him how much she'd enjoyed this visit and how glad she was that he'd brought her.

They'd been riding for over an hour, the late afternoon sun warm, the changing patterns and colors of the backdrop of mountains enthralling, the shifting shadows over the land so beautiful that it was breathtaking. She could understand why men like Quinn, like his father and Chet, would never be content to live anywhere else. This was their country, their land, they'd fought it and struggled with it and cursed it and hated it but they'd always loved it and they always would. It was a challenge they couldn't turn their backs on, and in their place Moria would have felt the same.

"Quinn?"

They'd been riding in silence for several miles, preoccupied with their own thoughts. "Would it be all right if I picked some of that lupine to take to Reba? She'll never believe I picked it in the desert! I don't think it's hot enough that they'll die before we get them back."

Just as Quinn had told them when they'd first come to the desert, it was carpeted with wild flowers, the brilliant blue of lupine, the bright orange of poppies, contrasting with cacti and mesquite and Joshua trees.

Quinn nodded. "I'll soak my bandanna in water and wrap it around the stems. I reckon they'll make it without wilting. But Reba's going to say that we picked them in Mattie's garden. She'll never believe all these flowers out here, unless I get her and Abe out to see Mattie before they die. They'll all be gone when the first real heat sets in."

Moria stripped off her gloves. The lupine stems were delicate, she needed her bare hands to pick them. They grew in clumps, a little distance from each other, and she was careful to pick only two or three stems from each clump in order to leave the rest to reseed even though it seemed that there were so many that there could never be any danger of them disappearing from the desert. She chose the freshest and largest flowers, still marveling, although her own eyes told her that it was so, that such beauty could blossom in this arid land.

Watching her, slumped in his saddle with one leg drawn up over the saddle horn, his hat pushed back on his forehead, Quinn thought that Moria picking the lupine was the most beautiful picture he'd ever seen. He fixed the grace of her movements, the shining concentration of her face, in his memory so that he would never forget it. A glance at the sky told him that they had plenty of time. The weather was perfect, there was plenty of daylight left.

Moria was moving farther away from him. It seemed as though

every time she came to a perfect clump, the one just beyond was prettier. She reached out, her bare fingers closing around a stem of one of the most perfect blooms yet, and then she froze as she heard a sound that she had never heard before. It was like the sound of dry beans or pebbles rattling in a gourd.

"Moria, freeze! Don't move a muscle, for God's sake, don't move!"

Moria froze. And then she saw it. The snake was coiled, its tail with a long double row of rattles vibrating violently, its wicked tongue darting in and out, its beady eyes fixed on her. Her face blanched, her mouth went dry, and she couldn't have moved, she couldn't have screamed, even if Quinn's warning shout hadn't told her not to.

Quinn was on his feet, his gun was in his hand. God Almighty, the rattler was only inches from Moria's outstretched hand! His own face white, beads of perspiration gathering on his forehead, Quinn knew that he had to make the first shot count, that he didn't dare miss. He didn't dare wait, either. If his hand wasn't steady, if his eyes betrayed him, he might hit Moria instead of the rattler. And even if he missed her, if he missed the rattler as well, it would strike. A diamondback, a big one, why hadn't he been more careful, why hadn't he warned her to keep a sharp eye out, why hadn't he stamped around before she'd started to pick the lupine, and made sure it was safe? He'd let his senses betray him into being careless, just because he'd been savoring every moment of being alone with Moria.

He fired. Moria screamed. She held her hand in front of her face, staring with disbelief at the long welt that creased the side of it, a welt already filling with blood. The face she raised to look at Quinn was as white as paper, her eyes almost black with shock and terror. But the rattler was writhing, dying, Quinn hadn't missed, even if it had been so close that he'd grazed her hand.

"Back off! Get out of its range, it's still dangerous!" Quinn barked at her. And then he fired again, and this time the flat, vicious head was shattered. Moria felt her knees go out from under her. The lupine was scattered at her feet, trampled as Quinn whirled to grasp her hand to calculate the damage.

The gouge wasn't deep. It would heal, and with luck it wouldn't leave much of a scar.

"You aren't going to faint, are you? Here, I'll carry you."

"I'm not going to faint. I'm all right."

"We've got to fix that up." His arm around her, Quinn supported her, her legs trembling so that they could hardly hold her up, back to the horses. They'd shied and pranced a few yards at the sound of the shots, but they hadn't run off, and Quinn blessed every hour he'd spent training them, blessed every bullet he'd wasted firing over their heads from the saddle to get them used to it.

Now he soaked his bandanna with water from his canteen and washed the long, narrow gouge on Moria's hand. She winced, her eyes wide, but she didn't whimper. He wrapped the bandanna around her hand in a crude bandage. "We'll have one of the doctors take a look at it as soon as we get back to town. At least he'll make a prettier bandage, so Reba won't go into a fit when she sees you."

Moria tried to smile, and something inside of him snapped. She was in his arms, he was holding her close, oh, God, oh, God, he might have lost her, she might have been struck by the rattler and died, she was so delicate, even lancing the punctures and sucking the poison out might not have saved her. And even if it had, Quinn had seen the results of rattlesnake bites, the blackened, rotting flesh, the weeks and months it took them to heal, the agony, the disfigurement. And if he'd missed the rattler and hit her, she might have been lying dead in his arms at this very moment, instead of looking at him with those huge, shock-darkened eyes.

His mouth came down over hers, he held her closer, until it seemed as if he were crushing her bones, as if he had to take her inside his own body to protect her, to hold her forever, never to lose her, not ever.

"Quinn, you're crying!" Moria looked at the tears on his face, her own eyes filled with wonder.

"You're damned right I'm crying! Hush up, don't talk." He kissed her again, and his body took fire and it spread to hers, consuming her, consuming him. This might be the only moment in all eternity that they'd be together, that they'd have each other, what had just happened had brought it home to both of them that any quirk of fate might separate them forever. "You belong to me, you're mine!"

As though she were in a dream, Moria thought, I never thought it would happen like this. In the middle of the desert, with clumps of wilting lupine for our bed, we're crushing them. Overhead, the sun was traveling toward the west, the shadows were lengthening, blue and lavender and purple, their beauty of color bewitching, carrying her away with the witchery.

And then she forgot the sky, the colors, the lupine, and there was only Quinn, and she gave herself to him with a cry of joy that was torn from her throat, wildly triumphant. And she learned what it was to love a man and be loved by him, she learned that what she'd known with Tony had been a sham, crumbs from the feast it should have been, because there had never been anything like this, she had never imagined anything like this, and she wept for all that might have been, that could have been, even as she embraced all that there was now, enough and more than enough to make up for all of it.

Later, much later, Quinn still held her close. "I never thought I'd see the day when I'd bless a snake. But we've got to go, Moria. Speaking of snakes, they come out at sunset. Can you ride, or shall I hold you in front of me on my saddle and lead Caballero?"

"I can ride. I could ride right up through that sunset, straight into heaven. I know the way now," Moria said.

Tomorrow, she might be sorry. Tomorrow, she might remember that she was still married to Tony, that she had no right to this love, to this joy. But it was still today, and Quinn, looking at her face, thought that if any angel were half as beautiful as this woman he loved, then any man would be a fool not to believe in God.

He kissed her once more, long and desperately, the sweetest kiss of all, and then he lifted her into Caballero's saddle and mounted himself, and they set their horses into a lope, and Moria scarcely felt the throbbing of her wounded hand.

26

If this were sin, then it wasn't any wonder that there were so many sinners. It would have seemed impossible to Moria, only weeks ago, that in a town the size of Phoenix, and living with Reba and Abraham, she and Quinn could find one opportunity after another to be together, to consummate their love again and again. Moria laughed, a small, silvery laugh. Wasn't there an old saying that love would find a way?

An abandoned Mexican adobe house a short way from town. A line shack on the open range. Or under the open sky, in the nearby low mountains, safe from prying eyes. It made no difference, as long as they were together. And if she was living in a false paradise, it didn't matter, because nothing mattered except Quinn. She belonged to him, she was his. There was only one thing she wouldn't do for him, and that was go through a false marriage ceremony with him, become a bigamist.

"Who would know?" Quinn raged. It was an old argument, they'd had it over and over again. "Who would it hurt? This skulking around is killing me, I want you with me all the time, I

449

want you for my wife. Your marriage was over years ago, a few words on a piece of paper wouldn't make ours any more legal in the eyes of God.''

"I'd know, and you'd know," Moria told him. "No more lies, Quinn, no more deceptions. I lived a good share of my life as a lie, and I can't do it again. There are still my children, and you can be sure that Jacob Vancouver would find out, and that he'd tell them. It would kill Reid." She didn't mention Gayle. Thinking that Gayle couldn't think any more badly of her than she already did was an ache that never left her.

Quinn argued, Quinn raged, and Quinn came back. If this was all they could have, so be it. This damned, stubborn, maddening woman had him in thrall. But he didn't have to like it. If Moria wouldn't see sense this time, then he'd keep after her until she did. Arizona, the West, was a place to start over, to leave the old behind. And God knew that Moria had more reason than most. But still she held out against him. She loved him, she'd go on giving herself to him but she wouldn't become a bigamist.

Reba and Abraham knew. Moria hadn't told them, they simply knew. They never mentioned it, they treated Moria as they had always treated her, with love and kindness. But their eyes held a new sorrow, grief for her because of the impossible trap she was caught in, so that she could never have the complete happiness that they would have given the last drop of their blood to buy for her.

As for the others, the single men who had beaten a path to their door, one by one they stopped coming as it got through to them that if Moria ever chose anyone, it would be Quinn. Only Lieutenant Daniel Haverly refused to give up. White-lipped, his body stiff, he also raged at Moria.

"If you love Quinn, why don't you marry him? There's something you're not telling me. I don't know what it is and I don't care. But if it's something from your past, if you'd trust me enough to tell me, I'd find a way to do something about it. I'd kill to help you, if necessary."

"Daniel, stop it! I think it would be better if you didn't come here any more. I know it would be better, because I can't give you even a drop of hope. I'll never marry, and I can't tell you why. Don't ruin your life over me, there are dozens of girls who would be proud to marry you, who'd give you the happiness that I could never give you. I don't want to see you again."

His face white, Daniel turned away. And Phoenix looked on and speculated. It wasn't natural for a woman as beautiful as Moria Donovan to hold out against both Lieutenant Haverly and Quinn Bradmore. The mystery deepened, with no more answers than there had been when Moria and the Greenbaums had first come to Arizona.

Wherever women met, Moria's name was mentioned, and not knowing the truth they invented every possible story to explain the phenomenon of a woman as beautiful as Moria who chose to live in the single state. She had some dreadful, incurable disease, or there was a scandal in her past. She was an unmarried mother, she was illegitimate, there was black blood in her veins, or Chinese, and she didn't dare marry for fear that her children would be throwbacks. No story was too wild to be examined and speculated about.

And if the women's tongues carried them away because of their very nature, a few of the men were nearly as bad. Ordinarily close-mouthed, drink had a way of loosening their tongues, especially the ones who had never had any chance at all of being in the running.

It was only a twist of fate that Daniel happened to be in the Last Oasis on the night Jesse Pickerel came down from the Tip Top mine to blow his wages on whiskey and women, only to find that his favorite saloon woman, Betty Christy, had already chosen another partner for the evening.

"Rough luck, Jesse! But there couldn't nobody blame Betty, you ain't got enough money in your pocket to make up for that ugly mug of yours, to say nothin' of the way you smell!"

"I smell good enough for Betty, damn you!" Jesse snarled. "She

451

ain't so particular. She ain't no spring chicken no more, she has to settle for what she can get!''

There was more than a little truth in that. Betty Christy was old for her profession, and she'd put on weight and her hips were so big that men joked about her when she walked away from them. She was avaricious, too, and she had a liking for married men because she wasn't above extracting a little extra from them to ensure that word of their activities wouldn't reach their wives. Her face was plump and pleasant under hair that had gone more white than brown, and she was sly enough to capitalize on her motherly appearance, offering sympathy to men who ought to be old enough to know better who thought that their wives didn't understand them. She persuaded them to confide in her, and more than one man had lived to regret it.

But Jesse, although he wasn't married and wasn't old enough to be a complete fool, was generous with his money when he was drunk, and gullible enough to believe Betty when she told him that he was virile and attractive and that every woman who had ever turned him down was a fool, so Jesse preferred her to the other, younger women who were by and large more honest. On this evening at the Last Oasis he was thoroughly furious because Betty had found another man before he'd arrived.

"It's pretty damned rough when even Betty Christy turns you down!" Jesse's tormentor mocked him. "Whyn't you go call on Miss Moria Donovan, maybe so she'd be more to your liking!"

Jesse drained his shot of cheap whiskey and hunched his thick shoulders, a scowl on his stubble-covered face. "Stow it! That Donovan woman, who'd want her? Stuck-up bitch, thinks she's better'n anybody else just because she's pretty and got money! Why, I heared stories about her—''

Daniel's chair crashed over as Jesse's voice carried to the table where he had been sitting alone in such a black mood, after Moria had asked him not to visit her any more, that the other men in the saloon had avoided him.

"Step outside," he told Jesse. "Now!"

452

"Lookie here, toy soldier, you'd better git on back to Fort McDowell and let yer captain tuck you in bed! Everybody here knows there's somethin' damned funny about that woman..."

White-lipped, his face gone deathly pale under his sun-browned skin, two white lines etched from his nostrils to the corners of his mouth, Daniel commanded, "Draw!"

Stunned, Jesse fumbled for his gun, his drink-fuddled brain telling him that it was kill or be killed. Men dived for cover, the proprietor yelped, "Not in here, dammit!" but his voice was drowned by the sound of two shots, and then a third. Jesse lay sprawled in front of the bar, blood spreading in a widening circle on the front of his checkered shirt. And Daniel slumped, one arm hanging useless as his shoulder was shattered by a shot in the back, fired by another man from the Tip Top mine, who had no special liking for Jesse but whose alcohol-fumed mind told him that one miner should defend another as a matter of honor.

Her face drained of emotion, only her eyes showing her torture, Moria told Reba and Abraham what she was going to do.

"Don't try to talk me out of it, because it won't do any good. Can't you see that I can't stay here? One man is dead, and Daniel's life is ruined. The cavalry meant everything to him, and now he's out of it, his right arm will never be any use to him again even if he wouldn't have been court-martialed and drummed out of the service for shooting a civilian in a barroom brawl! Reba, Abraham, it might have been Quinn! If it had been Quinn at the Last Oasis that night, instead of Daniel, do you think it would have been any different? If I stay here, it's going to happen again, sooner or later Quinn will feel forced to defend my honor just as Daniel did! And I can't let that happen."

"Then we'll go with you," Reba said. Her voice was calm, but her eyes, like Moria's, were filled with tragedy. She loved Quinn like a son, just as she loved Moria like a daughter. She'd grown to love this hot, dusty, alien Phoenix, she'd have to leave her kitchen, how many times would she have to leave her kitchen? But nothing mattered but Moria. She couldn't go away alone, not a young woman, a beautiful young woman, without the protection of a family.

"A store I can start some other place," Abraham said. "Where are we going, Moria?"

"You're not going. I won't let you. This is my problem, I'm ruining your lives as well as Quinn's, just as surely as I ruined Daniel's."

"Santa Fe would be nice. It's hot and dry there too, it'll be as good for Abe's health as Phoenix," Reba said. "Abe, I'll go with Moria and we'll find a place, and you can come when you've sold this house."

"Didn't you hear a word I said?" Moria had come to the end of her strength. "You aren't coming with me! I mean that, I'm going alone. I'll write to you, I'll always let you know that I'm all right, but I'm going alone."

"Papa, talk to her!" Reba begged.

"So I've talked. What can I do? She'll change her mind in a little while, when she's had time to get over her shock, and then we'll go where she is." Abraham struggled to keep his voice steady, but it shook anyway.

Moria stood up. She couldn't stand any more of this. Reba's face was killing her, Abraham's face was killing her. What would she do without them, how could she survive without their love and their unfaltering support? Wasn't it bad enough that she'd never see Quinn again, that he must never know where she was, never be able to find her?

The news of the gunfight at the Last Oasis had paralyzed her. A man was dead because of her, Daniel wounded, crippled, his life, his career, in shambles, shattered just as his shoulder was shattered. And always, the same question was in her mind, tormenting her, torturing her. What if it had been Quinn?

She grieved for Daniel. She would have given ten years of her life, more, if she could have prevented it from happening. And coming as it had, barely two weeks after another worry had descended on her with a precognition of doom, it had devastated her.

She was nearly a month overdue. She'd never kept particular track of her monthly periods. There had never been any need of it. But ever since she and Quinn had become lovers early in the spring it had always been in the back of her mind, and every month when her cramps had started she'd felt a prayerful, heartfelt relief. It was the irony of fate that the thing that would have made her happier than anything else in the world if circumstances had been different— giving Quinn the son he deserved, a son to walk in his own footsteps—should be a disaster instead of a blessing.

It might not be true. It was August now, and the hottest weather of the year had settled over Phoenix, relentless, unending. The temperature wasn't as high as it had been in July, but it was more oppressive, the humidity was higher from the storm clouds and the thunderstorms that moved in at this time of the year. Several times a week, nearly always right around sunset, the sky would turn black and a wind would come up, and the blackness was from massive areas of blowing dust, the dust storms that were so dangerous if you were caught outside in the open country and that even in town crept through every crevasse of the house and covered every surface with fine grit. Tempers were on edge, it was possible that the weather itself had been a factor in the gunfight that had brought her life tumbling down around her head.

But no matter what had caused the fight, Moria knew that it could happen again. She had to leave Phoenix and never come back. She'd manage to survive. She had money, several thousand dollars, because Abraham had insisted on giving her a share of the profits from the sale of his Chicago store.

"You'll have it all when Reba and I are gone, but I want you should have part of it now. It's yours, who's the head of this family that you should argue with me?" Abraham had demanded when Moria had tried to refuse the gift.

So she'd be able to live until the baby was born, if there were to be a baby. And after that, she'd find work. Miss Moria Donovan of

Greenbaum's Department Store of Chicago would be able to find work in any large city. It wasn't going to be in New Mexico because that was too close to Arizona, too near Quinn. And too near Abraham and Reba, as far as that went. How could she saddle them with an additional disgrace, with an illegitimate child?

My child! she thought, and her chin went up and a light of determination came into her eyes. Quinn's child and mine, and no child in the world will be better cared for, will have more love. She'd pass herself off as a widow. Her vow never to live a lie again would have to be sacrificed. Like a chameleon, she'd have to take on the coloration that would enable her and her child to survive. No one would know where she was or who she was except Reba and Abraham, and she'd swear them to secrecy before she left, and Rose O'Riley. Even Reid must never know, especially not Reid, unless Jacob traced her and made sure that he knew. If that happened, could he forgive her even this, or would she lose him as she'd lost Gayle, as she'd lost Quinn?

The last thing she packed was the pencil drawing of Liam that Reid had sent her. If her baby was a boy, she'd name him Liam.

She never knew how she got through that last evening with Quinn. They didn't go anywhere, there was no opportunity for them even to go into each other's arms. In the oppressive heat, she and Quinn and Reba and Abraham sat on the front porch to take advantage of any breeze there was, drinking iced lemonade.

"They aren't going to send Martin Fenway to jail," Quinn told them. Fenway was the man who had shot Daniel. "Daniel started the fight, even if it was a fair fight according to our customs out here, and Fenway was only trying to defend his friend."

"Thank God for that," Moria said, her throat tight. She couldn't forgive the man for shooting Daniel in the back, but for any man to hang or spend the rest of his life in prison would have been an additional burden of guilt on her shoulders.

"And Daniel's coming along. The company surgeon is sure that danger of infection is over, he's beginning to heal even if he has a long road ahead of him. He'll be going back to his family in

Georgia. Moria, will you, for the love of heaven, stop blaming yourself? It's time to put it behind you and forget it.''

"I expect you're right, Quinn. I'll try," Moria said. Did her voice sound all right, were her hands trembling? The lemonade was too sweet, Abraham had put more sugar in it after Reba had made it, while she wasn't looking. It choked her, she could hardly swallow it, but that was because of the hurting, aching lump in her throat. I'll never see him again, she thought. I'll never hear his voice again. I can't even say good-bye to him.

He left shortly before ten o'clock. It was a long ride back to the ranch. He only touched her hand before he swung into his saddle. "I'll see you in about a week," he told her. "Get some sleep, darling. It's over."

She watched him ride away. Reba came to put her arm around her, but this time again she knew better than to tell Moria to cry. She didn't say anything at all.

Reba had had every intention of keeping her promise and not telling Quinn anything at all except that Moria had decided to leave and that she and Abraham hadn't been able to talk her into staying. All of Quinn's shouting, all of his raging, left her shaken but stubborn. And Abraham was as bad. He spread his hands, his eyes inscrutable.

"So she's a woman, she does what she wants. I should argue with a woman? We couldn't stop her, shouting isn't going to change it."

Frustrated, angrier than he'd ever been in his life, Quinn rode to the Crazy C Bar M to vent his frustration on Mattie, the one he'd always turned to when he came up against an immovable obstacle.

"Dammit, Mattie, maybe you can get something out of them! You're a woman, you ought to know how to get Reba to talk! I'm going to find Moria if it takes me the rest of the year, but if I had some inkling of where she was headed it would be easier. She's had a week's start on me, she could be heading in any direction by now! Go to town and make Reba tell you where to start looking, so I won't be running around in circles!"

Mattie looked at this brother of hers and her heart twisted. There was something she suspected, although Moria had given her no hint of it when she'd seen her only last week when she'd ridden in to Phoenix, starting well before dawn to escape the worst of the heat, to add her common sense to Quinn's in telling Moria that what had happened at the Last Oasis hadn't been her fault. It looked like there was no end to trouble. Their father had become even more antagonistic toward Moria since the shooting, and he'd turned against Mattie as well for defending her friend. And as always, Willa Bradmore was caught in the middle. Women, Mattie thought wryly, had a way of always getting the worst of it!

Should she tell Quinn what she suspected? Or should her loyalty be to Moria, another woman? It wasn't her secret to tell, and she felt like a rat, but on the other hand Quinn had a right to know, if what she suspected was true.

"Quinn, when I saw Moria last week, there was something about her . . ."

"What the devil are you talking about? What was there about her?"

"I can't be sure, but I've had four children and I've seen plenty of other women who've had children, and there's a look about them, something no man could put his finger on but it's there. Quinn, I think she's pregnant."

For a long moment, like an eternity, Quinn only stared at her. And then his face went so white that Mattie could have bitten her tongue off.

"I told you I'm not sure! But maybe you'd better find her. Saddle my horse while I get into my riding clothes. If Reba and Abraham know anything at all I'll get it out of them."

They didn't know where Moria had gone, Mattie was convinced of that before she'd talked to them for five minutes. Reba, as innocent and unworldly as any woman who'd been married more than thirty years could be, didn't even suspect what Mattie suspected. And Mattie didn't tell her, because Reba had enough to bear without that.

458

"All right, then. I'll start looking," Quinn said. His face was grim. "And I'll find her. It'll just take a little longer."

It didn't take as long as he'd been afraid it might. No woman who looked like Moria could pass unnoticed. Ticket agents remembered her, and what tickets she'd bought. Any determined man could have found her, he didn't need to be a Pinkerton detective.

It was a little harder when Quinn got to Philadelphia. Of all places, he thought, why Philadelphia? But determined, relentless questioning of cab drivers—it seemed as if he talked to every driver who met incoming trains—traced her to a small but respectable hotel. She wasn't there, she'd checked out three days ago, but a cab had taken her to a modest rented flat. "Black hair? Real beautiful? Youngish, not a girl but really beautiful?"

It couldn't be anyone else, and it wasn't. Moria answered the door, and her eyes went wide, and she whispered, "Oh, Quinn! Why did you have to find me, why won't you give up?"

"I ought to shake your teeth out. I ought to beat you within an inch of your life. Damn it, Moria, what are you trying to do? Tell me the truth, and tell me now, are you pregnant?"

She didn't have to answer him. It was there in her face.

Quinn's rage didn't abate with the knowledge. "So you were going to keep it from me! You were going to cheat me of my child, my son! And cheat him of his father! Start packing. We're going home."

"Quinn, you're crazy! You're insane! How can I? Everyone will know . . ."

"Then let them know! But they won't know a damned thing. We'll tell them we're married. If they suspect, you can be sure they'll never let a hint of it drop! One way or the other, you're coming back with me. And if I have to tie you up to get you there, I'll do it, and don't get the mistaken notion that I won't!"

More lies, more deceptions. But Moria was beyond fighting now. Seeing Quinn, having him find her, facing his rage, rage that he had every right to feel, took the last of her determination to get out of his life out of her. She loved him, she needed him, their unborn child needed him. She'd cheated him all these years, she couldn't cheat him of this, and now that he was here she wondered how she had ever thought that she could.

And then she was in his arms, and he wasn't shaking her or beating her, and she knew that nothing would ever be able to take her out of his arms again. If this was the way it had to be, it was something that she had to face, and make the most and the best that could be made of it.

Willa Bradmore was wonderful. The thin, weather-beaten woman, her eyes surrounded with a network of sun- and wind-caused lines, welcomed her new daughter-in-law without reservation. Mattie was ecstatic, Reba and Abraham accepted the fact that the deception was something that couldn't be helped. They were only human beings, not God, it wasn't for them to judge, only to love. And in spite of Moria's qualms, Phoenix itself accepted them at face value.

Any whispering, any speculation, that might have been done was done behind closed doors. The Bradmores were important people, well liked, highly respected. And even in a town as small as Phoenix, other scandals came along, there were other things to talk and think about. Now that Moria was married, now that the single men had to give up hoping and the single girls no longer had to compete with her, she lost a good deal of her news value.

Quentin Bradmore kept his own counsel. He coped with Moria by ignoring her. What was done was done. At least Quinn stayed at home now, he wasn't forever off chasing after her, and a grandchild was a grandchild, illegitimate or not. He might have refused to allow Moria and Quinn to live at the ranch, the Bradmores could well afford to build a separate house for them, but that would have caused more talk, raised more speculation.

But he didn't like Moria, and he made no pretense of liking her. He never spoke to her. On the other hand, he didn't go out of his way to make her life miserable. She was there, like drought and hoof-and-mouth disease, like dust storms and flooding rains and heat, just one more thing that must be lived with because nothing could be done about it.

For her part, Moria was polite to Quentin, she stopped trying to win him over when she realized that no effort on her part would be of any avail. She had Quinn, she had Willa, she had Mattie and Mattie's brood, she had Reba and Abraham, and if she hated having to enter another life of lies and deceptions, she hid it from all of them. Her father had managed to wrest all the happiness he could from a situation worse than this, and so had Eugenia, and Moria understood now, more than ever, how much their love for each other had meant to them and how it had made everything else worthwhile.

It was in November, a beautiful, clear day, the sky so blue that it hurt to look at it, that Quentin spoke to her for the first time.

Moria was restless. She was used to being active, and her thickening waistline was an annoyance. She'd been riding every day, never giving it a thought. She'd ridden all her life, Caballero was surefooted and his gait was easy, as smooth as a rocking chair. She'd ride over to see Mattie. Quinn was out on the range, Willa was making baby clothes. Good grief, Moria thought, no one baby could ever wear all the baby clothes that this one was going to have, Willa hadn't stopped sewing since she and Quinn had arrived at the ranch after Quinn had tracked her down and made her come back with him. Willa made the little dresses and jackets and petticoats, and Reba took them home and embroidered them, ignoring the fact that all that embroidery might not be suitable for a boy if the baby didn't turn out to be the girl that Reba hoped for. But Mattie, thank goodness, didn't sew. And it was a perfect day for a ride.

She'd only gone for two miles when she heard a horse overtaking her, running all out. She pulled Caballero up, startled, her heart doing a flip-flop. Had something happened, had there been an accident? Quinn! Maybe he'd been hurt!

Quentin Bradmore pulled up beside her. His heavy, square face was set, his eyes were cold. "Get back to the house," he said. "Then get off that horse. You can ride again after the youngun's born."

That was all. He reined around and rode away from her without bothering to look to see if she was obeying him. Moria was torn between fury at being treated like a child, and going on to Mattie's, and even greater fury that this command was the first word that her father-in-law had ever deemed fit to say to her.

And then she laughed, that silvery laugh that was a legacy from her childhood. The man was human after all. He might dislike her, he might wish that she'd never been born, but he didn't want anything to happen to his grandchild. And she took heart at the thought that when her child was born, Quentin wouldn't let his dislike of her reflect on his treatment of her child.

Quentin was right. She could ride again after the baby was born. In the meantime, it was her job, her only job, to make sure that it was born safely. If she were to cheat Quinn of his son or his daughter, simply because she wanted to go riding, she'd never be able to forgive herself. Accidents could happen. She shuddered, remembering the rattlesnake that had indirectly been the cause of the child she was carrying right now.

At supper that night, Quentin ignored her as he always did. Moria had an impulse to stick her tongue out at him. Would he ignore that, too? But she quelled the impulse, along with the impulse to giggle because of her childish thought. As long as Quentin was going to accept her child, she could put up with him no matter how uncomfortable it was.

Her hand reached out under the table and sought Quinn's, and his returning pressure sent a flood of warmth through her. Oh, Quinn, will you ever know how much I love you? Will you ever know how my heart is breaking because things can't be perfect for us?

But he already knew. If he didn't, she wouldn't be here, she would still be in Philadelphia, awaiting the birth of their child alone.

She wrote to Rose the next day.

Pray for me, Rose. Because I can't help wishing, no matter how wrong and wicked it is, that that old man would die, that Anthony would get the money he wants so badly so that they'd let me have my freedom at last.

How can you bear it, how do you bear it, living in that house, taking care of that man, after what he did to Eugenia, what he did to Liam? You deserve your own freedom, you've earned it a hundred times over, you could still have years of happiness with Michael McCarthy if it wasn't for me, for wanting to protect me. I wonder if my father ever would have entered the deception if he'd known how things would turn out, that it would go on and on without end, that there'd be no way out?

Write to me. Tell me about Gayle. Reid still writes to me occasionally, from his school in England, although I know that it would do me no good to attempt to write to him. My letters would be confiscated before they got to him. In a way I'm almost glad because, like a coward, I can't bear to tell him the truth about Quinn and me. Maybe when the baby comes, I'll find a measure of peace in my love for it. But the waiting seems so long!

And the waiting was long, but on a February day Liam Quinton Bradmore came bawling into the world, and as Quinn held his lusty, red-faced son in his arms for the first time, his face was so awestruck that Moria had to laugh even through the exhaustion that was drawing her down into sleep. No matter what happened in the future, she had this now, she had Quinn and this beautiful new son, and nothing could take away this moment.

27

"Ma, somebody's comin'!"

Moria looked up from the mending she was doing, a three-cornered tear in the knee of a pair of Liam's denim trousers, which had to be patched. She'd always liked to sew, but that sewing had been on dresses, on beautiful creations that she herself had designed. Now, it seemed that all the sewing she did was to mend Liam's clothes, and there were always clothes of his that needed mending.

She wouldn't let Willa do it, her mother-in-law had other things to do and her eyes weren't as good as Moria's. Willa was nearing seventy, seemingly immortal in her energy and her ability to run her house as she had always done, but all the same Moria was gradually taking over, so gradually that Willa didn't seem to notice.

"Don't call me Ma," she said. "How many times do I have to tell you to call me Mother?"

"Aw, that's highfalutin!" At five, Liam was every bit of the imp that Moria had known he would be before he'd been six months old. "And somebody is comin! I don't know him, I think."

This in itself was enough to make Moria lay down the despised mending and go to the kitchen door with him, to shade her eyes from the sun and try to make out who the rider might be. Liam knew almost everybody in Phoenix, almost everybody in Maricopa County, at least everybody who was likely to come to the ranch. He had a lively interest in people and he liked them almost without exception.

She couldn't make out who the oncoming rider was, either. Who in the world would be coming to the ranch in the middle of the afternoon heat on this phenomenally hot day for early June? Whoever it was, he'd need a cold drink, and his horse would need attention as well. He was probably some drifting cowhand in search of work, although any Arizona wrangler should have known better than to be riding in the heat of the day unless it was vitally necessary.

"Who is it, Ma?"

"I don't know. He'll be here in a minute, and then we'll see." She waited, Liam beside her, still shaking her eyes as the rider drew closer. And then, when he was still fifty yards away, her heart seemed to stand still and her breath caught in her throat. There was something about him, something familiar, there was a look about him that, for no reason at all, no sane or sensible reason in the world, reminded her a little of Liam. His eyes were shaded by the broad-brimmed hat he was wearing, but there was a set to his shoulders, and the way he sat his horse, that plunged her back into the past with such force that for a moment she felt disoriented, as though she had been thrust into a rift in time.

The rider traversed the rest of the short distance and sat there, tall in the saddle, his hat pushed back now. A smile started at the corners of his mouth and spread to his eyes.

"I don't have to ask if I'm at the right place. Hello, Mother."

"Reid!"

The word was torn from her throat. She said it again, choking, she was screaming, she couldn't help it.

Tears streamed down her face in floods, and she couldn't help that, either. And Reid had dismounted between one of her screams of "Reid!" and she was in his arms, she was sobbing against his

466

shoulder, she was getting his shirt all wet and he was hot and tired and dusty and this was no way to act and Liam was looking at her as if she were crazy and she went right on crying, and laughing, and then crying again.

"I don't know you," Liam said.

"I know you. You're Liam. Mother, does he know about me?"

"Yes." That was one thing she'd done right. She'd insisted that Liam must know about his older brother, his older sister. Maybe he was too young to understand, but she couldn't have him finding out years from now, and having it be a complete shock to him. He'd been told that she'd had to go away from her former home and family, and that it was something that concerned only the immediate family and that wasn't talked about to others.

Liam had accepted it as children accept things, he hadn't even been much interested when he'd understood how much older Reid and Gayle were. A grown-up brother and sister he'd never seen weren't anywhere near as interesting as people he knew and saw all the time.

"You're my brother. Your name is Reid."

"That's right." Reid put Moria from him gently, only kissing her again and brushing at her tear-flooded cheeks before he swooped Liam up into his arms and lifted him so that their faces were level with each other's.

"You don't look like me," Liam said. And added, honestly, "But that's all right. I'm pretty homely, anyhow. Dan and Sam and Scott and Gloria say so, but they like me anyway, they're only funnin'."

"I never saw an uglier boy in my life," Reid said solemnly. "Maybe I'd better get right back on my horse and ride back to town."

"You can't. Your horse is too tired. It doesn't look like much of a horse, anyway." Liam was not the least perturbed by Reid's joke. He was used to that from his cousins, who'd rather tease than eat, but horses were a serious matter. "We better take care of him, 'fore he falls down. What kind of a gol-danged fool are you, anyway, ridin' in the middle of the day 'stead of early in the mornin' or after dark? Maybe Grandpop would lend you a horse but I'm gonna ask him not to because I want you to stay a spell.''

"Mother, will you please stop crying? And Liam's right, we have to look after this sorry nag I rented from the livery stable. I knew it was hot out here, but as Liam just said, I was a 'gol-danged fool.' Once I was this close I had to come the rest of the way. Liam, do you think the horse is in really bad shape?''

"Nope. He's in worser shape than one of ours would be 'cause he's old and not tough like ours, but I reckon he'll be all right.'' Liam spoke with all the seriousness of a grown man. "You talk funny. I never heard anybody talk like you.''

"That's because I've lived in England for a long time, and the way they talk rubbed off on me. Everybody over there talks funny. They'd think that you talk funny.''

"But, Reid, you haven't told me anything! How, why . . .''

"I had it out with Jacob.'' Reid's face, streaked with runnels of sweat through the dust, went hard. "I'm twenty-one now and they couldn't stop me from coming. Not that Father cared one way or the other, it was Jacob who raised the roof.''

Moria was well aware that Reid was twenty-one. She'd thought of him all day on his birthday, last month, and she'd had a hard time not letting her depression show through to the rest of the family. Reid's twenty-first birthday, and she couldn't share it with him! It was 1891, she was getting to be middle-aged, and her son was twenty-one!

Reid looked at Liam. "Will you show me where to take my horse? I'm going to stay a spell. It's time we got to know each other.''

It was Reid. It was really Reid. Her loyal Reid, who'd been proud when he'd learned that Liam, the Irish horse trainer, was his grandfather, who'd been proud to be Liam's grandson and her son, who'd never wavered in his loyalty to her over all these years, not even when he'd been told about Quinn and Liam. He'd written to her, from England, and said that he was glad that she was making a new life for herself and that he hoped that she'd be happy enough to make up for everything else that had happened to her!

"Of course you're going to stay. Quinn will welcome you, and he'll be glad."

"And Quentin?" Reid's look was wry. "I understand from your letters to Rose that Willa will be all right, but how about Quentin? And all the others, your friends, your neighbors?"

"It will be all right. When we decided that Liam had to be told about you, we let it be known that the reason I hadn't married Quinn a long time before I did was that I was a divorced woman and I thought that I shouldn't marry again." More lies, more deceit, but they had thought it was necessary, in order to avoid still more deceit to Liam by not letting him know that he had a half-brother and half-sister. Willa had been in favor of it, and even Quentin had nodded after a family conference had decided it. Moria's father-in-law still tolerated her only because it had to be done, but he loved Liam and he'd go along with anything that was for Liam's good.

The horse taken care of under Liam's watchful eye, the two of them went back to the house and entered the kitchen, where Moria and Willa, Willa's face shining with welcome, were making both hot coffee and cold lemonade and setting an apricot pie on the table. Reid would be thirsty and hungry, in that order, and he couldn't wait until supper.

Willa held out her hand, and her grip was firm. "I'm glad you're here, Reid. I'm mighty proud that you've come. Just sit down and dig in."

Reid looked into her eyes and felt warmth envelop him. Impulsively, he bent and kissed her cheek. Willa's eyes took on an added glow. "Eat," she ordered. "And don't be afraid to take seconds. There's plenty more where that came from."

The apricot pie was delicious. Reid grinned at his mother.

"Did you make this, or hasn't Willa been able to teach you how to cook? Liam's a nice lad. I'm glad you named him after our grandfather. He would have liked that, he would have been proud."

"He has my father's name, but he looks like his other grandfather,'' Moria said, half laughing, her throat still working although she had managed to stop crying. "That square face, and he's going to have the same build, heavier than Quinn, more powerful shoulders.'' And although she would have been almost too happy to bear it if Liam had looked like the older Liam, in a way it was a good thing that he took after Quentin, because Quentin had given his heart to him the first time he'd laid eyes on him, a husky mite of humanity with his own stubborn face.

Great heavens, she must look a mess! She scrubbed at her cheeks and eyes with the backs of her hands, brushed her hair away from her forehead because the high pompadour she wore these days, the height of fashion, had started to straggle from her impatient hands while she'd been struggling with the tear in Liam's pants.

"What must you think of me! I'm surprised that you even recognized me! Reid, I'm almost forty! It must have been a shock.''

Even as she spoke, she was studying Reid's face. She could see a little of Tony in him, but his hair was darker, although his eyes were the same brown with those long lashes that had driven women wild. But his mouth was Liam's, and the line of the jaw, and the expression.

"You haven't changed that much. You're still beautiful. I never forgot how beautiful you were, how much I loved you and how proud I was that you were my mother. Estelle sent me a picture of you shortly before she died so suddenly. She managed to send it to Rose through Jacob's messenger, without Jacob knowing, to be sent on to me.''

"I remember. Rose wrote me about it. Dear Estelle! If Jacob had found out, it would have gone hard with her.'' She brushed at her eyes again because they'd begun to sting with the memory of Estelle, and then they widened. "You haven't any luggage!''

"I left it in town. There's only a valise, I traveled light. I'll retrieve it tomorrow, now that I know I'm welcome to stay.''

When Quinn and Quentin came in at suppertime, Quentin's eyes measured him, missing nothing. An easterner, the grandson of a wickedly wealthy family, a man who'd gone to school in England!

What possible use could a man like that be out here? At least he could ride. Quentin knew from Moria that Reid had been all but born in a saddle. But that was eastern riding, on one of those pancakes that easterners mistakenly called saddles. He probably even posted, like the cavalrymen, a phenomenon that sent western men into paroxysms of mirth, bobbing up and down, up, down, up, down, instead of sticking to the leather when their horses trotted. But any man, easterner or not, deserved the chance to prove himself.

Reid drained his coffee cup and nodded as Willa refilled it. He couldn't seem to get enough liquid in him, it was as if all of his body fluids had evaporated and now his tissues were soaking up water like a sponge in an effort to renew themselves. "No more cake, thank you. I'm about to burst."

Quentin wiped his mouth. "Care to ride out with us in the mornin'?"

"There's nothing I'd like better."

"Daybreak," Quentin said, the word short. Reid kept the smile off his face. Daybreak was no novelty to him. At his English prep school, he'd been turned out at daybreak every morning, the beds to be stripped, the mattresses hung out over the windowsills to air, before the students dressed and went down to breakfast. Anyone who had survived a strict English prep school was qualified to make a stab at western life, no matter how rigorous.

"I'll send a man in to pick up your traps, he'll lead your livery horse back," Quinn told him.

"Tell him to be sure to pick up my drawing materials. Everything's in a flat wooden case."

"You still draw, Reid?" Moria's face flushed with pleasure. "The pencil sketch of my father that you sent me is still my proudest possession. It's framed in the best frame Greenbaum's had to offer, and hanging in our bedroom right now."

"I still draw. And I've gone into oils." Reid met Quentin's eyes without wavering. He didn't add that he could do a day's work even if he was an artist. Quentin would find that out for himself.

As tired as he was, as early as he had to get up the next morning, he and Moria sat up late, over still more coffee, long after the rest of the family had gone to bed. They had ten years to catch up on, and it couldn't be done in a moment.

"I thought Jacob was going to have a stroke and end up bedridden and paralyzed like William Northrup, when I told him I was showing the Vancouvers my heels and that I wouldn't be back," Reid told his mother. "His eyes bulged out so far I was afraid they were going to pop out and leave him blind. He shouted himself hoarse. Did you ever hear a man shout in whispers? I was a disgrace to the Vancouver name, I was betraying every drop of Vancouver blood in me. If I left, he'd disinherit me, it would all go to Gayle, providing that Father leaves anything to be left to her."

"Oh, Reid! Disinherited!" Even Moria, who couldn't have cared less about the Vancouver fortune, was shaken. "You gave it all up!"

"What did I give up? A life that sickened me, values that sickened me, treachery, deceit, downright dishonesty as long as it makes a profit! Hypocrisy, false values, shallow people who care for nothing except their family trees and the money in their banks! Mother, I hated it. There's more of Liam in me than any amount of Vancouver blood and Vancouver money could combat. But there wasn't anything I could do about it until I was twenty-one. Jacob and my father had full power over me; if I'd left, run away, they'd have had me traced and brought back and they'd have made me a virtual prisoner so that I couldn't do it again. So I spent the time as well as I could, I didn't turn down the education the Vancouver money bought me. There isn't much about high finance I don't know, even if I'd gag on it if I had to make my living that way. And I tried my darnedest to talk sense into Gayle, to make her see that her kind of life isn't any life at all. That was my biggest failure."

"Gayle." The words were laced with pain. "How is she?"

"She's beautiful," Reid said. "She's so much like you at that age that anybody would think they were seeing a ghost. You might have been identical twins. She's so graceful that watching her is like watching music take on material form. The whole of the Hudson River Valley is at her feet. She's had at least two dozen proposals, but so far, not one of them has been good enough, she and Jacob have high standards.

"But right now, it looks as if Martin Schuyler is running ahead of the pack. When I left, Gayle and Jacob were toying with the idea of announcing their engagement at an October ball that would make every other affair that ever took place in the Hudson River Valley pale by comparison.

"Young Schuyler has it all: family, bloodline, fortune, and he's darned good-looking in the bargain. There's nothing we can do about Gayle, Mother. I'm sorry, but you'll just have to accept that. We can only hope that she'll be happy, or what she believes is happiness."

Her heart aching, Moria brushed impatiently at a strand of her hair that had again strayed over her forehead. "And your father?"

Reid's mouth was grim. "He's just the same. He'll never change. He didn't care when I left, he only put up a token argument. He's too basically selfish to care about anyone else, even his own children. He drinks too much, he gambles, and he philanders. Veronica Curtis is still the mistress he goes back to after every new affair palls. It's a pity that they didn't marry each other, I can't think of two people who deserve each other more, but then I wouldn't be here, or Gayle, and you probably wouldn't be with Quinn and you wouldn't have young Liam, so there's no use speculating, is there? This is the way things are. At least I'm here now, and you're going to have one heck of a time getting rid of me if I don't live up to your expectations!"

Moria crept into bed, careful not to waken Quinn, but he stirred and his arms reached out to draw her close. "He's a fine boy, Moria. Are you happy?"

Safe in his arms, weeping with happiness, Moria pressed herself against him, her heart overflowing. She wouldn't think about Gayle. There was nothing she could do about her daughter. But Reid was here, she had Reid back, and she didn't need Rose to pray for her this time because her own prayers of thanksgiving would never stop.

* * *

Reid settled to ranch life with scarcely a ripple. Quentin watched him with dawning respect, driving him hard, and the hard, whipcord-tough cowhands did the same. The cowhands were positive that he'd crack, no easterner could measure up. And he didn't know beans about ranching, that was for sure.

But he was willing to learn, and he could ride. The tough cow horses, trained to stop on a dime, trained to turn so short that any inexperienced rider would go off, some of them buckers, some of them biters and kickers, didn't faze the dude from the Hudson River Valley, the dude from fancy English schools, for a minute.

What they didn't know and what Reid didn't tell them was that he had not only ridden almost before he could walk, but he'd ridden to hounds in England, and he'd played polo, and polo ponies could stop as short, could turn as short, and were as tough as any cow pony that had ever lived.

He had to learn to rope, to throw and tie calves, to use a branding iron. He had to to learn to cut one steer out of a herd, but here again his polo training made it easy; guiding his horse with one hand and his knees was as natural to him as breathing, dodging and cutting short angles and circles something that he didn't even have to think about.

He had to learn to live with the climate, to never start out without a canteen filled with water even if he expected to be back within an hour. He wasn't very good with a sidearm, at first, but practice brought improvement and he was a dead shot with a rifle. Something else they didn't know and that he didn't tell them was that he had shot quail in Scotland.

All in all, he measured up, and earned their respect, and was accepted, even if they were baffled at the way he never set out without his sketchbook tied to his saddle, and the way he sketched them at every conceivable chore, the lines so true and lifelike that you'd expect them to look up and cuss.

Abraham and Reba took him to their hearts and Reid felt the same way about them. How could he help it, these gentle, good people who had befriended his mother, who had taken her in and given her a home and a family when she'd been alone and desperate? He felt as though he'd known them even before he'd come to Arizona, through the letters that Rose had smuggled to him from his mother. He spent hours in Reba's kitchen, never in the dining room or the parlor, always the kitchen, Reba's ultimate acceptance, and automatically moved the sugar bowl away from Abraham if Reba forgot.

In 1886, a disastrous fire had destroyed one of Phoenix's business blocks, and Abraham had built a store on one of the sites after it had been cleared, buying out the merchant who had owned it. The new Greenbaum's was a far cry from Greenbaum's Department Store in Chicago, but Moria had come in to help him stock it, her sense of what the women of Phoenix wanted as keen as it had been when she'd known what the women of Chicago had wanted. The store had turned a modest profit from the start, and it was doing better every year. Abraham had expanded it in 1888, buying up another store next to it, and now he was one of the most respected merchants in Phoenix.

Reid spent hours at the Crazy C Bar M, accepted by Mattie as her nephew, accepting her as the favorite aunt he'd never had, delighted with the young Chamberses, those brown, hard and forthright western children, an experience completely new to him. Dan was already a man at sixteen, Scott and Sam weren't far behind, and ten-year-old Gloria still ruled the roost.

It seemed as if his sketch pad was always in his hands. Portraits of Reba and Abraham now hung in Reba's parlor, done in oils. Portraits of Mattie and her brood held the place of honor in Mattie's parlor, with Chet looking as shy and friendly as if he were going to speak to you to welcome you and ask you to set a spell.

Quinn and Moria had to sit for him, and young Liam, as he put it himself, came last, riding drag and eating dust. Quentin refused to pose, but Willa was working on him, and Reid's brush had caught Willa in a portrait that was a masterpiece.

And Gayle was there, done from memory, her pride, her haughtiness, a disturbing factor underneath the beauty that sent Reid's newfound friend, Hayes Taylor, into fits. Hayes's family had a neighboring ranch, and the young man and Reid had hit it off from the moment they'd met. Every time Hayes came to the Bradmore place, he ended up in the parlor, his eyes eating up the portrait of the girl he'd give his eyeteeth to meet.

But the most treasured of them all was the portrait Reid worked up from the pencil sketch of Liam. Moria couldn't pass it without touching that beloved and well-remembered face with her fingertips, brushing it with a caress.

Reid was an artist. Mattie's friends, Abraham and Reba's friends, saw his work and some of them asked him to do portraits of their families. A neighboring rancher commissioned him to paint, of all things, his prize bull! Reid did them all, as well as landscapes so real that you could taste and smell the dust of the dust storms he portrayed, you could shade your eyes against the sun reflecting on the cardboard mountains. One of the newspaper editors commissioned him to paint a portrait of his wife, which hung in the editor's office until his wife confiscated it for her parlor.

Reid pocketed his commissions, aware that he could earn his living, and a good one, by his brush. In the meantime he had his eye on property that would soon be reached by the irrigation ditches that were spreading in an ever-widening network over the arid land. The property could be bought for next to nothing now. He admitted, ruefully, that there was a little of Jacob in him after all, that he knew a good deal when he saw it. But the resemblance ended there, because Reid wanted the property not to sell for a profit, but to put under irrigation and grow crops. Citrus, he said. Quentin looked at him as if he were insane, but at the same time he wondered if maybe the boy was right. He could spare a little cash, the land was bound to increase in value even if the citrus died. And alfalfa would always grow, given water.

Moria was happy. It was only in her dreams that she sometimes wept, as she tried to find her daughter, who was lost from her, as she searched in every nook and cranny, only to find that Gayle wasn't there. And then Quinn would wake up and draw her into his arms and soothe her until she was calm again, until the dream faded and she could sleep.

She mustn't be greedy. She had Quinn and Liam, she had Reid back, she had so much! But always, sleeping or waking, there was an underlying sadness about the daughter she'd lost and that she had no way of finding again.

In the meantime, she made the best of what she had. And she prayed. She'd started going to church again, to the Catholic church in Phoenix. Her family didn't mind, even Quentin accepted it. It brought her comfort to return to her mother's faith, even though her first confession had been so hard that she'd hardly been able to face it. She couldn't die with so many unconfessed sins on her soul.

But her happiness, her contentment, were things that she couldn't accept as being sins, even though she was still living a lie. Like Rose O'Riley, she was convinced that Mary, being a woman, would understand.

28

Anthony Vancouver was drunk. He was often the worse for drink, his drinking had increased throughout the years until his capacity was phenomenal, but even he could miscalculate if the mood were right, and tonight the mood had been right.

It was his father, of course. The old man was driving him mad with his ranting and raving because Reid had defected, because Reid had turned his back on the Vancouvers and all they stood for. If Reid had been afraid that Jacob would fall into a fit and die from the shock, Tony had been no less afraid of the same thing.

It wasn't that he was so fond of his father, but that if Jacob were to die, then Tony would have to take over the helm of the family enterprises, and cut short the life of pleasure that was the only thing that really mattered to him. And Jacob was old, he was past seventy, and he was a heavy man. Years of overindulging in rich, heavy food had put a burden of pounds on him that was a strain on his heart. Even Gayle, who knew which side her bread was buttered on, couldn't persuade him to push his plate away before he had cleaned it.

You'd think that the old man would settle down and accept things as they were, but he hadn't. It had been months since Reid had left, throwing their name and their fortune back into their faces as if they were no more than dust, and still Jacob flew into a rage every time he thought of it. His eyes would bulge, his neck would bulge, his face would turn an alarming purplish red. Gayle was worried, and Tony was frankly sick and tired of the whole thing.

It was a matter of amazement to him that Jacob still lived, considering his temper and his weight, when Estelle had risen from the dinner table one night nearly two years ago and retired to har room, and died in her sleep without any of them having suspected that she was ill. Her absence had scarcely caused a ripple in the household. It had always been Jacob who was dominant, so that his wife lived in the shadows.

Jacob had been at it again tonight. He'd raged all through dinner, pounding his fist on the table so hard that his wineglass had danced and made the wine slop out to make stains on the linen cloth. Immediately after dinner, Tony had escaped to take refuge at his favorite local tavern. And tonight, after he'd escaped even farther, to New York City, he wished that he hadn't indulged quite so freely after he'd continued his drinking at his private club.

He'd heard from one of the other members of the club that Veronica's comic-relief husband was in Albany trying to straighten out some legal matter to the advantage of his business interests. It was a pity that he hadn't learned of it sooner, but it still wasn't too late. A cold bath and a pot of coffee would fix him up, and a message sent to Veronica would ensure that she would meet him at a discreetly elite hotel they had used on many occasions, where the hotel employees saw nothing and told even less.

Tonight he had a need for Veronica. He could talk to her, she'd understand what he was being put through, and afterward her arms, her sensuous mouth, her body that had grown even more voluptuous over the years, would bring him oblivion to everything else. Veronica had aged well. She knew how to take care of herself, and she had every means at her disposal to do so. Her only child, a son, held little interest for her, outside the fact that she used his difficult birth to hold her husband off.

Tony sent around the messenger before he bathed, to give Veronica time to make herself even more beautiful than nature had made her, and get to the hotel. He had no doubts that she would come. He knew that she was in between lovers right now, that the last one's wife had become suspicious and they'd had to break it off before she caused a scandal. That was one of the reasons Veronica was always available to Tony when he wanted her. Tony had no wife to become suspicious, no wife who might upset the applecart so that even Edward would be bound to learn of her indiscretions.

He took a cab to the hotel. He no longer enjoyed walking as he had when he'd been a younger man. All the same, he dismissed it a full block and a half from the hotel. It didn't pay to take chances.

He registered under the name he always used, Mr. Jonathan Whittiker. He knew that the desk clerks and the hotel manager knew perfectly well who he was, but they never failed to address him as Mr. Whittiker. And they never questioned the beautiful woman who entered the hotel alone, after Tony was in his room, and bypassed the registration desk and went up on the elevator as though she were a guest. They weren't in business to question things like that, they were in business to make money by being discreet.

Tony was pleased with himself as he adjusted his cravat in the hotel room mirror. The bath and the pot of coffee had gone a long way toward restoring him, and the block and a half walk from the cab to the hotel had finished clearing his head. He still had the old stamina, even if he had felt a little the worse for wear an hour and a half earlier. His hair was still so light that the first gray that was appearing was almost indiscernible. There was a slight sag to his jawline, but when he lifted his chin it smoothed out, and the faint beginnings of a paunch disappeared entirely when he tightened his stomach muscles.

A magnum of champagne reposed in a silver ice bucket. The lights were dimmed, the windows swathed in velvet draperies, the bed wide and inviting. One of the best things about Veronica was that she was never in a hurry, she didn't constantly have to get it over with as fast as possible so that she could get back to her own safe little world without being discovered. Veronica knew when to choose her times, when they could have all the time in the world, to reminisce, to savor, at their leisure, what was still to come.

She was at her loveliest when she slipped into the room when Tony opened the door to her knock that was so soft that if he hadn't been listening for it he wouldn't have heard it. The muted lighting became her. She was dressed in black, her best color, and wearing pearls. If there was any gray in her hair, only her personal maid knew it, and her face was still firm. She watched her weight, and she used every artifice to keep the years at bay. No wonder he always came back to her, no wonder she had succeeded in holding his interest for all these years!

He kissed her, and her response was more than satisfying. She'd been without a lover for over a month, and Edward Curtis wasn't enough of a man to satisfy her wildly hot blood. How she endured him, as little as he imposed himself on her, believing as so many fools believed that decent women were models of virtue whose delicate sensibilities must not be bruised any more often than necessary, was more than Tony could imagine.

"Champagne?"

"Of course." Veronica's lips curved, her eyes glowed. She wouldn't drink too much, that was another thing. She never drank too much, as some of Tony's other mistresses did, so that when they went to bed they were less than satisfactory, their senses dulled.

They each sipped at a glass of champagne, in no hurry. They had catching up to do, they hadn't seen each other for nearly three months. But that only made it all the more exciting. Anticipation was almost as great a pleasure as the bed itself.

She let him undress her. That was part of their ritual. Tony enjoyed undressing women, slipping their dresses down over their shoulders, slipping their undergarments off, his fingers lingering, savoring the curves, the satiny skin, his eyes drinking in all the delights that were his for the taking.

"I'm glad you came to town tonight, Tony. I was going mad in that mausoleum all by myself."

"You didn't have to be by yourself. There were any number of invitations you could have accepted, don't try to tell me otherwise."

"I didn't feel in the mood for social gatherings. I felt in the mood for this. Damn you, Tony, why do you wait so long between our meetings?"

"Usually because you're busy with similar meetings with other men," Tony teased her.

"But they aren't you. None of them are like you. You've always been the one for me, Tony. You're in my blood, no other man can touch you, you're the only one who satisfies me in the way I have to be satisfied! Dear God, think how it might have been, if you hadn't made a fool of yourself with that adopted daughter of the Northrups', and ended up being bullied into marrying her! We could have been together all this time."

"And probably ended up killing each other! I know your temper, my love. The first time I'd strayed, you would have stuck a knife in my ribs. It's better this way. Knowing that you have no claim on me keeps you reasonable."

"You're impossible! I don't know why I keep on bothering with you!"

"I do. It's because of this, and this, and this . . ."

Veronica moaned. Her fingers dug into his back, the nails hurting him, driving him into a frenzy. It was time, neither of them could wait any longer. He picked her up and carried her to the bed. He didn't turn off the lights. He wanted to see her, he wanted to watch her face as their ecstasy mounted, as their culmination drew near. She was still the most exciting, the most satisfactory woman he'd ever known.

On the ground floor, a small dapperly dressed man crossed the lobby. Like Veronica, he bypassed the reception desk, and as in Veronica's case, he wasn't challenged, even though the night clerk had never seen this particular man before. It was obvious that he was a gentleman and gentlemen were never challenged.

The gentleman had no need to inquire at the desk. Another gentleman, as impeccably dressed as this gentleman himself and appearing to be as much of a gentleman, had observed and relayed the information to him where he had been waiting in the contingency that this might be the night that such surveillance paid off. The second gentleman had also supplied him with a key that would open the particular door he had in mind.

He walked in a sort of daze, almost as though he were sleepwalking. His eyes in his nondescript, weak-chinned face were tortured, tormented. Even now, he didn't want to believe it. The man who had been watching his house, who had sent him word as soon as he'd followed his wife and noted which room she had entered, hadn't seen another man. He'd find out, as soon as he unlocked the door, that his wife was visiting some out-of-town friend who was in New York only for the evening, perhaps a lady and the lady's husband, no more than that. It was even possible that they were going out to dinner together, that his wife had met them here to save them the time and trouble of picking her up. And she would be furious, she'd never forgive him, and that would be almost as bad as finding something else behind that closed door.

All this time, all this expense. All this planning and deceit would all be for nothing and might even end his marriage. His hand was trembling so badly that he could hardly fit the key into the lock. In the bedroom, on the rumpled bed, the two occupants were too wrapped up in each other to hear the faint sound it made as the lock clicked back and the knob turned. The gentleman drew a deep breath and flung the door open, and a moan escaped his lips, the moan of an animal in agony.

Tony and Veronica heard that. They froze, their arms and legs still wrapped around each other. Tony's exclamation as he extricated himself and leaped to his feet was one of disbelief. This couldn't be happening, there was no way it could be happening.

Veronica screamed, so paralyzed with fear that she couldn't even draw up the sheet to cover her nakedness. "Edward, no! No!"

The gun in Edward Curtis's hand went off. It was a small gun, only a derringer, he had had to have one small enough to conceal in his pocket. The report wasn't loud at all.

Tony clutched at his stomach. There was no expression of pain on his face, it was too soon for that, the shock was too great. And then he began to crumple, his knees seeming to dissolve as he fell to them, his look of astonishment, of disbelief, still dominating his face.

On the bed, Veronica screamed and went on screaming. And Edward Curtis handed the derringer to the bellboy who came running to see what the commotion was, he made no resistance as the hotel manager burst into the room and grasped his arms and twisted them behind his back. He had no wish to get away. His life was over, all that remained was for the law to hang him by the neck until he could be laid in his coffin. His only regret was that he hadn't been able to bring himself to shoot Veronica as well, but the thought of marring her beauty, the beauty he had worshiped, had held him back.

Ironically, Edward did not pay with his own life for the crime he had committed. Anthony Vancouver, the last scion of Jacob Vancouver's uninterrupted bloodline, now that Reid had betrayed him, died two days later of internal bleeding and infection. The tiny bullet, from a gun that most men laughed at as a lady's toy, had penetrated his intestines. Mercifully, the doctors who had tried in vain to save his life were able to keep him so drugged with morphine that he was only dimly aware that he was dying.

The jury, after a short trial, returned a verdict of not guilty. Edward had only performed the prerogative of any man who had discovered his wife with a lover. It was still, in that year of 1892, called the unwritten law.

29

It seemed to Gayle that her life had come to a dead end, that fate itself was against her. She'd grieved over Estelle's death more than anyone knew, because Gayle had always kept things hidden inside herself ever since she had been a child. Estelle had been good to her, unfailingly kind, she'd done her best to try to make up to the little girl for the loss of her mother. She had seldom talked to Gayle about Moria, because Jacob had forbidden it, but Gayle had known that her grandmother had loved Moria, that she thought that her husband and her son had been unfair.

Gayle's life had been a series of losses, one after the other, each one hurting more than the last because each time she had been more vulnerable because of having been hurt so badly before.

Only she knew, not even Reid had suspected, how she'd wept when Liam Donovan had died when his cottage had caught fire in the middle of the night. Since the first day Liam had lifted her into the saddle of her first pony, terrified and determined not to betray her terror because her mother and Reid had been watching, she'd loved Liam. Liam's smile, his assurance that everything was all right and

Lydia Lancaster

that he'd see that no harm came to her, had calmed her fears and made her believe that maybe she could do it after all, maybe she could learn to ride without falling off and making a fool of herself.

She wouldn't have minded being hurt. It was having her mother and Reid, having Grandfather Jacob and her father, and all of their friends, find out that she was clumsy and stupid and not worthy of the Vancouver name, that had terrified her even more than her terror of horses.

From that first day, Gayle had struggled to make Liam approve of her, to learn to ride well enough to win one of his smiles. She'd respected him and she'd loved him, he had been a figure that was bigger than life, a hero. But she was a Vancouver, and Vancouvers did not love servants, especially an Irish horse trainer. The Irish were a despised people, little better than cattle or slaves—Grandfather Jacob and almost-grandfather William Northrup had instilled that in her as a toddler.

Every time Liam had complimented her, told her that she was doing well, had been a triumph. Every time she had failed to win a compliment from him had filled her with a grim determination to do better the next time, so that he'd like her as well as he liked her mother and Reid. And when her recklessness had brought a reproof from him, the genuine concern in his eyes had filled her with elation because it proved that he did like her a little, that if she tried hard enough, he might even love her.

She'd risked falls and broken bones to make Liam get that look in his eyes, and counted it well worth the risk. And no one, not even Liam, had guessed her terror of horses, had guessed the effort it had cost her every time she had jumped her pony over a fallen log or galloped around a bend that was too sharp. Born to the saddle, Liam had said, never guessing in his wildest imagination how she was shaking inside, how she was sick to her stomach every time she got up on a horse.

And then, overnight, Liam hadn't been there anymore, and her heart had been broken. Reid might have helped her, if he'd had any inkling of how she had felt. But Reid, who had loved Liam too, had become quiet, grieving his own grief, staying by himself or with Moria, assuming that Gayle felt no such grief. Reid's grief, and Moria's, had shut her out.

It had always been like that. Reid and her mother together, sharing everything with each other because Gayle had never known how to demand the love from them that she longed for with every ounce of her being. She wasn't good enough yet, she wasn't perfect enough yet, to demand that they love her as well as they loved each other. So she'd cried alone, with no one to know.

She'd never known how to handle things. How could she handle having a mother who was so beautiful, so perfect, that it had seemed to the little girl that there was no way in the world she could ever measure up to her?

And she had been expected to measure up to Moria, it was a demand made by everyone in her world except Grandmother Estelle that she must measure up to her mother, that she must be as beautiful, as graceful, that she must become as good a horsewoman, that eventually she must be acknowledged as a leader of the Hudson River Valley society as her mother was, and be as beautiful and accomplished in every way.

It had always been there, the terror that she wouldn't be able to do it. Everywhere she went, everything she overheard, only proved to her how impossible it was.

"What a lovely child! The very image of her mother! I wouldn't have believed it was possible that anyone could ever be as beautiful as Moria Vancouver!"

But she wasn't as beautiful, she'd never be as beautiful! She'd never be as graceful, as intelligent, as accomplished and admired as her mother! How could she be, when Moria was perfect, when Moria possessed not a single flaw? And so Gayle had tried harder, because if she didn't measure up, then she'd be despised and felt sorry for, she'd be dismissed as a nothing.

During all of her formative years, there had been just one thing that she was sure of, that had been given to her as her birthright, and that was the blood in her veins, the Vancouver blood. Grandfather

Jacob had made that very clear to her. He'd taught her to be proud of that blood from the day she could walk and talk.

Almost Gayle's first memory was of the huge, intimidating man who had regarded her with his protuberant eyes, fixing her with them as though she were a bug impaled on a pin. He'd frightened her because he expected so much of her. There had been no way for such a tiny child to know that Jacob Vancouver had turned to her because his son was a disappointment to him, because his grandson, although he gave him the respect that was his due, showed no inclination to take the Vancouver blood as seriously as it should be taken, preferring his mother's company and that of the horse trainer who had taught him to ride.

And Jacob had had no way of knowing, and he probably wouldn't have cared if he had known, that Gayle's attention stemmed more from fear of him than from caring about the things he drummed into her head to ensure that she, at least, would be appreciative of her heritage.

Gayle understood very little of what her grandfather told her, when she was very small. But she did understand that here, at least, she had all the attention of one of the God-like grown-ups, and that as long as she listened, and nodded, and said "Yes, Grandfather," Jacob approved of her, beamed at her, was delighted with her.

Her grandfather preferred her to her mother, preferred her to Reid, all she had to do was smile and say "Yes, Grandfather." In return he gave her a gift that was worth more to her than any toy, the gift of knowing that because she was a Vancouver, she wasn't completely worthless.

She had seldom seen her father for long enough periods at one time to get to know him. He too was bigger than life, hand-some, charming, witty, while she was the least of the family, the smallest, the youngest, insignificant compared to her mother and her father and Reid.

She never stopped striving for excellence, for perfection. She worked hard at her studies, but book knowledge came easily to Reid, while she had to struggle. Her mother never failed to praise her when she did well. But Moria would look at Reid's work, at his figures that were always right the first time, at his drawings that made the drawings that Gayle labored over look like meaningless blobs, and her eyes would light up and there would be so much pride in her voice that Gayle would turn away, a lump in her throat, and add another stone to the wall that she had built around herself to shield her from hurt.

The scandal that had broken over the Vancouver house when Moria had confessed that she was Liam Donovan's daughter had torn Gayle apart. Her grief over Liam's death had already been more than she could bear, and to learn that Liam hadn't been just a horse trainer, just a despised Irishman, but her grandfather, made it so much worse that she didn't have any idea in the world how to handle it. Without warning, the ground had fallen out from under her feet and she'd been left with no place to stand. And before she had had a chance to adjust, to learn to bear it, her mother had gone away.

And so she had retreated further into herself, taking out her heartbreak and frustration of not knowing how to cope with things beyond her ability to cope with them by showing more pride, more haughtiness, more pretending to be something that she wasn't. Reid had turned against her when she'd screamed out that it wasn't true that Liam was their grandfather, that she didn't believe it, and her mother and father and Grandfather Jacob had been so busy fighting with each other that they had hardly noticed that she was there. And when her mother had gone, and Reid had been wrapped in his own desolation and grief and too angry with her to notice that she was suffering as well, there had been nobody but Estelle, who had been ordered not to talk to her about it, and Grandfathar Jacob.

Because of Reid's loyalty to their mother, Grandfather Jacob had kept Gayle isolated from him as much as possible. If she'd had a chance to talk to him, to question him, to tell him how she felt, the rift between them might have been breached. But before that could happen, before Gayle could find a way to spend enough time with Reid—who was happy to avoid her—so that she could try to reach out to him, he'd been sent away, to England.

And so the wall she built around herself grew higher and thicker until there was no way she could climb over it or tunnel under it or walk through it. And inside her prison, she lived with the driving necessity to become perfect, to become everything that was expected of her, to become everything that her mother had been and more— the third jewel in the crown that had dominated the Hudson River Valley society for so long, the only jewel that was left.

Her mother had committed an unforgivable sin, so unforgivable that William Northrup had been struck down by it, left paralyzed and unable to talk, so unforgivable that Jacob Vancouver flew into a rage at the very thought of it. It was left to Gayle to try to make up for it, to do and be everything that was demanded of her. Eugenia was dead, Moria was banished, but they were still a legend. For the ten-year-old girl, the burden of losing both Liam and her mother had been devastating, and she had had no one to turn to but had had to pit her own will against her heartbreak and terrors.

And she'd done it, she'd succeeded, at a cost that no one else could know. There was no unmarried girl in the Hudson River Valley who was as beautiful, who was as accomplished a horsewoman, who was in such social demand, as Gayle Vancouver. Suitors besieged her door, she couldn't turn around without stumbling over some young man who was dying of love for her.

The small scandal of Moria's never having come back, after her physical breakdown after Eugenia had died, had faded to no more than a ripple. It was generally believed that after she'd recovered her health, she had run away with some man she'd met in Europe. A small hint here, a lack of denial there, had all but confirmed it.

A scandal still, but far less of a scandal than the truth would have been, and one that cast no reflection on the wronged husband and the deserted children. It was even rumored that Moria's lover was titled, because nothing else would have fit her image, while Anthony was admired for refusing to besmirch his family name with a divorce, for protecting his children from that ultimate scandal.

Martin Schuyler had come into Gayle's life like a savior. Four years older than Gayle, he'd been completing his education during the crucial years when Gayle had been coming out into society. Before that, she'd been too young, considered by males of Martin's age to be no more than a little girl. And after his education had been completed, Martin had spent his year on the Continent, taking the Grand Tour that was still highly favored for the sons of the privileged classes. It was only on his return from Europe that Gayle's beauty, her desirability that made every other girl pale by comparison, broke over him with full force.

A union between the Vancouvers and the Schuylers was highly desirable, approved by both families and applauded by the rest of the Hudson River Valley society. Gayle was by far the last to know that she and Martin were nicknamed the Prince and Princess, fondly by some, enviously by others.

Only Gayle knew that beyond her love for Martin, and she loved him with all her heart, there was an extra, added bonus that she could hardly wait to collect. Once she was a married woman, once she became a mother, she would no longer have to compete with one woman who was dead and another whose legend of perfection still circulated among the society in which she moved. As Martin's wife, as the mother of his children, there would be no more fears that she couldn't measure up. She intended to immerse herself in her new family, to go out into society as little as possible, and only marriage and motherhood could give that to her.

The plans had been completed, the engagement was about to be announced at a ball that Jacob intended should rival even the engagements of royal princesses. And then one more year of being always on display, of having never to let down her guard, and after that Gayle could be only herself for all the rest of her life.

That year of her engagement would stretch out endlessly, but she'd get through it somehow just as she'd always managed to get through things that were so hard for her that sometimes she wanted to simply give up. Just one more year, and the nightmare would be over, and she would be happy for the first time in her life.

Martin had called on her the evening before Anthony Vancouver had been shot in one of the bedrooms of a hotel that Gayle had never heard of, that she had no way of knowing was well known to nearly every wealthy man who liked to have a little diversion on the side.

"Does the time go as slowly for you as it does for me?" Martin had asked her. He'd been smiling, but his eyes had shown how much he meant his words, how he longed for the day when they could be married at last. "Every day drags. It seems as though the hours will never pass until I can be with you, and then when we're together it's almost worse because I know I'll have to leave you so soon. Do you have any idea what I'm talking about, or aren't girls affected as much as a man when they have to wait for something they can't bear waiting for?"

"Martin, don't be an idiot! Do you think girls aren't made of flesh and blood?" Gayle had flushed scarlet as soon as the words were spoken. No young lady talked like this, they weren't supposed to be aware of the demands of the flesh, the longing for consummation that men suffered before the marriage vows were spoken. "Oh, Martin, I do love you! You know that, you shouldn't even have to ask!"

They weren't supposed to kiss each other like this. Gayle knew that, too. No phase of her social education had been neglected, she knew that kisses like this weren't supposed to be indulged in until after the wedding, even if then! No decent woman was supposed to feel like this, that she was going to explode from the pressure of longing inside her, so that she ached and sometimes cried after they'd had to say good night and she went to bed with her lover's kisses still throbbing on her lips, and pounded her pillow and tossed with frustration before she was finally able to sleep.

But it would be worth it, any amount of frustration, of waiting, would be worth it when she and Martin finally belonged to each other, when nothing could ever keep them apart again!

She'd cried that night, as she so often cried after Martin had left her. And laughed at herself for crying, because she'd see him again the next evening. And, inevitably, the time would pass and she'd never have to go to bed alone again, Martin would be with her, and she'd never be lonesome again, never be alone against the world.

The house was strangely silent when she awoke the next morning. Gayle always woke up early, it was a heritage of having spent a lifetime riding every morning, and now that she no longer had anyone to ride with—she hadn't for years—she still arose promptly at seven, when Amy, the middle-aged woman who took care of her, entered with a cup of hot coffee to get her going, and laid out her riding clothes.

A glance at the bedside clock told her that it was ten minutes past seven. Amy was late. That in itself was so unusual that Gayle was slightly disturbed. Could she be ill? But if she weren't feeling well, one of the other maids would have come to help her dress.

She got out of bed and splashed cold water on her face to drive away the last of her sleepiness. She could dress without help. And she'd have to hurry. Jacob was also an early riser, and she joined him every morning for breakfast before her mare was brought around. He'd be displeased if she were late, and these days it didn't pay to displease him, the slightest thing could set him off and then he'd start raving again.

She was stepping into the skirt of her riding habit when Amy hurried into the bedroom, her face agitated. Gayle's heart skipped a beat. Something had happened or Amy wouldn't look like that. "Amy, what is it, what's wrong?"

"Miss Gayle." Amy's voice was choked. "Miss Gayle, there's been an accident. Your father has met with an accident."

"What kind of an accident? How did it happen, where? Is he badly hurt?" Gayle demanded.

"You'd best ask your grandfather. He's in his study." Twisting her hands in her apron, Amy refused to say any more.

Without waiting to put on her boots, Gayle ran stocking-footed down the stairs and to Jacob's study. Her grandfather was sitting at his desk, his head in his hands, his face white and his eyes staring vacantly at the opposite wall.

"Grandfather?"

He'd turned his head to look at her, his unfocused eyes gradually focusing. "Your father has been shot," he said. And before Gayle

495

could assimilate the shock, he'd brought his fist down on top of the desk, scattering the papers, and his voice became a roar, animallike with rage.

"Shot! Shot by the husband of the woman he had with him! What did I do to deserve a son like that, he's caused me nothing but trouble from the day he could walk! He had one affair after another, he married that woman, that daughter of an Irish horse trainer! And now this! The scandal will ruin me!"

All of Jacob Vancouver's money, all of his influence, couldn't completely conceal the scandal. He managed to keep all but the briefest accounts of it from the newspapers, but the accounts were there, and the scandal spread like wildfire. A man of Anthony Vancouver's wealth and social standing, shot while he'd been engaged in an illicit liaison with the wife of another figure almost as wealthy and prominent, couldn't be hidden from the world.

Veronica was ruined, her social position shattered. It wasn't that nearly everyone who knew her, who knew Anthony, hadn't been aware of their regularly recurring love affair, but that they had committed the unpardonable sin of being caught.

Stunned, scarcely able to believe it, Gayle wanted Martin, she needed Martin. She needed the comfort of his arms holding her, of his voice, his dear, dear voice, telling her that he loved her, that she wouldn't have to face this alone. But Martin didn't come. Where was he, why wasn't he here when she needed him?

It was shameful of her to be thinking of herself when her father lay in a hospital, dying. She should think of him, she should think of Jacob, of how old Jacob was, of how he must be feeling. But Jacob scarcely seemed to be aware of what was going on around him. His face stony, he sat at his desk in his study, his hands idle instead of toting up columns of figures, and when Gayle tried to talk to him, to reach him, he looked at her with eyes as expressionless as his face, and told her to come back later.

Gayle wasn't allowed to visit her father before he died. Jacob gave orders that she was not to be driven in to the city. There were newspaper reporters and people who were merely curious there who would be sure to recognize her, she'd be jostled and questioned, and Jacob didn't want her name to appear in print in any connection with this affair. He himself went only once, to take care of the financial aspects and to arrange for the funeral as soon as Anthony died.

The funeral was well attended. Gayle's Aunt Juliana and Aunt Kristina were there, but they arrived, with their husbands, just before the funeral rites took place and refused to stay overnight at Belvedere. They, even more than Jacob, wanted no part of this affair, they only attended because to have stayed away would have caused more talk than ever. Ultraconservative, middle-aged matrons, their heavy faces were expressionless but their eyes were cold with outraged disapproval.

The society of the Hudson River Valley and those people they were intimate with in New York City closed its ranks against outsiders to present normal faces to the world in the face of this scandal that had befallen one of their own. Every pew in the church was filled, the floral offerings overflowed every available space. At the end of the service they filed past Anthony's coffin, their expressions carefully noncommital.

Those closest to the family gathered at Belvedere afterward, just as was expected of them. And when this last decency had been observed, they left, drawing their invisible cloaks around them, to wait for the scandal to die down and be forgotten, although they themselves would never forget it or that the Vancouver name was now tarnished beyond repair.

But Martin wasn't like that. His and Gayle's love for each other had nothing to do with Anthony's disgrace, with scandal. They'd have to wait longer to be married, that was an inescapable fact. If only they'd been engaged, at least, this extra waiting would have been shorter.

Why didn't Martin come? He'd been at the funeral, along with both of his parents, but he'd scarcely had an opportunity to speak to Gayle afterward. It hadn't been the time or the place. But now the funeral had been over for nearly a week, and still Martin didn't come. Gayle was frightened. She felt as though she were somewhere in limbo, lost just as she was often lost in the recurring nightmares she'd had since she'd been a child, in which she was searching for her mother but never able to find her.

When Martin did come, a full week after the funeral, Gayle was in her room and didn't hear his horse. Amy came to tell her that he was there. She had to hold herself back, to force her feet not to run down the stairs. She was a Vancouver, she must behave with proper decorum even though she felt a rage to race as fast as she could and throw herself into Martin's arms, safe at last, awake from her nightmare because he was here at last.

She knew that something was wrong the moment she entered the drawing room where he was waiting for her. He was standing by the fireplace, his shoulders and back stiff, his jawline sharp with self-imposed control. He didn't hold out his arms and sweep her into them, he simply looked at her. Gayle felt something inside her curl up into a fetal position, shielding itself from light and hurt.

"Gayle, I can't tell you how sorry I am about your father. It is a dreadful thing to have happened."

"Yes, it is." Was that all he was going to say? Where was Martin, her Martin, why was this man in front of her suddenly a stranger?

"I'm afraid I have more bad news for you. I'm going to have to go away for a while, my father is sending me to spend a few weeks in several different cities to make myself familiar with our interests there. I'll spend however long I have to in each office to learn exactly how they function. I know it's a terrible time to leave you, but under the circumstances it's best that I should go now, as there is no way we can announce our engagement until the period of mourning for your father has passed."

Until the scandal dies down, Gayle thought, her mind, her body, so numb that she wondered if she would be able to speak or move at all. Or enough time so that there will be no speculation or gossip when our engagement is never announced, when we are never married at all!

She wanted to scream at him, to pound him with her fists, to claw at his face, she wanted to hurt him as he was hurting her. She wanted to force him to say that it wasn't true, that he wouldn't leave her, that she meant more to him than anything else, more than his family, more than scandal. She only stood there and drew a deep breath until she could control her voice and make it do her bidding, make it speak in a normal tone as though she were agreeing that the weather was warm or that it was raining.

"I expect that that would be best, Martin. As long as it's necessary for you to go, this is the best time."

"I'm glad you understand. I was afraid that you wouldn't."

Liar, hypocrite! What had he really been afraid of, that she would cry, that she would beg? Don't do this, her mind screamed. You can't, you love me, you promised me!

"Of course I understand. It's only practical. When are you leaving?"

"The day after tomorrow. I might not have time to see you again before I go, I'll be busy making preparations, getting my last instructions from my father."

"Of course. Then we'd better say good-bye now, hadn't we?"

"I'll write to you. I'll write as often as I can. Try not to miss me too much."

In another minute he was going to go to pieces. Martin wasn't made to lie, to cover up his true intentions with half-truths. He was ashamed, it was hurting him. But not enough to make him defy his father, defy his family, who had decided that a liaison between the Vancouvers and the Schuylers was impossible now that this scandal had rocked the Hudson River Valley to its core.

"Thank you for coming. If you can't come again before you leave, I'll understand."

He kissed her. He had to kiss her, it was expected of him, he was still a gentleman. He held her close and she could feel him trembling. That wasn't right, she was the one who was supposed to be trembling. She extricated herself from his arms, and smiled.

"Good-bye, Martin. I'll wait for your letters." The farce had to be played through to the end, because he was a gentleman and she was a lady.

"I'll write every week." White-faced, Martin started to take her into his arms again, and then his arms dropped to his sides.

He'd write the first week. And he'd write a few times after that. But the letters would become shorter, and they would become further apart. There was nothing wrong with Gayle's intelligence.

She walked with him to the door, watched while it closed behind him. She hadn't cried. She hadn't begged. At least she still had that. It was better than nothing, but not much. Too filled with grief and hurt to rage or cry, she went back upstairs, and faced the months and years ahead of her when she'd be entirely alone except for Grandfather Jacob.

30

Reid brought the mail from town, after he'd been to visit Reba and Abraham. A westerner now, he took care of his horse before he entered the ranch house kitchen. Moria looked up from stitching a new dress for Mattie, who had turned into a peacock ever since Moria had begun designing her clothes, blossoming out in her middle age as she never had as a girl.

"I never knew I could be so good-lookin'!" Mattie said frankly. "It took you to show me that a silk purse can be made out of a sow's ear, after all. Chet's actin' like we're newlyweds ever since you gussied me up, and I like it!"

Moria still loved to sew, as long as it wasn't patching or darning, and she particularly liked to sew for Mattie and Willa. Reba was impossible. She hardly ever got out of her housedresses, and when she did she hung herself with all of her Indian turquoise jewelry that she could find space for, as though she were a Navaho woman who carried the family wealth on her person.

"Well, are you going to tell me or aren't you? What's happened to tickle you so much?"

"Reba has a bicycle. And she's learned to ride it! She says that Abe never has time to take her out driving now that he has his store, and she's afraid of driving a horse and buggy by herself, how does she know what a horse might take it into his head to do? It might decide to run the buggy right into one of the ditches along the streets, that carry well water for the city water supply."

John J. Gardiner had installed the public water supply system back in '88. The ditches were open and Reba was convinced that buggies were going to go into them.

"Well, I never!"

"But Reba did! And now you're going to have to make her a bicycling dress so she won't kill herself by getting her skirts tangled, and then she can get around all she wants to without risking her life to a horse."

Moria didn't know whether to laugh or be appalled. She decided that she was more appalled than amused. Reba would kill herself! Whatever had possessed her?

"Why on earth did Abraham let her do such a thing?" she demanded.

Reid's grin intensified. "That's exactly why she did it, Abe told her that she couldn't, he made the mistake of telling that she was too old and that she was out of her mind. Don't worry, Mother. At least it isn't one of those old-fashioned bicycles with that huge front wheel, she'd have broken her neck on one of those for sure. This is a safety bicycle, and actually she's doing very well. I was treated to a demonstration. And everyone in Phoenix watches out for her, she won't be run down and horses aren't shying and bolting all over the place anymore the way they used to at the sight of one of the contraptions, they're getting used to them. She wants a bright red bicycling outfit, she says she wants to be sure that everyone will see her and give her plenty of room."

He broke off to reach into his pocket. "There wasn't any mail except a letter from Rose."

Mattie's dress slipped from Moria's lap into a heap on the floor as she jumped up and stretched out an eager hand. "Oh, Reid! Why didn't you tell me? Give it to me! And pour yourself some coffee, I'll read it aloud.'' There would be news of Gayle in the letter, Rose never failed to tell her anything she knew, and no matter how trivial it was better than nothing.

"Where's the Holy Terror? Reba was disappointed that I didn't bring him with me. There's a batch of molasses cookies in my saddlebag, I forgot to bring them in, I'll fetch them as soon as I've washed the dust out of my throat. Doesn't Reba think that you and Willa can cook? She started baking just as soon as she'd shown me how she can handle that machine of hers.''

"He's with Quinn and Quentin, over on the North range." Moria was already tearing open the letter.

The exclamation of shock that was torn from her lips made Reid pause as he picked up the coffeepot that was always on the back of the range, ready for anyone who wandered in needing refreshment at any time of the day.

Tony was dead! He was dead, he'd been shot, murdered, in a hotel room where he'd been spending the evening with Veronica Curtis! Edward Curtis had discovered them together and shot him!

Gayle! Moria thought. What had it done to Gayle, how was she taking it? Was she torn by grief, was that young man of hers, Martin Schuyler, giving her the comfort she needed? It was a full moment before the real impact of Rose's news hit her.

Tony was dead. She was a widow, she was free. She wouldn't have had it happen this way. She'd never wanted Tony to die, much less die in this manner, murdered, shot down by the husband he'd cuckolded, dying in a wave of shame and scandal. She'd only wanted him to set her free.

But the fact remained that no matter how shameful the circumstances, she was a widow, she was free.

"Mother, what is it? What's happened?"

Numbly, Moria handed him the letter. It took him only a moment to read it, and when he'd finished, his face was as stunned as his mother's.

"Mother, you and Quinn can be married now. Not that I haven't

503

always considered you as being married to Quinn. You had every right to do what you did, you had no alternative. But you and Quinn will want to make it legal."

Reid's own emotions were roiling inside of him, but that was where they would stay. He hadn't respected his father, he couldn't remember a time when he had really respected him. He'd known from his earliest boyhood that Tony was a philanderer, a womanizer, that he'd betrayed Moria again and again. He'd known that Tony was selfish and lazy, that he'd cared for nothing but his own comfort and amusement. He'd put Moria through hell, and when he'd made the final betrayal by refusing to stand by her when he'd learned that Liam Donovan had been her father, Reid had turned his back on him, never forgiving him. And he didn't forgive him now, he wasn't enough of a hypocrite to pretend that he did. But Tony had still been his father, and it was a shock, and there was Gayle to think of.

He'd have to write to Gayle, offer his sympathy, ask her if there were anything he could do. But he didn't actually expect an answer. Gayle was self-sufficient, she was a Vancouver, she had made it perfectly clear ever since her childhood.

His mother came first. Moria, and young Liam. He and Quentin could hold down the ranch while Moria and Quinn took a trip, while they were married in some state so far away that no rumor of it would ever reach back to Arizona. They must stay away as long as they wanted, have the honeymoon they'd been denied, reap the utmost happiness that they both so richly deserved and for which they had had to wait for so long.

"As soon as Quinn and Liam ride in, I'll take Liam to my room and let him daub with my paints," Reid said. "That'll keep him out from under your feet while you and Quinn make plans."

There was no need for Liam to learn that his mother and father weren't married, there should never be a need for him to know about it. Reid had felt a fierce protectiveness toward his young half-brother ever since he'd first seen him, as little as Liam needed protectiveness from anyone. Pure Bradmore, that boy, and Reid thought that it was a good thing because the Bradmores were tough, they were indestructible.

"Thank you, Reid. I think it would be best. I'm going to take the letter up to Willa now. It's time for her to wake up from her nap, anyway."

Willa's afternoon naps were a family joke. Moria insisted that the older woman should rest during the middle of the day, and Willa had rebelled against it with all the stubbornness of her grandson. But in the end, she'd conceded that maybe a few minutes of rest wouldn't do her any harm, it would give her a chance to catch up on her mending or reading. The fact that her eyes closed and she dozed off every afternoon was something that was never mentioned, but during the hour that she spent behind her closed door even Liam was quiet so that her rest wouldn't be disturbed.

Moria had sat down again, her hands folded in her lap. She still couldn't believe it. Married, she and Quinn could be married! She wanted to cry, to let her tears spill over and her shoulders shake. But she wasn't that weak, she never had been that weak and she hoped that she never would be.

Looking at her, Reid was making plans, remembering train schedules, remembering that he'd have to ride into town again tomorrow to tell Reba and Abraham. He imagined the joy on Reba's face, on Abe's, and it brought a lump to his throat. And after that he'd have to stay at the ranch until Moria and Quinn got back from their honeymoon, he and Quentin would have their hands full managing without Quinn. But he could handle it. He'd learned, to his satisfaction, since he had come to Arizona and taken on the coloring of a westerner, that he could handle anything that was thrown at him.

Moria wouldn't have believed that she could feel like a bride again, that she could feel as though she were a girl of seventeen or eighteen. Here she was, a woman staring forty in the face, a mother three times over, two of her children grown, and she was as excited as if this were the first time she'd been married.

In their hotel room in Chicago, she looked at herself in the mirror, and laughed to see that her face was flushed as she remembered the night before, her wedding night. Their marriage had been as simple as it was possible to be. With no family, no friends to help them celebrate their nuptials, they had stood in front of a priest they'd seen only once before—when they'd arranged for him to perform the ceremony—with the priest's housekeeper as a witness and a hastily recruited member of his parish for another. But their vows had been as sacred, as everlasting, as though they had been married with all the pomp and ceremony of a big wedding.

They'd had dinner afterward, at one of the elite restaurants where Quinn used to take her, where Reba, dressed in her best, had talked to Abraham in a voice loud enough to carry, pointing her out as she'd exclaimed, "That's Miss Moria Donovan of Greenbaum's Department Store! Look at that gown! She must have designed it herself. Everyone's going to her, and I can see why!"

No one recognized her now. She was older, there were a few strands of gray in her hair, and she wasn't dressed to attract attention but in a dress so elegant in its simplicity that only a few of the other women in the dining room recognized the genius that had gone into its design and looked at her with respectful envy. She looked the part of a wealthy youngish matron, her face still lovely in spite of the years that had passed, with the additional beauty of maturity to make it even more striking.

Quinn, too, had matured well. The life he led had kept his body lean and hard, and at forty-five he was so striking with his western coloring and broad shoulders that Moria thrilled to be seen with him. Compared to Quinn, the other men in the restaurant had seemed pale and without vitality. How fortunate they were, how blessed, that the years had been kind to them and that they had each other!

To Quinn, Moria was still the most beautiful woman in the world. Last night he'd proved it, with a fervor that had left her trembling and breathless, marveling that their belated honeymoon could be so perfect. After all their years together their passion for each other had grown until it was insatiable, their need for each other was as strong as it had been on the day on the desert when Moria had almost been struck by a rattlesnake and they had taken each other at last, so shaken by her narrow escape that there had been no turning back.

You ought to be ashamed of yourself! Moria told herself, but her laughing, shining eyes belied her unspoken words. She wasn't ashamed of herself. She was a married woman, wasn't she? Quinn was her husband, she was his wife, and it would happen again tonight, and tomorrow night, and the night after that. It would happen every night of their month-long honeymoon.

Quinn opened his eyes. "Up already? Don't you know that this is our honeymoon? Come back here!"

Moria hesitated, and then she steeled herself. "No. You get up. I'm ravenous."

"We can have breakfast in bed. They have room service here."

"I don't want breakfast in bed. I don't want to waste a single moment. I want to be out where the people are, I want to store up every minute of it to last me all the rest of my life. I love the ranch, but you have to admit that its population leaves something to be desired. I'm going to spend hours in every department store in town, I'm going to check on what's being done at Abraham's old store. And we have to go and see Reba and Abraham's old house, we promised them that we would, or don't you remember?"

"We don't have to do it all in one day. And it isn't Greenbaum's anymore, its name has been changed to Graham's."

"I know. I'm afraid I'll cry when I see the sign. But I'm going all the same. And if it isn't up to par, I'm going to beard the owner in his den and give him a piece right off the top of my mind! Quinn, do you think that any of the old help will still be there, that anyone will remember me?"

"Probably. You aren't an easy person to forget. If you were, I'd have forgotten you years ago and we wouldn't be together now. Come back here, dammit!"

Moria hesitated again, and then she capitulated. After all, Quinn was right. They had all the time in the world, the stores and the sight-seeing would wait, but this moment with Quinn would never come again.

Moria wondered if any other woman in the world had ever had a honeymoon as wonderful as hers, the joy of it all the more thrilling because she'd had to wait for so long. Married in Chicago, and the week there, and after that they were to retrace their steps back to Arizona over the exact route they'd taken when Quinn had come to force Abraham to move to the Southwest. They'd stop along the way in cities they'd touched only briefly, cities that had already changed, grown as the country was growing.

The culmination would be in San Francisco, that city of enchantment that she had yearned to revisit. This time she'd see everything, have time to savor everything to her heart's content, to store up memories that she would never forget.

"Don't you dare come back until you've had a real honeymoon!" Willa had told them. "You've earned it, and I want you to enjoy it. I'll ride herd on the menfolk here."

Liam had been a problem, wanting to go with them on their trip that he had no idea was to be a honeymoon. But Reba had taken care of that, by taking him for the duration of the trip and promising him unlimited use of her bicycle. Somebody had to get some use out of the contraption. She didn't really need it, she'd only bought it because Abe had told her she couldn't. Phoenix was a modern town now. It had streetcars, drawn on rails by mules, and riding the streetcars was one of the greatest pleasures of her life.

Phoenix was growing, and the country was so civilized now that Fort McDowell had been evacuated last year. Reba had seen the equipment that was moved being carted through town, loaded on carts three-tandem deep and pulled by ten-horse teams. The whole town had turned out to watch the end of an era, and Quentin had been disgusted because the fort itself and the land had been sold to the Department of the Interior for a little under seventy-five hundred dollars, a fraction of what it had cost to build. Government inefficiency and waste, Quentin had said sourly, adding that it only proved his point that the less government there was, the better. But Moria had remembered Lieutenant Daniel Haverly, and there had been a lump in her throat that had nothing to do with the fort being dismantled.

Going into Quinn's arms on that first morning of their honeymoon, feeling the hard length of him pressed against her, Moria shut everything else out of her mind. Nothing else mattered, all of the heartbreak, the troubles, she'd known were as if they had never been. As Quinn's mouth closed over hers, as his hands and body claimed her, she knew that this was the happiest moment of her life.

On that same morning, Gayle sat across the breakfast table from her grandfather, wondering how she was going to get through another day. Martin hadn't come to see her again before he'd left. She hadn't expected him to, but it still hurt. She hadn't known how much she could hurt and still go on living, still go on functioning. She should have known, she was familiar with hurt, with loss, they had been with her all her life, but she hadn't become immune to them, the hurt was as fierce, as unbearable, as it had been when Liam Donovan had died, as it had been when her mother had gone away.

"Gayle, hasn't it been a long time since your young man visited us?" Jacob asked. He seemed to have gotten over his first shock after Anthony's death, his stolid Dutch blood made it mandatory for him to go on. And his practical nature told him that although Tony had been his only son, he'd been far from a satisfactory son, that there had been no possibility that he would ever change.

It was over, and when something was over there was nothing to do but go on from where you were. He still had Gayle. Schuyler grandchildren would be acceptable. The behavior of his two daughters, Juliana and Kristina, at Tony's funeral had so enraged him that he had made up his mind to disinherit them and their children and leave everything to Gayle and the sons she would have when she and Martin Schuyler were married.

"Martin is away on a business trip for his father. He'll be gone for several months."

Jacob's protruding eyes protruded still more as he fixed them on his granddaughter. "He chose a peculiar time to go! He should be here, giving you the support that it's his duty to give you!"

"Grandfather, he won't be coming back. Not to me, at least. I don't have to tell you why."

Jacob's face turned purple as the implication of Gayle's words struck home to him. "Are you trying to tell me that you aren't going to be married, that he's jilted you?"

"That's exactly what I'm telling you. We aren't good enough for the Schuylers anymore." It was cruel of her, but Grandfather had to know the truth sometime and there was no use in putting it off. They both had to accept the facts and live with them, and it would be easier for him than it was for her. He had his business, his empire, always first in his heart, to comfort him. She had nothing.

For a moment, she thought that he was going to explode into one of his rages that would go on and on until the entire household would fear for his sanity, if not for his life. But Jacob only went on staring at her for what seemed an eternity, and then he got up from the table and went into his study and closed the door behind him.

At his desk, he began to formulate plans. The Schuylers would pay for this dereliction, they would pay dearly. Jacob had facts and figures at his fingertips. He knew exactly where Martin's father was overextended, exactly where the weakest links were, links that could be broken. It would take time, but the Schuylers' fortunes would come tumbling down to ruin.

And while that was being done, there was the matter of Gayle. He would take her abroad. There would be a title, the scandal of Anthony's death would not follow them there, and Gayle's beauty, her charm, her accomplishments, would attract suitors in droves. With his fortune in back of her, it was inevitable that she would be able to snare a title. She would be a lady, a countess. His grandchildren would have royal blood in their veins.

Nothing would satisfy him now but that Gayle should make up to him for everything else, for the disappointment Anthony had been to him, for his daughters and their husbands turning their backs on him. Gayle should marry so brilliantly that it would send the lot of them into confusion and make the Schuylers and all the rest of the Hudson River Valley society regret the day they had snubbed Jacob Vancouver and his granddaughter.

Titles could be bought. A great many noble families were hard-pressed for money, and Gayle was such a prize that they would feel no shame at the alliance with a commoner. A countess, even a duchess! There was no limit, outside of a throne itself, to what the combination of Gayle's beauty and his money could buy.

At first, Gayle thought that it was still the shock of her father's death that had affected Jacob, that as time passed he would revert to his normal self. Martin's defection had added to his anger about Juliana and Kristina, but as long as she and Martin couldn't have married for such a long time anyway he was sure to get over it. It would be another disappointment to him when he realized that she had no intention of ever marrying now, that Martin's desertion of her had left her so empty that there was nothing left of her to give to any other man.

"Grandfather, I don't want to go to England. I don't want to go to Europe. It would be in the worst of taste, anyway, so soon after Father's death. Traveling wouldn't change anything. We will just have to wait it out."

"There's no reason to wait. I do not wish to wait. You are at the peak of your beauty now, this is the time to present you to society in other countries. All doors will be open to you, I know how to arrange such matters. Is your wardrobe suitable, until we can supplement it in London, in Paris and Rome? You are to go over it immediately and report to me. A winter crossing isn't to my liking, and the year is wearing on. I wish for us to be settled in London before the season opens."

"There's no point to this discussion. I'm not going." Merciful God, was Jacob planning to put her on display, to auction her off to the highest bidder? Driven to the breaking point, she realized that that was exactly what her grandfather had in mind. She was to be put on the block, she was to buy herself a title! But she wouldn't do it, there was no way he could make her do it.

They quarreled. Jacob shouted, Jacob commanded, until the servants trembled and speculated on what the outcome would be. A few of them laid bets, although it was hard to decide which would prove to be the stronger willed. No peaceful day went by, and sometimes the battle between Gayle and Jacob went on far into the night.

Outwardly, she kept herself under control. Jacob did all the shouting, all she had to do was keep on saying no. But, inside, she was turning into a quivering mass of nerves, so that the slightest sound startled her, so that her head ached until she was almost blind with the pain, until her hands trembled unless she willed them to be still.

She thought about her mother constantly. Reid was with Moria now, in the Arizona Territory. He'd argued with her for hours, before he'd left Belvedere, trying to persuade her to go with him. The arguments had torn her apart. But there had been Martin, how could she have gone to live in Arizona and left Martin behind? She wanted to see her mother, she wanted it more than anything in the world except to marry Martin, to bask in Martin's love, and never have to compete again, never have to be something that she wasn't. She'd thought that she would die of grief when her mother had gone away, when Reid wouldn't talk to her about it because he was angry with her, when Jacob forbade anyone to talk to her about it. There hadn't been any way that she could cope with her grief, she'd been forced to withdraw even further inside herself, behind her defensive wall, to keep from being hurt even more.

But now that Martin had betrayed her, now that his love hadn't been strong enough to let him stand by her when she needed him the most, visions of Arizona, of her mother, haunted her. She had a compulsion to pack her bags and take the first train west. But her childhood terrors prevented her. It would only start all over again, the rending, impossible competition with her mother, the certainty that she could never measure up, that she would be found lacking. And Moria loved Reid the best, Reid would always stand between them, close to Moria, while she wept inside because she wasn't good enough. As bad as her present situation was, it was better than plunging herself back into that other situation where she'd always been a child crying outside of a lighted window, cold and alone and afraid, unable to find the key that would let her in.

Her one escape was to ride, but even that brought back memories that were too painful to be borne. Her mother on Jazir, Reid on General, herself on Firefly, her mother so beautiful on the great black horse that she had despaired of ever being able to match her. Liam riding with them, telling her to take care, telling her that she was too reckless, her mother shaking her head, her eyes worried even when she smiled with pride at a good jump, at a reckless gallop where the bridle path was too narrow and winding for safety. "Gayle, what are we going to do with you! Why can't you be like Reid, and show some common sense? You'll break your neck, do be more careful and listen to Mr. Donovan."

"Cut it out, Gayle! Why do you want to worry Mother? And what if you broke Firefly's leg, how would you feel then?"

The voices came back to her, the pictures superimposed on her brain. Would they never fade, would they never leave her in peace? Gone, all gone. Her mother in Arizona, living with a man who wasn't her husband, the mother of an illegitimate child! Her half-brother would be five or six years old by now. Did he look like her mother, did he look like Reid, did he look like Liam Donovan? Or did he take after his father, Quinn Bradmore?

Gayle knew about them, because Jacob had told her. There had never been a time when Jacob had not known where Moria was, what she was doing, and he had relayed his information to Gayle to ensure her complete loyalty to him. Every word had cut Gayle to the quick, inflicted wounds that had never healed.

Jazir was dead now, buried in the West pasture. Kamil, Eugenia's golden horse, was dead, buried at Retreat. And Reid was in Arizona, she'd never see him again, or her mother, or the boy who had been named Liam. Just as it had always been, they were close, there was no room for her.

She'd ridden Jazir after Reid had been sent to England. Something inside her had made her ride him, made her make sure that he was well cared for, exercised, kept in the best of condition. She'd gone on riding him until he had become too old and she had ordered him to be turned out to pasture. But she'd still visited him every day, she'd taken him apples and carrots and lumps of sugar. She'd pressed her cheek against his silky, familiar neck, the coat not as silky now as it had been when he was young, when her mother and Eugenia had been the two most beautiful women in the Hudson River Valley, riding the two most beautiful horses.

Jacob had bought Nefertiti for her two years ago, a blooded mare almost as beautiful as Jazir. Like Jazir, Nefertiti was black, as black as Gayle's hair. Unlike Jazir, she had a white star on her forehead. No woman in the Hudson River Valley had a more beautiful horse, no woman was a better horsewoman. Gayle, the third jewel, the jewel that must outglow Moria and Eugenia, that must surpass them in every way for the gratification of Jacob Vancouver.

"Mind you're careful, Miss Vancouver." Bert Parker, the stablemaster who had been at Belvedere since before Gayle had been born, admonished her on the morning she left the house after a particularly violent quarrel with Jacob at breakfast. "The going is treacherous after that rain we had last night, and it looks to be coming up another storm. If you was to ask me, I'd say to do without your ride today, miss."

"A little rain won't melt me." Gayle spoke more sharply than she'd intended. After Grandmother Estelle had died, she'd taken the reins of the household firmly in her own hands, and to the surprise of the servants she had been easy to work for, as firm as Estelle had been but never demanding or unreasonable. There was something of her mother in her after all, the staff had decided, all of them remembering Moria with affectionate respect as she had been before she had left Belvedere. And because Gayle treated them fairly and with the respect that was their due, they gave her their loyalty just as they had to her grandmother.

Parker started to protest again, but then he clamped his mouth shut. Miss Gayle was a grown woman and the mistress; if she chose to ride in the rain there was nothing he could do about it and probably she would come to no harm.

"It's all right, Mr. Parker. I'll be careful. If it starts storming I'll come back in."

The quarrel she'd had with Jacob the night before had left her so shaken that she'd hardly slept at all, and the continuation of it this morning had made it worse. Jacob was determined that he was going to bend her to his will, but she wouldn't have it, she'd die first. But the more she'd dug in her heels and refused, the louder Jacob had shouted, until in his blind rage he'd reminded her that she was dependent on him, that she didn't possess a penny of her own, that she'd do as he wished or he'd disinherit her as he was disinheriting Juliana and Kristina.

Ignoring the storm clouds that were gathering again and blackening the sky, scarcely aware of them, Gayle set Nefertiti into a trot and then lifted her into a gallop. Nefertiti snorted and tossed her head, uneasy because of the storm in the air, but Gayle's hands on the reins held her steady. Underfoot, the path was as soggy and treacherous as Parker had warned her, but she paid no attention to that, not even noticing when splattered mud flew up from Nefertiti's hooves to dirty her riding habit.

Let Jacob disinherit her, then! She loved her grandfather, he had always been good to her, he'd made her his favorite and she had needed that, no one knew how much she had needed it during all those years when she'd struggled against her terror that she'd never be able to measure up to her mother, to Eugenia, to Reid, when she'd felt alone and lost and insignificant. He'd given her a sense of worth, even if it was only from the knowledge that she was a Vancouver.

But as much as she owed him, as much as she loved him for having been her only haven during her childhood years, she would not go running off to the other side of the world to place herself up for auction in order to save his pride.

She'd be sorry to leave Belvedere, it would break her heart, the thought of severing this last blood tie filled her with such bleakness, such emptiness, that she could hardly bear it. All the same, she'd go. She wasn't a child now, she was a grown woman, she was capable of earning some kind of a living. Her mother had done it, going to Chicago and becoming Miss Moria Donovan of Greenbaum's Department Store. And now she would have to do it.

Her face grim, her eyes filled with determination, she made a mental inventory of her assets. Count money out. Like her mother, she'd have only a few pieces of jewelry to sell so that she could survive until she found employment. Grandmother Estelle had given her a pair of sapphire earrings on her eighteenth birthday, earrings that she herself had been given on her own eighteenth birthday. Gayle had no idea how much they would bring but the stones were large and flawless. She'd try not to sell them outright, it would be hard to bear if she couldn't get them back again, her only remembrance of her grandmother. Any other pieces she owned were nowhere near as valuable, and she wouldn't take them in any case because they had come from Jacob.

Like her mother, she would have to leave her true identity behind her. But that was no loss, because she felt that she had never had a true identity, that she had never been a person in her own right. Now at last she would either attain one, or she would go under.

Her education had been the best that Jacob's money could buy, but a post as a governess was out. She was too well known among families wealthy enough to employ governesses, she'd be recognized. A saleslady, then, like her mother, or perhaps she could realize enough on the earrings to go to one of the new typewriter schools and learn to operate one of the machines and find employment in a business office.

There was a crash of thunder, so loud that Nefertiti shied and reared. An instant later, a shaft of lightning streaked out of the roiling clouds and struck a tree just off the path, shearing off a limb that crashed almost underneath the mare's feet. Nefertiti reared again, and panicked, out of control.

Caught by surprise because she had been too immersed in her thoughts to realize how close the storm was to breaking, Gayle struggled for balance for one futile moment before Nefertiti laid her ears flat to her head and bolted, running blind. And another few instants later, even as Gayle fought to control her, she crashed into a tree and fell, with Gayle still in the saddle, trapped under her.

Nefertiti scrambled to her feet, limping, and headed back for the safety of her stable. Gayle lay on the sodden ground, unconscious, stunned by the fall, her leg doubled under her at a crazy angle, until the driving rain on her face brought her back to the world of reality.

The shock her body had sustained kept her from feeling pain until she tried to get up. With a dismayed cry, she sank back down again. There was no doubt that her leg was broken. The rain lashed down relentlessly, as though it were trying to drive her into the ground, as though it and the wind that was driving it were intent on holding her prisoner.

She had to get up, she had to get back to the house, get shelter, get help. Pressing her lips together, gritting her teeth, she tried again. But it wasn't any use. She couldn't walk, and her searching eyes could find no broken branch short enough and strong enough to use as a crutch.

She'd crawl, then. Sobbing with the effort, nearly blacking out from the pain that she could feel now, swamping her in waves, she began to inch her way along the ground.

Parker and the two stableboys found her half an hour later, sodden, exhausted, her face drawn with agony.

"Holy Mother!" Parker cried. "Miss Gayle, we're here, you're all right now." He sat down in the mud and lifted her head. "My jacket, you blithering idiot! Help me off with my jacket to cover her, and then run and fetch a shutter!"

Through her pain, Gayle tried to smile. "You were right, Mr. Parker. It's raining. I should have listened to you."

"Hush now, hush. Don't exert yourself. We'll have you back to the house in no time and the doctor fetched and you'll be as right as rain. . . ."

Horrified at what had come out of his mouth, he broke off, and Gayle's laughter rang out, laced with pain but still laughter, as silvery as it had been when she was a little girl, as silvery as her mother's had been when Parker had known her.

Gayle laughed then, but she screamed when she was lifted to the shutter. She'd taken a deep breath, the deepest one she could, to steel herself against screaming, and that had been a mistake because it only gave her more breath to scream with. And then she fainted.

Just before oblivion overtook her, one ironic thought crossed her mind. Jacob couldn't force her to go abroad now, she wouldn't bring much on the auction block with a broken leg.

31

Moria's first impulse, when she received Rose's letter telling her that Gayle had been hurt in a riding accident, was to take the first train east. But that would have been futile. What would be the use of standing on Jacob's doorstep and being refused admittance, as she surely would be? Gayle was receiving the best of care, Jacob's resources would buy the best. A broken leg could be a serious thing, but Gayle was young and there was no reason to believe that it wouldn't heal without complications.

All the same, Moria felt a deep, shamed guilt to think that the accident had taken place while she and Quinn had been on their honeymoon, having a wonderful time, while she had been happier than she'd ever been in her life. She'd been reveling in Quinn's love while her daughter lay injured, she'd been behaving like a bride, without a thought for the daughter she hadn't seen for so many years.

But Rose's second letter, received early in October, threw her into a panic.

Gayle had left Belvedere. Rose had been told that Gayle's leg hadn't healed as it should, but she hadn't wanted to worry Moria by passing along the information until there had been time for it to improve. Surely, with all the medical care she had, it would only take time.

Not only that, but the old man would give her no peace. He wanted to take her abroad and find her a titled husband now that Martin Schuyler had jilted her because of the scandal connected with Tony's murder. And Gayle refused to go. They were at it hammer and tongs, day and night, the servants at Belvedere said that their shouting sometimes went on until one or two o'clock in the morning. Rose had gone to Belvedere herself to find out just what was going on.

It was even worse than she had feared. Gayle was as thin as a rail, her face pinched, her nerves all but shattered. But she was determined to leave Belvedere. She'd given Rose the sapphire earrings that Estelle had given her, and asked her to pawn them for her.

Michael McCarthy had solved that problem. He'd brought Rose five hundred dollars and told her to tell Gayle that it was what he'd borrowed on the earrings, but Rose still had them in her possession. And Michael had waited outside Belvedere, in the middle of the night, until Gayle could creep out of the house so that he could take her to New York City, where he'd already rented a room for her.

So we know where she is. She's going to a typewriter school, to learn to become a typist. But there are two very real problems. Her leg hasn't improved, she walks with a distinct limp and it causes her a good deal of pain. And Jacob Vancouver has traced her down and he still gives her no peace. Michael has moved her twice, and even assigned a man to watch her building and follow her to and from her typewriter school, but outside of laying violent hands on Jacob there's no way he can keep Jacob from harrassing her.

We've told her and told her that you'd welcome her in Arizona, that you love her and want her and that there's no reason for her to go on alone, but she says that there's no way she's going to inflict herself on you or anybody else. She has

*courage, but it isn't right and it's time you knew just what is
going on.*

Reid's face was as grim as Moria's when they finished studying
Rose's letter. "That settles it. I'm going to New York. Mother, don't
look like that! I'm going to bring Gayle back here if I have to carry
her, and that's a promise!"

He left the next day. When he arrived in New York City Michael
was waiting for him at the station and took him to the rooming house
where Gayle was staying. It was in a poor neighborhood, because as
naïve as Gayle was about money she wouldn't have believed that her
five hundred dollars could stretch to cover a nicer place in a better
section of town, as well as pay her tuition and feed her until she had
learned to operate a typewriter well enough to obtain employment.

Waiting outside for Gayle to come home after her day's lessons,
Reid's heart twisted when he saw her walking toward him down the
street, limping badly, her face drawn and pale, set against the pain
and fatigue of walking on her lame leg.

For a moment, she didn't recognize him. He was deeply tanned,
he was wearing a western hat, his shoulders were broader.

"Reid! What on earth are you doing here?"

"I've come to take you home. No, not to Belvedere . . ." this as
an expression of alarm crossed her face, intermingled with the pain,
". . . to Arizona. Dammit, Gayle, you have a family that loves you!
If I don't bring you back with me, Mother isn't going to let me in."

Gayle's lips were as white as her face. "Mother has her own life.
She's found herself a man, and even had a child by him."

"You're darned right she has! And the man she's found is a good
man, a man who loves her enough to lay down his life for her, and
the child is the best kid you can imagine. It's a warm, loving family
and you belong in it!"

"No." Gayle's face was set. Oh, God, just for once in her life
why couldn't she be left alone to make it on her own, not to have to
compete with her mother, to be a carbon copy of a woman no other
woman could compete with? And now she was sick, she was lame,

she was exhausted, and it was too much, but she wasn't going to give in, not if she died for it!

"Go away. I don't need you. I don't need anyone."

"Like hell you don't! Everybody needs somebody. You're going to listen to reason if I have to shake your teeth loose to make you do it!"

If only she weren't so tired! If only her head would stop throbbing, her eyes would stop blurring! She tried to step back, to turn away from him, but her leg betrayed her and she lurched and almost fell. Reid caught her, and she collapsed in his arms.

The next day, with Gayle under the care of a licensed nurse, Reid went to Belvedere and demanded to see his grandfather. After being left waiting in the entrance hall for fifteen minutes, he lost what patience he had left and entered his grandfather's study without being summoned.

Jacob looked at him with his protruding eyes, his face registering anger.

"Get out of my house. I didn't ask you to come and I don't want you here unless you're ready to come back and take your place as a Vancouver. If that is why you're here, you must realize that you come back only under my terms, is that understood?"

"Listen to me, Grandfather." Reid felt a little sick. Gayle was right, the old man was hardly sane. "The terms I came to discuss are mine, not yours. Gayle is going back to Arizona with me, going to join her family. And I want you to understand, and understand very well, that while you may still be some kind of a power here in the East, your name and your money don't mean a thing in the West. Grandparents have no legal authority over their grandchildren as long as one of their parents is still alive.

"I'm only here to warn you that if you lift a hand to cause Gayle, or my mother, or any of us, any trouble, there will be serious consequences. We know how to deal with people like you, and the minions your money can hire, out in the Arizona Territory. There isn't a man in the Territory who won't stand behind us all the way if we have to take extraordinary measures to protect ourselves. Have I made myself clear or do I have to go over it again?''

Jacob rose to his feet. His protruding eyes bulged. "Get out! Get out of my house! You'll find that I'm still a power! You'll learn who you're dealing with . . ."

Reid left him, the old man still raging. There was no use in trying to talk with him or reason with him. He only hoped that he had made his message clear.

The moment he had gone, Jacob ordered his carriage. He spent the next several days battling with his attorneys, demanding that they find a means to make his granddaughter return to him. They told him what they had told him before, when Gayle had left his house. There was no way that it could be done.

Defeated, filled with impotent rage, Jacob watched Reid help Gayle on to the train a week after Reid had arrived in New York. They saw him, and Gayle felt a shudder pass through her body, so strong that Reid felt it and moved to place himself between his sister and the malevolent old man.

"Don't look back, Gayle. There's nothing we can do about him. He is as he is, and nothing can change him."

"He's old," Gayle said. "He's old and alone."

"And you're young, and if you waver now you'll be lost. No, don't look at him again. Look ahead, because that's where your future is."

Using all of her will, Gayle didn't look out of the train window at the old man who still stood watching as the train pulled out. She knew that Reid was right. As weak and ill as she was, Jacob would have had her back at Belvedere no matter how strong her will was, even though she had been doing well at her typewriter training school. Then she would have had it all to do over again as soon as she had regained her strength.

She'd left Jacob and Belvedere too soon, she should have waited until she was stronger before she struck out on her own. But Jacob had been driving her mad. She'd had to get away for the sake of her own sanity. And she still would have succeeded, if only Jacob had left her alone. It had been his continued harrassment that had driven her to the breaking point.

Now, on the train, she trembled to think of meeting her mother face to face again after all these years. She didn't want to go to Arizona, even though she was consumed with her inner need to see her mother, to see her young half-brother. But she didn't belong there. She didn't belong anywhere. She was only going because there was no alternative. As soon as she was well and strong again, she would leave, and build a life of her own or die in the attempt.

Rose was sitting with William Northrup in his room when Jacob forced his way into William's house. She'd been to see Gayle the night before, Michael had taken her, and she'd left messages to be carried to Moria, along with her deepest love.

Now she sat and watched this other old man who had spread his malevolence over everyone she had loved, who had tormented Eugenia and made her life a living hell, who had murdered Liam, who would have destroyed Moria and Moria's children if he hadn't been struck down before he could move to bring about their destruction.

Sometimes she thought that she was a fool to stay on here, to dedicate her life to watching him, guarding against any possibility that he might still recover enough to set in motion the forces that would destroy Laura Gateman and her husband and her family, that would destroy Moria and Reid and Gayle. But she knew that miracles do happen, and she was always aware of the strength of William Northrup's will. It was there in his eyes, the only part of him that was still alive, cold and fierce and radiating hate.

So she stayed on, and she would stay on until William Northrup died, because if he were to force his body to recover even enough to hold a pen, she'd have to find some way to prevent that pen from being put into his hand even though she lost her immortal soul in the doing. She didn't know what means she would use, she'd face that when it came, if it came, but she knew that she would do it.

Michael McCarthy, now. Rose's mouth curved into a smile. She, too, had had her life ruined by the man who lay in his bed, his malevolent eyes never leaving her face. Dear knew that Michael, the foolish man, needed a wife to restrict his diet, his paunch was getting more disgraceful every day, and he drank too much even if he insisted that no Irishman could drink more than God had fashioned him to hold.

Still smiling her wry, humor-laced smile, Rose nodded her head. Yes, she would have been happy with Michael. Michael had so many friends that there would always be something to do. Dancing, he told her. In all her years of service in this country, Rose had never been to a beer garden, and Michael's accounts of the happy, convivial people there made her ache to be a part of it. It would have been nice, she would have enjoyed it, and the devil take the man in this bed, who refused to die.

Not that she was asking for him to die. She'd not have that on her conscience. It would be enough on her conscience if she had to prevent *him* from using a pen, from using his voice, if he were to make any sort of recovery. But it would have been so nice if he'd died of his own accord, if she could be free to go to Michael, a wife at her age, the thought was enough to make her blush.

There was a commotion downstairs. Mrs. Lindstrom's voice was raised in protest, and then there were clumping footsteps on the stairs, not Michael's, because Mrs. Lindstrom wouldn't have tried to keep him out, and because Michael would never walk like that, heavy and slow, and no other man ever came into the house. Alarmed, she rose from her rocking chair and went to see who it could be.

Jacob reached the top of the staircase, with Mrs. Lindstrom directly behind him, still protesting, and that was peculiar in itself because Jacob Vancouver was a neighbor, a business associate of him there in the bed, and he might have some valid reason for this visit. But when she saw the expression on Jacob's face she understood. He'd come to make trouble, there was no other way about it, and now she herself barred his way.

"What do you want? My patient is resting, he isn't to be disturbed."

Jacob didn't answer her. He simply shoved her out of his way, and for all of his age his arms were strong and powerful so that Rose's ninety-seven pounds and five feet and a fraction of height were no match for him with his bulk and those arms.

There was no male servant in the house, only she and Mrs. Lindstrom were left. Two village girls came in once a week to help with the cleaning. The rest of the indoor staff had been dismissed years ago, when there had been no more need for them. There was still a gardener, an old man himself, who depended on village boys to help him keep the grounds in some kind of order.

"Mrs. Lindstrom, fetch Bates!" Rose cried, although what Elmer could do was beyond her, he'd be no more match for Jacob Vancouver than she herself was.

Jacob wasn't even aware that Rose was sending for assistance. There was nothing in his mind but rage against the man who had brought all this down on him, the man who had allowed his Irish horse trainer to foist his daughter off on him and then had foisted her off on his son, to the ruination of everything Jacob had.

Now he loomed over William's bed, his face contorted, his eyes bulging, the veins in them showing, as red as his mottled face.

"You!" Jacob shouted. "You deserve to die! It's only justice for you to die! Justice, I want justice!"

"Mr. Vancouver!" Rose fastened herself to Jacob's arm. "Stop it, stop it this instant! What are you trying to do?"

As he had before, Jacob shook her off without seeming to know that she was there. He bent over William's bed, his hands clenching and unclenching as though he were savoring how it would feel to have William's throat between them. Spittle had formed at the corners of his mouth, and sprayed across William's face as he resumed his shouting.

"Evil, wicked, bringing that witch, that daughter of an Irish horse trainer, into my life, foisting her off on me, and now my son is dead

dead as he wouldn't be dead if he'd married a decent girl! My family gone, my good name gone!''

In a frenzy of rage, he seized the bedposts and began to shake the bed. William's body shuddered as his paralyzed muscles made a last, desperate effort to come to life, to move, to escape from this danger that threatened him. His eyes were filled with wild terror. Watching, Rose's hand covered her mouth to stifle the screams that welled up in her throat. She had to do something, Jacob was going to kill him, and as much as she had wanted the devil dead all these years it would be murder performed before her eyes.

For a moment, it seemed as though her own body were paralyzed, that she couldn't force it to move. And then, almost without knowing that she had moved, the oil lamp from the table was in her hand, and she brought it crashing over Jacob's head.

And for a moment, it seemed as if the blow had had no effect at all. Jacob stiffened, shards of glass in his hair, on his shoulders, the kerosene dripping down over his face and soaking into his clothing. And then he staggered a little, and reached out to grasp the back of the rocking chair to steady himself. The chair, set in motion by his hand, moved back and forth, rocking, and Jacob rocked with it, stunned and disoriented. Rose watched him, not daring to reach out to steady him for fear that even a touch would make him fall.

He was still standing there, his body moving back and forth with the rocking of the chair, when Elmer Bates charged into the room, a rake in his hand. A rake! Rose had a hysterical impulse to laugh.

Then Jacob straightened and walked around to the front of the rocking chair, and sat down in it, his head in his hands. Elmer Bates stood uncertainly, the rake still in his hands but lowered now, not knowing what this was all about, knowing even less what he was supposed to do now.

But there was no need for him to do anything. On the bed, William's eyes rolled back in his head, the twisted, misshapen left side of his face was even more contorted than it had been before. He had suffered another stroke, and this time it had killed him.

There was an investigation, but it was brief. By the testimony of the only eyewitness, Jacob Vancouver had not laid a hand on William Northrup, but only shouted at him. And it was obvious that Jacob Vancouver had been under a mental strain, that he hadn't known what he was doing.

Now Jacob sat alone in his house at Belvedere, all of his interest in life gone, leaving his business affairs to his minions until his eldest grandson, Juliana's son, came to take the helm. Hans Vandyke was twenty-four, and some common ancestor had given him something of the look of Anthony when Anthony had been that age. But unlike Anthony, Hans had a keen business sense and he knew which side his bread was buttered on. He had only to insinuate himself into the old man's affections, and soon the whole of the Vancouver holdings would be his.

One grandson, Jacob thought, something inside him stirring. One loyal grandson! And old, his world shattered, he let Hans deceive him, he put his trust in this boy who looked like Anthony but who had his own keen mind, not knowing even if he would have believed it that soon this grandson would have him declared mentally incompetent and shut safely away in a sanitarium while Hans gobbled up his empire for his own selfish purposes.

William was laid to rest beside Eugenia. The Hudson River Valley society, as was their custom, drew themselves together to form a barrier against the rest of the world, and attended his funeral en masse.

To Rose, it was a travesty. Not only a travesty, but a sacrilege to lay *him* to rest beside the woman he had tormented. But Michael was beside her, and his supporting presence reminded her that Eugenia wasn't in the grave with its magnificent marble marker, Eugenia was in heaven, with God and the angels and Mary and all the saints, with Liam. Where *he* was, she didn't know and she didn't care to know. That was up to God. She had done her duty, she had kept her trust to Eugenia, and now at last she was free.

"And what excuse are you going to give me now, you stubborn woman?" Michael asked her when the funeral was over and the last of the mourners had gone.

"No excuse, Michael McCarthy. You're as good as a married man right now."

They were sitting in the drawing room, which had been divested of its dust covers and cleaned for the funeral. It was all right for them to sit here now, just as it was all right for them to be drinking a bottle of William Northrup's best brandy, because it all belonged to Moria now. Smiling at Michael, Rose felt the weight of years lift from her shoulders. A bride she'd be before the month was out, and a wife, and it had all been worth the waiting.

32

It took every ounce of strength that Gayle could call up to face getting off the train when it arrived in Phoenix. She was exhausted, the journey had drained more of her small store of strength than even Reid suspected, although he had coddled and fussed over her every stage of the way, insisting on frequent breaks to spend a night in a good hotel in cities they passed through, insisting that she take her meals in bed on those rest-breaks.

Her leg hurt, there had been muscle damage when Nefertiti had fallen on it, as well as the break that had healed improperly so that her broken leg was slightly shorter than the other, no more than half an inch but that was enough to make her limp noticeable when she was tired. Now, debarking from the train, she was terrified that it would give out under her and she'd fall and be humiliated in front of her mother and Quinn, who were waiting for them. She was thankful that Phoenix had a railway line now; Reid had told her that when their mother had come out they'd had to take a stage from Maricopa, and Gayle wasn't sure she could have faced that last leg of the journey bouncing along rough dirt roads.

She studied the people who had gathered to meet the train, but she didn't see anyone who could be her mother and the man she had married. She forced a smile as Reid handed her down, refusing to let the wince that rose up in her as her leg took her weight show on her face.

Where were they? Hadn't they come, after all, had Moria decided that she wasn't anxious enough to see her to come in to town, that she could wait until Reid delivered her to the ranch?

A woman rushed toward her, her face working, and Gayle froze. Mother? Was this woman her mother? This woman was *old*, a handsome woman, a beautiful woman still, but definitely in her middle years, a little gray showing in her black hair, fine lines around her eyes, her skin sun-browned where it had been translucently fair the last time Gayle had seen her. How could this be the woman to whom she couldn't possibly measure up?

"Gayle!" Moria's arms were around her, holding her close, her eyes were shining with tears. "Oh, Gayle! I'd have known you anywhere! I can't believe you're here, I just can't seem to make myself believe it!"

"Hey!" A little boy, his face square and determined, was trying to insinuate himself between Moria and Gayle. "Hey, Ma, give me a chance, I wanna see my sister!"

"Hold up, son." A strong hand, as brown as leather, planted itself on the boy's shoulder and dragged him back. "Give your mother and Gayle a chance to say hello to each other, you'll get your turn in good time."

"But I wanna see her now! I didn't never have no sister before!"

"You never had a sister before," Quinn corrected him. "Except that you did, you'd simply never seen her. And don't call your mother Ma."

Liam. His name was Liam, Gayle thought, and he was her brother, her one-half of a brother, as Reid had put it, but that half was enough to make up for, and more, the lack of the other half. Liam, named after her grandfather, although there was no resemblance to the horse trainer whom Gayle still remembered as vividly as though he had died only yesterday.

"Hello, Liam," Gayle said over her mother's shoulder.

Now that his sister had finally taken notice of him, Liam was struck dumb. But not for long. His eyes widened and an expression of total amazement came over his face. "My Gawd, you're beautiful!" he said.

"Liam!" Moria's shocked outrage at her younger son's choice of words changed into laughter.

"Can't say I blame the lad, Miss Moria." A man as tall as Quinn, a little taller than Reid but about Reid's age, removed his broadbrimmed hat, and with his own face alight and his hazel eyes shining, waited to be introduced. There were others standing near, all of them interested and expectant, all of their faces friendly, but this one man stood out as his eyes never left her face. It was as though he were mesmerized, and Gayle felt a faint embarrassment in spite of the fact that she'd been admired and her beauty extolled all of her life.

"Hayes, I'm sorry. I'm so excited I hardly know what I'm doing. Gayle, this is Hayes Taylor, he's a neighbor of ours."

"How do you do. I'm very pleased to make your acquaintance," Gayle said. Her hand was grasped in Mr. Taylor's hand, a hand that was as hard and brown as Quinn's, and for a moment she thought that every bone in hers was about to be crushed until he loosened his grip, his face abashed with excruciating embarrassment.

"Beg pardon. Did I hurt you? I didn't mean to, I was just so blamed anxious to meet you."

"It's all right."

"Hayes, back off," Reid said good-naturedly. "Gayle's tired, we have to get her home so she can rest. You'll be seeing her later."

"Yes, yes, everyone will see her later!" Moria said. "Liam, pick up one of those bags. Quinn, can you bring the buckboard around so that Gayle won't have to walk? Reba, Abraham, come over here!"

"I can walk . . ." But Gayle's words were lost as Quinn strode off to bring up the buckboard.

The team stood quietly for a moment after Quinn had maneuvered them into position, but then the train engine gave forth a burst of steam and they reared, panicked, their eyes rolling and their front hooves pawing the air. Quinn's hands, masterful on the lines, brought them under control, but Gayle's face had gone deathly white as her deeply buried terror of horses, the terror that she had had to fight as a child in order to measure up to Moria, and that had come back tenfold after Nefertiti had fallen on her and injured her so badly, flooded over her. It rose up in her like a wave, it engulfed her, and Liam cried out, "Holy Moley, look out!" as she crumpled to the ground at their feet.

She woke up in a strange bed in a room she had never seen before. An elderly face, filled with concern but the kindest face she had ever seen, bent over her. She'd seen the woman at the station, she'd been with an elderly gentleman but they had both held back while Moria had greeted her daughter. She'd known who they were, Reid had told her about them, Reba and Abraham Greenbaum, her mother had been introducing her to them when the horses had reared and she had fainted.

She was so filled with shame for her weakness that she wanted to sink through the mattress and never be seen again. To have disgraced herself within minutes of her arrival! How could she ever face her mother, how could she ever face Reid again, or Quinn, or young Liam? And unbidden, the thought came, what must Hayes Taylor have thought? She'd proved herself a weakling, a coward, in front of them all, they'd all be disgusted with her. All of her childhood terrors came back, the fear of not being able to measure up, and she wished that she were dead.

Her mother came into the room, followed by a man she had never seen before. Even as she realized that he was a doctor he picked up her wrist to count her pulse.

"She'll be all right. My guess is that it's nothing more than exhaustion. Her heart is sound enough, all she needs is rest and care," the doctor said after he'd listened to her heart.

"Thank you, Dr. Mills." Moria's relief was so great that she trembled. "And thank you for coming so quickly."

The doctor's tone was cheerful. "I'd have been at the station myself, if young Tim Wetherby hadn't run a splinter three inches long into his foot! Well, young lady, how do you feel now?"

"I'm all right. It was stupid of me to faint. I'm sorry I've caused all of you so much trouble."

"That's what a beautiful young lady is for. You just rest, and see that you eat everything Reba sets in front of you! It won't be a hardship; Reba Greenbaum is the best cook in Phoenix, as I know, to my contented stomach. I'll look in on you again tomorrow, but there's nothing to lead me to believe that I'll have a new patient."

Rest! Gayle wanted to crawl inside the word, pull it around her and snuggle in it. She was so tired, so dreadfully, terribly tired! She closed her eyes, hearing the murmur of male voices downstairs. What must they think of her, Quinn and Liam and Hayes Taylor? She wasn't going to cry, crying was a weakness. Grimly, she held back her tears.

"That's right, darling. Go to sleep," Moria said. "Sleep as long as you want. I'll just stay here until you feel well enough to go on to the ranch, however many days it takes. Reid will bring us in whatever we need."

Gayle slept, and woke and ate delicious food from a tray, and slept again. It seemed as if she couldn't get enough sleep. Her exhausted body, her exhausted mind, near the thin edge of a complete breakdown because of Jacob's harrassment of her when she hadn't been strong enough to bear it, demanded it.

When she awakened the next day, it was already nearly noon. Moria was sitting beside her, her hands busy with a dress she was making for one of the neighboring ranchers' wives. Her skill with her needle had brought her a good many lasting friendships, her willingness to share her unfaltering sense of design had put to rest any doubts or jealousy the other women might have had about her because of her beauty and her superior education.

"So you're awake at last! Reba and I thought we'd let you sleep as long as you could. Are you hungry? Reba will be up in a minute, and don't feel embarrassed if you can't eat everything she'll bring you. Our Reba seems to feel that the whole world would starve if she wasn't here to feed them.''

"I'll do my best," Gayle said. "What are you making? It's a pretty color." She felt totally inadequate, just as she always had in the presence of her mother, even though Moria was no longer the flawless beauty she had remembered. What was she to say to her, how could they make conversation? They had nothing in common, they were strangers.

"It is a pretty color. It's a dress for Emma Taylor. She's Hayes's mother."

"Yes, I remember him." Gayle didn't want to talk about Hayes Taylor, after she'd made such a fool of herself in front of him. "You sew beautifully."

"It's come in handy. It helped pull Abraham out of the red and put him in the black, back at his department store in Chicago. Do you sew, Gayle?" It was dreadful to think that there was so much she didn't know about her daughter, it would take weeks, months, for them to catch up.

"No. I never learned."

"Then I'll teach you, if you think you'd be interested. After you're well again, of course. Right now all you have to do is bask in luxurious idleness."

"I don't think I'd care to learn." Gayle flushed because she knew she sounded ungracious, but what would be the use of trying to do something that her mother did so much better? She'd only make a botch of it, she'd fail again.

Moria was disturbed. There was something untouchable about Gayle, so that she despaired of ever being able to reach her. Was it to be like this, then, was she never going to truly have her daughter back, was Gayle's resentment against her so deep that they could never become close? Desperately, refusing to give up, Moria tried another tack.

"I think you'll like the ranch. We have some of the finest horses you've ever seen. I can hardly wait to show Caballero off to you. He's a palomino, one of Kamil's blood line. If you decide you like him better than any of the others he'll be yours to ride. But you'll have your choice of them all. Quinn says you're to have whichever you like best."

"That's kind of him." Gayle's face was noncommital, but she was filled with panic underneath her calm manner. They'd expect her to ride. And she couldn't do it, she'd never be able to do it. She shouldn't have come here, it had been a mistake. The weeks and months ahead of her loomed like an eternity, until the time she'd be well enough to leave and strike out on her own.

During the next several days, Reba watched Moria and Gayle, her soft eyes filled with concern. There was something wrong, and some way, somehow, she had to set it right. But there was one thing she knew without being told. Gayle had been hurt, she'd been hurt so deeply that the scars hadn't even begun to heal, and if she couldn't be persuaded to talk about it, then they would never heal and the tragedy that had begun when Moria had been driven away from her children would never be breached.

"It's time you went back to the ranch," she told Moria. "You can't leave Willa all alone to cope with everything, and there's nothing you can do here. I could take care of Gayle with one hand tied behind my back. So go, shoo, and leave your girl to me, your menfolk need you and Gayle and I don't."

Heartsick, Moria went. In spite of all her hopes, all her fantasies, the years during which she and Gayle had been separated couldn't be crossed in a day. Her fear was that they would never be able to be crossed at all.

She didn't confide her fears to Reid, or even to Quinn. This was her problem, hers and Gayle's. There was nothing they could do to help and there was no point in burdening them with it.

Left alone with Gayle, Reba began her campaign by talking. She'd sit in a rocking chair beside Gayle's bed and tell her about the earliest days she and Abe had known Moria.

" 'Bankrupt,' Abe said, you wouldn't believe! Every time your mother had a new idea, a good idea, Abe would moan 'bankrupt'!''

"I never knew that."

"Of course you didn't, how could you?" Reba rocked, laughing. "The courage Moria had, you wouldn't believe! And all the time, she was breaking her heart over you and Reid, all the time she was fighting her broken heart because of her father. But she didn't let it stop her. She had to go on living because if she gave up she'd never see you again. She had to go on living the best she could with what she had, don't we all?"

There was so much that Gayle hadn't known! And she admitted, with complete honesty, that most of it she wouldn't have wanted to know, she would have refused to listen to, if she wasn't flat on her back in bed with no way to get away from this woman who insisted that she must know.

But now that there was no place to hide, no way of getting away, the wall she had built around herself began to crumble, stone by stone. Only a chip at first, when she learned for the first time how Moria had been stranded in Chicago with nothing but her wedding ring and her courage to stand between herself and starvation. And a larger chip, when she learned how Moria had been discharged from Marshall Field's and had bearded Abraham in his den and talked him into giving her a job when he had had none to give and was fighting to keep from going under.

Courage. Her mother had such courage! Courage that she herself didn't have, that she could never match, any more than she'd ever been able to match Moria in any other way.

"It's a pity that you were hurt so bad that after you were thrown from your horse you couldn't get right back on again," Reba said.

Gayle started. How had that subject come up? She was sure that they hadn't mentioned horses.

"I could hardly get right back on again, with my leg broken."

"And now you're afraid," Reba said. "Not that I blame you. I was never on a horse in my life and I'm glad I never had to be, I've always been afraid of them. With you it's different. You think you ought to ride again even if you're afraid.''

"That isn't true! Why would I be afraid? I've ridden all my life, I was riding when I was four years old, Liam put me on my first pony and I loved it! Riding is as natural to me as breathing. . . .''

She couldn't be crying. But she was. And not just crying, but blubbering, her shoulders shaking, all the agony of her pent-up fears tumbling out.

"How did you know?" she hiccuped, gulping, her eyes filled with resentment and anger and reproach.

"I have eyes." And Reba's arms were around her, Reba was holding her and rocking her, her arms a shelter such as Gayle had never known, a refuge from everything that pained and frightened her.

"Cry," Reba said. "Cry it all out. It's time."

There was no way to get away from Reba, even after the floodgates had opened and Gayle had cried herself sick. You strengthened your defenses on one side of the wall, and she pried another stone loose from the other side before you knew what she was doing.

"My, but I'd have loved to know Liam Donovan! To have a man like that for a grandfather, what an honor! What was he like, Gayle? Moria and Reid have told me, but everybody sees something that other people don't see.''

"He was tall, and his shoulders were broad, and he was strong and handsome. He was . . . he was . . .''

All of her tears had been shed, but the dam was filled again, and they came, flooding her face, flooding her soul. Gayle's voice was a wail, torn from her heart. "I never got to call him Grandfather! Not even once. . . .''

"I can't imagine what it would be like to grow up at a place liks Belvedere, to have all that money, all those beautiful clothes, everybody admiring me!" Reba said. "And such a beautiful mother, and you as beautiful. Like a fairy tale!''

"It isn't true! It wasn't like that at all! It was Mother who was beautiful, it was Mother who was perfect! Always so perfect, and I couldn't be that perfect no matter how I tried, and I was shut out, there was no place for me!''

And now Reba knew it all, and she pushed away the impulse to weep as hard as Gayle was weeping. The time for crying was over, the time for healing had begun.

"The bicycle," Reba said.

"What?" How was anyone supposed to keep up with the train of Reba's thoughts? Wasn't it enough that Reba had entered her mind, probed to the depth of places that no one else had ever been allowed to see? What bicycle, and for the love of heaven, why?

"My bicycle. You'll ride that."

"And that will teach me not to be afraid to ride a horse again?" Gayle's voice showed that she thought that Reba was mad.

"It will exercise your leg. And when your leg is strong again, you'll be able to ride. I always knew that that bicycle would come in handy some day. Something stood behind me and gave me a push when I looked at it and didn't want to buy it, so I bought it.''

"I don't want to ride a horse again. Where I'm going, making my own living, I won't have a horse to ride, anyway."

"Then maybe you'll want to ride a bicycle. Anyway, you have to get your leg strong again before you can think of going anywhere and finding a job. I can't wait for Papa to come home so I can tell him that the bicycle is going to be of some use after all." Reba rocked, smiling. And defeated, Gayle knew that she would learn to ride the bicycle.

"I never knew. I never had any idea. Gayle, I never had any idea!" Moria said. "Can you ever forgive me? I should have known, I was your mother!"

"It wasn't your fault. I was a prickly child. Just ask Reid. He says I was impossible. And I never knew about you, either, there was so much I didn't know until Reba told me. Mother, do you mind if I say we've been a couple of prize idiots?''

"I don't mind at all." They looked at each other, and because of

Reba, the gap between them had disappeared, all the years were spanned. "But it still kills me to think that you thought you had to compete, that you were afraid you couldn't measure up, and I never knew it. At least one thing is certain now, Gayle. You don't have to compete with me anymore! I'm a middle-aged woman, I'm not in the running and I wouldn't even want to be."

"You're still beautiful, you're still one of the most beautiful women in the world."

Moria laughed and made a face. "You're supposed to add, 'for a woman of your age'! No, Gayle, no more competition, real or imagined. I'm your mother, nothing more, and that's the way I want it."

"Mother, how does Reba do it? I've never talked to anyone the way I talked to her, she found out more about me in just a few days than anybody else ever knew about me in my whole lifetime! I told her things I'd sworn I'd never tell anyone, because I thought I'd rather die than have anyone know."

"It was the same way with me," Moria told her. "After Abraham gave me a job, it was only a matter of days before she knew my life history, and before I knew what was happening I was living with her and Abraham, I had a family and a reason to go on living. She's a wonderful woman. I think that love is the answer, pure and simple love. And we, both of us, were fortunate enough to have that love spill out over us."

Days of rest and Reba's good food had restored Gayle's strength more rapidly than any of them had dared hope for. Now Reba moved on to her second goal, to restore the strength and muscle tone to Gayle's leg. Every morning, she rode the bicycle, the first few times with Reid holding it up until she learned to balance it, with Liam running alongside shouting encouragement. "You can do it, Gayle! It's easy! Look, all you gotta do is keep pumpin' like crazy!"

For Gayle, keeping pumping was harder than it sounded. Her weakened leg protested, it ached and hurt, the muscles did their best to refuse to respond. But the bicycle had become a challenge. She was determined not to be a burden, to be able to pull her own weight at the ranch or find work in town, and she had to have the full use of both of her legs to do that. Abraham had offered her a job in his store, but she didn't want to accept a position that she knew had been created for her. A return to a typewriting school seemed the best alternative, in some city large enough to have one. Or a position as a saleslady here in Phoenix but in a store that Abraham didn't own.

After the morning session with the bicycle, Gayle would lie on her bed and Reba's knowing fingers would massage her leg, loosen the knotted muscles and stroke the circulation back into it. It hurt, but Gayle clenched her teeth and bore it. And little by little, she could feel new life returning to the limb she had been convinced would never serve her adequately again. She was able to ride the length of the block, then ride it twice, three times, four times, until she could ride all the way around two or three blocks and then do it again.

It was time for her to leave Reba and Abraham's house and go to the ranch. Her staying on, as much as they wanted her, was causing them problems. Now that she was up and well again, every young unmarried man in the vicinity was beating a path to Reba's doorstep, intent on beating the others out.

Abraham sat in the kitchen every night with his oversugared tea, mourning the loss of his tranquillity. He'd gone through this before with Moria, and while nobody would dare to tell him that he was old, he wasn't as young as he'd used to be and it was wearing. Gayle he loved, almost as much as Moria, but peace and quiet were nice too.

Reba would sit opposite him, hoping that when there happened to be more than one young man at a time, their rivalry wouldn't come to blows in her parlor. She didn't want her nice furniture or her vases and statuettes smashed, or blood on her beautiful rugs, even if she hardly ever used the parlor herself, still preferring to spend most of her waking hours in her kitchen.

Of all Gayle's suitors, Hayes Taylor was the most persistent, and he had the edge over the others because he'd been Reid's friend before Gayle had come to Phoenix. There was no use for Gayle to pretend that Hayes didn't disturb her. He was so completely different from any other man she had ever known! All of these western men seemed to be taller than life, to move like panthers, lean-hipped and broad-shouldered, their eyes keen and quizzical, exuding a confidence that came from their own confidence in their manhood. But Hayes was more so than the rest of them.

Gayle entertained her other callers in the parlor, with Abraham and Reba in the kitchen. But Hayes sat at the kitchen table, and Gayle already understood what that meant. To be accepted in Reba's kitchen was a mark of favor extended only to members of the family or to friends who were accepted as members of the family.

Gayle had never believed in love at first sight. Her mother had fallen in love with her father at first sight, and the result had been disastrous. So Gayle had been cautious, she'd held back from falling in love, until she'd become known throughout the Hudson River Valley as the girl who thought that no man was good enough for her. She'd known Martin Schuyler for nearly a year before she'd finally decided that he was the one for her, before she'd dared to let herself love him as she'd longed to love someone and make him her own.

Now, she couldn't help but compare Hayes and Martin, and she shuddered to think what a narrow escape she'd had. The man she had idolized had failed her just as her father had failed her mother. Even if her father hadn't died in a manner that had brought disgrace on the Vancouvers, a time would almost certainly have come in her married life when Martin would have failed her again.

And now there was Hayes, and she didn't want to fall in love with him. It was too soon, her emotional hurts over Martin still hadn't healed. But there was no way that she could keep from comparing the two men, to Martin's detriment. She knew, with a faith as sure as her faith in God, that Hayes would never let the woman he married down, that his love for her would be strong enough to surmount the greatest disasters.

But how could she marry him, even if she loved him so much that life would be meaningless without him? She was only half a woman.

She'd never been whole, a person in her own right, and now she was lame besides even though her leg had strengthened under Reba's expert manipulations. And above and beyond all that, there was still her terror of horses. How could she possibly be a rancher's wife, where horses were a part of daily life? She'd let Hayes down because she wouldn't be able to measure up.

It was time for her to move to the ranch, to continue building her strength until she could strike out on her own. Beyond that, she wouldn't even let herself think.

33

Gayle loved Willa from the start. The ranchwoman was something entirely outside of her previous experience. Looking at her, talking to her, Gayle couldn't help but compare her to the society women who had been a major part of her old life, and find the society women shallow and useless. Willa's strength of character, her integrity, her lifetime of doing what had to be done, set her head and shoulders above those others.

In return, Willa accepted her, and gave her the ultimate compliment of expecting her to do her share of the work. She didn't mind that Gayle was awkward at first, that she scarcely knew which end of a paring knife to use, that the first time she made a bed she couldn't get the corners smooth and straight. She taught her, and Gayle learned, just as she learned to darn Liam's socks and mend his perpetually torn trousers, freeing Moria from those tasks so that she could use her real talent of dressmaking without having to stop to do the mending.

Quinn was unfailingly kind to her. He accepted her because he liked her, not simply because she was Moria's daughter. She was part of the family, just as Reid was part of the family. The thought brought a lump to her throat. In all the luxury in which she had been raised, there had never been a sense of belonging, only of the importance of having the right blood in her veins. Like Willa, Quinn expected her to pull her weight to the limit of her ability, and it made Gayle proud.

But there were the horses, and there were Quentin's eyes on her when she flinched when she was taken to see them. Quinn's father made no comment when she said that she wasn't ready to start riding again, and his eyes were unreadable, but Gayle knew that she had failed to measure up. Liam was only puzzled. Being afraid of horses was something he couldn't fathom. When Moria and Quinn said that there was no hurry and it was of no importance, Quentin's eyes and Liam's puzzlement still gnawed at her.

All the same, she couldn't.

Rose's letter, followed by official documents, after William Northrup's death, took the main attention away from her for a little while. William's death had been a shock. It had seemed, as impossible as it was, that the malevolent man would live forever.

But now William Northrup was dead, and all of his estate belonged to Moria. There was a family conference while it was decided what to do about it.

Moria wanted nothing that had belonged to William Northrup. Quinn agreed with her, and Quentin and Willa followed suit. Only Liam was a little disappointed, dreaming of owning the biggest horse ranch in the world, and even that passed because, after all, no matter how many horses he might own if they had all that money, none of them could be any better than the ones they had right here.

"I want Michael McCarthy to use every penny to help the Irish immigrants," Moria said. "I'll send him my power of attorney and he'll take care of it all. He'll know what to do, and he's honest, not one penny of it will stick to his own fingers. Gayle, is that all right with you?"

Gayle's chin was up, her eyes shining. "I can't think of a better use for that man's wealth!" she said. It gave her and Moria the deepest satisfaction to know that William Northrup's fortune would be spent on the Irish immigrants he had held in such contempt, and they hoped that he was whirling in his grave.

Michael's letter confirmed their conviction that he'd be glad to follow Moria's wishes. And Rose's letter, enclosed with Michael's, told them that everything she and Michael owned had already been willed to Reid and Gayle and there was nothing they could do about it. "And there's money available, in a loan from Michael, for Reid to buy up more of that land he's convinced is going to be so valuable. Get it while the getting's cheap. It's what Eugenia and Liam would have wanted. Michael's by way of being a rich man but we're both simple people, we wouldn't want to live anywhere but in our nice homey flat and go out to the beer gardens with all our friends."

One more paragraph made Moria smile. "Dora Sisti has popped up again. Michael and I saw her in a soup line at the Salvation Army. Considering that she's been punished enough, having lived in mortal fear that Jacob Vancouver would have her killed because of what she knows, Michael got her a job cleaning one of the meeting halls. She almost turned and ran when she saw me, she was afraid I'd give her some more of what I gave her before, but I wouldn't dirty my hands on her. Still, I'd not see her starve. Her jealousy and spite ruined her life, so let her live in what peace she can find, with enough to fill her stomach."

Moria felt the same way, and after all these years she could even dredge up a little pity for the woman who had done her best to destroy her life. People bring their own punishment on themselves, she thought, and her eyes meeting Quinn's, she thanked God that she herself had found such perfect happiness.

"You're gonna be rich anyway!" Liam informed them, grinning. "Abraham told me that he's leaving everything to you and Pa. Maybe I'll get me that big horse ranch after all, only not for years and years and years because I'd rather have Abe an' Reba than all the horses in the world!"

Her eyes filled with tears, Moria hugged him until he squirmed, and then he howled with outraged protest when Gayle kissed him. Even if she was his sister, she was a girl!

But the distraction of having to decide what to do with William Northrup's fortune passed, and Gayle was faced with the dilemma of what to do about Hayes. He burned up the trails between the two ranches. Three or four times a week he rode over and stayed so late that he had to bunk down with Reid for the night. The other young men had tapered off, convinced that they were outmatched, although a few kept calling in hopes that they might get their foot in a crack of the door that Hayes had already breached.

"Now, honey," Hayes said, "of course you're scared of horses, after what happened to you. There's nothing to be ashamed of about that. I was shaking in my boots the first time I got thrown and staved in my ribs, I never would have got back on one of the critters if my brothers hadn't teased me till I had to in self-defense. You know something, after I climbed aboard the same critter that had thrown me, and rode him, I was so sick to my stomach I had to run behind the bunkhouse and heave my g—my insides."

"How old were you?" Gayle asked, her heart going out to him. Hayes's answer shook her.

"I was six." But she was a grown woman, not a child, and her fear had been with her all her life no matter how deeply she had buried it.

And she loved Hayes, there was no use in trying to tell herself that she didn't. All of her hurt when Martin had deserted her, all of her resolves never to trust her heart to another man, had flown out of the window as Hayes had continued courting her—his patience, his understanding, his pure masculinity, battering at her defenses until they had all crumbled to dust. Hayes was everything she had ever dreamed in a man, and more, everything that her love-starved heart had convinced her that Martin was and that he hadn't been.

But she couldn't marry him. There was no way that she could be the wife of a rancher. And she couldn't bear it. As long as she had this fear, she wasn't good enough for him.

"Gayle, you aren't being realistic. If one door is closed to you, then you find another. Riding horses isn't all there is to life. Hayes would still love you if you'd lost your leg in that accident, not just been slightly lamed and left with a very natural fear that will probably disappear gradually, given enough time," Moria tried to tell her. "You can't punish him, and yourself, by refusing to accept his love. You have to go on living, and I'm not so blind that I can't see that Hayes is your life and you're his."

Her mother didn't understand. And Reid didn't understand. He railed at her, his eyes filled with disgust.

"You're as stubborn and unreasonable as you were when you were an obnoxious little brat! What do you think you're doing to Hayes, even if you don't care what you're doing to yourself? He wants a wife, not a woman who can go out and take prizes at horse shows! So you're afraid of horses, so what? If I'd been bitten by a rattler, you wouldn't catch me sticking my hand in a nest of them just to prove that I dared!"

Quentin said nothing. His face gave no clue to approval or disapproval. In his seventies, he was still a big man, weathered, looking as strong as hickory, but he had slowed down, letting Quinn and Reid take over more of the work. He was still the head of the family, running the ranch with an iron hand. Gayle respected him for what he was, a man who would never give up as long as he could force flesh and blood to do his bidding.

It only made it harder for her. What must he think of her, a girl who couldn't conquer her fear of horses. It wasn't as if she wasn't capable of riding, of handling almost any horse that had ever been born, and that made her cowardice all the worse. But it was Liam's eyes, questioning, not understanding, that perhaps hurt her even more.

She wasn't good enough for them. She wasn't good enough for her family, or for Hayes.

"You're driving me out of my mind!" Hayes told her. "Dammit, Gayle, beg pardon, but you drive me to cussin! How many times do I have to tell you that you don't have to ride unless you want to, that it doesn't matter a hoot if you never ride again? You're the woman I want, I'll never settle for anyone else, so you might as well break down and take me because I'm not going to give up even if I have to kidnap you and drag you to Mexico and have some Spanish-speaking priest marry us with you not knowing what's going on!"

"Hayes, you idiot! I'm not that stupid, I'd know what was going on. Besides, I'm learning Spanish, Mother told me that it's a good thing to know out here, where there are as many Spanish-speaking people as there are Anglos."

"It comes in handy," Hayes conceded. "But there are only two words I want you to know, and they're in plain English, just 'I do' when the parson asks if you'll take me to be your husband."

"To love and honor and obey..." Gayle murmured, a lump aching in her throat, tears, unshed, stinging against her eyelids.

"Obey, hell! I'll make the parson take that part out. I don't want a woman to obey me, I want a woman to love me!"

Before Gayle knew what he was going to do, he had her in his arms, he was kissing her as she'd dreamed that he would kiss her, only it was a hundred times better, it shook her to the center of her being, left her breathless, gasping, clinging to him as if she must merge her body into his or die of the wanting. It hadn't been like this with Martin, it could never be like this with any other man, Hayes was her man, without him she was nothing, she didn't even exist.

They were alone in the kitchen. Everyone else had gone to bed more than an hour ago. The fall roundup was over, when there had been days on end when all of the men had been out on the range and she hadn't seen Hayes at all and she'd felt that she would die of not seeing him. What if something happened to him, what if he were gored by a steer, what if he were thrown and broke his neck, what if there should be a stampede and he were killed? Her life would be over as surely as his was over, without their having had each other.

Now, for this one, endless moment, Gayle gave herself to her emotions, to her love. Everything inside of her screamed to say yes, to say it over and over, to take what was offered her, selfishly and without regard for the consequences.

But she couldn't do it. Even though she felt as though she were dying, she had to say the words, she had to put an end to this before it destroyed them both.

"No, Hayes. I'm sorry. You'll never know how sorry I am that I'm hurting you! But I can't marry you. Don't ask me again, because the answer will be the same."

"Damn you!" Hayes pushed her away from him, and then, his jaw set, he pulled her into his arms again and kissed her even harder than he had before. "You can't say no! I won't let you, can't you get that through your head? I won't let some half-baked notion of yours ruin both of our lives!"

This time it was Gayle who broke the embrace, using the very last of her strength. "Hayes, I'm sorry. Please don't come over here any more. If you do, I won't see you." And with that, she eluded his reaching arms and ran out of the kitchen to take refuge in her own bedroom, while Hayes, cursing and damning all women in general and Gayle in particular, stamped out to the veranda to roll a cigarette and get himself under control before he battered her bedroom door down and Quentin Bradmore strung him up on the giant cottonweed tree that shaded the front of the house in the summer.

Finishing his cigarette, Hayes went to the corral and saddled his horse. There was no way he was going to spend the night bunked down with Reid, after what had happened. As late as it was, he'd ride home, and he'd be damned if he'd ever come back!

But he did come back. And Gayle refused to see him, just as she'd said she would. Moria tried to reason with her, Reid raged at her, Willa tried to talk to her and point out how foolish she was being. Quinn shook his head in perplexity, and Quentin kept his own counsel.

This couldn't go on. She was spoiling things for all of them. She didn't belong here, she had no place here. She'd have to make the break. She was strong enough now, and she still had the sapphire earrings that Estelle had given her and that Michael McCarthy had saved for her. Abraham would lend her money on them, it would be a business deal.

She'd go to some big city and find work. San Francisco was too close, Hayes would follow her there, and she couldn't go back to New York State and put herself in reach of her Grandfather Jacob again. She'd go into town tomorrow, she'd drive the buckboard, she wasn't afraid of driving, only of getting up on the back of a horse. Abraham would know what city she should settle in, although both he and Reba would try to talk her out of leaving. But her mind was made up. She was going because she had to go.

Running away! her mind screamed at her. You're running away! You can't measure up, so this is your defense, to cut and run. She was ruining Hayes's life and her own, she'd break her mother's heart, all because she was a coward!

Daylight was barely streaking the sky. She hadn't slept at all last night. The house was silent, even Liam wouldn't stir for another half-hour or more, and Reid had ridden over to the Taylor ranch yesterday and stayed overnight.

Her face white, her legs trembling, Gayle got up and dressed. The divided skirt that Moria had given her, in hopes that she'd wear it to try riding one of the gentler horses, was still in her room, a silent rebuke. Gayle put it on. Sick with fear, she let herself out the front door, the door that was virtually never used.

The horses in the corral looked at her as she approached them. There was the gentle mare that Quinn had assured her that she could ride, but her eyes passed over it as she studied the others. Most of them in the corral were tough cow ponies, Quinn's prize palominos were kept separate in another corral. Some of these range horses bucked, some of them bit, some of them kicked. And one of them did all three, and threw every cowhand at least once when he was mounted. The only reason he was kept was because he was fast and utterly tireless and too good a cow horse to get rid of.

Sidewinder. The cowhands cursed him, even threatened to shoot him.

The western saddle was heavy, bulky, completely unlike the small eastern saddle, the sidesaddle, that Gayle was used to. She'd never ridden astride. The stirrups were wood, rounded at the bottom. The cinch gave her trouble, although Liam had shown her how to fasten it, disgusted when she'd told him that in the East girths had buckles.

Sidewinder puffed out his stomach, filling it with air so that the saddle would loosen up when she got on. It was just one of his mean tricks. The bridle was single-rein, not double, as she was used to using, and the horse tried to bite her as she slipped the bit into his mouth. She cracked him across the nose, and felt the bitter bile of terror rise up in her throat.

Sidewinder knew that she was afraid. She had trouble mounting him, she'd never mounted western style before, facing the front of the horse. And there was that other thing, something unheard of in the East. When a westerner put his foot into the stirrup his western horse took off, and the rider had to swing into the saddle with the horse in motion. They were trained that way for working cattle.

Gritting her teeth, Gayle put her foot in the stirrup. It was bitter cold, the cold that cut through to the bone, the cold of the dry desert air that cooled off every night even in the middle of the summer and that in the winter dawn made her shiver and tremble. Her breath showed white as she breathed, and white plumes emanated from Sidewinder's flared nostrils.

She didn't know how she'd done it, but she was in the saddle. It was as if Liam Donovan were beside her, telling her that she could do it, that she had to try, that she had to give it her best.

Back at the house, Moria had started awake, feeling that something was wrong. And in the room he shared with Willa, Quentin had heard Gayle leave the house, his ears as sharp as they'd been when he'd been a young man and every sense had to be sharp in order to survive. Now, fully dressed, he appeared behind Moria as she opened the door to Gayle's room and found her daughter gone.

"She went out," he told her.

They hurried, but they were too late. Gayle was on Sidewinder, and Sidewinder had determined that she wasn't going to stay there. Moria started to run, she opened her mouth to scream, but Quentin's arm was around her, holding her back, his hand was over her mouth. She struggled, but he shook his head.

"Leave her alone. This is her fight."

Moria went limp, as if every ounce of strength had drained from her. That was Sidewinder, he'd kill her, there was no way Gayle could ride Sidewinder, as terrified as she was of horses. Didn't Quentin know that he'd kill her?

"She can do it. Even if she can't, she has to try. Leave her be."

In the corral, Sidewinder reared. Gayle stayed on. Every muscle in her body reacted to keep her in the saddle because she was a rider, she'd ridden all her life and she'd had the best teacher in the world, Liam Donovan.

Sidewinder's front feet came down with a spine-rattling jolt. And almost before they touched the ground, he leaped sideways, and fishtailed. Held back by Quentin's arm, kept from crying out by Quentin's hand over her mouth, Moria watched, despairing, as her daughter went off.

Gayle got to her feet. "Damn you! You ornery, cussed, no-good chunk of horsemeat, stand still!"

She almost didn't make it back into the saddle. Sidewinder jumped sideways away from her just as she got her foot in the stirrup. Moria made a moaning noise in her throat, but Quentin's grip didn't relax.

And Gayle was on. Her other foot searched wildly for the other stirrup and toed into it. Sidewinder tried to take the bit in his teeth, he fought her for it, plunging and jumping, pivoting and tossing his head, threatening to knock her out of the saddle as he brought it back with such force that Moria shuddered and felt the earth spin under her feet.

Gayle yanked Sidewinder's head down. She used her fist to whack the top of his head, with all of her strength and weight behind it. Sidewinder pivoted to the left; Gayle yanked him back into a straight line. He reared again, and she brought him down, her teeth banging together so that her head nearly exploded with pain. And then Sidewinder went straight up into the air and came down facing in the opposite direction and Gayle was on the ground again, the wind knocked out of her. In Quentin's grip, Moria was struggling wildly, but he only held her tighter.

"No. Leave her be."

She'd be killed. Her daughter was going to be killed, and Quentin would be her murderer! Damn him, damn him, Moria raged, as his grip tightened still harder.

And Gayle was on her feet again, she was in the saddle again, her heels caught Sidewinder and her knees gripped his sides, gripped down with a force that would have been impossible if Reba hadn't forced her to endure the pain of riding the bicycle, the pain of the massages and manipulations that had brought strength back to her leg.

"Go to it!" Gayle shouted, her scream a triumph of pure, primitive rage. "Do your damnedest! I'll ride you, damn you, I'll ride you if it kills me! I'll ride you if it kills you, so you might as well give up!"

Sidewinder had no intention of giving up. And neither did Gayle. The battle went on. Sidewinder plunged, spun, lunged, jumped sideways in the nasty maneuver that had earned him his name. Gayle stuck to the saddle like a burr. She used every trick, every skill, that Liam Donovan had taught her. It was all still there, a part of her. Her bones felt as though they were rattling, her spine felt as though it was cracking, and still she stayed on.

This was a fight for her life. Every second she stayed on, every time she refused to be thrown, was a blow against everything that had ruined her life. If she could win this battle, all of the old fears, all of the old hurts, would be conquered as well, dead and buried. No more running away, no more hiding inside of herself because she was afraid to fight for what she wanted. And little by little, inch by inch, she fought Sidewinder down, while the half-dozen wranglers who were at the home place straggled out of the bunkhouse half-dressed, their mouths hanging open, not daring to move to intervene because of Quentin's commanding gesture.

"Try it again, you misbegotten spawn of the devil!" Gayle screamed. "Try it again, you no-good, double-blasted snake! Damn your hide, you aren't going to get rid of me this time!"

And Sidewinder wound down, and straightened out, and she was riding him. Around and around the corral they went, Gayle straight in the saddle, her face flushed with a wild triumph. She was riding him, she had mastered him, *she had measured up!*

Moria was sobbing. Quentin held her in his arms, her face pressed against his broad chest. She realized, with disbelief, that her father-in-law was trembling.

"Thank God," Quentin said. "Thank God! For a minute there, I was doubtful. Go ahead and cry, Moria. I feel like cryin' myself. She did it, our girl did it!"

For the first time, Gayle realized that they were there. She reined Sidewinder to the corral gate, leaned over and opened it, and rode through, closing it behind her. She was already a ranchwoman, she knew better than to leave a gate, any gate, open. She rode Sidewinder over to her mother and Quentin. She was laughing, her eyes shining.

"How did I do?" she asked. "I think I'll just ride over to the Taylor place."

"Not on that horse," Quentin said. "I'll saddle Caballero for you while you get some grub inside you."

"Not on this horse," Gayle conceded. And she added, with devils sparkling in her eyes, "He's too tired."

"Mind your language while you're at the Taylors'," Quentin said mildly. "I never heard words like that come out of a woman's mouth before." And damned if he had, he thought, his eyes filled with pride and admiration.

Moria kissed his cheek. "Thank you," she said. After all these years! She was still shaken, still shaky, but she managed to smile.

"Look at me! In my dressing robe, and I'm half frozen! I'll make some pancakes and eggs. And I can ride with you, after we've eaten."

"She doesn't need you," Quentin said. "She knows the way. Slap some steaks on the griddle, while you're at it. I feel like a good breakfast."

They were out by the corral, Reid and Hayes, when Gayle got there. They saw her coming, sitting straight in Caballero's saddle, riding astride. Reid took one look at her, and one look at Hayes, and got himself out of the way into the bunkhouse.

Gayle slipped out of the saddle into Hayes's arms. Hayes's face was dumbfounded.

"I'll be doggoned! I'll be everlastingly doggoned! But I knew you could do it, didn't I always tell you you could? Only you shouldn't have ridden over here alone, you should have had somebody come with you!"

"I didn't need anyone to come with me. Anything I need to do, I can handle alone," Gayle said.

"If you aren't the stubbornest, most exasperatin' woman I ever knew!"

"You've said that before." She let him hold her. This was where she belonged, here in his arms, until the end of time. She was Gayle Vancouver, soon-to-be Gayle Taylor, a self-sufficient person in her own right, and she'd come home.

The chances were that she wouldn't ride for pleasure, at least for a long time. But if she had to ride, she could do it, and if she had to ride the most vicious, unmanageable horse in creation, she could do it. Knowing that, she knew that she could handle anything that being a rancher's wife threw at her, no matter how hard it was.

Yes, she had come home. It had been a long journey, it had taken her all of her life. But she was here now, where she belonged, and that was all that mattered.

ROMANCE...
ADVENTURE...DANGER

__TO THOSE WHO DARE
by Lydia Lancaster (90-579, $2.95)

They were society's darlings. They were born to marry for wealth and position, rear respectful children and take tea with the elite. But they chose love instead of prestige, principles instead of pride. In a growing town on Erie Canal, they dared to follow their dreams.

__THE MER-LION
by Lee Arthur (A90-044, $3.50)

In Scotland, he was a noble...but in the bloody desert colosseum, he was a slave battling for the hand of a woman he hated. James Mackenzie intrigued royalty...the queen of France, the king of Scotland, the king of England, and the Amira Aisha of Tunis. But James Mackenzie was a man of destiny, a Scot whose fortune was guarded by THE MER-LION.

__DAUGHTERS OF THE OPAL SKIES
by Aola Vandergriff (D30-564, $3.50)

Tamsen Tallant, most beautiful of the McCleod sisters, is ~~one~~ in the Australian outback. Alone with a ranch to run, ~~re~~bellious teenage nieces to care for, and Opal ~~'s~~ new head stockman to reckon with—a man whose ~~k~~ holds a challenge. But Tamsen is prepared for ~~for~~ she has seen the face of the Devil and he looks

DON'T MISS THESE EXCITING ROMANCES BY VALERIE SHERWOOD

BEST OF BESTSELLERS
FROM WARNER BOOKS

THE CARDINAL SINS
by Andrew M. Greeley   *(A90-913, $3.95)*
From the humblest parish to the inner councils of the Vatican, Father Greeley reveals the hierarchy of the Catholic Church as it really is, and its priests as the men they really are. This book follows the lives of two Irish boys who grow up on the West Side of Chicago and enter the priesthood. We share their triumphs as well as their tragedies and temptations.

THE OFFICERS' WIVES
by Thomas Fleming   *(A90-920, $3.95)*
This is a book you will never forget. It is about the U.S. Army, the huge unwieldy organism on which much of the nation's survival depends. It is about Americans trying to live personal lives, to cling to touchstones of faith and hope in the grip of the blind, blunderous history of the last 25 years. It is about marriage, the illusions and hopes that people bring to it, the struggle to maintain and renew commitment.

To order, use the coupon below. If you prefer to use your own stationery, please include complete title as well as book number and price. Allow 4 weeks for delivery.